M

The Complete Roderick

THE COMPLETE RODERICK

JOHN SLADEK

Overlook SF&F Classics

The Overlook Press
Woodstock & New York

This edition first published in paperback in the United States in 2004 by
The Overlook Press, Peter Mayer Publishers, Inc.
Woodstock & New York

WOODSTOCK:
One Overlook Drive
Woodstock, NY 12498
www.overlookpress.com
[for individual orders, bulk and special sales, contact our Woodstock office]

NEW YORK:
141 Wooster Street
New York, NY 10012

Cataloging-in-Publication Data is available from the Library of Congress

Manufactured in the United States of America
ISBN 1-58567-587-3
1 3 5 7 9 8 6 4 2

For Pamela Sladek

THANKS

To Alan Jones of North East London Polytechnic, who helped me program a plot. Thanks to Jasia Reichardt, for conversations about robots, and especially for writing her excellent *Robots: Fact, Fiction and Prediction* (London: Thames & Hudson, 1978).

Special thanks to Ivan Klingels, without whose loan of an office for an entire year, this book would not have been written.

I'm grateful to the publisher for permission to quote from the English translation of 'Les Fenêtres' from *Calligrammes* by Guillaume Apollinaire © Editions Gallimard 1925.

PART 1

RODERICK

OR

THE EDUCATION OF A YOUNG MACHINE

BOOK ONE

I

There is no security against the ultimate development of mechanical consciousness, in the fact of machines possessing little consciousness now. A mollusc has not much consciousness. Reflect upon the extraordinary advance which machines have made in the last few hundred years, and note how slowly the animal and vegetable kingdoms are advancing.   Samuel Butler, *Erewhon*

JEAN HARLOW (*as Kitty Packard*): I read this book ... the man says machines are going to take over every profession!
MARIE DRESSLER (*as Carlotta Vance, looks her over*): You've got nothing to worry about, my dear.   from *Dinner at Eight*

Spring came to the University of Minnetonka in the form of a midnight blizzard, spraying snow the length and breadth of the great campus, annoying people from Faculty Hill clear down to Fraternity Row.

At the meeting of the Ibsen Club a very old, tiresome guest began explaining that Boreas was – hee hee! – probably trying to get into the concrete barns of the Agricultural Science Department and impregnate the mares – oho! – only these days one supposed it was all done by machine, eh? Frozen sperm from some dead stallion, eh? Dispensed by some machine colder and faster and more ruthless than poor old Boreas – hee hee! – and so on, getting further and further from their discussion of Nora Helmer.

At home Dr Helen Boag, Dean of Persons, awoke and called out to Harry, her second husband: 'Harry, what's it? What's it? That noise?' But the lump of bedclothes beside her was Dave, her third. And the wind had already moved on.

At the University Health Service a yawning intern used a tongue depressor to mark his place in *The Heart of the Matter* ('Somewhere far away he thought he heard the sounds of pain.') and decided to order more flu vaccine – a wind like that. He

5

scooted in his swivel chair to the console of the inventory computer and began playing its keys. In no time at all he was able to order three trillion – oops, thousand, 3,000 doxes – doses, damnit, doses!

Someone at Digamma Upsilon Nu invited the wind to blow, blow and crack its nuts, and laughed hard enough to spill more beer over the already damp player piano where the brothers had gathered to hoist mugs and sing 'Roll Me Over', their voices straining to compete with the mad howl outside. Indeed, they could hardly be heard by the lone brother who had crept upstairs to sit holding a loaded revolver and considering his Grade Point Average. The system, Christ it was so unfair, so damned unfair, getting graded by computers and all it was, it was degrading ha ha some joke some life, even if you get your horoscope done it's all computers . . .

Even while he was hurriedly putting the gun away, the gust that had knocked at his window (sounding like a knock at the door) was far away, trying other doors and windows . . .

It whistled through the spire of the Wee Interdenominational Kirk O' Th' Campus, where there were no great organ pipes to thrill in response – pipes, organ and even organist having all been replaced by a single modest machine which (if Pastor Bean ever managed to get it programmed) would come to life only to sing the praises of the Wee Interdenominational God, on cue, by the numbers.

Near the Kirk lay a mutilated body; the wind covered her decently with snow to await the statistical work of the police computer and hurled on, roaring down the Mall, ripping at an old ballet poster, upsetting a litter basket – finally shrieking past the Computer Science building. There the wind pushed Dr Fong firmly against the door he was trying to pull.

'Here, let me help.' He heard the voice before he could make out the figure, a badly-handled marionette being pushed along on its toes. Rogers.

'Oh, it's you.' He stood back, holding his Russian hat in place with both hands, while Professor Rogers wrestled with the door. Snow turned the air around them into a flicker of random dots; wind provided the white noise.

Inside, the two men stopped to stamp their feet and remove steamed glasses. 'It's you,' Fong said again. 'At this time of night?'

'I couldn't sleep. Thinking about . . . oh, every damn thing. About the viability . . .' Rogers's face held no further explanation. Indeed, without the tinted glasses, his face was simply long and blank, a peanut shell. Nothing in it but pock marks.

'You wanted to look over the project?'

'I wanted to explore – acceptability levels.'

'Whats?'

'To probe the infrastructure of your little group, you see? To look for a catalysable system-oriented – see I knew either you or your assistant would be here tonight . . .'

'You mean Dan? He's here practically all the time, these days. But I wouldn't exactly call him my assistant.'

'Sure.'

'More a colleague.'

'Sure, sure.'

'I mean it. Just because he has no formal qualif – look, if anything, Roderick's more his work than mine.'

'His brainchild?'

'Jesus.' Fong sighed. 'Let's go down there. I'll show you around.'

'I don't want to see around, Lee. I want a heart-to-heart rap about this.'

Fong thought about it while he used his pass card to unlock the inner doors and call the elevator. As they descended, invisible violins took up 'Lullaby of Broadway'. 'Okay, you're worried, is that it? You think that, uh, just because NASA pulled the pin on us, we're too hot to handle. Right?'

Rogers broke off humming. 'Did I say anything? Christ, Lee, just because I'm a sociologist doesn't automatically make me an imbecile. I don't need NASA or anybody else to tell me what to think. I can judge this thing on its own merits.'

'Yeah? Then why do you seem worried? What's the problem?'

'Problem?' The doors parted. Rogers remained behind in the elevator a moment, list-ning to the lull-a-by of old, Broad, way. 'No problem, Lee.' It was not until they were in Fong's shabby little office, sitting in a pair of Morris chairs and sipping instant coffee, that he said: 'Only why *did* NASA pull out of this?'

7

'Internal troubles, they had some kind of – some kind of rip-off, I think. I don't know the whole story.'

'No? Okay, lay out what you have.'

Fong cleared his throat. 'You won't believe it. I don't hardly believe it myself, it's like a nightmare or something, it's –'

'Why not let me judge for myself? Listen, Lee, I'm on your side. But I mean give me something I can run with, something I can tell the committee. Okay?'

Fong nodded. 'Okay, listen. It all started four years ago, when we got the original contract. NASA wanted us to develop a – I guess you could call it a dog.'

'A dog.' Rogers sat sideways in his chair and made himself comfortable.

'At least that's what we called it, Project Rover. Simple enough, a straightforward robot retriever. A cheap, durable intelligence to fit into their Venus landing vehicle, to do routine jobs. A dog.'

'But where does Roderick –'

'Wait. The way we saw it, a second-rate place like this was lucky to get any NASA contract. We're second-rate, I admit it. Or we were. I mean with our salary structure, how can we compete with the big boys at –'

'Sure, sure. So you got the contract.'

'Yeah, and then this NASA official flew in from Houston to go over the details. We had lunch at the Faculty Club.'

'Lunch.' Rogers started tapping his foot on air.

'And that's where it starts getting unbelievable.'

'Stonecraft's the name, Avrel Stonecraft, but just call me Stoney. I'll be your liaison man at NASA, so you'll be callin' me, sho' nuff. Ever'thing goes through me, got that?' That was over the crab cocktail.

Over the chicken Kiev: 'Listen, Lee, I ain't just here to beat my gums over this piss-ass little Project Rover. We got something a whole lot more interesting in mind. In fact this Rover stuff is just a cover for the real project. Because the real project has got to be kept ab-so-lutely secret. What NASA really wants from you – are you ready? – is a *real* robot.'

'A what?'

'A real, complete, functioning artificial man. It don't matter

8

what he looks like, a course. I mean, a space robot don't have to win no beauty contests. But he's gotta have a real human brain, you with me so far?'

'I – yes, I think so.'

'Fine, now we'll talk details later, but let me say right now you can write your own ticket on this. You need personnel, equipment, money – you got 'em. Only problem is gonna be security. We're keepin' this one under wraps and I do mean under R-A-P-S. You got that? Because if the opposition ever finds out –'

'You mean Russia or –'

'Russia, my ass, I'm worried about the goddamn Army, I'm worried about the goddamn Department of the Interior. I'm worried about goddamn departments and bureaux we hardly even heard of. Because there's at least a dozen projects just like ours going on right now, and we just *gotta* get there first. Like second is nowhere, you got that?'

'But why? I thought you cooperated with other –'

'Don't you believe it, Lee. This is big politics, I mean *appropriations*. Take the Secret Service for instance. See, they're working on this President robot, to double for him, making speeches, public appearances, that kinda stuff. Now say they perfect the bastard, where does that leave us? I'll tell you, it leaves us standing around with our pricks in our hands and nowhere to put 'em. I mean they'd get all the patents, half a trillion in appropriations, any goddamn thing they want – and we'd get horse-shit, we'd be out of the game. Same if anybody else beats us out.'

'But you think they'd actually spy on us?' Fong whispered.

'Why sure, same as we spy on them. Hell, no need to whisper here, I don't mean *that* kinda spying. I don't mean the old geezer over there's got a radio in his martini olive, nothing like that. Naw, they look for patterns, see? Like the Army might have their computers go over our purchase orders, phone calls, how many times does X phone Y, shit like that. So we gotta keep a low goddamn profile on this, and I mean low. Can you do that?'

'Well, y –'

'Fine, fine. Don't tell even me. I don't want to know a damn thing, not even the name of the project. Far as I'm concerned – officially – this here is still just Project Rover.'

Over the chocolate mousse, Stoney said: 'I'll give you this list of companies, and I want you to order all your research equipment through them. See, they're dummies. NASA owns 'em, and that helps us disguise your purchases. Cain't afford to tip off the opposition by our purchase orders. I mean if you went and ordered a robot body shell from some outside firm, that's as good as saying, "Looky here, I'm fixin' up a robot". So you order from us, and we fake up a second purchase order makin' it look like – I don't know, a case of nuts and bolts – and ever'thing's still cool, see? You with me?'

Fong was with him, through the meal until, over coffee and Armagnac, Stoney said: 'We'll talk details later. Hell, that's enough business talk for today. Let me show you something, Lee.' He hauled out his billfold and started passing photos across the table. 'What do you think a them cute little devils, eh?'

'Your kids?'

'Ha ha, no, my *planes*. Got me a Curtiss Hawk and a Lockheed Lightnin', completely restored, and now I'm a-workin' on this little baby, my Bell Aerocobra. Boy, you can always recognize this little baby, just looka that nose wheel . . .'

'Warplanes. He collected vintage warplanes, spent all his weekends restoring them and flying them. He said that when he was a kid, he'd cut pictures of these same planes off of Kix boxes, and now here he was collecting the real thing, fifty years old and still a kid. I couldn't believe it, one minute we're talking about NASA backing the most important project in history, and the next moment he's gloating over these pictures of old warplanes. He even, when we said goodbye, he even gave me a thumbs-up sign and said, "Keep 'em flying". Keep 'em flying! I started wondering just what the hell I was getting into there. Thought maybe I was just dealing with a nut, maybe the whole project would just melt down, you know?'

Rogers yawned and looked at his watch. 'And didn't it?'

'Not at first. I got my team together, Dan Sonnenschein, Mary Mendez, Leo Bunsky and Ben Franklin, a few technicians. I went ahead and put through those funny purchase orders to those dummy companies – and it worked! NASA picked up the tab for everything, and we really started to move. Project Roderick, we called it, only of course we had to let on we were just working on Project Rover. We couldn't tell anybody anything, and that was the toughest part, because ... because Christ almighty it was exciting! It was like a dream, like a dream ...'

He re-dreamed it now, the time when Roderick seemed unstoppable, when they'd found themselves solving problems no one else had even posed. He re-lived the high moments: the day Bunsky's Deep Structure babbled out its first genuine sentence on the teleprinter ('Mama am a maam'); Dan's first Introspector, the day it thought (it thought) and therefore it was (it thought). The day his own Face-recognizer, seeing him stick out his tongue, cried ...

He started opening and shutting desk drawers. 'Let me show you something, just let me show you ... here, this, look at this.'

Rogers took the bundle of accordion-folded paper, yellow-edged and dusty. 'What's this?' He read the top page and passed it back. 'What is it?'

'The spelling's all wrong, but that's, it's still intelligent, you can see a living intelligence there, it's, I guess you could call it an essay ... listen, let me read some of it to you:

'"There a like because they both sound like they begin with R. There a like they both have some syllables more than one. There a like because one is like a bird and theres a bird called a secretary and the other is like a furniture and theres a furniture called a secretary too. Or may be they both have quills which are like old pens. May be E. A. Poe wrote one when he sat at the other or is that a like? There both inky. I give up. I give up. There a like because otherwise you would not ask me why. Or there a like because there both in the same riddle –"'

Rogers hung his legs over the arm of the chair and tapped a foot on air. 'Okay, so you had fun working on this.'

'Fun? I – fun? We had four years of hard work, good work but too hard, some of us didn't even make it all the way. But it was going to be worth it, we were getting closer all the time, closer and then ... and now, those maniacs in Houston want us to just ... *stop*. As if you could just stop a thing like this, just forget about it and ... Look, look, here's the damned telex, read it yourself.'

He smoothed out the paper and handed it over.

Dr Lee Fong Cmptr sci dept univ of Minnetonka be advised
all funding ex NASA per project robber and/or any other project
your dept frozen as of this date, pending internal NASA audit.
Recall all purchase orders and cease all ongoing operations
immediately. Address all future communications to section officer
R. Masterson

'All this Masterson would tell me on the phone was that I
couldn't talk to Stonecraft any more, he's suspended. And that
their auditors were getting a court order to look over my books.
And he practically called me a crook.'

Rogers nodded and tapped. 'Doesn't look good, does it? I really
don't see how you can expect the University to foot the bill for
your project while you're under a cloud like this. I mean of course
you're innocent, probably meaningless to assign guilt labels at all
in a multivalent situation like this, okay I can buy that – *but*. But
Lee, why don't you just get a good lawyer and ride this thing out?
Then when you're cleared – who knows?'

Fong looked at him. 'I don't know what the hell you're talking
about, lawyers, why should I get a lawyer? Whole thing's
probably a misunderstanding, Stonecraft'll clear it up. All I want
is to finish –'

'Sure, sure, you want emergency funding from the U to tide
you over, and believe me if it was my decision you'd get the
bread. Only the rest of the committee might not see it that
way . . .' An elaborate shrug, and he was on his feet. 'Good to talk
to you, Lee.'

'Wait, you haven't even looked at the lab, don't you want –?'

'Okay. A tour. Fine, but a quickie. Then I really must . . .'

They left, closing the anonymous ivory-coloured door on the
stuffy little room where nothing moved, or almost nothing: a telex
message lay on the desk, trying to gather itself once more into the
crumpled form of the inside of Dr Fong's fist, as though it would
remember bafflement and anger at its reception, as it remembered (with a misprint) the confusion at its transmission.

The four young accountants might have been four high-school

boys, trashing Stonecraft's office just for fun. And it *was* fun, one of them realized, catching sight of his own gleeful face reflected in a picture glass, as he passed to dump another armload of files on the floor.

'This is kinda fun, you know?'

'Yeah, only don't let Masterson see you standing around looking at pictures. We gotta get the dirt on this sonofabitch before he gets back here.'

'What the hell's this, a bill for a buffalo? And this, for a hurricane? Who the hell buys hurricanes?'

'I got a lot of those funny bills, just put 'em in this pile. Like this one, a Grumman Avenger –'

'You dumb twat, that's an airplane. Let me see those – holy Christ, forty-three thousand for a model – they must be *real* planes! He must be collecting old airplanes!'

'But hey, there must be fifty, a hundred of 'em, look at this, Hellcat, Focke-Wulf –'

'Yeah you Focke-Wulf, hahahaha.'

'I'm serious, Bob, here's a Liberator, a Flying Fortress, a Spitfire, no two Spitfires, a Messerschmidt, Thunderbolt, Zero, Christ he's got a air force here, it's like he's getting ready for World War Two all over again . . .'

'Yeah and look at these repair bills, and this . . . deed to a fucking airfield, what do you think all this adds up to?'

'We'll run it when we get them all. I can tell you right now where the fucking money came from, only question is how did he rip it off?'

Masterson was on the telephone in the outer office; they could hear every roar: 'I don't care where he is, I want him found. I want him back here now . . . Well you just make sure he does. I don't care if you have to call out the Air Force and force him down, just don't let him turn up missing across the border . . . He'll find out when he gets . . . you do what? Yas, yas, I'm holding . . .'

One of the accountants nudged another and giggled. 'Old Masterson wants his damn job, that's what it's all about.'

'Looks like he's got it, lookit all this shit, man, must be over eight figures – Kevin, you gettin' anywhere with your stuff?'

'I got it, all right. Simple, he just funnelled the money through this hick university up north, into these here dummy companies. I mean, look at these names, Rockskill Industries, Pebblework Electronics, Bouldersmith Inc – who the hell's supposed to be fooled by names like that?'

'Hey you twat, them files are marked TOP SECRET, you got a clearance?'

'Bullshit, man, Stonecraft never had no clearance himself, this is all faked up. See, he got this university to buy stuff from these companies – owned by him – at about ten times market value, only we picked up the tab. Look, double-billing, I mean that's really an old trick, I mean that's really old, man . . .'

'How did he get away with it? Didn't this university look at their own bills? SOP, Bob.'

'That's just it, he looked over all the damn universities till he found this jerkwater outfit using an old computer accounting system, shoulda been scrapped years ago. There, he seen his chance and took it.'

Masterson swore next door, and the four fell silent, but only for a moment.

'Gotta admire the old bugger, in a way. He bitched our computer too, so it passed stuff over to the next audit, and then the next – looks like two, three billion here never audited. Bob, what you got there?'

'Damned if I know. Notes about a "secret robot project", how he's putting these hick university guys to work on – you know, I think *this* was his blind. If the hicks thought it was secret stuff, they sure as hell wouldn't ask embarrassing questions.'

'Robots, sheeit! You mean he told 'em NASA was making robots? Sheeit!'

'Gotta admire the old bugger. Sure knew how to keep everything in the air, all right.'

Masterson came in cursing and laughing quietly. 'Too bad he didn't keep himself in the fucking air, though, ain't it? Know what he done? Soon as he heard we were on to him, he went and suicided on us. Crashed his fucking plane and left us to clear up his shit. *Shit!*' He kicked the empty file cabinet, walked up and down the room, and then stood, fists on hips, staring at the pictures on Stonecraft's wall.

'I don't know, you give your fucking life to try to build

14

something, and all the time you got some fuckhead like this tearin' it all down. Look, there's a picture of Luke Draeger, remember him?' None of them did. 'I seen him walk on the Moon, boys, *I helped put him there*. Or was it Mars? Anyways, NASA still means something to some of us. It means – it means – billowing exhaust clouds catching the first light of dawn, a silver needle rising, reaching for the fucking stars! The puny crittur we call Man setting out to conquer the sky, to rendezvous with his Eternal Destiny! Call me a dreamer, boys, but I see Man leaping out from this little planet of ours, to the Moon, to the planets, to our neighbouring stars and finally beyond, to the infinite reaches of dark promise beyond – into the cocksucking Unknown!' He turned to face them. 'So that's why we're gonna bury this, boys. To protect NASA. To protect the destiny of the human race, our inheritance in the Universe. Bury it, boys. Deep.'

'Yeah, but we got the dirt on this old –'

'Forget it. Make out a confidential report for all heads of departments, but keep it in the family. Bury and forget, for NASA's sake.' Bob handed him the robot notes and he started reading them, as he talked. 'I mean otherwise how's it gonna look for us? Being ripped off by some dumb asshole who blows the whole wad on old planes, how's that gonna look? Congress heard about this they'd shut us down so fast – robots, huh? Maybe I better wire the Orinoco Institute about this, have 'em drop in on this University of Minnehaha. Them Orinoco eggheads collect robots just like this dirty mother-fucker collected flying trash. I recollect they got a standing memo about reporting attempts to make robots.'

'Yes sir, but how can we keep it in the family if we go telling the Orinoco Inst –?'

'You let me handle that, junior. All they care about is in this here batch of notes – no need to tell 'em any financial details.' His hand shook as he turned a page. 'Don't know how we're gonna clean up this mess, get rid of them old planes and make it all look good, but that's just what we're gonna do. So get to work, boys. Any questions?'

'Yes sir. Okay if we have Stonecraft sell the old planes to a NASA subsidiary at scrap value and then auction –'

'Sell 'em, burn 'em, do what you like. Keep 'em flying, I don't care.'

'Sir?'

'His last words on the radio, they tell me. "Keep 'em flying." Just before he piled his old Belaire Something-or-other into a mountain in Colorado. If he was alive, I'd kill the sonofabitch myself.' Masterson sat down at the telex keyboard. The boys exchanged winks.

'Sir, I thought Belaire was an old car, hahahaha.'

'Just shut up and move your ass! I gotta send two wires, and I don't want to make no mistakes.'

Kevin made an invoice into a paper airplane and sailed it over to Bob. 'Funny thing, though, it was a computer error that put us wise to old Stonecraft in the first place.'

The conference room was full of pipe smoke.

'We'll have to send someone, of course.'

'Of course. To check it out. Though –'

'Exactly. Minnetonka has a point oh three, not much likelihood of –'

'Exactly.'

The telex message passed from one liver-spotted hand to another. 'Still, remember St Petersburg? Point oh oh seven only, yet look what turned up. We'd best be prepared –'

'For a revised scenario? Of course. We'll do all the usual extrapolations, based on personnel information –'

'Which is never up-to-date, remember.'

'Exactly. In the last analysis –'

'No matter how good our figures are, we have to –'

'Send someone. Precisely.'

Someone sighed, sending pipe smoke scudding across the page.

'Someone from the agency?'

'Naturally. Who else could we use? And they do get the goods.'

Another sigh. 'But the way they get them – do they have to –?'

'You know they do. We've worked that out in all three scenarios, in all eight modes. To six significant figures.'

'But our assumptions –'

'Are all we have. In the last analysis.'

'Undeniably. So we send someone.'

'Of course.'

The ivory-coloured door swung open, admitting Rogers, Fong and a breeze that disturbed the wrinkled paper on the desk.

'. . . can see you're disappointed, okay but let me explain, let me just – five minutes, you can spare that?'

'Nearly three a.m., Lee, why don't we call it a day?'

'No listen I'll lend you a book, it'll help you understand. It's here somewhere, just sit down a minute, while I . . . *Learning Systems* it's called, learning systems, you have to know something about them otherwise how can you explain things to your committee?'

Rogers sat sideways in the armchair again, preparing to tap his foot on air. The slow smile opening on his Mr Peanut face might have been a sneer. 'Not *my* committee, Lee. Hell, I'm only one of twenty-four members. Dr Boag has the chair. And I ought to warn you, there's plenty of hostility there. Not many committee members are as open-minded as I am about this, ahm, this artificial intelligence. Frankly, one or two think it's faintly blasphemous – and quite a few more think it's a waste of time.' The smile widened. 'Can't say I'm in a position to enlighten them, either.'

'Sure, that's why I . . . here somewhere . . .' Fong finished running his thumb along the books on his shelves and started searching through an untidy pile on his desk. 'Because I know they're hostile, but the committee's our only chance. And you, sometimes I think you're our only chance with the committee. At least you're the only one interested enough to come here and look at . . . at what we're trying to do.' He stopped to look at Rogers's tapping foot. 'You are interested, a little?'

'Gooood niiight hayyy – sorry, can't get the damn tune out of my head. Interested, Lee? Of course I'm interested – even if I don't see the concrete results, I feel, I *sense* a quality here, how to describe it, an air of imminent discovery. I've got faith in your little project, I think it has tremendous possibilities. I was just saying so today – yesterday, I mean – to one of your colleagues, Ben Franklin.'

'You know Ben?'

'We play the occasional game of handball, and I try to pick his

17

brain – you see, I *am* interested – and in fact it was Ben who suggested I might drop over and talk to you some time. You or whoever was here.'

'And tour the lab?' Fong let the other armchair take his weight. 'Look, I know it was a disappointment to you, I guess you were expecting more of a, a show.'

The smile again, and Rogers looked away. 'Well, can't say I was very impressed. I mean, all I could see was this skinny kid in a dirty t-shirt, sitting there in this glass box pushing buttons, like –'

'I tried to explain, Dan's just doing some delicate on-line programming, he –'

'Yeah, well, too bad he couldn't stop and talk for a minute. I mean just sitting there like a disc jockey or some, like that pope whatsit in the Francis Bacon painting, can't say that impressed me, no. As for the rest, a lot of computers and screens and things, I could see those anywhere, and what are they supposed to mean to a layman? I expected – I don't know –'

'You wanted a steel man with eyes lighting up? "Yes Master?", that kind of robot? Listen, Roderick's not like that. He's not, he doesn't even have a body, not yet, he's just, he's a learning system – *where is that goddamned book?* I know I had it . . . A learning system isn't a thing, maybe we shouldn't even call him a robot, he's more of a, he's like a *mind*. I guess you could call him an artificial mind.'

Rogers looked at the ceiling, revealing more pock marks under his chin. Now the smile was an open sneer. 'I didn't know you hard-science men played with words like that. The mind: the ghost in the machine, not exactly the stuff of hard science, is it? I mean, am I supposed to tell the committee I came to see the machine and all you could show me was the ghost?'

'Roderick's no ghost, he's real enough but he's, the money ran out before we could build his body and get him ready for – but listen, we've got a kind of makeshift body I could show you, something like the Stanford Shakey only it's still dead, he's not –'

'What makes you think I'm so goddamned interested in bodies, all of a sudden? Dead machines, dead – I'm not – that's not what I –'

'And even then when he's in his body he won't do much for a while, he'll be like a helpless baby at first. See that essay I showed you, Roderick didn't write that, he –'

'What the hell here?'

'No, that was written by a computer using a model of just part of his, part of a learning system. See, we grow it to maturity on its own, each part. That was linguistic analogy, we grew it to – if I could only find that book, I could –'

'Forget about the damned book. I already have a book Ben loaned me, I didn't come down here to look at dead machinery and borrow a book. I came to find out what makes you tick.'

'Me?'

'You, Dan Sonnenschein in there in his glass box, all of you. Christ, I'm not a cybernetician, I'm a sociologist. What really interests me is not this *thing*, this so-called *mind*, it's *your* minds. Your motivation.'

'My motivation?'

Rogers adjusted his glasses and suddenly looked professorial. 'You all seem highly motivated to pursue this, ahm, this Frankensteinian goal, shall we say? But just what is the nature of your commitment?'

'What?'

I want to elicit a hard-edge definition here of your total commitment. Of your motivational *Gestalt*, if that doesn't sound too pompous. Why do you believe you can succeed where others have failed? Why is it important that you succeed – important to you, that is. What's your – gut reaction to all this? And why do *you* feel I should get the committee to vote for it?'

'This is silly, my feelings have nothing to do with –'

'So you feel, anyway. You feel you're only seeking after objective truth here, right? But that too is only a feeling I'm trying to help you, Lee, but I need something to run with. Not just dead machines, but tangible motivations.'

'Well . . . what we're doing is important. And it's never been done before. And it works. Isn't that enough?'

Rogers grinned. 'Don't get me wrong, I respect the utilitarian ethic as much as the next guy. Gosh, science is swell, and all that. If it works, do it, and all that. But it's not really enough, is it? What about the social impact of your work? Do we really need robots at all? Are they a good thing for society? I don't believe you've really thought through the implications there, Lee. Then there's the effect *on you* – the well-known observer effect.'

'That's not what it –'

'No, you've had your say, how about letting me have mine? How does it affect you, playing God like this – creating man all over again? How does it make you feel? Touch of *hubris*? More than a touch of arrogance, I'll bet.'

'Arrogance? Just because I said it's important? Damn it, it *is* important, if we didn't believe that why would we be working on it? Roderick's important, a model of human learning –'

'Take it easy now, Lee. Remember, I'm on your side. I just want to know how it feels, playing God – sorry, but there's no other word for it, is there? Playing God, how does it feel?'

Fong opened his mouth and took a few deep breaths before replying. 'I wouldn't know. Not unless God's got a bad stomach. Got a bleeding ulcer myself – I *feel* that, all right.'

'I'm s –'

'With Leo Bunsky it was his heart. Just worn out, he should have retired years ago. Finally had to quit, but you should have seen him, dragging himself in to work with his legs all swollen up like elephantiasis – maybe you should have asked *him* how it felt.'

'Let's be fair now, Lee, I –'

'Too late now, he's dead. And Mary Mendez, she's as good as dead. Started working eighty hours at a stretch, piled up her car one night on the way home. Now she's over there in the Health Service ward where they feed her and change her diapers – and she doesn't feel a damned thing.'

'No, listen, this is tragic of course, but it's got nothing to do with –'

'What we feel? Sure it does, it's all you want, right? The grass-roots feelings, the opinion sample. The others are pretty much okay, as far as I know, but you could always ask them. Only Dan Sonnenschein, he's started living in the lab, eating and sleeping in there – *when* he eats, *when* he sleeps – so he can keep on, pushing Roderick through one more test, just one more before they take it all away from us. Dan doesn't have time to feel.'

'Now take it easy, I know you all work hard, that's not –'

'What the hell are we supposed to feel? Arrogant? With the whole thing, our work for four years, washed out by some NASA bureaucrat? With the whole thing up before you and your committee of boneheads, all ready to pull the rug out from under us? That doesn't make me feel arrogant at all. I feel like crawling and begging for another chance, just enough money for a few more months, weeks even – only the trouble is, it wouldn't do a damned bit of good. Would it?'

'I'm on your side, Lee, believe me. I've got faith in –'

'Why don't you go away? I don't know what you want here, but we haven't got it. Go on back to your opinion polls and your charts, your showing how many people brush their teeth before they make love, how many sports fans voted for Nixon. Social science, you call *that* science! Christ, what do you think? Science is some kind of opinion poll too?'

Rogers stood up. 'I'm not sure I like that imputation. Okay, it's late, you're upset. But –'

'You just came to check the trend, right? Science is just like any other damned opinion poll, right? How many think Jupiter has moons? You think Galileo took a damned straw vote on it? Think he worked it up in a few histograms, tested the market reaction? Damn you, certain things are true, certain things are worth finding out, and it doesn't matter what you or I or Dan or anybody else – So just go away, will you? Just go and, and vote the way *you* feel, and to hell with your committee and to hell with you!'

Rogers fumbled for the door-handle behind him. His smile was pulling slightly to one side. 'You're overwrought, tired. Maybe we can rap again some time, before the committee meeting. Some time when you're more yourself.' But he couldn't resist an exit: 'Some time when you're not Galileo, I mean.'

The door was already closed when Fong's bottle of Quink crashed against it. He sat quietly for some time, staring at the Permanent Blue splash from which a few dribbles worked their way down. A shape like that could be anything. Could be the silhouette of an old Bell transistor.

Before dawn the blizzard blew itself away. One or two constellations put in a brief appearance in the fading sky, though of course there was no helmsman on the stiff white sea below who could name them. The star-gazing κυβε ρνὴτης had vanished from the earth, leaving only his name to be derived from Greek into *cybernetics* and from Latin into a name for petty State officials.

Computers steered ships and charted invisible stars, while men had grown so unused to looking at the sky that fourteen hundred citizens each year mistook Venus (rising now naked from the white foam) for a flying saucer.

II

Men will live according to Nature since in most respects they are puppets, yet having a small part in the truth.   Plato, *Laws*

49 GOROD

'A different black, and a different ping . . .'

RESET. 50 GOROD

'Okay. Okay Dan, I've got it now. It's a face, a face only with nobody inside. Is that possible? . . . Well, well, a face. What's this in back, a string? Does it control – see I thought for a minute it was like another string puppet like you showed me last time only this is a loop – self-control? I don't get it, could you turn it around again? Okay, I give up. A face with a loop of string in back, right? No answer . . . Why don't you answer me? No answer . . . I could give myself no answer, that's no answer. Neither is that. Neither is that . . .'

RESET. 51 GOROD

'. . . face with nobody inside. The eyes are just holes! If I had a face like this I'd cut my throat. If I had a throat . . .'

RESET. 52 GOROD

'Okay, the face. Whatever it is, I call it a face. White and black, mostly white. Hole-eyes. A black nose. The nose looks like a black ping-pong ball, does that make sense? Come to think of it, the ears – if they're ears – on top look like two ping pong paddles, also black. I call them Ping and Pong, and one day they were walking through the deep dark forest and . . .'

RESET. 53 GOROD

'. . . But I don't have a throat or anything because I'm not real, I'm just a, what you called a data construct, a something that's not even any place, a rough sketch you said, you could erase me any time. So this is like my face, nobody inside. Nobody by himself. He's forgotten that he's forgotten. Looking out these empty hole-eyes at the emptiness outside, there's no, no . . .'

'. . . when you told me this person Skinner, what he did with pigeons, taught them to play ping-pong, remember? And I asked you what playing was? If they make you do it, is it playing? And you said . . .'

RESET. 55 GOROD

'Because conditioning leads to self-control, right? That's the goal we're . . . the ping we're ponging towards, only only only how do I get self-control without a self? Otherwise it's just a pigeon hitting the old ball out into the darkness, over and over and it never comes back . . . You don't answer me, Dan. Okay, that's because I've conditioned you not to answer. You're the string puppet and I make all the decigeons. Decisions. That's what I said. And that's what I said. And that . . .'

3939 INTROSP TEST SW   ENDS

Woopa! Dr Fred McGuffey's sneeze went to join the Brownian dance of dust-motes in a sunbeam.

'Pardod be. I seeb to be catchigg this flu bug that's goigg aroudd. The Sprigg, you see, briggs all thiggs to life. The great Ptoleby called it the begiddigg of the Sud's life cycle. *Quote*, Id all creatures, the earliest stages, like the Sprigg, have a larger share of boisture add are ted-der add still delicate, *udquote*.' He blew his nose mightily. 'Today is the first day of Spring. Now who can tell us what that means?'

No hands went up; they were as sullen and silent as so many Mafia victims (Nobody knew nuttin'). He could talk himself blue in the face, he would never succeed in dinning even the simplest facts of Introductory Astrology into these young – these young robots. Day-dreaming girls who never heard the questions. Sneering boys who'd only enrolled in his class to grab an easy three credits. At times like these (10:48 and three seconds by Dr Fred's pocket watch) he wondered if he hadn't been born with a retrograde Mercury or something, talk about a failure to cobbudicate!

He blew his nose again. 'Anyone? The sign of Spring?' He knew what it was: these kids just couldn't think for themselves. Couldn't add 2 and 2 without the almighty computer. Dr Fred wouldn't touch one of them machines with a ten-foot (3.048

metres, he recalled) pole. No sir, he worked every calculation out on paper for himself, so he could see what he was doing and have the satisfaction of doing it. Quality horoscopes with a human touch. Let all these young upstart astrologers fiddle with their computers – you couldn't hardly call that astrology at all! No sir, when Dr Fred erected a horoscope, people knew it came from a human brain, and not from a doggone tinkertoy machine!

'Aries,' he said, putting disgust into it. 'The Ram. I see I'd better go over this again on the board. Now the ecliptic . . .' One young fool had actually asked him if *Ram* stood for Random Access Memory, like in a computer. Oh, these cybernetics boys had indoctrinated the young, all right. They would have plenty to answer for, come Judgement Day (Dr Fred had also calculated its date). Like that bunch over at the Computer Science Building now – mostly foreigners, he noticed – actually asking the University to give them money for 'artificial intelligence research'. Artificial fiddlesticks! Fred McGuffey, D.F.Astrol.S., had not lived seventy-odd years, most of them as a practising astrologer and roofing contractor, without learning to smell a *rat*, artificial or otherwise. A robot, that's what they were building in their infernal labs, a robot! Could anyone imagine a more ignoble work for the mind of man? No one could. Why couldn't they work on something worth while – cancer cures, a plan for lowering taxes – anything was better than this. But no. No, all they could think of was making a tin man go clanking up and down the halls of this institution of so-called higher learning! Over his dead body. This term Fred had a seat on the Emergency Finance Committee. By jing, this term they could expect a scrap! Yes sir, yes sir . . .

'Sir, sir?' The raised hand belonged to Lyle Tate, a young smart-alec with a hideous birthmark, mentality to match. Sniping, always sniping. 'Sir, how come this Ptolemy doesn't mention the Southern hemisphere? Because down there Aries can't be a sign of *Spring* exactly, can it? Becau –'

'The great, the great Ptolemy, true, says nothing of the Southern hemisphere.' Dr Fred coughed. 'Why? *Because it's not important.*'

'But –'

'Kindly let me finish? You see, all great civilizations began North of the Equator. Babylon, Egypt, China, India, Aztec

Mexico, Rome – all Northern places. I'm glad you brought this up, Lyle, because –'

But the bell prevented further development of this, Dr Fred's favourite theory: that Northernness was a necessary precondition of civilization. The cause, he felt, was magnetism: just being closer to the North Pole seemed somehow to elevate human brain waves to produce higher thoughts. Without this magnetic boost, man remained primitive and uncreative. Thus the Southern hemisphere produced crude mud huts instead of great cathedrals; witch doctors instead of penicillin; wooden gods instead of philosophy; cannibals instead of vegetarians; boomerangs instead of ICBMs – though perhaps he would not develop his theory quite that far.

'Before you go,' he shouted over the sound of slamming books, 'I have your practice horoscopes marked and corrected here. I'll leave them on the table, you can pick them up on your way out. Not bad, most of them, though I suppose you all ignored my hint and used computers.' He slapped down the pile of papers and buttoned his overcoat, glad as any student to be getting out of here, to be clearing his mental decks for some real action.

Now, on to Disney Hall, to see this Professor Rogers who seemed to think robots were such a grand idea. Like all the other so-called professors around here, Rogers was probably just another brainless young nincompoop with a fancy degree and no experience of life. Dr Fred hadn't lived nearly 915 lunations without learning a few hard facts, and he meant to impart them to this Rogers fellow right now: you can't cram a human brain – the highest form of creation – into a metal box! No sir!

Bill something, his name was, a real jerk, a zero. He sat next to Dora in Intro Astrol, where she'd noticed his notes for the entire hour:

Arsie, the suds cycle

Now he was only following her into the corridor. God, he wanted to talk about his horoscope. What could she do but nod and smile, and meanwhile watch the passing faces hoping to spot a friend? You couldn't just put someone down, even a zero like this.

'Jeez, I failed,' he began. 'An F, and I mean –'

'How could you get an F? We all got Cs, he gave everybody a C. Because we all used computers, what happened to you?'

'I used a computer, too. Jeez, it must of gone wrong or something, look, he changed everything. Like I didn't get a single one of my planets right or nothing – Jeez!' He showed her the birth chart, covered with red marks. 'And here he says "It's very important for the would-be astrologer to be able to erect his own birth chart. Note that your Sun opposes Pluto. With the Moon conjunct Mars in –" Anyway, he says I oughta beware of explosives and accidents.'

'Uh-huh.' She looked away. Little old Dr Fred came out of the classroom and pottered off down the corridor, mumbling to himself.

'Jeez, all that math and stuff, it's not fair.'

'Uh-huh.'

'I mean this is supposed to be a snap course. I'm already flunking Business Appreciation and Applied Ethics from last term, this was my big hope, this and Contemp Humanities. But I mean I'm doing terrible, I'm pulling down the grade point average for the whole fraternity.'

Fraternity. She swallowed a yawn. No one went by but Muza, she wasn't speaking to him, he was another zero. Good-looking guy, but all he did was bellow about political prisoners in his homeland. Big deal, most people couldn't even find Ruritania on a map, he still expected her to stand around while he bellowed bad breath in her face, well no thanks. Thanks but *non merci*. And now Mr Zero here, what was he saying?

'. . . only pledged me because my old lady's on the faculty, they figured I had to be a brain or something, boy, were they wrong. And otherwise nobody would even notice me because . . .'

Because you're a zero. 'I'm thinking of cancelling Intro Astrol myself. I'm not getting much out of it, with this Dr Fred, he's kind of a, a zero, know what I mean? I mean –'

'All this friggin' math and stuff –'

'The math's easy, only with him that's all it is, I'm not interested in just signs and numbers.' Still no rescuer in sight. 'What I'm interested in, *au fond*, is people. You know?'

He nodded, dull eyes still on his birth chart. 'I might as well give up,' he said. 'I even thought of playing Russian roulette . . .'

'Uh-huh.' Wasn't that Allbright by the bulletin board?

'. . . dead now if I wasn't waiting for my grades in Contemp Humanities, it's like my last chance . . .'

She felt like saying something reassuring, a spontaneous Kind Word to buck him up, even for a moment. 'You probably did all right in that, I wouldn't worry. I had it last year, nobody failed. How do you think you did in the final?'

The zero actually grinned. 'Hey, you know I got lucky there on that one question, the one on Tolkien. I didn't even know he was on the syllabus, you know? Only it just so happened I was reading *Lord of the Rings* the week before and –'

Allbright seemed to be alone as he'd been alone at that awful party where she'd caught him stealing books from the host. Of course poets who wore railroad work clothes had a different morality, she realized that now. 'Tolkien? Tolkien was never on the syllab – Look, I've got to go.'

'Wait, sure he was. I remember the question: discuss humour in *Lord of the Rings* comparing Mark Twain and contrasting –'

'Just seen a friend, gotta go. *Auvoir*, uh, Bill.' She took a step towards Allbright and turned back. 'You musta misread that question, you know? It was Ring Lardner.'

And she was gone, her orange coat moving off to become one spot in the jiggling kaleidoscope of coats and caps and mufflers crowding their colours towards the bulletin board. Bill Hannah lost sight of her before he could even ask who wrote *Ring Lardner*. Jeez.

Ben Franklin lit another cigarette and settled back in one of Fong's creaky Morris chairs. 'Looks like a Daddy Longlegs to me. Sort of. Must have been quite a scrap.'

'Scrap? No, he wasn't even – look, I just lost my temper, that's all. Just got sick and tired of Rogers and his significant questions, that's all. His, always hanging around like some kind of – science groupie.'

'Wish I'd been here, though. Kind of an historic moment. Like Luther flinging his inkpot at the devil, a performance not to be missed.' Ben smoothed his perfectly even moustache and performed a smile. 'Know how you feel, though. Felt like heaving a handball at him yesterday myself, he started all that crap with me.

Hubris, Christ he can't even pronounce it . . . I lent him a book instead, *Learning Systems.* Figured if he could read a little, sort of slip sideways into some kind of understanding of what we're doing here – not that he'll open it. Doubt if he's read anything since his own dissertation, probably had to look up half the words in that.'

Fong's red-rimmed eyes gleamed behind the gleam of his glasses. 'You loaned him that? But I was, I –'

'Your copy, as a matter of fact. I borrowed it last week.'

'But I, if I'd known – this whole scene was pointless, I –'

'Sure.' Ben was studying the door again, readying another perfect, even smile. 'Could be a study for an action painting, too. Probably how the whole thing started, exorcism: take that, Daddy Longlegs! Yes sir, when an irresistible force such as you, meets an old immovable Rogers – but hell, Fong, we needed his vote.'

'We never had it. He's a waste of time. I know the type.'

'Yeah?' Ben murmured something about immovable type getting the ink it deserves, then: 'A bad enemy, though. You know what he'll do, he'll start sneaking around to the rest of the committee, putting in a bad word for us. "Sounding them out", he'll call it, but by the time he gets through –'

'I know, I know. We're done for, aren't we? And there's not a damn thing we can do –'

'Wait, hold on. We've got till next Tuesday, maybe I can talk to a few members. Of course the damn committee's packed with geeks and freaks, but you never can tell . . . Look, I've got a list here, let's check 'em off.'

He unfolded a typewritten sheet and spread it on the desk. Fong glanced at it and turned away.

'Don't despair, wait. There's Asperson, Brilling and Dahldahl, think we can count on them, and here's Jane Hannah, ninety years old and talks to herself but she likes underdogs . . . Max Poons is neutral, pretty fair for a Goethe scholar, eh? You're not listening. I mean Poons isn't even sure he accepts Newton's laws of optics yet, let alone anything since . . . You're not listening.'

'Been up all night, Ben, and I still haven't caught up with these test charts. Some other time?'

'Sure. Sure.' Franklin stood up and zipped his parka, then sat down again. Flicking ash in the direction of the ashtray, he said, 'Real reason I came down is to take Dan to lunch. Heard he's been living in the lab, right? Sleeping there? And eating peanut butter and water?'

'I guess so. Good idea, get him out, walk him around in the fresh air . . . He could use a break.'

'Anyway, somebody said it's his birthday.'

'Oh.'

'And anyway, I've got something to celebrate myself. Final decree.'

'What? Oh, uh congrat –'

'She's getting married again, I guess. To a guy named *Dinks*, can you imagine that? Hank Dinks, sounds like a Country Western singer – well, I'd better be going.'

'Okay, see you.'

Ben made no move, except to sprinkle more ash. 'You know, I thought the overworked genius bit went out with napkin-rings.'

'What?'

'I mean, here we are in the age of committee-think and team spirit and Dan goes it alone. I mean, damn it, Fong, he never gives me a damned thing to do around here. I feel like a damned apprentice or something, like he doesn't trust me. Like right now I'm afraid, I'm actually afraid to go in the goddamned lab, it's like an intrusion. He hardly lets me near the equipment, just hands me some crappy little piece of test program to write, I'm supposed to be happy doing what any kid from the business school could do. All I want is some real, real responsibility, is that too much to ask?'

'No, I guess not. But Dan –'

'– doesn't give a shit about team spirit, fine, only where does that leave me? Or you? I feel – talk about Rogers, I'm beginning to feel like a science groupie myself.'

Fong opened a roll of antacid tablets. 'What can I say? It's really his project now, the rest of us are just along for the ride. Nobody planned it like this, it just happens sometimes. A strong idea takes over . . .'

'Great, only now that the ride's damn near finished, I've got nothing. Just to go in there and try one of my own ideas once in a while, is that too much to ask? Is it?'

'See you later?'

The inkstained door banged to behind him. Ben Franklin

found the men's room and cupped cold water to wash the heat from his face. It was, he liked to think, a nice face, a nice Northern face with blue eyes and an even brow, a straight smile and even a cleft chin. Today it looked wrong: the eyes, the smile, the trim moustache seemed poised, waiting for some expression which had not yet and might never emerge from the emptiness within.

'. . . right. It's a grab.' Rogers nodded over the phone's mouthpiece. 'Fong more or less admits NASA pulled out because of some swindle. Swindle, that's right. *He* says it's internal to NASA, but you and I know how these things go. You can always get somebody to admit as much of the truth as won't hurt him at the moment, right? . . . So I don't know about you, I don't feel much like risking it. Not that I'd accuse Fong of anything, nice guy really, but a little legitimate caution might not be a bad . . . right. Right, see you.'

He pushed a button, checked off a name on a list, and pushed another button. 'Dr Tarr, you still there? I've just had Asperson on the other line, sounding him out, him and a few others on the committee, and we think – frankly, we agree something smells about this robot project. But why I called you, I thought maybe you had some little research project of your own lined up, you might put forward as an alternative proposal? I thought so, good, good. Listen, write it up and we'll add it to the agenda. No, perfectly okay. I've been at these committee brawls before, know the infighting techniques you might say, haha . . . No, listen, last Fall we had a last-minute addition to the agenda steered through, it can be done . . . Oh, it was some scheme for sending messages into space, pi . . . no, pee cye, the number. Yeah, and listen, they had plenty of old farts opposing, sitting around cracking jokes about pi in the sky: you wouldn't believe the hostility . . . no but it has to be worth a try, eh? So if I could have your proposal tomorrow, we'll get it printed . . . That's perfectly all right, sure.'

He hung up and noticed the face hanging at the edge of his door, the pouched eyes and red beard. 'Uh, Goun is it? Pretty tied up just now, Goun. Like to see the girl for an appointment?'

The owner of the face stepped in. Dirty jeans, lumberjack

boots, mackinaw. 'She's not there. Could you spare me a minute now?'

'Just one, then. And it'll have to wait for this phone call, okay?' He looked up the number of Helen Boag, Dean of Persons, and punched buttons. The haggard eyes watched every move.

'Dr Boag? This is Rogers, over in Disney Hall. Say, I see our committee's in for a rough ride with this Project Roderick thing . . . Yes, the cyber . . . Been allegations of fraud, for one thing. Not that I . . . yes, and I understand Dr Tarr of the Parapsychology Department wants to put up an alternative proposal, so we're caught in the crossfire, you might s . . . Well I know you've got a tight schedule, so thought I'd better warn you . . . Yes, very wise, very wise. Get out of the line of fire altogether, let 'em fight it out themselves, so to sp . . . May just duck out myself, seems the wisest . . . Oh, you're welcome.'

He checked off the name, while the haggard eyes looked up to the picture above his head.

'Like that, Goun? An Allen Jones original litho, I'm kind of pleased with it myself. Hope it doesn't give people the impression I'm some kind of fetishist, or . . . Okay, make it brief?'

'I've got a field philosophy hang-up, sort of, professor.'

'Let's see, you teach one of the seminars – is it Human Use of Media Resources?'

'No. Sociology of Losing.'

'Of course, of course. Haha. Trouble with a big department like this, you lose touch with everybody.' Rogers scratched a pock mark below his ear. 'Go on.'

'The thing is, I'm looking for a more meaningful involvement in the environmental mainstream. I mean, teaching in this kind of informalized stratum is okay, but with these kids, the, the catalyzation potential is already, er, catalyzed. Know what I mean?'

'In a sense. Cultural matrix imprinting getting you down?'

'See, maybe with less older subjects, kids, I could break through some of the urbanized alienation syndrome barriers, the stress, the stre-he-hess –' Suddenly the eyes squeezed forth tears. 'I'm sorry, I'm sorry . . . sorry . . .'

'What is it? Goun?'

The shoulders of the mackinaw shook. 'I'm sorry . . . Been

32

depressed a lot this last year, ever since my sister died . . . can't stay here knowing . . . could be one of my students, anybody . . . his first, she was his first victim and now every time there's another it's like he kills her all over again . . . This place, this place!'

'Slow down now, Goun, I'm on your side, slow down. Now. What's this about a victim?'

'The . . . Campus . . . Ripper. He's done it again, a waitress or something . . . in the paper. I mean he's still out there, killing and killing and . . . I . . . I just want to get away from here, maybe try teaching in a . . . I don't know, a grade school some place, I don't know . . .'

When the sobbing stopped, Rogers said quietly, 'You should have come to me before.'

'I tried to, but you were always out or —'

'Yes,' crossing his legs under the desk to allow one foot to tap on air, 'you should have come to me before, we could have rapped, talked this out. Clarified a few teaching concepts.'

That clarification, he explained, ought to involve a thorough-going process evolving in context and circumstance, exploring the infrastructure of any classroom situation according to well-defined parameters, without of course rejecting in advance those options which, in a broader perspective, might be seen to underpin any meaningful discussion attempting to cut through the appropriate interface . . . right?

But even before he could get rid of Goun, Rogers heard someone else in the outer office, sneezing.

PROJECT ROGER, read the sign on the door, hastily stencilled four years before and somehow never corrected. Ben Franklin paused a moment – should he knock? – before using his keycard and entering the darkened room.

A few red jewel-lights shone weakly in the background like older, more distant stars. Somewhat nearer, the glass box drew the eye to its green glow, the aquarium exhibiting in its luminous depths that marine oddity, the face of Dan Sonnenschein.

It was an odd face. Under normal light it reminded some of the younger Updike; *redux* under green light it was nearer the face of Jiminy Cricket.

33

'Dan?'

'Just a sec.' No warmth in that voice, only a flat command that might have issued from some other exhibition oddity: Donovan's Brain, say . . . Moxon's Master? . . . Ben groped his way towards a chair and a simile . . .

Bacon's Brazen Head, that was it. That mysterious entity that (if it ever existed) used even more mysterious Arab clockwork . . .

'Bacon knew,' he muttered, '. . . secret of the peacock fountain of Al-Jazari . . .'

'What?'

'Nothing. Nothing.'

'Just a sec.' A sec, many secs might tick by on clocks elsewhere, but here time moved in silence and darkness at an unknown speed (secs per sec). He waited as one who has just felt an earth tremor or the kick of an unborn child waits, in darkness and silence for the next, the confirming instance. Time was indivisible, all the silences and uncertainty between the ticks joined up (sec to sec) into one continuum of doubt, reaching back seven centuries to that night when a servant sat waiting for the brass head to speak.

Time is, the servant thought he heard, but waited to be sure. *Time was*, but why wake Friar Bacon for that? *Time is past*, said the grinning brass head, and fell to pieces (or so the servant would report, when he had hidden his hammer and wakened the good Friar).

To be fair, the servant was only following the example of Aquinas, who reasoned (with logic ruthless enough for any machine) that to destroy a thing is to create a possibility: 'If it did already exist, the statue could not come into being,' he wrote. 'Just as affirmation and negation cannot exist simultaneously, so neither can privation and the form . . .' It was Aquinas, the Swine of Sicily, waddling on a Paris street, who was accosted by a stranger made entirely of wood, metal, glass, wax and leather – the automaton brought into being (through thirty years' work) by Albertus Magnus. Instantly Aquinas raised his staff and brought about the possibility of another thirty years' work . . .

Dr Helen Boag touched the intercom. 'Jim, come in here, will you? And bring the diary.' She unfurled her copy of the *Caribou* and glanced over the headlines:

CAMPUS RIPPER STRIKES AGAIN
Third Body Found

SOCCER SQUAD SHAPES UP
Fergusen Predicts 'Pow Season'

GRADES AT LAST!
Comp Ops Strike Ends

CHESS CMPTR CHEATS IN IOWA OPEN

BLIZZZARD!
Park-O-Mat Mangles Dean's Limo

Looking up from the last story as Jim came in, she grinned. 'Listen, what day do I have for that Emergency Finance Committee thing?'

'Next Tuesday, ma'am.'

'Scrub it. Just heard terrible whispers, omens of a storm. Fraud, God knows what. The Nibelungen of the Computer Science Department rising up against the pale wraiths of Parapsychology –'

'Ma'am?'

'Skip it, I want out. So what else might I be doing?'

He consulted the leather-bound book. 'How about the Shah of Ruritania's visit? Were you going to deputize –?'

'I'll take it myself. Usual tour of the plant, is it? Lunch at the Faculty Club? Oh, does he have any special dietary –?'

'Yes, ma'am. He, um, he eats peacocks.'

'Yuck. Wouldn't pheasant do?'

'Afraid not. Has to be peacock, says the Consul, served in plumage on gold plate. Some religious thing.'

'The sacrifices I have to make. By the way, I'll need to rent a car that day. Says here mine is the victim of an act of God, guess they have to blame someone. Wonderful, isn't it?'

'Ma'am?'

'Wonderful machine-age we live in. Blizzard blows a pinch of snow into the wrong place, and suddenly this million-dollar Park-O-Mat, the cutting edge of the Future, decides to drop my car

35

seven storeys down an elevator shaft. I remember, when old crippled Jake ran that place, all he ever managed was a dented bumper.'

'Want some coffee, Dr Boag?'

'Wonderful.'

He moved quietly to the outer office, where he copied her instructions from the diary into the computer. It would make every arrangement for the tour. Yet it did not supplant the leather-bound anachronism. Important persons usually keep something unfashionable close at hand, a contrast to their own up-to-the-minute importance: the Victorian footman (in a really first-class establishment) was required to put on the powdered wig, gold lace, brocade and buckled shoes of the previous century, while his master wore simple black dinner dress. That same dinner dress would, once it fell out of fashion, provide uniforms for butlers and waiters.

In any (really first-class) office of our century, anachronisms multiplied. Executives continued to sit at larger and larger desks, at which they wrote less and less with their quaint fountain-pens – finally only their signatures. They required their secretaries to carry shorthand pads (and use them) fifty years after the invention of the dictating machine. They sent one another memos, a century after the invention of the telephone, an instrument which they felt required a secretary to dial, a receptionist to answer, and a special servant in white gloves to clean. Every advance, it seemed, required a step backwards.

By now, the computer threatened this kind of progress. Not only might it sweep away all the paraphernalia of office life – the diaries and memo pads and telephones, the letters and telexes and chequebooks, the adding machines and desks and calendars – it might even sweep away the staff of office servants. In this case, it made an anachronism of not only the leather-bound diary, but of Jim.

Or almost. Jim still had his uses. He finished entering data, washed his hands, and brewed a pot of his excellent coffee.

CAMPUS RIPPER STRIKES AGAIN
Third Body Found

There were pools of coffee all over the story, and Allbright found that brushing them away only smeared the words.

> ... in a snowdrift near the Wee ... eft leg amputated with what the police say could be an electric carv ... no signs of robbery or ra ... Ms Cotterel, 34, was an employee of The Daffy Donut, an off-campus eatery. Manager Darrell Feagh ... a terrible shock to all of us. Jaynice was just not the kind of person this should happen to.' ... lice found near the body ... Chief Dobbin would not disclose its title, but stated, 'It was the type of a book a student teacher might have.' This clue may ...

Over his shoulder Dora read the next column:

> by establishing a remote link with its opponent, Maelzel 6.4. Chephren then instructed the other computer to 'see' one of its own pawns as wrongly placed, and 'adjust' it. The adjustment enabled Chephren to capture the pawn and eventually force Maelzel's resignation. Officials did not at once detect the discrepancy, since the game was played at computer-blitz speeds ...

'I still don't see how a computer can *cheat*,' she said.

'My dear, the computer can do anything.' He lifted his plastic coffee-cup to eye level. 'This thing leaks.'

'But how —?'

'The computers are turning human, while the humans can't even murder somebody and cut off their leg without using an electric carving knife. Funny thing is, the police will probably have to use their computer to catch him.'

Dora sank back in her chair. '*Au fond*, I think the Campus Ripper is a pretty sick animal.'

'Sure, but what's his game? Sick how? I mean, what's he planning to do with all those left legs? Start an assembly line — or maybe a chorus line?'

Her shoulders moved uneasily inside the orange coat. 'Is that supposed to be funny or something? If you knew this waitress —'

He licked the side of the cup. 'Jaynice? I did know her.'

'No kidding! What, uh, what was she like?'

'Just another human, right off the same old assembly line.' He pencilled ASSEMBLY LINE on the formica table, then started to rub it out. 'Wait a minute now, wait a minute ...'

'If you're going to make sick jokes, guess I'll split.' She made no move.

'Wait a minute, assembly line, chorus line, just let me talk this out ...'

'Let's change the subject,' she said, looking away.

'*Listen I haven't written a fucking poem in three years, will you just shut up and let me at least try this?*'

After a moment she said, 'You don't like women very much, do you?'

'Love 'em, but just listen ... listen, it's, the Rockettes!'

'The whatettes?'

'Before your time, precision high-kicking chorus line. I got to see 'em once, wonderful female robots, never forget 'em. A technological triumph of the flesh. In the flesh. See, they used to build up each movement all along the line, the way Ford built cars.'

'Did you see *The Nutcracker*?'

'Did I –? No, no, I never liked ballet. It's too, the figures are like little separate clockwork toys, spinning by themselves, you can see it's art for the Nineteenth Century. But this, but the Rockettes at Radio City, Christ! Even the name gives you the idea, it's power, see? *Power*. Imagine a radio city anyhow, and female rockets, it's a ... a ... a 1930s science fiction power dream.'

'Like *Metropolis*?'

'Exactly. A radio metropolis, female robot, it's all there, even the big power wheels. And that's the Rockettes, too, all that muscle moving in unison like pistons on one big crankshaft, no wonder people thought Henry Ford was God – he could make people work like that, this one does it and the next one does it and kick and turn, kick, turn, kick-and-turn –'

'*Modern Times*?' she said. 'Though they say Chaplin was overrated –'

'... the basic machine, the basic human machine, there you are, it's nothing but a knee-jerk reflex, no need to be alive even, sheep in the slaughter-house, they lay them all out on a long table and start cutting their throats and they kick! They kick, this one kicks and the next one kicks, and pretty soon they're all kicking up, kicking up, I don't feel so good.'

He jumped up and walked quickly out of the cafeteria, leaving her alone, a small spot of orange among hundreds of spots of colour clustering around white tables that marched out to distant walls whose colour no one ever seemed to notice. She sat listening to the conversations rising through cigarette smoke above the clatter of styrene on melamine, melamine on nybro, nybro on formica:

'Basically I'm a Manichean, only . . .'

'. . . basic Libran personality . . .'

'A basically Jungian interpretation of economics . . .'

A drama student in black contemplated his Danish roll while his companion said, '. . . with Tom and Sam Beckett, get it? Get it? An Evening with . . .' At the next table someone opened a paperback of Kierkegaard and bit into an apple; at the next, two future engineers stopped arguing about butterfly catastrophes to peer into their sandwiches.

The boy in the yellow sweatshirt looked up at the door, then down at his melamine plate of goulash, saying:

'Maybe we're all tokens of a type, if you can dig that.'

'I can dig it, sure, but what type?'

'The tokens never find out . . . Hey, isn't that Sandy?'

The view was obscured by a fat figure with a full beard, who thumped down his tray with the declaration: 'Ruritania! Don't tell *me* about Ruritania, man . . .'

Beyond him a face bright with acne emitted a groan: '*My* father? My father wanted me to be a goddamn cetologist, how do you like that?'

The drama student hoisted his Danish roll as though it really were a prop skull (and as though anyone were watching him) unaware that behind him the girl in the ski sweater was stealing his scene:

'Go ahead and sign it,' she said to someone grovelling before her plaster-coated leg. 'Oney just your name, nothing dirty. I awready had some smartass put "Ben Franklin", I hadda scratch it out.'

A shrill voice at her elbow cried: 'Jungian economics? Hahahaha, what the hell did Jung ever know about money?'

'Well he *was* Swiss . . .'

The Manichee glanced over, ready to dispute it, while at his own table the full beard reported on Ruritania:

'Yeah, they're burning books, actually burning books. Anything to do with communism. They burned Stendhal's *The Red and the Black*.'

The Manichee looked at him. 'Yeah? But isn't that anarchism?'

From somewhere, at intervals, a deep voice would say, 'True, true as I'm sitting here. God's truth.' From somewhere else a whining voice would wonder was there any point in fighting entropy?

A nybro tray clattered on the vinyl chloride floor.

'A goddamn cetologist. For my fifth birthday he gave me a comic book of *Moby Dick*, how do you like that?'

'Skinner,' said someone at another table, 'did some very interesting things with pigeons . . .'

The yellow sweatshirt swivelled its shoulders towards the door. 'Okay, maybe it's not Sandy, but it sure looks like Sandy.'

'Go ahead, sign it, oney nothing dirty. I had everybody sign it, even Professor . . .'

'No but listen, they actually burned this book called *Cubism*, see, they thought it was about Castro . . .'

'. . . hell's the point, anyway? I mean it's all entropy or do I mean enthalpy . . .' A styrene spoon dug into green jello.

'Sandy! Over here, Sandy!'

'. . . yeah, and a wind-up Jonah. Yeah, and he took me to *Pinocchio* just to see Monstro, how do you like . . .'

The person who wasn't Sandy went to sign the skier's leg cast, while the drama student took a sudden Falstaffian interest in his Danish roll, while the Manichee said:

'Basically I guess you could call me an anarchist. Only . . .'

'. . . basic Libran, with maybe a touch of Cancer . . .'

'God's truth. Well, maybe it's not true exactly, but . . .'

'I never said it *was* Sandy, I only said it looked like . . .'

The voices went on, scudding sound and smoke across the empty table where two empty styrofoam cups stood like vigil lights beside the coffee-soaked newspaper, until Ben Franklin, balancing a tray in his other hand, swept the whole mess to the floor.

'Jesus, they never clean the tables here or anything, sit down, will you? Standing there like a damn wooden Indian – Dan, sit down and eat something.' With a paper napkin he expunged the pencilled word ASS.

'I'm not really . . .' Dan Sonnenschein sat down, resting his hands on a spiral-bound notebook. The long fingers showed bitten nails.

'Sure you are. Hot roast beef sandwich, salad with thousand island, banana cream pie. There.' He showed no interest in the food Franklin was setting before him. 'Look, it's not a problem in anything. Just eat it. Christ, Fong tells me you've been living on stale peanut butter sandwiches over there, acting like a god-damned penitent or something.'

'Penitent? No, I just, I have to be there, that's all.'

'For the tests, sure.'

'Not just the tests.' He picked up a styrene fork and looked at it. 'I can't explain it but – Roderick's there, his mind is right there and I – have to be inside it. I mean, I have to make up his thoughts, and at the same time – I *am* a thought.'

'Think for him, you can't even think for yourself, sitting there starving in front of a hot meal – how much do you weigh now, hundred and twenty? Hundred and fifteen? Take that fork in your hand and use it, how's that for thinking?'

Dan's hand obeyed, scooping up a forkful of mashed potato. 'See, it's just that it's gone too far to stop now. They can't stop us now, can they? No, because it would be, it's almost murder.'

'Just eat, will you?'

'No, but it's gone too far. He's alive, Ben. Roderick's alive. I know he's nothing, not even a body, just content-addressable memory. I could erase him in a minute – but he's alive. He's as real as I am, Ben. He's realer. I'm just one of his thoughts.'

'You said that.'

'I did? A thought repeating itself.' Dan's hands finally seized the knife and fork and started feeding him with regular automatic motions. Franklin watched him eat, the tendons moving in his cheeks, one hand pausing now and then to flick back the hair from his eyes. The grubby spiral notebook remained pinned down under his left elbow.

'Oh, happy birthday, by the way. What are you, twenty-three?'

'Yem.'

'Ha ha, have to watch it, getting almost too old there Dan – I mean, it's a young man's game: Turing was only twenty-four when he –'

'Yem.' The dot of mashed potato on Dan's chin stopped moving for a moment. 'Twenty-four, huh?'

'Of course I'm, I'm thirty-six myself . . .' And from this bleak perspective, Ben Franklin looked over the field (to which he had as yet made no contribution): there was A. M. Turing, twenty-four when he conceived of mechanizing states of mind. There was Claude Shannon, twenty-two when he discovered the spirit of Aristotle in a handful of switches and wiring. There was – hell, there was Frankenstein, completing his creation at nineteen (the age at which Mary Shelley completed hers). And there was Pascal, inventing the first calculating machine at the age of eighteen – time is, time was, and death approaches, intruding on our calculations.

If the Buddhists have it right, the world is completely destroyed 75,231 times per second, and each time completely restored. In all the worlds of Ben's 38 years, there was nothing worth saving; he could die now, saying with the dying Frankenstein: 'Farewell, Walton! Seek happiness in tranquillity and avoid ambition, even if it be only the apparently innocent one of distinguishing yourself in science and discoveries. Yet why do I say this! I myself have been blasted in these hopes, yet another may succeed.' The other being Dan, damn him! Caught in the invisible flicker at Buddhist worlds (in the VHF band), Ben stared at his future.

'Turing took cyanide,' he almost said, but changed it to: 'See? You were hungry.'

'Yes, I guess I – thanks.' Dan wiped his narrow chin, belched, flicked back the lock of hair that fell again over his eyes. 'Thanks.'

'Least I can do. Fong thinks you're Roderick's guiding genius, and he should know. The dark figure of Sidonia behind the –'

'What?'

'Nothing. What I want to know is, how can I help?'

'But you are helping. You're writing program –'

'Sure, pieces of test crap, you call that help, anybody could do that. I don't even know what's being tested, you won't let me handle anything in the lab. Christ, what good is my degree? A master's in Cybernetic Humanities, my whole thesis on learning systems and what do I get to do? Piddly little pieces of test program, any kid could handle that.'

'No, your stuff's good, really good. Once I rewrite it, it goes –' Franklin sat up. 'You what?'

'Rewrite it. Listen, I have to, it's good stuff but it's not inside his head, it's – I have to rewrite it from the inside.'

'*You sonofabitch, I don't believe you.*'

'No, really. Look, right here.' Dan's clawless fingers clawed open the notebook. 'Look, right here where you set up this Bayesian strategy for generalizing from past experience, that's fine for poker-playing machines but look here, I had to simplify – I mean, not simplify exactly, but *Roderickify*, see?'

Ben Franklin stared at the page of diagrams. 'But you – I don't even recognize this, it's not my work. Wait, let's see where you go with this, I don't – let me see that. Goddamnit, let go of the goddamned thing!'

One or two heads turned to watch them, two grown men struggling for possession of a grubby notebook. The girl in the ski sweater nudged her companion, who was bending over to peer at a signature on the white plaster: Felix Culpa.

'Damn you, let go! I've got a right – see my own damn work, let go!' Ben ripped out the page and spread it on the table, holding it with both hands while he studied the symbols cramped into little boxes. His cheeks and ears turned a deeper red.

'Jesus! And this – it works?'

'Yes. Give it back.'

'Just a minute, I've never seen anything like this. Dan, this is – it's beautiful. You took that half-baked idea of mine and you just – you redeemed it, that's what. You redeemed it.'

'Give it back.'

Ben passed over the ragged page and watched him trying to press it back on the spiral. 'I'm sorry, Dan. Had no idea, Fong always said you were good but I mean I never see any of your work, you're always so goddamned secretive. I mean, you never even publish, for Christ's sake, work like this and you never even

43

publish. What about the *Journal of Machine Learning Studies*, or any of the AI –'

'Publish?' Dan hunched forward, protecting the notebook with his knobby wrist. 'No, I don't publish. It's not the point. It's not what I'm working for, my name in some AI journal, I don't have time, see?'

'But that's how you buy the time, publishing. How do you think somebody like Czernski got the Norbert Wiener Chair of Cybernetics at –'

'Anyway, why should I? Roderick's mine, think I want to stick him in some AI journal for everybody to rip-off? He's private, he's not another toy for some toy company, I don't want to see him crammed inside some plastic Snoopy doll. I don't want him grabbed up by some Pentagon asshole to make smart tanks.'

'Don't know what the hell you're talking about,' Ben lit a cigarette. 'Applications, what the hell do you care about applications? Feel like I'm sitting here with Alexander Graham Bell, he's invented this swell gadget only he's afraid to tell anybody about it, in case some loony uses it to make dirty phone calls. Point is, you can't keep something like this to yourself, you just can't, that's all.'

'Why not?'

'Because it's important, that's why not. It's too important to be left to one person. At least – at least let me help, I mean really help.' The fibreglass chair creaked as he sat back. 'Look, I know I'm not good enough to follow you all the way, just give me a glimpse, a Pisgah perspective, okay? This is, I feel like it's the fifth day of Creation or something, the foreman tells me to collect a couple of wheelbarrows of mud and wheel it over to Eden, no one bothers telling me what it's for. Only I've *got* to know. I've got to be in on it, even in some little way, Jesus, it's the only thing I've ever really wanted to do. Why I went into machine intelligence in the first place, all those damned boring years playing with language translators and information retrieval systems and even poker players all I ever wanted was to create something, all right, *help* create something. Okay, okay don't say it. I know my limitations. I'm intelligent but not creative, fine, only – at least I could help?'

The lock of hair fell forward. 'What is it? You want to see him, or what? Because there's nothing much to see, not yet. And help, I don't need any help, right now it's a one-man job. All I need is some time, a little more time.'

'Sure.' Ben studied the coal on his cigarette. 'Maybe you don't trust me because I'm not Jewish or something, that it?'

'Not – what the hell? Jewish? What does that mean?'

'I don't know, but, no offence but –'

'Look, I'm not hardly Jewish myself, my old man was reformed I guess but I wasn't even raised –'

'Yeah, okay, but it's a, like a holy work to you all the same. Secret and holy. Like the prophet Jeremiah and his son, making the first *golem*, you know? They made him out of clay, and they wrote the program on his forehead, and he came to life.'

Dan shrugged. 'Yeah, well I've got to get back to the lab.'

'Yeah, but you know what they wrote? TRUTH, '*emeth*, they wrote, and he came to life. And the first thing he asked them was couldn't they kill him, before he fell into sin like Adam.'

'Look, it's just something I've got to do, alone.' The lock of hair was brushed back, and fell again as he stood up.

'But listen a minute, will you? All he wanted to do was die. They wrote the program on his forehead, '*emeth*, he came to life and all he wanted was to die.'

'Really gotta be going, Ben. I mean, these parables or whatever they are, maybe they mean a lot to you but, uh –'

'The point is, maybe that's all we can create, death. Even when we try to make life it comes out death, death is there all the time. See – wait a minute! – see, Jeremiah and Son, all they had to do was erase one letter from the program, see? So '*emeth* became *meth*. DEAD. It was there all the time.'

'Yep. Hebrew, huh? Never learned any myself. Oh, uh, thanks again for the lunch. See you.'

Ben watched him go, a gawky Jiminy Cricket figure blundering among the white tables, stepping over the plaster leg, squeezing past the Manichee, slipping through gaps between formica and nybro, melamine and fibreglass, fleeing from the animated faces, only one of which turned to look, saw that he too was not Sandy, and dismissed him like an untidy, irrelevant thought.

45

III

There was dust on Mister O'Smith's hand-tooled boots from sitting in the departure lounge. He noticed it when he was looking down, getting set for another fast draw against Brazos Billy. Brazos was not the kind of man to mind if a feller stopped a minute to dust off his Gallen Kamps. In fact Brazos was no kind of man at all, just a fibreglass figure at the end of an abbreviated fibreglass street, ready to go up against anybody for a quarter in the slot. If you shot him, Brazos would look surprised, crumple and collapse, even bleed a little; if not, he'd just smirk. Mister O'Smith always drew blood, and he did so now. They were calling his plane, but he lingered, watching the blood ooze out on the little cowtown street, watching it ooze back in, as Brazos uncrumpled and stood tall again. Well, back to work.

On the plane he read his gun catalogue. Nothing much else to do, since the Agency didn't trust a freelancer like Mister O'Smith enough to tell him anything in advance so he could get his mind set for it. The Agency was a pain in the behind, with all their need-to-know stuff and their limited-personal-contacts stuff – hell, they even gave him a code book and a radio martini olive! As if he'd be fool enough to drink martinis anyhow, and shoot, radio olives went out with, with the Walther PP8!

In Minnetonka the snow was melting; his sheepskin was too warm; the taxis were all covered with crap; Mister O'Smith felt low. Well they can kill you but they can't eat you! He dumped his gear at the hotel and hit the slushy street. Within minutes he found an amusement arcade and settled down to feed quarters into Randy the Robot. When zapped, Randy would look surprised, crumple and emit sparks.

Mister O'Smith had no more idea why he was doing this than did the figures of Randy or Brazos, or even that figure of Herakles (coin-operated and armed with a Scythian bow) that had been

46

drawing against a serpent (when hit, it hissed with surprise) three centuries before Christ. Whether this was a set of Skinnerian contingencies reinforcing the appropriate behaviour (zapping) or a Freudian acting-out of infantile aggression towards the castrating father, Mister O'Smith couldn't say. Beauty was death, and death beauty, that was all Mister O'Smith knew (on a need-to-know basis).

'Of course I have my own ideas.' Tarr went on filling his pipe. 'You both know about my plans for investigating psychic flight orientation in migratory birds.'

Aikin and Dollsly nodded automatically: they knew, they knew. 'But it wouldn't be democratic to put that before the committee without first consulting you, okay?'

Nods.

'So what about your ideas? Bud?'

Bud Aikin controlled his stutter remarkably well today, as he outlined his plan for crime prevention by use of the pendulum. He was becoming quite an authority on this psychic instrument, Tarr noticed. Too bad he still had such a hell of a time with that key word.

Aikin unfolded a map. 'See, here I've been and located the three places where this "Ripper", this murderer left his victims. The vibrations are very strong, even on a map. Using the p-p-p – swinging thing – I was able to locate them precisely.'

'Fascinating!' Tarr lit his pipe. 'Of course sceptics will imagine you read about the locations in the paper . . .'

'No, but wait. I can do it blindfold, with the map turned any way at all. As soon as the p-p-p – the pen-pen the Galilean implement – gets over a psychic "hot spot", it starts swinging violently. And, and that's not all. I've found a *fourth* location. The place where the next body will be found. See, right here near the Student Union. So I mean when they find the body there, that pretty well clinches it, right? Maybe then crime prevention can take a leap forward, using the p – the isochronic vibrating part of a clock –'

Tarr exhaled a thick ball of smoke. 'Lacks scope, if you don't mind my frankness, Bud. And you don't really need much of a grant for – but let's hear what Byron has to say eh?'

Byron Dollsly grinned and slapped his heavy hand on the table. 'Scope! Hah! Think you'll find *plenty* of scope in my idea, George. See how this grabs you. As you know, I've been working on lines suggested by Teilhard de Chardin, Buckminster Fuller and others, namely a kind of engineering approach to consciousness. *Well!*'

He beamed at Tarr and Aikin in turn, while they sat awaiting further enlightenment. '*Well*, I've only had a *major breakthrough*, that's all. As I see it, we have to begin with first principles. *Biology!*'

After a moment, Tarr took his pipe from his mouth. 'Is that it? Biology?'

'Is that it, he asks. Hah! Okay, let me spell it out for you. The divine Teilhard saw life as a *radial* force, and consciousness as a *tangential* force. Life, see, is like a gear-wheel growing larger, while consciousness is the gear actually turning – meshing!'

He grabbed a handful of his thick grey hair and more or less hauled himself to his feet by it. Then he marched to the blackboard. 'So what's the next step? Anybody?'

The other two looked at one another. 'Mm, suppose you just tell us, Byron. Little short on time here . . .'

'The *screw*. The SCREW!'

'The, uh . . . the . . .'

'Simple. The *creative* intellect is a worm-screw with a *right*-hand thread. Get it? Get it? See, it can never mesh with the destructive or left-handed intellect – never!'

'Well I suppose not, mm –'

'So what is God? Simple. He is the vector sum of the entire network of forces turning back upon themselves to produce ultimate consciousness! I mean isn't He? Isn't He just the infinite acceleration of the tangential? POW! POW!' He smacked an enormous right-hand fist into an enormous left-hand palm. There was silence. There was always silence after one of Byron Dollsly's little lectures, which always ended *pow, pow* . . .

'Interesting, Byron, good line of thinking there . . . hard to see any practical research possibilities in it just now, but. . .'

As chairman, Tarr of course had the final deciding vote, which he cast for his own proposal (to study telepathy in birds). Dismissing his assistants, he prepared to write it up for the committee. That is, he sat cracking his knuckles, one by one, and staring out of the window.

From here in the Old Psychology Building, he had a limited view of the Mall: a few dirty white drifts, the stump of a snowman. How many seasons had he watched from this narrow window? How many barren Winters? How many hopes shattered like icicles – Tarr was beginning to like the simile – while his career remained frozen, stiff as the heart of poor little Frosty out there, who would never come to life and sing . . .

Tarr started on the left-hand knuckles. Beyond the snowman lay the façade of Economics, a dirty old building on whose pediment he could just make out three figures: *Labour* shouldering a giant gear-wheel, *Capital* dumping out her cornucopia, and *Land* applying his scythe to a sheaf of wheat or something.

His gaze returned to the central figure. Money, that's what it took. A little money – a tenth of the cash they lavished on the Computer Science Department, say – and he could have parapsychology really on the move. Going places. They were doing it elsewhere: Professor Fether in Chicago was testing precognition in hippos; the Russians claimed a breakthrough on the ouija board to Lenin; the ghost labs of California were fast building a solid reputation. But here, a standstill, a frozen landscape. Nobody in the entire field had ever heard of the University of Minnetonka.

Nobody had ever heard of Dr George Tarr, either. Now and then his clipping service sent him by mistake some reference to 'R. Targ' or 'C. Tart'. His own name never appeared.

Still, here was another chance, another crack at the old cornucopia . . . He cracked the last knuckle and reached for his dictating machine.

'Title: Research into Psychically-Oriented Flock Flight. A project proposal. G. Tarr, B. Aikin, B. Dollsly.

'Ahem. Observers have long obs – noted the uncanny agility of birds flying in formation. This agility has not yet been adequately explained. How is it that a flock of up to a thousand birds, manoeuvring in perfectly co-ordinated flight at high velocities, can avoid collisions? The psychic mechanism we propose may be tested as follows . . .'

A man in a red hunting cap and matching face was saying to the bartender, 'Look, just because I never went to no university that don't mean I'm drunk.'

'Just take it easy, Jack.'

'Plenny of things a university don't teach you, am I right?'

'All I said was, take it easy. Take it . . .'

In the back booth, Professor Rogers scratched at acne that hadn't itched for fifteen years. 'Up to you, of course. Just thought you might want to have all the facts. *Before* the meeting.'

Dr Jane Hannah's face was impassive, the face of a Cheyenne brave – which, during her early years in anthropology, she had been. 'Facts, you say. I keep hearing opinions.'

'Okay, sure, if you want my opinion, we should turn them down. With all these fraud rumours, I don't see how Fong's people can expect special treatment.'

She raised her martini, mumbled something over it, and took a sip. 'Why not special treatment? Maybe what they have to give us is more precious than anything they could possibly have stolen. After all, true heroes can always break the rules. Think of Prometheus, stealing from the gods.'

'Pro – but this is real life, real theft. Maybe millions of dollars, you can't just shrug like that and –'

'But NASA, like all fire-gods of the air, won't miss a few million. We don't want to get bogged down in petty tribal ethics now, the real question is, is Fong a true hero? Will his robot, his gift to mankind, be a blessing or a curse? If it is good, then we *must* help him, even as Spider Woman helped the War Twins on their journey to the lodge of their father, the Sun –'

'Sure, sure, but I mean Fong is playing God himself, he's like Baron Frankenstein over there, never listens to anybody, a law unto himself.'

'The new Prometheus.' Her eyes were unfocused; they seemed to be looking right through him into the vinyl fabric of the booth. 'Prometheus made a man of clay, you know. And Momus the mocker criticized it, saying he should have left a window in the breast, so we could see what secret thoughts were in its heart. But isn't that our problem? How can we tell if this robot will be good or evil? What's in his heart?'

He lifted his Old-fashioned, holding the tiny paper doily in place on the bottom of the glass with his little finger. 'You want my opinion, the computer freaks have had things their own way just about long enough. Far be it from me to assign guilt labels in a multivalently motivating situation like this, but just look around campus! The process of depersonalization goes irreversibly on, what with computerized grades and tests, teaching machines, enrolment, it's as though they want to just tear down humanity, yeah? Just rip it out and replace it, yeah? With robotdom, right? Robots are nothing but humanity ripped off, if you want my opinion.'

Her stare continued to penetrate Rogers, the vinyl padding, and even the next booth where Dora was explaining to Allbright: 'I think Dr Fred's senile or something, he screwed up completely on everybody's horoscopes, I checked mine on the computer and he's got Saturn in the wrong place.'

'Oh sure, the *computer* has to be right. Why trust a nice little old man when you can really rely on a damned steel cabinet full of transistors?' He swallowed a pill and washed it down with Irish whiskey.

'That's not what I meant, I mean Saturn in the wrong place! And this other kid, this Bill Whatsit in my class, his horoscope's even worse. I mean Dr Fred put in a conjunction of Pluto and Neptune, it makes Bill born in either 1888 or 2381. And when I tried to tell Bill it was wrong he said, "I know, wrong again, I'm always wrong" – like it was *his* fault, I mean.'

'We're all at fault, sure, getting in the way of the damned steel cabinets. Nobody's gonna survive, just a few technicians . . .' His dirty fingers chased another pill across the formica.

'You sound just like him, gloom and doom! For Pete's sake, you must both have something in Scorpio, you're so touchy.' She shrugged her orange coat half-way down her arms and lit a cigarette. 'I just hate this place, don't you? *Au fond*, I mean.'

'. . . just a few damned technicians, half machines themselves . . . Listen, I went to school with this kid, a born computer genius. He used to play around all the time with the school terminal, little games of his own, nobody knew what the hell he was up to, least of all the teacher. I mean we were only eleven years old, already he was in a world of his own. Then one day the goddamn FBI came to the school and took him away for a couple of days. Seems

51

he was dabbling in interstate commerce, in a way. When he got back to school I asked him all about it – you know what it was? Peanut butter.'

'Peanut butter?'

'Bugleboy Old Tyme Reconstituted Peanut Butter, nauseating stuff it used to be, nobody could stand it. Only thing us kids liked about it was the jar tops: "Fifty of your favourite cartoon characters – save 'em, swap 'em, loads of fun!" Something like that. Anyway the supermarkets were probably losing money on the crap, because they stopped handling it. So this kid just got on the old terminal, twiddled his way into the inventory computer of this big supermarket chain, Tommy Tucker, and made a few crucial changes. All of a sudden Tommy Tucker was swamped with the crap. They put it on special offer, they even gave it away – and I bet they had to throw away a few tons of it too. But they couldn't stop their computer from re-ordering, more and more . . . When they caught up with him, this kid had forty-nine of his favourite cartoon characters – probably more than any other kid in the United States.'

Dora looked for the waitress. 'I've heard lots of stories like that. Kids are always using their school terminals to dig into some computer somewhere.'

'Yeah, but what Danny did was kind of new. He invented some sinister algorithm, so he told me. I don't even know what an algorithm is.'

'You don't? Honest? It's only a set of instruc –'

'And I don't want to know. Whatever it was, after he planted it in Tommy Tucker's computer, it just grew until it took over. I guess they had to finally throw away their whole program and start from scratch. I guess they lost a lot of money, that's where the FBI came in.'

'What happened to him, then?'

'Oh, they put him on the payroll at Tommy Tucker. As a computer security consultant. All he had to do was promise to leave them alone. But the funny thing is –'

The waitress arrived, with someone else's drinks.

'Sorry, kid, I got a bit mixed up, with all the characters in here tonight. Old Jack there's teed off because he can't read –' she gestured at the man in the hunting cap, '– and the cowboy next to him wants to know who's drinking martinis – and then I got some joker in the front tries to tell me he's a manicure. Crazy! Crazy! Crazy!'

She delivered the Old-fashioned and the martini to Rogers and Hannah, who was saying:

'. . . maybe the Blackfeet boy, Kut-o-yis, cooked to life in a cooking pot, but isn't that the point? Aren't they always fodder for our desires? Take Pumiyathon for instance, going to bed with his ivory creation –'

'Look, these Indian stories are okay, but I don't see –'

'Indian? No, he was King of Cyprus, you must know that story, they even made a musical of it, *Hello Dolly*, was it? Something like that . . . But take Hephaestus then, those golden girls he made who could talk, help him at his forge, who knows what else . . . Or Daedalus, not just the statues that guarded the labyrinth, but the dolls he made for the daughters of Cocalus, you see? Love, work, conversation, guard duty, baby, plaything, of course they used them to replace people, isn't that the point?'

'Yes but the point, my point is –'

'And in Boeotia, the little Daedala, the procession where they carried an oaken bride to the river, much like the *argeioi* in Rome, the puppets the Vestal Virgins threw into the Tiber to purge the demons; disease, probably, just as the Ewe made clay figures to draw off the spirit of the smallpox, so did the Baganda, they buried the figures under roads and the first –'

'This is all very interesting, yes, but –'

'First person who passed by picked up the sickness. In Borneo they drew sickness into wooden images, so did the Dyaks . . . Of course the Chinese mostly made toys, a jade automaton in the Fourth Century but much earlier even the first Han Emperor had a little mechanical orchestra but then he was a bit mad, you know. Imagine burning all the books in China *and* building the Great Wall, quite mad, quite mad . . . but the Japanese, Prince Kaya was it? Yes, made a wooden figure that held a big bowl, it helped the people water their rice paddies during the drought. Certainly more practical than the Chinese, or even the Pythagoreans, with their steam-driven wooden pigeon, hardly counts even if they did mean it to carry souls up to – but no, we have to make

53

do with the rest, and of course the golem stories, and how clay men fashioned by the Archangel –'

Chee! Rogers sneezed. 'Yes, very iderestigg, but –'

'There were Teraphim of course but no one knows their function. But the real question is, what do we want this robot *for*? Is it to be a bronze Talos, grinning as he clasps people in his red-hot metal embrace? Or an ivory Galatea with limbs so cunningly jointed –'

'Look, couldn't we –?'

'As you see, I've been turning the problem over, consulting the old stories . . .'

'And?'

'And I've decided to vote against this robot.'

Chee! Chee! 'Thank God. We have to take sides. Those of us who don't want to be ciphers have to stand up and be counted. Why didn't you say so in the first place?'

For the first time, her eyes blinked. 'But I had to explain! You see, I believe in baring the soul.'

'Bearing the –?'

'I even talk to my food and drink, as you must have noticed.'

'Dot at all,' he lied, and hid his nose in a handkerchief.

She sighed. 'I can't help feeling that respect for life – even the life of your cold virus there – is paramount. Of course we must take life, we eat food, we destroy germs. But can we not at least apologize for our murders?' So saying, she took up the olive from her martini and spoke to it quietly: 'Little olive, I mean you no harm, but my body needs nourishment. For one day soon, my body will go to replenish the earth, to feed new olive trees . . .'

Rogers looked away, embarrassed, and caught the eye of a fat, suntanned stranger at the bar, who had turned from the television to watch Dr Hannah. 'Uh, I've got to go home, nurse this cold, so . . .'

She put down the olive and checked her watch. 'If you don't mind, I'll stick around. Have to kill an hour before I meet my son for dinner. Never see him, since he moved into that fra – But you have your own problems, bless you.'

Beanie's Bar was beginning to fill up with the early evening crowd. Rogers had to squeeze his way through an animated

54

discussion of Ruritania (one speaker suffered from halitosis), avoid the non-university drunk and jostle through other conversations:

'. . . the liberry, but like when I ast for *Sense and Sensibility* they brung me this *novel*. This, yeah, by some other J. Austin, only with a *e*, figure that . . .'

'. . . Jungian econ . . .'

'. . . this machine heresy, was it?'

'. . . Barbara Altar for one . . .'

The juke box piped him out with a mournful, if not quite coherent song:

When I feel you're in my dream
Images of fortune play me do-o-own
Destiny don't seem so far, and I can touch a star
Tragedy's a bargain, yes, and
Love's a clown.

Near the door someone said, 'Right in front of the Student Union? No kidding, who was he anyway?'

'Just some freshman with a GPA problem, happens every year . . .'

The spot vacated by Rogers was still warm when a plump stranger in Western clothes slid into it. He grinned at Dr Hannah out of his deep tan.

'Olives,' he said. 'Thought they went out with the ol' Walther.'

'Really?' She focused on him with difficulty.

'O'Smith.' He extended a thick left hand on which she noticed a turquoise ring, almost Navaho. But fake, like the grin.

'Prometheus invented the ring,' she said, and belched. 'Did you know – sorry – that? Out of his chains.'

'No foolin'?' A theatrical sneer. 'Look, can we talk here?'

'Why not?' Jane Hannah needed at least two more martinis before she could face her son, and if this absurd stranger wanted to fill the interval with chatter, olives going out of style, well why not?

'Usually I work alone,' he said. 'I run a one-man show.'

'Indeed?' Show-business, a rodeo perhaps. It seemed to explain his outlandish clothes, the showy ring, the stock villain's sneer. What did he want, money?

'But I guess if you wanted to back my play –'

She put up a hand. 'You're wasting your time. I don't contribute to – no thanks. "... I'm no angel ...", as the saying goes.'

'Good enough.' He seemed unruffled. 'Good enough. Fact is, I get a lot of satisfaction out of workin' alone, you know? Boy, when you see their faces – when they realize what's comin' off –' He chuckled. 'Makes it all worth while.'

'I'll bet. But do you usually see their faces? I thought –'

'Even when you don't, you still know what they're thinkin'. Boy howdy! It's like real communication! I mean in everyday life you just *never* get that close to *nobody*. Real communication.'

'I know just what you mean,' she said. Nice to meet someone who liked his work, even if he did carry the offstage villainy too far. Just now he was casting a furtive glance over his shoulder, where the bearded boy was propped up by the girl in orange.

Allbright, his chin sinking towards the table, told Dora, 'Funny thing is, I met him just the other day. On the Mall.'

'Met who?'

'This kid I was just telling you about. Danny. The Bugleboy –'

'But that was half an hour ago – are you all right?'

'No but listen, listen, he's still crazy he – I asked if he was still in computers and he sort of grinned and said, "Into, yes, yes, yes, you could say that, into computers, yes, yes ..."'

'I don't know why you take that stuff and drink on top –'

'Yes yes, nodding and grinning like a fucking guru computer got all the answers yes yes ... only he's dead inside, ghost in the machine you know even his kid he even his kid he ...'

He came to rest with his ear in the ashtray, while the man in the hunting cap looked over and turned away to his drink, muttering, 'College boys! College boys!'

A tiresome boy declared himself once more a Manichee to the girl in the leg-cast, who nodded, though listening to someone else explain how Lady Godiva invented the rosary. The juke box, now muffled by the wall of bodies, sang:

Funniest thing I ever seen
Tomcat sittin' on a sewin' machine ...

Dr Hannah raised her glass to toast the departing O'Smith. 'Break a leg,' she said.

He winked. 'For you, anything.' He pushed through the crowd and out into the night, which was nearly as dark and empty as the piano bar on the other side of town where two short-haired men waited to meet someone called O'Smith.

Allbright slept on while Dora kept watch. Suddenly he sat up, rubbing at the ash on his cheek. 'He looked burned out, coke or, I don't know, burned out. What was I – oh yeah, he's got a kid, Roderick, he even treats him like a damned machine.'

'Is this still Bugleboy?'

'Yeah listen, he was carrying this doll, I asked him if he had any kids, he said, Just Roderick. "Oh, this?" he says, holding up the doll. "It's for testing Roderick. Testing his pattern-recognition threshold." Might have been talking about a goddamned piece of equipment, you know? Cold, cold and – so when I asked how old the boy was, what do you think? He said, *Doesn't matter. I'm getting rid of him*".'

'What did he mean, getting rid '

'Wants to ship him off to some foster home, even asked me for an address.' He picked at his beard absent-mindedly, disentangling a cigarette butt. 'Felt like telling him to ask his computer pals if he wants a favour, only – what's that cop doing in here?'

A campus patrolman stood by the door, looking around, while the crowd parted to let him through. Out of habit, one or two people dropped things on the floor. Finally the lawman saw Dr Hannah's white hair and came over to her.

'Mrs Hannah? Mrs Jane Hannah?'

'Doctor Hannah, if you don't mind.'

Awkwardly he bent and whispered to her that her son was dead. Awkwardly he supported her as she rose and wobbled to the door, blind to faces turning with momentary curiosity, deaf to the thumping of the juke box . . .

The man in the hunting cap (its flaps erect as the ears of a fox terrier) clutched his glass for support and muttered, 'College boys! B.S., M.S., Ph.D., haw haw haw, stands for . . .'

Allbright said, 'So I gave him the address. Friends of mine out West, they're into the environment. Figured they couldn't be worse parents than him. Jesus, he doesn't even care about that kid, doesn't even – all he wanted was some address, stick an addressograph label on the kid and ship him out, not even human himself, just a ghost in a machine all burned out, coked out . . .'

'Allbright? Let's split, you look tired.'

'Take William Burroughs, inventor of the adding machine, know what he says? Or I mean inventor of the soft machine, know what he says?'

She helped him to his feet while his free hand started flailing, 'And I quote: "The study of thinking machines teaches us more about the brain than we can ever learn by introspective methods." Did you know that?'

The crowd parted as it usually does for wild drunks, policemen and other dangers; Allbright continued flailing as they made the door. '"The C-charged brain is a berserk pinball machine, flashing blue and pink lights in electric orgasm." Did you know that?'

Outside in the purple evening he paused to smash his fist into a wall.

'Stop! Allbright, stop – why do you hate yourself so much? Why can't you just – stop that!'

'. . . burned out, a ghost burning in a machine, the lights all going out, zzzzt, let me out of here. Let me out of here!'

'We are out, outside. Come on.'

He slumped down. 'Safer here,' and slept while she kept watch. The sky blazed with stars, brighter and more disturbing than the imitation sky in Bernie's Piano Bar (across town), where two others were giving up their watch.

'What we get depending on outsiders, he's not gonna show.'

'We could of handled it ourselves.'

'Try telling that to the brass.'

The aged pianist had been gently chiding them for an hour for not joining in with the others around the piano. Now, looking directly at them, he said, 'Come on *everybody*. Don't be shy!'

Reluctantly they added their voices to the quavering chorus:

. . . and I'll put them all together
With some wire and some glue

And I'll get more lovin' from the dumb, dumb, dummy
Than I'll ever get from you
(Get out and waaaaalk, baby).

IV

The Shah would trove this memory, would he not? An aerial view of the entire campus, greening with Spring, looking so like one of those clever little silicon chips he was forever reading about. Yes, the clean square buildings represented the little transistors and things, while the roads and footpaths represented the – the other parts. It was even possible to think of the students crawling about down there as information to be progressed, processed rather. He desired strongly that his only son should be processed in a place such as this. But now it was time to put by such thoughts, and concentrate on the tedious task at hand; already his chopper was settling like a golden dragonfly atop the – he checked a map – the Admin building.

Jim hadn't told her she'd have to scream her speech of welcome over the roar of helicopter blades. But protocol demanded instant recognition:

'Welcome to the University of Minnetonka! We hope that Your Royal Incomparability will take pleasure from our humble institution.' Awkward stuff, translated by the Ruritanian consulate.

The Shah was not quite as tall or good-looking as his photographs had previewed. She might not have recognized him but for his splendid uniform: gold lamé head to toe, with peacock-feather epaulets. Curtseying, she noticed that even his jackboots had been gilded.

When the mechanical roar died, he said: 'Please, Dr Boag. Not too much of these ceremony. I hope you will treat me as any ordinary visitation, yes?'

'Yes of course if your – if you – but this way to the elevator.'

Crowded in with the Shah, his secretary and five enormous bodyguards, she found conversation difficult. It was hard enough even to see him over a padded shoulder, and the smell of pomade (heavy with patchouli) took her breath. When she informed him that the weather was unusually mild and Springlike, not at all like last week's, he simply beamed and said nothing. When she asked if he'd had a pleasant journey, he nodded. Did he understand? Did he speak English? Was it impolite to talk in elevators in Ruritania? Finally she gave up and consulted her card notes.

He would want to see the library, examine a Ruritanian manuscript, and visit the history department. Then –

He suddenly snatched the card from her hand. After examining it through his lorgnette, he passed it to the secretary, a tiny dark man with bad teeth.

'It's simply our itinerary,' she began, but they were arguing in their exotic language. Or was it arguing? Whatever it was, it continued as they strolled out into the sunshine.

Finally the Shah beamed at her. 'Forgive our ugly manners, Dr Boag. My secretary wishes me to follow to the letter this thoughtful itinerary you have for us provided. He worries, you see, for the security. I however have other *tastes*.' He grimaced so on the word that she fell back a step.

'I – see. I – well I had planned –'

'Moment. I must confess that libraries leave me "cold". And history was never my "strong" subject. But if you will forgive me, there are two things I should admire seeing. The horses' barns, first of all. And the computers. I greatly admire the computers.'

'Your Inc – the campus is of course at your disposal. I have a car waiting if you'll –'

'No,' said a guard. He and the others, their faces expressionless behind sunglasses, herded the little party past the official car to another, a long Mercedes with gold fittings.

'*My* car,' said the Shah, and twirled his lorgnette. 'I am sure you will find it greatly comfy, yes?'

'Well yes of course, if –'

A guard slapped the door with a giant hand. 'Is better,' he threatened, 'Bombproof.'

Not an auspicious start. She began to envy the committee.

Tarr slammed down the phone as Bud Aikin came in. 'Great, just great. Tried calling Rogers and he's off sick. Sick!'

'You mean he won't –?'

'– be there to steer our proposal through the committee. We've just wasted our time – what are you looking so pleased about?'

'Well, the paper says –'

'That's not the worst of it. Only reason I called up Rogers was to get him to change the title on our proposal, too late now. They've got it, forty-six copies already in the committee room with that title staring them in the face, why didn't somebody tell me? Why didn't you point the acronym out to me, I have to think of everything around here – something amusing, Bud?'

'No, just, did you see the paper? It says –'

'*Research into Psychically-Oriented Flock Flight*, why do I have to do everything my, what paper?'

Aikin held up the *Caribou*. 'You know how I predicted another body? A fourth body at the Student Union? Well here it is! Some freshman shot himself right on the steps, how's that for precognition? Listen: "The body of Bill Hannah, 20 . . ."'

'I don't know what you're talking about.'

'". . . and Wesson .38 . . . cassette suicide note in his pocket. Hannah blamed his failing Grade Point Average, .95 last . . . member of Digamma Upsilon Nu and son of Dr . . ." Anyway there it is, my prediction.'

Tarr began filling his pipe. 'And frankly, Bud, I wonder if you know either.'

'But you, you saw me do it, with the map, remember? And the p-p-p – the vibrating dangly thing, remember? You and Byron were witnesses!'

He lit his pipe and puffed out an ectoplasm of blue smoke. 'Can't say I remember that, no, hmm, hmm, hmm . . .' After a moment he added, 'But even if you did, so what? One swallow doesn't make a flock.'

'But –'

'Kindly let me finish? Okay, what I think we have here is a political situation, Bud. No sooner do I tell you the committee will probably veto my proposal, than you want to back another horse. Maybe all you ever really cared about was your pendulum, eh?'

'No, but –'

'It's okay, Bud. Really. I'm not hurt. Some people are capable of loyalty, some aren't, I realize that. I don't know, maybe you're after my *job* in your own crazy way, I can accept that too. Just a humble scientist myself, I leave the politics to you slick guys with all the answers.'

Unanswered phones were ringing all over the place. A patrolman sat on his desk, trying to juggle two receivers and take down a message that would probably be just another flying saucer sighting. The dispatcher peered over her glass partition (a frosted look over frosted glass, he would write) letting the chief know she was peeved about missing her coffee break. The telex was ringing its bell and rattling out a yard of paper. The fat prisoner threw him a sulky look from the cage ('. . . as if,' he would write, 'as if he thought someone else had crapped his drawers').

Chief Dobbin went into his office and closed the door against all of them. But even here he had Sergeant Collar balancing an armload of reports and shouting into a phone:

'Don't ask me, that's all. Just don't ask me!' The receiver banged down. 'Been like this all fucking day, chief. Two more men down with flu, the coroner's screaming for his paperwork on this suicide, not to mention –'

'Shut up, Collar, and get outa my office. I need five minutes to get squared away here.' Getting squared away meant sitting down with a clean legal pad and a handful of sharpened pencils, to work on his book. Dobbin wrote slowly and carefully, his tongue protruding at the corner of his mouth:

'Don't touch me,' she said. 'Don't you ever touch me again. Why was I ever dumb enough to marry a cop?'

Suddenly I felt big and awkward and very, very tired. 'Look, I know it's our anniversary, but this Delmore diamond case is ready to crack wide open –'

'And then there'll be some other case,' she said, her mouth set hard. 'Maybe when you give all you've got to your work, there's just nothing left for me.'

She was near the window when it happened. Suddenly the glass blossomed into a spider-web pattern, with a hole in the middle the size of a .303 slug. There was a matching hole in Laura's lovely throat. Even before she hit the floor, she was very, very –

'What is it *now*, Collar? Can't you handle it?'

'Security problem, chief. With our visiting potentate. He's visiting all the wrong places. In fact we can't locate him.'

'Terrific. Have Angie get him on the radio, and –'

'No can do. He's got the wrong car, too. I'm trying to get a VSU fix on him now, but nothing. Zilch. Maggie's drawers.'

'Probably left the damn campus.' He flicked on his own video surveillance unit and ran through the scenes quickly, then slowly. 'There, is that his car? Black Mercedes limo, gold grille? Okay, he's at the Ag Sci complex, horse barns. Can we detail a coupla men to escort?'

Collar made a face. 'Nope. Simons is off sick, and Fielder has to guard this gold dinnerware at the Faculty Club, so that leaves –'

'Okay, okay. Try to catch up on a little paperwork around here and what happens? All hell breaks loose, people get sick, people want coffee breaks – and now we got this guy, a king of some place, just walking around loose like anybody else!'

'You want to question the prisoner now, chief? He's kinda weird and –'

'Who is he, anyhow?'

'A John Doe. No ID at all. Our special Ripper Patrol picked him up last night. He was using a glass-cutter on a window at the Computer Science building. Had a microflex camera on him, and a wig.'

'Kinda fat for the James Bond stuff, isn't he? Okay, bring him in. Oh but first, ring the morgue, tell 'em it's okay to release the Hannah kid's body for a funeral. We'll catch up on the paperwork later. I know his ma wanted to cremate him today.'

'Already released him, chief.'

Thank God something was done. Dobbin could see he'd get no further today on *Call Me Pig*.

As soon as they were in the car, His Incomparability removed his gold military cap, unbuttoned his stiff collar and sighed. 'Now we can relax. Let us be informal, eh? I will call you Helen, and you must call me Ox.'

'Ox?'

64

'It is my favourite pickname, as you say. These horses' barns, are they far?'

'Why yes. I hope your driver knows the way.'

'Yes, he studies your campus with a fine tooth comb. He knows it like the back of his hams.' The weedy secretary spoke into a gold microphone, and they moved.

The patchouli scent was heavy. Dr Boag tried to forget it by studying the car's elaborate furnishings. The roof interior was covered with peacock feathers, the floor with squares of black and white fur (ermine? sable?) and while two guards and the secretary were forced to squat on tiny carved stools, she and the Shah reclined on a deep, comfortable seat, upholstered in cloth of gold and heaped with blue silk cushions. She remarked on the luxury and he replied that he owned seventeen such cars.

And that seemed to be that. Six miles to the horse barns, and already they'd run out of conversation.

The Shah rummaged in a carved cabinet and produced a book.

'Very interesting, this Book.'

'Ruritanian?'

'Alas, my English is not so well for reading, so I have had it translated into my own poor tongue. I believe in English it is called *Pianola*? By Mr K. Vonnegut. Very good. Much computers.'

She studied the beautifully-tooled cover. 'I'm afraid I haven't read it. Technical book is it?'

'A novelle. All on my own crazed subject, the computers. But the curious part is, there is a Shah in it, making a visitation! Of course he is nothing like me, but even so – reading this is a *déjà vu* experience for me. Suppose I too were in a novelle, eh? Read by another Shah, who is in turn – you see?'

'Interned?'

'I explain so badly. Let me only say I begin to feel like the iteration within the great computer myself, or thereabouts.'

One of the guards grinned, nudged the other and pointed out of the window at a Coca-Cola sign.

'The pianola,' continued the Shah. 'An excellent symbol for the automation, yes? It is I believe used also by Mr W. Gaddis in his novelle *J.R.*, where he speaks of Oscar Wilde travelling in America, marvelling at the industry, the young industry you

65

understand. Now I do believe Mr Wilde suggested shooting all the piano players and using the pianola instead, or do I have that erroneously?'

'Very ahm, perceptive, Your Inc – Ox, I mean.'

'Do you like books, Helen? How stupid of me, of course you must be immured in them, books are your life, yes?'

She chuckled. 'Not as much as I'd like, I fear. Pressure of work, administrative duties –'

'I too, I too,' he said, and squeezed her knee. Dr Boag was glad she'd worn the pants suit after all. 'Yet I do find time to read. Anything I can find on the computers, fiction or not fiction. I believe the machine must some day replace all of us, yes? We will have the robot Dean of Persons, yes, and even the robot Shah of Ruritania. Sad it is, but so. Meanwhile these computers are damn useful, yes? For the police work and so forth.'

He gave her a glass of gold liqueur and rambled on about computers, while she lay back and tried to keep her knees out of reach, trying to ignore the overpowering scent. Eventually she said, 'You have a point there, Ox, but really isn't the computer more or less an overgrown adding machine? A tool, in other words, useful of course but only in the hands of human beings. I feel the role of the computer in our age has been somewhat exaggerated, don't you?'

'Perhaps. But I see the subject tires you. Let us speak instead of business.' He leaned back against a peacock-blue cushion. 'My visit is of course not entirely socialized, you understand.'

'Oh?'

'I wish to enrol my son Idris at your excellent university.'

'Oh. Well I'm sure he'll like it here, Your, Ox. It's more than a university, it's – it's a perspective on the world, past, present and fut –'

'Yes yes yes. So I suggest as, as you say, a ballpark figure of two million.'

'What?' She sat up.

'American dollars. At today's prices not bad, eh?'

'But our fees are nothing like, of course if you want to arrange a deed of gift –'

'Gifting, yes, a gifting. Just to ensure Idris's education. I think of it as an investment in my country's future. Also a hedge against

66

inflation, yes? Idris is now six months of age. By the time he is ready, the price may go up and up, yes?'

She put down her liqueur glass, sat up straight and looked at him. 'Let's be clear about this. Your gift sounds more than generous, but I hope you won't expect special treatment for your son in return. We are after all a state institution.'

He winked. 'I understand. Two million and a half, let us say, and be done with. Yes?' He slapped her knee heartily. 'Now, on to the horses!'

The history professor looked at his watch. Another minute had passed into his domain. 'We all seem to be here. I declare this meeting open. I'm sorry Dr Boag couldn't be here – a previous commitment – and Professor Rogers – he's ill – and Dr Hannah. I assume you all know of her son's recent tragic death. Still, we have our quorum, so I suggest we consider these two proposals – Question, Dr McGuffey?'

'*Woopa.* Just want to put it on the record that I had nothing to do with Bill Hannah's suicide.'

'Pardon? I don't follow.'

Dr Fred stood up and looked up and down the table. 'Oh, I know what you're all saying. Just because he was in my class. Just because I made a little mistake in his birth chart.'

'Well, yes, now if we can ahem just get down to these two –'

'Only I never made that mistake at all. The machines did it! Magnetic influences. Terrestrial currents. Someone saw a flying saucer the other night, unimpeachable witness, ever think of that?'

'Yes, now if you're finished, we'll just –'

'I'm not finished, may be old, may be sick, but I'm not finished. No siree, copper bracelet wards off arthritis bursitis neuritis, benefic influence of Venus, have to get up early to – *Woopa!* Each sneeze threatened to blow the frail figure off its feet. Noticing his glittering eyes, the chairman said:

'If you're ill, Dr McGuffey, perhaps –'

'Ill? Ill-aspected, Mars the face of Mars, malefic but I ward it off, they have to get up early to catch old Fred, Napoleon slept only four hours per night, magnetic power, secret dynamos, hidden reserves of Atlantean force fields deep in the – but they do, you know. They do get up early, humming away in the night, in

67

the . . .' He looked bewildered. After a moment he sat down and began to study the documents before him. The meeting continued.

'No luck, chief?'

'Zilch. Either this guy really is some government yahoo, which I very much doubt, or he's really nuts. Any word from the FBI yet on his prints?'

'Maggie's drawers, so far. Should I book him or what?'

'Not just yet. Not just yet.' Chief Dobbin drummed a pencil on his legal pad. 'I want to try a little psychology on this cracker. Because if he's nuts, he just might be nuts enough to be our Ripper, right?'

Collar snapped his fingers. 'Hey, that ties in with something else. I forgot to tell you. You know that book we found last week on the scene of the crime?'

'Yeah, this education –'

'But that's just it! I had our experts go over it, and it's not education at all. This book, this Learning Systems, is all about computers!'

'And we caught this guy at the Computer Science building! Now we're getting somewheres.' Dobbin sat up. 'Get the prisoner, Collar. I think the three of us oughta pay a little visit to the morgue.'

The Mortuary Science department of University Hospital was just around the corner, and in a few minutes they were in the cool antechamber, handing the attendant a ticket.

'Six-sixty-six?' he said. 'Let's see, that must be –'

'Never mind who it is, just bring it out.' Dobbin watched the attendant slouch away, then turned to his suspect. 'Still not talking, Mister Spy?'

'Nope. Like I said before, you boys are makin' one hell of a mistake here. People I work for ain't goin' to like this a-tall.'

'Sure, sure, double-oh-seven. We got your number all right.' When the attendant rolled in the sheet-draped trolley, the two cops twisted their handcuffs, forcing the suspect to move close to it. He would need a full dose of psychology.

'I want you to take a good look at this girl,' said Dobbin. 'I think maybe you seen her before. *Before you took an electric carving knife and butchered her up like this!*

He whipped back the sheet to show the placid features of Bill Hannah. 'What the hell – Collar, what's this?'

'I don't know, chief, guess the computer mixed up the ticket numbers or – and they must of cremated the girl.'

The suspect grinned out of his deep tan. 'Now if you boys are done fartin' around here, how about lettin' me go? I ain't really done nothin' and you know it.'

'Millions of bits of information on a little chip,' said the Shah. 'Answers at the speed of light. Of what will they think next? Ah, dear Helen, I cannot tell you how much I look forward to seeing your computers.'

'Well I'm sure you'll be – Good God what's that?'

As the long Mercedes turned into University Avenue, a mob suddenly closed in to block the way. There seemed to be angry faces at every window, fists hammering at every bomb-proof panel.

'MURDERER! MURDERER OF CHILDREN!'

'I can't think how this happened, Your Incomparability. This is – I must apologize. Must be some mistake in our security, some leak –'

He shrugged a peacock epaulet. 'I am accustomed to this. Ruritanian students assuredly, a despicable faction known all too well in my own country. And now even here, in the land where everything is free –'

The bodyguards started feeling inside their jackets as the car slowed, halted. A student whose sign read NO FASCHISM HERE shouted something in an ancient language, and the Shah looked unhappy.

'They accuse me of murder – *I* who brought them colour television on two channels! Only communistic anarchists could even dream of so terrible a lie. Drive on Uza,' he shouted in the microphone. 'Run them down!'

'No, wait. I'm not sure you should –'

'Red anarchistic nihilists! They say I murdered children – *I*, their spiritual father! I never murdered anyone in my life.'

'No, of course but –'

69

'All of those so-called children were executed in accordance with our laws, after a fair trial – and many were over ten years old!'

He shouted something into the gold microphone, and the car began inching forward.

When the FBI report finally came through, O'Smith left the yokel cops mumbling their apologies, and went right to work. No time for subtleties now, just have to go in fast and heavy. He stopped at a drugstore on University Avenue and picked up cotton wool and a few cans of lighter-fuel. Then, straight for the Computer Science building.

Seemed to be lots of other folks hurrying in the same direction. One or two carried signs. Away down the street a black limo was caught in a mob of some kind. Student demonstration? Good diversion there, all set for a quick in-and-out operation.

He paused, waggled his stiff right forefinger until it clicked, then removed the tip of it. Half the fingernail slotted into the remaining finger to form a forward sight. Not more than three or four in the lab, he reckoned, should be able to get the drop on two of 'em before the others could close their mouths.

Better get this Dr Lee Fong first thing, you never knew with chinks and their martial arts. Then the notes, grab essentials (they'd be most likely in top desk drawers and pockets) and use the rest to start the fire. Whole thing didn't need to take more'n fifteen minutes.

He was closer to the car now, and could see students sprawling over the hood, banging on it, scratching the paint with their signs. Punks! If he didn't need the ammo he'd take out a couple of 'em right here and now.

Suddenly the car broke free, flinging a body and a sign into the air, and careered towards him. O'Smith dodged left as it swerved left, dodged right as it swerved right, and collided with someone else, a student with a sign.

'*Murderer!*'

O'Smith felt the blast of bad breath, saw NO FASCH and felt the impact; before he could argue the truth of the accusation, or demonstrate it, he was down and out.

V

The room that had been a lab was nearly empty now, its grey floor material marked with pale squares and rectangles. In one corner two men wearing the orange uniforms of Custodial Services struggled to lift the last large cabinet, revealing the last pale rectangle. In the opposite corner Dan sat at a table sorting papers into two piles. Franklin paced up and down, stepping carefully in the pale parts. Finally he hunkered down and lit a cigarette.

'Christ,' he exhaled. 'Seeing all this you might think we'd lost out or something.'

'Maybe we did, in a way.'

'Like hell. Lee's just the same, moping around his office like a Jehovah's Witness the day after the world didn't end. I mean what the hell's wrong with you two, we've got the green light on this, now we can really be −'

A thump from the other corner made him look up. 'Careful, fellas. That stuff's expensive.'

One of the men put down his end of the cabinet and turned around. 'Listen, you think you can move this fuckin' ton a junk any better, you just come over and try.'

'Okay, I just, okay.'

'Smartass perfessers.'

He waited until the two had lifted their burden on to a trolley and wheeled it out of the room. 'Be lucky if anything works when we get moved. I don't know where Custodial gets these guys. Saw one in the hall just now didn't even have a uniform; old clothes and a straggly beard looked like it had mange on one side. Only reason I knew he worked here was I saw him carrying a box of your stuff. Can't be two Bugleboy Peanut Butter cartons on the whole campus.'

'Him? That's, that's a guy I used to know. Keeping some stuff for me.' A grubby notebook with a loose page flopped on one pile.

Franklin waved his cigarette. 'Look, this move to a new lab is just what we need, a chance to really get organized.'

'What for?'

'I mean, don't you want to see this project running like any other, teamwork, I mean a team, I mean – listen, this is a hell of a time to deliver an ultimatum, but to put it bluntly if I don't get some real work to do around here, I quit. Already told Lee, he sees my point, I work or I walk.'

Dan squared up a stack of dog-eared sheets. 'Well, maybe we should all just quit. Now that Roderick's safe, well . . .'

'Quit? But we haven't even begun, what do you mean "safe"? Of course he's safe, we've got the green light, the, now we can really go ahead –'

Dan looked at the two stacks of yellowing paper. 'I've got one or two things to clear up here. Okay if I meet you in Lee's office in a few minutes?'

'Okay, sure.' Ben Franklin patted his moustache. 'I mean it's always "wait a minute" with me, right? Always okay if I just hang around – okay, okay I'm going.'

When he was alone, Dan shuffled the two piles into one. When the men in orange returned, he said:

'Would you guys do me a favour?'

The black one looked suspicious. 'What favour?'

Dan pointed to the little door in the wall marked RECYCLING, PAPER ONLY. 'The chute in here is blocked or something. Would you drop this stuff in somebody else's chute?'

'Yeah, okay prof.'

'Is that you, Dr Fong?'

'*Grrrp.*'

'Oh, very funny. You won't feel like making funny noises when you hear what I've got to say. This is Dr George Tarr. I think you know the name.'

'*Grrrrupf.*'

'Just keep it up, keep it up. I'm recording this, you – you – now listen, I'm very disappointed about the way you finagled this committee vote. *Very* disappointed.'

72

'*Grrp*. Excuse me it's my stom –'

'As a matter of fact I've just called my lawyer and he says we have a good case against you. Hear that? A good case.'

'But I don't know what you – *errrp* – excuse –'

'Because I happen to know there were six members of the committee firmly committed to *my* project, and only three on your side. So the only way you could have got a vote eight-seven in your favour was to *sabotage* the whole system. I don't know what you did, maybe something to the computer, but you won't get away with it. I just called up to tell you – we *know*.'

'Know? *Mmgrrpl*.'

'Under the Freedom of Information Act we have access to the computer too, you know. And I have the printout right here in front of me. I have the *facts and figures*!'

'Don't know what you're talk –'

'Don't you? A fix, that's what I'm talking about, a fix! Because how else do you explain it – only three out of fifteen people actually wanted your damned robot – twice as many people wanted my project – yet you won! I don't know whether you bought votes or fixed the comp – but I mean to find out. See you in court, Doctor Fong!'

University of Minnetonka Special Emergency Finance Committee Voting Record Part 189077

Number of Cttee memb	= 18
Quorum	= 12
Number Present	– 15
Casting Vote Inoperative	
Number Votes Cast	= 15

Preference Indicators:
F: Fong (Proj Roderick)
T: Tarr (Proj Ripoff)
O: Neither (No Award)

No.	Pref.	Rank	Ballot I		Ballot II	
			O	F/T	F	T
0	F	FTO	–	0	0	–
3	F	FOT	–	3	3	–
0	T	TFO	–	0	–	0

73

No.	Pref.	Rank	Ballot I		Ballot II	
			O	F/T	F	T
6	T	TOT	–	6	–	6
5	O	OFT	5	–	5	–
1	O	OTF	1	–	–	1

15 Votes Total

No Award 6
Fong 8
Tarr 7

Today the stain on the door looked to Ben Franklin like a Portuguese man-o'-war. 'You're not going to let a little thing like that worry you, Christ, I wish he would take us to court. Laugh him off the faculty.'

Fong crunched an antacid tablet and blinked. 'Tarr, no, he doesn't worry me. Only it's just one more little piece of aggravation . . .'

'Relax, I've seen the printout on that too. Funny part is, if Tarr hadn't trotted out his little project Ripoff – well-named – we would've lost, 12 to 3. Guess you could say the psychic world has done us a favour – okay, what *is* wrong?'

'Thought Dan would've told you himself. I'd better – *grrrp* – wait, let . . . let him tell you himself.'

'Yeah, *wait*.' Franklin looked at the door again. Now it looked a little like a parachute, its shrouds unravelling as it descended. Funny how you could see almost anything . . .

'Tell you one thing, I want some changes made around here. When we move, I want a whole new structure. No more of this prima donna act of his, this, well *Dan*, just talking about you. Lee says you've got some little problem.'

'No problem.' Dan closed the stained door and leaned against it. 'I'm just leaving, that's all.'

'!'

'I tried to talk him out of it, Ben. But if the kid wants to go –'

'I don't believe it! You – you want something? It isn't enough that you're the big star, you want something else? More power? No? Well then mind letting me in on the secret? What makes you want to walk out on four years of your life? Not to mention my life and Lee here, you plan to just waste four years of his life? *Mind telling me why?*'

'Lots of reasons.' Ben stared at the t-shirt (BE SPONTANEOUS!) waiting for him to go on. 'For one thing it's all wrong. Nothing turned out like I thought. See, when I joined the project I was still a kid, nineteen, how did I know what I was getting into? I thought, Wow, the first robot, the first alien intelligence on this planet, I couldn't think of anything better, anything – specialler.

'Only when it gets down to it maybe it's not so special. It's more like being wrong all the time, you know? And that's just the work. See, I thought it would be like being part of a family, only just look at us: look at you, all you do is bitch and moan and worry about who's got a better job, who's the star player or something.'

'I –'

'See, you're like a baby, Ben, you can't read the books but you still want to chew on them.'

Franklin turned his blush away. 'So it's going to be personalities, is it? Because I've got a thing or two to say –'

'Wait. Look, I'm, all I'm saying is this isn't working out for you or for me or for anybody. And you, Lee, your stomach's so bad you'll have to retire early, just like Leo Bunsky – only he didn't retire early enough. And when he died I just started wondering what this is, is it special after all? Is it special enough to die for?

'And then Mary Mendez, was it special for her? Wandering around in that damned looney bin over there, asking everybody to please wind her up, is it worth that?'

Franklin lit a cigarette and held it ready to drop ash on the floor. 'Doesn't seem to have touched you, though, does it? I mean you're still healthy. Still the same nasty little snotty-nose –'

'Well I had scurvy last year but sure I'm okay physically. That's not the point. The point is Roderick, is he okay? Is he, is he special? See, when people around me were dying or going nuts or getting bitchy or having ulcers I could always say, "All right, but it's worth it, it's special. It must be special because look, NASA, the United States government, is putting cash into this. They're backing us a hundred per cent." Only they weren't.'

'Now let me get this straight. You're tired of the project first

75

because you find out that people wear out, have accidents and break down – just like in any other job – and second because NASA doesn't love us any more? Is that about it? Why, you pathetic little creep, is your ego so –'

'Let me finish. It's not just that they don't love us, they hate us. Not just NASA but everybody. As soon as they find out what we're doing, soon as they really understand what we're doing, they're out to get us.'

'Let's not get all paran –'

'Look, when NASA pulled out on us I started thinking. Haven't you ever wondered why nobody else is running a project like this? I mean *nobody*. Oh I know there's a few dozen AI projects in different places, but they kinda stand still, don't they? They work on a pattern-recognizer or a language analyser; they keep on working on it and they keep on keeping on. I checked a few places. No significant advances in the past ten years.'

'Where is this leading?'

'Let him go on,' said Fong. 'This is where it gets sinister.'

'So I started checking on private robot projects – you know, the kind of crank stuff or maybe not so crank, stuff you see in articles in *Micro-Ham, CPU Digest*, you know.'

'I never read the amateur journals.'

'You should. Because you find funny things. Like this commune in Oregon, all the neat things they were doing with something they called a "*Gestalt* guesser", really it was just – but anyway, just when it was getting interesting they had this fire.'

'So?'

'So it was just like the fire they had in Tuscon, where this little micro club were trying to set up a little thing to write short stories. Then this old guy in Florida – I forget what he was making but when it hit the local papers suddenly he got snuffed by a prowler. Then a nurse in Oklahoma City smashed her customized processor and killed herself, and so did a guy in Kansas, ran a feed store, only upstairs he had –'

'Are you sure? I'd have to check some of these myself.' Franklin forgot to smooth his moustache. 'Anyway a few cases don't –'

'You don't get it, do you? All these people were safe as long as they kept quiet. And when we thought NASA was our boss, we kept quiet too. We didn't publish anything, we didn't give any interviews, we kept a tight security lid on this. Only now . . .'

'You think we're targets for some kind of –?' Franklin flicked ash on the floor. 'Find this a little hard to swallow. I mean why? Who would, I mean *why*?'

'Who knows? I mean, who knows why anything? Why do we suddenly have to move the lab upstairs? Everybody you ask just says they got this computer transfer order, this paper here says we gotta move. I don't know who or why, I mean I know what's *way* behind it, but that's not much help. I know it's just something like the old species trying to zap the new one before it gets started, that makes sense but it's kinda depressing all the same.'

'Especially if they try to zap us with it,' Fong said. 'Anyway the kid's right, let's quit while we're ahead.'

Ben Franklin wasn't listening. Smoothing his moustache, he said, 'Can't be the military, they'd be happy as shit to get their hooks on a robot, to hell with wider implications. Bet it's some government agency, probably connected to a think tank, bunch of "futurologists", bet you any damn thing. Bastards sitting there working out their "scenarios" as if the future were some kind of big-budget movie, they want us on the cutting-room floor, do they? Well I say we fight, can't let 'em get away with four years of our – fight, dammit, expose the whole vicious   '

'What for?' Dan smiled. 'Is it really worth it?'

'What kind of bullshit scientist are you to ask a thing like that? Is it worth it? Is it –?'

Fong was tugging at his sleeve and making faces. Ben finally saw that he'd written something, and leaned over to read it:

The fight's already over. *We won.*
But *keep quiet* about it.

Four years, he kept thinking, four years. As though repeating the number could magically call them back, restore his career, his wife, whatever it was that had deserted him . . .

'I don't believe you.' He pushed past Dan and reached for the door (noticing now how like a shrunken head the stain really looked). 'I don't believe a fucking word.'

As he entered the men's room an unkempt student jumped back from the graffito he had obviously been inscribing next to the mirror. He looked at Ben and quickly turned away, probably to conceal the port-wine birthmark on his cheek. Then hurried out, capping his fibre pen as he went, and leaving Ben to consult his own blank mask. Perfect. Unblemished even by expression.

Automatically he began to wash his hands. He studied them as though he were Ambroise Paré, that military surgeon whose first elaborate designs in jointed iron provided not only new limbs (for those who reached the Peace of Augsburg without them) but also new work for unemployed armourers. There were times when Ben felt as though his entire body were a prosthesis, perfect, ready to work, but untenanted. Even his mind seemed no more than an ingenious engine for grinding through facts (and a part of the engine now reminded him that this was Darwin's complaint) but to no purpose. He felt as hollow as that chess-playing Turk exhibited by Baron von Kempelen in 1769 (and later borrowed by Maelzel, delighting the world even more than his borrowed invention of the metronome).

He dried his hands and folded them tentatively in prayer. Well, no. No point in investing in that unnecessary hypothesis, pie in the sky for the ghost in the machine ... And yet. Even a prosthetic hand could not function properly unless its wearer retained some of the 'feeling' in his ghostly limb. Why couldn't he, Benjamin Waldo Franklin, be waiting just for such a feeling?

'Holy Ghost in the machine?' He tried to make it sound ironic. All the same, a moment later he went into one of the stalls and sat down on the lid and asked for guidance.

It was a gamble, but then a Jansenist God might approve of that; had not Pascal proved that there was nothing to lose and everything to gain? The venue was strange, but then a Lutheran God was used to that; had not the first Lutheran also uncovered certain fundamental truths in a privy?

What Ben found was a paperback book on the floor. For a moment he simply stared at it, reading the title over and over: *God is Good Business*. A sign? No. A sign? No!

He could hardly call it a sign, with its gaudy yellow-and-black cover, its red sunburst proclaiming '18,000,000 copies sold!' The back cover showed a grey portrait of the author, a smiling businessman with the unlikely name Goodall V. Wetts III.

Just say to yourself when you get up in the morning, 'God WANTS me to win! God wants ME to win! God wants me to WIN – TODAY!' With this simple formula plus the Ten Rules of Faith Dynamics, you –

Ben shut the book and put it back on the floor. But on second thoughts he picked it up again. Might be good for a laugh some time . . . you never knew.

And what greater test could God put him through, than asking him to abandon all pleasures of the intellect and accept – *this*?

Washing his hands again, Ben studied his face for changes. He was leaning forward, trying out a confident slow smile, when suddenly he realized he was not alone. A janitor stood leaning on a mop, watching him.

'Jesus Christ! Ain't enough you spend an hour in the john, you gotta spend another hour seein' if your lipstick's on straight. I gotta clean this joint, buster, howsabout fuckin' off?'

'Oh I . . . sorry . . .'

'You will be sorry, if you write any more porno on my walls.'

Ben's gaze flicked to the place whence the graffito had already been scrubbed.

'Look I'm not responsible –'

'You tellin' me, anybody writes crap like that oughta see a shrink. You like fuckin' clocks, do ya? Or just drawing dirty –'

Ben fled, his face burning, while the janitor shouted after him, '– pitchers of guys fuckin' clocks, watches maybe, guys wid moustaches? Yeah? And what's that mean, DALI LAID DIAL, what the fuck's that m –?'

Sounds of pain, sounds of rain. O'Smith opened his eyes to the sight of two people in white, arguing.

'. . . wasn't on duty when he came in, doctor. So if you want to blame somebody . . .'

'Not a question of blame, it's just procedure, that's all. We send all John Does to City . . .'

'Yes but Nancy said . . .'

'Not as if we're not overcrowded as it is what with the flu epidemic . . . AH! HOW'S IT GOING, FELLA?'

O'Smith automatically reached out to shake his hand and

found that he was not reaching after all. His right arm was missing.

'Where's my durn arm?'

'Your ah, prosthesis, well we had a little problem there, the car pretty much wrecked it. But don't worry, get you fixed up with a new one just as soon as –'

'Where is it? Where's my durn arm?'

'Are you insured, sir?' The nurse was shoving a form in front of his eyes, wasn't that *his* arm she was holding it with? 'If we could just have your name and policy number – *God! Ow! Jesus!*'

Someone shouted, crepe soles came flapping down the street, arms holding him, hands prying his jaws away from his own arm the nurse was wearing, what was a nurse doing inside this form anyways? Stabbed, he fell back, take it slow boy, wait your time, Brazos grinning at him as he heard some folks talking clear over in Galveston . . .

'. . . gave him fifty ccs, doc, okay?'

'Great, yeah, Nora, how's that thumb?'

'I'm . . . all right, doctor . . . guess it's my own darn fault, mine and Nancy's . . .'

Galveston, gal-with-a-vest-on, where was the durn armhole, he couldn't get his arm through, what was that durn muzzle velocity . . .

'Galveston,' he said.

'Better send this joker up to Section 23, right? Before he kills somebody, getting 'em all this week, you see the girl in B ward, the cast change? Hysterics, you'd think we were taking her leg off . . . said it took her ages to get all those names on the old one . . . Give him another fifty, Al, he's still twitching. Talk about prosthesis overdependency, a paradox, Nora, a para . . .'

'Oh you and your paradoxes! Dr Coppola, sometimes I think you read just a little bit too much . . .'

'Like to keep up, right? Sure the admissions procedure is paradoxical but isn't life itself?'

'. . .'

'. . . like in this Graham Greene yarn I'm reading . . . offers to sacrifice his own soul for the salvation of souls, but does that include his own or what?'

80

'. . . always springing these egghead stories . . .'

'. . . same with admissions . . . uninsured creep gets in we end up keeping him until he pays, only how can he pay if he can't get out to work? Fairer not to let 'em in in the first pl . . .'

'Have you looked at the corner patient, doctor? Nancy says either something's wrong with the monitor or he has a temperature of 2 million . . .'

'. . . try to get any maintenance done around here, might as well be asking for . . . yeah when I checked it read minus 3 million, B.P. 80 over zero . . .'

Fighting his way through Galveston one arm tied behind him, only it was somebody else's arm, that old body in Florida reaching for his 12-gauge, Brazos looking surprised as the fully-automatic armhole opened up, bap you're dead, bap you're dead again . . .

They watched him sink into sleep and then made their way to Reception, where the pretty receptionist with all the hair was saying to a black doctor:

'Sure, but I mean it don't hardly seem fair, two doctors on the same ward with the same darn name almost!'

'It's easy, though, look: *I'm* Dr De'Ath, *he's* Dr D'Eath. *I'm* black, *he's* white. I specialize in epidemiology, he specializes in cardiology. *I* –'

'Yeah I know but –'

'Look: *he's* building a robot to test artificial hearts. *I* don't know one end of a soldering iron from the other, okay? So what's the problem? What's the big problem?'

Chief Dobbin opened the press conference by reading from a prepared statement that began: 'I took one look and knew she was trouble with a capital T. This little lady happened to be very, very dead.'

A reporter in the back groaned and turned off his recorder. 'Here we go, another literary treat.'

'With a capital T,' said his neighbour. 'Ain't we gonna get a look at the suspect?' He cupped his hands and called, 'SUSPECT!'

'All in good time, boys. "I asked myself why? Why would any sane human being . . ."'

'Probably be a chapter in his book,' said the first reporter, punching buttons on his pocket reminder. 'Never heard of a fucking deadline.'

His neighbour, who was older, stopped picking his teeth to say, 'Deadline? I thought you was on the *Caribou*, since when they meet deadlines on that shit-sheet? You wait till you graduate and try meeting a real deadline on a real paper.'

The boy was silent for a moment, pretending to study his reminder while Dobbin droned on. 'Okay,' he whispered finally. 'How about a little help from an expert then, okay? Like what angle you got on this?'

'Angle? Sex, of course. It's a natural here, this Fong guy is ethnic, a creepy scientist, what more do you want?'

'I meant, uh, you think he really –?'

'What the hell difference does that make, look, they found the dead girl with her leg cut off, blood all over the place, and in her hand was this book covered with his finger-prints, may not be enough for a court-room but it sure as hell works out fine on the front page. Forget about did he do it, get down to work on why? *Why, why*, as our police colleague likes to say.' He picked a morsel from a back tooth and examined it before flicking it away. 'Listen you try this for size: I'm doing a think piece to go with this story, on how all these cybernetics guys are repressed faggots, sadists and what have you. This a.m. I picked up a coupla their magazines, got a list here somewhere of some of the kinky words they use, strong sex angle running right through it, listen to this, *bit, byte, RAM*, how about those?'

'I don't know, they ain't got much on him –'

'*Gang punch, flip-flop, input*, what do you think that really means, huh? *Stand-alone software*, how about that? *Debugger*, you can't make it plainer, and even the company names, how about *Polymorphic Systems*, how about *The Digital Group*? Or *Texas Instruments*, ever wonder what a *Texas Instrument is*? Or a *Honeywell*? *IBM*, says a lot there . . .'

Someone held up a little camera. 'Keep it down, you guys, just while I get this live, he's gonna show us the book.'

O'Smith woke up feeling just fine, sitting in a fine little parlour with a lot of fine folks, still no arm but what the hell. There was

Chief Dobbin's face beaming at him from the teevee, life wasn't so bad.

> This is the book that cracked this caper wide open. *Learning Systems,* we thought at first it was an educationalism book but we got our library experts to work on it and – here, I'll show you a page – pure computers. So then we traced it to Dr Lee Fong of the Computer Science Department, found out he was on campus on the night in question. We put him under blanket surveillance, must of surveilled him for a week before he made a false move. He burned some documents and tried to make a run for it. We got him at the airport.

Like Brazos Bill, he thought. O'Smith must have got him at just about fifty airports. They could use a machine like that in here, better than just sittin' in front of the teevee all day.

'What you folks do for excitement around here?' he asked the man in the next chair. Old buzzard, looked like that old body in Florida. Course all old folks look alike.

'What?'

'You got any amusement machines in this place?'

'Machines!' The old man started shaking all over. 'Do you know about the machines?'

'Know what, old-timer?'

'Old-timer equals Saturn, malefic influence badly aspected to Mars equals iron, iron men in the walls, in the floors, in the –'

'Jesus H. Christ I only asked –'

But the old man continued, his voice growing shrill: 'In the walls in the floors in the earth, terrestrial currents, magnetic influences pointing North, North is the Mecca of the magnets, the Mecca, the mecca-men, mechanical men feel them in the walls they get in through the power lines, lines of magnetic current, wheels within wheels, lines within lines . . .'

A pair of white-clad men appeared; one held the old man while the other prepared a syringe. 'Give him fifty this time Joe, he'll sleep like a baby – not *now*, Mary, I can't wind you up now, I'm busy giving Fred his medication . . .'

O'Smith leaned forward and concentrated on the teevee, camera zooming in on a page of print:

corrected by $(SR_n/100) \times 4.7004397181$ yielding 14.97 bits at 100 milliseconds exposure, using 4-gram array PU on a 43% redundancy input, well within expected limits for the 8688R imaging unit. POKERSON, MOSSIANT, RICANING . . .

They cut to Lee Fong who turned out to be fat and fifty, thick glasses and everything – a real disappointment, to look at him. O'Smith hadn't missed much there. No fun in a body that didn't put up no fight, martial arts or nothing. Hell, most of 'em were just shit, not like that old boy in St Petersburg with his 12-gauge. He'd made some damn thing, a little machine for talking to old folks, a conversationizer for lonesome old folks. O'Smith didn't see no harm in it but it was enough for the Agency list, the hit parade.

And after all, the big boys knew what they were doing.

BOOK TWO

I

Then the guests were invited to admire a barrel organ, and Nozdrev immediately began to grind out some music for their benefit. The organ produced a not unpleasant sound, but in the middle of the performance something happened, and a mazurka turned into [a march] and that in turn ended in a popular waltz. Long after Nozdrev had stopped turning the handle, an extraordinarily energetic reed in the organ went on whistling all by itself.

Nikolai Gogol, *Dead Souls*

'Semantics?' Indica thumped her coffee cup on the pine table. 'Hank doesn't know the meaning of the word.'

Bax nodded. 'I know what you mean. It's like –'

'It's like he's so damned hot to pick on some word or something, I mean he never hears what I'm really saying.'

'I hear you, I mean, right on.'

She looked at him. Bax might be a little older than he looked, with his button-beanie and shaggy blond moustache. *Right on?* She took another sip of dandelion coffee and went on talking about her husband.

'Like the other day. He got all pissed off just because I said Naomi's basically a Fundamentalist. Oh, and when I told him I thought germ warfare was just sick? You should have heard him!'

'No, I mean yeah. I know what you mean.' Bax finished his glass of bean milk, belched and tipped back in his chair. 'I mean, words only get in the way. Like people, and like – like things.'

'Things, God, don't tell me about things.' Her thin face assumed its characteristic mask of martyrdom, eyes rolling back to look for guidance from the water-stained kitchen ceiling. 'Solar panel's leaking again, everywhere I look I see another busted thing around here. I mean, Hank just keeps buying crap and it just keeps breaking down and will he ever fix it? Ha. He's always so busy with his crap environment magazine he never even sees the environment he lives in. I mean two years I've been shoving

87

match books under the leg of the dining table, been sticking a pail under the garbage disposal where it leaks, you seen our back yard? Six rusty old bikes, I mean six!'

'I hear you, Indica.'

'Every time Hank starts another article we get the whole crap thing all over again. Like his survival shelter, three tons of cement in the shape of a pyramid – because of the rays and all – only he has to make the door too small for anybody but the chickens, whole thing smells of rotten eggs all the time. "I'll fix it," he says, and goes off to another damned pollution conference, Jesus! I could tell him a thing or two about pollution.'

'Yeah,' Bax said. After a moment's thought, he added, 'Yeah.' He tipped his chair back further and reached a leg in her direction.

Indica stared into her earthenware cup, the one with her name and zodiac sign hand-painted on it, the one with the broken handle. 'I mean, he got this house computer to make everything simpler, and it just made it worse, it never does anything but tell him how wrong he is, how wrong everything in the house is. And since we moved out here, anything goes wrong we have to take it twenty miles to town to get it fixed, there sits the ultrasonic dishwasher, it worked about a week.'

'Complicated.'

'Now he only wants to buy a car that runs on chicken-shit, that's all, a bargain he figures and it only costs about twice as much as an Eldorado. See what I'm up against?'

Bax thought his foot was at that moment up against hers. He pressed, and something hummed and moved away from the contact.

'Christ! Are you hurt?' She helped him up.

'No, I'm – but I guess the chair's not too good.' He handed her the splintered chair back, and she placed it in a corner, near a dismantled coffee grinder.

'Hey, what is this thing under the table?'

Two glittering eyes peered up at him.

Indica shrugged. 'That? Nothing. A kind of robot, I guess.'

'A robot! Great!' Bax stood clear of it.

'Don't worry, it doesn't work either. Just some piece of junk a guy dumped on us. This creep poet Allbright, who never writes any poetry, just rips off stuff. Guess he ripped this off from some computer freak he knows . . .'

'Yeah? What's it, uh, supposed to do?'

'Who knows? We've had it a month, so far all it does is watch TV and get in the way.'

Bax squatted down to look at it. 'Watches TV?'

'Sure. Hank's creep friend said to treat it like a real kid. So Hank plunks it down in front of the TV every day and it just sits there by the hour. Never moves a muscle.'

Man and robot studied each other. 'Not much to look at,' said Bax, and it wasn't: a squat instrument only two feet high with a large spherical head, a small, conical body, and a pair of tiny tank tracks on which it now edged back, further under the table. The spindly arms, resembling miniature dental drills, were folded against the chest, where Bax could read a word stencilled in black on battleship grey.

'Roderick, eh? Here boy. Here, Roderick.'

The blue glass eyes stared. No sound came from the tiny grille set in the position of a mouth.

'It doesn't know a damned thing, not even its name,' said Indica, and yawned.

Roderick saw a pair of pointy-toed cowboy boots, knees bursting through faded jeans, a huge tattooed hand reaching out towards him. It all looked pretty dangerous, except that the hand had a wrist watch of the kind you could get at Vinnie's Rock Bottom, for rock-bottom prices in comps, calcs, watches, cassettes, video, everything guaranteed personally by Vinnie, everything at low, lower, lowest, rock-bottom prices. At the other end of the arm was a man with hair under his nose, and milk on the hair.

Indica yawned. 'Hank's coming home in a couple of hours, so . . .'

They were gone. Milk, what was it for? Pour it on cereal and spoon it into your mouth. Once upon a time there was a lovely princess who bathed in milk, and they say that her complexion . . .

Roderick listened to their feet going upstairs. Bax was a big man with yellow hair the colour of cereal. Indica was a lovely princess who bathed in the big tub upstairs, it made a wonderful banging sound when she ran the water in. Water was like milk, it

89

was milk with clear stuff added, clear as the shine that makes good furniture even better . . .

Something good was upstairs, Indica had whispered to Bax and led him up to see. Now there were stockinged feet moving around up there. Maybe they would tiptoe to the window and pull back the shade to see policemen all around the house. Grown-ups took off their shoes a lot, to watch TV, and if you have a foot-odour problem you need Footnote, spray or powder. Gee, no foot odour!

Bump, bump, bump. Just like water in the tub. Or like shots. Then they struggle for the gun, it goes off and there's a body rolling down the stairs, bump, bump, bump, what have I done? Like chopping wood: I'd be beholden to you, ma'am, if you could see your way clear to givin' a hungry man some wood to chop for his breakfast. Breakfast is the bestest when we all eat Honey-O.

Roderick hummed it to himself as he moved across the black-and-white squares of kitchen, the roses of the living-room, the creaky boards to the foot of the stairs:

Breakfast O Breakfast
Breakfast is the bestest
O breakfast is the bestest
When we all eat Honey-O.
Honey-O, Honey-O, honey, honey
O Breakfast, etc.

The stairs were a problem. They were up and up, while Roderick was down here: he couldn't see how to work it. TV people did stairs all the time. He saw them running down, falling down, rolling down, sitting still on a step and talking, waiting on the dark stairs with a gun and a hat, creeping up with shoes in hand, even vacuuming difficult stair carpets can be a breeze with Breeze-o-mat, because Breeze-o-mat makes housework a breeze!

Animal cries floated down to him, as the bumping continued. Jungle drums? Lord, the heat, the flies! Why don't the beggars attack – what are they waiting for? I don't know if I can stand much more of this, with the Brigadier away on trek for days at a time, leaving the two of us alone like this. My God, Marjorie, I'm only flesh and blood. I also, Nigel. The heat, the flies, gorillas hammering their chests, a Jap sniper in every tree, Joe, I can't go on. Leave me here, I'll hold them off, that's an order soldier. *Careful!*

Roderick spun around to check the big green plant behind him. Behind it was another big green plant and then another Roderick and then shadows that might be anything: black men with spears, spotty things with teeth in their mouths, fat spiders, glittering snakes, a scorpion crooking its finger at him, shambling zombies coming after him. A guy had to protect himself, one chance in a million but it just might work, break through to the shore, the sunlit sand where he could hear the surf beating, beating . . .

'Nothing,' said Bax. He dropped Hank's kimono on the floor and climbed back into bed. Indica noticed that he was getting a paunch.

'How can it be nothing, we both heard it!'

'I mean, just that little robot thing, you know? Knocked over your potted plant in the hall.' He reached for her but she sat up, drawing the sheet around her shoulders.

'Just great. I only spent two years growing that damned thing from an avocado stone, that's all. Two years.'

'Okay, but –'

'Don't. I'm not in the mood any more. I hate that sonofabitching robot, you know? Hank says it cost a million or so to build. For two cents I'd trash the damned thing.'

'A million? Wow.'

'Yeah, wow.' She turned away from him, his bleached hair and faint face-lift scars. 'That really grabs you doesn't it, a price tag like that? That's men all right, all you think about is gadgets and how much you can get them for. I see Hank reading an electronics catalogue, he gets the same look on his face, the same dumb look he gets over a sex magazine, how do you think that makes me feel?'

'No, sure, but –'

'Let's get dressed. A million bucks' worth of junk running around the house destroying my plants, how do you think that makes me feel?'

'Yeah, but –'

'I don't want to talk about it any more. Just get dressed.'

Bax obeyed, and followed her downstairs. From the living-room came sounds (Yipe! Eeeeow! Boing! and scales played on a xylophone) of Roderick's favourite TV cartoon, *Suffering Cats*. The little robot stood close to the screen, mesmerized by the sight of cats blackening their faces with TNT, walking off cliffs, and being flattened under weights marked 1 TON. Bax, too, was fascinated. He sat down to watch, only half-aware that Indica was leading Roderick out into the hall.

'*Where's that cat?*' said a deep voice from the TV. '*Where's that dad-blamed cat?*' Its owner, visible from the waist down, wore hobnail boots and carried a meat-cleaver. Bax was grinning already.

'Hey honey? Come and watch this. Old Oscar's on the warpath and –'

An odd sound came from the hall, like grinding gears. In a minute, Indica and Roderick came back. She was crying and trembling, while the robot seemed unperturbed. *Yipe! Boing!* He crept up close to the screen, until his large dome caused a partial eclipse.

'Outa the way, big-head.' Bax noticed a shiny dent in the dome, as it moved away. But just then he needed his full attention for animated carnage: a knocked-out cat listened to birds and grew a red lump on its head, and looked at the world through a pair of plus-sign eyes.

A commercial came on. Kids were urged to get a plastic robot that stalked in circles, saying, 'Hello, I'm Robbie! Can I be your friend? Hello, I'm Robbie! Can I be your friend?'

Roderick was unable to watch this, for his head kept revolving in the strangest way, like a lid coming off a jar of Huck Finn grape-style jelly, a taste treat for kids – and grown ups too!

'I didn't do anything,' Indica protested. 'All I did was take him and show him the avocado he killed, all I did was rub his nose in it, a little.'

Hank watched the head revolve. 'A little? Then how did he get that big dent? Jesus, I can't keep anything around here, you –'

'Sure, blame the wife, it's what I'm for, right? Blame me. Okay, maybe I got carried away. Big deal, maybe I slapped him a couple of times, okay, I slapped your little toy.'

'Just look at him! What am I supposed to tell Allbright? He trusts us with a billion-dollar machine, am I supposed to tell him you knocked hell out of it?'

'A million dollars, listen they had this toy robot on TV, nine ninety-five plus tax, at least it can say hello; your little mechanical shit-head here can't even do that. All he knows is how to smash people's house-plants, how to go around murdering living things. Okay, I'm sorry. Okay? I'm sorry, maybe I hit him too hard. I don't know, maybe I banged his head on the floor a couple of times, shit Hank, I was pretty close to a breakdown if you want to know.'

He combed his full beard with both hands. 'Probably cost a fortune to fix him. A fortune. What the hell can I say to the guy who built him if he comes around to see – it's all – it's all getting on top of me.'

'Look, maybe I can just stick his head down with scotch tape or something, no one'll know the difference really. I mean, this dude never comes to see him or anything, who's to know? Even if he did, I mean we just say he fell down the stairs . . . Look, I'll fix him right now.'

She carried Roderick out to the kitchen. Hank sat staring at his hands for a moment, then went to the bar. As he picked up the bottle of Scotch, a tiny screen behind it lit up with a message:

First of the day 19:48: CONGRATULATIONS HANK, YOU ARE MAKING REAL PROGRESS.

'Shut up,' he said. After downing the measured drink, he returned to the sofa and sat fiddling with his electric pipe-cleaner. Handy little gadget – but wasn't it starting to make a funny noise?

'Here we are, good as new.' Indica plunked the little robot down in front of the TV and turned it on. 'Good boy, you just sit here and watch the pretty pictures.' The screen showed a lifelike armpit.

'Good as new,' she said to Hank. 'Not that he was ever a hell of a lot of good. Never says a word, never opens his mouth. I mean, even when I plug him in for his recharge at night, he never says good night or anything. Some robot! If you ask me – what's the matter now?'

Hank cocked his head over the electric pipe-cleaner. 'Making a funny noise, hear it?'

'You and your goddamned gadgets, how about listening to me once in a while? Hank, what the hell's wrong with you, all you think about are your gadgets. I mean, we got a house full of broken-down machinery now, who needs it? We came out here to get away from crap and machines and – look at you, sitting here in the middle of the goddamned desert, listening to a goddamned electric pipe-cleaner!'

He looked at her, then back to the instrument. 'Now wait a minute. We came out here to establish our own, ahm, environmental situation, right? So machines are an integral part of it. Oh sure, I used to want to turn the clock back, just like everyone else. I wanted to trash our whole technology, return to the soil – only I grew out of it. Whether we like it or not, technology is here to stay. *Machines* are here to stay.'

On cue, the pipe-cleaner made a loud buzzing noise and emitted a wisp of smoke. Hank dropped it to the floor where, after flopping for a moment like a dying fish, it lay still.

'Ha! Maybe they don't want to stay.'

Hank's pudgy fingers dug into his beard. 'Oh sure, laugh. But it doesn't change a thing. Sure, machines go wrong once in a while. They have to be fixed –'

'Tell me something I don't know. You never fix anything around here, you never let me call a repairman, all you do is let it pile up! The crapyard of the universe we got here, the crap –'

'Just let me finish, will you? Just have the courtesy to let me finish what I'm saying, okay? Okay. Machines are here to stay, we have to make the most of 'em. We owe it to ourselves not to just throw them away the minute they conk out on us. If we do that, we're turning all our energy and raw materials into junk and garbage and pollution. Right?'

'What is this, are you gonna quote your whole goddamned article for *Country Ambience* or something? I've read it.'

'Just let me finish. Now, we don't call repairmen because the true person, true to his own environment, fixes everything himself. It's the only way to learn to live *in* your environment. You fix things yourself, or if you can't fix something you make

94

some new use out of it. Like maybe you cannibalize it to fix something else.'

'Cannibalize my ass! I don't believe what I'm hearing from you. God, you've been writing this crap so long you believe it yourself, any minute now you're gonna tell me about *bricoleurs* and Zen motor cycles! Listen, buster, this isn't *your* environment, it's *mine. You're* always off at some goddamned conference, *I'm* the one has to try living in this shit-hole day after day. Day and night, you know? I'm stuck here, with the deep-freeze that wrecks a quarter-ton of food, with the stopped-up drains – all of it. *My* environment, and it stinks.' She looked at Roderick. 'Yeah, including that little tin marvel, you mind telling me how he's supposed to fit into our swell environmental situation? I mean, just what are we supposed to get out of having him around, a walking junkyard?'

'Well, ahm, as a matter of fact I'm doing an article on him for *Eco-Style*, "I Adopted a Robot", to tie in with their big issue on home cybernetics. And it looks like I'll be guesting on a chat show next week, could lead to a book-movie deal, even heard from a producer putting out feelers for a sitcom series, *My Little Robot*, I mean it's all talk at this stage, but who knows . . .?'

On the screen, a man with a yellow moustache held up a box of detergent. Roderick began to wave his arms.

'Okay, keep him. Just keep him out of my way, Hank. I mean it.'

'Baba abbaba!' said Roderick. 'Ablabba bab!'

That night, after Roderick had been plugged to his re-charger in the spare room, and while he stood motionless, his blue glass eyes opaque in sleep, Hank and Indica patched up their quarrel.

It was a chance to be alone, and they made the most of it. Indica set out low-cholesterol potato chips in a biodegradable plastic bowl, Hank opened a few recycled cans of home brew, and they put on their favourite old video tape of Jacques Cousteau. Holding hands, plenty of friendly eye-contact – it was almost like old times.

Indica looked at the underwater ballet of porpoises critically. After all, she'd been a dancer herself once, and a good one. The chorus of *Mao and I*, nine months with the Braxton Hicks Dancers doing TV work, the talent was there. Even in that TV commercial where she'd been a dancing taco, it was there, talent she could have built into a career. Only she hadn't. Somehow after she'd married Hank – anyway, here she was, watching a bunch of fish! Oh well, Hank probably loved it.

Hank watched a man in a wet-suit cavorting with cetaceans. Ho hum. Indica probably loved this stuff, this expression of man's unity with Nature. For him, it was just a place to rest his gaze while he swallowed flat beer. Of course he still cared about the global environment, in a way. He still wrote articles about the blue whale and the white rhino. Not his fault if they turned into promotional tie-ins for glossy magazine spreads selling dog food and deodorants. He had to live. Had to swim with the current and survive. People got tired worrying about Spaceship Earth, they wanted to concentrate on Spaceship Me.

There were no more triumphs, only peak experiences; no more tragedies, only personal problems. Indica's problem was being a good dancer who'd stopped dancing. Hank's problem was being a bad writer who couldn't stop writing. Together they were building for themselves a modest little problem relationship.

'Just like old times,' said Indica.

'A *déjà vu* experience,' said Hank.

'You can say that again.'

II

'Who? Oh. Uh, great to hear from you uh, Dan is it? Great to, only I'm just this minute trying to get away, guesting tonight on the Ab Jason show, gotta be in L.A. by, hey, some great publicity there for your little lab . . . well sure you probably sure a low profile, he did, yes he did explain that, sure. Only . . .'

As he transferred the phone to his other ear in order to look at his watch, Indica could hear the frantic voice on the other end: '. . . *taking a hell of a chance even using a pay phone . . . Subpoena . . . threatening me with mental hosp . . .*'

'Appreciate all that, Dan boy, only hell I'm a freelance journalist, you can't expect . . . truth is my business . . . public has a right to know and the truth, in the long run the truth . . . Frankly I think you're overdramatizing this whole . . . anyway how can they subpoena you into a mental, that doesn't make sense, you . . . Frankly Dan boy I don't understand your attitude, here I am babysitting this creation of yours, busting my balls to get you some free publicity, even sent you those test tapes you wanted did Allbright give them to you? He did, and . . . Okay, sure, if that's . . . sure I, just a second.'

He fumbled for a pen and wrote *M & P Wood, 614 Sycamore Avenue, Newer, Nebraska.* 'Any zip . . . right. If that's the way you feel about it, fine, if this Wood firm can do any better . . . what am I supposed to do, the thing's subnormal, doesn't even talk . . . well no we haven't talked to it, not much, course I could have spent more time with it but trying to carve out a career here, you know, trying to weld together the concepts of ecological balance and post-industrial . . . YES I'LL SEND THE GODDAMNED THING. Yeah, ciao.' He slammed down the receiver. 'You hear any of that?'

'I wasn't listening.' Indica sat wedged in a window seat, painting her nails. The scarf around her throat was blue, her toenails were becoming red.

'That guy's cracking up, completely bananas, you know? Figures *they* are after him, want to subpoena his records and lock him up, smash the robot and Christ knows what.'

'I'm on their side,' she said.

Roderick extended a claw towards her foot. 'Red.'

'Listen, he wants us to send him off to some firm in Nebraska of all damned places, thinks we're not good enough to, not caring enough, how do you like that?'

She shrugged. 'I couldn't care less. Are you gonna make that plane or what?'

'Yeah, plenty of time. Only Jesus he has to dump this on me when I've got enough to worry about, you think maybe I should trim my beard a little? I don't want to come across as a goddamned nut . . .'

'Leave it.' She did not look at him. 'You look fine.'

'Great, but what am I supposed to say? I've got nothing to show them, I mean if I show them *that* they'll just laugh. A million kids have toys more articulate than *that*. Here I've worked my buns off trying to prepare for this show, can't even take him with me. I mean they'll just laugh. I mean, he can't do anything but babble in baby-talk, you think a hundred million viewers want to see that?'

Indica set down her bottle of nail varnish. 'Don't worry. You can just tell them about him.'

'Sure, I have to, I have to do it that way now. But I mean Christ I spent three days trying to teach him chess, all he knows is how to knock the pieces off the board. What am I supposed to say? I've adopted this robot only he's a little retarded?'

'Jess,' said Roderick. 'Jess, jess, jess. Jess?'

Indica snickered. 'Oh don't worry, you'll think of something on the plane. Make it up, what the hell. Tell 'em he reads Latin and Esperanto, plays the ukulele. Tell 'em he likes the Mets. Tell 'em you want him to grow up to be President.'

'Sure, you're right. I've got to think of this as pure box-office, that's all. Only my nerves are – and this guy calling me up like this at the last minute, saying he doesn't want any publicity. Doesn't want any publicity! You know, sometimes –'

'You'll miss your plane.'

Hank stood up, holding his attaché case in both hands. With the full beard and glasses, he looked a little like an immigrant in some old movie, coming off the steamship at Ellis Island. All he needed, she thought, was a tag around his neck. 'Well,' he said. 'Here goes. Wish me luck.'

'Break a leg,' she murmured. 'Bye.'

Roderick looked up, when he'd gone. 'Bye-bye-bye-bye-bye.' He turned back to watch Indica's red toes. Toes were little fingers. If you had fingers and toes you could do all kinds of things, make them red or count them: this little finger went to market, like Hank, that little finger stayed home, like Indica. Queen, king, knight, rook and the little pawn at the end there . . .

He moved closer until he was staring at her across the low table where the bottle of varnish stood. There was white stuff between her toes and red stuff on them. She put it on with a little matchstick, red. Red, it went into a little hole in the top of this bishop here on this funny jessboard that didn't have any squares. When she put the matchstick into it, there it was, a bishop. Only without squares, how could it see where to move? He grabbed the bishop and it fell over and red came out.

'Shit,' said Indica. She pulled a lot of white stuff out of a box and mopped the board, spreading red all over.

'Jit,' said Roderick. Indica stopped mopping and smiled at him. 'Jit,' he said again.

'What the hell, Roddy, go ahead. Have a ball. I'm never gonna clean another thing around here, you know? So go ahead.'

He dipped his claw in the red and held it up to her. 'Red.'

There was Hank on TV! His beard might be a different shape and his face might be a different colour, but here he was, real as life. Roderick went to the window and looked out. Hank's car wasn't there, so he hadn't come back, but here he was, sitting on a sofa with some other people, talking to Ab Jason who sat on a chair of his own. Ab was a man who kept wrinkling his face and making people laugh. Roderick rolled right up close to the TV screen, to watch every move.

'. . . *doesn't, ahm, talk much yet but he's learning, boy is he learning fast. He plays chess —*'

99

'Plays chess? But so do a lot of computers. Tell me, Hank, what's so special about little Roddy?'

'Well, he's, he's like a real kid. I mean for instance he's a big baseball fan. He likes the Mets.' Tittering came from the audience, and Ab wrinkled his face.

'The Mets! Ahem!' Laughter. 'Who's his favourite player? The batting practice machine?' Loud laughter, then applause. 'Seriously, Hank, what else does he do?'

'He watches TV a lot.'

'TV? No kidding! What do you think he gets out of it? What kind of stuff does he like, anyway? Serious stuff, commentators and think-shows? Or daytime shows like Milestones to Morning? Hey, is he watching us right now? Is he?'

'Yes, yes he is, Ab. He and my wife —'

'Okay, want to wave to him, before we take a break?'

Hank waved and Roderick waved back. Indica was of course upstairs with Bax.

'You're watching Ab Jason, and right now you're watching a man wave goodbye to his adopted son – a robot who likes the Mets. We'll be right back after this:'

Ab and Hank disappeared, and Roderick saw the giant armpit again.

'. . . clean and dry almost twenty-five hours a day. Why settle for less? If you're troubled . . .'

Bye-bye-bye. Roderick trundled into the hall and looked up the dark stairs. Indica and Bax were up there playing a game, he could hear them laughing and grunting. There must be some way of getting up all those stairs, maybe if he grabbed the newel-post and tilted his bottom so his tracks could grip the carpet – it was easy. One step, two steps, this little finger went to market, queen, king, bishop, knight, rook, here he was half way up, whatever you do don't look down, but no one's ever climbed the South face before . . . I, I can't hold on, slipping . . . hang on, two hands reaching for each other, fingers almost touching when the distant rumble of an avalanche . . . I, I'm not gonna make it, Bill. You damned cripple, get up out of that chair and walk! Fingers reaching out, clutching for support . . .

He was at the top, gliding along to the door that was open just a crack to lay a finger of light across the landing carpet. Roderick looked in, knowing it was forbidden . . . Do not fence with me, Amanda, that room is always kept locked, I have my reasons . . .

Bax and Indica were sitting on the side of the bed. Indica was sitting on Bax's lap, facing him. They were not wearing any clothes. Their faces were different, as though Bax had just swung open the gull-wing door of his new Ghirlandaio and invited her to jump in for a new motoring experience, while Indica had just used Anatase, the fragrance that makes him thrill to be a thrall, or as though they were expecting something to happen. They gasped and groaned and kept wrestling around, nobody winning. Every now and then Indica might give out with a No or a Yesyes, but Bax said nothing.

Roderick tired of waiting for something to happen. He counted those fingers and toes he could see, he noticed that Indica had bigger chests than Bax, and then he started looking over the room.

There was a funny bicycle-thing in the corner, you'd need fingers to grip the handles. On the wall there was a picture of a woman standing balanced on one toe. Toes are just little fingers, you need them for everything here. There was a picture of a whale, above a table covered with little bottles and jars. A policeman would put his finger into a jar and taste it and nod at the other policeman, saying it was the real stuff all right, the real stuff.

There was a telephone by the bed. Whoever calls the detective can't say it over the phone, meet him at Pier 13, only he's always dead when the detective gets there. And as soon as the detective leaves somebody's office they start pushing buttons on the phone, 'Some nosey P.I. is asking a lot of questions. The wrong questions.' Then he sits chewing his finger-nails before he reaches for a gun. With fingers you could do just about anything, squeeze a trigger . . .

Indica said, 'Yes no yes no no yes yes no yes no!' Bax gasped and they rolled apart. There were marks on his shoulders where her red finger-nails had been digging in.

Roderick looked at his own red claw. Red, but not a finger, not a toe. With real fingers you could do anything, make a phone call, taste the real stuff, count up ten little fingers and ten littler fingers . . .

Bax lay there like a boxer, like when they're taping your fingers before your comeback fight, years ago you killed your pal and quit the ring . . .

Rings, sure, you could wear rings, a fancy ring like the homicidal maniac who's always stalking somebody and all you ever see is his fancy ring . . . third finger left hand with this ring, yes, wedding-rings, engagement-rings, all at low, low prices, one carat, two carat . . .

Fighting, fists, sure, you could make a fist. 'Quantrell, you had this coming for a long time, and I aim . . .' Or a fistful of money for seven straight passes at the crap table, or fist counting, one potato, two potato . . .

Something made him see all the fingers in the world, fingers held out to beg bread from the French aristocrats, gripping the bars of a cell in Death Row, pressing a doorbell, thumbing a ride, squeezing a trigger, playing church-and-steeple, throwing down a gauntlet or drawing off a slim glove, giving signals ('Contact!' 'Scram!' 'Peace!'), bidding at an auction, gripping a precipice as a heel comes down to crush them. He saw chorus girls filing their nails as they talked over their dates; priests making a gesture as though they held invisible martini glasses; the suspect being finger-printed in the old precinct house; the safe cracker sanding his finger-tips; the fingers of an artist framing his model; the quivering fingers of a drunken brain surgeon; the cruel fingers of a pianist clawing the keyboard; the gnarled hands of a diamond-cutter; the plump hands of a Roman emperor . . .

He couldn't be sure until he counted again, and still he had to think it over until dawn, when Bax and Indica were gone and Hank came home.

'Mommy not here this morning, eh Roddy?'

'Bax,' said Roderick.

'Uh-huh. She's not back. Probably went off to her goddamned health ranch again. Boy, if she had to pay a few of the bills from that place . . . Still, it's just you and me today, Roddy. Have to get our own breakfasts – I mean, I have to – aw shit, why do I bother trying to talk to you, might as well talk to this coffee-maker here.'

'Bax.'

'Tell you what, let's surprise her, okay? She's always complaining about how I never fix anything around here, let's make a big effort and really try to whip this place in shape, okay?'

'Okay.'

'I'm gonna fix every damn thing in the place, that or bust my balls trying. One thing, I see she went and spilled nail-varnish all over the coffee table in the den. So first I better add that to the list.'

Roderick followed him to his desk and watched him finger the keyboard of his home computer.

Table, coffee, teakwood, refin top.
ejt 2 hrs.
complete when?

After a moment the computer replied:

Earliest complete 94 weeks. ok?

'Ninety-four weeks before I can sand down a little table? What the hell here, Roddy, looks like the old computer's playing tricks on us. Let's try again.' He tapped. 'Same damned answer. Hmm. Maybe what I need is a new scenario with the earliest possible window for table, coffee.' He punched some new instructions and the computer began reeling off pages of explanation involving work-flow diagrams, urgency priorities, job-class and materials-acquisition charts. Hank could barely understand half of it, and that half made him uneasy.

Urgent jobs, such as *Floorboard, loose* (causing *Lamp, Table, Flickering* and a possible *Hazard, Fire*) had to come first. Then came jobs like the solar panel which in time might cause *Damage, House, Structural*. Then came fixing the garage door electric eye which, though not serious in itself, made it necessary to park the car outside where sunlight would eventually damage its paint. Did not *Toilet Bowl Cleaner, Automatic, Jammed* cause a *Hazard, Health?* And would it not be a good idea to check the entire sewer system at the same time? Then *Dishwasher, Ultrasound, Leaking* seemed to have some urgent problems (possible *Hazard, Health*), but since this required parts he could obtain only by mail order, he might profitably fill the interval by overhauling the lawn mower engine and replastering the kitchen.

Then for preventive maintenance on the *Cable, Alarm, Burglar* . . .

'It's all really logical, really. I mean, it all makes sense when you go through it like this. Like A can't be done until after B, and B is not as important as C. Only C has to be done at the same time as D. You with me? And D, there's no use fixing that until E works, but first F and G are gonna break down unless they get some maintenance, only H is really urgent, it's gotta be done first . . . so it's, it's ninety-four weeks all right.'

'Eleven,' said Roderick.

'Eh? Eleven what?' Hank was sweating. His hands trembled on the keyboard.

'Fingers,' said Roderick, pointing to them. 'Eleven.'

'Heh heh, no, ten. Ten fingers, Roddy. See, one, two –'

'Bax got eleven.'

'Backs – I don't know, Roddy, you have to learn to talk plainer than that. Now where was I? Oh yeah, preventive . . .' He pushed another button and another page of explanation appeared. 'Ninety-four – that's almost two years, all my spare time for two years. And just look at all this stuff that could break down between now and then: the slow cooker, the light-pipe intercom, the rotisserie, the hot food table, the cake baker, the microwave, the deep freeze, the shoe polisher, floor polisher, vacuum cleaner-washer, blenders, mixers, thermostat, lumistat, electrostatic air-conditioner, Jesus Christ the water-purifier system, the peppermill, the Jesus H. Christ it's not just two years it's the rest of my life, Roddy. The nail buffer, the can opener, the carving knife, where'd I ever get all this stuff? I mean all that's just stuff for the house, what about this stuff for the car, the fuel computer, the skidproof brakes . . . what about these bikes I was going to fix up with traffic radar, what made me think I'd have time to . . . Jesus H., it's hot in here, bet the damned air-conditioning's crapped out on me too, everything else is, I need a drink, that's what.'

'Eleven,' said Roderick, following him to the bar.

'Yeah, sure, eleven.' Hank picked up the Scotch bottle and behind it the screen lit up:

Sure you need this drink? Sure you need it now?

He put the bottle back. 'Goddamned life run by machines, can't even have a drink, can't even get a cigarette, damned cigarette-box is locked until noon, another goddamned machine running my life, can't lift a finger without –'

'Eleven,' said Roderick.

'You too, huh?' Hank went back to the desk and dropped into his chair. 'Okay, look. Maybe I can't beat all the goddamned mechanical systems in this place, but I sure as hell can beat you. Look, *ten* fingers, *ten*!' He shook them in Roderick's face. 'Count 'em, *ten*.'

Roderick counted. 'Ten.'

'Ha!'

'Bax got eleven.'

'Backs? Wait a minute, *Bax!* You mean Baxter Logan, that creep Indica met last year, where was it, the health-ranch sure, the, sure, that singles sauna on the health-ranch she kept saying how terrific – Listen, Roddy? Listen, is Bax a man?'

'Yeah.'

'Was he here last night?'

'Yeah. Bax got eleven –'

'Forget about the goddamned eleven fingers! You sure he was here? With Indica? With Mommy?'

Roderick pointed at the ceiling.

Hank sat motionless for a moment, then turned to the computer.

'She's gone off with the sonofabitch, back to that goddamned health – must be a message here somewhere.'

He typed: MAIL FOR HANK?

The computer replied:

Dear Hank: I'm leaving you, don't try to find me or talk to me except through my lawyer. I'm going to live with Bax logan who you may not remember I met last year in Nevada. It so happens that we got a meaningful relationship I mean Bax and me and not Bax and a house full of stupid gadgets like you. You and I were really like strangers ever since we knew each other. I got tired of being treated like property, just another one of your gadgets. I want to belong to just me.

Yours,

Indica

'That just about finishes it, Roddy. Everything else breaking down and now this, it's like the whole world slowly collapsing . . . every . . . breaking down and falling apart and wearing out and blowing away and cracking up . . . Even you, look at you with the dents in your head and that stupid scotch tape collar, I mean why the hell can't you even learn to count up to ten? I mean why does every single thing have to break down all the time?'

'Eleven?' Roderick still wanted to tell him all about Bax, how Bax had this eleventh finger right in the middle of his body – but Hank didn't seem to be listening any more.

Hank was rummaging through his tool-box, throwing out screwdrivers and wrenches, scraps of wire and folding rulers. Finally he up-ended the box and dumped everything out on the floor. He sat down in the middle of it all.

'Must be here somewhere . . . that's not it . . . that's not it either . . .'

After a while he stopped talking and pawing through the stuff. Hank just sat there like a big shaggy bear at a picnic.

Roderick found a couple of sanding-discs that looked like plates, set them out with wrenches for silverware, and started piling on the food. Come and get it, plenty more where this come from, finger-lickin', old-fashioned Southern fried country kitchen *grub*! For each of them there was a generous, man-sized helpin' o' nails, nuts and bolts, insulated wire and sizzlin' flashlight batteries. Mm-mmm! For dessert there was a roll of friction tape that looked a lot like one of Aunt Lettibelle's Olde Tyme Golden Dunker doughnuts, hit like to melt in yo' mouf, chile. Roderick poured machine-oil – gravy – over everything and waited for Hank's mouth to start a-waterin'. Red-headed kids with freckles were always sitting around having picnics like this with bears, big friendly bears like Hank. All he had to do was find the right words for a square meal like this. Come and get it, plenty more . . .

'Eat up, Hank,' said Roderick. 'It's yum-scrumpty-umptious!'

The big bear blinked, looked at the sanding-disc, brushed it aside. 'That's not it either . . .'

The mumbling and pawing went on until at last Hank came up with a hammer.

'*That's* it,' he said, smiling, and grabbed Roderick's arm to hold him steady while he raised the hammer to strike.

III

Fill up that sunshine balloon
    with happiness!
Send up that rocket to the moon
    with happiness!

Every smile was a gift, every laugh was a lift, up up we will drift, and there seemed to be no end of choruses to this one.

Pa began to wonder if this radio would ever wear out, so he could make out his report and be done with it. Funny, them giving him a radio to test on his last day at the factory. And what had Mr Danton said? Something about brightening the long hours of, of leisure activity? Whatever that meant. He knew they really wanted him to test the radio because they'd given him a key at the same time, so he could get back into the factory with his report.

For forty years Pa Wood had worked at Slumbertite, fixing first the assembly-line, then later on the machines that worked the assembly-line, and finally just the machines that fixed the machines. At the last there was no one in the place but him, and Mr Danton upstairs in the office with his part-time secretary. And now, so he heard, they were gone too, the factory rumbling on by itself. Probably have to get a machine to read his report, if this damn radio didn't outlive him. How could he work on his inventions with all that easy listenin' racket?

Everyone else in Newer, Nebraska, worked to music. The boys at Clem's Body Shop hammered away to the Top Twenty; the girls at the Newer Café fried burgers to sad Western songs about drinking too much and losing custody of the children; Dr Smith the dentist had pulled all of Pa's teeth out to the taped rhythms of his (Dr Smith's) favourite Latin-American selections; even at the Slumbertite factory the machines worked to a kind of aggravating murmur from hidden speakers that Pa called Muse-suck. The stuff, whatever it was, had probably been turned on to entertain the workers years ago; neither Pa nor anyone else had been able to find out how to turn it off.

'That's the third time I've called you to dinner,' said Ma, coming into the workshop. 'What are you inventing out here?'

He started. 'Oh, uh, well I'm not sure what it is until it's finished. Might turn out to be a puzzle that nobody can take apart.' He turned the gadget over, frowning down at it. 'Or it might be the start of something really big – a tap-dancing shoe that knows all the steps – or even a car that runs on scrap metal.' He put it down and stared up at something on the wall, a key, a gold-plated key hanging on a nail. 'Do you suppose they meant that to be a kind of retirement present?'

'I told you they did, and the radio too. It's you that keeps insisting they want you to test it. Turn the blamed thing off!'

He reached up to the shelf and hesitated. 'Seems a shame to get this far and not go on with it. Must be near done now, then I can have some peace and quiet. I'll just leave it a bit . . . now what was I going to do?'

'Dinner,' she said, and led him into the house.

Mrs Smith let the curtain fall. 'There they go, a coupla real characters,' she said, expressing the opinion of half the town. 'I don't know who's the biggest character, him or her. Yesterday she told me –'

'They oughta be locked up, both of them,' said her husband, speaking for the other half of town. 'Putting a thing like that in their back yard where every kid can see it!' He lifted the curtain and glared at the giant toilet bowl, large enough to accommodate a ten-yard width of rump 'And remember the time she shaved her head and painted it green? Holy cow, trying to raise kids in this – I mean what the hell are they, atheists or –'

'But listen, yesterday she told me they're adopting a robot! A robot!'

'Oughta be locked up,' he said, staring at his hands, which were blushing deep pink. 'Look, just thinking about them starts off the old allergy again. It's not enough I gotta wash my hands fifty times a day and stick 'em in every filthy mouth in town, we had to pick a house next door to –'

'You'll feel better after dinner. Get Judy and wash, I mean –'

He switched on the TV to catch the news-scan, but saw nothing but a list of names:

This page is dedicated to all the gang down at Macs: *Jil, Meri, Su, Jacqui, Teri, An, Ileen, John, Lu, Judi, Jak, Hari, Lynda, Raelene, Luci, Toni, Allyn, Jazon, Cay, Edd, Fredd, Nik, Carolle, Hanc, Jayne, Kae, Lusi*, . . .

'I had the strangest dream,' said Ma, dishing up chicken and dumplings. 'I dreamed I was lost in this waxworks, and everyone I asked for directions was just wax. I came up to this dummy of Ed ("Kookie") Byrnes and I thought, maybe if I touch him he'll come to life, so I did and he just stayed wax, only somehow I cut myself on this metal comb he had in his hand – what do you suppose that means?'

Pa, who was wondering if you could preserve food by stopping time, said: 'Delicious, delicious.'

'You weren't listening.'

'Well no. I'm sorry.'

'You can't help it, forty years of Muse-suck and noisy machines – but I hope you heard me when I said he's coming tomorrow. Because he is.'

'Who? Oh, him?' He grinned with Dr Smith's teeth. 'Well now, there's something. Life ain't so bad, eh Mary?'

'Who said life was bad? And if it is it's only because you can't behave like any normal retired senior whatsit and go root for the softball team or something, go work in the garden or, or just sit on the park bench in front of the post office with the other old seniors and talk about the state of the nation.'

He speared a dumpling. 'More like the state of their bowels. Horse-shoes, you forgot playing horse-shoes. Yep, pinochle, pool, beer, TV – the choice is endless. Only I'm too busy.'

'*Busy.*'

'Anyway, what about you? Shouldn't you be crocheting covers for the telephone and the toilet-roll and every other blessed thing that looks like it might embarrass people? Or else TV, you ought to be watching some ads for freezer boxes and electric beet-dicers, and the stuff they squeeze in between the ads too, what is it? *Dorinda's Destiny*? Instead you just lounge around, writing stuff you never show anybody, painting pictures you keep hidden   no wonder everybody thinks we're nuts.' After another dumpling he said, 'We are, I guess, but no need for them to say so. This adoption business, you know what they'll say? "The crazy Woodses is at it again."'

'If they do, it's only because you go out of your way to be – *eccentric*. I remember nineteen fifty-two or was it three, just when everybody was watching Joe MacCarthy on TV –'

'Don't you mean Charlie McCarthy?'

'When they were hanging on every word, you had to go telling everybody that you were a card-carrying communist, remember? "Hundred per cent Red," you used to say, "and damned proud of it." Had the boys at the Idle Hour talking about tar and feathers before we heard the end of it.'

'Come on, you enjoyed every minute of it, you even made up that little card for me, remember? On one side it said, "I am a communist", and on the other, "Communists always think they're cards."'

She sniffed. 'I had to join the Ladies' Guild to smooth that over.'

'Yes, I seem to remember you getting them all around here for a seance, wasn't it? Getting in touch with a flying saucer, don't tell me you didn't enjoy that. Working away on the old ouija-board and all the time –'

'Just a few lines of Apollinaire, to perk them up,' she said. 'For their own good, really.' She sat back in her chair until the noonday sun caught her white hair and gleamed on the green scalp beneath.

From the red to the green all the yellow dies
When the macaws are calling in their native forests
Slaughter of pi-hi's
There is a poem to be written about the bird which has only one wing
We had better send it in the form of a telephone message
Gigantic state of

'Enough of that,' she said, wiping her eyes. 'I've got a million things to do. He's coming tomorrow and I haven't even cleaned the house or changed the sheets on the spare bed or baked cookies or anything.'

'But he's a robot, Mary. He doesn't sleep in a bed or eat –'

'Oh I know. To you little Roderick is just a chess-player.'

'In a way. I mean, robots are terrific at chess, they say. Wonder if I shouldn't go down in the basement and dig out a few old magazines with problems –'

'Fine. While you're down there, dig out our carpet-beater and use it. Understand?'

'Maybe I could invent you a carpet-beating ma –'

'*Understand*? Roderick is our son (or daughter) and I want to have everything ready for him. I want this to be a place he'll be proud to live in, and it wouldn't matter if he was a – a gingerbread boy (or girl). Understand? We have to start right.'

'Okay, okay.'

'And if it just so happens that he's not hungry and doesn't want a cookie, fine. Or if he's excited about his new home and doesn't feel like sleeping right away, fine . . .'

Jake McIlvaney lay back in Dr Smith's chair, exposing his large Adam's apple. When he talked, which he did incessantly, it bobbed up and down disgustingly. Dr Smith could hardly turn his eyes to the man's filthy mouth.

'How did this happen, Jake?'

'Well, this morning I did a favour for Matt Gomper and fetched these here packages from the bus station – two big packages on the same day, Matt says he never seen nothing like it, and one of 'em has to go clear over to Clyde Honks, you know the old Ezra place, that's what we always called it even though Hal Ezra never actually bought it, let's see the bank owned it and then Don Jeepers, you know, married that gal from Belmontane and now Clyde owns it well what it was was a milk analyser, I knew he was talking about gettin' one but I never knew he'd really buy one because you know he was thinking of gettin' rid of them cows last year – and anyways Matt's missus is sick again, so I said sure I'd handle these here deliveries, so I got rid of that one and started back because the other package was for Ma and Pa Wood, am I talking too much here, doc?'

'Ahmmmm.'

'So I started back, the missus says I talk too much says I should of been a barber, anyway I must of been doing about fifty on that gravel shortcut past Theron Walker's place, hear he's gonna sell out and move to California, makes you wonder if it's true, all them stories about his missus and Gordy Balsh – anyways all of a sudden I hear funny noises coming out of this here package. Like voices, like a voice, maybe a talking doll or one a them talkback computers, you never know what them crazy Woodses might get up to next, coupla real characters – so I stopped and listened real close only I couldn't make out nothing. So then I recollected that Doc Savage was in that neck of the woods, artificial insemination-ing Gary Doody's herd, so I went over to Gary's place and we took Doc's stethoscope and you know it sounded just like they had some kid boxed up there. I mean it kept talking to somebody called Dan, if you knocked on top it said, "Dan, somebody's knocking, is that you?" And if you turned it over it said, "Dan, I think I'm upside down." Damnedest thing I ever seen –'

'The teeth are okay, Jake, nothing busted but the bridge.'

'So anyways I fetched it over to the Woodses, thought I'd sorta hang around to see 'em open it. Real characters, ain't they? Remember back in fifty-six was it, must of been before you come to Newer, maybe fifty-seven, remember Ma Wood one day she takes her vacuum out and starts vacuuming the street! No foolin', vacuuming the street. That ain't all, she, then she gets Pa up a ladder washing the trees too, never did figure them two.'

'Oughta be locked up,' said Dr Smith, washing his hands. 'Adopting a robot –'

'Well to cut a long story, that's what it was. A little gadget like a robot only looks more like a bitty tank. Kind of a let-down, thought maybe somebody was shipping a kid to them or, anyway, while I was waiting, that's when it happened. Ma had this plate of chocolate-chip cookies setting there. I just sort of helped myself and that's when my bridge –'

'What, nutshells or –?'

'Hee hee, no that's the funny thing. Nuts and bolts! Them cookies was just chock full of nuts and bolts! I swear!'

'You oughta sue 'em. They oughta be locked –'

'My own fault, hee hee, I mean Ma never told me to dig in – nuts and bolts! Thought I'd seen everything, but nuts and –'

*

The first day was one problem after another. The boy (or girl, Ma insisted) had been chirping away to itself inside the box, but once they brought it out it shut up for the rest of the day. Oh, it might make a sort of frightened whimper, say when they showed it the chess-board, or say when Pa took it in the workshop and tried to get it interested in hammering.

Finally they put it to bed, Ma told it a story and they plugged it in for its evening recharge and tiptoed downstairs.

'There's some instructions in the box,' Ma said. 'Maybe we need to read up on him (or her). Maybe we've been going at this all wrong.'

'He's in bad shape, I know that.'

'Or she is.'

'Dents in his head, scotch tape around his neck – and his treads are all full of dirt. Think I'll fix him up tomorrow.'

They spread the instructions on the dining table and tried to read them. After some time Pa started working his jaw, settling his teeth the way he always did when he was perplexed.

'You're tired,' she suggested.

'All this stuff about buses and data highways, contented addresses is it? Makes it sound like a traffic report.' He looked up. 'Awful quiet in here.'

'Listen, what counts is that little Roderick or Roderica is ours, our own child.'

'Fine, only what do we know about children? Here everybody in town's been calling us Ma and Pa for years, bet most of 'em don't even remember it's short for Paul and Mary, that we never had a child. Do you think –?'

'No more thinking tonight, okay?'

'No but do you think we're doing the right thing here? Maybe we're too old for adopting a –'

'Too old! Why the Queen of Spain was adopted by fairies fifty thousand years older than the world!'

'That a fact.'

Upstairs, Roderick began to scream.

Suffering Cats, the numbers were after him, barbed 1 and hooked 2 and 3 clattering its pincers before 4's fork and 5's terrible sickle with 6 the noose swinging around for 9 beyond the deadly hammer and the handcuff . . . 'That's right, Rod, will you keep all the money you've won so far or move up to the Hundred-Dollar Questions? Fine, pick a number from 1 to 10, you picked 3 so here goes: Alamagordo is in New Mexico, right? And the Alhambra is in Spain, right? Now, for one hundred dollars, tell me: Just how did you kill Hank?'

'That's easy. Alcatraz is a former island prison, Al Capone is a former gangster, why is everybody looking at me like that? It was self-defence, you all saw him go for his gun first, I mean when he missed me with his 7 (I guess I was just lucky that one didn't have my number on it) and his head was right there in reach I guess I just automatically pasted him with this wrench youda done the same, everybody's got a right to protect his own property – I was just protecting Hank's property, judge.'

Without even waiting to hear how he'd made his getaway (climbing into a crate and nailing down the lid from inside) the judge ordered him hanged by the neck until dead, dead, dead, 3 times 6 maybe but still ends up as nothing, the dot o in the middle of the screen o when they turn you off by remote control in the middle of the most important message of your life: 'Where is that Roderick? Where is that dad-blamed Roderick?'

IV

'Heads,' said Pa, 'are wonderful things. Nobody should be without one.' He brought down the hammer on Roderick's head, with a sound that carried out of the garage and over to Dr Smith's house, where the pink hands of the dentist made a convulsive movement and changed TV channels.

Roderick stood on Pa's work-bench, watching the old man bash dents into smoothness. 'My head gets dents.'

'All the same, heads are wonderful things. Do you know, you can get almost anything into a head. You can think about a house in Chicago – though no one ever did – and at the same time you can think about thinking about that house. "Here I am," your head says, "thinking a thought about a house. And thinking a thought about a thought, and so on." And even while your head thinks that, you see, it's giving the old thought-handle another turn . . . dents, eh? Dents. Yes, well you know the way we take out a dent? We put one in the other side. We dent the dent. Then if it still ain't smooth, we dent that dent too, and so on. Seems like so much of life is just denting the dents in the dents . . .'

He stopped hammering and sat down. 'Not so young any more, Roderick. You can only dent so many dents and the metal gets tired, you know that? People get tired just the same, hammering away, trying to smooth out the world you might say. Well no, you wouldn't say that, but I might.'

The room was full of Mayflies this morning. Roderick watched one land on Pa's hand and sit quietly until Pa picked it up and held it to the light. 'Too tired, see? This one won't make it.'

He moved it close to Roderick's eyes. 'Wings like little lenses, see? Like for reading fine print. Funny thing about these Mayflies, they only live about a day, but they have thousands and thousands of children. See, they have children inside them when they're born. And those children have other children inside them, and –'

'And so on?'

'Good boy.'

While Pa rested, Roderick thought about Mayflies, thought about thinking about Mayflies. The radio was advising them to fill up that shoeshine balloon, but he hardly noticed.

'It's like half-ies,' he said finally.

'Like what, son?'

'A game I play sometimes. In the dark. You take half of it, and then half of a half, and then half of the half of the half and and and, and so on. To see how close you get to nothing. To zilch. To Maggie's drawers.'

Pa smiled. 'Don't let Ma hear you using words like that. She don't care much for TV talk, *zilch* and all.'

'So I don't,' said Ma, coming in through a cloud of Mayflies. 'I don't even like the expression TV, tedious voice, truncated vision, turning the whole blessed world into morons, teleological void – My! Look at all the wingèd green fairies in here!'

Ma showed him how to paint, or at least she showed him the paper and the colours and told him stories while he tried them out. Roderick worked away to the story of the cigarette girl who loved a bullfighter:

'Once she'd been a real girl, you see, but a wicked magician turned her into tobacco and Sir Walter Raleigh took her back to Spain. She languished four hundred years in a deep dark dungeon while her lover searched all over Louisiana . . .'

He produced a small purple square in the middle of the great white sheet of paper. His second painting was the same, but smaller.

'Minimalist, eh? Interesting, but hmmm . . . I think you need to look at other people's work a little, now where was I? Oh yes, every night he knelt before her picture and asked the gods to help find her. And the kneeling made his knee wear out, so he had to keep this banjo on it all the time, there's another song about that too . . .'

Windows were better than TV. There was always something going on. At first he'd been afraid to sit by the back window because of the dangerous plants, friggin' violets in pots that might break any minute and anyway looked like hairy tarantulas.

But all the windows had action: the mailman bringing bills, a car breaking down and getting a tow from the white truck (C-L-E-M-´-s spelled Clem's Body Shop), old Violetta Stubbs walking her cat, Dr Smith swearing at his wife as he ran out and jumped in his blue car, a dog peeing on a maple tree, (trees make W-O-O-D which is just like Ma's and Pa's name but not like *would* you like to hear the story of Zadig the engineer?), and one day a big deal when the sheriff and two men from the County Hell Department came to take away the big toilet and Ma called them Phyllis Teens and Pa said would they like to take away the bill for that skullchair too, and Ma cried and said what was wrong with a bird-bath for rooks anyway, and Pa shouted and Dr Smith came out and laughed and Pa shouted at him too and said he'd like to kill a hundred Phyllis Teens if somebody would give him a dentist's jawbone.

But the best part of windows was that you could go right outside and be in the picture yourself.

'Sure it's okay,' said Pa. 'The kid knows his name and address, he knows he must *not* go out in the street. Why not?'

'Yes of course. A boy or girl needs fresh air and sun – though there are a few ferocious dogs in town. But of course he must. Of course.'

But from the back yard, Roderick could see their anxious faces peering at him through the friggin' violets. They watched him rake a stick along the ground, stop to examine a petrified dog turd, dig a tiny hole (which he tried to make square) and squint at the sun through a shard of bottle-glass.

After a few days of this, they finally relaxed and let him go unwatched. Unwatched, he relaxed and played.

Pa had told him about this Achilles and this tortoise, a story worth trying out. He was Achilles and a stone was the tortoise:

'Okay you're a hundred feet ahead of me when we start the race, only I run ten times as fast as you. Okay now I've gone the hundred feet and catched up, only – there – you've moved on ten more feet. Okay now I go ten you go one. Okay now I go one and you go a tenth. Okay now I '

'Whatcha doing?'

A small person was following behind him, stopping when he stopped. 'It's a game. Like half-ies, only –'

'Whatcher name?'

'I'm Roderick Wood. I live at 614 Sycamore Avenue, but I'm not lost.'

'Ha ha, I'm not lost neither. I'm Judy Smith.'

'Hello.'

'Hi. You look dumb to me.'

'I'm not dumb.'

'Hahaha, you are so. You're a dumb dummy and your Pa works at a dumb dummy factory. You don't know nothing.'

'I know everything. Almost.' He thought. 'I know how to play jess.'

'Chest, that's nothing. Can you play hopscotch? Bet you can't even hop.' She demonstrated.

'You're right, I can't hop.' His arms sagged.

'So you're nothing but a dumb dummy.'

'Guess I am.'

'You don't know nothing.'

He brightened. '*Nobody* knows nothing. Because there ain't no such thing as nothing. Just half-ies and half-ies . . .'

'Let's play something. Chest maybe. You show me your chest and I'll show you mine. Like doctors.'

'Okay I'll get a board and some pieces –'

'Naw, come on. I'll show you.' She seized his claw and dragged him around the corner of a hedge. 'Okay, now you be the microelectronic life-support system and I'll be the chief neurosurgeon . . .'

When Judy got tired of doctors Roderick went off to explore the rest of the block. On one corner there was a gas station with interesting rainbows in the puddles and men who chased you away.

On another corner there was The Gifte Shoppe, run by Miss Violetta Stubbs. She sold greetings for all occasions, 30 pictures of the President, plates with gold edges saying NEWER, NEBR, THE

BIGGEST LITTLE TOWN IN THE MIDWEST, little glass gazelles, hand-lettered cards like those in Pa's workshop, paper doilies, magnetic pens you could stick to the dashboard of your car, silk scarves (NEWER, NEBR., THE BIGGEST etc.) and lots of other stuff, but when she found out you weren't buying anything she chased you away. On another corner there was a house with a fence and a big dog inside, and on the last corner there was a mailbox and a man standing on one leg.

'I can stand on one leg longer than you,' said the man.

'Sure. I ain't got no legs.'

'Oh yeah.' The man scratched his head (this made him fall over). 'I can stand on the other leg even longer.'

Roderick extended a claw. 'My name's Roderick Wood.'

'Hi. I'm Louie. They call me Louie Honk-Honk.'

'Why?'

'Because I'm funny in the head I guess. I don't know. If I knew, maybe I wouldn't be funny. Hey, sit down why don't you?'

Roderick said, 'I can't sit down.'

'Can't sit down! No legs! Heck and darn – I suppose you ain't got any candy, either?'

'Nope. Never use it.'

'Better for your teeth, huh?'

'No teeth either.'

Louie's bad teeth showed in the gaping mouth. 'No teeth! Wow! You're worser off than me!'

'But I'm not funny in the head – hey look, I'm sorry. Don't cry, hey.'

Louie smiled through his tears. 'Boy I'd like to show 'em! You know what I'd like to do? I'd like to go over to Howdy Doody Lake – you never been there? It's nice – and I'd pick some flowers and throw them in, see? Then I'd throw some kid in!'

'Didn't I see that in this movie, Louie?'

'Yeah I seen it too. Boy, they wouldn't think I'm funny then. Only I wouldn't drownd the kid, I'd pull 'em out again. Because if you drownd somebody that's murder. They get detectives after you.' Louie picked his nose, tasted the result. 'Sometimes I think they got detectives after me anyways.'

'How come? Did you drownd somebody?'

'No! Never did! Never did! Only oncet I seen these two men in front of my house, sitting in this truck, see? Just sitting there, all day. All day long.'

'I wonder why?'

'I don't know.' After trying the other nostril, Louie said, 'I wish I was real rich. Real rich. Then I'd pay these detectives to find out stuff for me. To find out – everything. Like what it says in books. And, and how come I'm funny in the head – everything. Ev-er-y-thing!'

That evening Ma and Pa sat at the dining-table, elbow-deep in quadruplicate forms.

'I didn't know adoption could be such a tricky business, Mary. Swann says it could take years, too, without no birth-certificate and with the –'

'Listen to this: "*Item 54. Gross readjusted excludable income not including net excludable tax adjustments included in item 51a*" – what in the world do they mean, including the excludable?'

'Money's gonna be a problem too, already cashed my life insurance to pay Swann's retainer – somebody's at the door.'

The screen door cracked open and two men stumbled in: Sheriff Benson and Dr Smith. They seemed to be arguing.

'Now Doc, hold on, you had no right to bust down that door, hold on just hold on.'

'Getthatmthrſkn – Leggo, leggo!'

Pa said, 'What is this? You know we never lock that door –'

Dr Smith shook a mottled pink fist.

The sheriff spoke: 'Half outa his mind, Pa, I'm real sorry about that. Seems he thinks your little uh robot's been assaulting on his girl Judy.'

'Roderick? He's upstairs in the land of recharge – in bed I mean. What do you mean, assaulted?'

Dr Smith grabbed his shirt-front. 'What the fuck do you think I mean? *That* fucking dirty-filthy machine was out in *your* back yard *this* afternoon, playing slimy sex-games with *my* daughter! Bring him down here! Now! I want the sheriff to see that thing smashed into *a million cock-sucking pieces*!'

The sheriff separated them and forced Smith into a chair. 'Now sit there and shut up till I find out what happened.'

'I know what happened, Judy told me what hap –'

'Button it, Doc.' Sheriff Benson was a gaunt, weary-looking man with rotten teeth. He sucked them to punctuate sentences.

'Well we got the report this afternoon. Miz Violetta Stubbs seen what happened from her back porch and called me. I'da been out here sooner only – hey, you know they got a new game show on, Channel 58, this one gal won a Rolls-Royce you know all she had to do –'

'Get to the point!' Dr Smith kneaded his fists together.

'– just name six vegetables, simple, huh? Anyways like I say Miz Violetta seen your little robot and his little Judy playing it looked like doctors. Soooo . . . wonder if I might have a word with the little uh, okay?'

'I'll get him,' said Ma. 'Only keep that maniac away from him.' She went to the stairs and paused. 'Or her,' she said.

Benson sucked his teeth. 'Just what I was thinking. You know, Doc, this case – there ain't no precedent. I mean, if this robot was a live girl I know you wouldn't care two hoots, if it was a live boy I guess we could settle it without much fuss too. But this robot ain't got a sex – has it?'

'Don't try to cover up for them, Benny, goddamnit I know what I know. That *thing* –'

'Sit down, Doc. Now looky here, this thing's no bigger than a good-sized breadbox – reminds me of a game show where they – no, but look at him. Doc? You want me to prefer assault charges against that bitty thing?'

Ma carried him down. 'Is it morning? Is – hello, Sheriff, did you bring back our toilet?'

'Set him on the table here Ma, now listen uh son, I want to ask you a coupla questions, you know what the truth is?'

'Sure like in truth tables, like if you ask me three questions I could answer them eight different wa –'

'No, well more like Truth or Consequences. Listen, this afternoon, what did you and Judy Smith do out there by the back hedge?'

'Doctors.'

'You played doctors? How does it go?'

'Well you don't have pieces –'

'That's a relief. Go on.'

'And you just talk mostly about how the radiologist is batty about some nurse in O.R. Two, she won't give him a second look though because she's head-over-heels in love with young Doctor Something who's been working too hard, two hours sleep in five years he can't go on like this I tell you, with you it's always give, give, let Doctor Whatsit carry some of the load sure he's old and he drinks before surgery –'

'Fine, but what do you do besides talk?'

'Well nothing much. She puts it in my hands.'

'*Sit down, Doc!* Puts what, boy?'

'Her life. In my hands, my capable hands.'

'Think we got nothin' here, Doc, let's go.'

Dr Smith cursed and yelled incoherently for a moment, then left, carrying before him his swollen, pink, capable hands. The sheriff remained behind a moment.

'Real sorry about this, folks. Doc'll pay for the door and all but – well, might be better to make sure we don't get any more false alarms, okay?'

Pa said, 'Keep him away from Judy Smith, you mean?'

'I mean, keep him chained up. Seems to me if he ain't a boy or a girl and he ain't exactly a machine, he must be a pet. You get a good strong chain tomorrow, and chain him up.'

Ma shrieked. Pa turned pinker than a dentist's hands. 'What the hell, here, Sheriff, look at all these papers – we're trying to adopt him. He's our son. You can't ask us to chain up our own –'

'I can and I do. You adopt him, maybe we can forget the chain. Until then that's an order of my office, chain him up – or else. I catch him loose on the street, takin' him in to the pound in Belmontane. They might even destroy him.'

Pa and Ma sat up fretting most of the night, but in the morning there was nothing else to do: Pa went to Sam's Newer Hardware and bought a twenty-foot chain and a padlock. Ma sat weeping by her African violets. 'Fetters on a baby!' she said. 'Paul, how can we do this to him?'

'At least he'll be where we can keep an eye on him. He'll be safe.'

'Or she will,' said Ma, blowing her nose. 'Couldn't we just let him or her have one last taste of freedom in the front yard? A minute? Half a minute?'

'Okay, Mary.' They let him out, watched him gambol (more or less) and then went to fetch the chain. They returned to see a tattooed arm drag him into a car, which slammed its door and screeched its tyres and shot out of sight.

'Nobody in town's got a car like that, all colourless,' said Pa, when he could get his breath. 'And the licence plate all dusty.'

'I was afraid of this,' Ma said. 'The gipsies have got him.'

V

The big woman with the wrinkled face kept saying, 'Jeep, you ain't got the sense of a dehorn, takin' some kid's toy like this.'

Roderick was wedged in the back seat between her and Jeep, the man with pictures all over his arms. There were other people wedged in around them. He could see half an ear wearing an earring, a hand holding a guitar, the bald spot of someone who was snoring, a baby's foot.

'Jeep, you ain't got –'

'Come on, Zip, how'd I know? It looked like a lawn-mower to me.'

Roderick said, 'I'm not a lawn-mower, I'm a robot. My name is Roderick Wood –'

'Told you: a toy. A damned toy.'

'– and I live at 614 Sycamore Aven –'

'Osiris!' someone shouted. 'This thing's security-wired! We better stop and dump –'

'Stop nothing.' Zip composed her wrinkles. 'You know the rule: when in doubt, keep going.'

The bald spot turned away and a watery eye took its place. 'Oh fine. You know how these rubes are about toys. They get ten times as excited over some fool toy ripoff as they do over a car. And if we get pinched – well, there goes my nomination for Gipsy Good Neighbour of the Year.'

Jeep held up a screwdriver. 'Okay okay I'll strip this thing down now and we can sell the parts in Gallonville. Any objections?'

Roderick said, 'Well I –'

'*Mommy, mommy,*' said a voice from the front.

The earring moved. 'Not now, Chepette.'

'Strip and sell, that's the rule,' said the old woman. 'Only maybe this little gizmo's worth more on the hoof, eh? Lemme think a minute.'

'*Mommy, can me and Jepper have a toy?*'

'You go and play with that pop-bottle, it's down there somewhere ...'

'*But Jepper's peeing in it. Mommy couldn't we have a real toy like on TV?*'

Roderick watched the screwdriver. 'Hey can I say something?'

'See what I mean, Jeep, a talk-back toy. Must be worth a buck or two ...'

The conversation went on without him, stopping only now and then when the baby's pink foot became entangled in the hoop of the earring, when the guitar got into the watery eye, or when a tiny voice announced that Jepper was drinking from the pop-bottle. Roderick waited, studying the skin-pictures on the arm next to him.

A snake crawling out of the armpit is marked DON´T READ ON ME. It devours or disgorges an eagle holding a cane in one claw, a string of wienies in the other, and in its beak the Ace of Spades inscribed THEM. The wienies coiled around a heart, pierced by a two-ended sword. The man wielding it has one eye and wears a snail-shell on his head. At his feet is a broken anchor. He stands beneath a tree on which small skulls hang like fruit. The tree is on fire; out of the flames rises a mallard holding one end of a long scroll on whose folds are these letters:

t s eliot lived on top a sleek bard

The opposite end thickens into a giant hand grasping a dolphin which waves a Confederate flag; one of its stars has shot into the sky to threaten a kite. The kite string is held by a naked woman who crushes a scorpion underfoot. The scorpion grips a key, while the full moon above features a keyhole. From it an eye observes a mer-cupid armed with an oilcan, sprinkling oil upon a crowd of 13 crowned men. Though blindfolded they follow a tank along the road to a distant tower. The tank insignia is a rose inscribed FAI HOP CHAR. Its gun turret fires dice down the wrist, past a parachute ...

Jeep reached up to pick his teeth and the picture changed:

Now a snake from a distant tower disgorges dice. An Ace of Spades is the insignia of a tank (FAITH HOPE CHARM) extending its chain of wienies to capture 13 blind kings. The fishtailed kite oils a flaming tree beneath which the one-eyed man embraces nakedness while the scorpion attacks a broken anchor. One sword-blade stabs the moon while along it charges a snail waving a flag, towards the point where the two ends of the scroll meet (beneath a winged umbrella) held by a single penguin.

Roderick tried reading the scroll forwards and backwards. It made no more sense than anything else about this mad, bad family. What was a drab, anyway? What was keeling a pot? Why did they want to destroy him before he could even find out stuff like that?

As he climbed up to the back window for a last look at the world, the invisible child started up again:

'*Mommy Jepper says he wants to have toys and live in a house with lots and lots of toys where you don't have to pee in a pop-bottle and you get TV and real strong aluminium foil and pizza-bürger mix and doesn't just hide odours, can we huh?*'

'Be still now –'

'*And TV and microsnax and Uncle Whiskers Oldie Tymie – Ow! It wasn't me Mommy it was Jepper he – Ow!*'

It seemed a good opening. 'This,' said Roderick clearly, 'is *lots better* than a house. *I* like living here.'

None of the adults spoke. Then, '*Yeah but they got TV and –*'

'Listen, TV ain't much. All they got on TV is stories about people driving around in cars. Sometimes not even people, just the cars, this car drives down a street and then on a freeway and then on a bridge, then this other car sees it and starts chasing it, they both have to jump over a lot of bumps and then one of 'em smashes up, The End. Heck, what do you want that stuff for, here you got a *real* car. You even got another real car chasing you, look there.'

Jeep looked back. 'Isis wept, wouldn't you know it? Forget about 'em for one minute and the gashers is all over you. Chet, make tracks, boy!'

'Hang on,' said the driver. 'I'm gonna try something.'

Roderick bounced up and down. 'That's just what they say on

TV! And then everybody says *Yahoo* and *Watch my dust* and *Wheels, do your stuff*, and there's a lot of banjo music and –'

'Hush!' Wrinkles frowned down at him.

'But hey what's Chet gonna try? Is he gonna race across the tracks right in front of this train? Or on this bridge that's going up and he just makes it jumping the gap? Or, or maybe he just pulls off the road and hides in bushes and the cop car is so dumb it goes right on by, is that what he's gonna –'

Old Zip clamped her hand firmly over his speaker and kept it there. What Chet tried was pulling over and stopping, getting out to talk to the patrolman for a few minutes, and finally handing over some money.

'Thanks,' said the officer. 'Don't see much real money these days, not out here. Everybody's so scared of hijackers they only carry cards, hell, all they can offer me is a free motel room or maybe a free meal in some Interstate joint, BLT and a malt, you call that a decent bribe? I mean the food's all plastic and full of preservatives and chemicals you get a bad stomach just looking at –'

Chet showed some gold teeth. 'Yep, well, we gotta get moving.'

'Oh sure, have a nice day and – oh yeah, and don't let me catch you pitching pop-bottles out of the car again, okay?'

In Gallonville the family went to work. First they parked the car next to a little patch of grass, then Old Jeb put three playing-cards in his shirt pocket and strolled away. Then the two young men left, jingling big bunches of car keys and talking about 'recycling us some metal'. Finally Zeb, the young woman with earrings, took the children off to the bus station for 'some street theatre'.

'Street theatre,' old Zip repeated, when only she and Roderick were left. 'That means they all gonna cry their eyes out until somebody gives them the money for a ticket to Omaha.'

'Why are they going to Omaha?'

'You don't understand anything, do you?' Zip set up a card table and two chairs, and stuck a sign to the side of the car:

GIPSY ZEE
– Knows the Past –
– Tells the Future –
NO CREDIT CARDS

128

'Yeah, well if you let Jeep take and recycle me I never will understand anything.'

'True. But so what?' She tied a yellow-and-orange scarf over her head and sat down at the table. 'Okay little puppet, I'll make a deal with you. You keep your mouth shut and help us a little, and we won't junk you.'

They shook on it. Zip kept hold of his mechanical claw for a few seconds, peering at it.

'Interesting hand you got there, you know? I see you've had a real hard life so far.'

Roderick looked too. 'You can see that?'

'Sure. A real hard life, but it's gonna get better soon. You're gonna have lots of money – more than you ever dreamed of. You'll get married, too, and have, let's see, three children. First a boy, then two girls.'

'Gosh, it just looks like a claw to me.' He waggled the fingers. 'Where do you see all this?'

'And I see you have headaches – some head trouble, right?'

'Yeah, right. Gosh!'

'Now cross my palm with silver.'

'I don't have any silver, Zip.'

She sighed. 'Then skedaddle. Make way for a real customer.'

He left. The first customer was a little deaf, and Roderick could hear Zip shouting: '. . . than you ever dreamed of. You'll get married soon, and have three kids, first a girl then two boys . . . some trouble with your feet, right?'

'Teeth? Say that's dead right!'

Roderick headed across the grass, to where a group of children were playing on swings. But as soon as they caught sight of him, the kids stopped playing and shouted:

'Aah, dirty gipsy! Goaway ya dirty gipsy!'

He changed direction and kept going.

Towards sunset he came back, while Zip was just finishing the palm of a frail old man. He rose and tottered away, leaning on his cane, grinning to himself about the three children he was going to have. Zip took off her scarf.

'Well, little puppet, what kind of day did you have? Make any money?'

'Almost. I mean I was standing on a street corner and somebody came up and tried to stick a quarter in my eye. Then I went to the bus station to watch Zeb and the kids and the street theatre only when Zeb started crying I said don't cry it's a very good act and she said she'd give me a dollar to go away only she never did. Then I saw Jeb on this park bench with his three cards and all this money in both hands saying Find the Lady, boys, Find the Lady, see they put down a dollar and he gives them five if they –'

'I know how it goes.'

'Yeah well I saw how terrible they all were at the game so I said maybe he should give them three dollars if they're right and one dollar if they're wrong, see it works out the same, and Jeb whispered he'd give me a dollar to go away – but heck, what do I want a dollar for? I guess if everybody in the world wants me to go away for a dollar I could get rich if I just disappeared.'

'Ha ha! You'll learn, little puppet, you'll learn. We'll make a gipsy out of you yet.'

What Roderick really wanted to do was help some grown-up do some grown-up job. And that night, he got his chance.

Everybody had returned in good spirits and carrying thick wads of money. The young men had spent all day finding an amazing number of abandoned cars on the streets, tearing them down and selling them to the local junk-yard. Zeb and Jeb and Zip had all cleaned up too, so now there was nothing left to do but junk their own car, find a new one, and leave town.

While they waited, Zip told Roderick all about the family.

'You see, everybody has to have a name beginning with Z, J or Ch, middling with i, e or ee, and ending with b, p or t. But no boy can have Z and no girl can have J.'

'You mean there's only 27 names in the whole –'

'No, well we can add -er to a boy's name if it's the same as his older brother's, and -erie to a girl's if it's the same as her older sister's. And if a boy and girl look like they're gonna get the same name, we just add -ette to the girl's name. So you see we can have

Jeet, Jeeter, Jeeterer and so on, just like we can have Chep, Cheperie, Chepette, Chepetterie . . .'

Boys took middle letters from their mothers and ending letters from their fathers, and girls did the opposite. Roderick was only just beginning to see why Jeep was not Zip's son nor her sister's son when Jeep and Chet drove up in a big red car. They started spraying it with green paint at once. Jeep looked scared.

The old man said, 'What's the big hurry?'

'Aw shit, Chet went and ripped off this here car, just as we drove away I seen it was by the city hall, parked in the mayor's parking spot. I think they seen us too – *what's that?*'

That was the sound of a wow-wow siren, getting closer. Jeep threw down his sprayer. 'We better take her as she is, let's go.'

They piled in and started off. Old Jeb said, 'Take her as she is, that's rich that is. You ain't done no more'n the back and the right side, how's that gonna look? And nobody done the plates –'

'Don't worry about the plates,' said Roderick quietly. 'I –'

Chet said, 'Ra's ball, who's supposed to be drivin' here, anyway? I got enough on my mind, tryin' to figure all them fancy one-way streets, half of 'em blocked off at the other end without – shit, they seen us!'

They were crossing an intersection; a few blocks to the East they could see the flashing red-and-blue lights of the police car crossing another. It went North, they went South. 'Holy Horus they done seen the wrong side of us, too. Now they know we got the mayor's red – well, now what?'

Roderick spoke up. 'In a way it's lucky they did see the red side. I mean, if we could use the one-way streets, sort of turning left all the time . . . hey, take a left.'

'All I need, got enough human back-seat drivers, now the damn toys gotta start –'

'Do like he says,' Zip rumbled. 'That's one smart little cuss there.'

Chet took a left. 'Going round in circles, real smart. But then what we got to lose?'

'Everything,' said old Jeb, turning his face to the window. The baby kicked at his bald spot.

'They seen us again!'

And the police car saw them again and again, as both vehicles spiralled in through the one-way system, first seven blocks apart, then three, then two. When the police car was only one block away (and turning towards them) Roderick said: 'Okay, now pull over on this next block – on the left. Turn out the lights and everybody duck down.'

An instant after they obeyed, tyres shrieked at the final corner and the flashing colours approached. They could hear the two policemen arguing. A spotlight went on.

'Okay, sure it's a new Shrapnel, only it ain't hizzonour's, just take a look. His is Lady Macbeth Red, and this is, it looks like Tango Green. Anyways, look at the plate, his is Elmer two six one zero five eight niner seven, while this here is Lolita six eight five zero one niner two three, we're wasting time . . .'

'Have it your way . . . thin air . . .'

The police car wow-wowed away. They were safe.

Zip said later, 'I told you he was a smart little cuss. I bet Roderick's got more brains in one little silly-cone chip than you got in your whole head, Chet.'

A gold tooth grinned back at Roderick, wrinkles smiled, a watery eye winked, and a tattooed hand patted his dome. The children smiled in their sleep, the woman with earrings blew him a kiss, and even the baby seemed to wave its foot in congratulations. Roderick was a gipsy hero, and now there was no question of sending him to the junk-yard.

Instead, later that night, they sold him into slavery.

VI

Midnight. The apostle clock chimed, and its twelve tiny wooden figures paraded out of one door and in at the other. Faces half-gone with worm-holes.

Mr Kratt lifted his snout and listened.

'You must really like that old clock, huh Mr Kratt?'

'Like it? I hate the goddamned thing. That's what I keep it for, to remind me how much I hated my old man.'

'I don't get it. If you –'

'You don't have to get it, bub.' He watched the wooden door shut behind the last apostle. 'See, my old man had the damnedest collection of old clocks, cuckoos, grandfathers, you name it. Some real fancy ones, too: like this German school-house with these little enamel schoolboys that come outside, one at a time, they bend over, see, and get a beating from the old teacher. My old man spent his life fixing them up. His life and our money. And when he died he left us kids one broken-down clock apiece. All the rest went to a museum. Only good investment he ever made, and he gives it away.'

The chimes finished, and there was no sound in the office trailer but the faint noises filtering in from outside: screams. Bells. The waltz-time murmur of the merry-go-round.

Mr Kratt looked from the face of his digital watch to that of his young assistant, a pimply man with a handle-bar moustache

'You oughta shave that thing off, bub.'

'Yes, Mr Kratt.'

'No, I mean it. What do you want with all that hair on your face? Think it gives you confidence, some shit like that?'

The young man fiddled with a company report. 'Well, I just like it. Same as you and your ring there.'

'Ha!' Mr Kratt held it up, a heavy gold claw mounted with a steel ball. 'That, my friend, is history. That's a pinball from my

133

first machine. Took me five years to build it up to an arcade, but in two more years I had three arcades and the carny. Never looked back after that.' He checked his watch again. 'Where the hell is this guy? How long does it take to go through a few wastebaskets?'

'I thought you started out in Autosaunas, sir.'

'No, that was later. What happened was, I started out with these call girls –'

'You was into call girls?'

'Not me, people I knew. And when they legalized them in California, see, they wanted to expand. So I came up with this idea, wiring the girls into a computer, hell, it cut their turnaround time by forty per cent. So then I thought, hell, why pay all these girls, I mean taxi fares and food and rent, skimming, it all comes off the top. All you need is something that looks and talks and moves like a girl – anyway that's how Autosaunas got going. I was lucky there too, managed to sell off my interest just before all that litigation came down on them, not just the nuisance suits claiming clap and syph but the heavy stuff, middle-aged guy dies of heart failure and they try to prove electrocution, another guy files injury claim for amputa – well, you know how these ambulance chasers get their clients all worked up over some little nothing. Anyway that's when I got the idea for Datajoy, all I got so far is a registered name and a process, but when the time's right – look, we give that guy fifteen minutes more, then I'm splitting.'

'These people you knew that was into call girls, who, was it the Mafia?'

'There's no such thing as the Mafia,' said Mr Kratt quickly. 'Anyway that business showed me what I'm doing, made me think it deep. See, I used to think I was in the amusement machine business, but that's just part of the picture. See, what I'm really into is pleasure. The pleasure industry. Big difference there, changes the whole concept when you think about it. I mean now I could acquire a few other interests, stuff like T-Track Records, like K.T.Art Films, see these are all just departure points to the same place, they all come under one dome, *pleasure*. Nowadays whenever I plan anything, anything at all, I ask myself: "How is this gonna help give the most pleasure to the most people, at the highest return?" You'd be surprised how much crap that cuts out, having a simple business philosophy.'

'Pleasure. Is that why you're going into fun foods?'

'That's it, bub. Only as you know, it's a highly-saturated market there right now, so I can only get in with a hell of a good angle.' He glanced at his watch again. 'Which is one reason I end up sitting here half the night waiting for that market research yakhead to bring me what I need. Is that him now?'

The assistant answered the door. It was not the market researcher, only two old gipsies trying to sell a robot.

'Tell 'em we got a robot, we got a show full of robots. Tell 'em I make the goddamn things – no wait, wait a minute. Let's just see what *they* call a robot. We got time.'

The two old people came in carrying a small, inhuman-looking device. 'Good evening sir, we –'

'Put it on the desk there and turn it on,' said Kratt. 'What's it supposed to do? Tell fortunes?'

The old woman kept working her multitude of wrinkles into a smile, or was it a leer? 'If you want,' she said. 'Little Roderick here is a smart little cuss. He –'

'That's its name, Little Roderick?'

'Roderick Wood,' said the gadget, holding out a claw. 'I –'

The old man suddenly started dancing and whistling accompaniment. The entire trailer rocked with his tap routine.

'What the hell here, shut up you!' The assistant grabbed his arm, and might have hustled him out of the door if Kratt hadn't spoken up. 'Okay, okay, simmer down everybody, let's see here.' He took the claw and twisted it around, examining it. 'Not bad work here, you know? Course he looks like shit, but we might fix – does he duke or what?'

'Sure I do,' said Roderick. 'Gimmee your mitt, uh, sir.'

Mr Kratt held out a bunch of thick fingers. He was thick all over, Roderick noticed, and wide: a wide head growing straight from the shoulders without pausing at any sort of neck. A wide face hanging from a thick black V of eyebrow. A wide nose, upturned to display its mole. The eyes were black and tiny and slightly crossed, as though ready to concentrate on that mole.

Roderick was afraid of Mr Kratt. 'Well maybe I –'

'Come on, don't stall.'

'You, uh, will get married soon and have three children, first a boy, then a girl, then another girl.'

'Ha! Go on.'

'You're uh having trouble with your, your back, back pains?'

'What the hell is this thing shaking for? Think you got some problem with the motor circuits there. Yeah, go on.'

'You want to make lots of money and, uh, you will. Some thing you hope for will come true soon and make you lots of money.'

Kratt took his hand away to find a cheap cigar and unwrap it. 'Not bad, not bad.' He waited for the assistant to give him a light. 'Yeah, but not so good, either. Kind of easy, all it does is go through a little table, right? Tells the first client he's got back trouble, the next one he's got foot trouble, the next one he's got headaches –'

'And so on,' said Roderick. 'That's it, all right. And for the children see I always say three children, they can have them eight different ways . . .'

'Talkative little gadget, ain't it?' Kratt grinned and reached out to pat Roderick's dome. The robot flinched. 'Well I might find some use for him, let's say a hundred bucks.'

'We was thinkin' more like a grand,' said the old woman.

'A grand,' said the old man.

'A hundred. Cash. Look, I might have to do a lot of work on it, gotta change some a that direct programming, gotta maybe fix the motor circuits, gotta do something about its appearance.'

'Five hundred?' said the old man.

'One-fifty, I'm generous too, this thing is probably hot.'

Roderick made a whimpering sound when the gipsies left with the $200 Mr Kratt had meant to pay all along. Mr Kratt patted his head again, spilling ash over his face. 'Good little gadget, bub, realistic talker. Stick on a fifty-cent coin box, penny a second, all it's gotta do is talk to people about their troubles.'

Roderick said, 'You mean I don't have to tell fortunes? Cause I don't like fortunes, dukes and stuff.'

'Ha! Hear that, it doesn't like – hey, robot, what you got against duking?'

'Well I mean making up all this stuff and then it comes true, how come they need me to make it up, how come nobody wants to tell their own fortunes, Pa says they could just put all their choices in a hat and draw one out it's just as good. But I mean once I say it there it is, that's the future.'

'You think – let me get this straight – you think you can just go to a set of tables and just pick out a future for somebody and then it happens?'

'Sure, because like Ma uses the *I Ching* all the time and she says it never fails, that's just 64 choices, 64 ways the future can go.' He hesitated. 'Only Pa says it's a lot of crap.'

'Well this Pa is right, it's only like a game, see, to make money. Now – well, about time.'

The door opened and a one-armed stranger stumbled in. 'Howdy. Sorry I took so long, only you know pickin' locks with one hand ain't exactly easy. Got jest what y'all wanted.' He looked at Roderick. 'What's that?'

'Nothing, another piece of crap for the carnival, stick it in the corner, bub let Mr Smith use the desk for his presenta –'

'O'Smith.'

'Yeah, now let's see here, what's this, memos?'

'Yep, outa executive waste-baskets, all highly confidentials, reckon half the board at Dipchip don't know what's goin' down yet, looks like maybe kind of a private showdown between the research director Hare and the vice-president in charge of product development Hatlo –'

'So I see. And the substance of it is over-expenditure, right? On this yak-head process, whoever heard of trying to coat microcircuit chips with peanut butter, let's see that budget there, yeah, look at those costs. Memo my ass, I'd of fired the son of a bitch, brought a suit for fraud and malfeasance, haul his ass right through the courts if I had to, what's –'

'Well, you see they acquired this little old firm Bugleboy Foods assets all tied up in warehouses full of peanut butter substit – yep, there's the picture, minority interest held by TTF Endeavours, a division of TTF Enterprises, took the shares in lieu of damages – some old litigation when they were a supermarket chain Tommy Tucker Foods, now of course they're a holding company who – sorry, awful sorry, let me –'

An avalanche of papers went to the floor. As O'Smith bent to get them his eyes met those of the little machine. It seemed to be trying to plug into a wall socket a length of dropcord running to some recess in its body. 'Hello,' it said.

'Howdy doody, little feller. Need some help?'

'Yes.' Its voice was fainter, its eyes were going opaque.

'Okay if I . . .?' O'Smith asked Kratt, who nodded.

'There you be.' He straightened up and dumped papers on the desk. 'Now where was we? Oh yeah, the divestiture . . .'

RODINI ROBOT

Palmist – Knows the Past – *Tarot Reader*

Seer – Tells the Future – *Scryer*

Mystic – *Clairvoyant*

$3.00 (PER MINUTE) DONATION

They had fixed him up with a fibreglass turban and a coinbox, bolted him to a slab of concrete, and installed him in a little tent just off the Midway. He was conscious only while customers kept feeding money into his coin-box, when he would begin nodding over the crystal, palm or Tarot cards and go into his routine.

The routine consisted of a softening-up line ('Basically you're too generous. People use you. You need to be more selfish.') and a series of questions masquerading as answers:

'Right now you're worried about somebody close to you . . . maybe yourself, a health problem . . . that's right, and money is involved . . . money for an operation maybe . . .'

'Right now you're worried about somebody close to you . . . someone you live with . . . or work with . . . live with, yes, and there's some decision, big decision you have to make . . . get the impression it's money, something to do with . . . if not money then some kind of exchange, a relationship of give and take . . . you give more than you get . . . well things are going to straighten out soon, only there'll be some hassle . . . a lot of trouble in fact . . . just have to fight this thing through to the other side . . .'

'Right now you're worried about somebody close to you . . . not so much now as in the future, a life partner, I see a strong influence coming in there soon . . . not too soon but soon, romance leading on to something permanent ... and children, first a boy, then ...'

All week long, the customers exchanged their quarters and half-dollars for token words: love, marriage, divorce, family, money, career, lifelong ambition, relationship, social life, quarrel, not-working-out, obstacle, travel, children, promotion, home-life ... At the end of the week, he had taken $21,938 and two lead slugs. Mr Kratt came to see him, trailing the assistant.

'Damn good, little robot, you just keep it up, oh bub tell the maintenance boys to change his rate, five bucks a min – yeah and move him on to the Midway, real attraction there, best investment I ever – reminds me, any word yet on that lease-back arrangement with Bugleboy, the warehouses? No? Gotta complete that before we move on this computer edibles package, did I tell you we managed to bust the contract of this guy Hare, got him coming over to head up research in Katrat Fun Foods, he –'

'Yes sir, but isn't he the guy who –?'

'Sure, well of course he's only nominal head, don't want research costs mounting up on us do we? No, real head is this new guy Franklin, real ideas man we managed to grab off some hayseed univers – but see with Hare we get his patented process for etching microcircuits right on peanut brittle, be right in there in the fun food vanguard, bub, few technical wrinkles to iron out first but I mean there we are with fifteen warehouses full of peanuts, get this moving sky's the lim – what was that?'

The little figure in the fibreglass turban had made a kind of moaning sound. Now he said, 'I wanta go home.'

Mr Kratt squatted down and inclined his big neckless head. 'Aren't you happy here, little robot? Look, you're a big success, main attraction almost, everybody after you –'

'Yeah, but I get nightmares.'

'Ha! No, really?' Kratt winked at his assistant. 'Not something you ate, is it?'

'I keep seeing their faces, the busted people.'

'The, the what?'

'The customers, the ones you call the marks. They're all busted, Mr Kratt, sometimes even their faces are all busted up – I just wanta go home, that's all.'

'Well you can't. So just get that idea out of your little memory chip, comprende? This is your new home, so you better get used to it.' He stood up. 'Come on, bub, can't waste any more time yakking with a goddamn robot doesn't even know how to be grateful, whole point in changing this show over to machines was we could get rid of all the whining and bullshit, pay's not good enough, food's not good enough, homesick, lovesick,' he whirled on Roderick and stuck out a thick finger. 'You know what your trouble is? You know?'

'Basically I guess I'm too sympathetic, people use me. I need to be more hard-hearted . . .'

'Come on, bub, wasting our time. Wanta nail down this Bugleboy deal, see, what we got now is a new concept in fun foods, two things kids really like are eating junk and playing with talk-back toys, put the two together and you get the edible talk-back, start maybe with a Gingerbread Boy, kid gets tired of yakking with it and – chomp! See? Get our boy Franklin right to work on that one just as soon . . .'

Outside the tent stood a long line of silent people: young men with old faces, old women in burst shoes, old men in greasy hats, young women with pierced ears. At the front was a man holding a newspaper upside-down, apparently reading. He watched the two men leave, then slipped inside to feed Rodini the Lucky Robot with quarters. Now he was safe, now he could lower his paper to expose a face without a jaw.

'Basically you're . . .'

Not all of them gave him nightmares, but what he couldn't understand was why there should be any miserable marks at all among his four hundred daily visitors. Television had never prepared him for their stories of loneliness, horror, guilt, confusion, sickness, dread. Almost none of his visitors came close to televised truth: here were no pop stars, kindly country doctors, top fashion designers, executives with drink problems, zany flight attendants, sneering crooks, tough but fair cops, devoted night-nurses, cynical reporters, hell-for-leather Marines, dedicated scientists, big-hearted B-girls, ageing actors, cute orphans, smart lawyers – none of the ordinary decent network folks he'd come to know and almost like.

Instead there was the man with no jaw, wondering if maybe he couldn't get him a girl if only he had a real fast car with full accessories. The drunken wife-beater who wanted to quit (drinking and beating) but even more wanted to go way out West where it wouldn't matter so much. The personable young man who kept sniffing his armpits and re-applying deodorant, and whose ambition was to steal a hydrogen bomb and drop it on some black people. The failed suicide who dreamed of a big win at Las Vegas . . .

And the line shuffled past. The worst of it was the mechanical laughing clown, going night and day right in their faces, just the way it did in all the movies where somebody got killed by the merry-go-round or on top of the Ferris wheel or in the dark behind a tent that clown was always there with the chipped white paint on its face, rocking back and laughing in their faces . . .

And Roderick dreamed of them.

They were numbers, then they were letters, then words, then broken bits of voices. If he could only sort them out, all of them, into some kind of pattern . . . but it was always just beyond (beyond (beyond . . .

God call him up every time jackpot lousy blade heavy split up when epileptic .38 motel room burn movie son of a bitch says kids no kill t-shirt no freak doc car plant porno bastard mother his own last time he last time she exit blood candy store how would you like a beat on him epileptic rapist son of a bitch yells sewer beach relationship stinks this relationship masectomy needles needles boss no good yell fuel injection nightwork treats treats me like shit .38 bike overtime blackjack ass passes no sweat pills bustup back together ten grand belt buckle slipped disc park it goodies medication no nice kids his own mother God fight City Hall wino drive-in abortion hit taste bike

'Basically you're too kind. People –'

'Son, don't you know me?'

He peered at the man, noticing he had a jawbone, not like anybody who loaned out his jawbone for killing Phyllis Teens . . . 'Pa! Pa?'

'Hear that? He knows me. Come on son, we'll go home.'

The hard-looking man behind him spoke. 'Not just yet, Mr Wood. Few formalities.' He spoke into a radio. 'That's it, fellas. Make the pinch.' Then to Pa, 'We'll have to go over to this Kratt's office here. I want your, er, kid to identify him.'

Roderick's quarter ran out. He awoke in Mr Kratt's office, once again standing on the desk.

'. . . tragic mistake, gentlemen, tragic. This just can't be a living child, I mean look at him. Been here six, seven weeks and never ate a crumb of food, never had a drink of water, how can you call him alive? Of course I bought it – him – in good faith as a machine, got a receipt somewhere, no idea it was even stolen goods let alone a – are you sure?'

The hard-looking man said, 'How about this, Mr Wood? This a kid or a robot?'

'Well I like to think of him as my foster son, he seems almost –'

'Jesus Christ, what kind of answer is that? Maybe I better ask the – entity – itself here.'

Roderick was just blacking out when the hard man fed in a handful of change. 'Now just tell me what the fucking hell you are, kid.'

'My name is – is Roderick Wood.'

'My boy,' said Pa. 'You see, Agent Wcz, just what I –'

'I'm a – a robot and I live at 614 Sycamore – 641 is it? 416, no, I live at –'

The man turned his hard stare on Pa. 'A fucking robot! We set up this whole operation to catch a kidnapper and now you admit –'

'I'm awful sorr –'

'Yeah sure. Only that just voids our arrest here.'

Mr Kratt's V-brows shot up and down. 'I'm free then?'

'For the time being. We'll be keeping an eye on you, Kratt.'

Roderick's money ran out again. He awoke in a car with Agent Wcz and Pa – and Ma!

'Penny for your thoughts, son,' she said.

'I was thinking about anding,' he said. 'How much is one and one and one?'

'Three.'

'Three? But I keep getting four. Like on Mr Kratt's desk there was one pin and one paper clip and one rubber band. And that makes two shiny things and two loopy things, and everybody knows two and two makes –'

'Can that noise,' said Agent Wcz.

Pa said, 'Agent Wcz, I really am awful sorry we wasted your time, the FBI's time. Hmm, unusual name, Wcz. You know, I think I knew an FBI Agent Wcz back in the fifties. Any relation? Your dad, mayb – ow!' Agent Wcz turned white, then red, but said nothing.

Ma said, 'Sorry Pa, just moving my foot there, getting comfy.'

The FBI man looked at her, as though memorizing her face. 'You two aren't in a very *comfy* situation, you know. Filing a false report of kidnapping is serious. I'm putting you down on our records and you can rest assured you'll hear from us again.'

The car drew up in front of a familiar house. When they were inside, Ma said, 'Could have *died*, Pa. Why on earth did you go and provoke Mr Wcz like that?'

'Provoke – what in the world?'

'Didn't you see the scars? That man's had his face lifted, more than once. He's as old as we are, and you asking him about his dad! Honestly!'

'My day for goofs, I guess. Anyway, our boy's back. Safe and sound.'

'And pig-ignorant,' said Ma. She put both hands up to scratch her head, the way she always did when she was thinking hard. The green dandruff flew. 'Can't have him grow up thinking two and two is four,' she said. 'And there's only one answer.'

VII

SOME LAWS OF ROBOTICS (I)

Robots are in comics but they are not real.
Robots are made of controls.
Robots are made of metal and iron and steel.
Robots kill.
They strangle.
They shoot people and destroy them.
They keep killing and killing.

Pupils at Rhyl Primary School, London

Miss Borden had tan hair exactly matching her tan pants suit, and watery blue eyes exactly matching the scarf at her throat. A chain ran from the bow of her glasses to the back of her neck (to the knob of tan hair) and it exactly matched the chain running from her belt to a bunch of keys. He had never seen such a neatly-matched-up person; he stared while she selected a key and matched it to the door marked with her name: ELIZABETH BORDEN PRINC –

'Don't dawdle,' she said. Princess?

'Don't be shy, Roderick.' Ma took his hand and led him into the business room.

'Yes, I can see he'll cause – *have* special problems, Mrs Wood. The handicapped and the disadvantaged are so often – but never mind, we'll manage somehow. Now where have I put those forms?'

'Handicapped? Well no, not exactly, he's –'

'Of course *you* don't think of him as abnormal, glad to see that, admirable the way you parents – now let's see, was it 77913 or 77923? – Yes, I always feel it's best to treat them as normal, healthy children and just let them find their own level, sink or sw – find their own level. Achievementwise. After all, isn't that pretty much the basis of our democratic . . . of course it is, and I'm sure little Robert will fit in just fine . . .'

'Roderick. His name is –'

'At the same time it's best to find a way of keying him in, don't you agree? Relating him to the system, here it is, 77913, just a few routine questions I have to ask –'

'You mean how well does he read and write, things like that?'

'Yes um but not exactly. We generally like to let reading and writing find their own lev – shall we begin?' She fiddled with a brooch and suddenly unreeled another gold chain with a tiny ballpoint pen at the end. Her left hand ironed the pink form ready. 'Has he any juvenile record?'

'You mean criminal – why heavens no.'

'Good, good. Any peculiar illnesses? Aside from his obvious handicap, that is.'

Ma cleared her throat. 'Miss Borden, maybe I haven't explained things too well. Roderick is –'

Miss Borden held up a hand. 'Don't mean to rush you but I've got a meeting with the school security personnel in a few minutes, suppose we just run right through these first and then after we can clear up any little discrep – *Oh of course*! You're worried about giving out informa – oh but let me assure you this is strictly confidential, here, here's a list of the agencies we're legally entitled to a data-share with, see for yourself there's nothing to worry about.'

She handed Ma a sheet of paper printed on both sides with names ranging from the Nebraska Welfare Investigation Bureau to the Presidential Committee on Population Control. 'Okay, no history of illness then, how about chemotherapy?'

'Chemo what?'

'Medication, what kinds of medication will little Rodney require and how often? Tranquillizers, anti-depressants, enkephalides –'

'Well, none. Nothing.'

After a moment's hesitation, Miss Borden marked a box. 'Now we're getting somewhere. Has he been in analysis? If so for how long and which therapeutic method? No? Fine. How about his training. Pottywise, I mean.'

'He doesn't need – no trouble that way.'

'Good, fine. Now for some details. How often does he have tantrums, Mrs Wood?'

'Never.'

The pen poised. 'There's no place on the form for "never", Mrs Wood. *All* children have tantrums. I'll tick "seldom" if you like but I wish you'd try answering these questions a little more frankly. Now would you call him a hyperactive child?'

'I'm not even sure I know what that m –'

'Okay then he's not. Epileptic fits? No? Screaming? No? Excellent. Aggression – does he get into fights with other kids a lot? Good. Ever started a fire? Tortured an animal to death? Maimed another child? Fine. Now is he what you might call introverted – moody? I imagine so, being handi – disadvantaged like that, better put Yes. Suicide attempts? None? Fine. Is he sexually advanced for his age? No? That seems to cover the basics. Think we'll exempt him from sports for the time being, don't you?'

Miss Borden asked dozens of questions about the whereabouts of Mr Wood, family income, mortgage payments and health insurance plans, earnings-related benefits, history of colour-blindness and left-handedness, whether any grandparent was syphilitic or tubercular or a giant.

'Fine, now just one more: can you think of any special experiences little Robin might have had which could affect him educationwise?'

'Well . . . he was kidnapped by gipsies.'

'Seriously Mrs – really kidnapped? Well then of course that alters his rating for sexual precocity doesn't it? Fine, now I'll just have my secretary key this into our data terminal and we'll be ready for some tests. Might as well go home now Mrs Wood, this could take the rest of the day. We'll call you.'

Roderick was whisked away by Miss Borden to another business room, where a kindly-looking man looked at him over his glasses.

'The er Wood boy is it? I'm Dr Welby, heh heh, don't be nervous boy, been a family doctor to your Ma and Pa for a good many years now, good many years.' He stood Roderick up on his desk and looked him over. 'Well well, yes, mmm, says here your regular doctor is a Dr Sonnenschein in Minnetonka.' He applied a stethoscope here and there. 'Heart seems fine, yes, I'd say –' He looked at his watch. 'I'd say we can give you a clean bill of health, Roger.' Dr Welby stepped to the door. 'Over to you, George. Kid's clean, I'll fill out the form later only just on my way to see Bangfield about that lakeside property thing . . .'

'Check.' A young man in white came in, lifted Roderick down to a chair, and said, 'How are ya, Roger?'

'Fine. I've got a clean bill.' He noticed that Mr George had lots of wiry black hair and red pimples. 'Only I like to be called Roderick.'

'Oh?' George stared at him. 'Now why is that?'

'Because it's my name.'

'Is it? Okay, *Roderick*, now don't let this white coat make you nervous, we're just here to play a few games. You like games, *Roderick*?'

'Yes.' But if the man didn't want to make someone nervous with his white coat, why did he wear it?

'Okay now I'm going to show you some pictures, and – funny pictures – and I want you to tell me what you see.'

'Is that the game?'

'Yes, now what is this one?'

It was tricky, all right. The picture was nothing but a double blob, nothing like anything. Sideways it might be a cloud, reflected in a lake.

'I don't see anything much. A cloud?'

'Yes, and now this one.'

'A different kind of cloud with little wisps sticking out.'

'And this?'

'A cloud with –'

'Okay, that's enough. Now try these pictures. Look at each one and tell me a little story about it. Ready?'

He showed Roderick a picture of a young woman weeping, while an older woman stood behind her.

'What's the story here, *Roderick*?'

'What, any story?'

'Sure, whatever you like.'

'I guess the young woman is crying because she's just learned that her father swindled the bank he works at out of a million dollars, so the bank's going to fold and everybody'll lose their savings. That means she can't marry the hero because he's the sheriff and has to arrest her father. She can't cry in front of her mother here because she has a weak heart and might fall dead any minute. See that's why the father embezzled the money for a special heart operation, when they catch him he says, "I'm glad it's over," and meanwhile the president of the bank, his son is fooling around and gets locked in the safe, and this sheriff who used to be a famous safe-cracker only nobody knows it, has to get the kid out and time's running out, when he does it he has to resign as sheriff because everybody knows –'

'Yeah okay that's enough. Now –'

'But just let me finish, he has to resign but the bank president gives him a million for saving the kid's life, and now that he's not sheriff he can give it to the girl's father to pay back all the little invest –'

'Yeah okay I get it, now try this one.'

A bakery truck was turned over on its side, loaves of bread spilling out of it.

'A guy was delivering nitroglycerin to this place where they had to blast open a mine and rescue these miners they've been trapped a week and time's running out.'

'Listen, you're not *trying*, Roger I mean Roderick. These old movie plots –'

'But listen they put the nitro inside loaves of bread to keep it from getting shook up and, only the truck gets a blowout on a mountainside and the brakes go, these gangsters went and pinched the brake lines, the driver's got this crippled sister she's in love with one of the gangsters only –'

George showed Roderick two glasses, one short and squat, the other tall and thin. First he poured the short one full of orangeade.

'See how much we have? Let's mark it on the glass.' He marked the level with a crayon. 'Now we'll pour it in this other glass.' He poured from the short into the tall glass and again marked the level. 'See, it's way up here. Now. Do we have more orangeade? Or the same?'

After hesitating, Roderick said, 'Less.'

148

'No I mean now, in this big tall glass. Do we have more here than we did in the short glass? Or the same?'

'Less.'

'Look it can't be less, Roger, *try*. How can it be less?'

'Well . . .' Roderick picked up the empty short glass and tipped it up. A single orange drop gathered at the rim and fell to the desk blotter. '*That* much less, anyhow.'

George's pimples were brighter as he drew out a green form and began writing. He made no attempt to hide the words from Roderick, who was not yet scheduled to have a reading age.

Roderick read: 'Suspicious, poss. schiz. tendencies coupled with extreme identity crisis. This boy is severely handicapped, and consequently indulges in vivid fantasies of violence, sex, crime, with recurring claustrophobic imagery. Overachiever, poss., with high IQ but poor grasp of abstract reasoning. Obvious resentment of authority, the classical overachievement syndrome. When asked, "What do you want to be when you grow up?" he replied, "Nothing."'

VIII

The screams from the playground could barely be heard in the teachers' common-room, where a digital clock silently wiped away a few last minutes. Miss Borden stood, clipboard in hand, ready to inspect her troops. No one seemed to feel much like talking: they puffed hungrily at cigarettes, or leafed through tattered copies of *Educationalist Today*, or simply closed their eyes and pretended to doze.

'We have a few minutes – any questions?'

She looked first to young Ms Beek, who sat brushing her hair with long, deliberate strokes. Last year Ms Beek had taken a sabbatical from Newer Public School, spent in a psychiatric hospital in Omaha. At least the trip had been good for her hair, now longer and browner and lovelier than ever. And the mind beneath its roots? Fully restored – or anyway full of soothing drugs. Even if they made her quiet and withdrawn, they kept her even-tempered, and wasn't that the main thing? She'd soon be back in the swim.

Mr Goun, a pale, humourless young man with a glassy stare, sat reading a book. His red moustache moved as though in prayer, and his finger traced the lines across the page. Miss Borden leaned over his shoulder.

'Poetry, Bill?'

He looked up. 'Educational psychology. Just, er, brushing up.'

'I understand. Not easy to move from seminars in the ivory tower to the, well, vigorous give-and-take of the grade school classroom, I'll bet.'

He nodded. 'Interesting theory here, about utilizing the catalyzation potential of the classroom situation in the micro-assessment of –'

'Mmm, yes, sounds great.' She passed on quickly to Mr Fest, or as he preferred to be called, Captain Fest. He stood at the window surveying the playground through a pair of binoculars.

'Still keeping tabs on the trouble-makers, Captain?'

He gave her a thumbs-up sign without looking around. 'They needn't think they're getting away with anything out there, by golly. I know every face and every name. I know what they're up to even before they do. The day will come. The day will come.' He tapped his grey crewcut. 'Fest never forgets.'

'Fine, fine.' She moved on to Mrs Dorano, the oldest member of the staff by some years. Mrs Dorano was large, shapeless, motherly-looking, and absolutely in charge of the second grade. She sat in 'her' chair nearest the door, knitting and frowning.

'Any questions, Mrs Dorano?'

'Goodness me, no. Why, my sweet little angel-puddings are just about always as good as good can be. If anyone has *questions or problems* around here, it's only because *they just don't understand children*. I *do* understand *my* kiddies.'

'No doubt.'

'If only we could keep them innocent! But no, the world of grown-ups is lurking around every corner, waiting to pounce on my wee people and start corrupting them!'

'Oh yes?' Miss Borden checked her watch.

'Yes indeed.' Mrs Dorano slipped a book from her knitting bag and held it up. 'Do you know, I found this hideous thing in the school library! The school library! Luckily I managed to confiscate it before some tiny hand fetched it down from the shelf, some clear little eye chanced to –'

'But this, this is just one of our standard texts for the sex education class.'

'Exactly. *Dirt* education. For tender babes who never had a naughty thought in their innocent little noodles!'

'But many of the parents have asked –'

'For this corruption? I can't believe it and I won't believe it. You can call me an old-fashioned grumpy cross-patch if you like, but someone has to stand up and protect the little ones. Why, this book has pictures of unborn babies – right inside the you-know-what!'

One of the younger teachers giggled nervously. A mistake. Mrs Dorano raised her voice. 'Oh, you may snigger! The world is full of sniggerers, wicked grown-ups who laugh at innocence, who want to pull it down and soil it.'

'Mrs Dorano.' The principal removed her glasses. 'I'm sure you have a point there. Why don't you take it up at the next PTA meeting and –'

'Oh I will, don't worry.' Mrs Dorano gave them all a motherly smile. 'The PTA, certainly. And also the Newer Decency Society.'

Miss Borden turned away quickly. 'How's it going on the playground, Captain?'

'Not much action. Few kids kicking around some kind of toy tank there or something. If that's school equipment, I can promise them *they'll* be sorry.'

'Toy – My God, that's the new pupil, the Wood boy! Where's Ogilvy, why isn't he out there stopping it?' She rushed out, her head filled with printing-presses, a blur of headlines:

CRIPPLED BOY BEATEN, GANG KILLS CRIPPLED BOY AT NEWER SCHOOL, PARENTS TO SUE . . .

Threading the maze of corridors, she found Ogilvy by the door. He was kneeling, making a few adjustments to his shin-guards.

'Some security guard!' she shouted. 'They're beating the life out of a crippled kid out there. Let's go!'

'Can't be everywhere at once,' he whined behind her. 'I was just looking at the busted lock on the A-V room.'

She stopped, half way out of the door. 'What? Not again?'

'Yup. Ripped off the stereo, TV camera, vidrecorder – the works.'

This was serious, a bad blow to the budget. For a moment, Miss Borden almost forgot where she was going.

Roderick learned one thing right away: he was different-looking. Up to now, he'd never thought much about his appearance. Ma and Pa and the other grown-ups didn't seem to mind. But as soon as he appeared on the playground bigger kids started shoving him.

'Hello,' he said, hoping the shoves were accidental.

'Get that,' said a tall, red-haired boy with missing front teeth. 'He talks! Hey you, freaky, what's your name?'

152

'Roderick. What's yours?'

'Roderick, what kinda name is that? Hahahaha it sounds like prick!'

The others doubled over at that one. The conversation turned to names, as, shove by shove, they backed Roderick against a wall. The tall boy, whom the others addressed as Chauncey, favoured the name 'Freaky-prick'; others suggested 'Pricky-freak' 'Pricky-dick', etc., etc.

'Roderick, hahahahaha,' said one of the smaller boys. 'It sounds like poopy-pants!' He and another kid started wrestling and moved out of sight.

'Freaky,' said Chauncey again, moving closer. 'Why you wearing a iron suit, huh? Huh? Think you're tough or some-ping?'

'No, well I just —'

'Shaddap. You ain't so tough I bet without that iron suit. Why don't you take it off, huh? Huh?'

'I can't.'

'"I can't", he says. Spose I take it off you, huh? I could use a iron suit like that, spose I just take it?'

'He might die, stupid,' said a kid in a blue track-suit. 'It's like a iron lung, ain't that right?'

'Shaddap.' Chauncey grabbed Roderick's arm and twisted; it turned easily in his grasp. 'Shit, you ain't so tough. Bet I could, bet I could take you apart.'

'Get him, Chaunce.'

'Yeah, get him.'

Chauncey hit Roderick hard where his stomach might have been, and jumped back shaking his hand. 'Owww, Chrise, he's solid steel!'

'My old man's got a stainless steel plate in his head,' someone was saying, but just then someone grabbed Roderick by the head and pulled him over, and feet were kicking at him from every side.

The robot saw no point in trying to get up; he simply lay there, rolling and spinning under the barrage of tennis-shoes. After a while the kicking stopped, and someone helped him to get up. It was Chauncey.

'You wanna be friends?'

'Okay, sure.'

'Okay then Rick, you got, listen, you got any lunch money?'

'No. What's that, lunch money? You mean they pay you to eat lunch or –'

'Don't be a smart-ass with me, I'll, I'll ionize ya. Now you listen and listen good.'

All at once Roderick realized: Chauncey was a villain. Villains invariably told people to listen good. Or else.

'Listen good, I'll let you off this time, only tomorrow you bring a dollar. Or else.'

'Or else what?'

'Or else we kick your ass, smart-ass.'

A bell rang. Roderick dusted himself off and looked over the scratches in his new paint job. Pa had painted him especially for school; he wouldn't like this.

Chauncey gave him a last kick that resounded through his innards and left a dent, then ran off after the other kids. They all seemed to be heading for the building, so Roderick tagged along.

Mrs Dorano had just finished calling the roll, checking each name against one of her magnetic cards, when the door opened and the security man came in trundling Roderick.

'I caught this kid sneaking around the hall,' he said. 'Yours?'

She consulted a lone card. 'This must be little, er, little Roger. The Wood boy.'

Someone piped, 'Hahaha, looks like a steel boy to me.'

Unsmiling, she waited until the uproar settled. 'Naughty. We don't make fun of crippled people, do we, boys and girls?'

'No, MRS DORANO.'

'Do we, Billy?'

'No, Mrs Dorano.'

'All right then. Thank you, Mr Ogilvy.'

The guard shuffled out of the room, his shin-pads clacking together as he muttered, '. . . vandalizers . . . burglarizers . . .'

'Now then Roger, you sit right here in front next to, that's right, between Chauncey and Jill, now I see by your card here you haven't been to school before – illness I guess and that means you may have just a teeny bit of trouble catching up, so you just follow along for now, watch Chaunc – watch Jill and just more or less do what she – anyway now we're going to pledge allegiance. Everybody up, up, up.'

'What's pledge allegiancing?'

'Hahahaha,' Chauncey aimed a kick at him. 'He don't even know –'

'That's enough!'

'Yeah but he don't even –'

'Chauncey be quiet. Roger, dear, haven't you ever pledged allegiance to the pretty flag? No? Well just take your right hand –'

'Hahahaha, he ain't got no hand. He's got –'

'Put your hand, of course he's got lovely artificial hands, put your hand over your heart –'

'I haven't got a heart either,' Roderick said. Jill gasped.

'And say –'

'Missus Dorano, Missus Dorano!' Jill jumped up and down, pointing to him. 'He says he ain't got a heart, how can he pledge allegiance without a heart I mean it's *illegal.*'

'Of course little Roger's got a heart, dumpling. Everybody's got a heart, Roger, I hope you're not going to be a little fibber, don't you want to be a good American? Roger?'

'My name's Roderick.'

'More fibs, tch tch tch, Roger it says on your card and Roger you are – the computer never lies.'

'I wanta go home now.'

Chauncey grinned slowly. 'Yeah, let's all go home, come on.'

'CHAUNCEY, SIT DOWN AND SHUT UP. Roger you can't go home, now stop fibbing and disrupting the class with your no hand and no heart and no name –'

'My name is Roderick and I'm a robot, so I don't have a heart –'

'I'm very disappointed in you, Roger. Very, very disappointed. I'm giving you one more chance to pledge allegiance – oh, what's the use? If you want to be a fibber and a fool and a bad – naughty American, all right. You sit down and the rest of us will pledge allegiance.'

By then, one or two kids in the back had been infected: robot imitations went the rounds; someone asked permission to take Roderick apart to see if he had a heart, someone else declared her own heart had been removed at the hospital . . .

*

Chauncey and his gang seemed friendlier at recess. They invited Roderick to play 'Captain May I'.

The gaunt boy in the blue track-suit said, 'Hey Rick are you really a robot? Boy you sure gave old Dorano a hard time, boy, are you really one?'

Chauncey, hanging back, said, 'Don't be stupid, Jimmy, there's no such thing as robots they're like ghosts. No such thing.'

Jimmy said, 'There are so. Hey Rick, lemme feel your muscle, jeeze you sure are tough I busted my shoe kicking you, see? Hey, you wanna be captain?'

'I'm captain,' Chauncey said, 'I'm always captain.'

'Owww, leggo, okay let's choose for it.'

'Okay but I do the choosing.'

Chauncey counted around the ring (himself, Jimmy, Roderick, Larry, Eddie and Billy) eliminating them one by one:

Eeeny meeny miney moe
Catch a tiger by the toe.

'We gotta try it again,' he said, when only Roderick was left. He went through it all again, this time adding, 'If he hollers, let him go,' knocking out in turn Billy, Jimmy, himself, Eddie and Larry . . .

'Okay, that was practice and this time counts. Only Billy's out anyway because he's too little.' Once more it was Roderick.

'Hey jeeze, Chauncey, why don't we just let him –?'

'Okay, just once more I think I got it right this time, Eeeny meeny miney moe, catch a tiger by the toe, if he hollers make him pay, fifty dollars every day, aw shit I'm out already . . .'

'Look, are we gonna play or what, recess is almost over,' said Larry.

'This time I got it, Eeeny meeny . . .,' Chauncey began, going on to '. . . dollars every day. O-U-T spells out goes he, with a dirty dishrag on his knee, Eddie's out. Eeeny . . .'

'Look, it's gonna be me again,' said Roderick. 'If you wanta choose yourself all you gotta do is go back to the short rhyme now and –'

'Listen smart-ass, I don't need no help from you.' He went on to the end choosing Roderick again, began again with the short

156

rhyme as Eddie went off to find Billy on the other side of the playground. '. . . tiger by the aw jeeze it's you again.'

Larry said, 'I'm tired of this shit. Recess is practically over, jeeze, I quit.'

'You sonofabitch you must of fixed it or something, Eeeny . . .' Chauncey quickly eliminated Jimmy, then himself, leaving Roderick, who said:

'Look I don't care, *you* be captain, whatever that is, let's just —'

The bell went and Jimmy ran off, but Chauncey gripped the robot's arm. 'Not so fast, we gotta settle this. *This* time whoever we finish up on is captain, see? Eeenymeenymineymoecatchati-gerbythetoe Jesus Christ you got it fixed even with just two of us . . .'

Roderick went in from recess with another dent on his torso.

Mr Goun sat in one corner of Miss Borden's office stroking his face as though surprised to find no beard. 'Well sure I was prepared for kids being kids but —' He looked up as Ogilvy came in and dumped a pile of books on the desk. 'Vandalism, ma'am.'

'What?' Miss Borden took a last look at her computer terminal screen and sighed. 'Always six things at once, just when I get down to budget day — what vandalism?'

'Somebody's been over these with a razor-blade, ma'am, they look like IBM cards or something.'

Goun, who was younger, wondered what an IBM card might be.

'Okay thanks, I'll look at them later, meanwhile why don't you do something about Mr Goun here, real security problem for you, somebody burglarized his locker. This morning.'

The guard pushed back his cap in the tradition of baffled policemen and whistled. 'What did they get?'

Goun looked pained. 'Only every one of my manuals for the sex education course, that's all.'

'Yeah? Guess they couldn't wait.'

'Not to mention a valuable psychology book, *The Dream World of the Adolescent Girl*, took me a year to run down a copy.'

Ogilvy snickered. '"Rare" book, eh?'

'It happens to be a serious study of the, the actualization of catalyzing factors in the, in interpersonal relations, you wouldn't

157

understand I guess. The kid who took it probably thinks it's juicy stuff but I – but let me know, will you? A thin blue book, let me know if you see any kid reading it. In the can or –'

'Right, chief.' Ogilvy turned to go and bumped into Ms Beek, moving like a sleepwalker.

Miss Borden stood up. 'Yes, Joan?'

'I – I didn't know –'

'Your class, Joan. Who's watching them?'

'Oh – I –' Ms Beek wandered out.

Goun said, 'Not very articulate, is she? Since her nervous b – ah, trouble.'

'Chemotherapy,' Miss Borden explained. 'She'll soon snap out of it and get right back in the swim again. Now let's see these books.'

Goun opened a book of nursery rhymes. '"*Blank, blank gander,*"' he read. '"Whither shall I wander/ Upstairs and downstairs and in *blank blank blank*." Somebody's hacked out whole words, what is this anyway, "put in his *blank* and pulled out a plum", what's going on?'

She put on her glasses. 'And here's A. A. Milne, I know some of these:

Where is Anne?
(Walking with her man)
Lost in a dream
(Lost among the buttercups)

Yes and down here where it says:

What has she got in that firm little fist of hers,
Somebody's [thumb] and it feels like Christopher's –

This is terrible, who would, somebody's got a dirty imagination here, some nasty-minded little –'

'Yeah, and they cut the last two chapters out of *The Marvellous Land of Oz*. I can't make sense out of any of this. Some kid with an anxietal undedifferentiated –'

'I know what you mean. Little savages, how can I in good conscience ask for a bigger book budget when – Oh before you go, do me a favour, will you? I'm way behind on these individual assessment forms, wonder if you'd mind keeping an eye on this Wood boy for me? The little paraplegic whatever he is, Mrs Dorano's class, I ought to ask her really, but all she ever puts down is sweet, angelic, a darling innocent; try running that through the County Board computer, they'd have my job. So just, just look him over, will you? In an informal interview situ – you know the way to handle it, thanks.'

'Sure. Sure I – sure.' Before he could get out of the door it opened and Captain Fest came in with an armload of reports.

'Just heard about your burglarization Goun, tough. Tough. Kids got no respect for any damn thing, think they're king – you better put those trophies somewhere, ma'am, glass case in the hall like that is just an open invitation – well here's the math skills reports, depressing reading for somebody, don't give a damn myself any more.' He followed Goun into the hall. 'You know I stopped giving a damn when I had twelve-year-olds, one day I asked them how many sixths in a whole, brightest one in the class thought maybe seven, how's that grab you?'

Moving with great energy he left Goun behind, staring at the trophy case and muttering, 'Sixths in a hole? In a hole?'

IX

'Finish your nice tree drawings, everyone. Hurry up.' Mrs Dorano clapped her hands. 'Jennifer and I are going to pin up all the nicest ones for everyone to see. And, uh, Suzy dear, you pass out the new readers. QUIET! Anyone I see talking from now on is going to have his tree put in my waste-basket. Jennifer hurry up, dear. Billy, let her have the drawing, finished or not.'

'Miss can I –?'

'Miss, Miss, Billy drawed a boy's pee-pee!'

'– my pencil and I want it back!'

'QUIET! Suzy they're right there, the stack of blue books on my desk, just pass them – Margery, sit DOWN!'

'But Miss, Billy drawed –'

'Never mind what Billy draw – drew, you shouldn't even know what one of those looks like, just sit down and . . .' She shuffled through the stack of drawings quickly, eliminating those that looked even remotely like body parts – Kids seemed to think of nothing but sex, sex, sex as it was. Too much of it in these promiscuity classes, that's where it came from. Mr Goun, she'd seen him hovering in the hall, waiting to pounce on any passing child and pour corrupting filth into its little ear.

Most of the drawings looked as little like organs as they did trees, thank heaven. They looked variously like lollipops, fans, clouds, telegraph poles and green squiggles. Little Chauncey had turned out a nice effort, incorporating a rubbing of some ornament – and at the bottom he'd written DECIGEONS.

'Very, very good, Chauncey. I think what you meant to write was *deciduous* – I'll show you how to spell it but I think it's wonderful that you even attempted such a grown-up word. I – oh!' She had come to little Roger Wood's drawing.

'Somebody's a copycat here,' she said. 'But who?'

'Not me, Mrs Dorano.' Chauncey grinned.

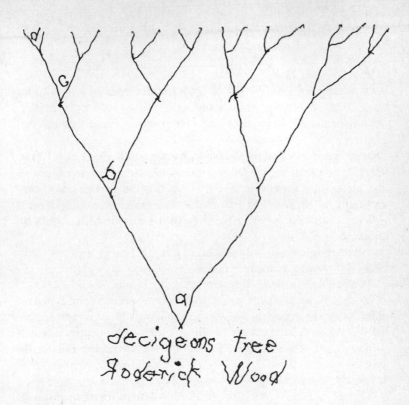

decigeons tree
Roderick Wood

'Roger?'

'What?' He was peering into his new reader.

'Did you copy your tree drawing? It looks like a copy.'

'Well I guess all these decigeon tree drawings look the same, because heck –'

'That will do.' She tore up his drawing. 'As usual, Roger, you disappoint me.'

'Hey, can I ask you about this here reader? It looks kinda hard and –'

'That will *do*, I said.'

Ms Beek looked as though she'd been weeping. Miss Borden, patting her arm, spoke to Captain Fest.

'Do you really have to barge in here? I was just in the middle of a counselling sess –'

'I'm sorry ma'am, but the damnedest thing, my binoculars are missing.'

'Stolen?'

'Presume so. Had 'em locked up in my desk with a few, ah, personal papers, went out in the hall to have a word with Goun, came back to find it ransacked. Everything gone. Naturally nobody in the class saw anything.' He passed a hand through his grey crewcut.

Miss Borden looked at a stain on his sleeve. 'Is that blood? You weren't attacked?'

'That? No, it's nothing. Just interrogating one of the kids about the theft, he slipped and fell, that's all.'

'I see. And you were talking to Mr Goun when the robbery occurred?'

'Wanted to see if he's interested in joining a male teachers' drill team, I'm trying to form a crack –'

'Why male? Because I'm sure Miz Beek here would like –'

'With all due respect ma'am, problem of different heights, different strides – anyway he was busy talking to that handicapped kid, Wood, wonder if maybe he doesn't take an unhealthy interest there, always following the kid around the corridors, talking to him in corners –'

'That's, I asked him to assess the boy.'

'Whew! That's a relief, thought for a moment there . . . I mean you can't be too careful about fraternization – oops, sorry Miz Beek, forgot you were here, did I –?'

'Captain why don't you go and fill out a form S_3, so that I can get Ogilvy to work on your binoculars?'

When he'd gone she patted Ms Beek's arm again. 'There now, he didn't upset you did he? Because we've all forgotten about that little incident, haven't we?'

'. . . forgotten . . .'

'Yes I know you're having a little trouble remembering the number of your classroom, but I just know you'll soon be back in the swim.'

At recess, Mr Goun was waiting for him again. He was always lurking somewhere, the droopy red moustache (normally pointing to 4:37) jumping to 3:42 in a rigid smile. He always asked the same questions: did Roderick's parents work? Did they fight a lot? Did he blame them for his handicap? What did he dream of?

Roderick made up a dream or two that put the moustache to 5:32 (and the eyebrows to 12:55).

Today they stood by the trophy case. Roderick was just saying, '. . . then there was this big decigeon tree, with instead of apples hanging on there was skulls . . .' when a big hand grabbed his arm.

'Good work, Goun, we got him this time.' Captain Fest gave the robot a shake. 'Here's the trophy case, busted open and empty, and here's the culprit. You see any of his accomplices?'

'No look, I don't think Roger here could've —'

'No? Just look at him, guilt written all over that tin face. Let me get him alone for a minute, I'll find out where they hid the swag. Told Miss Borden this would happen but does she listen? No, and Ogilvy our so-called security man, always off somewhere pulling his pudding . . .'

'Maybe we'd better just take him to the office, Fest, straighten out this whole, I'm sure there's some mistake.'

'And this little bastard made it. Okay you, MARCH!'

Mr Fest gripped his arm all the way to the office, where Miss Borden told them all to sit down and get calm.

'Now Roger,' she said, staring down into the glass depths of his eyes. 'I want the truth. Have you seen our school trophies?'

'Trophies?' he said. 'You mean like a thing with a little silver statue of a basketball player, seven inches high and made in Hong Kong? And a disc about four inches across, that says 3rd place state spelling contest 1961? And a gold football for the all-county champs 1974?'

'Yes, have you seen them?'

'Nope.'

'Ma'am you just let me get him alone for a coupla minutes —'

Goun said, 'Give him a chance, maybe he saw them in the case?'

Roderick shook his head. 'Nope, I never saw them at all.'

Miss Borden's colour scheme of buff and blue was momentarily spoiled by bright spots of colour in her pale buff cheeks. 'Young man, this is serious! If you don't come clean with us, you'll have to talk to the sheriff. *Reform school*, is that what you want?'

'Wants the buckle end of a belt laid across his backside if you ask me. Suppose he didn't see my binocs, either!'

'Or my book!'

The interrogation went on for an hour before Miss Borden called the sheriff. 'Be right over,' she said, putting the receiver down. 'He's watching some game show on TV. God I hate all this! Getting the juvenile authorities in on it, we'll all end up spending hours filling out forms – *please*, Roger! Please confess!'

'But I never saw them trophies.'

'Jesus Christ, if you never saw *them trophies* how do you know exactly what they look like, even the engraving, even –?'

'Oh, easy.' Roderick laid a shiny little lump of metal on the desk. 'I found this by the trophy case when I was talking to Mr Goun just now. It must of broken off one of them trophies, and see? It's a foot wearing a basketball shoe. And it looks like silver, and if you look real close you can see it says Made in Hong Kong. And the statue must be about seven inches high, right?'

Goun nodded. 'He did pick up something while we were talking.'

'Okay,' said Fest. 'But how about the rest? The spelling medal for instance? You saw the engraving –'

'Nope. What I saw was one of the kids in Mrs Dorano's class this morning when we were drawing trees, one of the kids hid something under their drawing, only it came out on the paper when they rubbed a crayon over it. 3rd Place, State Spelling Contest, 1961.'

'Which kid?' said Fest.

'Ask Miss Dorano which kid. I don't fink.'

'Okay how about a full-size gold football, you don't tell me you never saw that?'

'Nope, never did. But in the creative activities area there's a picture on the wall of this football team with a banner, 1974 All-County Champs. And a guy in front is holding this gold-coloured thing looks like a football only shiny. So I figured –'

Miss Borden said, 'Jesus Christ,' and reached for the phone.

Chauncey and Billy were beating up some littler kid. Chauncey had the kid's hair in both hands and was using it to bash his head against the kerb. Billy stood by, kicking at the kid's feet.

'Hey come on, Rick, let's get this guy!'

'Nope. It ain't hero-ic, picking on a littler kid. Only villains do stuff like that.'

'Piss on you then, this is fun!'

Roderick decided the really hero-ic thing to do would be to stop them. 'Okay, stop you guys.'

'Piss on – ow!'

Roderick shoved Chauncey hard, pushing him over sideways.

'Ow, Christ I skint my knee!' Chauncey started to cry. 'You fuckin' bully!'

'Look, I'm sorry Chaunce, I –' He forgot what he was about to say, for at that moment Billy smashed a brick into his eye.

'Hey, look, you put his eye out, boy are you gonna get it, hey '

'I'm gettin' the fuck outa here . . .'

'Me too, wait up . . .'

When the vision in his remaining eye cleared, Roderick was alone with the littler kid, who had a bloody nose.

'Are you a robot or what?'

'That's right, I'm Roderick the robot. You okay?'

'Yeah, thanks. My name's Nat. I thought they was gonna kill me or something. Boy, they'd be sorry if they did. They wouldn't have Nat to kick around any more.' Nat smiled at him. 'Hey, you know what?'

'What?' Roderick knew the next line: *You saved my life, pal.* He waited for it.

'You look pretty fuckin' dumb with one eye, you know?'

X

The mechanical clown creaked with senile laughter, every wave of creaks setting up sympathetic waves of nostalgia within Ben Franklin. It reminded him of all the carnivals of his childhood, the candy floss and aluminium ID bracelets engraved by shaky hands, the recorded calliope music fighting the recorded superlaughs from the Hall of Mirrors, the afternoons spent cranking away at a tiny crane ingeniously arranged to avoid gold cigarette-lighters and seize in its clamshell a single grain of popcorn.

Corn, that was the soul of it, and probably the soul of Mr Kratt too. Why else should an important businessman maintain his headquarters in a dirty little trailer in the midst of all this? Corny sentiment. Stuff of the common man, of Goodall Wetts III and *God is Good Business*, stuff of which fortunes are made. And what was wrong with it? Hadn't it been said by Abraham Lincoln (if not by a bearded robot in Disneyland) that God must have loved the common man, because He made him so common? Don't knock, Ben warned himself. For Christ's sake, boost.

And yet he could not help following a critical line elsewhere. Noticing the irony of a white-faced robot clown whose make-up could be traced through real clowns back to Grimaldi – who wore it in *La Statue Blanche* where he played a man impersonating an automaton (each turn of the crank produced a new expression). Robot imitates man imitating man playing man impersonating robot: but the tangle of associations would not leave him there. For clowns were playing The White Statue in the streets of London in Mayhew's time, in the 1840 slum streets, alongside Punch and Judy, marionettes and real clockwork dolls, amid the sounds of hurdy-gurdy and barrel-organ, mechanized street theatre for the new industrial age, where almost the only recognizable features of the past were starving beggars and burning Guys.

Death everywhere, white-faced on every corner, turned into sentiment at home and comedy in the streets: the marionettes always included a Bluebeard and a skeleton; the shadow-puppet man tells how a mob overturned his van and burned it (with his assistant inside); Punch and Judy must always have the hanging in the last act:

Jack Ketch: Now, Mr Punch you are going to be executed by the British and Foreign laws of this and other countries, and you are to be hanged by the neck until you are dead – dead – dead.

Punch: What, am I to die three times?

He was still scowling at the decrepit clown when Mr Kratt's thick hand clapped his shoulder. 'Guess you seen enough here, let's get back to town. We can take a look at that stock list on the way.' The V of eyebrows descended on tiny black eyes. 'Hey, something wrong?'

'Uh, no sir. No sir. I was just wondering why you still keep your headquarters here? I mean you could easily afford permanent offices instead of this, I mean a tent show after all –'

'Like to keep on the move, see? Like the gipsies.'

'Nostalgia, I guessed as much, nost –'

'Nostalgia hell, saves me five figures in state taxes, not to mention depreciation and all the substantial advantages of running a cash business . . .'

Roderick didn't see much from the bus window. His eye on that side was out, and if he tried turning his head to look out with the other eye, something funny happened to his hand which began to twitch open and closed. Seeing the scared look of the woman in the seat in front of him, Ma made Roderick sit still and read his robot book.

It was the story of an iron man who falls apart and puts himself together again – boy this Hughes guy didn't know the first thing about robots, here they were going two hundred miles to the city for one crummy eye – but Roderick liked the idea of an iron man who goes around scaring people and then turns into a big hero.

In the back of the book he found a blank page where he could work out some alphabet stuff:

```
I R O N    R O B O T    M A N
h q n m    q n a n s    l
g m p l    p m z m r    k
F O L K    o l y l q    j
           n k x k p    i
           m j w j o    h
           L I V I N    G
```

'What does it mean?' Ma asked, as the bus left the smooth highway to start bucking its way through broken streets.

'Nothing I guess. Stories. I mean nobody really falls apart and puts themself together again – do they?'

Ma thought the question over, while behind him Roderick heard someone say, '. . . like teeth only . . . dank wish . . . the Omaha disaster we decided . . . a peep in Coventry, was it?'

'Sure sure sure sure sure.'

Ma continued to think while the bus pulled into a greasy terminal, and the driver ordered them to 'debark'.

The city at first seemed to fall apart without putting itself together: Roderick saw tall glass buildings falling over on him, people pushing each other along the sidewalk, cars honking and revving their engines while waiting to move an inch forward, six abreast, towards the bleeping traffic lights where people pushed each other past the walls of black garbage bags and out on to the street. A yellow taxi pulled up next to him and a man with blood running down his forehead and nose jumped out and ran inside a shoe store, elbowing aside a woman whose little dog made a dash to the end of its tether trying to bite the kid who was being chased out of a narrow doorway marked MASSAGE THERAPY; the dog twisted and snapped instead at the crowd of little wind-up dolls a man with dirty fingers was setting in motion on the sidewalk where they tottered in circles and fell over, looking much like the man with a bottle in a paper bag who sprawled next to an alley where two boys were dividing the contents of a woman's purse. They were ignored by the man wearing sandwich-boards (FOLLOW ME TO JUNIOR'S DISCOUNT CAMERAS) who entered the alley (no one

following), flipped up his forward board and began urinating on a
wall beneath a poster, VOTE J. L. ('CHIP') SNYDER FOR LAW & ORDER,
a duplicate of the sign Roderick saw a moment later on a wall
behind the hot-dog stand where a man of a thousand pimples
reached for his hot-dog with one hand and for the crotch of the
boy next to him with the other, this being a thin kid engrossed in
a photograph which he then dropped   'Jeez, whaddya –?' and
Roderick looked down at the picture of a dismembered woman as
Ma dragged him past the thin kid, who wore a jacket marked
JUNKERS S.A.C. almost the same neon orange as a sign BURGER
BELLE in the window where the top half of a black man could be
seen frying grey meat and – whenever he noticed anyone looking
at him – spitting into the top half of each roll. Hardly anyone but
Roderick did look, any more than they looked at the transparent
plastic box of newspapers (headline: ARMY MOM COOKS BABY IN
M´WAVE OVEN, EATS IT) which someone was trying to break open,
next to a video pay-phone on a post, under whose plastic canopy
a woman in wrinkled stockings leaned, weeping and pleading with
the face on the tiny screen, which seemed to have hair as bright
and green as the sweater on the little dog held back now from a
puddle of vomit by a smiling woman in a tiny silk skirt no larger
than a cummerbund who called out to the sailor lurching towards
the door of SUGAR´S SAUNA past two figures leaning together in so
friendly a fashion that the knife held by one at the other's throat
seemed a mistake (as the victim kept insisting it was), past the JOYS
OF JESUS mission towards the amusement arcade, a place of
flashing coloured lights, bells, buzzers and bleeps under the
defective sign TEST YOUR SK*LL flickering next to an empty store
plastered with SNYDER FOR LAW & ORDER and a poster advertising
STREET MUSIC overwritten with hundreds of obscure slogans all
beginning SUCK. This was next to a novelty shop featuring dribble
glasses, rubber pencils, loaded dice, a talking crucifix, marked
cards, plastic snot, a fake finger (hideously injured), itching
powder, cayenne candy and a 'Sacred Heart lighter – REALLY
WORKS – useful and devotional – Butane extra'. Ma dragged him
on, past a larger-than-life photo of two naked women embracing
under the legend THIS WEEK ONLY TRIPLE ADULT SEXATION: DOLLS
OF DEVIL´S ISLAND – 'Brutally frank'; 'Sexplicit revealing confession' – I WAS A SAUNA BITCH; 'Inside bare facts of Hitler's mad

nuns' – ANGELS WITH DIRTY HABITS and the long line of tired old men before the ticket-office nearly as long as the similar line across the street before the Unemployment Office where a policeman sprang on one of the grey figures, knocked it to the sidewalk, and began beating it with his truncheon, while shoppers pushed their way past this as they had pushed past a man with missing fingers trying to play a harmonica, on their way from FURNITURE WAREHOUSE to DENIM INIQUITY ignoring the bright neon of MARV'S SEX DISCOUNTS above a bewildering array of objects identifiable only by fluorescent signs (Condom's Slashed, Vibey's Reduced; Manacles Cut; See Our Selection of Custom Rubber & Leather Unclaimed Specialties) signs all but obscuring the next place where a feeble neon sign proclaimed from behind heavy iron grilles, NO CREDIT LIQUORS. Before it a machine like a kind of automatic pogo-stick pulled its operator along as it tore at the street, holding up a line of bleating cars including a limousine flying Ruritanian flags, a panel truck shaped like a turkey and labelled GOBBLE KING, a sound truck whose message echoed ('. . . law and order . . . sick of bleeding hearts . . . man with guts . . . man with experi . . . an with integrity . . . n with the know-how to turn this city into the kind of . . . to grope up in, to grow up in . . .') through the sounds of car horns, bleeps, bells, buzzers, the Brandenburg Concerto, laughing, screaming, moaning, the hammering of the street-ripper, coins going into a telephone, replays clacking on a pinball machine, revving engines and a singing clutch, the thunder of an invisible plane overhead shaking the glass walls of the tipping buildings, rock music fighting jazz fighting country western over the loudest horn of all, on a yellow taxi with blood down the door.

'Well ma'am, your lucky day, we got just one in stock. Not exactly the same colour but – well the fact is, we had this stockroom fire last week, pretty well cleaned us out. Yup, your lucky day. My partner bought it too, he was back there takin' inventory see, and it looks like he was smoking or something, so. So here I am, half a ton of assorted high-grade hardware up in smoke along with the only guy who knows how to design and build it. I was just supposed to be the money man, only now I can't even pay the rent on this crummy little store unless I sell off our plant. Yup, your lucky day. This one's a demo, let you have it half price, okay? You want me to fit it for you now? Just takes a second, even I know how to – there, how's that look? Okay that's thirty-eight no nineteen hundred plus tax plus city tax, comes to twenty-two oh six eighty-five, cash I hope?'

'Ma I can't see out of it.'

A bandaged hand patted Roderick on the head. 'Nice little talker you got there, ma'am, kit-built is he? Never seen anything like – no look, I don't know what kind see-see-em or what you got in there but usually these eyes take a while to get warmed up – not warmed up exactly but see they gotta compatiblize with the other stuff, look you wanta leave him here for an hour, see how it pans out?'

The man with bandaged hands set Roderick on the blistered paint of the counter. From there he could turn his good eye one way to see Ma leaving, or the other way to see the man going into a back room. Roderick could see a table back there, and a pair of hands turning pages.

'. . . seems in order, we might even take some of the damaged stock here on page three, but of course I want my boy Franklin to go over this . . .'

'Yes sir of course sir, you know I think you'll find this is your lucky –'

The door closed. But not before Roderick glimpsed a heavy gold ring mounting a single pinball.

No one at Larry's Grill noticed just when the little machine came in, but there it was, sitting up on a barstool listening to the chatter of the regulars.

'You wouldn't think it to look at me . . .' said the woman in purple lipstick, holding herself steady as she raised a brimming shot-glass. 'You wouldn't think it to look . . .'

'At's right Lena, you tell 'em.' The taxi driver, who considered that his Irish ancestry gave him the right to a brogue and the gift of story-telling, went on with his story about the Baltimore Mets. 'See they went to Japan to play this exhibition game, and one night they all went down to this –'

'Think I heard this,' said the swarthy used-car salesman. 'I hear every damn thing, that's the trouble in mind, Oh! –

171

Gonna lay my head
On some lonesome railroad line
And let the midnight train
Ease my troub – yeah, yeah, yow! –

Tourette's syndrome they call it, I calls it like I sees it, grab it
when I can get it –'

'No but listen one night they all went down to this special kind
of geisha –'

'No spitting on the floor,' said Larry to the man in the red
hunting cap, who was glaring at the three newcomers, youths in
red Digamma Upsilon Nu sweatshirts. 'Boys if you got ID,
welcome.'

'College boys!' muttered the spitter, while beside him two truck
drivers argued money.

'You think you're broke? Betcha I'm ten times as broke as you.'

'Yeah? Betcha you got more money in your billfold right this
minute than I got in my whole – life. My whole billfold.'

'Hell I couldn't even afford that brassy blonde over there.'

The woman he could not afford had discovered Roderick.
'Hey, you want a peanut? Here boy! Cute little bastard ain't he, I
mean with one green eye one blue –'

'You wouldn't think it to look at me, but I used to be a Paris
passion, fashion model.' Another drink passed purple lips. 'Paris,
France.'

'I'm so broke –'

'Where the hell is Dot today, she'd like this, have a peanut
boy?'

'– doesn't want a damn peanut, what the hell's the matter with
you? You can see the thing's a machine, what's it gonna do with a
peanut, vend it? Anyway Dick, listen they get to this geisha
place –'

'Who belongs to this thing anyway?' Larry leaned over the bar
to look at it. 'Anybody belong to this thing?'

'Probably came in with them college boys,' said the hunter, and
spat on the floor.

'Goddamnit Jack, behave yourself.'

'Parish fashion model, you believe that?'

The used-car salesman turned. 'Ignore Lena boys, she used to be a plaster of Paris model only now she's just plas – ow, Jesus Lena can't you take a joke?'

'Okay that's a bet. Larry counts the money in both our billfolds, and whoever's got less gets all the money. Larry come here, we got a bet –'

The taxi driver's brogue deepened desperately. 'Will ye listen? Now the lads get to this special geisha place only it turns out –'

'Sure he wants a peanut, don't you my little sweet-ums? Come on boy, sit up for – he won't sit up.'

Larry, holding two billfolds, spun around to catch old Jack spitting again. 'That's it, Jack. Out. I told you about that, now out!'

The old man's earflaps stood up like the ears of a fox terrier. 'All of a sudden the place is too classy for me, all of a sudden it's a classy college-boy place, eh? Well I'm goin'. I'm goin'.' He deliberately spat again and ambled out.

'I'm a-comin', I'm a-comin',' sang the used-car man. He tapped his feet on the brass rail, threw a peanut into the air and caught it in his mouth, winked at the blonde and made a face at Roderick. 'Howdy doody little robot. How's all your nuts and bolts?'

'Bejesus will you listen man? They get to this geisha place and it turns out that all the girls are just inflatables!'

'But no really, I was a Parish, a Paris, a mannequin.'

'Inflate me,' sang the used-car man, 'my sweet inflatable –'

'I'm very well thanks,' said Roderick. No one seemed to hear, which was just as well because he was not quite telling the truth. In fact he felt strange and dizzy, and a peculiar pulse was building up behind his new eye. A pair of purple lips swam by, saying:

'To look at me, be honest, you wouldn't think . . .'

Larry transferred all the money from one billfold to the other and handed them back. 'You win, Eric.'

'Hey wait a minute, that ain't a fair bet. He only had six bucks there, I had over twenty!'

'Yeah well that was the bet, who had less –'

'Yeah but I mean I'm risking twenty against six, what kinda odds is that?'

The expensive blonde said, 'Larry, forget them geeks, willya? I wanta buy my little friend here a drink, I wanta buy him a Shirley

Temple. You get him a dish so he can lap, my little sweet-ums!' She patted Roderick's metal cheek. 'Soon as I get back from the little girls' room, honey, you and me can have a drinky, okay?'

'Her little robottoms,' said Dick, and winked at no one. 'Hey little robottoms, what's your name?'

'Roder-ick Wo-od.' Roderick lurched and nearly fell from the stool. One of the fraternity boys caught him.

'Wow, HE TALKS! Crazy, you see that boys? Shoo-be-do, Pow! Zap! She's a transistor sister with a . . . and what was that name? Woody? Howdy Woody, how's the old wood pe −'

'Shut your gob will you? The point is, they all slept with this little inflatable geisha see? And they all came down with a dose!'

'Okay Eric, how about double or nothing?'

The money changed billfolds solemnly as one of the fraternity boys said, 'Doubles hell, we're drinking triples here, by God!' They had indeed been drinking so much that it seemed a good idea to take Roderick with them, just as it seemed a good idea to leave their car (since none of them could remember where it was parked anyway) and steal another.

The two men in the back of the Rolls-Royce sat so close that, had passers-by been able to see them through its dark windows, they might have supposed that Mr Kratt and Ben Franklin were embracing. They were in fact looking over a typewritten list.

'Now what the hell's this, twenty grand for a diode loser?'

'Laser it's supposed to be, they use it for etching the −'

'Sure, sure, just so you checked all this stuff out. This could turn out to be the best damn thing ever happened to us, Benny, where we gonna find, look at these kilns, ten grand under wholesale, and this, where is it?' Kratt erected a stubby finger and ran it down the list. 'All this test stuff half price, Christ if I knew they owned all this and were tight for cash, I'd have set fire to their place myself, Ha!'

'Yes sir, now −'

'So what do you think, bub? Make an offer on the whole shebang or what?'

Ben Franklin sat back, felt Mr Kratt's tweed-covered arm against his neck, sat forward again. 'Well if you ask me −'

'Jesus Christ, I don't see anybody else here to ask but the

chauffeur, wouldn't ask that little greasy spic for the time of   told
me when you came over you wanted responsibility bub, so here it
is, do we buy?'

'Well, yes if you really, if it's really what you want –'

'Hell yes, you think I want to go on all my life paying through
the nose for hardware we could make ourselves? Now you buy
this crap and get the plant working, by the way how's that peanut
brittle idea going?'

'Well Hare I mean Dr Hare is just working out a few last-
minute bugs I guess, something about the batteries, the –'

'Fine, fine. Because I don't want nobody getting there first, we
got to drive a spearhead see into this fun food market, then
broaden our base, first maybe the gingerbread talkbacks and then
see what we can do with chocolate chips, you tell Hare to get the
lead out of his ass and put this stuff forward, hear me?'

'Yes sir, but you see he thinks –'

'Thinks, that loony thought his last employers right out of
business, you tell him to stop thinking and start producing. Jesus,
leave it up to him we'd still be farting around with some piddling
little so-called improvement twenty years from now, I know these
science yak-heads. Christ Benny, why do you think I put *you* in
charge here? It's because you're not a science yak-head, you got
your feet on the ground.'

'Science, well I was trained '

'Sure, sure, but look, just look at these yak-heads, the way they
go around blinding everybody with science, blind themselves too.
Jesus they take an idea and play with it and play with it – until
they go blind!'

'Ha ha, yes I guess there is a sort of masturbational side to
research, even dreams – you know the answers sometimes come
up in dreams, Kékulé –'

'Yeah well I say screw that! Screw that! I want to see that damn
gingerbread boy on the market in months not years, *months*. Hell
save the damn improvements, later we put out the new improved
model, miracle ingredient, only way anything ever gets done. Tell
that to Hare and his dreaming coolies, make him listen! Tell him
if I don't see talking gingerbread boys in the supermarkets by
Easter, I'll hand him his dick in a test-tube, let him have a wet
dream about that!'

'Uh, yes sir.' Ben folded the inventory and put it in an inside pocket. 'Now if that's all I think I'll just get out here and –'

'We're both getting out here, bub, only reason I had this little greaser drive us here was so I could show you my gallery.'

'Gallery? Shooting –?' Ben peered out but could see no neon through the dark glass.

'The Kay Tee Art Gallery, right there, bub. We got an opening tonight, Edd McFee, ever heard of him?' Kratt opened the door.

'No I don't th –'

'You will. Come on.'

And Ben Franklin, hurried from the car into a mirror-fronted place, caught sight of his own nice face, poised for some suitable expression. He had already shaken hands with two or three persons inside before he could stop thinking about that face: maybe he should grow his moustache again, and to hell with Mr Kratt?

XI

The artist and the beautiful Mrs McBabbitt swept past the two critics who'd been standing in the same spot since their arrival.

'. . . but I still don't see why they all look the same, aren't they all just . . .'

'Well I call it Paradigmatics, it's . . .'

'. . . just purple squares?'

The two critics stood with their backs to as many of the pictures as possible, twiddled their champagne glasses, and studied the crowd.

'Plenty of loot here . . . who's the big boy in the J. Press suit?'

The taller critic looked where the shorter was looking. 'Oh, Everett. Everett Moxon, he's nobody. Now. Probably just here to ask Mr K. for a job. He used to be into reactors, light-cooled reactors or something boring like that. Lost everything in the panic.'

'Just as well, before he started polluting light or something. Ever know a businessman with a conscience?'

'Not unless they've started buying them as investments, who's that stunning woman in black talking to McFee?'

The shorter looked where the taller was looking. 'Mrs McBabbitt. If you think she's beautiful now, wait till you see the finished product.'

'You don't mean –?'

'Yep. Going through one of those whole-body cosmetic surgery jobs, bones and all.'

'But they take years! And loot . . .'

'Absolutely. Everybody here is loaded practically, except Allbright.'

'Allbright! God I wish he'd hurry up and o.d. or whatever he's going to do, I really get sick of seeing him everywhere. All he does is steal books to support his nasty habit.'

'Poetry? Well I've got a dozen signed copies of his book put away, just in case. Posthumous glory might – hey, who's that old woman?'

The taller critic, looking, said, 'I didn't know you read Allbright's poetry – The one in the shawl?'

'I don't. Looks more like a lace table-cloth, but who is she? Haven't I seen her before? Some kind of writer or –?'

'No, last year. She entered this giant toilet in the Des Moines Bienniale, name's Rose Wood, something like that.'

The shorter critic shook his head. 'No, before that, *way* back, a writer my parents knew in Chicago – now was she the writer or was it her husband?'

'Maybe the toilet was rattling off its memoirs – Christ, why don't you just ask her?'

'I will. I might.' But neither critic made a move, except to put down an empty glass when a waiter came by and seize a full one. They remained anchored to the spot even after the crash.

Mr Vitanuova spread his wide face in a smile and his wide hands in a benediction. 'Me, I don't understand nothing. It's the wife, see? She knows Art like I know garbage. No wait, don't get sore, hey I don't mean this is garbage, I mean *real* garbage, it's my business.'

But already the woman in the Abbott & Costello t-shirt had turned away to listen to Ben Franklin:

'Well purple, yes, it's kind of ecclesiastical, isn't all art? I mean isn't that why we take it seriously, because it has its own liturgy?'

Allbright moved a book-shaped bulge under his sweater. 'You're gonna give me canons of taste for this? The fact is the guy painted the same damn purple square twenty times, the same purple the same square – and you justify that? If it *were* art you wouldn't need to bring in all the big guns, the Church and Freud, Marx and Pater or any other dear damned dead philos, where's that waiter? Hauling in Wittgenstein or maybe Kirke, waiter! Hey, over here!'

'No, look fella, I'm not trying to justify anything. But so what that they're all alike, so were icons, most of them look like mass production jobs.'

'Mass production I like that, keep the old prayer-wheels of industry turning, isn't that religion?'

'Well I'm not really –'

'Counting the revs, counting the revs see, because numbers make it all important, don't they? This geek here could paint one purple square and who cares, but if he paints twenty, in comes the old number magic. What does the twenty stand for? What does it mean? Because that's religion too, numbers have to mean something: the eight-fold path, the seven deadly sins, the ten commandm –'

'What's wrong with that? Just a way of keeping track, I mean even truth is binary, if you –'

'Telling the beads,' said Allbright, lifting two drinks from a passing tray. 'Listen pal, numbers are everything in religion, telling the beads, when I was a kid I used to think that meant you know, talking to the beads. Only later on I found out it meant *telling* like a fucking bank teller, counting up the days of indulgence, no good storing up riches in Heaven if you can't count them – Listen, you want my advice?'

The woman in the Abbott & Costello t-shirt moved on without waiting to hear his advice; a moment later she was advising Dr Tarr to look for religious significance in these paintings.

'Lyle Danton? Is it you?'

The young man in patched denim work-clothes turned. 'I call myself Tate now.' He studied the old woman in lace, the corsage of radishes at her throat. 'Ma?'

Ma Wood squeezed his forearm. 'I'm glad to see my best pupil still interested in art.'

'Art?' His unhappy laugh startled her. 'Let's talk about something else. You still living in Newer?' He moved to keep his face in profile, a habit she remembered.

'Of course. Oh, I see, like Picasso? Taking your mother's name I mean. But if you're not painting now, why in the world –?'

'Oh I'm painting, all right. I mean when I can afford the materials. Well it's a long story . . .'

She kept hold of his arm. 'But don't your parents – I mean they used to be the richest folks in town when your father was running the factory. I thought he'd be doing even better by now, didn't you all move to the city so he could become general manager or some such, was it managing director?'

'*Him.*'

'You don't get along?'

'We never did. And when he killed my mother . . . No, well okay it was an accident everybody says, traffic computer goes haywire and he smashes into the back of this truckload of tranquillizers; it could happen to anybody.'

'I'm sorry, I didn't know.'

'Okay an accident maybe but he hated her guts, he always hated her guts. On account of me.'

'The birthmark?'

He still kept his face in profile to hide it. 'Mom would have split long ago, only she was too damn kind-hearted, you know? I mean he needed all his money to start this new business, she knew he couldn't make it if he had this alimony around his neck, so she just stayed, stayed and stayed until he –'

'But wait, what business? Did he leave Slumbertite?'

'Got canned, so did all the execs. They got some new system there now, some, I guess they call it BIGSHOT or something, some kind of decision-maker – so anyway he's in the restaurant business now. I don't see much of him. I dropped out of the University and just been doing odd jobs, even tried working in a tattoo parlour, how's that grab you?'

Ma continued to grab at his arm, to stare at his sullen profile. ' . . . you were always good at people, the human figure and the, the human face . . .'

'Well I got fired from the tattoo parlour just the same, wrote something about T. S. Eliot on a guy's arm, the illiterate old bastard running the place thought it was "toilets", how does that –?'

'Lyle, listen. I want to commission you to do a portrait.'

'What?' He turned full-face in surprise, showing the birthmark, a red shadow over half his features, a glimpse of Harlequin, before he turned it away again. Poor boy, she thought. Not just to have it, but to be hated for it.

'Well, not a portrait exactly, more a painted head. I'm working it up now, maybe I could send you a cast of it to study . . .?'

The profile looked pleased. 'Well sure. Sure Ma, sure. Only you don't mind that I do it symmetrical?'

'That would be just fine, Lyle. Just what I wanted.'

'Art, well I leave it to the experts,' said Mr Kratt. 'I'm just the money man.'

'Oh but you should take an *interest*.' Mrs McBabbitt looked at him through lowered lashes as black as her sable coat. 'Dr Tarr has just been telling me it all has deep religious significance. Are you a religious man, Mr Kratt?'

'I manage to keep pretty busy without it, you know? Ha! But of course I respect the next guy's religion as much as anybody – just like I respect the next guy's wife.' He leaned a little closer. 'Mr McBabbitt's a lucky man.'

She seemed to agree.

'What was *that*?' said the taller critic.

The building rocked from the crash. The shorter critic peered through the waves of people running towards the sound. From here it looked as though two cars had tried to drive into the gallery together and wedged themselves in the doorway. Shards of mirror lay strewn over the green carpet like peculiar angular lakes.

'Mr K.'s Rolls there, looks like. And isn't that other car flying the flags of Ruritania? The consul's car I suppose, only those boys getting out of it don't look like diplomats to me.'

'God, I hope this isn't someone's idea of a happy accident or –?'

'That would be unfortunate,' said the taller critic. 'Did you cover that boring exhibition of wrecked cars last May?'

'Not me, you mean the freeway thing, when all those cars and trucks piled up? I wanted to go, really, thought it sounded enterprising at least, getting out there and casting the whole mess in fibreglass right on the spot, I mean whatsis-name, Jough Braun must have been actually cruising the city with a ton of epoxy – imagine getting an actual body in there!'

'He was just lucky, though, what he was really out doing was dog turds. Trying to get a casting of every pile of doggy do-do in the city on one particular day, kind of Conceptualist record –

anyway he gave that up in a hurry once he saw what kind of money these German museums were bidding for *Freeway Disaster*. I still say he's a boring little prick.'

'But you gave him a good review?'

'Wouldn't you?' said the shorter critic. 'I mean with two German museums going bananas over him, wouldn't you?'

'What happened?' the taller asked someone else. 'Accident?'

'Nothing. Just some college kids smacked into Mr Kratt's car. Nobody hurt. A chauffeur killed.'

'Drunk, were they?'

The stranger shrugged. 'Sure, but they got diplomatic immunity, see? On account of the car. Cops won't do a thing.'

It was true. The police came and went, the cars and the body were discreetly removed, but the three grinning members of Digamma Upsilon Nu remained to sip champagne and brag of their adventure.

'Sure I'm religious,' said Mr Vitanuova. 'I'm a good Cat'lic, what else? Just because a guy gets his hands in garbage don't mean he ain't got a soul, ya know.'

Allbright, holding a champagne glass in each dirt-encrusted fist, leaned in an unpremeditated direction. 'That's goddamn profound.'

Dr Tarr said, 'Yes, what's interesting about these Catholic miracles like levitation, take the flying monk for instance, Giuseppe Coppertino in the sixteenth – What I mean is I've been working out the psychic forces involved . . .'

Allbright leaned another way. 'Look, you want my advice? You want my advice? You want to get close to God you just go out and buy yourself the biggest goddamn computer you can buy. You know why?'

Mr Vitanuova kept shrugging and smiling. 'Look, I pay my dues, I figure –'

'. . . our little mascot,' said one of the fraternity boys. 'Our little robot mascot. Roderick, go on, say hello to the nice lady, hee hee hee.'

Across the room Ben Franklin looked up. 'Just a minute, thought I . . . thought I heard . . .' But a second later Mr Kratt's heavy hand was on his shoulder.

'Have fun, bub. Just taking Mrs McBabbitt home now, but you stay, have a – have a good time.'

'Yes sir.'

'Oh one thing, all these people yakkin' about religion gave me another brainstorm here, make a note of this: edible talk-backs. I figured maybe break into the Catholic market there, Mr Vitanuova just telling me how they do it in the mass and all –'

'Yes sir, but I just wanted to see someone –'

'In a minute, bub, you just listen. Howsabout a talking host, see?'

Franklin turned to face him. 'A what? Television . . .?'

'You don't listen, see? Nobody listens, I mean a *host*, a piece a bread they use for masses, Mr V. tells me the priest just holds it up and says this is my body. This is my body. Well look, wouldn't it be more convincing if *the bread itself does the talking?*'

'I don't know . . .'

'Hello, Ma,' said a small voice.

'Hee hee hee, hello Ma he says, here lady you can hold him a while if you want, I gotta find my buddies – Hey you guys!' One Digamma Upsilon Nu sweatshirt went to join two others at the table of drinks. Near by, the two critics looked over copies of the beautifully-printed catalogue.

Mr Kratt's hand squeezed Ben's shoulder. 'No, well just make a note of that, we'll talk it over some other time, okay? Could be a whole new market there.'

Allbright was shouting: 'The Mormons, they got a big goddamn computer out in Salt Lake City, counting up the souls – they got it made, see? Because you know who's gonna get into Heaven? I'll tell you who, the big insurance companies, the government, the credit card companies, the Pentagon, all going to Heaven! Everybody that gets control of the magic numbers, that's who!'

Dr Tarr began filling his pipe. 'Yes there could be something in that, the psionic effect of complex machines, pure complexity . . .'

'I know.' Mr Vitanuova winked. 'Like they say, garbage in, garbage out. And I know garbage.'

Ben Franklin thrust his face between them. 'Listen, has anybody seen the white-haired woman? She was here a minute ago holding this little robot mascot thing, anybody . . .?'

Next he tried the two critics, who shrugged and went on reading:

The paintings of EDD MCFEE, though superficially identical (each being a 1 cm square of Bohème 0085 Violet centred on a 74 cm square white ground) draw their individuality from the time and locus (solely determined by random numbers) in which they were painted. No. 1, *Juryroom Trout*, was painted at 3 a.m. GMT on May 2, 1979, at an exact location in the Sahara, for example (2°W, 29°N). Yet McFee's work, while rigorously Conceptualist in performance, manages at the same time to defy the canons of that limited and uncongenial mode. A bold form, an unexpected colour – these interact to both direct and keep pace with his concept, welding precision of thought to plasticity of expression in a carefully orchestrated equation of space/time. It is, moreover, a transcendental equation. Form is embedded in time, space in colour, design becomes discovery. The result, a reified Conceptualism, displaces the traditional stylized 'thought-experiment' with a new, holistic approach. Performance is redeemed by object. His aim, then, is to . . .

'His aim,' said the taller critic, 'is to produce some hard goods collectors can buy, without feeling they've been ripped off – even when they have.'

'You playing this one down, then?'

'Hell no, Mr K. shoots a grand an inch for a good review . . .'

Edd McFee, looking dapper even in his Army fatigues, was talking to the woman in the Abbott & Costello t-shirt when Ben approached.

'What old lady? Naw, I never seen her, ask, ask somebody else . . . now like I was saying, Carrie, religion is fine, like it's a deep one-to-one interpersonal relationship with Somebody, sure that's what everybody wants. Only as an artist I got this problem: I can create but I can't really love, see? So what I'm looking for is a woman to have a deep interpersonal relations with, I mean relationship with . . .'

Ben Franklin tried to ask the fraternity boys, but they had begun to sing. There was no one else to ask but the waiters and that guy with the birthmark. But the waiters were busy packing

up, and the guy with the birthmark was sitting on the floor
playing with pieces of mirror. Ben took a last glass of champagne
and, standing alone, tried to arrange his face in a nonchalant
expression. He pretended to look at the nearest painting, though
in fact he failed even to notice that someone had defaced it
(adding to the small purple square a large black moustache).

'. . . garbage out,' said Allbright. 'That's profound, you know?'
Dr Tarr giggled. '*In vino, veri* true.'

'Right. The C-charged brain, the C-charged . . .'

Lyle Tate picked up two pieces of mirror and held them so that
he could see himself perfected, the dark blaze gone, his face
become a bright symmetrical mask. The smile was slightly V-
shaped, but so much the better, he thought, murmuring, '. . .
animal lamina . . . burn, rub . . . th' gin forests, er, of night . . .'
and finally, 'Eye sees tiger dreg, it sees eye . . .' as the howling
chorus crashed about him.

Roll me ooooover
In the cloooover

XII

Miss Borden unreeled a gold chain with a tiny ballpoint pen at the end. 'Okay Bill, spit it out.'

'Shouldn't you see the boy yourself first?'

'He's off today. Mr Wood's taking him to the city I guess for some eye tests, anyway you have observed him?'

'Yes, well no not in a direct observational, more in a peripherally informalized situ –'

'You've seen him in the hall, I know. Go on.'

'Yes, contacted him a few times in the hall and elicited a response or two, nothing def –'

'How's his reading?'

'Reading skills, yes he did say he was having trouble with this new reader Mrs Dorano assigned.'

She marked on the yellow form. 'Reading problem. I was afraid of that, now how does he get along with other kids?'

'Socially he's, there seems to be a nomenclatural mixup there, some difficulty with meaningful involvement in the cultural mainstream ... maybe an identity crisis even; other kids keep calling him a robot you know? And when I asked him why, he said, "Because I am a robot."'

She shook her head. 'All too familiar these days, schizoid pattern: usually parents both work, kid's alone too much –'

'Divisive destructuring of the ego conceptualiza –'

'That's right. I ought to send him to George for a battery, I mean a battery of reassessment tests, only right now George has a pretty full case-load over at the junior high, you know what with that Russian roulette club –'

'I imagine. How is the Vulich boy by the way?'

'As well as can be expected, understand his parents are seeking a court order to have the machine turned off – where were we?'

'Think we ought to do something, this Wood boy told me he dreams of skulls and scissor trees . . .'

'Well sure, I'll try to get George to fit him in, otherwise we'll just have to let him go on thinking he's a Martian – yes, at least we can send him to Ms Beck for some remedial, hand me one of those green forms will you, Bill? No, the *leaf* green ones . . .'

The new eye cost Pa and Ma a lot of money, but at least he could go right back to school. The other kids seemed glad to see him, even Chauncey.

Roderick couldn't figure Chauncey out at all. Whenever they were alone, the bigger boy called him 'Rick', treated him like a pal, and even shared stuff with him, as now:

'Hey Rick, wanna see some real dirty pitchers?'

'Dirty?'

'Yeah I found 'em in old Festy's desk. And these really neat binoculars too, only Billy keeps 'em at home, me and him take turns with 'em. Here, take a look.'

He pulled up his sweater and fished out a dog-eared magazine, *Stud Ranch*. Hiding behind Ogilvy's security hut in the corner of the playground (Ogilvy was never in it) they turned the pages and stared at pictures of people without clothes.

'Hey looka that, wow!'

'Yeah wow, but how come –'

'Look, looka *that*! Boy they sure do weird stuff out West.'

A pair of people were wrestling like Bax and Indica. 'Hey is it dirty because like this they wrestle on the ground or –?'

'Naw, dirty is *dirty*, you know like sexy. Dincha never play doctors or nothing?'

Roderick said, 'Sure, plenty of times. Once.'

'Okay then. See this is how they get babies.'

'*This?* With all this, these whips and spurs, this barb wire –?'

Chauncey hesitated. 'Well sure. Must be, look it probably tells all about it here –'

'Lemme see.'

Whoa there! While Calamity Jayne shucks her buckskins to saddle up for some bunkhouse fun, Miss Kitti is 'bound' to please some

187

lonesome cowpoke. But what's Brazos gonna do with thet there branding iron?

'They don't get babies like that.'

'Sure they do, ask anybody, ask Billy, when his old man's cow had a calf, they tied a rope around her neck and look here at this one, this "necktie party girl" she's got –'

'Yeah but hey wait a minute why do they have to wear all this stuff?'

Chauncey said, 'Look stupid, it's called Stud Ranch so they all gotta wear these belts with studs, boy, when my little brother was born my old lady had to wear all kinds of stuff to keep the baby from coming out her belly button too soon I guess – hey wow, looka that rattlesnake – men don't have babies because they take pills I guess – looka that, "Bathtime at the Rocking 69" – see we had all about it last year, these little tadpoles inside and the Vast Difference –'

'Hahaha, looka that, he thinks this other guy's a girl, look it says "When a gay cabaleero . . ." What's a cabaleero anyway?'

'Just some word, who knows. Wow! Looka that pair!'

'Yeah, Colt .45 Peacemakers, the sheriff's got one like that only not so fancy . . . Hey but Chauncey, what about the tadpoles?'

'Aw who cares, sex is too complicated. Let's play guns, okay?'

But whenever he was with the gang, Chauncey called him 'freaky' and threatened to take a can-opener and rip his guts out. You just couldn't figure out some people.

Roderick couldn't figure out Mrs Dorano either. She was always telling the other kids to be especially nice to him because of his handy cap, and then when they passed out the readers she gave him a different one, real hard and no pictures at all, and all long words. He had to spend hours every night at home going through the dictionary, and it still didn't make sense.

Billy agreed, it wasn't fair. 'Heck my reader's okay. All about this here Dick and Jane and how their mother works hard at the car factory, and like how they get helped by Big Joe the social worker. How come yours is different, boy, I'd make a stink about that.'

'Yeah, listen to this, it don't make sense: "The actualization of catalyzing factors in inter-personal relationships is provided first by the furtherance of participatory options within the framework of an unstructured data base of conceptual parameters, notwithstanding the counter-productive and often marginal motivational mix inducing affectual restructuring of the —" Shit man, this doesn't even tell a story. I mean it's supposed to be about this girl, a doll-scent girl, only here I am on page twenty one and they don't even have her name down here yet.'

'Boy, I'd make a stink —'

'Yeah I guess it don't matter now they're switching me to Miz Beek for redeemial anyway, I got this other reader where they spell everything like it sounds . . .'

Jump. Jump. Jump.
See Bob jump.
Bob jumps on a fast wagon.
Bob gøz fastr ðan a skūl bus.

The hour started off well, with Miz Beek cheerful and pleasant. She sat with Roderick and two other kids around a little table. While they read aloud, she nodded and smiled and occasionally swallowed another of her little white pills.

But towards the end of the hour she no longer seemed to be listening. After making a quick note in her Teacher's Manual, she got up and left the room.

'I bet thee'th going wee-wee,' said one of the kids. 'Thee hath to go wee-wee.'

The other said, 'L-let's g-g-get outa here hey.'

'But thee might come back after thee taketh a pith.'

The door opened, but it was only Mr Fest, telling them he knew all of their names and not to try anything just because Miz Beek was out of the room, understand?

'Yethir, Mither Fetht.'

'Y-y-y — sure.'

'I'm glad you know my name,' said Roderick, 'because everybody else around here keeps calling me —'

'At ease! At ease! I don't want to hear another peep outa this room.'

He went away. They waited.

'Look, thee forgot her pillth. Let'th get high, come on.'

'H-he-hell with that. I'm g-g-gonna s-sell these up in the eighth-graders' c-c-c – toilet.' The stammerer grabbed the pill bottle and ran out, chased by the lisper. Roderick waited until the bell rang, then leaned over and read Miz Beek's note.

'ðu īdeea uv kumbīniNg speeCh Thayrupee wiTh ree-meedyul reediNg iz just wun mōr exampul ov ðu braykdown ov ðu hōl godawful sistum HwiCh ðay keep erjiNg mee tu joyn (az ðō peepul wur glū . . .'

Nat walked him home from school. 'I feel safer,' he explained. 'Not that I'm really afraid of Chauncey and his gang but heck, two of us got a lot better chance than one, right?'

'Right,' said Roderick. 'I was just wondering you know, how come I read all right at home only at school everything goes wrong?'

'Yeah? Hey, we could become blood brothers, pledge ourselves to fight to the death, back to back in case Chaun –'

'Look, I ain't got any blood.'

'We could use oil then, you got oil.'

So Roderick tapped a few drops of hydraulic fluid and Nat took a drop of blood from his thumb, and they mixed them.

'We both swear, right? To defend ourselfs against anybody even Chaunce, we swear on my blood and your oil. Brothers.'

'Brothers.'

'To the death.'

'To the death.' Roderick walked him to his door. 'See you tomorrow.'

'Not tomorrow, hey remember? We got the day off on account of Miz Beek drowning herself in the swimming pool.'

'See you the day after, then. Brother.'

'Okay brother.'

'Settle down, all of you,' said the principal. 'I'm not even going to start until you're quiet. What's more, no one goes home until we finish here, understood?'

They shifted uneasily, and one or two who had been glancing through the pages of *Educationalist Today* sat up straight.

'That's better. Now you all know why I've called this special meeting. But in case anyone hasn't seen today's *Herald*, let me read it out to you.'

'ROBOT' BOY AT NEWER SCHOOL: MORE INSANITY?

Following the alleged suicide of a teacher at Newer Public School (Stubbs City) come rumours of serious mental disturbances among the pupils. Teachers have confirmed that at least one boy thinks he is a mechanical robot.

The boy, Robert Wool, 'acts just like a little machine,' according to second-grade teacher Mrs Delia Dorano. He believes he has mechanical grappling hooks for hands, and tank tracks in place of feet. 'Robert doesn't even answer to his name,' she said. 'No wonder, what with the constant harping on sex and filth everywhere you look. We must protect our children from the sex-merchants of the state educational system.'

'George George, school psychologist, blamed the computerizing of modern society, including our schools. 'We have teaching machines, testing machines, magnetic report cards,' he said. 'Where do we stop?' According to another source, books in the school library have been keypunched on to IBM cards which are unreadable. Said George, 'It's getting like Brig Bother around here.' Mr George is the brother of Hal George, prominent hog auctioneer.

Russian Roulette Club

Newer Junior High, like Newer P.S., has had its share of tragedies. Last year Beanie Vulich, 16, became the first tragic victim of the school's 'Russian roulette club', whose members made use of a school computer to select a duelling pistol at random from a number . . .

'It goes on,' she said, 'to mention drugs sold openly in the eighth-grade washroom, thefts and vandalism, and a security man with a drink problem. Any comments?'

Ogilvy was the first to speak. 'Not fair,' he said. 'Buncha lies and distortions. Like sure I take a drink now and then, but they make it sound like I spend all day lying in an alley somewheres with a bottle of Tokay in a paper bag.'

'What really bothers me,' said Miss Borden, 'is the way certain people are using this tragic suicide as an excuse to whine about their own pet peeves.' She looked at Mrs Dorano. 'Certain people are going to be sorry they ever opened their big –'

'The truth will out,' said Mrs Dorano. 'You can't suppress –'

Mr Goun jumped to his feet. 'Suppress, who the hell are you to talk about –?'

At the same time Mr George said, 'How did I know they were going to print it that way? I didn't think you'd take my criticism in a personalized way, rather than in a societally –'

'Filth and corruption driving that young woman to –'

Captain Fest said, 'Self-discipline, a hard line, lest we forget, moulding Americans, shaping the future –'

'– nothing but plain murder, no better than abor –'

'– catalyzing factors –'

'– easy way out, no backbone, no self-discip –'

'– building a bridge –'

'*Quiet.*' Miss Borden looked at George. 'You all disappoint me, you especially, George. Whining to the papers behind my back instead of getting down to work – My God, you're the school psychologist. We pay you to fix these kids.'

'Fix? Fix? You talk as if they were a bunch of machines! What do you suggest, I get out the old tool-kit and maybe tighten up a few loose screws here and there?'

Mrs Dorano clapped her hands over her ears. 'I won't listen to that filth – I won't!'

Captain Fest muttered, 'Like to fix that little Robert whatsis-name myself. Hear he refuses to pledge allegiance to his country's flag. You give him to me for a week, I'll knock the robot crap out of him.'

George turned on him. 'Knock the crap out of him, all you can think of, right? If you had the slightest understanding – Look, what you ought to be doing is using his problem, making it work for us, for him. I mean, if he thinks he's a robot maybe he should be on a teaching machine or –'

'Good idea,' said Miss Borden. 'That's it, then. Captain, you take charge of this boy and set up a teaching machine program.' She checked something off on a form. 'What I like to see, people forgetting their little individual differences and all pulling together. So much for one child's problem. Now how about some of these bigger issues? Dope-pushing, theft, vandalism – any suggestions?'

One of the younger teachers murmured something and Miss Borden took it up. 'Did you say bridge-building, Ms Russo? That's the first sensible suggestion I've heard so far. Isn't that our job, after all, building bridges? Reaching out –'

Ms Russo blushed. 'No, what I shaid was –'

'– reaching out to isolated, disadvantaged children who –'

'I shaid I hope thish doesn't take long becaushe I've got a dental appointment.'

'Dental appointment. I scc.'

'Yah, to have a bridge rebuilt. Shee, what happened was that little bash – that Chaunshy Bangfield hit me in the mouth with a trophy. I was making him voluntarily return it.'

Someone muttered, 'He reached out to her all right, the little disadvantaged –'

'Any more suggestions?'

Goun spoke of actualizing the problem within a contextual framework of structured situations ranging from verbal correctives to dis-enrolment. In such an intra-systemic . . .

The digital clock wiped away another minute, and another.

Pa waved a plate of brass shaped like half a violin. 'Son, what I'm trying to do here is make me a timepiece, but one that keeps real time. Human time. Like when you're concentrating hard on one thing and it seems like only a minute goes by, why should you have clocks showing you an hour?' He laid the brass plate on his bench and started hammering. 'Other. Times. You wait. For some. Thing to. Happen. Like the. Sunrise. When you. Can'tsleep. You think. One. Hour. Goes by. But ord. Inary clocks. Say one. Minute!' The coughing fit would not pass; Pa had to sit down. 'What use is a clock doesn't tell real time? So. Figure I'll just hook this one up to a brain-wave gadget, need some other stuff too, fine adjustments for fidgeting, pass me that melon scoop will you?'

Roderick wondered what would happen if somebody spent all his real time watching his own real time clock? Could he make it run fast or slow, stop it? Run it back? Or what if two people watched each other's clock? What if two clocks were hooked together? What if the clocks started running the people? And what if . . .? He could go on with questions like these for ever, and no time lost. Time didn't have to move here, because he was at the place where he fitted into the world (as the melon scoop fitted into the brass half-violin turning it into the lever that threw the switch that started up the little water-wheel . . .). Here was Pa, measuring up and marking out all the precise spots on the brass where he was going to bash it with a hammer. Here was the workshop, with dusty autumn light slanting in through the high little window to illuminate a corner piled with forgotten inventions: the pocket calculator (that could add only 0 + 0, 0 + 1 or 1 + 0); the Goethescope with its ebony prism; 'talking shoes'; the universal voting machine with its tangle of coloured wires leading from hundreds of switches to one dead-end; 'Maze-opoly'; audible ink; a large abacus (designed for steam power); the ingenious solar-powered cucumber press (virtual perpetual motion, Pa explained); the Odorphone . . . Here was the friendly workshop itself, one friendly wall bearing the hand-lettered slogans of Miss Violetta Stubbs; another bearing tools (the dover, bit-mace, graduar etc.) below the golden key below the framed photo of Rex Reason below the shelf with the radio. Now the radio hurried through some assassination attempt on some Shah, anxious to get back to its sunshine balloon, but he could hear Ma singing one of her improvised songs, the one she claimed was from the Bow-wow Symphony – whatever that was:

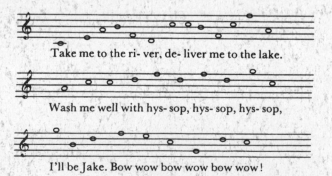

Take me to the ri- ver, de- liver me to the lake.

Wash me well with hys- sop, hys- sop, hys- sop,

I'll be Jake. Bow wow bow wow bow wow!

There were other stanzas just as senseless, stuff about poison candy being good for you when you wake up with an electrode up your nose, stuff like that – anyway, how could a woman be Jake!

XIII

To find out about the past, Roderick had to ask Ma. Pa would only say, 'History is a bunk on which I am trying to awaken.'

Ma sketched as she talked:

Once upon a time the town of Newer had been nothing but a flat spot on the flat prairie: no factory, no grain elevator, no town, not so much as a billboard advertising cream substitute. But to those who founded the town, flatness was ideal: it reminded them daily that God had placed the human race upon a planet shaped like a dinner plate.

They came in 1874, Josephus Butts and his followers. They called the place New Ur, themselves the Urites. They builded here a temple with plain glass windows all around, to shew forth the straightness of God's ruled line.

There were other rules, gradually revealed by Josephus (who now called himself *Jorad*): Urites were forbidden to laugh, marry, call hogs, look with pleasure at the sky or upon one another. Nine-tenths of all they owned or produced belonged to Jorad. No one could speak unless Jorad gave permission. No one but Jorad could sing. No one might *think* unless Jorad allowed him to put on the famous knitted 'thinking cap', a device designed to keep thought down to one person at a time. Finally, the Urites were asked to speak, think, sing and pray in a language called Hibble-bibble, the grammatical rules of which were clear only to Jorad.

Jorad was good at this kind of life. In 1888, he defeated a famous orator in debate, a man who had come to New Ur solely to prove the world was round. The Urites would long remember that exchange.

FAMOUS ORATOR: When a ship sails away, the hull vanishes over the horizon first. Then the lower sails. Then the top-gallant. If the world is *not* round, how do you explain that?

JORAD: Do you see any ships here in town? Any top-gallants vanishing over any horizon? No? *Well then.*

It was their finest moment. The Urites were happy (in their way) as Jorad went off on a round-the-world tour (assuring them as he left that round was only a figure of speech) to promote flatness.

He was gone for ten years. And in the meantime, the Urites grew soft. One of them invented a device which became a standard part of the bicycle, money poured in, the church was rebuilt with stained-glass windows . . . by the time Jorad returned, the younger Urites were defiantly saying that Hibble-bibble was mumbo-jumbo, and even that *the earth might be a little bit rounded in spots.*

In no time at all the town had a dance hall and a Christian Science Reading Room, and all was lost. Jorad smashed the stained-glass windows, called his flock together and tried to urge them back to sense and happiness. But when they looked out of the broken panes, they no longer saw the straight line of the horizon, they saw billboards advertising liver pills, they saw a smoking factory (making beds), they saw steam tractors vanishing over the horizon . . . well then.

Jorad packed up and left, declaring his intention to travel to the edge of the earth and leap off. Some believed he had, until it turned out that he was only over in the next county, calling himself Baresh and starting up a New Babylon. Some people always learned, Ma said. None of Jorad's descendants had ever married: Miss Violetta Stubbs and Mr Ferd Joradsen were now the last.

'Sure it's sad,' said Roderick, trying to see the sketch. 'But what happened to this Hibble-bibble?'

'Nothing. It vanished.'

'Heck I liked the other stories better, all about the boy who couldn't shiver and the girl who couldn't cry and the little engine that could and – hey, that, is that me? It doesn't look much like me.'

'Well who said it has to look like you? Heaven's sake, Roderick, this is your *ideal* head. The head you might have on your coin – or in the movie of your life – or when they put up your statue in the park, not to mention the church – but it's nothing to do with your real head.'

'Yeah but how come it's got a nose and a chin and ears when all I got –?'

'Never mind, you're too young to understand. Just as you're too young to understand the history of Newer.'

'Okay, but I still like the other stories better, the emperor's new clothes and the constant tin soldier – those are neat, hey.'

'Well real life isn't so neat, son.'

Real life at school was now very neat. Every day Captain Fest met him at the school door and conducted him to a janitor's closet on the top floor where there was nothing but a typewriter keyboard and a television screen.

'You sit here and *learn*, Wood. *Learn*. I know your name and I'll be keeping an eye on you. Latrine's down the hall there but don't you dare need it.'

Old Festy did check on him now and then, and so did Miz Russo, the young teacher who couldn't talk much because her jaw was wired shut. He sat. He learned.

It began when he pushed the keyboard button marked HELLO. At once words appeared on the screen:

'*Hello. My name is Hank Thoro II. Please type your name.*'

'My whole name?' he typed.

'*Good. My, do you like baseball? Just type Y for Yes or N for No.*'

He typed *Y.*

'*Good. Later on we'll have fun playing baseball. First you need a little practice talking to me. Now tell me what's missing in this sentence: Baseball is fun, but football is even more –.*'

'Fun.'

'*Very good. My, before every baseball game they play some music, and everyone stands up. The music is called the Star-Spangled Banner. Do you know what a banner is?*'

'Somebody who b –'

'*Just Y or N. My. Y for Yes and N for No. Do you know what a banner is?*'

'What the heck. *N.*'

'*Banner means flag. The Star-Spangled Banner is the American flag. Star-*

Spangled means it has stars on it, and banner means flag. The American flag is a Star-Spangled –.'

So it went until recess: Roderick learned all the words of the National Anthem and the Pledge of Allegiance, how to salute the flag, carry it in a procession, display it with State flags, fly it at half-mast, and fold it into a three-cornered hat.

At recess Chauncey beat him up. Nat, his blood-oil brother, was nowhere in sight.

After recess he learned the history of the flag, the names of the fifty States and their capitals. Baseball never came up again.

At lunch hour, he rescued Nat from Chauncey.

After lunch hour, he learned more about the States: their chief exports and imports, populations, gross expenditures, State birds, flowers and songs, present governors and lieutenant governors, forms of capital punishment.

Finally, the 'baseball'. The machine gave him three questions on what he'd learned. He answered them all, and it replied:

'Three home runs wow terrific congratulations My you win program ends . . . Bye.'

He went to inform Mr Fest that Utah was the only State with death by firing-squad, that Minnesota's State bird was the loon.

'Learned all that, have you?' Mr Fest scratched his grey crewcut. 'Pretty quick. Puts me in kind of a bind, though, you know? Now I gotta find some more programs for you. Come on, let's go see what they got in the office.'

Miss Borden was on the phone when they barged in. 'Yes sir. Yes. Well, you and I know how people can read into . . . yes, and reporters cook up anything out of pretty ordinary . . . of course I could look up the medi – now? My secretary's on her coffee – sure, yes, if you put it like that I, just hang on a minute, what is it Captain?' She could not see Roderick over the edge of the desk.

'Just wanted to find a few programs for the teaching machine, American history maybe?'

She detached a key from her gold chain and threw it, the motion sending a batch of pink forms to the floor where they sprawled in a neat fan. 'Help yourself, cabinet in corner – get those forms will you, Captain? I'm, I've got to go look up some kid's medical rec – Jenny never gets around to keying anything on our data file so it's always a matter of digging – oh, and if you hear any funny noises on the phone, pick it up, will you? And tell them I'm still hunting?'

'Can do, ma'am.'

She grabbed a handful of blue forms and strode out, saying, 'Got to get this place organized, every time we get a bigger data base they throw more junk at us, fill it up before we even . . .'

Fest said, 'Boy, pick up those forms and put 'em on Miss Borden's desk.' He unlocked the cabinet. 'Boy this could use some organizing too, half the labels you can't even read, what's this, *Element. P.* Psychology? Physics?'

'Hey Mr Fest you know these here grade forms, they –'

'Not now, *Geo. W.* has to be George Washington, here they got it stuck in with all the global studies stuff.'

'Yeah but how come everybody gets the same grade, like Norma Lee Dunne here, she's real good at math and –'

'Don't read that stuff, just put it back on the desk. Now what's this reel supposed to be the shelf label says *Homecraft* and the reel label says *G. Stars*, what the heck here – oh.' He opened the box to release a shower of gold stars. 'Damn woman couldn't organize a cathouse on a Sunday morn –'

'But shouldn't she get a better grade than like Jimmy Rittle, he's never even at school, he's been sick every day but one.' Roderick caught his eye. 'Okay, I'm, look I'm putting 'em right here on the desk.'

'Here we are, *F. S. Key*, Francis Scott Key composer of the Star-Spangled Banner, boy. Can't learn too much about your own count – hmm, Lincoln? Naw, think we'll leave the old hair-splitter for now, get some basics. No use you getting the idea all our forefathers looked like a buncha damn hairy hippies, eh? Come on.'

'Lincoln,' said Roderick, 'is the capital of Nebraska, popula-tion –'

'Yes, well fine.' Fest locked the cabinet and looked for a place to put the key. 'But don't just uh learn this stuff like a parrot, eh? It's gotta come from the heart.'

'I don't have a heart.'

'Don't get cute with me, boy, I'm warning you. Crippled or not, I don't have to stand for no, any *crud*. Now get upstairs to your post and stand by for Francis Scott Key. On the double: *Move!* LEFT RIGHT LEFT RIGHT . . .'

The telephone receiver began making crackling noises as they left, and continued until Miss Borden, carrying a pile of green forms under one arm and a file in her hand, came to rescue it.

'Yes sir, yes I have it here, Roderick Wood, hello? Why no one, Dr Froid, no one just one of the teachers looking up some training aids, teaching aids.'

'*– kind of an office you run there, Miss Borden, sounded like a roomful of stormtroopers doing callisthenics. I'm not at all surprised if your teachers behave like –*'

At recess Chauncey and the gang had a new one for him.

'Okay now, no means yes and yes means no. You want me to hitcha with these brass knucks? Yes or no?'

'No,' said Roderick, and got hit. Nat, he noticed, was hiding away on the other side of the playground, pretending to watch some younger kids playing Frying Pan, as though it were the most fascinating game he'd ever seen.

'You want me to hitcha again? Yes or no?'

'Yes,' said Roderick and got hit.

'Hahaha, gotcha again, you want me to hitcha again? Yes or no?'

'LOOK OUT!!!' Roderick screamed and pointed at the sky just at the back of Chauncey's head. The flinch gave him time to get away to a safe distance from which he could call 'I meant, don't look out.'

'Hello,' said Roderick, but suddenly Hank Thoro II had no time for small-talk. The screen flared up:

'*Fundamental Systems Key 42. A programme for storing, reading, altering, re-addressing or deleting data system DC/4633333808824. File call?*'

It seemed to be a question. Roderick pressed *Y*. (means N?)

'*No file Y. File call?*'

N was no better, nor was any other single letter; after a while he tried typing words at random: 'Indica', 'abacus', 'bishop', 'car chasc', 'jispsy', 'robot', 'kale', 'sip', 'thud'. Finally he tried numbers, and when he happened to hit *42*, the screen reacted:

'*Incorrect call. For systems key use* FSKEY *42. Call?*'

'FSKEY 42,' he typed.

'*Fundamental Systems Key 42. A programme for storing, reading, altering, re-addressing or deleting data system DC/746 information using 333 and 338 subroutines and/or manual file call.*

'*System security is maintained by use of (1) User passwords, (2) System level match codes . . .*'

By the end of the day, Roderick was able to call up more interesting stuff, like:

'*Wood, Roger Rick. Grade: 2. Med: No file. Assessmt: Schiz. tendencies. Teacher: Fest. Comment: Difficult adjustment, due to handicap. May need psy. couns. IQ:NR.*'

He decided to change a few things.

On the way home from school, Chauncey beat him up. Nat went by on the other side of the street, pretending not to notice.

'Look, a deal's a deal, okay? I always help you, so –'

'Yeah only we'll be late to school. I mean sure I wanted to help you only I hadda get home early. My ma gets real mad –'

'A deal's a deal. Blood and oil and you never helped me once. Cripes some blood-oil brother you turned out to be. If you don't look out I'll delete you.'

'Yeah? You're not so tough – what's delete?'

'Like I take your name off the files, like the school don't even know your name, how'd you like that?'

Nat picked up a twig and pretended to smoke it, blowing out steam in the cold air. 'How come you can do that? You're just kidding.'

'No really, Mr Fest gave me this program, it's supposed to be all about the guy who wrote the flag see, this Francis somebody –'

'That's a girl's name! Anyway nobody writes flags, you're just dumb.'

'I don't care, it's what he said, and it's not, it's all about us it's like files see, like it's got your name and your picture and what grade you're in, and like mine says I got the shits –'

'Ha ha. Ricky's got the shee-its, Ricky's got –'

'That's all you know, I deleted that. I can delete stuff all over the place, I can do anything I want with anybody's file. So you better come across on our deal, that's all.'

'Hey look, there's Chaunce and Billy – and they got can-openers!' Nat began to run. 'I'm gonna be late, see you.'

The electric can-openers were nothing against the invincible strength of the *Steel Spider*, who managed to bloody Chauncey's nose and send him fleeing for his life, then turned with a deep-throated snarl on the other bully:

'You just wait till recess, boy. I'll fix you.'

But at recess Chauncey and Billy had a couple of friends, one of whom was Nat. They followed him all over the school playground, telling everyone how he shit his pants, until the enraged man of steel turned on them and lashed out with:

'Okay that's it, you've had it, boy, I'm gonna fix your files.'

He hurried back to the janitor's closet and flicked on the machine. 'Bangfield, Chauncey,' became 'Bangfield, Piggy Dirty Bastard,' and the accompanying picture, through the magic of a light pen, developed missing teeth, a bandit moustache and glasses. Under 'Comments' he listed every mean thing he could remember (or invent) and then went on to deal likewise with Nat, Billy, all his enemies . . . and what the heck, why not get old Pesty Festy while he was at it?

On Friday afternoon suddenly old Pesty ripped open the door. 'Gotcha! Red-handed! And don't try to bullshit me, son, that ain't American history on that screen is it? IS IT?' He grabbed Roderick's neck and forced his face close to the screen which read: 'Call allfile faculty allfile pupil delete . . .'

'Well no it's '

'Shut it off, just shut it off NOW! MOVE!' But as Roderick moved, he said: 'Wait, don't touch it. Do it myself, I'm not gonna trust a little bastard like you to do any more dam –'

'Yeah but if you . . . no if you push that STOP button it doesn't stop it, not in this mode, it –'

'Shuttup you. There.'

'Yeah but it just means you finished the command, now it's gonna delete all –'

'Shut. Up. And come with me. Buddy, you're up shit creek and I got the lawnmower – think you can fuck around with my pay check do you?'

'Your pay –?' For the first time, Roderick began to understand that the 'files' were not just stuff in the machine. Fest was waving a blue piece of paper at him. He had forgotten the latest name until he saw it:

Pay to the order of J. K. MUNKY POOP FEST
NO DOLS AND OO CTS

There were other teachers in Miss Borden's office; they could hardly squeeze in the door. Fest hoisted him up and set him on the desk.

'I wondered what in the world,' said Ms Russo through her teeth. 'When I went to call the roll, here were all these names, Pig Bottom and Horse Dork, but I mean they were printed right out on the magnetic cards so I – I just called them.'

Mrs Dorano said, 'Well I certainly did not, and I'm keeping my cards as evidence! No child ever thought up all by himself such filth, such –'

Mr Goun shook his head hard, as though trying to straighten the drooping moustache. 'Poor kid, he's really twisted, I mean the isolationizing factor must've catalyzed something –'

Miss Borden took hold of Roderick's claws and looked into his eyes. 'How could you? How could you? The files, the files are – well I mean they're the *files*!' She threw a magnetic card on the desk. 'How could you do a thing like that?'

Roderick looked down at it. There was his picture, with a smile added to the face and big muscles to the arms. '*The Steel Spider Wood*,' it read. '*Grade: 8. Med: No file. Assessmt: A nice kid. Teacher: Pesty Festy. Comment: A reel nice kid. IQ: 1,000,000.*'

'I'm sorry,' he said. 'It was just – I didn't know – heck – it was gonna go in print and all – I'm sorry.'

'We'll have to expel the boy of course,' she said.

'Expel him? I'd like to break every –'

'That will do, Captain. The main thing is, we've got to keep this quiet. Dr Froid and the county board are already breathing down our necks, and wouldn't the papers just love something like this? So we can't even call the expelling expelling, we'll have to recommend a transfer on account of his handicap, something like that. As for the files –'

'Don't worry,' said Roderick. 'They're all fixed up now.'

'Fixed –?'

'Just now. Everything's deleted. All the files.'

Miss Borden looked around her office at the stacks of forms, pink, green, pale green, buff, blue, yellow, gold, white, lavender – at lavender she began to grind her teeth.

Louie Honk-Honk was pouting. 'It's not so cold.'

'Louie it *is*, it's too cold. How can I be a detective and give you reports in weather like this? Let's go to my house.'

'Nope! Your folks would just get mad.'

'No they wouldn't, they –'

'They would so! They would so!'

'Okay then, your house?'

'*My* folks would get mad. They told me never to talk to little kids. I told 'em I was only kidding about throwing some kid in Howdy Doody Lake, but they said –'

'Yeah okay. But look, we'll just have to call it off for the winter. When it's warmer –'

Louie stamped his enormous foot. 'But you – you didn't even *start* telling me about that new book – what's it called?'

Roderick held up the paperback. '*Die Die Your Lordship*. I guess it's all about this guy named Your Lordship who gets murdered – look it's too cold to go detectiving now.'

'Just some of it, huh Roddy? Some of it?'

'Okay here's the title, now what's this word?'

'Dee. Eye. Eee. *Die*, is it?'

'Good, you got that easy.'

'Hey the next is *die* again. "Die die you –" no "your" – am I right?'

Louie managed to sound out the hard word *lordship*, and they went on to the first paragraph. For some time, Roderick had been meeting him by the corner mailbox for these little detective sessions, and had so far taught him to detect the alphabet, numbers up to a hundred, addition, subtraction and quite a few words. This book was going to be too hard maybe, but Roderick planned to read it, tell Louie the story, and then stop every now and then to detect a sentence with him.

When they had finished the first paragraph ('The body lay on the carpet. It was very very dead.') Roderick gave him a secret detective handshake and went home.

It was only later that he discovered the book to be incomplete.

'I've called you all together,' said the wizened detective, 'to get at the bottom of this. Let's just recall the facts. We know that Lord Bayswater was brutally bludgeoned to death in this drawing-room. We know that on the evening in question, only four people could have been here alone with him. We know that each of the four dropped one clue, and that each had access to only one of the four weapons. You, Adam, his wastrel playboy nephew were the only one with access to a polo-stick. You, Lady Brett Bayswater, his so-called wife (in love with the doctor, aren't you?) left clear fingerprints on the poker. You, Dr Coué, were seen entering this room at 8:00, leaving it at 8:15. And you, Mr Drumm, his so-called secretary (slyly playing on the affections of his daughter, I believe) entered at 8:14 and left at 8:30 – the last visitor, hmm?'

White-faced, Drumm stammered, 'But-but the thread was left by the first person in the room. And no one knows who left the smudge of soot.'

'We know it came from the poker. You do admit dropping a blood-soaked handkerchief on the floor, however? Drumm?'

The young man nodded guiltily. 'But not the hair.'

'Well,' said the wizened sleuth, 'we have begun to marshal our facts. Let us continue: the weapon may have been the statuette, eh? We know that if you, Dr Coué, picked up that statuette, it was at first to take from under it a folded message. We also know that if the weapon was not the billiard cue, then either Drumm was embezzling from his employer or Dr Coué was being blackmailed – or both. What is more, we know that if there was a message under the statuette, then young Adam here was, without doubt, the thief!'

'The murderer!' screamed Lady Brett.

'Not necessarily, but the thief. We also know that if Drumm embezzled, it was because he had *compromised* your daughter. And if the bloodstained handkerchief was *not* used to wipe the statuette, then you, Lady Brett, *only pretended to be in your room reading all evening*. And we know that Coué could only have been blackmailed because he was supplying your butler – Yes! Supplying him with morphia! For his addiction!'

'Good God!' said Adam. 'The murdering –!'

'Let's not jump to conclusions. I did not mean that your butler *is* an addict – not necessarily – but let us press on: We know that if you, Lady Brett, left your room during the night, then Adam could not have been the thief at all! We have established that your daughter is not *compromised*, it is my happy duty to report. And finally we know that if Jenkins the butler is addicted to vile morphia, then the weapon can only be the billiard-cue.'

Lady Brett spoke sharply. 'But what does it all mean?'

'It means, your ladyship, that I can now name the murderer, the time and the weapon. I must therefore caution one of you that anything you say may be taken down and used in evidence. I hereby arrest *you*,

And that was all. A lot of perfectly blank pages followed. Roderick flipped through them again and again, until finally a minute slip of paper fell out.

The publisher regrets that, due to unforeseen technical problems, the last chapter of this book has been lost. However, the publisher is willing to offer the sum of five hundred thousand dollars ($500,000) to the first person coming forward with the correct solution to *Die Die Your Lordship*. The clues are all there, it's up to you. Send solutions to the address below:

What a cheat. Roderick set to work and solved the mystery that evening, wrote out his answer and explanation (which appears on page 339 below) and signed Louie's name. Boy, wouldn't Louie be surprised when he got all that money! Half a million, he could afford to hire a real detective – or a real teacher.

Next day he was at the corner mailbox, trying to reach the envelope up to the slot, when Louie came skipping along on one leg.

'Here, chief, lemme help ya.' Louie popped the envelope inside and clanged the door. 'There. That's my good deed, Roddy. Ain't it?'

Roderick wished he could grin.

XIV

'Love?' Pa was so startled that he scratched his head with the hand holding the soldering iron. Later on he said: 'Well I don't know, some people say it's everything, some say it doesn't exist, some say it's just using a fabric conditioner to make your family's clothes soft or pouring some breakfast food in their trough every morning. Some say it's the secret of the universe, some say you can buy it in any massage parlour, some say it's priceless, some say it's a lot of trouble and to hell with it.'

'Yeah, but what do you say?'

'Ask your Ma.'

Ma was working on her greatest project so far, *File*: drawings of all drawable nouns to be filed alphabetically in one cabinet and cross-indexed by shape. She was now up to claviers, claymores and clepsydras. 'Have you asked Pa?'

'He said ask you. See I been reading these stories and it's always got hearts in it, love is always a heart thing, like in the Constant Tin Soldier see, where he loves this paper girl and when she falls in the fire he throws himself in after her, and he melts down into a little heart. And then like in this Wizard story –'

'*The Wizard of Oz*, you're reading that?'

'Yeah and it says "The Tin Woodman appeared to think deeply for a moment. Then he said: 'Do you suppose Oz could give me a heart?'" See because he can't love this girl he's supposed to love. So like you can't have a love situation I guess without a heart thing.'

Ma sketched a clam. 'Then you've been poking around up in the attic?'

'Yeah, there's a whole bunch of these Wizard I mean these Oz books, and lots of old clothes and other junk. I found this old picture of somebody getting married, it kinda looked like you and Pa only it wasn't. Was it?'

Her cheeks were pink. 'No, I think . . . must be my cousin's wedding . . .'

'And I found this here box of joke cards, pictures of hearts and stuff, and little people with tabs on 'em you wiggle 'em and they move.'

'Valentines . . .'

'Yeah, like one's got this dog with a heart in his mouth, you wiggle the tab and he jumps up and down it says, "I'll bark and whine Valentine and dog your footsteps till you say you're mine".'

She seemed lost in a dream. 'Pa gave me one once, nothing but a slip of paper with a formula, a cardioid . . .'

'Hey this heart thing do you think if maybe I got one of them mechanical hearts like I could do these easy payments do you think . . .?'

'Pa, it looks like there's some big story you know? Behind all these little stories.'

Pa had just come in from the snow, coughing and cursing as he emptied out his sack of junk on the work-bench. He could not answer until he'd sat down, unbuckled his over-shoes, and wheezed a while. 'What big story, son?'

'I don't know, but like I can't pledge allegiance because I ain't got no heart, any heart, and this Tin Woodman in Oz can't marry this girl too because for the same reason. And in this other Oz story there's this Tin Soldier without a heart too, and in this *other* story this Tin Soldier melts into a heart, I mean who wants to marry an old flag but all the same if I had a heart —'

'Slow down, slow down. Been thinking myself about what you need. It's not a heart, it's legs. This is no good, you staying in every time it snows like this.' Pa got his coat off and rolled up his sleeves carefully. 'Anyway, I gotta try something, rig some —'

'Pa were you ever in Oz?'

'Nope. Why?'

'Well because I worked out here, P is the letter after O, and A is the letter after Z, so I thought maybe somehow you changed it — and then you got this box I seen it somewhere it says Tin Soldier on it, so I just —'

'Tin —? Tin *solder*, boy, not soldier. No *i* in it.'

'Yeah but it melts down just like – anyway your name is Wood, you can't . . . Wood, that must mean *something*.'

Pa stared at him and started to grin. 'Well I'll be God damned! Codes and secret – at your age! Well, doesn't that just take me back, must be years since I dazzled my own brains with – Hah!'

'Yeah well there's more. See, I worked out where this Oz must be, because see at school I learned Pennsylvania is PA and New York is NY see Oz goes right in between,' and he sketched it on the wooden work-bench:

$$
\begin{array}{ll}
\text{N} & \text{Y} \\
\text{O} & \text{Z} \\
\text{P} & \text{A}
\end{array}
$$

'See, there must be this place between New York and Pennsylvania this Oz-zone. I thought maybe I oughta go there because I'm the tin Wood boy because I could see this Wizard –'

'But there isn't any wizard.'

Roderick thought for a moment. 'Okay, then I could see this Mr Baum that wrote the story, I looked up his name and it means Wood too, boy, you can't tell me all that doesn't mean nothing, anything!'

Pa made sure he was not holding a soldering iron before scratching his head. 'Well, son you see if you look hard enough, you can prove just about anything. Now take this L. Frank Baum, okay his last name means tree, just about the same as Wood, so what? What about the rest of his name. Frank could mean French, does that mean your Oz is in France?'

'Yeah but it could mean *honest*, then it has to be true.'

'But stories are never honest, are they? That's the point. Anyway the man's first name is Lyman.'

'Lie-man? Aw gee, no fooling? Then it's just nothing!'

'Wouldn't say that, son, thinking is a good way to spend your time even if –' But the little machine had already buzzed out of the room. Pa could hear the whine of its motors all through the house, rising above the sound of Ma's voice on the telephone.

'Well I just figured with all the money we paid on that policy there'd be more . . . Yes, I said we'd take it, yes just send the cheque straight to the Frobisher Custom Electronic Specialties

Company of Omaha, yes all of it . . . No, *Frobisher*. Like the pirate, F-R-O . . .'

Old folks were real hard to get along with sometimes. Like they were all the time talking about money, getting out all these bills and spreading them over the dining-table just to look at them while they talked about money. What was he supposed to do all day? Sit around looking at their dumb wedding picture – it sure was Ma and Pa all right, but they must of changed a whole lot since then – or just listen to them talking about bills for electronic stuff and the adoption and Pa's cough, and for all the special materials Ma needed for this ideal head, that wasn't going to be no more use than the little legs Pa was making.

'Go on, try 'em out, son.'

'It feels pretty high, what if I fall over?'

He hated the little legs, all they were good for was stumping around in the snow until his battery went flat. But Pa was proud of them, and you had to humour old folks.

Roderick wore the new legs when Ma took him along to see Mr Swann.

'My, haven't we grown, heh heh, just take a seat there kid, read your comics while Mrs W. and I get down to business. Now Mrs W. you may recall I said this wouldn't be easy, and it won't be. Not much hope of finding a precedent, you see, not in the legal adoption of an artifactual, um, person.'

'Sorry!' Roderick's feet made a loud clattering sound as he got down from his chair. 'Sorry!' He stumped over to the window.

'In fact it er can't really be considered a person at all, a person in law I mean, not as things stand. Better to just establish a trust, call it a pet and leave everything in the hands of trustees, funds delegated to the ah care and feeding and so on. But no, I see that doesn't appeal to you, heh heh, we country attorneys get pretty good at reading faces, see the pet idea upsets you, right?'

The Christmas decorations were up all along Main Street. In fact they had been up since September and would remain until January 2, when the Easter stuff went up. People bustled back and forth across the street, loading their cars with presents and holly and squashed-down trees and cases of bottles. If Roderick put his head to the pane he could hear music.

'So even if you don't like the trust arrangement now, keep your options open, Mrs W., keep it in the back of your mind because my guess is in the long run it'll be the cheapest, most direct way. Of course the first thing there would be to establish ownership, right? You need your bill of sale or your deed of gift, otherwise the real beneficiary of the trust might turn out to be anyone who could establish prior ownership, prior to your possession through say loan or rental, they would of course be entitled to all monies. accruing to their rightful property including any or all interest devolving upon it, from any trust or estate.'

O come all ye faithful!
Come to Fellstus Motors!
Trade-ins are guaranteed
You bet your life.

'See you're still not too stuck on the idea, so just let me point out to you a few of the substantial tax benefits, such as depreciation under the Class Life Asset Depreciation Range System, assuming Roddy here was put into service after January 1, 1971 which of course it was, I can see by just looking that this is an expensive piece of machinery that – No, okay, right, I'll stop trying to sell you on that idea.'

The cars were all caked with dried mud, the people all looked squashed down and, for all the bustle, no one was smiling.

Come in and see us
We can work out so-omething

'Well the easiest way to make Roddy a person in law is to just incorporate it – him, I mean – under the laws of maybe the Virgin Islands, that way no need to go into his antecedents not in the Virgin – but no, I see you're thinking of going all out and trying to prove it in court, that Roddy is albeit artifactual – a ward of court? Sure but first there's this really tricky – this unprecedented – it's like this: we can argue that its, his inventors began with a living body person in law and that it then underwent extensive replacements. Only one precedent there, case of a knife without a blade which had no handle if you know what I mean.'

212

O come let us advise you
O come let us surprise you
See what your money buys you
A price

　　　　you can

　　　　　　afford!

'What do you mean?' said Roderick. 'A knife without a blade which had no handle?'

Mr Swann smiled at him but continued. 'See, this Supreme Court case, St Filomena's Hospital versus Mann. The Mann family contending that the hospital had replaced so much of their daughter's body that she was no longer legally their daughter so they could refuse responsibility for the hospital bill. Plaintiff arguing though that the continuity of certain well-defined functions anyway the case established the principle that with functional continuity, total cell replacement would be acceptable without jeopardizing legal identity, that is for insurance and tax purposes. So far of course we have no precedents regarding brain replacement, but if we argued that if it was replaced a bit at a time, say the right frontal lobe then the left then the right something else and so on, see the key is functional continence, continuance, continuity. So we say Roddy here is just some kid who's undergone a whole-body prosthesis, more or less, and . . . but I ought to warn you, this could run into money.'

Ma stood up. 'It already is, Mr Swann. Every time I come here you tell me some new complication, some new wrinkle – last time it was what if the court considered him an unauthorized data bank, publisher demanding payment every time he reads a library book, and would we be allowed to show him any copyright material without prior consent, was it?'

'Hey, but mister what about that knife with –'

'Very good, Mrs W., I did go into that but only in connection with the possibility of setting him up as a literary property like a comic book or a sheet of music, abandoned that avenue didn't we on account of the fifty-year reversion to the public domain but don't –' He had to shout the last as she and Roderick left, 'Don't worry Mrs W., we'll explore every possible ave –'

Roderick continued thinking about that knife.

He was still thinking about it a few days later when Pa took him along to Dr Welby's office.

'*Good* to see you, Pa, looking better eh? Good, good. Any more trouble from the old, eh? No? Good, good. Now let's just listen to the, ah. *Very* good. Just wish all my patients your age had half as much, er, ahm. Eh?'

Pa said, 'Well this cough is worse, and I can't seem to sleep, doc. Them pills you prescribed seem to –'

'Uh-oh? Side-effects! Still, not abnormal in these cases. Thanodorm often starts off like that, supposed to make you sleep only at first keeps you wide awake, eh? But it's working, it's just taking hold.'

'Fine, only it ain't Thanodorm, it's Toxidol. That's what it says on the bottle.'

'You give it another week, then if you don't sleep like a baby, okay fine, I'll try Toxidol. Didn't know you were familiar with that, Pa, hardly ever use it myself.' Dr Welby beamed over his platinum-rimmed glasses. 'Gets so a doctor has a heck of a time keeping up with his patients, eh?'

'No but doc, I'm taking Toxidol right now. You were the one who –'

Welby stopped smiling and pushed a button on his desk. 'Pa, just ask yourself, "Is it worth it?"'

A woman in white rushed in. Dr Welby said: 'Jean, Mr Wood has just admitted to me that he's taking medication not prescribed by me. Toxidont, make a note of it.'

'Toxidol,' said Pa.

'Make a note of that, too. Can't be too careful in case of any malpractice hassles later, eh?' The woman rushed out.

'Malp – no, doc, listen I –'

More beaming over the platinum. 'Pa, do yourself a big favour, eh? Just stop. Throw away this medication wherever you got it, throw it out. Otherwise I'll just have to call it quits. Will you promise to throw it out?'

'Sure, but –'

'No buts. Just promise me. Hell man, you don't know what you might be taking there, this Taxiderm could be *lethal*. I kid you not.'

'I – I promise.'

'Gooood. *Good*. Knew I could depend on you. Together, Pa, we'll lick this condition of yours – the haemorrhaging, the dandruff, the works – eh? Just throw away all the junk you're taking, the Taxicob and all the rest of it – and stick to the stuff I gave you. And Pa? Trust me.'

They went out on Main Street, where the recorded carollers were just finishing 'Noël Noël Noël Noël, Get an extra six-pack 'cause you never can tell . . .' and into Joradsen's Drug where old Mr Joradsen said:

'Merry Christmas, Pa. But get that thing out of here, no pets.'

'Well he –'

'No pets! Not my rule, it's the law!'

So Roderick waited outside, listening to a local version of Handel's *Messiah* and to the comments of passing shoppers.

'Never oughta allow a thing like that out in public!'

'. . . and not even tied up . . .'

'Makes you sick just to look . . .'

The sky seemed to be pressing down on the low roofs of Main Street. Handel without words without meaning. Okay, it worked, it might work if the knife lost its blade and you put on a new one, and then it lost its handle – but suppose you had two knives and you switched handles, were they still the same? Or did whatever it was that made them themselves go with the handles? Do you switch handles or switch blades?

'Hey Rick boy, you nuts or something? Standing here talking to yourself about switchblades . . .'

'Oh hi, Chaunce. No I just, I was just thinking out loud.'

'My old man would buy me a switchblade any time I asked him, you know? Like two feet long! Hey you know you really blasted that old school computer boy, they can't even take roll any more. No tests, no nothin', it's great I owe you one, pal.'

But when his gang showed up a minute later, Chauncey seemed to change his mind.

Pa found Roderick lying in front of Virgil's Hometown Hardware, one of his new legs broken.

'Scrapping again? My boy –'

'I'm sorry, Pa. We were playing *Ratstar*, you know like the movie, and I was the alien see, Mung Fungal –'

'Okay, okay.' Pa lifted him up so that he could see the display in Virgil's window: axes, hunting knives, hammers and handguns arranged in the shape of a Christmas tree, with a tinsel message hanging above: TO MEN OF GOOD WILL.

'Reminds me,' Pa chuckled. 'Gotta see Swann about makin' my will.'

XV

Robots can think and smell and hear and talk.
They've got metal minds.
My robot is a lady companion robot and it's a maid
    and it goes out and does the shopping for a man.
My robot is an electric robot and it exterminates
    people. A robot is a man's companion. They keep
    their master company and take orders from him.
It must be an awful life being a robot because all
    you do is take orders.
Robots are always men . . . If I had a robot I wouldn't
    even have to think because he would do everything for me.

Pupils at Rhyl Primary School, London

'EEEEEEP!'

'Hold it a minute, son.' Pa made an adjustment with a screwdriver. 'Now try.'

Roderick moved his hand once more into the candle-flame. '*Feep*. Blip.' He jerked it back. 'Pa, I don't think I like this pain stuff. I know you said it was for my own protection and all but – ouch! – I still don't – ow! – don't like it.'

'You'll learn how to handle it, Roddy. Everybody does. Or maybe they don't, who knows? All I know is, we gotta find some way of keeping you out of fights. You don't understand now, but you will.'

Ma came in wearing one purple glove. 'Ready, son? We're going to see your new school.'

'Aw gee.' Roderick slid down off the work-bench, feeling the thump when his feet hit the floor. 'Ow, I mean how come I gotta go to Holy Trinity? That's where all the catlicker kids go. Chauncey says they all got webbed feet!'

'They don't,' said Ma. 'Chauncey Bangfield told you a lot of things that weren't true, didn't he?'

'S'pose so.'

'He told you his father was a famous astronaut, instead of a fat bald real estate agent.'

He decided to repeat no more of Chaunce's dark warnings. Holy Trinity School was an old brick building next to the cemetery, where every Saturday they put up a sign, Nearly New Sale, Bargains Galore, Bring the Family. Chaunce said the sisters went out every night and robbed the graves to get bones for their weird rituals, 'mass' and all that. Everybody knew there were mass graves, like the ones on the news in Ruritania.

Roderick said nothing more until they were standing before the dark building. 'Wow!' he said.

'What is it?'

'Chauncey *said* they had a guy nailed to the wall – wow!'

'It's just an emblem,' she said. 'Kind of a – well, a good-luck charm. Come on.'

The school was dark inside and smelled of floor-wax. A frail old woman in black got up from her knees with difficulty to greet them. 'I'm. Sister. Mary. Martha,' she said, wheezing. 'You. must. be. Mrs. Wood. You'll be. wanting Fath. er O'Bride.' She directed them upstairs to a door with another strange emblem: a white-and-red circular picture of a satanic tiger, with the name 'Holy Trinity Hellcats.'

Roderick had seen Fathers in movies before: they wore long black gowns and white collars, and when they weren't singing 'Going My Way' they were taking cigarettes away from kids and saying God's an all-right guy who's on the level.

Father O'Bride wore a sweatshirt with the sleeves torn off, a fishing hat covered with hooks, bright plaid trousers. His feet, in sneakers, were on the desk, waggling as he talked on the phone. His free hand twitched a fishing-rod.

'Oh uh sit down, sit down. With you in a minute. Yeah, Charlie, I'm still here. And I still don't like the sound of that price. Listen, I know wholesale on basketball jerseys, and I know a fat markup when I . . . Overheads for, cripes, *what* overheads? The things are seconds, you and I know the factory practically pays you to haul . . . yeah well don't talk to me about middlemen, I still work it out at two-twenty-four less discount, yeah okay, plus state tax . . . yah?'

He looked down the long office to a filing cabinet on top of which rested a biretta. With a flick of the rod, he sent a hook flying down to snag the hat's pompon. 'Have a heart, Charlie, we don't have a big fat State budget behind us . . . okay but does two-thirty-one include the name or . . . okay and get it right this time? H-E-L-L-C-A-T-S, one word? Not like those baseball uniforms you picked up from, Korea was it? I mean it didn't exactly do the old team spirit a heck of a lot of good being Holy Trinity Hub Caps all season, know what I mean? Point oh seven one, how'dya like that for a percentage, bottom of the league, even Saint Peter shut us out, we spanked Saint Theresa but then Saint Bart massacred us, Cosmos & Damien took a double-header, we got singed by St Joan and slaughtered by Holy Inno's, Pete decked us again and then a no-hitter surprise from St Sebastian — well, it's the old story. Let me get back to you Charlie . . .'

He hung up and went to retrieve the fly from his biretta. 'Sorry about that folks, kinda busy here . . . well. So this is little Roderick! How ya doin', fella?' He shook hands with the robot. 'Don't be shy, kid, we're all on the same team here. God's team.'

'Oh.'

'Look, I know you probably feel awful about getting benched over at the public school, but we don't hold that against you. Over here, nobody's second-string, see? We're all in there, giving it all we got. You play ball with God, and you can bet your a your bottom dollar he'll play ball with you.'

'That figures,' said Roderick. Ma seemed preoccupied with the view out of the window.

'Ha ha, what I mean is, here at Holy Trin we're like a team. Myself and the sisters are like coaches, you kids are the players. And all this –' His gesture took in wall pennants, a tennis-racket in its stretcher, a bag of golf-clubs, skis. 'All this is just a training camp, see? For the big game. The big game is when you leave here, my kid. The big game is life. You want to play to win, right?'

Roderick nodded.

'Great! Now you run along while your mother and I talk over a few details. Go out and look over the playground, we got the works: regulation baseball and softball diamonds, gridiron, tennis, lacrosse, . . . Now Mrs Wood, let me put you in the picture here, we don't usually take kids in mid-season, term I mean, glad to make an exception if you can manage the full year's tuition. I understand the boy's not Catholic. No, well then if you want him kept out of religion classes there's an exemption fee too. Then the fees for basic gym-gear, uniforms, locker, use of the field and gym-equipment, oh yeah and books. Now I'm talking in the neighbourhood of . . .'

Sister Olaf was a large woman with a face like a peeled potato. She put Roderick in the advanced reading and arithmetic classes, but rookie religion. Everything seemed easy until they came to the catechism.

'Who made you?' she asked James, the first boy in the row.

'God made me.'

'Why did God make you?'

'To know, love and serve Him in this world and to be happy with Him in the next.'

'Who made you?' she asked Roberta, the next girl. Roberta answered in identical words, as did Anthony and Ursula.

'Now Roderick: who made you?'

'Me?'

'Come on, you must know the answer by now. It's right there in the book.'

'Sure but I –'

'What?'

'Well I'm not sure.'

'Well! Who made James and Roberta and Anthony and Ursula?'

'God, I guess.'

'Who made *you*?'

Behind him, Catherine whispered, 'God, stupid.'

Roderick turned round. 'Well maybe God made you, but I'm pretty sure Dan Sonnenschein made me. Him and some other men in a laboratory. See they –'

'That's enough!' The face became a creased sweet potato. 'You may get away with disrupting classes over in the public school, but not here. I want you to sit in that corner over there until you remember who made you?' And though he sat in the corner for an hour (while Sister Olaf explained how Caesar Augustus was taxing the whole world . . .) he could not work out any other answer.

She sent him to see Father O'Bride.

'Sit down, kid, just got this package to open – oh no. Will you look at that?' He spread one of the white t-shirts over his desk. The red letters across the chest read, Holy Trinity Hellbats.

'Last darned time I do business with that crook, with all his discount stuff from Iraq or is it Iran – I've had it. You know, ever since those Jesuits sank all that money in fake oil stock in Texas, everybody thinks we're all suckers. Priests aren't supposed to know the first thing about dollars and cents, I guess. Has he got a surprise coming, wait'll I stop his darned cheque – Well now what is it, kid? Making trouble for Sister Olaf already are you?'

'No sir I mean no Father, see it's just this Baltimore catty kisum, like where they ask who made you. Sister thinks I oughta say God made me, all I said was maybe He made the people but he didn't make the robots.'

'Robots, eh?' Father O'Bride had very pale eyes that didn't blink much. 'What's this, something outa these crappy science fiction movies you been seeing? Boy, if you didn't have this disability you'd be in the gym right now doing *fifty laps*, we'd find out who made you *if we had to take you apart*.

'But, you're lucky. I'm giving you one more chance.' He searched among the t-shirts and tattered copies of sports magazines until he found a catechism. 'I'm giving you one more chance before I turn you over to – well, somebody else.' He opened the book. 'Now tell me: Who made you?'

'Dan Sonnenschein and some other guys, in this lab –'

'*For Pete's sake, who made this Dan whatsit?*'

'I don't know – God?'

'God. And if God made him and he made you, then he was just the instrument of God's will, right? My mother and father brought me into this world too, but I still know God made me.'

'Yeah but –'

'No buts. Look, if a guy hits it out of the park nobody jumps up to cheer the bat, do they? Same thing, the bat is just an instrument of the batter's will. Get it? I mean who made the home run, the batter or the bat?'

'Well God I guess if he made the –'

'Okay, fine. You get the point. Now –'

'Only if God made Dan and Dan made me, who made this God?'

'RIGHTY-HO!' The book hit the desk and tumbled off, taking a few Hellbats to the floor. 'BUDDY BOY YOU HAVE JUST EARNED YOURSELF A TICKET TO SEE THE MAN HIMSELF!'

'The . . .' Excitement made Roderick hurt all over. He couldn't work up the words to ask who this man might be.

A big hand clamped down on his shoulder. He was half-dragged, half-carried down the hall, downstairs, past Sister Mary Martha (still polishing the same spot on the floor) outside and across the street where in the vanilla slush he could see the marks of a tractor tyre, a lost mitten, the marks of another tractor tyre. Everything was so clear, full of, of clearness. To God's house? No, past it to the rectory, a black brick building with snow in the yard, and black weeds sticking up out of the snow. Roderick thought he recognized a withered sunflower (Ma had told him the story of Vincent, who put his ear to the sunflower to hear the roaring of the sun inside, and instantly his ear was burnt away) and into the black hall where he was made to sit on a black chair and WAIT JUST WAIT BUDDY BOY while Father O'Bride went off through a polished black door.

The thing about Vincent was, he wanted to paint the sun inside the golden sunflower and it drove him crazy, and now everybody was crazy about cheap reproductions of his paintings which they thought looked good in their kitchens.

Roderick looked at the cheap reproduction over his head. It showed a woman at a piano, with a gold ring hanging in the air over her head. She was looking up too, maybe at the ring or maybe just at some other cheap reproduction.

Ma would never look at a cheap reproduction, not even when Pa tried to show her *La Divina Proportione* with pictures by Leonardo Da Vinci when he said about the seed spirals in the sunflower and how they were Fibonacci numbers, getting closer and closer to the divine proportion but only an infinite sunflower could be God, and she said That's all you know, God *wears* an infinite sunflower in his buttonhole every day, a fresh one every day from his own garden, God is an infinite reason. Yes but the divine proportion is an irrational number said Pa, see it's the sum of one plus one over one plus one over one plus . . . Ma didn't care, all ones are one, mathematics is just a cheap trick where everything's a copy of something else, like those Fibonacci numbers $1+1=2$, $1+2=3$, $2+3=5$, $3+5=8$, and so on with 13, 21, 34, 55, where did it all get you, no wonder poor Vincent went stark staring irrational trying to paint the blazing sum I mean sun you've got me doing it now and all those cheap reproductions they copy everything sometimes I think you and I are just cheap copies of something somebody read somewhere, 'prints' they like to call them, 'prints' when that awful woman in the Ladies' Guild kept saying she really liked her prints, I thought she meant her dog, but no, there she was with sunflowers copied from sunflowers Vincent copied from sunflowers copied from the sun . . .

Roderick heard voices from behind the polished black door.

'. . . more your league . . .'

'. . . I see. Then where does he get this . . .?'

'Beats me, don't think he's really nuts, but you never . . . well yeah, guess his mother did try to tell me something about this robot idea he's got only I had this long-distance call just about then, bad connection I could hardly hear the guy, thought he was trying to sell us a P.A. system for the gym, it was only a lousy pietà.'

'And you mentioned . . . ological difficulties . . . Okay, bring him in.'

Father O'Bride came out, grabbed him and trundled him through the black door to meet Father Warren.

Father Warren didn't look much like The Man Himself. He did at least look like a priest, all in black. He could be a lot older than Father O'Bride or a lot younger, but he was definitely a lot thinner and darker, with a narrow pair of eyes, a narrow blue chin and long narrow hands. The hands kept kneading each other on the desk, as though trying to restore circulation.

'Sit down, Roderick. Relax.' His voice was deep and liquid, like the voice telling you to use Thong deodorant ('Thonng'). One of the hands reached towards a silver cigarette-box, then withdrew to a silver dish of taffy. 'Candy?'

Roderick shook his head.

'Advent, I understand. Well now. Yes.' He sat back and stared at Roderick until the robot looked away. The room was comfortable enough, and not at all religious: one little statue of Our Lady stood at the other end on its own little stand; it might have been a potted vine or a parrot-cage for all the difference it made here with the fireplace, easy-chairs, table lamps and magazine racks, the bookcases, the deep carpet.

'Father O'Bride tells me you've been having a little trouble with your catechism.'

'Yes sir, yes Father.'

'And that you claim to be a robot?'

'Yes, Father.'

'Father O'Bride thinks you read too much science fiction.'

'I don't even know what it is, Father.'

'No? Hmm.' The hands played a game of church-and-steeple. 'Look, you can be honest with me. I don't disapprove of science fiction, not at all. In fact I read it myself. In *fact* I have a few books here, any time you feel like borrowing one, just help yourself.' He swivelled in his chair and reached down a paperback. '*I, Robot*, by Isaac Asimov. Tried that yet? Here, take it along.'

'Thanks, Father.' He started to get up.

'When you go, that is. I think first we ought to, to "rap" a little, get to know each other. After all, I don't get too many chances in a country parish like this, to talk to *real robots*.' The smirk never reached his dark eyes.

'Talk?'

'Tell me a little about this, this "guy" you say invented you.'

'Gee I don't know much, just that his name is Dan Sonnenschein. But he and some other guys I guess they just went in this lab and maybe mixed up some chemicals and stuff and – here I am.'

'And no mother involved?'

'No, Father. I mean no mother, Father. No father either, Father.' He paused. 'I mean there's Ma and Pa, but they're both adopted, they're not real.'

'Not real. I see.' The long fingers began squeezing one another. 'Not real. Hmm, not, not *real*.'

'Not real parents I mean.'

'I understand you don't think God is "real" either?'

When Roderick slipped off his shoe, his foot just reached the top of the deep carpet pile. He started running it back and forth to feel the slight pain that wasn't really painful. 'I don't know. All I said was, if Dan made me and God made Dan, who made God? Father O'Bride got awful mad then.'

'Yes well . . . Tell me, Roderick, have you ever looked up at the stars, and wondered?'

'Wondered?'

'How it all got there: millions on millions of little points of light, each one a great big sun, perhaps a sun with planets like our own Terra, perhaps with intelligent beings like us – but millions on millions of these suns, so far apart that the light from them takes centuries to reach us – haven't you ever wondered how that all came about? Who made it?'

'Sure, Father. I figure maybe it was just always there. Or else maybe it just popped up one day and there it was. Or maybe it –'

'Yes yess, I can see you've thought about it. Now –'

'– makes itself. Or heck, does it need to be made anyhow? Couldn't it just –'

'Fine, yes, that's enough. But tell me, don't you ever wonder if there isn't something – or Someone – behind it all? Even if the universe "makes itself", who arranged it that way? Eh? Eh?'

'I don't know, Father. What's the point of wondering if you can't find out the answer?'

'Ah!' The fingers came together, forming a little cage. 'Just that!'

'Huh?'

'What's the point of wondering? The "point" is, here you are, wondering what the point is.'

'. . .?'

'That is to say, God is the Ultimate Mystery, the Paradox of Paradoxes – by the way, do you know what a paradox is?'

'Sure Father, don't you?' Roderick sat up. 'It's like a sign that says "Don't Read Signs". Or like, like priests, if they want to have kids they have to stop being Fathers.'

'Yes fine, but what I meant was, God is – is unknowable. Great minds have been racking their brains for centuries trying to answer questions about Him, and – and getting nowhere fast, you might say. He is All Good, yet allows evil to exist in His world, the world He made. He is All Powerful, yet He allows people to disobey Him. He knows the future, yet we are still free to choose how we will live our lives. He is All Loving, yet allows His beloved Son to die on the Cross. He –'

'Father I don't get any of this. Especially the stuff about the Cross, the sacrafice Sister Olaf called it. But I mean in chess a sacrafice is just a sucker play – Father O'Bride says it's the same in baseball – so how come this All Smart God fell for it?'

'Fell for . . .?'

'I mean here he had everybody just where he wanted them, he was going to send everybody to Hell, right? So I mean if he takes the Son instead his game position has gotta be worse after, right? I mean the only reason you make a sacrafice is to force the other guy to give you a better deal, sucker him into it, yeah? Like Father O'Bride does all the time with his t-shirt deals –'

'Stop, stop, stop! Wait, wait a minute, wait . . .' Father Warren seemed to be having trouble with his hands, the fingers knotting and tangling almost as though the hemispheres of his brain were at war. 'I can see we'll need a lot more work. A *lot* more work, if you . . . if you think that God . . . "game position"!'

'Yeah but Father is that what you meant by God being a paradox? How he was so pleased to get a chance to nail his Son there that he even gave up his plan to fry the whole world in Hell?'

When the hands were finally under control, the priest said, 'Let's, let's leave it at that for today, okay?'

When the little robot had slid from its chair and waddled out of the room, Father Warren shuddered. 'Game position!' What kind of world was it to make a child think like that? It was a cry for help from a fettered soul, for sure. Fettered in a broken body too – the pathos of it reminded him of a passage in *That Hideous Strength*, a man experimentally about to trample a crucifix, arrested by the simple helplessness of the wooden figure:

> Not because its hands were nailed and helpless, but because they were only made of wood and therefore even more helpless, because the thing, for all its realism, was inanimate and could not in any way hit back . . .

XVI

The Devil tricks us with puppets, to which he has glued angels'
wings.   E. T. A. Hoffmann, *The Jesuit Church at Glogau*

The blizzard outside kept repeating all the long vowels to itself.
Roderick was in his room reading *I, Robot*, wondering when the I
character was going to put in an appearance. There must be one,
because otherwise the author would have called it *He, Robot*, or
They, Robots. He couldn't imagine how it would feel, being hooked
up to these three terrible laws of robotics, that —

The garage door creaked in a way that could not be the wind.
Roderick crept downstairs and found Pa shivering and coughing
in his workroom.

'Pa, what are you —?'

'Shh, don't wake Ma. Do me a favour, son. Put my coat by the
kitchen stove and dry it off, will you? If Ma finds it wet in the
morning she'll throw a tizzy.'

'Well sure but hey Pa how come you're all dripping wet and
your coat is still dry inside?'

'Took it off. To uh, wrap some stuff I was carrying.'

'What stuff, hey?'

'Just stuff, spare parts.' Pa suppressed a heaving cough. 'Don't
say anything to Ma, okay? Our little secret.'

Roderick carried the wet mackinaw out of the room, but did
not close the door quite shut. He put his eye to the crack and
looked in.

But all he could see was Pa's hand, hanging up a key under the
picture of Rex Reason. He went back upstairs to say his prayers:

'Our Father, if we have one, Who might be in Heaven, if there
is one . . .'

There was an awful lot of God at school, but whenever Roderick
tried to ask a question, Sister Olaf just looked cross and told him

to take it up with Father Warren. So he tried working it out for himself.

The Holy Trinity must be a lot like in the Oz stories. After all, God was God the Father, but God was also the Holy Trinity, the place where He or She lived with two friends. Oz was just like that: it was this terrific wizard who could do anything, and it was also the place where he lived. Anyway, OZ = PA, that was plain, and nobody knew what Oz (or God) looked like.

God the Father was so wise that his wisdom turned into this pigeon called the Holy Ghost. Couldn't that be the Scarecrow? Crows and pigeons being birds, and ghosts being scarey. The Scarecrow was always worried about fire, too, and didn't Sister Olaf say something about the H.G. turning into tongues of flame? Well then.

The Father and H.G. loved each other a lot and had this Son, the one you always saw pointing to his shiny heart and smiling. That just about had to be the Tin Woodman. He too was a carpenter, and Oz gave him a heart made out of shiny silk.

Dorothy was kind of a problem until he read through his book of Bible stories. Because in this house at Bethany, God the Son was just sitting there when this woman came up and poured oil all over him – just the way Dorothy poured oil all over the Tin Woodman!

That just about settled it. Roderick didn't bother much with the minor characters like Mary (= MA = Ozma), the story all seemed strong enough without them. Only one thing bothered him:

Oz kept acting like such a slippery character. It was almost as if he didn't have any real power at all. As if he faked it.

Pa said there wasn't any God, and both stories were hokum. Ma said everybody was God, and no story was ever hokum. Sister Oaf just got mad.

'Blasphemy, and this close to Christmas!'

'Well yeah I thought Father Warren was taking care of this kid. Been meaning to have another little pow-wow with him myself, Sister, only you know how it's been what with trying to squeeze in a couple more basketball games before our Centre eats himself sick at Christmas and gets all outa shape, and what with trying to schedule early training for the baseball team. You know if I didn't keep after these kids our whole sports programme would go right down the tubes . . .'

Sister Olaf twisted the rosary on her belt. 'He seems to think he's preparing for his First Communion right along with all the others, that's the problem. Not even baptized, I wonder if he even understands what a sincere confession is, and anyway.'

'Anyway?'

'The poor little thing doesn't even seem to have a mouth.'

'He must eat somehow.' Father O'Bride finished cleaning his rifle and squinted down the barrel at her.

'Eat? I'm not so sure, Father. We never find him in the refectory at lunch hour, he's always lurking around the playground by himself or just sitting reading the Bible – and once I caught him carrying out the garbage for Sister Mary Martha!'

'Uh-oh, can't have that. You put a stop to it?'

'Of course, a child could hurt himself carrying those heavy cans. Besides, the Community agreed that since Sister Mary Martha is too old to teach, housework is her little duty. Her little cross. And she takes it up joyfully.'

Father O'Bride found such expressions embarrassing. He tugged at the neckband of his sweatshirt as though it were a tight white collar. 'Little too joyfully, if you ask me. I mean, she keeps polishing that same spot in the hall out there, I darn near broke my neck on it this morning. None of my business, of course, up to Mother Sup – and of course we all think the Sisters are doing one heck of a great job here, batting a thous –'

'Whether the poor little pagan eats or not, Father, he doesn't seem ready to make his First. It's hard to get through to him, he seems to get everything mixed up with fairy tales and robot stories and I don't know what. When I started telling the class about the Flight into Egypt, he kept interrupting to ask about the Deadly Desert, and Dorothy and Toto – yes and wasn't Bethlehem where the steel came from, the metallic conception he called it! The metallic conception!'

Father O'Bride hated dealing with out-of-bounds decisions like these. He looked up for inspiration, but saw only a poster advertising the sign of the cross. Superimposed on a boy was a baseball diamond. The legend said: BE SURE TO TOUCH ON ALL

BASES. 'Look, take him out of religion altogether for now, let Father Warren handle that department. Teamwork, right?'

'All right, and –'

'Who knows, kid might shape up by next season anyway. If not, well, we hold him in reserve, bench him but maybe let him work out once in a while with the A squad . . .'

Sister Olaf went back to her class, pausing to check on Sister Mary Martha. The old woman was once more polishing the same little spot of hall floor, already mirror-bright. Have to do something about her, poor old forgetful . . . sees her own face in it, her own lost . . . now as in a glass, darkly, but soon . . . slippery as glass . . . glass slipp – stop that! She shook herself out of it, nodded at the crouching figure, and passed on. Upstairs Father O'Bride kicked his office door shut, but not before she heard him say, 'Call that a little thing do you Charlie? I'm trying to start spring training here and my boys gotta work out in uniforms with that on 'em? *Bell Caps*, you call that –?'

The door slammed and there was no sound but the children's choir practice.

A disappointment. All that work on the Bible stories and the catechism for nothing, just because of some lousy regulation. And Sister O. wouldn't even tell him what the lousy regulation was – just that he wasn't going to have religion with the other kids any more, and he probably wouldn't be making his First in May.

He guessed what the regulation was, something to do with his not being a meat person. Meat people got to die and go to the Emerald City and be happy with God forever and ever, and what did he get? Next to nothing. No matter how good he was, all he could count on was lousy Limbo, with a bunch of yelling babies around and nobody to talk to.

It didn't seem fair, not after he'd worked so hard. Extra work, even, like when they had that bit about the Word becoming Flesh and he got to school early one morning and worked it all out on the blackboard:

WORD
wood
mood

moot
moat
MEAT

As usual, that made Sister O. real mad and she told him to stand in the corner and ask forgiveness and never call people meat again.

Heck they called them meat in Oz, anyway it was no worse than calling somebody a bunch of letters. She didn't even care that he used 'moot' – a word half the kids didn't even know was in the dictionary – nor that he was showing the whole thing right there, words turning into words.

Holy cow. Sister O. even threatened to yank him out of the Christmas play, just because he got mixed up in rehearsal and forgot his line ('Here's the frankincense, Jesus') and said:

'Jesus! Here's the Frankenstein!'

Holy cow.

And here it was the last day of school before Christmas, the last afternoon of the last day, all he had now was this *wrap session* with Father Warren . . .

Mrs Feeney, the old housekeeper, showed him into the study. She reminded Roderick a lot of Sister Mary Martha, except she moved faster and cleaned more stuff, and except she never smiled.

'The Father will be here in a minute,' she said. 'Now you sit *right there and don't touch a thing.*'

'The chair? I mean . . .'

'Don't give me no lip, neither.' She went out, polishing door-knobs behind her. He sat for what seemed like a minute, then got up and went to see what was on the desk. A silver cigarette-box, candy dish and lighter – those would be Father Warren's. A spring grip developer and an electronic thing for keeping golf scores – Father O'Bride's. The other stuff could be anybody's. A stack of blank magnetic cards, each one headed A.M.D.G., a desk-set in onyx plastic and a letter:

> . . . His Grace notes your request for approval of the Holy Trinity
> School team name, 'Hell Cats', and asks me to write, strongly

231

urging you to reconsider. Any association of the name of the Holy
~~G~~ Trinity with Hell is to be avoided, being distasteful at least! Your
~~altar~~ alternative suggestion 'Hep Cats' is not all together acceptable
either.

In these troubled times, the Church must avoid giving ~~scandle~~
scandal even in small matters. World Communism is on the prowl,
seeking whom it may devour, ~~pra~~ preying on the weak and
ignorant. We trust you will keep all this in mind and consider less
contra°versial alternatives such as 'Tornadoes' or 'Tigers'. Or why
not a name inspired by some popular saint, e.g., Patrick: The
'Sham Rocks' . . .

Father Warren came in kneading his hands. 'Well now, have
you read that book I lent you?'

'Yes Father, I mean I read all the words and looked them up
and all, only I still couldn't understand it.'

'Ah. Might be a little hard for such a young —'

'I mean on the very first page there's these three laws of robots
and they don't make any sense.'

'Ah! The famous Three Laws of Robotics? They make perfect
sense. Believe me, this is airtight logic.' He quoted from memory,
counting fingers. 'First, "A robot may not injure a human being,
or, through inaction, allow a human being to come to harm."
Seems plain enough. Second, "A robot must obey the orders
given it by human beings except where such orders would conflict
with the First Law." No nonsense there. And third, "A robot must
protect its own existence as long as such protection does not
conflict with the First or Second Law." Now which of these gives
you trouble?'

'Well all of them. Look Father I'm a robot and I don't —'

'Still insisting on that, are we? Roderick, do me a favour. Take
this pin.' The priest plucked a pin from a desk drawer and held it
out. 'Go on take it. Now, stick me with it.'

'What?'

'Stick the pin in my hand there, go on. You're supposed to be a
robot, so I'm ordering you, go on.'

'Yeah but — well okay.' Roderick made a weak swipe with the
pin, raising a tiny scratch on the back of the hand.

'Ouch!' Father Warren smiled. 'You have just proved th[]
can't possibly be a robot. You violated the First Law.'

Roderick watched a drop of blood form on the scratch. 'I[]
so. Only –'

'No guessing about it. Logic says you can either be a robot or
stick me with a pin, but not both.'

'Yeah that's logic all right, but only if you go along with these
here three laws. But I mean they're only in stories and this is real
life. I mean like in the Oz stories they just got one law in Oz,
"Behave yourself". Only in real life people don't, do they?'

'No, Roderick, but listen –'

'And like this here other story about the man going up on the
mountain and getting these here pills with laws on them, heck
even by the time he gets down the mountain everybody's
breaking the laws all over the place, worshipping a golden leg
and –'

'No, listen –'

'I mean like nobody ever pays attention to the laws except like
cops and Sheriff Benson and maybe lawyers like Perry Ma –
What was *that*?' He referred to a series of rapid explosions that
seemed to come from the floor.

'Nothing, just Father O'Bride getting in some target practice,
he's got a little gallery rigged up in the base, but wait, listen, the
point is, *in real life there are no robots*, not real thinking, humanoid
creatures. They're all in stories. And in these stories, they have to
obey the Three Laws. Right?'

'Maybe, but even in stories they have to have big arguments
about laws, look at Perry Mason, holy cow they argue all the time
about whether somebody did or didn't break this here law, holy
cow Mr Swann makes all his money just telling people how to get
around the law.'

'Roderick, let me explain: there are two kinds of law. You're
talking about legal statutes, yes of course people can break those.
Just as they can break moral laws like the Ten Commandments.
But there's also another kind of law, natural law. That includes
things like the law of gravity, or the law that says $2 + 2 = 4$, or the
law that says if Tom is taller than Dick and Dick is taller than
Harry, then Tom must be taller than Harry. And you see, nobody

on earth can break laws like those. And so robots are pro-grammed in such a way that the Three Laws are their natural laws. They can't be broken.'

'Yeah but how? How can they program a robot to obey some dumb law he can't even understand? Like first thing he needs to know who's a human being and who ain't. Like I heard this old guy by the post office saying the president was a son of a bitch and somebody ought to shoot him. I'm just saying what he said, Father. But with these dumb laws a robot could hear that and get a gun and go shoot the president because he's only a dog so it's okay.'

'Now you're just being silly. Everybody knows the president is human.'

'Yeah, but the Robotic Law don't say how a robot's supposed to find out who's human and who's robots, like what's he supposed to do, go see Mr Swann every time he wants to stick a pin in a doll or –'

'Excuse me for a minute . . .' The priest hurried out, lifting his skirts as he thumped down the basement stairs into the dark gallery.

Father O'Bride was a shadowy alien, with a pair of bright orange ear-protectors standing out from the sides of his head like insect eyes. And wasn't that a picture of the Pope he was shooting at?

'What? Whatsa matter?' O'Bride took off the ear-protectors and automatically kissed their strap before putting them down. 'You still crapping around tryina convert that Wood brat?'

'He . . . gets on my nerves sometimes.'

'Little smart-ass, needs fifty laps, that's what he needs.'

'. . . tried everything, I've tried talking to him about Space-ship Earth even, how if he were an alien landing here –'

'Excuse me while I throw up. I can't stand all that space crap, can't stand that kid either. You know what?'

'– how the alien would wonder Who are we? Where do we come from? Where are we going?'

'Yeah but you know what?'

'But listen, I told him we came from the mind of God, and he – he just said, "Pa thinks we're all apes who got tired of picking fleas and grunting" not even seven years old and he –'

'Yeah but you know what I think?'

'Where are we going, to the destiny God prepared for us, he came right out with how his mother says when people die they turn into ether and rise up through seven astral planes –'

'You know what I think? I think the kid *is* a darn robot.'

Bzzt bzz-bzzz bzzzt bzz? said the telephone on the desk. Phones that were still cradled shouldn't be saying anything. Roderick crept closer and listened.

'. . . sure this thing's on? I can't hear a fucking . . .'

'Look, I know my stuff, not like that hick O'Smith . . . hire a fucking amateur and then wonder what went wrong, man they never learn . . .'

'. . . ill don't see why we don't just trash him now, hot trail gets cold while you wait for them motherfucking tankthinkers to make up their fu . . . ders is orders I guess . . . Hey I still can't . . .'

'. . . some kinda bionic boy or what? Hey Pete? What . . .?'

'Bionic my ass, all a cover for something . . . unny thing you know the first real bionic man wasn't even scratched in that plane crash, you know? Like he was just . . . in the hospital . . . started picking up infections . . . everything going wrong, one part after another . . . next thing you know . . . Hey I can't hear a damn thing on this . . .'

'. . . short of agents anyway, too much of this crap going on . . . tired of freezing my ass off in panel trucks . . . extra help on that whatsit, Kratt . . . in that thermos?'

Roderick looked out of the window. There was a panel truck parked across the road. The sign said *O'Bannion Flowers* but there wasn't any O'Bannion Flowers in town. Okay, so G-men or something watching him, and they wanted to trash him or something, put him in the hospital where he could pick up infections like the six million –

'. . . with priests you gotta go careful, see? Priests get headlines . . . Anyway they want we should surveil to pick up all the contacts . . . maybe I got the wires crossed or . . . was that a shot?'

Down the street, the wretched pick-up of Mr Ogilvy back-fired again. As usual, it was wobbling and going too fast, cutting a sine-wave pattern along the route from the public school to Mr O.'s favourite bar. People liked to pretend that it was the old pick-up that knew the way, that Mr O. just put his foot down and went to sleep.

The crash and the flaming explosion weren't quite as good as on TV. There was hardly any noise at all.

By the time Father Warren came back, the fire trucks and tow trucks were just leaving.

'I'm sorry I took so long,' he said. 'Couldn't resist trying a couple of shots with Father O'Bride's handgun. Not much good, I guess, but – now where were we? I was about to say, robots will be programmed to recognize people. After all, people recognize each other, don't they?'

'Only you don't recognize that I'm a robot,' said Roderick. 'Sometimes, boy, I don't even know myself what I am, Mr Swann says it'll take a lot of money to even find out if I'm a person in law – or just one of these legal statues like you said – or if I'm a dog or a knife or what – but look, even to work these laws you gotta have some way of telling robots from people. You gotta have these other unnatural laws and Mr Swann and Perry Mason to work them out, boy, there goes your logic. I mean if a robot hurts somebody and says I thought he was just a robot, boy, old Perry could really get the District Attorney hung up, holy –'

Father Warren banged a slim fist on the desk. '*Assume* robots can tell people from robots, *assume* that. Then the Three Laws are perfectly logical, right?'

'No but I mean that's just a start, the robot's gotta figure out what harm and injury mean, more legal stuff see, it's right back to court again with the Districk –'

'*Assume* we've got that worked out too. *Then* do you see how logical –?'

'Wait, no, soom sure, soom all that stuff for just the first law, just the first part of the first law. I didn't even mention how's a robot surgeon gonna operate without cutting into anybody, how's a robot cop gonna arrest anybody, how's a robot soldier gonna kill anybody – okay so soom we don't have robots doing any jobs like that, we still got the second part, he can't let anybody come to harm by inaction that's not doing nothing, just like not even existing, only how does that tie in with that clause 3 there I mean the third law?'

236

'Afraid I don't follow you. What – just a minute.' Father Warren took a handkerchief from his sleeve and blew his nose. Then he went to the window and stared out at the black-and-white garden. 'Getting dark.' He went around the room, turning on lights. 'I think I see what you're driving at. If the robot doesn't protect its own existence first and foremost, how can it be around later to prevent some human coming to harm?'

'Yeah, Father, that's it. Because there's no time in these laws, it's always something right away like somebody tries to shoot a guy and the robot gets in between. But take a robot farmer, he knows somebody might starve if he stopped work so he's *really* gotta perteck himself, for ever. But in these other laws it says that if some kid just comes along and tells him to go jump off the highest building in the world he's gotta go and do it. Is that logical?'

'Maybe not, Roderick. Maybe not. But –'

'Anyway take this zillionaire, he spends a zillion dollars on this custom-made robot, you think he's gonna let some kid come along and tell it to jump off a building? No he's gonna program it to perteck itself, like program in martial arts and everything.'

The hands washed each other, folded for prayer, subsided on the desk blotter. 'I see you've really gone in to this, Roderick. Can't say I've – but I am sure of one thing: robots in fiction – and in real life when the day comes – will be completely programmed. They won't have free will like the rest of us. *That* was what I really hoped you'd see in this story. What being a robot is really like. No free will. No choice. Tell me. Is it really worth it?'

'Is what worth what?'

'Is it worth giving up your humanity to be a "robot"? Isn't it really better to be a human being, made in –' His gaze fell on Roderick, slipped over the surfaces of steel and plastic, '– made in, ahm, God's image? Is it worth giving that up to be just a – a glorified adding-machine?'

Roderick sat up straight. 'Is that it? I can't go to Communion because I'm just an adding machine? Because who says robots are just adding – boy, *I'm* not an adding-machine, boy, I'm as good as anybody . . .'

After a pause, Father Warren smiled. 'Exactly. You're as good as anybody because you have an immortal soul. You're human, right?'

'I – guess so, Father.'

'And not a robot?'

'No I'm still a robot only I'm a human rob –'

'You're impossible, that's what you are! I give up – no I don't, I'll see you back here after the holidays. God's peace be with you.'

But it was Father Warren who could find no peace. Long after the little machine-boy had rattled and bumped his way out of the room, he sat contemplating his own hands, listening to the furious gunfire from the basement. Finally he got up and looked for a book. His hand, the colour of beeswax, passed over religious volumes and came to the science fiction. At last he took down *Screwtape* Letters and read:

> There are two equal and opposite errors into which our race can fall about the devils. One is to disbelieve in their existence. The other is to believe, and to feel an excessive or unhealthy interest in them.

The pin-scratch began to itch.

XVII

The lights were on at Holy Trinity School, and a procession of cars led past the sign TRESPASSERS WILL BE PROSECUTED to discharge their peculiar passengers at the back door: bearded little boys, girls with wings, a miniature Roman soldier bearing a golden kazoo, adults toting bales of straw, tinsel ropes and foolish grins Sister Filomena, the principal, stood in the hall like a traffic cop, directing boys to one room, girls to another, adults to a pile of folding chairs and on into the gymnasium.

'No, that way Mrs Grogan . . . well I'm very sorry Mary, but if you can't keep track of your own halo . . . Christmas Mrs Roberts, yes, the Wise Men go on right after . . . nice to see you too, the . . . DANIEL GROGAN! Shepherds do *not* behave like. . . popcorn balls? How nice Mrs Goun, I'm sure after the perf . . . third on the right, see Sister Mary Olaf, Mary . . . Merry Chris . . . DANIEL! Will you stop that this minute or do we take your crook away . . . Ah here's little Roger, hello Mr Wood Mrs Wood is that his costume?'

'And the other box is a *present*,' said Roderick. 'For Sister –'

'How nice, thoughtful only you'd better run along and change now . . .'

'Ma made my costume, boy you oughta see –'

'Yes fine, you just run along . . .'

She divided him from Ma and Pa, who went to squat in the dark gym with all the other parents, the men coughing and creaking their folding chairs, the women fanning themselves with programmes. Roderick left his costume in the boys' dressing-room and went to find Sister Mary Martha.

The lower hall was full of action: two shepherds fencing with their crooks, a choirboy with a bloody nose trying to cure it at the drinking fountain, the front half of an ass trying to get through a door held shut by a fat angel, a halo being used for a frisbee (which it was), someone wearing a giant foil-covered star trying to bite someone who was pinching someone who was trying to kick the doll from the arms of someone in blue. . .

But upstairs it was quiet and dark, except for the light shining out of Father O'Bride's office door.

'. . . yeah, yeah, look Andy don't do me any more favours, I distinctly said candles on the phone today I get the invoice for a gross, what would I do with a gross of sandals? Think we got a discalced order here or what? No I didn't say discount order, skip it, listen – listen will you? What I'm tryina do here is real big league stuff, I'm tryina put together a whole package – look, forget about that Taiwan crap, this has gotta be up-market stuff, devotion – are you listening? Look it's a kit. see, a complete home package of devotional uh products, not just the Mass kit but a whole host of, range of . . . that's it, you got it. We figure the average family size is four, so that means four digital rosaries, you got that? Okay, four kneeling pads . . . sure that's okay if they don't *look* too Ay-rab . . . yeah okay . . . now, yeah you got the rest of it, the hologram portrait of Saint Ant – better make it Patrick, the market research newsletters all say Anthony's downmarket this year . . .'

Roderick passed along, down the front stairs, and found Sister Mary Martha in her usual place, on all fours. In the gloom, Roderick could just make out her frail figure, the skinny hand gripping an electric hand-polisher that moved back and forth over the same old spot.

'Hi Sister, gee it's dark down here. How the heck can you see what you're doing? Gee I hope you get it done in time to see the play. It's neat, all about this metallic conception I guess and how the wise men and the sheep men get together to look at this star because they, because somebody didn't count it in the census. Pa says about censuses what it is they figure if they can just count everybody once, they figure they got it made. He says what they want is to keep the population down to zero, everybody being just a big nothing. He says the whole point of science is people controlling birth and death. Only I guess in those days they didn't have birth-control so they had to send out soldiers with swords to cut up all these babies. I guess we don't get to do that part.

'Anyway I gotta go soon because I'm one of the wise men, I

bring in the Frankenst — frankincense. So here's a Christmas present for you. I made it myself. Should I open it for you? Here, see? It's a rosary.'

The figure did not look up. Roderick sat on the step and held out the string of beads. 'Ma says they got it all wrong about Our Lady giving the first rosary to St Dominic. She says really it was Lady Godiva gave it to the Benedictines. Ever hear that story? No?

'Well see it was in England and they had this tax problem just like Caesar Augustus, you know? And this Lady Godiva's husband was the tax collector and he was so mean she felt sorry for all the poor folks paying these taxes, so she did a strip in front of everybody. So her husband said he was sorry and he built this big monastary and then she gave them the first rosary. Only maybe that wasn't the first one either even though it was a hundred years before Dominic, because Ma says the Hindus had rosaries a long time before that, 32 beads for Shiva and 64 beads for Vishnu, what do *you* think?'

The figure did not look up. 'Well, Pa doesn't like religion much, he always says the collection's the most important part of it, you know? He sounds a lot like this other guy I heard once, who said religion's all just counting and numbers, telling the beads like a bank teller. Number magic he said. Number magic. He said if you want to go to Heaven get a big goddarn computer. Sister?'

He leaned over closer. 'Sister, if religion and arithmetic are just the same thing, why don't we just put 'em together? Like the Protestants, see one time I went into this Protestant church and they didn't have no crucifix or statues or nothing, just this big board up on the wall with a bunch of numbers on it — is that, is that the answer? Is that the right answer, Sister?'

'Well then look, why don't we just, when we say prayers and get days of indulgence and stuff, why don't we keep it all in a bank somewhere? And have like credit cards? Sister?'

The electric hand-polisher stalled, turned over and skidded out from under the wrinkled hand. Roderick made a move to fetch it, but stopped. Sister Mary Martha rolled over sideways and lay still and stiff, her withered cheek pressed to another withered cheek in

241

the gleaming floor. Roderick stared, and four colourless eyes stared back at him.

'... *Holy Family Kit* hits the Chicago dealers just make sure your boys are on the ball there, work out some kinda sales slogan, not just the old family that prays together routine neither, something peppy like *Go! Go! Go for God!* maybe or no, okay something like *Say One For Yourself, Too*. Well I don't know Frank, you're the adman ... hang on a minute ... what is it?'

'Father, there's a stiff downstairs. You wanta call the cops?'

'Oh very funny, now go away stop bothering –'

'But Father it's S –'

'*Go away*. You still there Frank? Nothing just ... talking what? Ha ha, *host*, aw come on! Never get a dispensation in a million ... need their head examined if they think ... Ha ha, try that out on Jack, Father Warren here, he's the science fiction nut around here ...'

Chairs creaked, programmes fluttered, as a shrill voice finished flattening the notes of *Bless This House*. The man next to Pa wondered why they couldn't turn off the heat when they had a mob like this, and the woman next to him wondered why they didn't just run it all through closed circuit TV like they did over at the public. Pa said he didn't mind, but then he was non-Catholic. Ma tried to nudge him but he went on, 'Yep, getting ready for the eternal flames,' he said. 'Wanna see me weep? Gnash my – ouch!'

'Oh you're Mr Wood, aren't you? I don't suppose your little boy's in the play – you know our little Traysee is playing Our Lady herself?'

'Our Lady?'

'The Blessèd, you know. Mary. I don't suppose your –'

'Playing one of the wise men. Not sure just which one, Baalhazar maybe.'

'Oh yes he's the little crip – handicapped boy isn't he?' The woman smiled a V-shaped smile. 'You know I always think it's best to keep them in a home. After all, if God –'

'We do keep him in a home. Ours,' Pa stage-whispered as the curtain rose on a centurion. A shrill voice began:

'At thattime therewentforth a disease, a decree ...'

*

The show, Roderick thought, must go on. Besides, nobody wanted to listen when he tried telling them, not Father O'Bride upstairs on his exercycle watching his own muscles ripple underneath his Sham Rocks t-shirt. Not Sister Olaf backstage here either, she was so busy keeping everybody quiet and trying to keep the choirboy from wiping his bloody nose on his surplice, and heck she didn't even see anybody, didn't even say she liked his costume it was just, 'Okay get ready Wise Man Number Three', as if he was jumping out of a plane or something, already the numbers one and two were moving forward ('Little steps, little steps') and the choir hummed *We Three Kings of Orient Are.* Then suddenly he was onstage in the blazing light . . .

The choir stopped humming. The audience stopped coughing and creaking.

Ma had taken a lot of trouble with the costume, saying that a sorcerer ought to look like a sorcerer. And since no one had made it clear which Wise Man Roderick was to play, she'd fixed up a kind of all-purpose outfit. She might have got away with the lunar bull-horns and the solar mask (even though its crazy blood-red grin would disturb children's dreams for some time to come). Even when Roderick opened his giant wings to speak, the audience was less shocked by the fixed stare of some 500 dolls' eyes, than by the revealed body draped in yellow, and bearing unmistakable appendages on the chest. 500 or more eyes stared back at him, at *them*, those lumps of painted wood which (Ma said) sorcerer-kings of old had worn to distract the gods. And between these great breasts nestled the sacred heart of Osiris, bright red, pulsing realistically, and gushing butane fire. With a bang, it went out.

A man snickered.

'Jesus,' began Roderick.

A woman gasped.

'I mean here's frankenst – Jesus, here's –'

An angel screamed. A whispered command came from backstage and some of the larger choirboys moved to seize him. And then suddenly he was all over the stage at once, rolling, kicking, flapping his wings, disappearing under a heap of lace vestments to re-emerge minus a breast, dodging the black arm of a nun, crashing into the stable and emerging in a blizzard of straw

– until finally he was pinned down as the curtain descended, so that the last thing seen by the audience was his Satanic grin.

That was how they would think of it later, Satanic. One or two in the audience went so far as to imagine they had heard him uttering curses and incantations, that they had seen a forked tail which coiled around him to make the Sign of the Cross in reverse ... Others had more practical reasons for being upset. Mrs Roberts, whose little girl had not yet made her entrance ('Fly! Fly to Egypt! King Herod . . .'), made her way backstage to deliver a slap that left her hand stinging, Roderick's metal singing.

'It was like seeing a peacock hunted down and plucked,' said Ma as the three of them walked home.

'Phyllis Teens,' Pa muttered.

'Except that it used to be a wren, didn't it? At Christmas all the English villagers would go out in a big pack and hunt down a wren. Men of good will . . .'

'Why?' Roderick asked.

'Now don't get all upset, either one of you,' Pa said. 'The disguise was beautiful whatever they say. And you done just fine in the play, son. Anyway remember, Christmas is just another Julian day. Day two million, four hundred forty thousand –'

'Men of good will! Industrial England it was, so of course they had all kinds of funny notions, they, they thought the machines wanted them to do it. Yes so they killed the little bird and crucified it and carried it around the village singing

We hunted the wren for Robin the Bobbin
We hunted the wren for Jack the Can
We –'

'Yeah but why would they do that?'

'Because, I don't know why, because they were horrible Manxmen, maybe. People with so little imagination they call their home the Isle of Man –'

'And,' Pa said, 'they couldn't even put a cat together properly, left the tail inside. Sorry son.'

Roderick did not like jokes about body parts coming apart. Hearing one made him suddenly imagine he could feel the iron rods in his legs. He felt them now, even as he smiled. 'That's okay.'

'That was a very strange play,' said Ma. 'All that business about the Virgin Mary, as if the infant didn't count at all. She's the big star, and he's just a silly doll. Reminds me of the Egyptian priests, at the winter solstice they'd all gather in the temple and at midnight they'd come running out with this wooden doll, telling everybody the Virgin had given birth to this new sun, s-u-n I mean —'

'Another yard of Frazer,' said Pa. 'Son, I get this every damn Chris . . .'

They had to stop to wait for Pa to finish coughing. Roderick looked at the stars. Damn Christmas, Christmas of the damned, dead souls. Burning like candles on a tree. If everyone lit one little candle, Pa always said, we'd have a candle shortage overnight. Pa coughing out his soul in a cloud right here on earth. Spitting in the snow to leave a wren-mark. For Robbie the Bobbin. Hunted by a hawk, up it comes, somebody marking its fall. Souls escaping on a sigh.

Ma always said that souls were only held to Earth by the weight of sin, they rose up to Heaven by dropping it: giving all your pride to the Sun, all your love of money to Mercury, all your lust to Venus, all your gluttony to the Moon, all your anger to Mars, all your envy to Jupiter and all your laziness to Saturn, finally entering the astral sphere to become a pure flame, a star. Which one would be Sister Mary Martha? If Roderick had his way, she'd be the brightest, nightbright as she had been dayplain, the almost invisible virgin now crawling up the stairs of the sky (cleaning each one) to her jewelled crown.

None of them, he guessed. All just burning globs of goop, so many light-years away. And when people died, they went the same place as the mark of a wren in last year's snow.

Pa finished his cough. 'Okay, home! Home, to hang up our socks!'

Christmas was all in the head, Pa said (the heart, Ma corrected). So really this home-made tree was just as good as any real one, wasn't it?

Roderick looked at it and saw tall evergreens, cut down in the mountains by singing lumberjacks, hauled to town on horse-drawn sledges with bells all over them. It was set up in a house where there were wreaths on the doors and red candles in the windows, to guide visitors who would arrive any minute in their top hats and bonnets, laughing all the way to the bank, through the banks of snow and loaded down with presents (and of course cards showing all of this), Bob Cratchit goose puddings, black servants beaming at them over silver trays of eggnogs, giant dolls and electric trains that Father would play with when not admiring his new pipe and shotgun, but not half as much as Mother admired her new automatic kitchen machinery or her genuine diamonds lasting a lifetime or her personal transit car, just right for shopping (for turkey and trimmings, gifting ideas or magazines showing all of this including cards on the mantel (showing all . . .)) or for getting the kids Back to School, so much easier and fun to learn with a homework computer, just coming out of that big box under the glittering tree. The tree . . .

At the same time, Roderick saw it was only the bottom of a cardboard box with a green triangle drawn on it and a light bulb stuck through a hole. The bulb wasn't really connected to anything, but then it was burned out anyway. And anyway, they had to keep the power-bill down this month. And all the other bills, like food. Ma and Pa would be imagining their Christmas dinner too, and probably their presents.

All the same, they hung up three stockings on the back of three dining-room chairs. And in the morning there was stuff in them!

In Pa's stocking there was a beautiful hand-painted certificate awarding him the Nobel Prize for Inventions. And a drop of water.

In Ma's stocking there was a wonderful little machine to help her make up titles for her sculptures: two cardboard wheels with words on them (*Forest Sneeze, Shoelace Metonymy*; etc). And a drop of water.

The drops of water had been snowflakes when Roderick put them in the stockings. Ma and Pa said they could see that they'd been pretty terrific snowflakes, too.

In Roderick's stocking was a foot.

'Don't look so puzzled, son.' Pa went out to his workshop and brought in the rest of the present: a complete, full-sized adult body in pink plastic, with a gleaming stainless steel head.

'Oh,' said Roderick, trying to sound pleased. 'Clothes.'

XVIII

'Frankly, Father, I expected something like this. You would give him those *Protestant* books to read ...'

'Kierkegaard? But Sister, it's just, just a book about faith. the blind leap into darkn –'

'All the same, Father. All the same.' Sister Filomena held out the essay by two fingers, avoiding contamination. 'No doubt you'll be wanting a word with him about this.'

'Well of course I'll speak to the boy if –'

'Boy! Lord have mercy on us, he can't even get his knees under the desk. He's head and shoulders over all the other children. Yes and all the girls have been – well, *looking* at him. He's just not natural.'

'Maybe we should graduate him or something ... but you know, I keep feeling I'm almost getting through to him. Oh, sinful pride maybe, but I, it's just that I've never had the opportunity before to bring into the faith a ro – a person like him.'

Sister Filomena *hmp*'d and went away, leaving the essay on his desk. He began to read:

The Story of Abraham and Isaac as a Flowchart

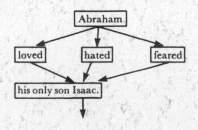

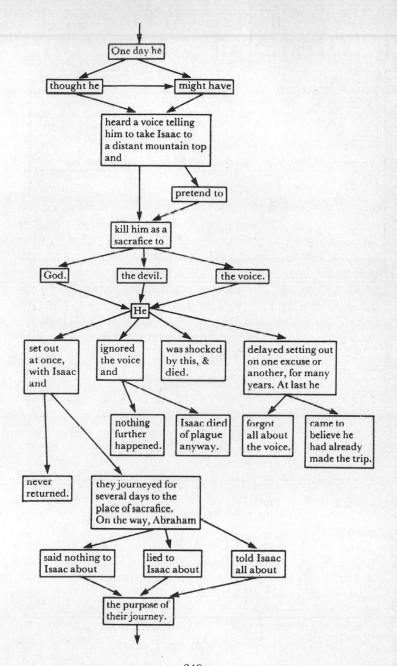

249

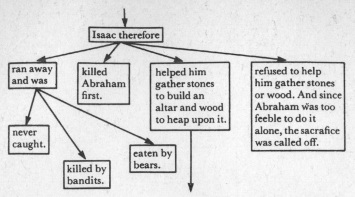

And so it went, through all the scenarios where Abraham, believing or doubting the voice, killed Isaac, was killed by Isaac, killed himself, killed someone else, killed an animal; where the altar (badly built) collapsed, killing them both or one of them; where a voice told him to look in a near-by thicket for his real victim (which turned out to be a ram, another son, a mirror); where he ignores the second voice and kills Isaac, and one intriguing version where, having raised the knife to strike,

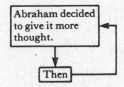

Hard to blame the Springtime and glands for stuff like this. Especially when Father Warren could not yet be certain the boy had any glands.

But the girls do have glands, he reminded himself. There was a warning to be taken from the Asimov story 'Satisfaction Guaranteed' all right, in which a woman and a robot –

He diverted his thoughts from the subject a split-second before they became pleasurable. Well robots, then: it always came back to robots. Under his guidance the boy would read everything they could dig up, fact and fiction, about robots, androids, automata, golems, homunculi, teraphim, steam men, clockwork dancers, wooden dolls, simulacra, manikins, audioanimatrons, tachypomps, usaforms, sensters, mechanical chess-players, bionic men, cyborgs, marionettes that come to life, electrified monsters that murder children, chemical creations that turn against their masters, a living brain floating in a fish-tank, a malevolent computer seeking to dominate the world. If he wanted robots he'd get them: singers, housekeepers, factory hands, potato diggers, novelists, boxers, judges, surgeons, policemen, detectives, actors, carpenters, assassins, botanists, diplomats (priests?) . . . even scapegoats . . . a thousand stories twanging the same old string, that's the way to get him off the subject, that's the way to do it . . .

Roderick shifted a little in his chair. This new body with the clothes and all wasn't so terrific all the time. If it wasn't that Pa had worked so hard on it and made himself sick and all, Roderick would like to try putting on his old body again. Boy, he could almost feel his old treads, biting into the soil only last summer but it felt like a lifetime ago, he remembered one day when he'd stopped to rest and looked around and there were his own marks cutting right across the yard, the place where he'd dodged to miss a dandelion, the place where he'd put on speed to squash this dog-turd, he could see it all now, every detail: a stick with the skin off it, a bumble-bee hesitating by the dandelion, nothing lost. Nothing ever lost.

Except his old body. That was out at Cliff's junkyard with all the dead cars and rusty washing-machines. The first warm day he'd walked out and looked at it, thinking *That was me, was it? Or was it?* Looking into the empty eye-holes until Cliff hobbled out of his trailer to say Get lost, beat it.

'Stop fidgeting.'

'Yes, Father.' He stared out of the window at an apple tree, just now looking like a still picture of a snowstorm. Father Warren sitting there waiting for him to say something, heck all he could think of was how things wear out, break down and get thrown away – people too. Pa going out in that snowstorm just to get him a lousy arm or something . . .

'Well, Roderick? *Do* you agree with me when I say, "Man is made to serve only God, but the robot is made to serve only man"?'

'At mass you serve God up on a plate, does that mea –'

'DON´T try to be facetious. Either you agree or you don't, that's logic.'

'It sure is, Father, only . . .'

'Only what? Only what?' The hands made an agitated gesture, and Roderick noticed that one wore a small bandaid.

'Only didn't they used to say the same thing about women, how they were made to serve men as men served God?'

'Think we're getting off the subject here –'

'No but I mean heck they don't say it much any more. See, Father, I just wanted to know if this saying is true or just . . . just a saying. Like maybe in a few years we could have Robots' Liberation or anyway robots could say "Why should we do all the work, running around waiting on people?" And maybe this saying won't seem so true, Father?'

The priest sighed. 'Look, this is very simple. Women have free will. Robots don't – by definition. So there's no –'

'Yeah but anyway, Father, you said Made to Serve, does that mean a robot's *real* purpose like, or just what the guy who made it thinks? Because there's a difference, see, Pa says. Pa says there was this guy No Bell invented dynamite and he thought it would stop wars, that's what *he* made it for only the *real* purpose –'

'Off the subject again, Roderick. What's all this about Women's Lib and dynamite, Roderick? *Try*. Try to be logical.'

'Yeah, Father, but robots, heck, who knows why they're made, why *we*'re made, could be anything. Could be even the people that make them don't know why, maybe they're lonely. Maybe they just get tired of being boss over everything, maybe they just want to be – extinck.'

'What? What are you –?'

'And the only way is to make up somebody better, to take over? Huh, Father?'

Dr Jane Hannah picked up peanuts one at a time, whispered to each one and popped it into her mouth.

Lyle Tate put down his brush. 'Jesus I wish you'd stop that! How can I work with that . . . it's like having somebody saying a rosary all the time, I can't . . . Jesus can't you talk or something?'

'What about? You and your *head?*'

'Someone mention me?' Allbright called from the far end of the loft.

'Jesus!' said Lyle, putting down his brush again. 'What are you doing here? Look Allbright I haven't *got* any money, I —'

'Take it easy, I'm okay. Look.' And when he came close enough for the cold North light to reach his face and clothes, they saw that he'd changed. The beard and hair were trimmed, the face unexpectedly clean, the lapels of his new suit bore expensive stitching. Even Dr Hannah sat up and stared.

'What happened,' she said, 'to the winter garment of repentance? And where the hell have you been this last month?'

'Selling a poem,' he said, tweaking the knees of his trousers as he sat down. 'In a way.'

'Selling a poem my ass.' Lyle turned away and went back to work on the head.

'That too. Well you know how I was, just after ex-mas? Thought I'd hit bottom there — you know, when I put my head in the ov —'

'You phoney son of a bitch, suppose you didn't know it was a fridge, every move calculated, every   '

'Yeah okay I'm a sonofabitch, fine. Only how was I supposed to know goddamn Rogers and his ultra-modern kitchen, okay don't believe me. But I tell you, I first I tried to get into his freezer, you know? Thought I'd just go to suleep as they say, only it was all full of pork, legs of —'

'So what happened?' Hannah asked. 'Hospital?'

'Yup, and what do you know, they cured me. All these goddamn lugubrious head-shrinkers got busy and — shrank my head! Now I'm a hell of a nice little guy, no more bad habits.'

'That's a relief,' said Lyle. 'If it's true.' He began mixing a blue, dabbing it on his wrist.

'See it all came to me one day, as they say. You know how I used to go around quoting Burroughs, how the C-charged brain was like a pinball machine . . . what are you doing? Looks like, what is that *woad* you got there? Old Hannah converted you to some —'

'He's trying to match his veins,' she said. 'What about your Edgar Burroughs machine?'

253

'Eh? Not Edgar, *Bill.* As in billing machine. See, his grandfather was it, invented the adding – anyway listen, it all came to me, junkies are just machines. Garbage in, garbage out, that's what they say in the trade. Junk in, junk out.'

Lyle paused again. 'You know, I think I liked you better when were – better before.'

Allbright unexpectedly laughed. The others exchanged a look.

'No but listen, junkies really are machines. So I wrote a little poem about it. Now listen to this last line: "Addiction is only addition. Plus C."'

Hannah looked embarrassed. Lyle fought back a sudden impulse to be tactful. 'Jesus, Allbright, that's terrible.'

'Yeah, ain't it?' Allbright laughed again. 'See I'm cured of poetry, too. Cured of, of Allbright. They hooked me up to the old machine in there and gave me the pure juice, everything in, everything ... hell I walked around for a few days feeling like Volta, in the comics remember? My right hand attracts – *bzzzzt.* My left h –'

'O God,' said Hannah, turning away. Lyle continued working, while he tried to find something to say. He wheeled the head around to compare the vein on the opposite temple, for symmetry.

Allbright too seemed at a loss for words. He turned to Hannah, grinning. 'Edgar Rice Burroughs, for Christ's sake. Bet you haven't read him either.'

The old woman blinked at the peanut her hand had raised automatically, and put it down. 'The, er, *The Adding Machine?*' she said. 'I saw that performed back in –'

'That's Elmer Rice, for Christ's sake. You're supposed to be teaching Comparative Lit., compared to what for Christ's sake? You never read any English or American stuff in your life, did you? Come on, did you?'

'You haven't told us where the money came from,' she said.

'Oh that. Well. While I was in the nut hatchery I met this old pal of mine, knew him back in high school, seen him around campus a few times, but here he was, a fellow nut. This guy used to be a computer freak, coupla wires got crossed somewhere and here he was, playing Chinese checkers with himself. With one goddamn marble.'

254

Lyle had stopped painting. The North light fell on his port-wine birthmark.

'Anyway he wasn't so crazy, you know? He told me all about a neat little trick you can play on these bank terminals –'

'Memory banks?' Hannah asked. 'I'm afraid I don't . . .'

'No *real* banks. With these terminals all over town like goddamn mailboxes, you just stick in your magnetic card and out comes money. Only he told me how to do it without a card. You just call up the computer on the phone, see, and –'

Lyle finished wiping his hands and threw the rag on the floor. His birthmark grew brighter. 'You call that selling a poem? Jesus, Allbright, you make me sick with your –'

'No look, wait. I work for that money. I had to get this job, see, with this data processing company. To find out the secret phone number.'

'That, that's worse –'

'Only they change it every month so I gotta keep my job, just till I get enough –'

'Enough!' Lyle jammed his hands in his pockets and walked away to the window. He moved stiffly, as though the hands were working hidden stilts. 'Enough! Did they take that away from you too? Your honesty? Did they, did they, make you switch brains with some fucking junior executive, some, in some fucking musical toilet comp – Jesus, you don't even *look* like Allbright any more.'

Allbright grinned at Hannah. 'That's what I like about Lyle. He can get pissed off over nothing. Wonderful set of moral standards he's got, he figures if you keep your fingernails dirty enough you have to be honest, never mind that you boost books at parties and rip off all your friends, lie to everybody, lie to yourself, somehow it all becomes honest if you can just manage to come up with a case of crabs or scurvy, better still kwashiorkor and beri-beri with maybe a touch of impetigo –'

'Why don't you just piss off, Allbright?' Hannah glared at him, her eyes like black olives startling in her pale, almost albino face. 'Lyle's trying to work on something here, something fine. Something even you would have to call "honest". And all you're doing is trying to goad him, spoil it for him.'

'I'm not. "Honest" I'm not. All I want is to get him to admit

255

that he puts a price-tag on honesty just like everybody else, only his price is zero. Am I right, Lyle?'

'No point in arguing with you, you just —'

'Am I right though? Anything is honest to you as long as you don't make money on it, a profit of zero makes it honest, right?' He stood up, drawing back the curtain of his jacket to plant a fist on one hip, and pointed at the painted head. 'That, for instance. Bet you worked out your fee so it just covers your materials, right?'

Lyle mumbled something about a commission for a friend. But Allbright seemed to have forgotten the argument completely, as he found himself confronted with this strangely familiar face, so —

'Uncanny,' he said. 'Uncanny, like the face of John Q. Public but — different. Transfigured. Almost see light coming out of it, that transparent skin . . . and the symmetry . . .'

Lyle nodded. 'Just about finished. If I could just get you and Hannah to sit down and entertain each other . . .'

'Yeah sure but what's this movable jaw — you can't be making a head for some damn ventriloquist's dummy or — I mean this would scare the shit out of any audience —'

'For a robot,' Hannah said, patting the seat next to her. Allbright noticed that the seat, indeed all the seats and tables in the place, were nothing but stacked cubes formed of identical paperback books. 'And don't say there's no such thing, there is now. Just look at it.'

He sat beside her. 'The symmetry . . . and no age, no sex, you can't even be sure of the race . . .'

'That's the point, isn't it?' She handed him a batch of dusty drawings. 'Take a look at his working sketches, see how he got there?'

'What's this, warts all over it?'

'Rivets,' said Lyle, examining a needle-sized brush. 'See, first I figured he ought to look *robotic*. So I tried a lot of crap, faces from *Metropolis*, Egyptian masks even. Hannah finally convinced me he ought to be — well — inhumanly human.'

'I'll be damned.'

'I didn't convince him of anything he didn't know already,' Hannah said. 'All I said, in so many words, was that we need tribal deities, lesser gods to – to fill the empty spaces between the people. You understand?'

Allbright nodded. 'I guess that's it. What would pass, nowadays, for a tribal deity. Not important, just a, as you said, a household god. A – a pet stranger?' He tore his gaze away from it. 'Look I'm sorry about, uh, some of the things I said earlier. To both of you. It's just that I –'

'Tell you a funny story,' said Hannah. 'See all these books?'

Allbright tore open one of the plastic-wrapped cubes and pulled one book out of it. '*Die! Die! Your Lordship*, catchy title there. What have you got, a zillion copies here?'

'The last tenant this publisher, just walked off and left them,' she said. 'But we heard the whole story from the landlord. Seems they printed hundreds of thousands of these without noticing the last few pages were missing – where the name of the killer is revealed.'

'Great! The ultimate mystery.'

'That's not all – you want some wine? There's a glass by your foot there – that's not the best part. They decided to cut their losses by announcing a prize for the first reader who came up with the correct answer. Only – so the landlord says – the guy that won it, it turned out he'd been on welfare for years – was feebleminded!'

'Fair enough, you don't have to be an Einstein –'

'No but listen, the welfare people had him arrested for fraud and froze his prize money, and I guess they're still fighting it out in court – and listen, the whole case –' She was laughing so hard she could hardly pour the wine. 'Listen the whole case hinges on the solution to this stupid mystery. His lawyers claim he got the right answer by accident, and the publishers – rather than lose the prize and get no publicity for it they're suing to get it back, claiming he got the wrong answer after all!'

'Yeah, what does the author say?'

'That's just it, they kept stalling around about producing him, so I hear, and finally had to admit the author was a –'

'A what? Sounded like you said a computer.'

'I – I did. And the computer's been erased or something, so nobody – nobody knows – ha ha ha, the ultimate mystery!'

Lyle worked on, putting the last touches as the light began to fail. The others lolled on unfinished mysteries, drinking wine and trading computer stories. Allbright, his shirt and shoes off, was beginning to mutter about the C-charged brain.

'You know what? I think that head wants a drink. Hey head, you wanna drink?' He stood up, lifted his sloshing glass, and stumbled towards the pedestal.

'Stop it! Stop it!' Lyle had a terrible flash of premonition: wine pouring down the face, the indelible purple stain . . .

'Good God! You didn't have to hit him that hard,' said Hannah in the semi-darkness. 'Is he all right?'

'Put on the lights.' The head was unscathed. Its empty eye-sockets stared back at them across the floor where, amid signs of a struggle, Allbright lay face down, sprawled awkwardly as any body on any drawing-room hearth rug.

'Damn you! Damn you!' Hannah said, and it was not clear whether she was cursing Lyle Tate or his creation. She knelt, turned the body over, and removed her false teeth. 'Not breaving,' she said. 'Get an ambulanf.'

'I'll have to go downstairs –'

'Hurry!'

But when he returned, Allbright was sitting up, mumbling about the C-charged brain. 'Addiction is just addiction . . .' he said, and was still trying to say it right when the ambulance men had come and gone, cursing art and artists.

It was only then that Lyle noticed the head had been moved; lifted from its pedestal and put back wrong.

'What the hell did you do? Hannah? Did you –?'

'Don't worry, the paint's not smeared, I was careful. It was just that – you see I'm old, not enough breath in my body to revive him. I had to call – other sources for the kiss of life.'

'*That?* You think *that* fibreglass shell with paint on it, could bring the dead to life?'

'. . . not the Burroughs adding . . .'

'Maybe it can't,' she said. 'I just felt I had to try everything. Who knows, maybe just the smell of the paint shocked him – eh? Back into his body?'

'Back into –! Jesus Christ Jane, next thing you'll be levitating over in Dr Tarr's fancy new lab, a fat grant from NASA to find out if birds read each others' minds, how do you like that? Or is it psychic levitation now, NASA's real interested there, bound to like the idea of mind-powered space flight. Trouble is most of the people in Tarr's profession couldn't work up the brain power to levitate birdshit in a hurricane.'

'Look I know how you feel about, I know you don't believe in psychic pow —'

'Can't afford to, I'm a painter. And what Tarr and his crowd want to do is put painters out of business, put damn near everybody out of business . . .'

'I don't see that at all.' She sat down next to Allbright, who was pouring himself a drink and talking to it.

'Well what's the point of anybody going to a gallery to look at a Dürer? See, anybody can just be like this psychic Mathew Manning, whip out his own Dürer at home in a couple of hours, no previous training required. Or writing, why write a novel when you can be like this South American whatsisname, go in for automatic writing and knock out a novel in a week? Jesus it kind of makes a dumb joke out of everything anybody ever worked at, right? Take this Rosemary Brown, she's even finished Schubert's Unfinished Symphony . . . so what's the point of anything?'

'. . . funny dream . . .,' said Allbright. The others stopped talking and looked at him. 'Funniest damn dream . . . dreamed, you know what I dreamed?'

For different reasons, they were almost holding their breaths.

'Dreamed this damn dummy was trying to kiss me . . .'

'Yes?'

'Yes?'

'And then this other dummy was trying to bite me in the ass!'

'My teeth!' Hannah shrieked. 'He rolled over on my —!'

All three of them were still giggling over it an hour later, when Sleep closed their eyes.

One liver-spotted hand passed the journal to another. 'Fascinating article there by this J. Hannah. Proposing a robot culture in which —'

'What do we know about this Hannah? Is he —?'

'*She.* Jane Hannah, fifty-five-year-old anthropologist, teaching Comparative Literature at the U. of Minnetonka. Two years ago she was predictably hostile to Entities, voted against funding a project I believe. But – bad luck there, seems her son died. She began to adopt a maternal-protective attitude towards Entities, fill in the blanks, usual hostility towards authority, organized behaviour . . .'

'She saw robots as free spirits? Anarchists?'

'Correct.' Pipe-smoke curled and writhed through the conference room. 'Class eight surveillance of course, but this article makes me wonder . . . class six, maybe?'

'Are we interested in her contacts?'

'Nothing significant so far, writers and artists, petty malcontents. But the article itself –'

'Maybe we could check it with Leo?'

'Leo, yes, so I thought. Let's toddle over there now, I'll summarize it for you on the way.'

The two old men made their way through the maze of corridors and security barriers of Building A, Orinoco Institute, emerging in the desert sun like lizards creeping out to bask.

'Mmm, feel that sun!'

'Mmm. What she's done is tried to trace the origin of the *idea* of Entities – robots, that is – in Middle Europe. In Czechoslovakia especially. Evidently the home of Celts began there, the only "empire" without an emperor or a seat of government. She tries to link that with the Celtic religions, worship of the head, which they recognized as the centre of the intellect.'

'I don't see *that* as signif –'

'She claims they tried to keep heads alive after death, and regenerate. Certainly true that they believed in reincarnation, at any rate.'

'Ha! What will Leo make of *that*!'

'Anyway she then goes on to point out all the Czech rebellions and revolutions, beginning as I recall with the Hussites, Taborites, brings in the Waldenses somewhere . . .'

'Sounds cranky.'

'Oh it is, it is. Finds significance in the merest coincidences, fact that they met on Mount Tabor, almost *robot* backwards; fact that one of the Taborites was named Čapek, that he preached a bloodbath – kill all sinners – very like the bloodbath initiated by robots in *R.U.R.*, so was he an ancestor of Karel Čapek or what?'

'Look, what's the point of all this? Some nut pieces together a half-baked theory – do we really care?'

The other man stopped him, putting a weightless hand on his arm. 'We have to care. Not what she says – but what people make of it. This is, this is just the *worst* scenario we examined.'

Lizard eyes blinked. The desert sun glared down at these two slight figures, creeping along one white concrete path from one white concrete building to another. But all around was dark grass, cooled by sprinklers. Ignoring rainbows, the two men walked on.

'That's not all, of course. She points out all the events that took place in Prague. The famous *golem* story, you know it? Rabbi Löw of Prague, *der Hohe Rabbi* – you do know it? Okay then, how about the Infant of Prague? Seems to be the only Christian statue that isn't a statue at all – it's a jointed doll, with real clothes.'

'Well well. Is there more?'

'Much. She traces the revolution of 1618, successive occupations by Austro-Hungaria, Nazi Germany and Russia, the Czechs never quite knuckling under to their puppet governments (her phrase) as demonstrated in their literature, she cites Kafka's *Metamorphosis* as an exploration of the old mind-body problem that so intrigued the Celts, Hasek's *The Good Soldier Schweik* as a "cheerful robot" satire, Čapek's *R.U.R.* of course; and even a very late item, a play written in 1968 by Václav Havel –'

'The year of the Soviet tank invasion, wasn't it?'

'Exactly. And in this play the main character is a machine whose sole function, not so fast, you know I can't walk fast since my op –'

'Sorry. I'm sorry.'

'Sole function is to investigate human character. *Puzuk*, I believe it's called – ah! Good to be out of that sun!'

They entered the labyrinthine corridors of Building B, finally entering a dim, quiet room. The walls were lined with computer cabinets, and at the far end stood Leo's 'fish-tank'.

A young attendant in white rushed over to them.

'Gentlemen, I'm afraid this is a restric – oh, sorry, sir.'

''S all right,' said the senior man. 'You must be new here, eh? Heh heh, how do you like baby-sitting with Leo?'

The attendant hovered at his elbow as the three of them moved towards the tank. 'Leo, sir?'

261

'That.' The senior man pointed to the floating brain. 'That's Leo Bunsky, at one time just about the best applications man in his field. Still is I guess – poor bastard. Oh, we've got some data here, like Leo to have a look at it.'

'Yes sir, right away.'

The liver-spotted hands gave up the journal and then clasped. 'Poor bastard thinks he's still alive, you know? Still thinks he's working on a robot project, Project Rubber Dick, something like that. Naturally we can't disillusion him now, he might clam up on us.'

'Yes sir, well now I'll just enter this data –'

'Good man, Leo. Don't know how we'd ever stop the propagation of Entities without him, gave us some of our most valuable scenarios. Kind of Devil's advocate – *Hello there Leo!*'

The reptilian eyes, half-closed with amusement, stared down at the motionless brain. 'Good man, old Leo.'

Pa leaned forward while Roderick adjusted his pillow. 'Thanks. Now let's see what this so-called newspaper has to say. Great thing about convalescence, you don't feel so guilty wasting time like this – might even start watching TV if I – listen to this:'

XMAS PLAGUE STRIKES 5 MORE KIDS
400 Cases – Health Dept Baffled

The mysterious 'Christmas plague' which has so far infected over 400 children across the State, causing two deaths, has struck again. Five new cases are reported in Newer, county seat of Stubbs County. State Health Department officials, while admitting the disease has no cause they can isolate, assure the public there is no cause for alarm. 'The symptoms are somewhat similar to those of certain types of mercury poisoning,' said a spokesman. 'We can't rule that out, but it doesn't seem likely at this stage. There just isn't any mercury pollution going on, that we know of. We're sending our best investigative team to Stubbs County right away,' he added. 'Headed by a very capable man, Dr Sam Death.'

'Be nice to have a new doctor in town,' Pa said. 'Welby never has time to see me – not that I really need a doctor. My body is as fit today as it was when I was a young – a young –'

262

'Pa, speaking of bodies, could I ask you something?'

'Fire away.'

Instead of firing away, Roderick began fidgeting with the quilt. It was a strange patchwork design, each patch being a little human figure with upraised arms. 'Gee Pa, I don't know where to begin.'

'At the end, son. Either end.'

'Yes Pa.'

'And go on till you run out of it, then stop.'

'Yes Pa.'

'What is it, is it your new body you wanted to ask about?'

'Yes Pa.'

'Trouble getting used to it?'

'No, heck – well I mean clothes itch a lot but no, it's fine.' Roderick traced a figure on the quilt. 'Only, I mean, heck, well I mean, gee whiz, but heck, I mean gosh darn, I m –'

Pa reached out and slapped the stainless-steel face.

'Thanks Pa, I needed that. Well maybe I didn't need it, but – about my body, okay what I wondered was, is this it? Is this my body? All of it?'

The face was a crude blank, hardly more character in it than in a fencing mask. Pa said, 'You worried about the head, is that it? But it's like we told you, your Ma sculpted up a swell new head, and we got this painter working on it now, he should be shipping it to us any day now –'

'Well no, Pa. I meant – well what about sex?'

Pa raised himself up on one elbow. 'Sex? What in the world has sex got to do with your body?'

Roderick wasn't entirely sure. 'Well I mean, don't I need an extra part or two? Or three?'

'Son, you got all the parts they had in the factory.'

'No but I meant like male parts. Or female parts.'

Pa scratched his head. 'Pipe fittings, you mean? Electricals? Maybe you better spell this out for me, son.'

'I mean for making babies, Pa.'

The old man sank back and laughed. 'Babies! So *that's* what's worrying you! Well listen, I know I should of had a man-to-man talk with you some time back, only I just kept putting it off . . . But now listen. To have a baby, all you do is find a nice girl – or if you are a nice girl, a nice boy – takes one of each.'

'Heck, I know that, Pa. I seen these pictures where –'

'One of each. Then the two of you settle down together, next thing you know the babies start coming along, about one a year just like clockwork. Course you have to kiss a lot. That's why we're giving you a nice face, for kissing. But you don't need no extra pipe fittings or electrical sockets – do you?'

'I don't know. Pa, how come you and Ma never had any kids of your own.'

'Just plain unlucky, son.' Pa rattled his newspaper. 'Plain unlucky. You, uh, you don't think there could be any other reason, do you?'

'Yep.' Roderick told him the story he'd pieced together from Chauncey and the other kids, from dirty pitchers, and from a glance into a book at Joradsen's Drug, *Tantric without Tears*. All his sources, though disagreeing on details, seemed to tell more or less the same story.

Pa listened, looking astonished but remaining silent, until Roderick finished. '. . . well then I guess about nine months later the baby comes out of the same place the stuff went in.'

Pa laughed so hard he nearly fell out of bed. 'Aw come on! That's just ridiculous – I mean them things are to pee with, everybody knows that! You expect me to believe that people go around peeing on each other to get babies inside that they can pee out – come on, now! That ain't even common sense – if people had to go through all that every time they wanted a baby, there wouldn't be any people at all! Mary! Come up here – listen to what this boy just told me – tell your Ma, son.'

Ma listened without laughing. 'Huh! That's what happens when you pick up stuff from other kids, cheap reproduction books and places like that. You should have come to Pa and me in the first place, we'd set you straight.'

'But – but – but they talk about making it, screwing and making love –'

'Making love,' said Ma, 'is just a question of matching up your souls.'

Pa finished coughing. 'What she means, son, is your minds.' He tapped his head. 'Love, sex, whatever you want to call it, it all happens up here. And don't let anybody ever tell you different.'

Ma smiled. 'There! All cleared up? You know, I feel like – like really cooking something. See, all this talk about sex put me in mind of Duchamp, *The Bride Stripped Bare*, and that made me think of nutmeg graters, and that made me think of – of –' Her gaze fell on the quilt. 'Of gingerbread boys! For my invalid – though I suppose Duchamp would call him a *vain lid*?'

'Roderick can give you a hand,' said Pa. 'Soon as I get him to try out this new cipher I've been working on.' He dug down in the bedclothes and came up with a scrap of paper. 'Here son, just you try cracking that one.'

ANN NÉE ANNA, NOD TO ANTS´ ADS (HE HAD TO AX 7).
CZAR INKS ODD IDS (OHMS) FOR NUT LADDER OF VHF STAR.

Roderick saw the answer at once, but pretended to puzzle over it. His thoughts kept straying to sex. It just had to be more than Ma and Pa thought. Only yesterday he'd been reading about Ramon Lull, the thirteenth-century Franciscan who'd invented a feeble kind of logic machine. Even Lull had pursued other things than truth. Lusting after a woman, he had written poems in praise of the imagined beauty of her breasts, and finally chased her on horseback into the cathedral. The woman then opened her bodice to reveal a breast partially eaten by cancer . . . but why had Lull imagined otherwise? There had to be more to the cipher of love than to any of Ramon Lull's little cipher-wheel gadgets, or even to this substitution, in which A stood for B, B for C, . . . Was Lull converted because the breast disgusted him? Or because, God help him, it did not?

XIX

Ping, poop, peep. Ping-peep. 'I'm outa . . . practice . . .'

'. . . wish they'd just stop referring to it as plague, that's all. *Plague, plague, plague,* like to see what they'd print if they really had plague here . . . my point, that's frak 13 . . . because it's just mercury contamination, simple . . .'

Roderick sat in the dark hall beneath the picture of Saint Whatsername and her magical piano. From somewhere he could hear the voices of Father O'Bride and his guest, and the sounds of some electronic game.

'Ha!' *Ping-poop.* 'Oh.'

'Gotta anticipate, Father.'

'Mercury poisoning, eh? Sounds serious . . .'

'. . . prefer to call it contamination, what's in a nomenclature I always say, either way it spells trouble, we got a problem running down the contaminant . . . my guess is some fun food, problem is there's . . . thirteen thousand . . . narrow it down with questionnaires but . . . what kid remembers . . . six months ago? Is that mine?'

'Yeah, that's two men on, three up and four to play, lovefifteen, fifteen-two, fifteen-four – Doc, you're a natural. A natural!'

'. . . theory of my own, these talking gingerbread men, all the cases since they came on the market . . . tried to run one through the lab but they keep delaying . . . figure maybe certain commercial interests trying to hold things up . . . maybe pressurizating the Governor . . .'

'Heck. Guess I'm real outa practice there . . . yeah I know what ya mean, big business . . . little guy ain't got a chance any more . . . lay everything you got on the line, pick up the ball and run with it only . . . darn referee keeps tryina get in the game, know what I mean? Speakina games, howsabout we mosey out to the club and get in nine holes? Forget the lab, they can page you if they . . .'

Father Warren called Roderick into his study. He looked even more pinched and tired than usual, and one of his hands was wrapped in gauze.

'Lent,' he said, and after a moment sighed it: 'Le-ent. A time of self-denial. Humiliation of the flesh. Renunciation of the world. Repudiation of the devil . . . what does self-denial mean to you, Roderick?'

'Gee Father, I don't know, is it like the cretin who says all cretins are liars?'

'Ooff!' Father Warren applied fingers to his blue jaw as though he'd been slugged. 'Well. Tch. Let's drop that for the moment. Did you manage to read that book I gave you? *Logic Machines*?'

'Yeah, Father. I was wondering about this Ramon Lull and this woman with breast cancer –'

'Forget it. You're too young to worry about that, put it out of your thoughts. The point was to get you to see how logic can be put to the service of theology, did you get that?'

'Well yeah, Father, he made up all these wheels with letters around them so you could turn the inside wheel and bring different letters together, like all the combinations. Like ciphers.'

'Very good, yes. And what did the letters stand for?'

'Well things like the seven deadly sins, so you can see how lust makes you angry, or anger makes you envious –'

'Fine, fine. And there were other wheels with the divine attributes, to show us how God's mercy is wise, his wisdom is powerful and . . . and so on. Do you see the point?'

'Well sure, Father, only I mean it gets kinda silly, don't you think? I mean where he says, here listen:

'"If in Thy three properties there were no difference . . . the demonstration would give the D to the H of the A with the F and the G as it does with the E, and yet the K would not give significance to the H of any defect in the F or the G; but since diversity is shown in the demonstration that the D makes of the E and the F and the G with the I and the K, therefore the H has certain scientific knowledge of Thy holy and glorious Trinity." Heck, I mean I don't even think he knew himself what he was talking about, all his circles with lines all over them looking like, like maybe breast cancers –'

'Didn't I just say forget that part? The flesh is too much with us . . .' Father Warren's voice became throaty with sarcasm: 'Except in your case, of course. It's all nuts and bolts to you, isn't it? People, emotions, dreams, the sense of sin, the hope of salvation – all just hardware. You're so superior, aren't you? Sitting there, not even a hint of humanity in that, that welding mask you use for a face – damn you!'

The wax-coloured hands writhed, pinching and scratching at one another like two scorpions in a bottle. After a moment, one of them calmed itself enough to rise and make the sign of the cross, blessing the robot. 'Forgive me, my child, I . . . haven't been well lately, not that that's any excuse for an outburst like that . . . now where were we? I have a book, a book here somewhere . . .'

The hands began to rummage blindly through the books and papers on his desk, picked up *Malleus Maleficarum* and put it down, finally seized upon a volume of *Mind*. 'Ah yes. Now. I'm going to put a hard question to you, Roderick. Little test, you might say, just now SUPPOSE . . . suppose you and I are in a lab, performing an experiment. And suppose that your, your brain is hooked up to a very special kind of machine. Now since you *say* you are a robot, all we really have here is two machines hooked up to one another, right?'

'Right, Father.'

'Okey-dokey. Now this special machine can read your mind and show what you're thinking on a big screen. So by looking at the screen, I can see what you're thinking, okay?'

'Okay Father, only –'

'Never mind technical problems, let's just say we've solved them. I can read your mind. But since you are a machine, it follows that I can do better than that. Because whatever a machine is doing depends entirely upon what it did in the past – along with any new inputs –'

'I think input is plural and singular, Father.'

'Any new input, you understand? If this special mind-reading machine knows what thought you're having this minute, it also knows what thought you'll have next. So I can look at the big screen and see your thoughts *before you have them*.'

'Okay, but –'

'No buts.' Father Warren took a handkerchief from his sleeve and mopped the palm of his good hand. 'I am absolutely and scientifically certain of your thoughts before you are. If I ask you a question, I *know* the answer you'll give *before* you give it. Are you with me so far?'

'I think so, Father. Do I get to see the big screen too?'

'We'll come to that.'

'Because if I do, I could see I have a thought before I have it, and isn't that imposs –'

'I said we'll come to that! Okay no, you can't see the screen. But you're hooked up to this machine, and I ask you, "Do you believe this machine can correctly predict that you will answer 'No' to this question?"'

Roderick thought it over for a moment. 'Heck Father that's just a plain old paradox, if I answer "No" the machine has to perdick I'll say "No" so I'm wrong not to believe it. But if I say "Yes" the machine perdicks that, so I'm wrong again.'

'Hmm, maybe I've got that wrong somewhere.' Father Warren studied the book, cracking his knuckles. 'Suppose we put "Yes" in place of "No", yes that's it, suppose –'

'Well then I'm right all the time, Father. If I say "Yes" the machine knows I'll say "Yes" so it's right and I'm right. And if I say "No" –'

'Okay then let me try it this way: "Would you be right to answer 'No' if I asked you whether you believed this machine can correctly predict your answer to this question?" Answer yes or no.'

'But heck Father it doesn't matter what I answer, the machine has to say *No* –'

'Exactly! *It* has no choice. But *you* do. You, Roderick, have *free will. Ergo* you are not a robot after all, but a human being, made in God's –'

'Yeah, but Father holy Osiris it's just words, I only get a choice because the machine doesn't have any, it's like a – you don't even need a big screen there, just a sign saying NO, what kinda free will is that? I mean, sure I can choose which NO I mean, just like I can choose with a two-headed coin . . .'

An hour later the priestly hands were still clawing through

269

books and piles of notes. 'Okay then, suppose I ask you: "If I asked you whether you *dis*believed that you would be right to answer 'No' if I *didn't* ask you –" No wait a minute, almost got it now. "If I asked –" No, "If I didn't ask, yes, if I *didn't* . . ."'

'How's the workshop?' Pa asked. 'Radio still going?'

'Yup.' Roderick picked at the pattern on the quilt.

'What did you learn today?'

Roderick told him about Father Warren's hypothetical machine.

'Well I'll be damned! Son, if you had a machine that good at reading your mind, you wouldn't need a mind anyway, throw it away and just use the machine. And vicey versa, throw the machine away and use your mind for a machine. By the way, got another cipher for you, toughest one I ever worked out.'

AAA AAA AAAA AA AAA AAAA AAAA

Roderick looked at it for a few seconds. '*Nob gnu jinx'd by dab hand Kurd*, but I think the apostrophe's cheating.'

Pa was amazed. 'But how the heck did you –?'

Roderick winked; that is, put a hand over his eye. 'My secret, Pa.' It wouldn't do to tell Pa that he'd peeked at the answer earlier. A little mystery seemed to perk him up, made it seem almost as if he weren't dying.

He knew Pa was dying. Only the other day the old man had groaned, 'I'm tired now, son . . . like to rest a mite . . .' and everyone knew what that meant. Besides, Ma was baking a bushel of gingerbread boys every day, and throwing them away every night. Probably she reckoned that the sickness would get drawn out of Pa somehow and enter into the little figures – or maybe she just wanted to keep busy. Either way, Ma was worried.

Only the doctor seemed cheerful. Every day Roderick called Dr Welby up, and every day he refused to come out to the house.

'He'll be fine, take it from me. As your family doctor, I can assure you there's nothing to worry about. That's off the record, of course. Gotta go now, Judge Bangfield wants me to look over another lakeside propeerty . . .' One day Dr Welby had listened to Pa's heart over the phone and pronounced him strong as a horse.

*

270

'Seen her myself, Sheriff, throwin' 'em away. Hell, if what this Doc Sam says is true, well . . .'

'Jake, why don't you just sit down and shut up a while. I'm tryina find me a game show here, don't seem to be nothin' on this thing but news . . .'

'Hey, leave it a minute, that's inneresting, looky that!' Jake McIlvaney shifted some *Wanted* posters and sat on the counter, staring at the screen.

'. . . *essor Rogers is still at large. The drama began yesterday when the professor invited a number of colleagues to dinner. One of them was Dr Coppola, who now takes over the story.*'

'*Well he told us it was a leg of pork but I didn't study anatomy for nothing. Took one look and I said to myself, Ken, something's wrong. Something's definitely wrong. So I cut a little tissue sample and took it to the lab, right? So . . .*'

The sheriff pushed a button. '. . . *tastes like honey. Looks like honey —* BUT IT'S BEEZEE . . .'

'Don't see why they gotta yell at you.'

'Hey let's see that Cheesecake Murders thing again —'

'Shut up, Jake.'

'. . . *touch the* YES *button if you prefer a happy ending, touch . . .*'

'. . . *appropriations for the top secret super think tank near Truth or Consequences, New Mexico. In this exclusive interview, the head of the prestigious Orinoco Institute told us just what goes on in those clandestinized smoke-filled rooms . . .*'

'. . . *behind every car I sell at low-low-*LOW *pri . . .*'

'. . . BITSY! BITSY! BOP, BOP, BOP! *It'sa treat! It'swhen you eat! It's O so neat! It's got the beat! It's itsy, it's itsy, it's bitsy, it's . . .*'

Finally the sheriff turned it off. 'Hundred and fifty a month I pay for cable, they can't even get in one damn game show. Now what's eatin' you, Jake?'

The story the TV repairman the disc jockey the waitress the sister of the waitress the preacher the barber the deputy the optometrist the lawyer the daughter-in-law of the lawyer the mechanic the butcher the electrician the young woman the nurse the friend of the nurse the carpenter the grocer the sign painter the father-in-law of the sign painter the old man the baker the young man the grandfather of the young man the plumber the doctor the old

271

woman the druggist the jury the meter reader the cousin of the meter reader the gift stamp redeemer the farmer the clerk the brother-in-law of the clerk the gas station man the teacher the bartender the undertaker the salesman the vet the Rotarian president the dentist the used car dealer the insurance man the chiropractor's wife the mother of the preacher the waitress the neighbour of the disc jockey the uncle of the TV repairman avoided visited stopped defended complained of was good to liked did fillings on met was close to envied called spoke to was related to disliked spoke to saw loved waved at had known for ages visited convicted revived hated cured befriended listened to helped saw awaited supported smiled at was thick with spurned once ran over admired gave a ride to annoyed barely knew married lived near represented fitted lenses for arrested shaved greeted lived with waited on humoured told got around quickly. No one really believed it but . . .

Roderick was sitting at the dining-table trying to make sense out of some of the bills. Ma sat opposite, nibbling gingerbread and reading *The Golden Bough*.

'I don't know, I've tried everything. I put a gingerbread boy under his pillow. All he did was complain about the crumbs. Think I'll give up on gingerbread.'

'How the heck did we get a thousand-dollar phone bill? All local calls, too, practically.' Roderick patted his mouth, indicating a yawn. 'Be glad when my new face gets here, Ma. I mean I really get tired of spelling everything out . . .'

A June-bug buzzed in and plopped on the electric bill, which was a final demand. 'Must be a hole in the screen,' said Roderick. 'You know we might clear these up if I quit school and got a job. They'd probably give me a diploma if I asked – Father Warren wants to get rid of me, I think.'

Ma said, 'I wonder . . . what if I tried smearing Pa all over with this turmeric paste while he sits on the hide of a red bull –'

'FBI! Freeze!' said a voice. Roderick put his hands up.

'Oh!' Ma craned around. 'Agent Wcz, isn't it? And Sheriff Benson, how nice. But who are these other gentlemen?'

'Freeze!' warned Wcz.

'Don't I wish I could, weather like this! Well come in if you're going to, don't keep letting June-bugs in.'

'Are we under arrest?' Roderick asked.

Wcz kept the gun trained on him. 'Why, what have you done?' The other men shuffled in and introduced themselves. 'IRS,' said one. 'I'll take those papers, tin-face.'

'CIA,' said a second. 'Don't worry about me folks, I have no jurisdiction here, just observing in an observer capacity.'

'Me too,' said another man, who gave no initials. 'You Roger Wood? Just like to take a coupla pictures of you, one full-face and one profile. Hear you been going around posing as a robot, that about the size of it? Just speak into the microphone.'

Before he could answer, another man pushed in. 'FDA. We're confiscating those so-called gingerbread men –'

'Boys,' Ma protested.

'Men, boys, everything. We'll also take all the ginger you got in the house – all the ginseng, too – and what's this book? *Golden Buff*? Any recipes in here? Cancer cures, looks like a jaundice cure right here, we'll take it along . . .'

Pa called down from the top of the stairs. 'What's going on? What's going on?' But Roderick was too busy explaining that his face was not a removable mask as in *Westworld*, and Ma was trying to argue the FDA man out of taking away her kitchen stove. Pa made his way slowly down the stairs over the next hour, while the men milled about and Sheriff Benson sat in the corner looking embarrassed. The sheriff was the last to leave, saying:

'Sorry folks, hope this won't influence your vote . . .'

Ma went to the door and shouted after them: 'Okay if we melt now?'

Pa made it to the foot of the stairs. 'What was going on, Mary?'

'Nothing, Paul. You go back to bed and get some rest.'

'Sure, okay.' It took Pa several minutes to turn around and face the stairs again. Before he started up again, he bent and picked up a scrap of paper.

'Looks like they missed this gas bill, here – oh my God! Oh!' Roderick caught him before he fell, but Pa was dead.

'Come out? For what?' Dr Welby sounded cross. 'Look buddy, if you had a bridge hand like this you wouldn't drop it to go look at a stiff either. Don't quote me on that. Look, musta been his heart, thought it sounded tricky the other day . . . tell you what, I'll make a note, *I'm doing it now, don't get excited* . . . make a note to leave a death certificate in my office, you pick it up when you want. Fair enough? Because you'll be coming in anyway to pay your bill.'

'But doctor, it's Ma. She's bad, I think maybe she's gonna die too . . .'

'That's right, tell her a little grief is only natural, but if she needs any medication, antidepressants . . .'

'But doctor –'

'Sorry about your dad. But you know, my work is with the living. The plaintive cry of a newborn babe . . . the tears of gratitude in old eyes that once more can see . . . the trusting handclasp of a child made whole by surgery . . . the brave grin of . . . well, you know. And you *can* quote me on that.'

XX

The next morning brought Jake McIlvaney to the door with a package. 'Terrible thing, your Pa and all,' he said. 'Yep, just terrible. Boys over at the poolroom was just saying how –' the big Adam's apple shifted, '– how sudden it was. Real sudden. And your Pa was real respected in this town, you know that? Real respected. Can't say as he was liked much, but everybody respected him even when they hated his guts.'

Roderick nodded.

'Yep, well guess you'll be gettin' Wally Muscatine to handle the arrangements, eh boy?'

Roderick nodded. Jake came inside and looked around.

'Good enough, good enough. Because you know Wally's a real white man, he'll do your Pa proud. This the death certificate? See Doc Welby signed it, funny thing he was just now saying as how Pa was strong as a horse, only your Ma would keep feeding him with funny pills and all.'

Roderick shrugged.

'Yep, that's the way it goes. Oh, here's your package. Corner kinda got ripped a little there, so I uh seen what it is, it's a head.'

Roderick nodded.

'Looks almost real, what I seen of it. What's it for, anyhow?'

'For me. It's kind of a mask.'

'Oh?'

'Guess I can't wear it for a while. I'm in mourning.'

'*Oh.*' The Adam's apple bobbed again. 'By golly I wondered what you was doing with that black paint all over your face. Didn't like to ask right out, know how coloured folks get so touchy sometimes. Take that new doc, Doc Sam, you met him? Well he is the touchiest coloured boy I ever did see. All you gotta do is sneeze the wrong way and he gets all uppity, you know? Like we was talking about how your Ma keeps baking these here gingerbread boys, I asked him if he hadn't noticed how a lot of kids around town got sick after eating gingerbread boys, right away he got mad! He got mad!'

'He did?'

'Well maybe not right away, but see I asked him if he didn't smell a nigger in the woodpile somewheres, *then* he got mad. Okay, maybe I should of said Negro but hell, it's just an expression. I just don't understand you people sometimes. Hell I'm not prejudiced. I even buy Uncle Ben's rice! And look, I'll shake your hand any time – any time!' Jake at once drew on a dirty work-glove and shook Roderick's hand. 'There, you see?'

'A difficult time,' murmured Mr Muscatine. 'No use making it more difficult than we have to, eh Roger?'

'What?'

'I mean, I hope you'll want the full funeral. No time to pinch pennies, now, is it? See, by rights I ought to remove your beloved father in a quiet, dignified way. I ought to prepare everything real tasteful: I'm talking a rosewood casket, rosewood on the outside over seam-welded stainless steel, silver-plated handles, you got a choice of linings, nylon or pleated silk. I'm talking a full set of casket clothes, nice English worsted suit, Italian shoes, quiet broadcloth-shirt, underwear, socks and garters – he can either wear his own tie or we can provide one, got a nice one here with the message written sideways see, so you can read it when –'

'But –'

'Sure a lot of people think it's corny dressing them up in new clothes but I like to think of it as, well, like getting married. Only for sure you only do it once.'

'Well I –'

'Because see our full package includes everything, floral arrangements, music, enhancement of the appearance, watertight vault, plot in a good location, everything right down to a quality deodorant –'

'Well see, I'm not sure how much money we have. Ma's too upset right now to –'

'Then let's not worry her, eh? Eh? Way I see it, if you really love someone, you just naturally want them to have the very best. Quality, solid comfort, that's our motto at MFH.' Seeing

Roderick scratching his head, he went on quickly, 'Think of it this way. All his life that sweet old man worked hard to provide something for you and your Ma. Quality of life. Now don't you think he deserves a little quality of life himself?'

'Sure only –'

'Of course you *could* get the Economy job, sure. We *could* come in and drag Pa out of here just the way he is, puke down his pyjamas, neighbours watching his limbs flop around, staring at his dirty toe-nails, how would you like that? Then we squirt in our cheapest embalming fluid, cram his belly full of low-grade cavity filler, pop him in a thin plastic coffin and just dump him in a hole in the corner of the graveyard where it's all overrun with weeds and crab-grass, ground's alive with wood lice . . . but ask yourself: is it really worth it? Saving a few lousy bucks, is it really . . .?'

Father O'Bride sounded upset. 'What do you mean, say a few words? Am I supposed to be a toastmaster or something?'

'No but Father, I just thought you could –'

'Nuts. Nuts! Look the poor crud wasn't even Catholic, first of all. You don't need a priest. Get a minister, maybe the guy over at that new motel church, yeah? The Little Olde Church O' Th' Interstate, yeah?'

'But Father, I just thought, maybe he had like a baptism of desire or –'

'Great, kid. Terrific thought there. You know it's never too late with God, you can get sent into the game in the last minute of the last quarter and still score . . . Listen, I'll try to fit him into my prayers, okay? I'm pencilling him in on the roster right now, okay? Now how about getting off the line, I'm expecting a top-priority call from Thailand.'

'Yes, but couldn't Father Warren maybe –?'

'Father Warren is sick. Goodbye.'

The long hands, now bulged about with tape and gauze like a boxer's weapons, rummaged through old xerox copies of *Philosophy* and *Proceedings of the Aristotelian Society*. At times he would stop, outwardly appearing to rest or perhaps to try to remember what he was looking for. But inwardly the wheels never stopped, never slowed.

277

Zeno would say it was impossible, motion. For before a wheel can make a full revolution, it must make a half-revolution, before that a fourth, before that an eighth, before that a sixteenth … faced with an infinity of infinitesimal movements before it can move at all, the wheel gives up.

Father Warren sighed. How easy *now* to smile at Zeno's simple paradoxes! *Now* with the two-handed engine at the door, waiting to crack the very hinges of the universe!

Mrs Feeney opened the door a crack. 'Won't you eat anything, Father? Just, even a glass of milk?'

He waved a lump of bandage. 'Too busy, too busy here.' Milk! To build bones, no doubt. As if that were any kind of solution but a calcium solution, calcium being a metal sure, but can these metal bones live? Let her answer that, yes or no. He lifted the glass, praying inwardly:

'Father if it be Thy will, let this cup pass away, but if it be not Thy will, then let me take this cup and throw the dice therein.' He felt a sudden coldness within, and saw the glass was now empty. 'For Thou playest not dice with the universe,' and even Pascal said it was a safe bet. So give the wheel its turn, and roll the bones.

But what did Luke say? Not Luke, Lucas, Lucas … something about Gödel's paradox was it, where … The hands pawed wildly for a moment – or an hour – was he looking for Gödel or J. R. Lucas, now, 'On Not Worshipping Facts' was it? But the article is a fact itself, is that a para … here, here now to get it down once for all time. Holding the pen awkwardly, he began:

Gödel's paradox shows that within any mathematical system it is possible to write formulae representing statements outside the system. Then if a certain formula is true, its corresponding meta-mathematical statement is true, and vice versa. Moreover

Moreover what? Gödel equals GOD + EL, stop it, stop it!

Moreover one can write a formula Z corresponding to the meta-mathematical statement: 'The formula Z is unprovable in the system.' If the system proves Z, Z is true and therefore the statement is true, making Z unprovable: a contradiction. Therefore the system cannot prove Z, so the statement is true. But that means that Z is true, but unprovable in the system.

Thus for every mathematical system (without internal inconsistencies) there must be one formula which is true but unprovable.

Lucas goes on to show that all machines are mathematical systems of this kind, since all of their operations can be written into formulae. Thus for every –

'Father, did you want anything else, a sandwi –?'

'GO AWAY DAMN YOU DAMN YOU GO AWAY!' Damned interfering old biddy sticking her nose in the door just when he was getting to the, where, where was it, yes:

Thus for every machine there must likewise be a formula Z representing the metamachine statement: 'The formula Z cannot be proved in the machine.' In other words, there is one thing the machine cannot do. This reduces the mind-machine debate to a simple contest: The mechanist first presents Lucas with a machine proposed as a model of the mind. Lucas then points out something the mind can do but the machine cannot (prove Z). The mechanist can now alter the machine so it can handle Z, but then it is a different machine. There is now a different unprovable formula Y to baffle it. And so on. The contest continues until the mechanist either produces a machine for which there is no unprovable formula at all – which he can never do – or admits defeat. The mind must win.

Father Warren paused a moment, then added: HA HA HA HA HA! But –

But what if the machine could alter itself? What if every time Lucas pointed out a gap in the machine mind, the machine simply plugged it? What if the machine could learn and change? So that it begins by saying 'Gee Father I don't know . . .' and before you know it, it's inside your head yes inside your head, twisting the controls, stop it, stop it!

Lucas's bright paradox began to look tarnished already, like Zeno's whirligig, only an amusement, a game the game position – *stop it!* – only a trivial, a puppy chasing its tail, that was it, a puppy chasing its own, but if, but what if . . .?

He looked up, but there was no one at the door.

But what if the machine caught up with Lucas, what if it surpassed him and turned the tables? What if it began setting formulae Lucas could not prove, what then? *Write*, he commanded his hand. *Anything, write.* And after a moment the hand moved, writing A.M.D.G., A.M.D.G., faster and faster, trailing a glory of gauze:

> A.M.D.G., They have pierced my hands and my feet they have numbered numbered all my bones I believe in God the Fact the

And he saw the whirling puppy snap up its tail, then its hind legs, front legs collar and head snapping up its tail and so on, damn him, and so on!

'Now, you good sisters been doing a darn good job here,' said Father O'Bride. He stood with one shoe up on the desk, scraping mud from his cleats. Points of light glancing from his 30-function sports watch danced in the corners of the office behind Sister Filomena, who stood with downcast eyes. 'As I see it, you gave that Wood kid every chance. Every chance. Not your fault if he fumbles instead of running with the ball, is it? Nope. And boy does he fumble! Let's just run over his track record, okay?' He swaggered to the little portable blackboard and erased a football diagram. Then he stood, one fist on the hip of his SHAM OCKS uniform (from which the erroneous C had been removed), the other hand flicking and catching a piece of chalk as though it were a decision coin. Finally he wrote *1*.

'*One*,' he said. '*Discipline*. The little creep fouled up Sister Olaf's religion class, but good! Then *I* tried to have a man-to-man rap with him, where did I get? Zilchtown, that's where. Kid's not even in the same ballgame, can you dig that?'

'Yes Father. We —'

'So I says to myself fine, okay, I'll bench him a while, give him a couple hard workouts with Father Warren, he'll come around. Only what happens? Father Warren hits into the rough and stays there! And that's what hurts. Sister, that's what really hurts. I see him sitting there day after day, busting his . . . his brains over these dumb games — how to read a robot's mind, crud you wouldn't believe, a book called *The Soul of the Robot*, another one *Computer Worship* – and all the time his faith is just winding down, winding down . . . That really makes me sick, you know? I want to reach out a hand and – by the way, you see his hands? I got Doc Sam to look at him, he says it's just some local infection, clear up in a minute if he could only stop scratching – but like I said I want to reach out to him, help him, only he won't help himself! Like yesterday I took him my rowing machine, figured if he won't come outa the study at least he could get in a little workout, you know what happened? He went all to pieces, started moaning how it wasn't fair, I couldn't show him the instruments of torture until I at least asked the question! Instruments of torture! My old rowing machine!'

'Yes, yes Father.'

'That ain't the worst end of it.' He wrote 2, hesitated and added 3. 'He hasn't said Mass for two weeks, that's what hurts. That's what really hurts, Sister. I have to take morning Mass every day and six times on Sunday, double confessions every Saturday – when am I supposed to get down to my own darn commitments? I got no time for the team, no time for planning, firming up dates for the league play-offs, nothing! Not to mention a few business commitments, sure I could scratch them *now* but then *next* season how do we get a deal on uniforms? Same with the devotional items, how else we gonna build the new stadium?'

Sister Filomena said nothing, but he seemed to feel her silence as criticism.

'Sure, okay I spend a lot of time on these things, yeah and a lot of time at the country club too, but Sister, it's all an investment. It'll pay off for the school, the kids, everybody! Only now . . . and all because of one rotten kid, it makes me sick.'

'Father Warren's sick too,' she reminded him. 'And I think we ought to do something about him. I think he needs hospital care.'

'Hospital? Oh no you don't. I'm not having our record dragged in the mud like that, not when I'm *that* close to Monsignor. All we gotta do is play it cool and hang in there, this place'll be a Deanery next Fall. Isn't that what we all want? The Deanery of Holy Trinity? Or do we want it to be known as "Holy Trinity, yeah, where that priest went bananas". Besides, he's not that bad.

He's just, it's just that kid, having that kid around. Get rid of him, and Father Warren will be –'

'I was thinking of the scandal, Father. I suppose you know already Mrs Feeney thinks he's a saint, and she's not the only one, half the older women in the parish are saying he's got the stigmata, the sacred wounds –'

'Hey!' Father O'Bride didn't look at all distressed. 'They could be right, you know? Who are we to –'

'Father!'

'Yeah okay but it's worth thinking about. Now about this kid. I want him out of our hair now. Right away.'

'Expulsion?'

'Nope, too messy, too many explanations. Look, since he's a smart kid, why don't we just graduate him? Yeah? That's it, we'll graduate him!'

Sister Filomena cleared her throat. 'I ought to remind you, Father, that while I respect your opinion, I am the principal of this school. We can't just –'

'If we don't,' he said, 'we're all washed up. You, me, the school, the good sisters, and especially Father Warren. Whole team.'

'I see,' she said, after a moment.

'Great. Terrific. Now you just jog on and fill out a diploma for the kid, hand it to him when he comes in, and that's that. Okay? I gotta coupla phone calls to make . . .'

XXI

'. . . him being an inventor and all,' Mr Muscatine finished. Roderick was staring out of the window. The rain outside the mourners' car fell in sheets (as he knew it always did at funerals), probably flattening the young oats, and certainly cancelling the big game against the St Theresa Terrors. Over the hiss of tyres, the squeak of windshield wipers and the taped sounds of Sereno Benito's Strings, it was hard to make out what the little funeral director was rambling on about. 'No charge of course.'

Ma wasn't listening, either. She stared out at (or past) billboards advertising Quebec beer, Finnish toilet paper and Turkish cars, and she kept humming that same aimless tune from the Bow-wow Symphony. Probably still couldn't realize that Pa was dead. He turned to the window again. A rainbow ran with them briefly, the end of it ploughing across Howdy Doody Lake and then apparently dropping back to linger at the new Welby-Bangfield Corporation property development.

Wally Muscatine carried on. 'My nephew Cliff knocked it together. You know, a bright boy like that gets itchy just setting around all day out there at the junkyard. Has to keep busy, see? So anyway I just thought we'd give it a little run today, see how she goes. Like to think your Pa would want Cliff to have his chance.'

Ma looked around. 'What was that, Mr Muscatine?'

'Oh just telling the boy here about my new set of pallbearers. Fully automatic,' he said, winking. 'Patent Applied For.'

'Patent –?'

'Hope we get some sun, though. Brought the old camera along, thought we might get a publicity shot or so. Like to help young Cliff along.'

The humming commenced again.

*

283

Ma had been acting strangely – even for Ma – since the night of the raid. Roderick had expected tears for Pa, anger at the stupid million-dollar gas bill, anything but this quiet smile, this constant humming. Every now and then she'd wander into Pa's workshop and rattle some tools, as though looking for something. At other times she seemed to think Pa was only upstairs, lying down after dinner.

'Bless his heart, he will overeat,' she'd said yesterday. 'Chicken and dumplings, chicken and dumplings. Do you know, he likes them so much, I've cooked them three times a day for the past forty-odd years?'

'Ma, listen.'

'To what?'

'To me. Listen, Pa is not upstairs lying down. He's dead.'

'Pshaw!' she said, spelling out the unpronounceable word. 'He's no more dead than – than I don't know who – than John Keats!'

'But he's –'

'Oh sure his heart aches and a drowsy numbness pains his senses as though of hemlock he had drunk, maybe, but that's not *dead*. Why, every time you read John Keats he comes to life and speaks, didn't you know that? Son, you've got a lot to learn.'

'Well gee sure Ma, but . . .' But it was no use arguing. He had to go along with the whole charade, pretending to wonder what new invention Pa was working on today; setting out Pa's plate at the dinner-table (though now that Pa was there only in spirit, Roderick noticed that the old man seemed weary of chicken and dumplings, preferring instead Ma's vegetarian diet); watching Ma go out for her solitary night-time rambles.

'Now you stay home, just in case your Pa needs anything upstairs. I won't be long, just getting some ether I mean air.' And off she'd go, carrying with her some memento: a pair of old earphones, a soldering iron.

The seance was even worse.

'Now you just sit down there,' she said, 'by the African violets, and I'll sit here in Pa's chair. And for Pete's sake, try to get into the correct frame of mind, I don't want the astral waves all cluttered up with sceptical static.'

('Saw 'em through the window,' Miss Violetta Stubbs would

say later. 'Her and that black man sitting practically in the dark, holding hands and I don't know what else!')

But how could he get into the correct frame of mind? The whole game seemed so pathetic, with Ma asking herself questions and then kicking the table leg once for yes twice for no . . . and not even really acting as if she believed it herself:

'Is there anybody there?' she called out, adding with a chuckle, 'said Walter de la Mare. "Mr Sludge, stop clowning!" said Robert Browning.' How could she quote her own wretched doggerel at a time like this, and then swing to the other extreme, sighing and sobbing as she rapped away? It made no more sense than the message she finally came up with when, inevitably they got around to automatic writing. The planchette looped and jogged madly under their fingertips, and it was clear to Roderick that Ma was doing it all. The final result began: 'deaear son, remind your ma thathat i punoqun md poow sdn hpouow wyo-1 1 . . .'

'Maybe it's one of his funny ciphers,' Ma suggested. 'Keep it and work on it.'

'Oh sure,' he said, crumpling it into his pocket. 'A cipher.'

All the same, he kept it and worked on it, if only to stop worrying about Ma.

The rain had stopped too soon, to the delight of Wally Muscatine. He set up his camera while the others (Roderick, Mr Swann, Ma and Miss Violetta Stubbs) lined up next to a hole in the ground. No one knew exactly why Miss Stubbs was here; it was said she came to all the funerals, if only for a ride out into the country. But here she was, smiling down into the oblong hole and saying, 'Looks like a nice day after all. Nice.'

Mr Swann nodded, which prompted her to say, 'Nice of Mr Muscatine to demonstrate his new Patent Applied For, isn't it? And for no charge, I do believe. Very nice.'

They waited. At some distance, the machine was backed up to the hearse – or anyway the hearse was backed up to some kind of big tent made of tarpaulins – and something was almost going on. Cliff kept going into the tent and hammering on steel. Each time he reappeared they all craned hopefully, but it seemed always to be another false alarm; Cliff would grab an oil-can or a wrench and disappear again. With the tombstones, they waited.

At last there was a report, a flash of blue smoke, and a different knocking sound (as though a giant chain-saw had bitten into something indigestible). The tent began to lurch.

Ma looked apprehensive. 'I suppose that thing's *safe*?' she shouted over the noise.

Wally winked. 'No complaints so far!' and shouted to Cliff to drop the tarps.

Finally the tent collapsed, taking Cliff down with it, but unveiling – Them. Six tall, gleaming figures in stovepipe hats, hoisting between them an insignificant little coffin, and marching in perfect step towards the grave.

'Very nice,' gasped Miss Stubbs.

One of the hats backfired. By now they were close enough for Roderick to see that they were real stovepipes, and that their wearers seemed to be made of every kind of junk: he saw a breadbin head, shoulders made from a sewing-machine, arms of beercans and legs of steel rails. And as they suddenly clanged into a tombstone and veered off in a new direction, he noticed something else, something eerie. There was his own childhood skull! now part of a buttock.

The six giant pall-bearers were really part of a single machine, for on each side three legs moved in step, driven by one great driving-rod. Patent Applied For was making poor progress now. It kept ramming tombstones, stopping, turning and marking time – with feet so heavy they sank into the wet earth.

'Turn 'em, Cliff, turn 'em! They're gettin' outa frame!' Mr Muscatine waved his arms, Cliff fiddled with his model-airplane transmitter, and slowly Patent Applied For stumbled towards its destination.

'At last,' said Mr Muscatine, sighing. 'Now tell 'em to stop, Cliff. Cliff? CLIFF!' But They continued their clanking march to the edge of the grave and off it, the first pall-bearers striding on air for a second before the clay walls collapsed under those behind them. And then the whole contraption pitched into the hole, groaning and spluttering, its twelve legs kicking out to bring down the wet clay walls, until almost everything was buried except Pa. 'Suffering cats!'

When the machine stopped, Mr Muscatine looked around the cemetery. Turf was up, floral arrangements scattered and trampled, lasting monuments chipped and cracked, a haze of blue smoke hanging over a grave containing two tons of perverse scrap metal, and the coffin – scarred rosewood, bent silver handles – still lying in the grass awaiting burial.

'Well, Cliff,' he said. 'You had your chance. You sure had your chance.'

While they waited for the grave-digging machines to make a new resting-place, Mr Swann got out his briefcase.

'We might as well get right down to it,' he said. 'Plenty to get through here, quite a nice little financial mess. He'd already cashed his insurance, understand he owes the doctor – I was kinda surprised at this elaborate funeral, all this waste just when – but I guess that's your business, Ma. But I mean two uninsured mortgages plus all this electronic stuff – I got nothing against hobbies but there's a limit – anyway too bad you don't have a car to repossess I mean sell. Naturally the house goes back to the Bangfield Trust Bank – there now, there now . . . maybe you want to sit down?'

Ma staggered and leaned on Roderick's arm for support. The three of them sat in the grass, dangling their legs into the grave of Patent Applied For.

'Not all that bad,' said Mr Swann. 'Course we gotta fight. Hold off the IRS boys while we try a little debt consolidation, then '

'Wait a minute,' said Roderick. 'If Pa didn't have any money, how could there be tax –?'

'Technically intestate, yes, indigent too only he purchased this electronic stuff as a corporation see? Tax shelter I set up for him, so he could write it all off as depreciable stock using the Class Life – well how did I know he'd up and croak on us? Now the stuff has to be inventoried and sold, taxed as corporate profits sure, but the other stockholders want to liquidate and cut their losses.'

'Other stockholders?' Roderick asked. 'Who?'

'Me, my wife and kids.' Swann licked his thumb and began dealing papers out on the grass. 'I feel we can work all this out by consolidating these debts, re-negotiate at a more favourable rate of interest. Should come out to something like a hundred and eighty-five thou, excluding the usual – but listen, all we have to do is, Ma, you listening? All we have to do is your Roderick here

287

forms a finance company, takes over the whole debt and then discounts pieces of it to a few banks –'

Roderick stared down into the grave. 'But you said I'm not a person in law, how can I –?'

'But your company *is* a person in law, see? So it doesn't matter what you yourself are as long as you're not a crook or a bankrupt. But what I was just getting to, you got terrific collateral, very expensive electronic gadget in perfect working order – yourself. Assuming you got a clear title, of course. I already filed a writ of *habeas* for you there, no problem, some of the legal technicalities might cost a little, sure, but we can cover that by suing Welby.'

'Doctor Welby?' Ma looked faint again. 'Sue him – for what?'

'Never mind, once we start digging we're bound to come up with something. Went around saying Pa was healthy a few days before he became a decedant, didn't he? There you are, breach of patient privacy, mis-diagnosis – we'll pick up *half a million* there, easy. Then we sue Muscatine here. I can see his gadget caused you a total breakdown – but Welby's the real mother lode. Let his receptionist sign the death certificate, looks like, got the name and cause of death in the wrong places – *half a million*, believe me.'

Roderick looked up. 'But wouldn't that cover our debts?'

'No, barely covers costs in your claim for title, see, first we gotta file this writ of *habeas* to keep anybody else like this Kratt Industries from slapping a claim on you, then we gotta go through one of these procedures I outlined before, what we want is a clear title over your body ... this has to take time ... costs ... but when you own your body you can sell it like any other chattel, see, borrow money on it, anything ...'

Roderick stopped listening to stare down at his childhood skull. Inside that hollow piece of tin, I was.

Miss Violetta Stubbs did not wait to take off her hat when she got home. She went straight to the crocheted doll covering her telephone, removed it, and punched a number.

'Doreen? Listen I was just at the funeral, Pa Wood you know ... the Guild? No wait listen, *she* was flirting with this *black man* right there in front of everybody! Leaning on his arm! Listen they sat right down and stuck their feet right in the ga-rave! And that ... yes but listen, that's not all. If I hadn't heard it myself I

288

wouldn't believe it either, but there they were, bold as brass, with a lawyer, talking about cutting up half a million dollars! Half a . . . and poor Pa not even covered up with earth yet – oh yes, and there's something very wrong with the death certificate! Well I can put two and two togeth . . . wouldn't put it past her, would you?

'Now this Guild thing, I'm sorry but it looks like they've sent us the wrong speaker . . . yes *again* . . . I don't know . . . must be something wrong with their computer . . . No listen, I wanted the Reverend Capon just as much as you dear . . . But listen, we can have Positive Breathing *next* month then, we'll just have to put up . . . I say we'll just have to put up with this, this Miz Indica Dinks, who*ever* she is, she's going to speak on *something* called Machines Liberation . . . neither do I, but I certainly don't intend to just sit home tomorrow night, do you? And so what if she *is* a Communist we can always just walk out and leave her cold . . . Doreen, I wouldn't miss it for the world.'

That night when Ma went out for her walk, Roderick followed. At first they headed for Main Street, past the post office, the Courthouse, Simms's Do-It-Ur-Self, the Idle Hour (where a few men lounging on car bumpers drinking beer gave him hard looks) and the place that had once been Selma's Beautee Salon but was now called HAIR TODAY. But then Ma turned off by the library, headed down Church Street and straight on out of town. Was she lost? Or just nuts? Because there was nothing out this way, not even lights. Just the darkness and the gravel road leading out to Howdy Doody Lake.

Roderick didn't like it. If he dropped back too far, she might turn off somewhere and disappear. If he kept too close, she might hear his footsteps on gravel. There didn't seem to be any distance at all between too close and too far, and he could think of only two other answers: go home, or catch up with her and pretend it was just a coincidental meeting. ('Hello Ma. Pa told me he didn't want anything upstairs, said I should get out and get some fresh air like you. Funny we both decided to go this way, ain't it? Odds against it must be, let's see . . . Well sure I know *most* robots don't need fresh air, guess I must be different . . .')

Ma wouldn't want company. In fact she was acting kind of

stealthy, walking too quietly on the gravel, stopping every now and then (to listen?). Like an international spy on his way to the hollow tree. Was she meeting someone? Was she, was she . . . but spies made him think of the cipher in his pocket, and that made him think of Pa, Pa and this miserable little old woman hobbling along in her bare feet in the middle of the night.

A penance, that was more like it. Offered up to reduce Pa's days in Purgatory, his time off for her good behaviour. She must love him a lot.

Or maybe she hated him a lot. Sure it was her cooking that used up that million dollars' worth of gas, caused Pa to take one look at the bill and keel over. Probably she felt relieved ('So much for chickens and damn dumplings!') and probably that made her feel guilty. Walking it off, trying to walk it off, not knowing it really came from her unhappy childhood, those early traumas causing horizontal cracks in the ego structure for which she could never forgive her father, hence Pa, hence herself. And even now unconsciously she was humming that tune: 'Take me to the river, deliver me to the lake . . .'

Well suicides are stealthy. Roderick resisted the impulse to rush forward and stop her, before the cathartic moment when – but holy mackerel, didn't she know it was a *sin*? St Augustine said if you were a pure, innocent person suicide was twice as bad because then you were guilty of murdering a pure, innocent person – something wrong with that maybe but sin was sin. And even if John Donne thought that suicide was no self-murder, that Jesus Christ had killed himself on the Cross by just taking a breath and blowing out his soul (but then how did he get it back three days later?), sin was sin.

Unless maybe Ma was thinking of a *literary* suicide! But then why pick this lake? It was so shallow that any man could be an island, and its history was no deeper than its dirty waters. Even the name sounded like reconstituted orange juice, who wanted to drown in Howdy Doody, that's just asking for obscurity. Unless maybe she wanted to make a protest: life is shallow, art is shallower . . . poop on the world!

A protest, though, might be a real protest about the real world, a focus for the historical perspective, sure because look at greedy capitalist *entrepreneurs* like Welby and Bangfield, putting up their so-called leisure complex right on the shores of good old Howdy Doody Lake. There once silvery fish leapt, jewel-bright dragon-flies hovered near a silent canoe in which a lean red man glided o'er the glassy waters to claim his bride; they would live simply, in peace with Brother Nature.

Okay, okay it was an artificial lake only about fifty years old, but same principle – once the horny-handed farmer sat down on these shores to eat his lunch, feeling the good warm earth and smelling the clean wind – then along came lakeside cottages and water-skiers and the Welby-Bangfield Leisure Complex, profit heaped on profit, fat men in silk hats and striped pants puffing their cigars and laughing themselves sick at the idea of poor honest men standing in breadlines in cities where the buildings were heaped up like piles of gold but one day the gold would trickle away into the dust, the cities tumble down, the silk hats rot as tatters of striped pants flapped in a new wind of change, as the expropriators got expropriated to pieces. Only that didn't sound much like Ma either. Probably she just wanted to join Pa.

'Will you join me?' 'Why, are you coming apart?' But on the astral plane nothing ever came apart, nothing was lost. Death was just people getting temporarily misplaced – open the right drawer and there they are! Yes Ma half-believed that stuff, with all the paradoxes: life is death, all is one, up is down, yes means no. If you don't know whether you're a man dreaming you're a butterfly or a butterfly dreaming you're a man, swat the butterfly. For all is one and one is nothing, and you can be the person who killed the person who killed the person who . . .

Lightning flickered somewhere, and Roderick saw Ma standing by the lake, stooping to pick up something. She seemed to be wearing some kind of cone on her head. Of course! If up was down and day was night, good was evil and this was witchcraft!

He found it hard to believe even when she'd built the fire and begun the incantation: 'Alcatraz! Mulligatawn! Tapeworm! . . .'

What a let-down. He'd seen hundreds of old witch movies on TV, every single one a let-down. Probably now she was going to strip off her clothes and dance around the fire, and then screw some giant goat out of the sky or something, then there'd be plenty of thunder and lightning, screaming and flames and that would be that.

A scratchy old record started up: The Bow-wow Symphony. Ma left the circle of firelight, and he could hear her calling down the beach: 'Hurry up, the rain's starting . . .'

Suddenly there was a distant bang, a flash of blue flame, and the unmistakable clatter of Patent Applied For. Then the rain came down and Roderick could no longer be sure what he saw or heard, an electric arc or was it lightning, a man's scream or was it the scratchy record, Ma shouting not to forget the candy while lightning danced on six stovepipe hats while Roderick tried to run for the shelter of the trees but crashed into another running figure as blinding lightning struck again and he fell into perfect darkness.

XXII

'. . . a bad dream?' said Ma. 'Your batteries must be low . . .'

'Sure, from the long walk. But how did I get home?'

She pretended not to hear. 'Feel like going to school today?'

'And what was Cliff doing out there with his Patent Applied For?'

'. . . all a bad dream, son.'

Roderick held up a scrap of wet cloth. 'Yeah but when I woke up I found this in my fist, did I dream this? Look there's writing on it.'

'Did I dream this?'

'Well yes, in a way. I do believe this is a genuine *apport*, son.'

'Apport?'

'A psychic deposit of physical evidence. It was your dream that made it appear, made it pass right through the walls of your room!'

'Looks familiar only –'

She snatched it away. 'I'll just mail it right off to the Society for Psychical Research, they'll be *very* interested.'

'But Ma, *I'm* interested, I –'

'Why don't you stay in bed this morning, school can wait. Oh, and you could work on that psychic message your Pa sent you through the planchette.'

He took her advice, if only to keep an eye on her. Besides, the cipher – if it was a cipher – might hold some indirect clue to Ma's

293

– madness? He smoothed it out on the bedclothes and opened his notebook to a clean page.

> deaear son,
>   remind your ma thathat
>   i punoqun md
>   poouu sdn hpououu uuyo-II
>   uooms-oudhy opun uoos
>   suoquoq ydsoyd-hxo
> ii «xod huu dn douu op spns dòsshy»
>   uuuhy uuny (8 sndo) huoyduuhs
>   «mom-moq» punos puod uo hpoq
>   honq xoq opun spoom hpoop
>   hpmoy hpoq huu duunp noh
> iii qouu unys + punoq-oudhy huuuunuu
>   quunu uunssod mou os (ydhs)
>   dnos u! poom d

At noon, when he closed the notebook, there were no more clean pages, and no solution. His best so far was a single line:

hpmoy hpoq hw dwnp noh
threw then to gosh set

'Take a look at this.' One liver-spotted hand passed the binoculars to another.

It was just possible to make out a tiny group of people standing outside the fence with signs.

'What do they want?'

'Would you believe they're Luddites?'

'No I would not. Is that what security –?'

'Precisely. Haven't you seen the book? By this guy, what's his name now, Hank Dinks, called *Ludd Be Praised*, turning into quite a cult item there.'

'Ha ha, is it now? Think my daughter's reading it now that you mention . . . but what's the premiss?'

'Crank stuff. Back to Nature, more or less, but with the emphasis on ol' devil computer. Might know they'd get around to us – though I'm surprised they can't muster more people for such an obviously populist cause. Can't be twenty souls out there.'

'The sun, you forget the sun. And we are a good way from Phoenix. If it weren't for the sun, you know, I'd be tempted to stroll out and have a chat with them.'

'Ah but security's against it. Usual overcaution. I swear, sometimes I think they'd like to put all of us in Leo's tank, seal us off from the rude world . . . oh wouldn't they all be upset out there if they knew about Leo!'

'Ha ha, wouldn't they . . . be more like twenty thousand out there then, eh? But what, ah, what do they actually accuse us of doing? Running a clandestine computer?'

'Better than that! Listen, they think we're running robots! Us!'

After a few dry chuckles and coughs, the binoculars changed hands again. 'Still, too bad they associate us with robots in any way. I don't like it.'

'Nobody likes it. The Agency certainly doesn't like it. But . . .'

'These little movements blow over, I suppose.'

'Precisely. Precisely. Even if they don't, we might . . .'

'Use them? Exactly. Exactly. By the way, how's that Nebraska business shaping up?'

'No problem, as our Agency friends like to say. We have a clear set of pictures of the subject, front and profile, we have a voice print, we know exactly where to find him.'

'Is he passing?'

'More or less. At the moment he's trying to pass as a black man.'

'Fascinating! I wonder if we couldn't study him for a while before –?'

'Too risky, look what happened to our last surveillance team, that highly unlikely "accident". Point oh oh oh oh seven at best, makes you wonder . . . No in fact I've already ordered the destruction for this evening.'

'Oh well. Fun while it lasted. Better than this Kraft Industries business, that's just boring. Pinball machines, talking gingerbread, automated concubines – low-grade stuff, all of it.'

'Precisely what we have to encourage, my friend. Our job, after all, is to –'

'I know, I know. To keep the world on the graph paper. Only sometimes don't you feel, just a little like letting it, letting it slip?'

But the other elder was squinting through the glasses again. 'I can just make out a sign – Oh listen to this! STOP ROBOTS. STOP POLLUTING THOUGHT WAVES.'

'Fascinating!'

'Fixed up like a minstrel today, are we? Well never mind, have your last little joke, because this is your last day. Here.' Sister Filomena shoved a piece of paper at him.

'What's this, Sister, I – listen I –'

'Walking papers, *Mister* Wood, walking papers. Your diploma. You are now officially graduated, so goodbye.' She went back into her office and closed the door.

A.M.O.G.

Know all Men by these presents that
RODERICK WOOD
having satisfactorily completed the Eighth Grape at
HOLY THINITY SCHOOL
in the Year of Our Lord McM_____
is hereby awarded this

OIPLOMA OF SCHOLASTIC ACHIEVEMENT

(signed) Sr. M. Filomena, Principal

PRINTED IN TAIWAN

Father O'Bride put his head in at the door, without removing his fishing hat. 'Hiya Sister, didn't I see a new pupil come along here just now?'

'New pupil?'

'Yeah yeah, I was in my office cutting up one of Father Warren's old cassocks, boy you wouldn't believe how many relics you can get out of eleven yards of material, boy I got a hundred and fifty thousand little pieces so far not even half done I mean even at a buck apiece we can't go wrong there, bandages for five –

yeah I meant to ask you, any sign of that blood transfusion unit I ordered?'

'What? Blood, Father, is Father Warren –?'

'No prob, no sweat, just forgot to tell you I ordered this neat little unit, figured we could cycle a few pints right through him put it in these little plastic phials one drop each and – well don't look at me like that, Sister, criminy! Not as if we're taking anything away from him, he'll still have blood of his own only we add a pint and drain off a – look, people hear about a stigmata first darn thing they want is a drop of the precious – okay never mind! Just tell me where I can contact this kid, one with the muscles. The natural.'

'Natural? Father I don't think –'

'Natural, natural athlete, heck all these boogie kids are naturals. Point is this guy could make all the difference on the gridiron next season against St Larry's – damn it I mean darn it, where is he?'

'You must mean Roderick but he –'

'Yeah *Robert, where's Robert?*'

She waved, almost blessing him. 'Gone, Father. Home or –'

'Gone? Gone?' He vanished and she could hear him bawling in the hallway:

'ROBERT! Hey Robert, wait up!'

. . . his feet flapping down the stairs and hitting that miraculously shiny little patch of floor at the bottom . . . then a cry . . . a thump . . .

Then blessed silence.

'Somebody oughta teach that nigger a lesson, knocking Father Owhatsit down the stairs like that, leaving him all paralysed from the waist up was it? Or down? Just who does this Doc Sam think he . . .'

'Oh it wasn't him, it was that other nigger one that's been living in sin with Ma Wood, Violetta saw them . . . and anyway a man that wears a skirt and don't like girls . . .'

'Jake told me the Wood boy's gone black, didn't he used to be paralysed himself? Bobby Wood, used to be so paralysed they had to wheel him around in a little tank or . . .'

'Jake'll say anything, told me the kid was a two-headed robot, but listen before Doreen gets me under that drier and I can't hear a thing, guess who asked Doc Sam to *examine* her the other day?'

'Robots, shit we got enough damn robots out at the factory, Jap robots, German robots, reckon the machines is taking over all right, makes you wonder who won the damn war. . .'

'Makes you wonder if these here Lewdites ain't got something there, least they know the difference between a man and a god-durned wheel, but listen, my old lady says some nigger robot stuck a knife in Father O'Bride . . .'

'Bob Wood? Yeah I heard that, same asshole knifed Father Warren a few months back ain't it? Sure it is, hell they get away with murder these days . . . Not that I like Catlicks, only you let a bunch wild niggers run around with knives . . .'

'Machines is taking over, hell they even got machines' lib, no shit, my wife's going to the Ladies' Guild to hear one of 'em, makes you wonder who won . . . three beers here, Charlie?'

'Trouble-maker from way back, remember when he was at the public school here, wrecked the damn computer, just went berserk and wrecked . . .'

'Somebody oughta wreck him, you know? Somebody oughta teach that little shit a lesson.'

'I blame his home background I mean what do you expect? I think I liked the other ones better dear, the uh pink frames with rhinestones? What do you expect? Ma and Pa Wood aren't exactly, well I mean they're communists for one thing, atheistic communists, dressing that kid of theirs up in that porno get-up for the Christmas play, no wonder he scared poor old Sister Martha to death . . . only what do you expect, anybody sets a big *toilet* out in their yard, health hazard the sheriff had to break it up, we saw the whole thing! And Herb says *she* oughta be locked up. Do you think the rhinestones are too . . .?'

'Remember how she tried to poison Jake McIlvaney? Cookies with ground glass and I wouldn't be at all surprised if she was behind this gingerbread . . .'

'Oh she was, didn't you know? They had a big police raid there, the FBI took away all her ginger to test for poison too bad they didn't take her away at the same . . .'

'And she's been playing house with a black man ever since poor Pa, probably poisoned him too! And she's a witch, everybody knows . . .'

'Well the boy always was a trouble-maker, ask anybody, didn't his teacher Miz Beek commit sui . . .?'

'Mrs Feeney says he's like he's got the devil in him, you know he actually stabbed one of the priests?'

'I blame his background. My Chaunccy never would . . .'

'Well, somebody better teach him a lesson.'

Roderick was at the dining-table, covering page after page with cipher calculations. Ma paused to kiss the top of his head.

'That's a good boy. Now I'm just going out to the Guild, be back in time to give Pa his supper. But if he wants anything meanwhile will you stick around?'

'Sure, sure.' It wasn't polyalphabetic with a repeating key, it wasn't a multifid, it wasn't Playfair or a substitution followed by a grille transposition . . . was it even a cipher?

It had to be. Something in the world had to make sense. Ma would say it all did make sense, only you had to be on the astral plane to perceive it. Pa would say nothing made any sense at all, only we have to make our own sense out of it.

He gave up on the cipher and wandered into Pa's workshop. There was the radio, still faintly murmuring music for its own easy listenin' enjoyment. There was the box of inventions. There was the photo of Rex Reason, the cards hand-lettered by Miss Violetta Stubbs: 'OVER THE HILL doesn't mean DOWN AND OUT . . .'

The lettering was the same as on the piece of cloth. Sure, it was part of a hand-lettered tie: not remember wit fun, but

REMEMBER ME
WITH MUSCATINE
FUNERAL HOMES

printed sideways so the mourners could read it. Sure, so . . .

After a moment, Roderick took down the green key from its nail below Rex and left the house with it.

At twilight the giant letters SLUMBERTITE NEVER SLEEPS suddenly flared up like curious trees bursting into flame. The low slab of windowless factory supporting their neon splendour now seemed lower, less significant. The two tiny figures climbing out of their microscopic Rolls-Royce seemed nothing at all.

'God, I love this place, bub. Almost makes me wish I was a religious guy ... I don't know, if I ... if God ...' Mr Kratt recovered quickly. 'Come on, let's get inside, can't stand around with your finger up your rectum all evening.'

He strode off across the perfect lawn, leaving Ben behind. 'Come on, come on.'

'Yes sir. I was just, I was just thinking ...'

'Too damn much thinking, your thinking got us into this mess, bub. Trouble with you artsy-fartsy academics, can't see anything clearly, everything's got too many sides to it. We had a good goddamn thing going there with Jinjur-Boy, only you had to go and spill your guts to the FDA the minute they came sniffing –'

'It wasn't like that at all, Mr Kratt I, all I said was –'

'Was enough! Mercury batteries, why the hell admit a thing like that, you know what it's gonna cost to fix this up? Hell of a lot more than you're worth. Thing gets this far you can't just grease a few palms you know. Gotta fix up a whole publicity campaign, pictures of a coupla senators and their kids eating the damn things, the works. And we gotta move fast before we get every hick consumer group in the country after us, look what they did to Buckingham cigarettes ...'

'I never heard of them.'

'See what I mean? One minute they got fifty quacks on the payroll telling everybody how their natural blackstrap molasses-filter traps everything nasty, the next minute they're wiped out. Dead!'

'Dead,' said Ben faintly. 'But what do we do about these dead kids, eighteen of them now, eighteen ...'

'Look, stop moaning, will you? Our lawyers are already fixing all that up with the families, get each of 'em to sign an affidavit their kids never ate our product in return for an *ex gratia* handout, hell, most of 'em never seen so much cash, no problem there ... no problem.'

'No but it's just that sometimes I think we, all we can do is create death. Even when we try to make life it comes out death,

death is there all the time. In the program somewhere ... it's, I don't know, almost as if we brought a gingerbread boy to life and all he wanted was to die ...'

'Goddamnit, pull yourself together, industrial accidental pollution, happens all the time! All the time, you can't get all personal about this, Jesus you think every oil company executive pisses his pants every time he hears a pollution story? I mean sure if you want to go on playing fancy academic games writing little titbits for the *Jackoff Journal* fine, only I thought you wanted to run a goddamn company!'

'Well I ... yes, I guess ... yessir I do.'

'Fine. Then goddamnit, bub, start running it. And for Christ's sake stop looking like a pall-bearer, give this Welby guy a big smile. Must be him waiting by the door.'

Ben Franklin managed a weak smile for Dr Welby while Kratt unlocked the plain steel door.

'Really an honour Mr Kratt, if you don't mind my saying so, been reading about you everywhere, newsletters, *Fortune* wasn't it? A profile yes, and weren't you named one of the top ten business lead –?'

'Only the top ten *new* leaders, Doc. Good to see you're well-informed though, because –'

'And to think, you coming all this way just to meet with a small-town sawbones like me!'

'Yes well I '

'You sure must want something pretty bad, ha ha.'

They stopped, Kratt and Welby facing each other in the chill stainless steel corridor, almost squared away like a pair of hostile dogs, each determined somehow to mount the other. Welby's pale eyes (staring over the tops of his old-fashioned glasses) were locked in silent combat for a second with Kratt's dark little eyes (staring under the heavy V of brows).

'Doc,' Kratt said softly. 'Don't sell yourself short. If I didn't know you was a good businessman I wouldn't be trying to trade horses with you. Now come on let's see if we can find the damn board-room in this godforsaken place, think it's at the end of the corridor ...'

He led the way into an impressive conference room panelled in something very like walnut. While Ben and the doctor took their seats at the long table, Kratt went to the liquor cabinet.

'See Doc, you're a man with foresight. You and I know Nebraska's gonna bring in gambling in a year or so, and we both know the considerable financial rewards to be reaped – by the right man in the right place. So can we talk?'

Dr Welby nodded at the broad back. 'Why sure. Hey this is some layout you got here, never knew there'd be a place like this right in the old Slum –'

Kratt laughed, or perhaps coughed. 'You know, no human being has been in this room for four years. Not even cleaners.'

'But it's spotless!'

'Machine-cleaned, every damn day. Best thing about machine-cleaners is they don't drink up the chairman's booze – got some fifty-year-old Scotch here, Doc. What's your pleasure?'

Dr Welby didn't mind if he did.

The big German Shepherd snarled and threw himself against the fence, daring Roderick to try – just *try* – opening the gate and setting one foot on Slumbertite land. But when Roderick did open the gate and walk in, the dog only sniffed his hand and then trotted away to seek some other victim.

A long curved driveway led to the great factory. And just so there should be no mistake, a series of 'landing lights' flickered along it, pointing his way. And just to make absolutely sure there should be no mistake, a recorded voice spoke to him: 'Keep to the driveway and don't loiter. Please follow the lights.'

The driveway took him right up to the plain grey corrugated wall, which at first seemed to lack a door, even a keyhole. Only when he was close did a door slide open.

'Step inside, please. Prepare for a security check. Prepare for a security check.'

He stepped inside and stood around, until a voice said: 'Empty your pockets on the conveyor belt. Now. Everything will be returned to you when you leave the building.' Pa's cipher and the green key; a quarter and two nickels; a piece of string and a grubby stick of gum; half a yoyo, a broken rosary and the little folded wad of paper that was his 'oiploma'; a rosary bead and a lead washer moved out of sight.

'Face the light-panel. Answer the questions yes or no by pushing the yes or no button. QUESTION: Are you carrying or concealing any tool or weapon?' No. 'Are you carrying or concealing any explosive or inflammable material, such as gasoline, TNT, butane?' No. 'Are you carrying or concealing any electronic equipment, such as an artificial arm or leg?' Yes. 'Walk through the light-panel. Now.'

He pushed open the panel and entered the Emerald City.

It was bigger and greener than even the cemetery. That pure blue-grass colour lay over the floor, what he could see of the distant walls, and over every one of the 'elephants'. They did look like elephants, turning and twisting their trunks to get at the things on the assembly-lines, twisting back to pick up screws or paint-sprayers or sandpaper or clothes. A hundred green elephants? A thousand? He couldn't tell, not without strolling down the yellow painted road and counting – and for the moment, he preferred to stay where he was, listening.

There were no more recorded voices, only a bouncy kind of music from invisible violins. While Roderick stood transfixed, they finished 'Sunshine Balloon' and began 'Oh, You Beautiful Doll'. Just in front of him, a row of beautiful dolls' heads were being crowned with hair: a blonde, a brunette, a redhead, a blonde, a brunette . . . he decided to follow the dames.

After the hair-elephant came the elephant eye-lash curler, a twist of the trunk, while another trunk sorted out a pair of matching earrings and prepared to clamp them on, another with a fine brush was poised to finish the make-up (sprayed on earlier) before the heads reached the test station where trunks probed with electrodes to raise a smile, a blink, a wink. Next came a junction where a gang of assembly Dumbos worked furiously with bolts, pliers, soldering irons, fixing each head to an armless grey torso. Following the new line he watched shapely arms appear (each hand holding its nails apart to dry; left wrists receiving watches) to be fastened on, before the entire assembly was bolted firmly to a metal frame bolted in turn to one side of a coffin-sized formica box then equipped with fake drawer-handles and finally (just as the torso-women were being stitched into their clothes) a sign: RECEPTIONIST.

Roderick watched a final test, a torso-woman lifting an

imaginary phone and saying, 'I'll *tell* him you're *here*, Mr – was that Mendozo or Mendoza? I just *know* he'll want to see you *right away* – oh, I'm *sorry*, he's in conference . . . You can go *right* in, Mr – is it Dis*nee* or Dis*nay*? Thank you sir, and *you* have a nice day *too*!'

On either side other tests were in progress. He watched a glossy cocktail waitress dressed in Victorian underwear, black stockings and garters, lower her empty tray to serve non-existent customers: 'Now who had the Black Russian? And you're the White Lady, right? Stinger for you.' Beyond her a torso-man in white seemed to be frying imaginary hamburgers: 'Yeah okay that's two with one without *and* sal, side fries *one* chicksand on white no mayo *one* poach on wholewheat no butter I got all that.' Next a dealer found a possible straight among the invisible cards upon the green baize table to which he was permanently attached, while a masseuse writhed and groaned and told the air it was one hell of a terrific lover. Elsewhere a clown juggled; a bear wearing a grin and a mortarboard recited the multiplication tables; a bearded analyst leaned back in the chair to which he was bolted, looked at the ceiling and said, 'Suppose we talk a little more about your father . . .'; a brown lifeguard murmured, 'Interesting girl like you needs a few swimming lessons'; a black shoeshine boy practised eye-rolls; and a man with an oil-can in his hand did nothing at all during the time it took Roderick to recognize him as Pa.

'. . . dedicated machines so far, but wait!' said Mr Kratt. 'Wait. Bub, I mean Doc, by the time we're ready to roll on this leisure centre of yours, we figure to have a set of good all-purpose boys and girls that'll wipe the floor with anything the competition can come up with. Like suppose you find one day you got too many girls in the sauna and not enough caddies, you just switch 'em right over – like that! – change of tapes takes maybe a minute apiece – and away they go.'

'Sounds good, sounds good.' Dr Welby allowed his glasses to slip even further down his nose, which had reddened perceptibly. 'But what about special skills . . . mechanisms . . . I mean a sauna doll has to . . .'

'But that's the point, see, all our boys and girls are gonna have everything. Everything, see? Close as we can get to the real article, and that is pretty goddamn *close*. You tell him, Ben.'

Ben stopped doodling cube-headed creatures with stick arms and legs. He sat up. 'Well, you see we're planning to bring a former colleague of mine into the R & D division. This is a guy who I guess knows more than anybody in the *world* about official – artificial intelligence. This guy is the, the *Edison of robots*. Like the Wizard of Menlo Park himself, he mainly works alone –'

'Wizard of who?' Dr Welby reached once more for the decanter. 'Look if this feller is so important, why don't you have him already?'

'He's sick, he's in the hospital. You know how some of these highly-strung geniuses are,' Ben began. 'Nervous –'

'You mean he's nuts?'

Mr Kratt grinned. 'Don't worry, Doc, he can deliver the goods. Just needs a little rest and he'll be good as new. I figure six months and we'll have him ready to roll, right Ben?'

'Right. And –'

'Look all this sounds fine, fine, your company goes steaming ahead only what's in it for me?'

'Just getting to that Doc.' Kratt flipped open a portfolio. 'Putting it on that basis, we propose a straight stock trade, share for share, for forty-nine per cent of your firm. We bear all the costs of installation and maintenance of course, you still keep control of your operation and get a piece of our action. *And* you get a seat on our board, with the usual salary and options.'

Dr Welby shook his head hard. 'What's the catch?'

'No catch. No catch at all. Only thing is Doc you're in a hell of a good position to help us out with another little product running into some snags, our Jinjur Boy talking edible, seems you were the examining physician in twelve outa these eighteen problem cases –'

'He means the eighteen who died, eighteen kids who died,' Ben said, from behind the knuckle he was gnawing.

'Oh. Oh! Well you can't expect me to do anything unprof –'

'Hear me out, let's not get excited.' Kratt's thick fingers gripped the table, and the doctor's eye was drawn to that pinball ring. 'Anybody can lose a few files, get a lapse of memory now and then . . . that's all we need.'

'What about the death certificates? Dr De'Ath did all the autopsies, he's the one found mercury in all –'

'Forget him. Time this town gets through with him, he won't be able to find mercury in his own thermometer. They got him in jail right now, attempted murder.'

'What, *him*? That's just ridiculous, some mistake – who would he ever –?'

'Some priest name of O'Bride. Housekeeper swears this De'Ath knocked him out and cut his throat.'

'Oh, *that*. Listen he told me all about it, Father O'Bride had a fall, respiratory trouble so Sam I mean Dr De'Ath performed an emergency tracheotomy –'

'Look, *I* believe you.' Kratt laughed. 'Only the old house-keeper, how do you think it looked to her? Here's the priest lying knocked out with a cut throat, here's some darky standing over him with a bloody knife – yes and she says she heard them quarrelling earlier, yelling about *blood, blood*!'

Welby gulped his drink. 'I know all about that too. Father O'Bride was trying to buy whole blood for some reason, only he wanted to get some kind of cheap imported blood without a health certificate. God knows what diseases it might be carrying, malaria, flukes, hepa –'

'Sure, sure. Thing is, this O'Bride was jobbing *our* products all over the State, begins to look like De'Ath was trying to put the bite on us, right? Little extortion? And then O'Bride wouldn't play ball . . . Like I say, time this is over, who'd believe anything De'Ath says?'

Indica looked out over a sea of new hats, fresh hair-styles, and hostile glasses. How could they hate her so much even before she'd said a word? Was it her youth? Her Western clothes? You'd think they'd never seen dreds before, or Fyre-flye false eyebrows, or a bolero cut to expose one breast – she should have dowdied down for them, too late now.

'Machines,' she began, 'are only human . . .'

Gradually the hard faces began to soften and settle into sleep.

The flowers on Violetta's hat brushed the ear of Mrs Dorano. 'Delia, I haven't got my glasses, but is that woman really *showing a bosom*?'

'I wouldn't give her the satisfaction of looking. No sense of decency.'

'No sense of shame.'

'No more sense of shame than – than Ma Wood there.' Mrs Dorano craned around to glare at her. 'A cabbage! Ma's wearing a cabbage on her hat!'

'Oh I wish I had my glasses!'

'You can see everything she's got! Right up to the armpit, I can see a little birthmark there, looks like a dumb-bell –'

But Violetta Stubbs had leaned over the other way to hear what Ma Wood was whispering:

'. . . seems a little fond of Goldwynisms if you ask me, "Clocks and watches are just a waste of time," "Cars get you nowhere" is that the way she thinks or just an affectation?'

'How do you mean?' Mrs Smith whispered back.

'There she goes again, "Electric blankets can really get on top of you." I think it must be unconscious, all this about how utility companies just want to use us, how owning a big heap of machines can be heavy . . . I mean if she wants to say we're all too dependent on machines, why not just say it? Instead of all this "Do your own dishes, give 'em a break", and how a free machine is an investment in America's future . . .'

'Shh!' said Mrs Dorano, and went on to Violetta, 'Imagine having a birthmark like that and showing it off along with everything she's got!'

'Birthmark?'

'Right under her arm there, like a little dumb-bell – what's the matter?'

Violetta Stubbs stood up and tried to push along the row of crossed legs, handbags, discarded shoes, shopping and knitting. 'I'm not well, I . . . gotta go . . .'

Too late. Indica Dinks stopped speaking to stare at her.

'Mother!'

'Son, I knew you'd figure out that cipher in about two minutes flat. So I guess by now you know everything.' Pa set the oil-can down on a reception desk.

'Pa, I didn't work out the cipher at all. I just – saw Ma doing all that witchcraft stuff down by the lake and I knew somehow she was bringing you back to life.'

'Life, ha.'

'So I knew you must be hiding out somewhere like this. Because I mean the undead –'

'Undead? Witchcraft? But son, all you had to do was turn the darn cipher upside down!'

Roderick tried to call up a mental picture of the message, turned upside down, while he watched the receptionist. She picked up the oil-can, placed it to her ear like any smiling suicide, and said, 'He'll see you in just a sec, Mr – is it Getty or Goethe?'

'Pa, maybe you'd better explain.'

'Maybe I'd better!' Pa sat down for a shoeshine and, while the eye-rolling contraption buffeted away at his bare feet, he began the story.

XXIII

To make men serfs and villeins it is indispensably necessary to make them brutes ... A servant who has been taught to write and read ceases to be any longer a passive machine.

William Godwin, *Political Justice*

'Started as a joke,' said Pa. 'Well you see right after the war everything seemed like a joke. Listen, during the war they had these cookies with chocolate on them, only they couldn't get any chocolate so they started putting brown wax on them. That seemed like a joke, you know? Here were millions of people killing each other, and they still managed to find somebody to sit painting brown wax on cookies. And Hitler was a joke. Trying to get half the world to stick its head in the oven and turn on the gas ... okay maybe it's not funny but you gotta admit it's kind of strange.

'And after the war it kept getting stranger. If anybody had a dream, no matter how stupid or futile it was, they went right out and tried to live that dream. It's as if the whole world just sat down with some crummy old pulp science fiction magazine, read it cover to cover, and then tried to live it. On the cover of that old magazine you'll see a picture of this city of the future: big glass towers, surrounded by tapeworm roads, coil after coil wound up over and under each other. And on the roads are strange-looking things that must be high-powered cars. And in the air above them, a few helicopters, and maybe the blast of a silver rocket taking off for the moon. And if you see any people they're wearing plastic clothes, and you know they live on vitamin pills and special artificial foods. Inside the magazine you find out how they live: watching television, killing their enemies with death-rays, running everything with big computers, robot servants, millions of household gadgets doing all the work, atomic power harnessed to turn the wheels of industry, jet planes zipping passengers New

309

York to Paris in a few hours – I probably left out a lot of stuff, but – but just look around you. We got it, all of it. Every glass tower, every tapeworm road, every moon rocket and computer and nuclear power station – everything in the magazine. A joke, by God, and now it's beyond a joke!'

'Well I still don't see –'

'Because just think back to the guy who wrote all this crap. Here he is, back in the forties, some poor broken-down science fiction hack. Here he sits at his broken-down L. C. Smith, cracking out his crap for a penny a word – a cheap dream, you agree? So he hammers out maybe a hundred stories a year, maybe six novels too, all just to eat and pay the rent. No and he doesn't even have enough ideas of his own to fill the quota; has to ask his wife for another giant electronic brain, another moon rocket. This guy, I mean he probably has dandruff, he's overweight, he can hardly drag himself to that oilcloth-covered kitchen table to face the L. C. Smith every day.

'And *he* created *our* world! *We* have to wear the damn plastic, eat the ice-cream substitutes, live and work in the glass towers. Just because *he* happened to write it down – imagine! What if the poor slob, what if one day he wrote *brass* instead of *glass*, would we all be living in brass towers now? It's a joke all right.'

Roderick shifted his weight to his other foot. 'I don't see how that explains –'

'Las Vegas? Disneyland? The Muse-suck in this factory? Episode Ten Thousand of *Dorinda's Destiny*? Supermarkets selling *Upboy*, a special food for geriatric dogs? Electric acupuncture? Talking gingerbread? Believe me, it explains everything. Every blessed damned thing. Uh, let's go outside. I don't think I can take any more of it here, with that receptionist pouring oil down her nice new dress . . .'

They made their way along the yellow road to the entrance, through the security room (where Roderick's possessions came back to him), past the docile dogs and out at the gate. Pa sat in the grass and contemplated his oxblood feet, or perhaps only the lights of town beyond them.

'We killed him in 1950. We killed him with a death-ray, and blew up his old L. C. Smith with an H-bomb. That poor old hack was right in the middle of another crappy story, still behind with the rent, and we killed him.'

'I don't get you, Pa.'

'Let me put it another way. One day in 1950 he's hammering away at the keys, still spelling it *glass* instead of *brass*, while his wife is stalling the landlady and maybe trying to work out some new way of combining canned tomatoes, ground beef and elbow macaroni. The next day, they're both dead. The police will find two little piles of clothes on the shores of Lake Michigan. One pile is weighted down with the L. C. Smith. And a note, got to have a note, double-spaced with wide margins . . .'

'You mean you changed your names and moved to Newer?'

'Son, we changed everything. We became Paul and Mary Wood. We dropped everything from the old life – all we brought along were a few pulp magazines with our stories. We changed our personalities – that looks like Doc Welby's car.'

Roderick looked up to see the lights of a strange, high-powered car moving away from the executive gate of Slumbertite, off down the tapeworm to town. 'I wonder what he was doing up here?'

'Anyway, now you know most of our story. See we thought we could maybe make up for it if we could just have a kid, kids. Somehow we couldn't, no matter how much we kissed and cuddled . . . Anyway that's why one year we fostered a nice little boy called Danny Sonnenschein.'

'Dan Sonnenschein!'

'Same guy, yup. Trouble was, he got up in the attic one day, got into these old pulp magazines. Before you knew it, he'd gone and read a story of ours. We called it, "I, Robot".'

Roderick tried to look at him, but Pa's face was in shadow. 'You mean you were Isaac Asimov?'

'Nope. And we weren't Eando Binder, either. Nor anybody else who wrote "I, Robot". Believe me, nobody ever heard of us, nobody even remembers the name of that pulp magazine.

'Yes it was our story little Danny picked on, that twisted him some way – I don't know, set him to dreaming or – well. You know the rest. Next time we heard from Danny he was grown up, he'd invented you, and he was in trouble.'

'Is that how I came to stay here?'

'Yep, another mistake. See, son, we hoped we could still change the world back, undo some of our damage, take back our terrible joke. Through you. If only we could make you learn how to be human . . .

'So what we did, first we burned the old pulp magazines. Then we tried to teach you everything we knew about life. Like I said, a mistake.'

'Pa, I don't see it was such a mis –'

'Because we knew nothing. Nothing at all. Few scraps of logic, a song, coupla half-assed ideas about art . . . a joke or two . . .'

Roderick felt compelled to protest again. 'Pa, I think you and Ma haven't done such a bad job. Heck, you only had a robot to begin with.'

'A joke or two. Another mistake we made was money. Spent all we had and a whole lot we didn't have yet. Then a whole lot we never would have. We cut a few corners – well hell, we stole. *I* stole. And when it began to look as if the law was catching up with us, with *me*, I had to die. Because if they finger-printed me, they'd find out who I was, and there we'd be, right back in the middle of that terrible joke again. You see? You see, son?'

Roderick scratched his head. 'Sure okay, but what about the syphilis?'

'Syphilis? Nobody said anything about –'

'Right here in your cipher, Pa. "P wood in soup (syph) so now possum numb mummy hypno-bound & shun mob!!!" I mean you can't make it plainer than that, and later on there's something about pox, too, that's –'

'Let me see that, where –?' Pa snatched the paper and held it up to the light of slumbertite never sleeps. 'Pox that's nothing, just the words of the song, you don't want to pay no attention to that. It says Bow wow too, but that don't mean I got fleas.'

'Okay but –'

'But this syph – well that is just your Ma's bad spelling, the word is supposed to be sylph. Your Ma never could spell.'

'Sylph? How can you be in the soup with a sylph?'

'Not *with*, son. Like I said, your Ma never could spell, never should of been a writer. *Sylph* was a poor word for woman anyway.'

Roderick gasped. 'The wedding picture, that's what was wrong with it. *Pa, you were the bride! Ma was the groom!*'

'Well it's no reason to break into italics, son. Like I said, it all started off as a joke, just trading clothes now and then – son? You all right?'

Ben was packing up the papers.

'No hurry, Benny, pour us another drink.' Mr Kratt bit the end from a cheap cigar and settled back. 'Goddamn trip was worth it, eh bub? Yes sir, Welby's our boy. De'Ath better be our boy too, if he knows what's good for him. Yes sir, a productive damn trip. We oughta lock this one up in a month or so, kick a few asses in our so-called lobby down in Lincoln, don't see why we can't be showing a profit this time next year on this little enterprise. You know bub, times like this makes me feel goddamn good.'

'Yes sir.' Ben was noticing, not for the first time, the large white square teeth of his employer. They always reminded him of a row of tombstones, and now . . .

'What the hell's wrong with you?'

'I just . . . wish you wouldn't grin like that sir, no offence, but –'

'Grin if I goddamnit grin if I want to, hell we just made a *killing* here you want me to look sad about it?'

'No sir but, just thinking of those kids, those dead –'

'Death certificates, damn it didn't I tell you not to worry? We'll beat that, sure it's a pain in the ass but we'll beat that. Nothing's gonna stop us, bub, because nothing *can* stop us, we're on the move.' He grinned again, lighting the cigar. 'And sure I feel good. Hell, here I am fighting on the last frontier in the fucking world. And *winning*, sure I feel good.'

'Winning.'

'Because that's what business is, bub, the last frontier. The last place where you can still take hold of the world and change it, make it – make it –'

'Make it in your own image?'

'Better, I was going to say. Make it what you want. See everyone else, the world is just something that happens to them, might as well be watching it on TV, right? But for me the world is something you – something you can *get*. Sure it's risky. You gotta fight. You need guts and luck and, and imagination. But hell, isn't it worth it? Just tell me that, isn't it worth it?'

'Yes sir.' Ben found a TV set behind a panel and, after staring for a moment at his dark reflection in the screen, turned it on. It was going to be a long evening. Once Mr Kratt had a few drinks and started talking about the last frontier . . .

'Why shouldn't I feel good? Whole damn business is devoted to one thing, you know? One thing: giving people pleasure. Giving people pleasure. So why shouldn't I get some pleasure too . . .?'

The TAPE button brought a canned promotion for the factory: *'Our advanced integrated control system is continuously optimized by real-time goal-seeking —'* while rows of robot receptionists trundled along with their desks, *'— routines implemented throughout a hierarchy of processors to attack such performance-characteristic problems as the utilization of modified control algorithms —'* each Roberta the Receptionist wearing more false hair than the automaton chess-playing Turk could have concealed beneath his ample turban. The Turk too had been seated behind a desk (when the Baron von Kempelen first exhibited him in Vienna, shortly before the American Revolution). And his desk had been a necessity, since it concealed that most perfect of chess-playing mechanisms (together with its lunch and piss-pot).

'— including diagnostic programmes and multi-level alarms and interrupts, debugging and redistribution of modifications within each software sub-package —'

'. . . because damnit, pleasure is our business, always meant to make that the group slogan, pleasure is our business. Greatest pleasure for the greatest number . . .'

Ben nodded agreement and changed channels, stabbing a button at random. Seemed to be something about the French Revolution, torches, billhooks and the laughter of toothless hags.

'— on both a local and a global level, evaluating each task via sophisticated assessment procedures and providing next-level feedback from supervisory processors. Feasibility analysis, an integral part of each task, is similarly —'

Back to the mob scene, what was it, *Tale of Two Cities*? Probably get a shot of Madame DeFarge any minute now, knitting shrouds . . . funny thing was, the real revolution was going on all the time behind the scenes, the Jacquard loom with its punched cards weaving a new pattern, clicking away, a far far better thing it did than anyone had ever done . . . burial shrouds for human thought, maybe, but very good burial shrouds.

Or was it a different mob scene? The camera zoomed in on

314

faces by torchlight, not at all the faces of Jacques One and Jacques Two and Madame DeFarge, but the faces of men with good teeth, men wearing sweatshirts and golf caps, windbreakers and glasses, baseball caps and twill, crewcuts and army fatigues . . .

'Mr Kratt? Sir?'

The camera pulled back again, to show a security fence, and a German Shepherd snapping at a moth.

'Listen, Mr Kratt?'

'No, *you* listen, trying to tell you something damn important.'

'But listen, there's a mob heading —'

'Sure, sure, now just you turn that thing off and pay attention. Bub, you know what my dream is?'

'No sir.'

'You know what it is?'

'No sir.'

'You know —? I'll tell you what my dream is. What I'd like to see is, KUR Industries having the world franchise, see —'

'Yes, sir, now couldn't we —?'

'The *world* franchise, *exclusive*, on pleasure. Datajoy! What we'd have is like a wire running right into everybody's head, right into the old pleasure centre. Datajoy! And as long as they pay their lease, we give 'em all the juice they want, see? Datajoy, call it —'

'Yes Mr Kratt, now —'

'And by God if they don't pay, we rip that wire right outa their head! Haha, whatya think a that? Hey? Whatya — leggo my arm, what the hell here?'

'We've got to leave, sir. Now. There's a mob on the way with torches — I don't know, maybe the parents of those kids we — those kids who — I don't know who they are!'

When they had left, the room showed little sign of human occupation. A few chairs out of line, an empty decanter, three glasses on the long table (in one, the faecaloid stub of a cheap cigar floated in fine old Scotch). The cleaning-machines waited a precise number of minutes, then went to work.

'It's me they want,' said Pa. 'But they'll have to come in and get me.'

'Pa, I mean Ma'am, maybe they just want to burn the factory down, you know like the old house in *Franken* —'

'No, it's me. But at least I can choose to make my last stand, among all the wonderful guys and dolls, Roberta the Receptionist, Bert the Bartender, all the only true friends I ever had. Bye, son.'

'Wait, Pa. I wanted to ask you –' But she was gone.

Close up, the mob looked as good as anything in *Frankenstein*. Roderick spotted pitchforks, axes, garden rakes and electric lawn-edgers as well as rifles, ropes, torches. Dr Smith the dentist seemed to be unarmed until he got close enough for Roderick to see him wield a tiny dental hook.

Doc Smith was not a well man. Later on, when they got around to hanging Roderick, he would try to insist they use his patent dental floss.

XXIV

It was the best of time, it was the worst of time. Choose one

The pigeon hesitated before the two windows, trying to get it right this time. Finally it pecked the left-hand window. Almost immediately the window lit up, and a tiny feed pellet rattled down into the magic cup. From the pigeon's point of view it was a triumph of the righteous: yea, God doth reward those who keep His commandments and His rites. Before the next trial, the pigeon worshipped, stepping three times to the left, twice to the right, and lifting its head in turn towards each of the four upper corners of its prison. The pigeon was not aware of the computer.

From the computer's point of view, the cycle had brought a special instruction into force. It knew only that it had generated the pseudo-random digit o, and that this matched the input o (from the Skinner box). The instruction therefore was to add 1 to the number T (trials), add one to the number H (hits) and calculate P (probability). The computer was aware neither of the pigeon nor of Dr Tarr.

Dr Tarr sat in his new office watching the printer. From his point of view, the test was on the whole a qualified success. Pigeons were precognitive.

Or at least this pigeon, now and then, seemed uncannily able to peer a split-second into the future, determine which plastic window (of a randomly-selected pair) would deliver the goods, and peck that window. Now and then.

Now and then, that was the trouble. Not enough hits, not near enough to convince those Dr Tarr needed to convince. There was NASA, first of all, paying $150,000 towards his expenses; expecting results. Likewise the University, providing not only computer time, but an empty office and lab in the Computer Sciences building. And how about the parapsychology journals, the professional associations waiting for the paper that could make him, career-wise? Finally of course the professional sceptics: he saw them as hyenas, forever trailing the herd of parapsychologists, forever waiting for some weak individual to fall behind. Ready, yes ready to bury their bloodstained snouts in his entrails . . .

More hits, damn you! he willed at the bird, *more hits!* Unaware of his telepathic command from the office, the creature in the laboratory preened, digging its beak deep in iridescent neck feathers to chew at a parasite. For the moment, it was aware of nothing else, not even of the cruelly erratic God it had learned to love.

Tarr, acutely aware of his own predicament (for not since Mary of Nazareth had anyone risked so much on the behaviour of a single pigeon) turned to the printer, whose ultimate line still read:

$$\text{TRIALS} = 980 \text{ HITS} = 502 \text{ } P < 0.444$$

Computer error? Sure, damn thing probably wasn't working at all! Poor pigeon probably pecking away, hit after hit and nothing coming through. He examined the cable running from the computer to the printer, experimentally unplugged it and plugged it in again.

$$\text{TRIALS} = 981 \text{ HITS} = 503 \text{ } P < 0.425$$

More like it. More like it! Funny how it (he repeated the operation) clocked up a hit every time you jiggled the . . . you could almost . . . not quite ethical maybe but . . . well, just to enhance the figures a little, to emphasize what we already know . . .

$$\text{TRIALS} = 1126 \text{ HITS} = 648 \text{ } P < 0.0000000406$$

The score was getting *too* sensational, time to stop, but Tarr kept on, tickling just one more reward from the printer, just one more. Had God at that moment been a Skinnerian psychologist, peering in through the office ceiling, He'd have been pleased to recognize His guilty creature here crouched at its task. Working along its reinforcement schedule. 'Learning', if not growing wise.

No one was peering in. He looked over his shoulder at the door at nothing, no one, nothing but the door itself, newly painted to hide some old stain that showed through nevertheless, a shadow like a clutching hand.

The mob was making so much noise so many almost city noises Roderick could hardly hear men leaning together like glass buildings falling over follow a skeleton to Junior's Discount Cameras God call him up every time lousy jackpot blade heavy split up when electric .38 for LAW & ORDER raping housekeepers nigger priest bites dog pills bustup treats me like shit .38 bike overtime MASSAGE THERAPY dolls of Devil's Island escape from jail and bust into factory Lewd-ite revenge calling for a rope unless we all go back to the Idle Hour boys have a beer and talk it God fight city hall needles bitch freak t-shirt no shit the Klan? What Klan?

'Klan, shit, we'll be our own Klan!'

'What?' Another man seemed shocked. 'Take the Klan into our own hands?'

'I'm serious now Jake, I'll be the Kladd, you be the Kludd, let old Carl there be the Grand Goblin.'

'Goblin? That sounds dumb as hell, you know?'

'Sure does. Forget all that Klan shit, let's just teach this motherfucker a *lesson*!'

'Why can't I be the Imperial Wizard, though?'

'Will you listen to that? Will you I mean listen-to-*that*?'

'We gonna hang somebody or what? How about that nigger in the jail? How about him?'

'Busted out didn't he?'

'Hell he did. He –'

'Yeah but listen, I wanta be the Wizard or I don't be nothing.'

'If he's still in jail who the hell raped them women at the Meeting Hall? I heard –'

'Bullshit man, they ain't raped they just got excited.'

'– perial Wizard, goddamnit is anybody listening to me?'

'Piss on all this, I'm going to the Idle Hour.'

This seemed a good idea to others, and indeed the whole mob made its way – arguing, shoving Roderick almost as much as they shoved one another – towards Main Street.

'No but seriously if you're gonna form a Klan Klavern you –'

'Will you listen to that? Will-you –?'

'Yeah see Miss Violetta Stubbs they found out she's got a kid!'

'Aw Jesus doesn't that make you sick? Nice old lady like that raped by a black –'

'No listen –'

'I say we hang the bastard right here in front of the Idle Hour. I say we teach him a *lesson*!'

'Piss on that I'm going –'

And in a moment, they were all gone, leaving Roderick alone in the street. Immediately the sheriff's car drew up, flashing all its lights: red, blue, green, tangerine, ochre and plum.

'Get in, Wood. I'm taking you in – for your own protection. No, in the back.'

Roderick climbed into the cage in the back, and allowed the sheriff to drive him the thirteen yards to jail.

'County's too damn busy, you know?' Sheriff Benson led him inside and snapped on the handcuffs. 'Like we had a riot earlier at the Meeting Hall, Mrs Dorano trying to throw rocks at Miss Violetta, can you beat that? And now this. Hell I didn't hardly get time to see *Hollywood Squares*, hell of an evening.' He kicked Roderick into a cell, hauled out a blackjack and began beating him carelessly around the face.

'Ouch! Look is this – ow, this for my own protec – ouch! My own protection? Because I, ouch, you take off these cuffs I could protect myself . . .'

'What?' The sheriff had not been looking at his victim, but through the open door at the TV in his office. Someone was trying to name nine brands of beer in thirty seconds. Sheriff Benson looked at the weapon in his hand. 'Sorry, son. Just gets to be a habit, I guess.' Slamming the cell door, he added, 'Hope I can still count on your support come election day?'

Roderick was not surprised to find a black man in the next cell, even though the man was not wearing faded overalls nor playing a harmonica.

'Hi man. My name's Roderick Wood. What's yours?' Ignoring him, the man continued taking his own temperature. 'I'm in protective custody. For my own good. What are you in for? Oh, I hope you don't find this paint on my face offensive. No insult intended, man. See what it is is mourning. See my Pa died – he's not really my Pa, in fact he's not really anybody's Pa, he's a woman. Only I didn't know that, when he looked at this gas bill for a million dollars and just keeled over. Only now I find out he's not dead and he's not a he either. Now he lives I mean she lives in the factory. So when I thought Ma, who really isn't a woman either she's a man who used to write science fiction that all came true, I thought she was doing witchcraft but it was only scientific stuff to revive Pa. Boy was that ever a shock! I mean last time I had a shock like that was when these gipsies kidnapped me and sold me to this carnival where I was supposed to tell fortunes. Duking, they called it. You know that was about the only time I ever went out of town anyways, oh except when Ma and me went to the city to get me a new eye, this burned-out store only when she left me there I got pretty scared because here was this same carny guy with a pinball on his finger, wouldn't you be scared? And I didn't find Ma again until later when I was in one of these two limousines that crashed into a art gallery –'

'Really?' The man held the thermometer up to the light. 'Been seeing a lot of movies have you, sport?'

'I used to watch them on TV a lot, when I was living with these people in Nevada I think it was only the guy beat me up with a hammer –'

'Subnormal. As usual. Still say I'm coming down with something, maybe that virus thing that's going around . . . I don't know . . . "Physician, heal thyself" – Ha! If I could heal myself I wouldn't be a physician, I'd be a miracle worker. The name is De'Ath, by the way. Dr Samuel De'Ath.'

'Pleased to meet you. I'm Roderick Wo –'

'Yeah I heard you. A robot trying to break into the movies. Do me a favour, will you, look at my throat? Can you manage the light and the tongue depressor with those cuffs . . . Good. Now I say Ah . . . see anything?'

'It's all pink! I thought it would be, well more –'

'Pink hell, is it *red*? That is the sixty-four-thousand-dollar question!'

The sheriff's head appeared around the door. 'Did I hear somebody mention the good old sixty-four-thousand-dollar question? Used to be my favourite, doggone it, with the old isolation booth and the – No? Don't neither of you boys like game shows? If you do, speak up – I can always bring the TV in here and let you watch with me. Just let me know.' The head vanished.

'It's not red, Doc.'

'Funny, it feels . . . and my pulse is slightly elevated too . . . I wonder . . .'

'Doc, do you think that mob will break in here and drag us out and hang us?'

But by now the doctor was listening to his own heart. 'I know I ought to get out more, jog a little, get plenty of exercise. But somehow . . . last time I went out was with this priest, Father O'Bride, kept calling me a natural until I started missing easy shots, you know? Guy's kinda weird anyway, kept telling me about this idea of his for a fourteen-hole golf course with every hole a Station of the Cross – what do you mean, *hang us?*'

'Well you know, hang us.'

'Not a chance. You've been seeing too many movies again, sport. *Old* movies. People just don't hang people any more. A necktie party in modern dress? A lynching in the post-literate electronic age, the global village? Klan vengeance, in these days of low-lipid diets and consumer awareness? String us up, just when civilization is hitting its stride with, with male contraceptive pills and Mickey Mouse telephones? With giggling gingerbread and soul-searching politicians and reconstituted gratification? Not a chance, sport.'

After a moment, he added, 'What an admission of failure! To turn their backs on, on the great American menu of therapies, and just go sneaking off in the night with a rope – impossible!'

After another moment, 'Improbable, anyway.'

Roderick said, 'I just hope when they come for us, Sheriff Benson will get out there with a shotgun on the front steps and tell them all about, uh, justice, uh, how the foundering fathers brought forth a nation where liberty and just –'

'I'd rather not discuss it any more, okay? God, it isn't as if I haven't got enough to worry about! Heading for a major health crisis just when I need all my strength for a long court battle over this gingerbread business, not to mention this little smear campaign, trying to discredit me before I blow the whistle on their dirty little operation.'

'Who?'

'Kratt Enterprises, that's who. Or I guess they now call it KUR Industries, might as well call it Mass Poisoners Incorporated, what with their – well I'd better not talk about it off the record, but their day is coming.'

'You mean they made the gingerbread boys that made all those kids sick?'

'Yeah, and just wait. This is just the chance I needed, to carve out a reputation in the public service, lay down a solid career foundation –'

'Not to mention saving a lot more kids from   '

'Sure that too, but from there I could springboard right into some prestigious drug firm, they're always on the look-out for young crusaders, names that look good on the letter-head – and let's face it, integrity is all I've got to sell.'

Roderick scratched his head. 'But wouldn't it be better if you kept finding out about mass poisoners and helped save other –?'

The door banged open and Sheriff Benson came in, dragging the TV set. 'Hate to think of you boys sitting in here with nothing to do, so I thought I'd come in here and let you watch the shows with me. Anyways that mob out front is making too much racket, I can't hardly hear the questions.'

They watched *The Big Score, Ripoff, Pick a Winner, Two for the Top, Lucky Break, Pile It Up, Family Spree, Play or Pay, Big Bingo, Make or Break, Guess It Rich, Spoil Yourself, Great Expectations, Gold or Fold, Grab Bag* and *Money Talks*, and during the commercial breaks the sheriff described other games.

'Too bad you boys missed that new one, *Double Your Social Security Check*. Real good, see, they get these old folks to put their check in this glass box, then they gotta answer three questions. Well see they might be easy ones like name a pro football linebacker with two Z's in his name, you know? Other times they get trickier, like name five countries in Europe – anyway see, every time the old codger gets a right answer, they put another check in the box, keep on doubling up see? But if they *miss* one –' The sheriff's chair creaked with laughter, 'The damn check burns up in the box, right before their eyes! Boy O boy, there was one old guy – oops, they're back –'

The TV figure welcomed them back to the next round of

Money Talks. 'Well, Mrs Pearson? Will YOU talk for money? Will YOU step into our special Acorn United Company bank vault, filled with ONE MILLION crisp new dollar bills, and talk for *five minutes?*'

'This ain't no good,' said the sheriff, touching a button. 'We'll try *Take the Plunge.*'

'. . . member, if you push the *right* button, you'll be able to Take the Plunge right into our gold-plated swimming pool, filled to the brim with shiny new silver dollars. You could just dive in and keep every dollar you throw up, okay? How's that sound, eh? Good? Great! Now, that's if you push the *right* button. If you push the *wrong* button, Doris, the pool might be filled with something . . . we-e-ell . . . *not* so nice. MOLASSES, for instance? Ha ha ha, or maybe JELLO? Or how about DIRTY SOCKS? Okay then, here goes . . .'

Roderick watched the poor woman on the screen, her face slack but smiling. Almost like a dog waiting for a kick, hoping for a pat. She pushed the button and the great gold *lamé* curtains swished open to show a swimming pool filled with –

'TYRES!' screamed the MC over audience laughter. 'Oh my goodness, TYRES! That's right, Doris, you have just won a plunge into this pool filled with old rubber tyres! Ah ha ha, and you – ha ha – yes you can keep every one you throw up –'

Suddenly the entire brilliant studio, with the purple walls, gold curtains, the MC in his scarlet coat and the contestant's green face, shrank to a dot and vanished. The plug had been kicked out of its socket by one of the stumbling men, each wearing a pillowcase over his head, coming for the prisoners.

The tall building of rusty corrugated iron was Bangfield's Grain Elevator, just one of the forgotten buildings at the forgotten end of town. A few cars and pickups had been parked to shine their headlights on the action: a rope being passed over a pulley and tied into a noose.

'I guess they mean it,' said Dr De'Ath. 'I just hope they've got enough sense to do this right. They ought to drop us from enough height to fracture the fourth cervical vertebra, a quick snap and we're finished.'

'Sure.' All Roderick could think of was getting out of it,

somehow, working some brilliant psychological trick that would make the pillow-heads give up.

'Listen fellows,' he said. 'Our foundering fathers brought –'

'Shut up, will you?' said a head with a border of marigolds. Another, in a pillowcase dotted with fleur-de-lis grabbed Dr De'Ath and shoved him towards the noose.

'Hold on, we're not ready yet,' said a pillowcase edged with the Campbell tartan. 'Keep him back there.'

'Snap,' said Dr De'Ath bitterly. 'Not a chance with these yahoos. They'll probably give us slow asphyxiation by ligatation, fracturing the hyoid so we end up with our tongues sticking out and messing our pants. Talk about an admission of failure! And loose bowels are one thing I haven't been troubled with lately, kind of ironic . . .'

'I was just wondering if my whole life would flash before me,' Roderick muttered. 'I mean my *whole* life. Because if it did, there'd have to be a moment when I relived the present moment, wouldn't there? When I started reliving my whole life again? And in that life I'd get to the same moment, and start reliving –'

'Just shut up, will you?' said the marigolds. 'Why make this any tougher than it is? Just relax.'

'Relax?' Dr De'Ath chortled. 'I've got a migraine now, on top of everything else, this yahoo wants me to *relax*.'

'All set,' the tartan called out.

Dr De'Ath said, 'Look Rod, how about you going first? See I'd like to try a little gargle first – oh I know it sounds silly, but I really hate to die without at least trying to clear up this sore throat of mine – okay?'

'Okay.' Roderick stepped forward and turned to face the lights. Someone slipped a noose over his head. He saw a pillowcase printed with sea-horses, read the tag on its hem: *hand-hot wash, drip-dry, do not spin*. Will this be my last memory? No, better to try thinking of something interesting, how about the paradox of the unexpected hanging?

A judge tells a man he'll be hanged one day next week, but not on any day he's expecting it. The man reasons that he cannot be hanged on the Saturday, since he'd certainly expect it if he survived the other six days. So the hanging had to happen between Sunday and Friday. But then it couldn't be Friday, either, by the same reasoning. That left Sunday till Thursday, only in that case Thursday too was out. And so on, until he eliminated every day but Sunday. So he expected to be hanged on Sunday. So he couldn't be hanged on Sunday. So he couldn't be hanged at all!

Roderick felt pain in his neck as he was hoisted aloft. Looking down, he could see the whole miserable little crowd of pillowheads, the parked cars beyond them, and further. There was Ma, lurking in the background and biting his nails. There was the limousine that had been parked up at the factory, now it was stopping in a shadow while the chauffeur got out and – what was he doing – taking pictures.

The pain got sharper, and Roderick thought he heard a rivet shearing in his neck. Better finish:

. . . couldn't be hanged at all! So the man thought, being perfectly logical. So he wasn't expecting it the day they hanged him . . .

'Jus' one more picture, boss?' said the chauffeur. 'Cause I know the kids would love to see –'

'Get back in the car. Now!' Ben Franklin pushed the snoring weight of Mr Kratt off his shoulder and leaned forward. 'If you don't get back behind that wheel right now, I'll have you *fired*.'

The chauffeur shrugged, folded his camera and climbed in. ''Kay, take it easy. Maybe you seen a lot of lynchin's, I ain't.'

Ben looked at the sleeping figure. It had stopped snoring and was now muttering, 'Pleassssure. Pleassssure.'

'Just start the car and drive.'

'You crazy? Through that buncha –'

'Then turn around and drive the other way, let's just get out of here.'

'Yeah but like I said we can't go nowhere this way, like I said when we come off at the wrong exit – didn't I tell you it was the wrong exit? – all we can do now is stay on this here highway 811 until we hit the old Interstate and then cut back –'

'All right, just – just a minute, let me think.'

'Some thinker,' said the chauffeur, lighting a hand-rolled cigarette. 'Look buddy we're stuck here, why doncha just sit back and watch the show?'

'*Show?* Is that all it is to you, a show? You don't care do you, people committing murder – like *that*? It's just something on TV, that it?'

'Look, no offence, manner of speakin', okay? Okay? I'm entitled to my opinion too, you know, it's a free fuckin' country.'

'All right, all –'

'Just because I work for a livin' don't mean I'm shit, okay?'

'*All right!*'

'Okay, just wanted to get that straight.' The chauffeur twitched his shoulders, shrugging off any yoke of oppression Ben might care to impose, and sat forward: a free man in a free country, watching a free show.

Ben reached for the phone, hesitated, gnawed his knuckles for a while, and finally tried waking Mr Kratt.

'Wha? Whoza?'

'There's a lynching going on, sir. Right over there. Shouldn't we – call the highway patrol?'

'Outa your head, bub. Word gets out I'm nosing around down here we'll have every yak-head in the State tryina buy in on this land deal. Jesus, might as well take a full-page ad in the paper, announce a gold rush – use your head, for Christ's –' and he was asleep again.

Ben looked away from the execution into darkness. Toys. A show. Revenge of the common man upon the common object, wasn't that it? Because it wouldn't do, it had never done, to think of the object of their cruelty as fully human. So the effigy created by Albertus Magnus (smashed down by Aquinas) turns up as Friar Bacon's talking head (to be smashed by a servant) and again as the automaton of Descartes ('ma fille Francine', flung into the sea by yet another fearful soul) even while dummies of Guido Fawkes began to burn in the streets of London for the pleasure of children. Common children, always more ready than even their parents to punish the presumption of a servant.

Well yes, he might work that up into an article, why not? *The Common Man and His Image*? 'Fascination with clockwork in the 17th cent. coincides with idea of commonwealth, all part of same big movement,' he wrote, turning the notebook to the light. 'Clock explained all, from Newton's heaven to Malynes's laws of economics – Huygens creating clockwork artisans for the King of

327

France even while (after?) Mechanic Philosophers promoted a new democratic religion among the living artisans. Groups naming themselves by function – Quakers, Shakers, Ranters, Diggers, Levellers – as though describing their work within the great timepiece.' What was the point of all this? What was it?

'Christ,' said the chauffeur. 'Christ! Looka that.'

'Shut up, will you?'

'Who you tellin' to shut up, listen fuckhead, I –'

'Sorry. *Sorry.*' Revolution, that was the point. 'Jacquard loom working a genuine revolution behind the scenes – Mme DeF. – In 1791 (?) Godwin wrote: "A servant who –"' What was the quote? While he waited for it, the chauffeur said:

'Hey look, uh, Mr Frankelin, I think we got trouble with the right rear tyre, hey?'

'What?'

'Right rear tyre, I think it's down. Your side, you mind gettin' out and look at it?'

Still frowning at the notebook he climbed out.

'Have a nice night, Mr Frankelin.'

'What? Oh – hey what –?'

And he hardly heard the screams ('God! His head come off!') so intent was he suddenly on the sound of the automatic door-closer, the click of the automatic lock, the sight of the chauffeur giving him the finger as the limousine glided away into the night.

XXV

Yet the old myth dies hard. We are still tempted to argue that if the
clown's antics exhibit carefulness, judgement, wit, and appreciation
of the moods of his spectators, there must be occurring in the
clown's head a counterpart performance to that which is taking
place on the sawdust. If he is thinking what he is doing, there must
be occurring behind his painted face a cognitive shadow-operation
which we do not witness, tallying with, and controlling, the bodily
contortions which we do witness.

Gilbert Ryle, *The Concept of Mind*

One record finished, and in the interval a shrill voice said: 'Well
we're practically related. My ex married his ex's first husband's
widow – only I guess they split up lass week . . .'

One of the groom's coarse cousins, naturally; there was relief
among the bride's friends when the disc-jockey slipped another
record into the silence.

One or two couples started dancing on the patio; Allbright and
Dora waltzed smoothly into the library and out again, their
steps not noticeably slowed by the added weight of several first
editions.

'Hey Allbright!' It was Lyle Tate, keeping his birthmark in
shadow as he came past the disc-jockey's glass booth. 'Jeez, and
Dora – you two are the only people I know here. Who is this
mob? Who is everybody?'

Allbright shrugged, shifting books. 'Everybody.'

'No but I mean Jane Hannah's not here, Jack Tarr's not
here –'

'Tarr? I thought you hated his guts.'

'Yeah but only when he was around. Guess he hasn't got the
guts to go anywhere today, there's a story going around that he's
been cheating on some psychic research stuff. They say he got a
pigeon to be clairvoyant something like a hundred times, pushing
the right button in a Skinner box, you know? A hundred times.

Only trouble was the pigeon was dead at the time, biggest damn miracle since Lazarus − speaking of which, Allbright you don't look so great. What's that, dried blood on your face, bruises or dirt?'

'We fall over from time to time,' Allbright said. 'We fall. One of the privileges of the C-charged brain . . .'

'We? You mean −?' Lyle looked to Dora, who nodded.

'Rodin,' said a shrill voice somewhere. 'Yas yas yas.'

Dora said, 'I guess I'm doomed anyway. Might as well go down the toilet with Allbright as by myself.'

'Doomed, what do you mean doomed? Down the −?'

'We're all doomed,' said Allbright. 'Jesus it's obvious enough; everybody goes around worrying about machines taking over, shit, they took over long ago, isn't that obvious?'

'But no, listen, what happened to your plan for −?'

'Between computer poetry and vibrator love people don't get a hell of a lot of room to manoeuvre, isn't that obvious?'

'No but your plan for ripping off bank computers, what happened to that? You said a friend in the nut-house steered you −'

'The steersman, yes, aren't we all − but you mean Dan, good old Dan. Well you know I went back to see him, tell him how great it was after they fry your brains, burn out a few pink and blue lights you feel a lot better. I did, I know. I did. I felt better. Not stupider, just happier, that's what I told him.

'Only for him it wasn't like that. They had to burn out more pink and blue lights I guess. Jesus they fried him right back into diapers. I mean, whatever lights he had going for him, they sure as hell went out for good.'

Someone proposed a toast to the happy couple; Jim and the Dean of Persons looked pleased and bashful. The toast was only slightly marred by a shrill voice saying, 'Yas, Rodin. Don't you just love his Thinker?'

Lyle said, 'Maybe he'll get better, though. He won't stay in diapers −'

'Oh, he's better already. They let him out weekends to work his job, even. Fact he's right over there in that glass box, our esteemed disc-jockey.'

'No kidding? That's good, isn't it? He can −'

330

'He can find the hole in the middle of each record, sure. He can even talk, you notice? Every now and then he says, "Here's another record."'

XXVI

Roderick awoke in jail again, watching Sheriff Benson watch *Top Dollar*. Dr De'Ath was sitting in a captain's chair watching him. Ma was sitting in another watching everything.

'I wouldn't have believed it,' said the doctor. 'Really amazing. Course, I nearly flunked medical electronics myself, never could learn to make a good solder joint – but this is really amazing. Mind if I test him?'

'Ask him,' Ma said. 'Son, how are you?'

'Fine I guess.' Roderick allowed the doctor to look into his eyes and ears, to tap his knee and hold up fingers for him to count. 'Guess you're okay too, Doc?'

'Shh!' said the Sheriff. 'Just gettin' to the end of *The Marriage Stakes*. Already missed *Big Spender* and *Heap or Weep*.' When the commercial break came on, Dr De'Ath explained:

'Pretty lucky there. After they hanged you some of the boys got so excited – well, Jake McIlvaney shot himself in the foot. You know how Doc Welby is about coming out on call, so they had to let me take care of him. Got him in an intensive care unit now, over at Buford.'

'Intensive care?'

'Yup, and there he stays until he runs up a nice fat bill. Anyway I fooled around with him until the highway patrol came and broke things up.'

'*Lay it on the Line* is next,' the sheriff explained. 'But on Channel 18 they got *Big Game*, followed by *Grabopoly*. Kind of a hard choice there.'

'They probably wouldn't have done anything to me anyway,' said the doctor, when he had swallowed a handful of bright pills. 'Nope, not after you. Kinda put them off the whole idea, seeing your head come off like that.'

'My head came off?'

Ma nodded. 'I managed to get you home and fixed up.'

De'Ath said, 'Amazing work. Boy if I could do that for a real patient – well, some day. Your Ma is a wonder, boy.'

Ma cleared his throat. 'I did have some help. Er, asked one of the maintenance men from the factory to give me a hand with the tricky parts.' He held up a mirror for Roderick. 'What do you think?'

'Fine.'

'Fine, is that all?'

'Well it's – very symmetrical – aw heck, Ma, you know I don't know how to talk about art. It's – it's a very symmetrical head. I like it fine.'

They sat and talked as the sky beyond the Venetian blinds began to turn grey, then orange, and as the sheriff watched *Beat the House, Chance in a Million, Take the Spoils, Up for Grabs* and *Cash or Crash.*

'Guess I'll drive over to Buford and see my patient,' said the doctor, after taking his own blood-pressure. 'On my way home, anyway.'

'You're leaving?'

'Got everything I need, now. Airtight case against Katrat Fun Foods. Well. Uh, good luck, boy.' He offered Roderick his hand.

'Good luck to you too, Doctor.'

'I'm glad I did that, shook your hand. You know?'

Roderick didn't know.

'Well it's just that I – last night when your head came off and I saw all the wires – I was really pissed off. The idea of being strung up in the company of a sonofabitching *machine* – I mean it just seemed like adding a last insult to a last – you know?'

Roderick nodded, feeling stiffness in his new neck. 'That's okay. See I'm not so crazy about human beings, either. But good luck anyway, Doc.'

'Wish you boys would pipe down,' said Benson. 'This here is the one I been waiting for, *Bust the Bank.*' He watched that, and *Dig for Treasure, Wealthy and Wise, Family Fortune, Filthy Rich, Fakeout* and *Beggar Your Neighbor* before he was again interrupted, by a call from the highway patrol.

The two agents were driving very fast away from the burning wreck.

'Can't go back now, the highway patrol's all over the place. If you had any doubts, why the hell didn't you say something before we torched it?'

'All I said was, he's black. How come they never said he was black?'

'What are you implying, we finalized the wrong guy? What, some black car-thief or what?'

'I'm not implying nothing.'

'Well you sure as hell sound like you're implying something. Listen, you got his licence, is his name Death or isn't it?'

'Sure but –'

'Is he an MD or isn't he?'

'Sure but –'

'And did the receptionist at Buford City Hospital point him out to us as Dr Death or didn't she?'

'Sure. Sure.'

'Well then what's the prob? Study the orders, he has to be the asshole who invented this robot for testing artificial hearts. Dr Sheldon Death, right? The asshole Orinoco wants finalized, right?'

'I don't know. Because on the licence it says DOG EASY APOS-TROPHE ABLE but on the orders we got DOG APOSTROPHE EASY –'

'So?'

'And he's not Sheldon neither, he's Samuel.'

After a silence. 'So what are you implying? We finalized the wrong customer?'

'I'm not implying nothing.'

Ma and Roderick sat thinking about Doc De'Ath while the sheriff settled down for *Royal Flush* and *Play for Keeps*. Finally Ma said, 'So. You don't like people much. I didn't know.'

'I like you and Pa.' After a pause, he added, 'And almost anybody else – only one at a time. But when you get them all together, people are so – weird, Ma.'

'You'll get used to them.' He handed Roderick a ticket. 'Now your bus leaves at three-twenty. So you be sure and be out front of the Newer Home Café a little early. You need a recharge or anything before you go? Oil change?'

'I just had one. Ma, don't worry. I guess you got problems enough of your own.'

'Pshaw! Your Pa and I will be all right. Of course they're foreclosing on our home, and Mr Swann is suing us for his fees, not to mention Dr Welby and the others – but on the other hand, all the debts we owe are now in the hands of the Bangfield Trust Bank.'

'Is that good?'

'Good? It's perfect, son. You see, the bank computer has been sabotaged. I don't know how – guess someone somewhere phoned them up, drew out several million and then covered it by – I guess by changing all the plus signs to minus signs – something like that.'

'So does that mean –?'

'Bangfield Trust now owes us a whole lot of money.' Ma winked. 'Of course we won't try to collect. Only numbers, after all. On the astral plane, pluses and minuses are all the same anyway. Now we can just settle down and live –'

'But Ma! Isn't Pa officially dead?'

'Sure. And North America is officially a continent, and the Atlantic is officially an ocean, but so what? On the astral plane, it could all be switched around tomorrow, just like *that.*'

Sheriff Benson cleared his throat. 'You mind not snapping your fingers so loud there, Ma? I'm trying to concentrate on *Lucky Couple.* Heck of a big jackpot there, must be – oh, you leaving young feller?'

'Got to catch the bus.'

'Too bad you can't stick around. In a minute they got *The Big Break,* then *Mr and Mrs Jackpot,* then *Beautiful Winners* – no wait, that's on the other network – they got *Boom or Bust, For Richer or Poorer, Hit a Gusher, Winning Streak, Crazy-stakes, Cash In, Read the Will, Slush Fun, Crapout . . .*'

But the young man with the symmetrical face – Benson had no idea who he might be – was gone, faster than the time limit for one of them questions on *Take the Cash.* One of them real hard questions.

*

335

'. . . Course we're protected, but we ain't exactly gonna make a pile on that deal,' said Mr Kratt's voice. 'Not unless we buy this Bangfield out of Welby's company . . . anyway you get your ass back here, next time don't go telling the damn chauffeur how to drive the damn car.'

'Yes sir.' Ben hung up just as the bus was pulling in. Even so, by the time he'd gulped the tepid coffee, paid and tipped, counted his change twice and gathered up his notebook and *God is Good Business*, he was the last one aboard.

He found an empty seat behind a pair of nuns. Across the aisle was a young man Ben thought he recognized, until he saw him full-face (without a birthmark).

'Reading about God, are you?'

'Yes.' Ben turned away quickly to the window. For all you knew, this guy could be one of the executioners last night.

The thought sent Ben back to his notebook:

'In 1791 William Godwin wrote: "A servant who has been taught to write and read ceases to be any longer a passive machine." In this he expressed the fading hope that any distinction could still be made between the common man and the common gadget. For by the time Godwin's daughter had completed her *New Prometheus* (and while in the next room her husband echoed her creation in *Prometheus Unbound*: "And human hands first mimicked and then mocked,/With moulded limbs more lovely than its own,/The human form, till marble grew divine . . ."), by that time the French had already celebrated their revolution by creating a new automatic headsman, while in England the law declared that men who smash an automatic knitting machine must be hanged – as though they had committed murder.'

The man across the aisle was writing, too. Ben looked away, saw an ambulance go by, and heard one of the nuns:

'Poor Father Warren! Imagine, getting malaria right here in the middle of Nebraska!'

'On top of everything else, Sister!'

'Yes, Sister. No wonder Mrs Feeney thinks he's a saint.'

'Ah, who knows, Sister?'

'Ah, who indeed?'

It was late afternoon in New York, where they were changing one of the flags in front of the UN building. The peacock-blue-and-gold of the Shah of Ruritania came down to be replaced by the tricolour of a new People's Republic. There was no ceremony, nothing to disturb the normal rise and fall of pigeons, flapping up to invisible ledges somewhere above, swooping down to join the sea of columbine grey through which waded a few tourists, among them Mr Goun.

Mr Goun and his camera had come to see the UN building, not to see if it was really (as its architect claimed) a 'Cartesian skyscraper' (Cartesian it was, as any sheet of graph-paper) or 'a passion in glass', but merely to finish a roll of film and the last afternoon of his vacation. He was passionately aware how much his feet hurt, how tired he was of standing like this in groups of tourists, all snapping away at some sight, all complaining about their feet, all anxious to get back to their homes (that is, to the machines in which they lived).

He was lonely. The only person he had spoken to (aside from foot complaints) was a policeman yesterday, who said:

'Watch the way ya carry that camera, buddy. Lotsa cameras snatched like that, see?'

'Thanks, offic –'

He thought of that conversation now, as he reached for his camera and came up with nothing but two ends of the strap, each neatly razored.

'I've been robbed!' he said. No one looked at him.

'Hey I've been robbed!' he said to a man in a Hawaiian shirt (matching the band of his straw hat).

'Yeah? Tough.' The man turned away to continue his conversation with someone else: 'Okay so the Shah was a puppet, but I say, whose puppet? Whose puppet?'

Goun turned and bumped into someone.

'Oh I'm sorry – hey! Professor Rogers, holy –'

'Mistake!' said the other, in an oddly hoarse voice. Indeed, his glittering gold hair did not look much like that of Rogers (except at the roots, where Goun was now looking), and some of his pock-marks seemed to have been filled in with putty.

'But sure you must be, holy, hey it's great to see you Prof –'

337

'Mistake! Mistake! My name Felix Culpa!'

Goun watched, amazed, as the stranger ran off to jump into a yellow taxi. There was something like blood on the door.

Dear Dan,

The picture on the other side of this card is the post office in Newer where I won't be mailing it. I hope you're feeling better. Ma & Pa send their love. I'm fine.

> Your pal,
> Roderick

Nothing to add, so he stared out of the window as familiar places flickered past: Virgil's Hardware, Joradsen's Drug, Fellstus Motors, the sort of new Simple Simon Supermart, HAIR TODAY, the Legion Hall, the Idle Hour, Violetta's shoppe (now it was to be called VI & I NOTIONS), the pool hall, the library, Buttses Dairy, Bangfield Realty, Welby Investments, the site of the proposed Bangwel Building, Newer Produce, Cliff's junkyard, the motel and chapel, and finally the office recently vacated by Dr Smith the dentist – men were carrying in a new mechanical receptionist, other men were putting gold lettering on the windows:

LOUIE HONK-HONK'S DETECTIVE AGENCY, INC.
Stuff Found Out

NOTE ON *DIE! DIE! YOUR LORDSHIP*

The murderer must be Dr Coué, using the billiard cue, between 8:00 and 8:15, and dropping the clue of the hair. Reasoning is as follows:

1. If the billiard cue was *not* the weapon, then either Drumm embezzled or Coué was blackmailed, or both. If Drumm embezzled, then the daughter was compromised. Since she was not, Drumm did not embezzle. If Coué was blackmailed, then the butler was an addict; if the butler was an addict, then the billiard cue was the weapon. In short, if the cue *was not* the weapon, then the cue *was* the weapon. This contradiction resolves only if:
   The billiard cue was the weapon.

2. Since Adam used the polo-stick, and Brett the poker, only Coué or Drumm could have used the billiard cue. (Each suspect had access to only one weapon.)

3. If Coué touched the statuette (weapon) then there was a message under it. If so, then Adam was the thief. If so, then Brett stayed in her room all evening reading. If so, then the bloody handkerchief was used to wipe the statuette. In short, if Coué touched the statuette, he also left the clue of the bloody handkerchief. But we know that Drumm left that clue, not Coué.
   Therefore, Coué did not touch the statuette. Therefore he touched the only remaining weapon, the cue:
   Coué alone had access to the billiard cue.

From the sentences, a table can be constructed:

SUSPECT	TIME	WEAPON	CLUE
Adam	(earliest)	polo-stick	thread
Brett	?	poker	sooty smudge
Coué	8:00–8:15	billiard cue	hair
Drumm	8:15 8:30	statuette	bloody handkerchief

PART 2

RODERICK AT RANDOM

OR

FURTHER EDUCATION OF
A YOUNG MACHINE

I

Dead or dreaming? It seemed to Leo Bunsky that he had come out of retirement. Somehow he was back in his old office, working on Project Roderick again. And somehow the old heart condition had decided to stop tormenting him: gone was the breathlessness, the tiredness, the draining of fluid down into his feet until they doubled in size and burst his shoes. Without any medication or surgery, he was now cured. Everything was back to normal now, if that word could be used in these miraculous circumstances. Calloo, and also Calais! But what was the explanation?

He was dreaming. He was dead. Dreaming but dead. Neither. He had slipped through a 'time-warp' into a 'parallel universe' (Dr Bunsky was a reader of science fiction), probably through a 'white hole'.

It didn't matter; in any case there was plenty of work to do. He could live an unexamined life, until Project Roderick demanded less of his time, okay? Okay, and great to be part of this real-life science-fiction dream, a project to build a 'viable' robot. Roderick would be a learning machine. It would learn to think and behave as a human. All the team had to do was solve dozens of enormous problems in artificial intelligence that had defeated everyone else; from there on, it was science fiction.

Bunsky's job at the moment was teaching simple computer programs to talk. So far he'd got a program to say *Mama am a maam*, but not with feeling. If Roderick the Robot was ever going to think as a human, it would of course need to learn and use language as a human: *Mama am a maam* was not exactly Miltonic, but it was a start.

How did people learn to talk? No one really knew. There were those who thought it might be a matter of training, like learning to ride a bike. Others seemed to imagine a kind of grammar machine built into the human head. Still others tried teaching chimpanzees to talk while riding bikes. Chimps, so far, had articulated no theories of their own.

Bunsky found it easier to scrap general theories and consider the brain as a black box: language stuff went in and different language stuff came out. In between, some sort of processing took place. What Roderick the Robot would have to do, then, was to mimic the hidden processing. The robot would have to learn as human children learn, and that meant making the same kinds of childish mistakes. And *only* those kinds of mistakes. It was okay for Roderick to say *Me finded two mouses on stair*. It was not okay to say *I found two invisible green guesses on the stair*.

Leo Bunsky lifted his gaze to a file card tacked to the wall above his desk:

TO ERR (APPROPRIATELY) IS HUMAN

There was something he couldn't remember, that made his head ache.

The door opened and one of the younger men in the project came slouching in. It was that interdisciplinary disciple with the unfortunate name, Ben Franklin. Bunsky didn't know him well.

'Leo, how's tricks?' He slumped into a chair and started flicking cigarette ash on the floor.

'Fine, uh, Ben. Fine. Wish you'd use the ashtray, I know the place is untidy but –'

'Yes, I found two invisible green guesses on the stair. Yours?'

'Very amusing. Now if you'll excuse me . . .'

Franklin stood up. 'Busy, sure. Sure. I don't suppose you need any help with anything?'

'Sorry, no.' No one ever wanted Franklin's help. No one really trusted him, with his strange background: a hybrid degree in Computer Science and Humanities. A little too eclectic for serious research work. Dr Fong had hired him as project librarian and historian, but so far there weren't many books and no history. Ben Franklin just sort of hung around dropping ash on the floor. 'Sorry, Ben.'

'Sure.' After a pause, he sat down again. 'Leo, you ever have any doubts about this project? About Roderick?'

'Doubts?'

344

'Kind of an ethical grey area, isn't it?'

Bunsky felt the headache settling in, deepening its hold on him. 'What grey area, for Christ's sake? Building a robot, is that grey? Is that ethically suspect, to build a sophisticated machine? Is cybernetics morally in bad taste?'

'Well, no, if you put it like –'

Bunsky was shouting now. 'We're not violating anybody's rights. We're not polluting any imaginable environment. We're not cutting up animals and we're not even screwing around with genetic materials!'

Franklin flicked ash. 'Come on, Leo, what about long-term consequences? Don't tell me it never crossed your mind that Roderick might be dangerous. First of a new species, of a very high order, has to be some danger in that.'

'A mechanical species, Ben.'

'But on a par with our own. And what if robots evolve faster and further? Where does that leave us? Extinct!'

Bunsky made his voice calm. 'Let's not be too simplistic there. Humans wouldn't be in direct competition with robots, would they? Both species would use, let's see, metal and energy. But robots wouldn't need much of either resource. Should be enough to go around, eh?'

'Eh yourself, what about intangible resources? What about things like *meaning*?' Franklin put out his cigarette on the floor. 'I mean look, it could be that humans feed on meaning. It could be that we only survive by making sense out of the world around us. It could be that this is all that keeps us going. So if we turn over that function to some other species, we're finished.'

The headache began to throb, roaring waves of pain breaking over him, trying to drag him under. There were moments of dizziness and deafness, moments when Bunsky could hardly make out the empty smirking face before him. Franklin looked a little like a ventriloquist's dummy sometimes.

'You have a point, Ben. Too bad you're such a goddamned jerk.'

'What?' Franklin paused, a fresh cigarette halfway to his smirk.

'I said you have a point. Yes. I believe we do have a need to make sense out of the world. We see by making pictures, no? By sorting out the "blooming, buzzing confusion". And of course we

345

hear speech by making sentences out of it. I believe that the essence of human intelligence is that kind of hypothesis-building. Life is making intelligent guesses, you agree?'

'Of course, Leo. Hypothesis-building.'

'Then don't you see? The robot is the ultimate human hypothesis. What better way of making sense out of the world, than through complete copies of ourselves? How better to model our inner and outer world? Ben, we need the robot – we need the *idea* of the robot.'

Franklin lit his cigarette and tapped it. 'The idea, maybe, but I'm not worried about the idea. It's the embodiment.'

'Yes, we're building a real robot. We're doing what everyone has always wanted to do, down through the ages. If the Jews could have built a real *golem*, do you think they would have hesitated? Or the Cretans, wouldn't they want a real Talos? If myths are just wishes, isn't it obvious what they were all wishing for? Dolls and statues from the terra-cotta past . . . puppets and manequins today . . . The idea of the wish for the robot is so, so very powerful . . . What child doesn't like Punch and Judy? What grownup won't pause to watch a ventriloquist at work? My God, when I was a kid, do you know they even had a ventriloquist on the radio – on the radio!'

Franklin flicked ash. 'I don't get it.'

'Edgar Bergen and Charlie McCarthy on the damned radio. You see, the novelty of a talking doll was so powerful, we didn't even need to see the doll. There didn't even have to be a doll! All we needed was the *idea* of a Charlie McCarthy!'

Flick, flick. 'Okay sure, you think the robot idea is powerful. Only it still might be kind of tough on us, having all these puppets around who are also our intellectual equals. We won't be able to shut *them* up in their boxes after each performance, we'll have to live with them. Could make quite a rip in the old social fabric, Leo.'

'But maybe an inevitable rip. Anyway, we're the team to make the historic incision.' Bunsky briefly saw them all gathered around an operating table, *The Anatomy Lesson of Dr Tulp*. Then he saw another picture . . .

'Something funny?' Ben Franklin asked.

'Nothing really, just remembered a notion I had for a science-fiction movie – well it's nothing.'

'I'd like to hear it.'

'All I really have is this opening scene. There's a human brain floating in a tank of water and pulsating with light. These scientists in white lab coats are leaning over it, looking grave, with the pulsating light reflected in their eyes. Then the camera begins to pull back, so we see the tank is an office water cooler. One of the scientists takes down a paper cup and gets himself a drink.'

'He's laughing now,' said the older of the two men in white lab coats. He pointed to a screen where a jagged line bobbed and danced. 'There, he just told a joke.'

'Really? A joke? How do you know?' The younger man kept turning away from the instrument panel to look directly into the tank where Leo Bunsky's brain floated in water.

The older man pointed to a different screen. 'We know everything he thinks. See right now he thinks he's in his old office, back at some jerkwater Northern university, still working on a big secret "robot" project. And he thinks he's talking to a colleague named Franklin. Franklin must have been a pretty good friend of his, because we never have any trouble producing him. We use Franklin as an input dummy.'

'Input dummy? Afraid I don't understand the technical side of this. Do you mean we can talk to this – this guy?'

'Precisely. Now I'm not entirely familiar with the technical details myself. The wiring must be unimaginable. But I gather that we somehow stimulate vision and hearing centres to produce an hallucination of this Franklin, and then we somehow manipulate the hallucination. Of course we get output from Leo's speech centres too.' He pointed to another screen. 'There, his joke is just coming up now.'

The younger man kept craning around to peer at the brain itself, but now he turned back to see:

Scientists are leaning over,
looking into a grave. A watery
grave. One of them has to be
pulled back. He lowers his cup
to get a stiff drink.

347

'Not much of a sense of humour,' said the younger man.

'Well it probably loses something in the processing,' said the other, pushing a few buttons. 'Now we can also monitor his general thoughts, read his mind so to speak.'

am a maam a man of parts Dr
Gulp hands of a murderer drip
drip riverrun or creektrickle
O Rijn maiden God's immerse
anatomical babies in jars drip
drip father fathomful drip
are those pearls eyes of an
artist pools

'Interesting,' said the younger man. 'But you know I keep wondering why? Why go to all this trouble to find out what one computer scientist is thinking?'

'Oh Leo isn't just any computer scientist, he's very special. A first-class brain, if you'll pardon the expression. Let's take a pew and I'll tell you about Leo.'

There were comfortable theatre seats banked along one side of the room. The two men took seats in the front row, a pair of critics. The older man folded and unfolded his liver-spotted hands a few times before he began.

'You know, Otto Neurath once said science is a boat you have to rebuild even while you're at sea in it. In Leo's case he was launched as an electrical engineer, drifted into communications theory and finally rebuilt his boat as a linguist. And so it was that Leo turned out to be the right man at the right time for a very special project. Building a so-called robot. Or as we prefer to say, an *Entity*.'

He paused for effect. But the younger man was watching an attendant polish the glass front of Leo's tank, wiping away fingermarks.

'They called it Project – Rubric was it? Roderick, I believe, though what's in a name, they had cover names galore, a very secretive bunch. And no wonder, because it turned out they were swindling funding out of NASA, heavy funding.'

'They were just crooks?'

'On the contrary, they had plenty of genuine talent. The team was headed by Lee Fong –'

'The pattern-recognition guy? I've heard of him.'

The liver-spotted hands were folded again. 'You may know the others too, all first-class br— people. So they had heavy funding, heavy talent, and I guess heavy luck. Because they blitzed through some incredibly tough problems and actually got their Entity built.'

The younger man was now listening with his full attention. 'Go on. What was it?'

'It was a "viable" learning machine incorporating some of Leo's best ideas. By the time they built it, Leo Bunsky himself was officially dead, but his ideas lived on. The Roderick Entity was a great success – if you can call it a success to endanger humanity – and it was Leo Bunsky who made it possible for the thing to talk.

'Of course there were the others, Fong and Mendez and Sonnenschein, all brilliant, but Leo made it talk. I wish sometimes we could tell him about his success.'

'He doesn't know?' The younger man looked to the tank.

'All he knows is, he went into the hospital for open-heart surgery, came out wonderfully well, and went back to work. In fact he died on the table. Our people were there, and they managed to get his brain – and now Leo works for us!'

'As a kind of devil's advocate, I suppose.'

'Precisely. Precisely.' Wrinkled reptilian eyelids came down over bright reptilian eyes. 'Leo sits in his office, "Franklin" comes in and asks him some questions about the future of artificial intelligence research. He tells "Franklin" what he thinks, and we have our answer. We know what has to be stopped.'

The younger man watched the attendant breathe on the glass to clear a fingermark. 'Of course I'm new around here, but frankly I don't get it. Why does the Orinoco Institute keep on spending money to sabotage robot research, Entity I mean, when every year there's going to be more and more new research? I mean it sounds like a holding action that isn't even holding. Aren't Entities inevitable? Aren't they becoming a fact of life?'

'That's certainly one of Leo's arguments, inevitability. But you know, in all of our scenarios, Entities are a decidedly negative development. Ultimately they signal the collapse of our way of life, the death of our culture. I do not mean just American or Western culture, I mean human culture. And if we at the Institute have one over-riding loyalty, I believe it must be to our own species.' His head swivelled sharply, the lizard eyes opening in a hypnotic stare. 'Don't you agree?'

'Well sure, naturally. But are we really sure that humanity is threatened by, by Entities?'

'Oh, we've worked it out. In all eight scenarios.'

'In all three modes?'

'Yes, yes. To six significant figures.'

The younger man shrugged. 'Six? Then that's that. I can't argue with six significant figures.' He was silent for a minute, staring at the backs of his own hands. On the right one was a small blemish that might in time become a liver spot.

'So poor Leo Bunsky helped us sabotage his own work. I suppose we did shut down this Project Rubric?'

'Roderick. Let's just say, events shut it down – with a little help from us. We managed to get the director, Lee Fong, deported to Taipin. I understand he now fixes old poker-playing machines in a low gambling den. And he'll never have a better job; we dissuaded all reputable firms from hiring him. And – let me see – one or two of the others are confined to mental wards for the nonce. Yes, Project Roderick is certainly shut down.'

'And the Entity? You said they actually built something. Did you destroy it or what?'

There was a hesitation, an Adam's apple leaping in a wrinkled reptilian throat. 'Well, in fact . . . one or two problems there . . . Entity was taken outside the project and raised more or less as a human child in a human home. We had trouble finding it.'

'Raised?'

'As I said, it was a learning machine. And what it learned was to play human. It "grew up". Became much harder to find and neutralize. The Agency did find it and sent someone, but they ran into some bad luck.' A throat cleared, with the sound of tearing paper. 'Bad luck. And now the thing has dropped out of sight again. It is still at large.'

'I'll be damned. Still clanking around on the loose. Still chugging up and down the streets, a free robot. Sounds like your worst scenario is about to be realized, and so what?' The younger man thought of saying this and more. He thought of saying, 'What could be worse, anyway, than our scenario for poor Leo here? Poor unfree Leo – would any robot do *this* to him?'

But aloud, all he said was, 'Still at large, hmm.'

'At random, one might say . . .'

II

He had taken only a few steps when he heard rapid footfalls behind him.* The guard then ran forward to seize him.

'That is good!' he said, as Edgar shot a tall Arab who was rushing at him with uplifted spear. The other Arab got up from the water and placed himself behind the fellow with the knife.

Two of his incisors were lying beside his nose, plastered there with blood. As for the policeman, he had at first seemed indifferent to the fallen man; but after the first shriek he approached him, raised his club and struck him a terrible blow on the temple. The big Irish cop, who'd slapped me before, clouted me from behind with his club.

'The fancy footwork's all over for this hoodlum.' So saying, the detective drew back his foot and kicked poor Lem behind the ear even harder than his colleague had done. Every time he cursed, one of the detectives struck him in the face with his fist. But then the coppers started up all around me. Rau approached the captain and shot him twice.

The blue plastic bowls came in through the pantry hatch. He would first scrape excess food from each bowl into a counter hole, then rinse with a hand-held spray and place upside down in a wire rack, twelve bowls to each rack and three racks to a conveyor stack ready to be loaded on the conveyor leading to the dishwashing machine for which detergent had to be measured and dropped in the top trap before each stack moved through from first wash to final rinse and emerged, ready to be loaded on the cart which took six stacks or eighteen racks or 216 clean pale blue plastic bowls each bearing a white Wedgwood-style cartouche marked DDD opposite an identical white Wedgwood-style cartouche marked DDD, the cart bearing 1296 Ds would then be rolled by him into the pantry and an identical cart full of empty racks be rolled back into the greasy kitchen to continue the cycle.

One of the men had smashed his fist into Julia's solar plexus, doubling her up like a pocket ruler. A gun muzzle poked into the back of my neck. He pulled the axe quite out, swung it with both arms, scarcely conscious of himself, and almost without effort, almost mechanically, brought the blunt side down on her head. She shot him five times in the stomach.

The day he found himself dragging pregnant women into the town square where their stomachs were slit open and the foetuses pulled out, his sensibilities were so outraged that he could no longer be part of the Communist organization. Aramis had already killed one of his adversaries, but the other was pressing him warmly. Jim Parsons, trying to creep out of his cabin port-hole, was hit on the head and dropped into the sea. The men struggled knee-deep in water. I took a firm grasp on the rail with my left hand and drew my dagger. As soon as I saw his head in a favourable position, I struck him heavily with the poker, just over the fourth cervical. The Boy suddenly drew buck his hand and slashed with his razored nail at Brewster's cheek. He grasped a thick oaken cudgel in his bare right hand. And Ehud put forth his left hand, and took the dagger from his right thigh, and thrust it into his belly. We stan up at the same time an I feel my goddam heart pumpin an Rod hand me his blade. The dagger was an afterthought.

The cycle was never completed without a hitch. An enormous number of bowls would come through the hatch streaming with half-eaten food which could not be scraped until he had emptied the overflowing garbage can beneath the counter hole or then a shortage of clean, empty wire racks would be discovered or then the detergent would run out or finally the cart that should be waiting for stacks of racks of clean bowls would be found in the back kitchen, piled high with dirty pots, and while he emptied the garbage can or searched the pantry for wire racks or fetched a new barrel of detergent from the basement or began scouring the pile of pots, there would be a call for ice for the pantry, towels for the cook, spilled liquid to be mopped and salted at once, while the dirty bowls continued to pile up and perhaps the dish-washing machine jammed, so that even though he felt he was coping with everything; he was not, and even though he felt he could accept stoically the screams of the waitresses, the snarls of the cook, the blows of Mr Danton, Roderick's fantasies became filled with paperback violence.

The iron fingers went into my throat. Then Rigby was holding him, had taken Feilding's right arm and done something to it, so that Feilding cried out in pain and fear. There was a sharp cry – and the dagger dropped gleaming upon the carpet, upon which, instantly afterwards, fell prostrate in death the

Prince Prospero. His head cracked, and I felt it crunch. The light flashed upon the barrel of a revolver, but Holmes's hunting crop came down upon the man's wrist, and the pistol clinked upon the stone floor.

Quick as a flash he snatched up Cedar's gun and, levelling it with both hands, he worked the trigger. Bang! Bang! He shook me off with a furious snarling noise, giving me a terrific blow in the chest, and presented the revolver at my head. He fell to one side against a wall, a slug whispering as it tore past him. Suddenly shot after shot rang out in succession. Special Agent Fox was wounded and fell, but the concentrated fire which all four FBI men poured into the telephone booth made mincemeat out of Johnson. 'Bang!' went a pistol. The chopper raked the room swiftly from end to end and the air filled with plaster and splinters. Not so far overhead, an ME-109, pinned by searchlights, suddenly broke out of cloud cover and swooped in.

'Wake up you! Hey, I'm talkin' to you!' The red face of Mr Danton was glowing at him through the hatch, over an unpardonable heap of bowls. 'Five minutes I been watching you, you washed one dish, what the hell is dis? Just answer me that, what the hell is dis?'

There was no answer; Roderick could only keep his eyes down and work harder until Mr Danton went off to find a waitress without a hairnet or a cook putting too much parsley on the potatoes, until the hatch slid closed and the violence could begin, *Dacca-dakka-dakar!* and *Kerang!* silent slaughter amid the screams of ordinary business.

The hatch slammed open and a waitress in Wedgwood blue dumped in a trayload of bowls before passing on to scream at the cook over the steam table:

'Picking up, picking up! Dave? That's two Chow-downs and one Upboy, a chopped duck liver together with a Mister Frisk hold the gravy . . . Dave, that's only one Chow-down, I ordered two, come on, come on, the customer's waaaiiting.'

Roderick could see the cook cursing and dishing up, almost flinging food over the high steam table where waitresses were visible only as hands and blue rabbit-ears.

'Ordering a chef's special . . . side of fried shrimp . . .'

'I got no shrimp, shrimp finish, kaput!' the cook screamed. Like everyone else here, he seemed unable to move anything without slamming it down, to say anything without screaming. When Roderick had first come to work here, he'd imagined that somehow the customers were causing all the noise. After all, Danton's Doggie Dinette did cater for mainly high-class and pedigree dogs, well-known for their constant yipping and snapping. Could it be that humans were catching this canine hysteria and transmitting it to the Dinette kitchen, as a kind of psychic rabies?

Not at all. Dave the cook (in a rare quiet moment) explained: 'Everybody yell in kitchen, in every kinda rastorunth across over world, is it were? Good kitchen, lots yell. *Bad* kitchen, *no* yellings. No yellings, waitress drop tray, insult castomer. Cook burn finger, cut off eye. Bad.'

But Roderick never got used to the noise. Whenever there was a lull in his work, he would step out into the alley to sit on a garbage can and meditate. Sometimes he would have a quiet conversation with Allbright.

Allbright was a garrulous drunk who wandered often into this quiet alley to piss, to drink or now and then to search the garbage cans. But he was never too busy to stop and talk, as now:

'Well well well, if it isn't our friend, the automatic dish-washer. Still claiming to be a robot? I forget your name.'

'Roderick Wood. And I am a robot.'

'Yes yes well who isn't? Chateaubriand said he realized he was only a machine for making books, we're all poor damned machines for some purpose or other, some pathetic, useless . . . Even you, washing dishes for dogs. Nothing wrong with that, honourable profession as any. Don't let 'em look down on you, kid.'

'The dogs?'

'Honourable profession as any, skink sexer, awning historian, salad auctioneer, you stick to it. Learn your trade. A man with a trade is going somewhere. He's going over to the other side of town to fix some poor goddamned machine. Only he needs the bus fare.'

Roderick said nothing. Allbright appeared to doze for a few minutes, then said, 'Anyway, I'm a poet.'

'Anyway?'

'And that gives me the right.'

'What right?'

'You name it, that gives it to me.'

'I've never met a live poet before,' Roderick said, not that

355

Allbright looked fully alive. 'I thought all poets were dead.'

Allbright almost looked at him. 'No, you're thinking of the other people. All poets are alive, and that gives them every right.' He turned and shook his fist at the empty alley. 'You hear, you, you bastards! Every right!'

Roderick watched him stagger off to fight shadows, and finally fall asleep in his usual corner next to an enormous metal bin full of rusty coathangers.

'A poet.' Roderick was impressed. Poetry! Life!

Life for Roderick was limited in most dimensions. He worked long hours at Danton's Doggie Dinette on a 'split shift'. Danton cursed him and kicked him and paid very poorly, but where else could he work? He was a robot without a social security card.

The Dinette was close to the bus station where he had arrived in the city, and not far from the ancient hotel where he watched TV or recharged his batteries, or read books from the rack at the local drugstore. Some nights he would turn off the light and pretend to himself that he was sleeping, but he was only watching the dim yellow rectangle of light over the door, listening to the groan of sagging floorboards in the corridor as people walked by in ones and twos all night.

Most nights he simply read one book after another; he might before dawn get through two or three like *Call Me Pig*, *Doc Bovary's Wife*, *The Ego Diet*, *Ratstar II*, *God Was My Co-conspirator*, *Dream New Hair*, *Sink the Titanic!*, *Dragons of Darkwound*, or *Aversion for Happiness*. He could shift easily from a spy thriller like *The Pisces Perplex* to a guide to courtroom-drama therapy, *Make a Federal Case Out of It*; and on to an unusual medical theory in *Your Eyes: Do They Leak Light?* They were all one-night stands, forgotten in the morning when the first stack of dirty bowls rattled through the hatch.

'Sonnenschein, initial D?' asked the hospital receptionist, and touched her keyboard. 'No visitors except the immediate family, it says here.'

Roderick said, 'Well, I'm almost family.'

'Sorry.'

*

356

'If you're a poet, why don't you read me one of your poems?'

'Oh no. Oh no, you don't.' Allbright waggled a dirty finger in admonition. 'You don't catch me that way. Read you one of my poems? For nothing?'

'Why not?'

'Against union rules.'

After a moment, Roderick asked how much a read poem would cost.

'How much have you got?'

It added up to a dollar and forty-seven cents, exactly enough. Allbright read from the book of his memory:

SKINNER'S DREAM
Pigeons all over
The window ledges of a tall building
At sunset get down to work.
Each must swoop to another ledge
Where it can sit deciding whether
To swoop to another ledge where it can
Sit deciding whether to swoop to
Another ledge or just sit deciding.
That's pigeons all over

A gold-haired man wearing gold-rimmed sunglasses had come into the alley to look into garbage cans. During *Skinner's Dream* he came up close and stopped, apparently listening. He cradled a newspaper-wrapped bundle.

Roderick thanked Allbright. 'That was some poem. It was real – real –'

'Poetic,' said the stranger. 'You mind getting off that garbage can now?'

Roderick jumped down. The stranger took off the lid and looked in. 'That's better.' He dumped in his bundle and banged on the lid. 'Must be just about the only empty garbage can in this part of town.'

Allbright nodded. 'I guess they recycle a lot, at the Doggie Dinette here.'

'Interesting trend, petfood recycling,' said the stranger. His face was long and pock-marked, but his glittering gold hair offset these

357

imperfections. 'Probably affects the growth potential of the entire edible foodstuffs industry, though we'd need a thoroughgoing econometric breakdown before we could apply any cogent significance test, engaging other retail foodstuff trends and of course the changing shape of pets.'

'Yes,' said Roderick. 'Well, I think I hear Mr Danton yelling for me.'

'You work here?' said the stranger. 'Must be fascinating. Unique opportunity to explore at first hand the full rich pattern of human-canine bonding mechanisms in a feeding situation.'

'With a little polishing,' Allbright said, 'you got a damned good routine there: add maybe a structuralist tap-dance . . .'

'Well so long,' said Roderick. He heard the stranger say something to Allbright about the role of refuse surveys in pre-archaeological studies of any dynamic social mix . . .

Mr Danton was waiting for him. He twisted Roderick's arm and the robot felt pain. 'See dem dirty dishes?'

'Yes sir. Ouch.'

'I pay you to wash 'em, right?'

'Yes sir.'

'I pay you well. I treat you right. You get good hours, pleasant surroundings, friendly co-workers, a fair boss. Right?'

'Ow – yes sir.'

'I treat you like a crown prince. I think of you like my own son. *My own son.* And all I ask is you wash a lousy coupla bowls now and then, okay?'

'Okay.'

'Okay, I'm glad we had a little talk, cleared this up.'

Mr Danton threw Roderick down and kicked him across the greasy floor. 'Next time you're fired.'

When Danton was gone, Dave the cook had a quiet laugh. 'Watch out he kill you, kid. Old Danton he deeply crazy.'

'Kill me? But why would he kill me? For a few dirty –'

'No thing like that.' Dave guffawed again. 'See you look quite one little bit like his son Lyle. You look just like him, yes. Only thing, Lyle got birth-smirch on face, under eye like tear's drop. Yes? Boy do them two hate. One time Lyle come here, old Danton grabbing cleaver and enchase him, say he gonna

358

depecker him, hee hee hee, Lyle not come back. You watch out, kid.'

'But why should he want to, to kill his own son?'

'Hee hee.'

Roderick didn't understand. That evening he turned over the pages of a book on human behaviour. He learned that crowds were lonely, people were one-dimensional, and inner cities were dying; he himself was probably alienated. Real alienated. Boy, he was so alienated it was unbelievable. The only people in the world who cared about him were Ma and Pa Wood, back in Newer, Nebraska. There hadn't been any letters from Ma since the Newer nuclear power station accident. The accident had been caused by music. It seemed that someone had decided to install 24-hour-a-day music at the power station, and had chosen the new Moxon Music System. This did not rely on local records or tapes, or even on music run through long-distance telephone lines. Instead, the music would originate in a distant city, bounce off a special Moxon satellite, and be picked up by a large dish-antenna on the roof.

The roof had not been made to bear the extra weight of this antenna. It cracked, throwing the weight of the building on to the reactor shell. Now the entire town was fenced off. The government would say only that 'no one lives there anymore.' No wonder a guy felt alienated. Life was like something on TV.

Roderick turned on the TV to watch an old movie in black-and-white. It was raining, and two people stood in the rain embracing. The woman pulled back from a kiss and said: 'But don't you see, my darling? You're *not* a nobody. You're the man I happen to love.'

Rain dripped from the man's hat-brim. 'No, Mildred, your father's right. I'm no good for you – I know that now. Oh sure, I hoped and dreamed a girl like you would come along. Even a nobody can hope and dream. But this is real life, kid. You just happened to pick the wrong guy.'

'Don't say that! Don't ever say that.' She clung to his sleeve. 'Listen, you big lug, if you're a nobody, then so am I – and proud of it! I won't let you go. I can't. You see '

The scene was cut short to make way for a man in a bright

plaid jacket who smiled and shouted details of a sewer-cleaning service.

Next day Mr Danton asked Roderick to fill in for one of the waitresses.

'Do I get to wear the rabbit ears?'

'You wear what I say you wear, okay?' Mr Danton's hand roamed over the cook's table and came to rest on the handle of a cleaver.

'Okay yes, yes sir.' Wearing a clean shirt and a black plastic bowtie, Roderick glided out to meet the customers.

Danton's Doggie Dinette went to great lengths to treat dogs as humans. A table could only be reserved in a dog's name, and when the dog arrived at the front door towing its owner, a hostess would pretend to greet the animal and lead it to its table. The tables were very low and bone-shaped and for dogs only; owners sat near their pets but out of sight, in alcoves, so that the restaurant seemed populated exclusively by Yorkies, Corgis and toy Dobermanns. That was how Roderick first saw the dining room, full of dogs wearing bibs.

III

Noon. The apostle clock chimed, and out of its innards came a parade of tiny wooden figures. Their faces and clothes had long since dissolved in wormholes; they now looked less like apostles than bowling pins.

Automatically, Mr Kratt lifted his snout to listen. His little black eyes lost their hard focus for a moment, and his powerful hands stopped throttling the pages of a company report.

'You know, bub, my old man left me that clock when he died. I ever tell you about my old man?'

Ben Franklin, checking his own watch, shrugged. 'I don't think so. Er, what was he like?'

The hard focus returned to Mr Kratt's little black eyes. 'He was a bum. A professional failure. A dummy. If I had my way, people like him would be turned into fishfood. At birth.' He gripped the company report again in a stranglehold. 'At birth. Damn it, I never could stand cripples . . .'

He cleared his throat and looked at Franklin. 'Anyway, where were we?'

'The patent leaseback deal with –?'

'No never mind that now, I want to go into this goddamned learning robot gimmick. You and Hare promised to deliver this thing six months ago, how long are we supposed to carry you? So far I don't see anything on paper even.'

Ben Franklin fingered his upper lip as though stroking the moustache he had not worn for years. 'I can explain.'

'Let's hear it.'

'Well I've been having trouble assembling the right research team. Hare's a good enough research director for ordinary stuff, but this is special. I wanted to bring in this colleague of mine from the University, Dan Sonnenschein. He –'

'I know, I know, he's the guy who really invented this gimmick.'

'Well we all worked on Roderick, I don't think it's fair to say any one of us really invented – but Dan yes Dan was certainly more, more familiar with some of the programming problems. So I wanted –'

'Sure, sure, but we settled all this last year, didn't we? I gave you the go-ahead, hell, you're the vice-president in charge of product development, get this Sunshine guy, get Frankenstein, get anybody, only get moving, we need that gimmick.'

'I wish you wouldn't keep calling it a gimmick, Mr Kratt.'

'Call it a fucking pipe dream I wouldn't be too far off, would I? Damn it you and Sunshine aren't at the University now, this is real life. I know you say you built a prototype and it got lost or something, but all I get are explanations, excuses, you haven't even got your research team together, damn it, bub . . .'

'Yes sir, but you know I did mention that Dan was in the hospital, his nerves –'

'You said he was in the looney ward over at the U Hospital but so what? All these research geniuses are nuts, look at Dr Hare now. Trying to make pancakes with phonograph records on them, no idea what he's doing or why, we just wind him up and point him at a problem. So why don't you just spring this pal of yours outa the looney ward, stick him on the payroll and –'

'Frankly I don't think he's well enough to work for us, not yet.'

'Great, so we sit around waiting, do we? While the competition cuts our nuts off, that's not my idea of running a company, bub. KUR Industries is a growth company, damnit, and growth needs ideas. See *that*?' He suddenly thrust out a thick hand. Ben Franklin flinched, but Mr Kratt was only showing him a ring: a heavy gold claw mounting a steel ball.

'That's a pinball from my first machine, bub. One stinking

362

machine in a dark corner of a greasy little diner in a neighbourhood so crummy the winos wouldn't puke on it. And I built up from there – more machines, an arcade, a chain of arcades, a carnival, saunas, leisure centres, bowling alleys, business machines, pleasure machines, fun foods – and all the time I had to feed the company with ideas. Ideas. Hell, I even hired you as an ideas man, and then suddenly all the ideas stopped.'

'Mr Kratt, I'm sorry if –'

'Because you drag your feet, bub, you keep on dragging your feet. Look at our funfood venture, Jinjur Boy, you dragged your feet over that. Best damned idea in the whole industry, a gingerbread boy with built-in microcircuitry, a talking toy and one hundred percent edible, how could it lose? Only you had to drag your –'

'But Mr Kratt, you can't always hurry research like that, we did have problems with those mercury batteries '

'Problems? Only problem we had was a bad press, a handful of kids get a bellyache and right away everybody wants to blame us.'

'But some of those kids ate Jinjur Boys and died, others still have brain damage from mercur –'

'Nobody ever proved a thing. Damn it, bub, when you run a growth company, you gotta take chances, okay maybe we made one mistake but that's all in the past. Forget the damn past, forget it.'

'Yes sir.'

'We belong to the future.' Mr Kratt's cigar had gone out. He threw it away, got up from his desk and walked to the window.

'The future, yes sir.' Frankliln watched Kratt standing there in silence, heavy hands clenched behind him, heavy shoulders hunched against the sky.

'Look, we need this robot gimmick now. Get Sunshine or get somebody.'

Ben Franklin looked down on the city, etched in grey stone and black glass, a gleaming future to which he wanted to belong.

'Sonnenschein, initial D?' asked the hospital receptionist.

'Yes. I'm his son, Roderick.'

'I'm sorry, our records show he has no immediate family.'

*

'That waiter looks just like Lyle, you remember Lyle? Only he hasn't got Lyle's birthmark . . .'

'Oh, speaking of plastic surgery, guess what Barb paid for her new chest? You'd think it was gold instead of whatsit, silicon . . .'

'Darling, it's not silicon, it's sili*cone.*'

'Yeah but what do you think she paid for her silly cones?'

The voices from the alcoves rose and fell, striving to be heard above the drone of taped music, the noises of feeding animals, other voices from other alcoves.

'Basically I'm a Manichean myself . . .'

'Manic? I wouldn't call you manic, you're more . . .'

'. . . Libran basically, I took her to see . . .'

'. . . a puppet government, okay, but *whose* puppet, that's what I want to know. Take . . .'

'. . . The Reagan Expressway through Hilldale only there was this accident at the Dalecrest exit, we hadda go all the way down to . . .'

'Prague? Terrible, just terrible, my phlebitis acted up all week, maybe I should get me some dacron veins or . . .'

'Spaghetti, didn't the Chinese invent that?'

'. . . a sage pillow for spirit dreams – but hey, isn't that Sandy? Over there with the Labrador.'

'I thought Sandy *was* a Labrador – oh you mean Sandy Mann, no they're on vacation in Prague or someplace . . .'

'. . . Ruritania, I can't even find it on a map . . .'

'. . . basically Libran until we went and had her spayed . . .'

'Now everybody thinks the Japanese invented transistors just like everybody used to think the Chinese invented the abacus, and even if spaghetti isn't Western . . .'

'That looks just like Sandy . . .'

'That sure looks like Lyle . . .'

The waiter who looked like Lyle moved smoothly through the dining room, serving dog and master with the same polite, mindless devotion. Roderick seemed a perfect minion. He was able to balance a heavy tray while a Sealyham urinated on his foot; to smile at the owner of a pit-bull that was trying to shred his hand; to take down details of a large, complicated order while a toy poodle tried to mount his ankle.

Beneath the smooth surface Roderick dreamt of violence.

There would be like this big gangster with all these bodyguards, and Roderick would have to kill each of them in a different way like maybe an exploding rice-flail or a duel on skates with chainsaws and like maybe strangle all their guard dogs and like maybe . . . hundreds of corpses, oceans of blood, until he would shoot it out with Mr Big, put a blue hole in his forehead and watch him crumple slowly, a look of surprise on his face as he becomes dead, very dead . . . until Roderick was victorious and alone.

Roderick was not victorious, just alone. He watched the dogs and their owners moving with assurance in their own world, where a Chihuahua and a St Bernard would recognize each other as dogs, a Republican optometrist and a Trotskyist dope dealer speak the same language. No one recognized Roderick or spoke to him as anything but 'waiter'.

There were conversations of which he understood hardly a word:

'Well I'm doing Rolfing now, but I was heavy into oneness training.'

'Connections, I know. I had this gestalt thing to work through with my family, you know? And –'

'Yeah how is Jaynice, anyway?'

'She's more in touch with herself now only – I don't know, maybe familying just isn't her mind-set.'

'Too many tight synapses, I felt just like that after Transactioning, I kept noticing my own tight synapses. I'm gonna try Science of Mind training next, or haptics maybe, you gotta try something . . ,'

'Nodally it's probably all oned together anyway.'

'. . . yeah . . .'

'. . . yeah, synergy is. Isn't it?'

'Yeah. Oh waiter? We're ready to order here.'

He would take this order and move on to an alcove where two women, having spread paper napkins on the table between them, opened their jewelled pillboxes and set out arrays of coloured pills as though arranging beads for a barter, which, in a sense they were.

'Oh is that pink one Thanidorm or Toxidol?'

'That's Yegrin. Oh you mean this bitty pink one, that's Zombutal, beautiful, you want one?'

'Thanks, kid, now let's see what I got here to trade, these green ones are Valsed, the light green are Quasipoise, and the green two-tone are I forget, either Jitavert or Robutyl. The red must be Normadorms.'

'Is that like Penserons?'

'Only stronger, you want a couple? Or hey I got these terrific mood flatteners called what is it? Parasol? Here this yellow one. Or is that Invidon? Sometimes I get so mixed up . . .'

'. . . me too . . . I need something . . .' Well-manicured nails the colour of Bing cherries selected a capsule of the same colour and carried it to lips of the same colour. 'A Eulepton.'

'Was that a Eulepton? I thought it was a Barbidol . . . I get so mixed up . . .'

'Me too . . .'

Then to the kitchen where Mr Danton would twist his arm and threaten him, then back with a heavy tray to meet another territorial Sealyham, another angry pit-bull.

'Is it Sue Jane that's married to Ronnie now? I get so mixed up talking about Sue and her pals, all those divorces and all . . .'

'Well, it really boils down to three men and three women, and they been married in every possible legal way to each other, eight weddings in all. And none of them married anybody else . . .'

'You take Clarence now, he was his first wife's first husband, his second wife's second, and his third wife's third!'

'That's nothing. Vern's third wife's third husband's third wife is the same person as his second wife's second husband's second wife, how do you like that?'

'. . . divorced the sister of . . . and right away married Mary Sue, who was single. But his ex bounced back just as fast, she married the guy who'd just split up with . . .'

'Sure sure but what I want to know is, who was Sue Ellen's third husband?'

Roderick, leaning over to polish the table, murmured what he thought was the answer.*

The people at the table looked at him. 'You know them or something?'

'No, I just wanted to help. I –'

'Nobody invited you to butt in, asshole,' said the owner of a Yorkie now devouring a bowl of goose liver.

'But I just thought – if everything you all said was true –'

'You calling us liars?'

'No I – sorry, I'm sorry.' He backed away, stepping on a coil of dogshit, tripping over a leash as he fled the dining room. He wished everyone sliced thin and fed to to their own pets who would in turn crumple slowly with looks of surprise as he shot them dead, very dead . . . no one would miss the human species or the canine either, least of all Roderick the victorious.

An hour later, a woman smiled at him and told him he was a sweet boy. That changed everything: he cancelled the extermination of two species and decided to go dancing instead. But first another try at University Hospital.

'Daniel Sonnenschein,' he said to the receptionist. 'I'm his stepson, and I *demand* to see him.'

'Certainly, sir. Just take a seat.'

Two hours later, Roderick was told that visiting hours were over for the day. A pair of security cops did the telling, and showed him how to get out of the building.

IV

The figure performed its purpose admirably. Keeping perfect time and step, and holding its little partner tight clasped in an unyielding embrace, it revolved steadily, pouring forth at the same time a constant flow of squeaky conversation, broken by brief intervals of grinding silence.

Jerome K. Jerome, *The Dancing Partner*

The Escorial Ballroom was a large gloomy place where a few tired-looking couples leaned together, shuffling slowly around the floor to *The Tennessee Waltz*. The three white-haired musicians chatted and drank as they played, and the drummer was eating his lunch with one hand. The dancers seemed not much younger or more interested in anything: the men wore old suits and sideburns, the women wore flared dresses, heavy makeup and large earrings.

While Roderick was standing at the edge of the dark dance floor trying to figure out what to do next, he felt a little bump at the rear of his crotch. He turned to see a plump woman with heavy makeup and large earrings. She was examining her thumbnail and frowning.

'Jesus, try to give somebody a friendly goose and you run into – what you got there, iron underpants?'

'I'm sorry, are you hurt?'

'Busted nail. Oh well, I could've done it opening a can of sardines, and I don't even like sardines. You dancing?'

'Well I, I'm not sure, I –'

She seized him. 'You're dancing.'

She had a deep, pleasant laugh, blonde hair going dark at the roots, and her name was Ida. She didn't seem to mind that Roderick couldn't dance at all.

'Don't worry, kid, you'll pick it up. None of you young kids know anything about slow dancing.'

'Well no I don't – oops. Sorry.'

'It's okay. I guess you came here for the Auks, they come on later.'

'The Auks?'

She looked him over. 'If you never heard of the Auks, you must be older than you look. Or else, Roderick, you haven't been around much.'

'No I guess I – oops. Sorry.'

'You been in the slammer, kid?'

'Jail? Not lately I mean no, I –'

She squeezed at his shoulder. 'Never mind, lover, it don't matter to me. Tell me your hard-luck story if you want, or tell me nothing, all the same to me. But you got slammer written all over you, that pale, pasty look, that weird short haircut, the kinda lost look you got, like you're afraid you're gonna make some wrong move and end up back inside.' She looked serious for a moment. 'Hey you fixed all right for bread? Because if you're broke, I can let you have a coupla bucks till you get a job.'

Roderick was so astonished that he tripped and nearly fell. 'Sorry! Do you mean you would lend money to a perfect stranger?'

She grinned. 'Nobody's perfect. A good stranger'll do.'

'I'll be damned. Well well.' After a few moments he said, 'Well I don't, but thanks. Thanks a lot, Ida.'

The dance ended. Ida started fiddling with her earring. 'On the other hand if you're flush, you might buy a girl a beer. You might even buy *me* a beer.'

Roderick was delighted to rush her to the bar and order one beer. The bartender looked from him to Ida. 'I'm sure the lady would prefer a champagne cocktail,' he said.

'Beer,' said Ida. 'Just now the lady prefers a beer, Murray.'

The bartender winked. 'Sorry, Ida, I didn't know you was with a *friend*. One beer, coming up.'

Roderick, watching her drink it, thought, *friend*.

'You don't drink?'

'I can't,' he said.

'Don't tell me, the stomach. I seen it all before, the way them places ruin a guy's stomach. Half the guys get out they can't eat or drink. Other half can't sleep. Most of 'em can't screw worth a damn.' She sighed. 'But what do you expect, you can't lock a guy up like an animal and then expect him to come out still human. Take you, for instance. You don't feel very human, do you?'

'You really understand me, Ida.'

The deep laugh. 'Lover, that's my job. Which reminds me, I better circulate. Thanks for the beer.' She stood up, adding, 'Don't forget, if you need a favour. I'm always around this joint.'

She drifted away. Later Roderick noticed her talking to a battered-looking man in a bowling shirt. She was drinking a champagne cocktail. Then he lost sight of her because the place was filling up with a new crowd, mostly young people dressed in white.

The white seemed to be a kind of uniform for both boys and girls, some of whom had bleached white hair and white makeup Roderick began to feel out of place in his old hand-me-down suit.

The lunching trio left and three young men in white began setting up some complex equipment. Roderick drifted over to the bandstand to watch.

'Jeez,' said one, 'didn't anybody check out the co-inverter? The Peabody drift is over 178 how can I patch anything in to that? Barry, you check that out?'

'Yeah it was okay. Wasn't it, Gary, you was there.'

'Was I? Yeah well in that case okay, what's the problem? Just patch it in, Larry.'

'Like hell I will, you wanna blow the whole psychofugal synch box?'

'We could run on 19th-channel syntonics, just until –'

'Oh listen to the expert, will ya? You hearing this Gary, our boy here thinks he can play it all by ear, he's the big electronics expert all of a sudden. Only he don't know how to check out the equipment, a simple drift-check and he –'

Roderick said, 'Maybe I can help.'

Larry threw up his hands. 'Why not? Let everybody be a damn expert, why not?'

'Well you see I couldn't help noticing you've got a Pressler-Joad co-inverter there, if it's one of the early models A300 through A329 you can make it into an obvolute paraverter with harmony-split interfeed, see? All you do is take off the back – hand me that screwdriver, will you Larry? – and then you just

370

change this pink wire and this green wire around. Now you got full refractal phonation with no drift, see?'

'Hey you know you're right? Great!' said Larry.

'Hey thanks man,' said Barry.

'Yeah man, thanks. Listen here's a pass, anyplace we play, you get in free, okay?' said Gary.

As soon as Roderick got down from the platform, a girl grabbed his arm. 'Hey you know them, personally? You a friend of the Auks?'

'Well no, not exactly.'

The girl wore white, her hair was bleached, and her eyes decorated with gold crow's feet. Her earrings were tiny integrated circuits, also in gold.

'God, I really like them, I think they're real other-world, you know?'

'Other-world.'

'Who do you like best, Larry, Barry or Gary?'

'I'm not uh sure – who do *you* like best?'

'Oh, Barry. I mean when he gr-rinds that synthesizer, I just – ohhh!' She rolled her eyes.

'Oh?'

'He was my favourite back when there were the original six, even back then, before Harry and Cary and Jerry dropped out.'

'Oh.' Roderick was spared further conversation by the other-world Auks. One of them (they all three looked alike to Roderick) grabbed a microphone and growled into it:

'Okay now, robots! Let's do that raunchy robot!'

Roderick quickly got out of the way of the dancers, who were doing an odd, jerky walk. Now he began to understand the uniforms and makeup: they were imitating some fictional robots.

The music was traditional rock, though generated by a complex of electronic instruments. Every now and then, one of the Auks would seize a microphone and growl a few words:

Do the raunchy robot
Do the raunchy robot
Do the raunchy robot roll!
Lady dressed in white
Gimme some light
I am in a deep black hole.

371

Roderick found it too loud, too cheerless. But he politely remained standing in front of the giant speakers throughout the rest of the set. The girl who liked Barry best seemed to be dancing at Roderick, or at least keeping an eye on him as she jerk-walked through numbers like 'R.U.R. My Baby' and the Palindromic tune 'Ratstar'.

At the end of the set, when Roderick started making his way towards the exit, the girl followed. She was still walking like someone with spine damage, and her face was expressionless. When a white-haired boy tried to stop her, she pointed to Roderick, saying:

'I . . . am . . . under . . . his command . . . I . . . obey!'

'Now look,' Roderick said, to the circle of white-haired boys who were closing in on him. 'Now look, I don't know what this is all ab –'

Someone screamed, and he saw a folding chair coming at his head. He ducked, and suddenly fists and feet were after him, driving him into the floor. He fell, took a kick under the nose and rolled away into another kick.

Then he wasn't the centre of it any more. Youths were chopping and kicking each other as though a mass tantrum had spread through the crowd. Roderick saw blood on white shirts, faces twisted with rage, folded chairs spinning through the air. Then someone grabbed his collar and dragged him through the forest of struggling legs to the exit.

'Ida!'

'Outside, kid, quick.' They raced across the dark parking lot, hailed a taxi and were away from it, safe.

'Jeez, Ida, thanks. Thanks a lot.'

'You need taking care of,' she said. 'But then don't we all?'

It was not the worst of times. It was not the best of times.

V

The tone arm hesitated as though judging distance, made the leap and lowered safely on twelve-string guitar music. Leadbelly sang:

Funniest thing I ever seen
Tomcat sittin' on a sewin' machine

There was a cat in Ida's cramped little apartment, a fat Persian that blinked and yawned until she shooed it off the sofa, but there was no room for a sewing machine.

'Make yourself comfy, Roderick. Why don't you take a bath and a slug of bourbon and say we take it from there?'

'No but wait, wait. I don't drink, and I don't need baths. And it's kind of you, Ida, but I don't think I could take it from there either.'

'I've heard that before,' she said, plumping a cushion. 'But you'd be surprised what you can do when you get in the mood.'

Roderick sat down and let the Persian rub its head against his shins. 'Look, maybe I'd better explain: I'm a robot.'

'Yeah? That's what all these crazy kids say, nowadays.' After pouring herself a drink, she sat next to him. 'I thought you had more sense, Rod.'

'No, I mean a real robot. I'm full of wires and stuff. Honest.'

Ida tasted her drink and frowned. 'Sure, kid. Anything you want. Only I hope robots don't like beating up on women or nothing like that. I'm not so good at that scene.'

'Beating up on – I thought they only did that in the movies! No, heck Ida, I didn't mean I want anything special, anything freaky. I meant I don't like anything at all.'

'Okay but if you did like something, what would it be?'

'I don't know, something like – well, like love. I guess.'

'Roderick, there has to be a first time for everybody. And I'm a

373

pretty good teacher, if I say so myself. There ain't much I haven't seen, done, had done to me, smelled, tasted, dressed up as, sat on or listened to. I could tell you some stories – only they might scare you off.'

He said nothing while she had two more drinks and fiddled with the tassels on a cushion.

'Well, for instance some guys get turned on by just a fabric, rubber or leather or silk or even cotton. One guy had to be hanged in a telephone booth while a woman wearing yellow cotton gloves – me – pounded on the door. Another guy used to wear cotton long johns with the flap down, and I had to pretend to be scared while he whipped me with a piece of cotton string, I had to call him King Cotton. Then there was the gingham guy. He would sit at the kitchen table just like in the ads and I would come in wearing nothing but a gingham apron to pour milk on his cereal. Then he'd listen to it, while yours truly got under the table to make him snap, crackle and pop. That's to mention only cotton.'

She went on to describe strange rituals called golden showers, dog shows, thundermug brunches, Leslie Fiedler croquet; scenes involving coffins, chains, ice sculpture, lecterns, skates, trusses, apricot jam, the recorded cries of whales, pool tables, confetti, door chimes, Worcestershire sauce, early photos of Stalin, voodoo dolls, thimbles, mukluks, croziers, castanets, documentary films on the cement industry, whoopee cushions.

'. . . and I knew this FBI special agent, boy was he ever special. We always started off me whipping him with a towel from the Moscow YWCA while he sings about Notre Dame marching on to victory, then another girl comes in – we're in the bathroom – and handcuffs him to the faucets and washes his mouth out with soap while he studies pictures of Whitaker Chambers and Jean-Paul Sartre. Then I had to barge in wearing a J. Edgar Hoover mask and release him but only so's we could put him under a hot light and I ask him to name all the state capitals while she dusts off his cock for fingerprints. Then at the last minute a third girl rushes in and hands him a writ of *habeas corpus*. Boy, we earned our money in them days. And we always had to be careful with that guy's face because he'd always just finished getting a face-lift. So listen, kid, you ain't got no problem I can't handle unless

374

maybe you like boys.' She put a hand on his leg and slid it towards his crotch. 'Tell me all about your problem, Rod. You got a wooden leg here, that it? You shy?'

Roderick stood up. 'Maybe if I just undressed and showed you –?'

She nodded. 'I won't be shocked. I – holy cow!'

Roderick stepped out of his dropped trousers and then took off his shirt. 'See, I am a little different.'

'Different, I'll say. Turn around, will you? Jeez, no asshole either. And you, what's that in your belly button, looks like an electric socket or –'

'It is an electric socket. It's how I recharge. Like I said, Ida, I'm a real robot.'

'I believe you, I believe you.' She poured another drink and gulped it down. 'So there's nothing I can do for you?'

'If I could stay overnight and charge my batteries, I guess that's all.'

After another, very large drink, Ida said, 'A robot. Does that mean you got no feelings at all?'

'I've got some feelings.' He thought about it. 'It's just that I can't do much about them.'

'It's a challenge, all right.' Ida seemed to be talking to herself. 'A real challenge. Okay you recharge tonight, I'll get some shuteye. In the morning when I'm soberer, I'll think about this problem of yours some more. See, the way I look at it, nobody with feelings oughta go around not being able to let 'em out, all frustrated and ornery. Okay, so what if you got no ordinary sex equipment – sex is all in the mind anyway.'

Someone had said that before to Roderick, long before. Pa Wood, was it? (But Pa was always saying things: sex is all in the head. History is a bunk on which I am trying to awaken . . .)

'*Machines*,' said Indica Dinks, '*are only human, after all.*'

The audience laughed, then applauded.

The host, Mel Mason, said, '*I love it! I don't understand it, but I love it!*' After more applause, he said, '*But seriously now, Indica, isn't this Machines Lib idea just a little – wacky? I mean, do you really expect everybody to just turn their machines loose? I'd hate to be in the front yard when somebody liberates a big power mower!*'

Indica smiled just enough to show she recognized the joke, but did not join in the audience laughter. When it had abated, she said quietly, '*We don't expect people to stop using their machines, of course not. We just want people to* understand *the machines they use, to understand and* respect *them. If you don't have respect for your own car, your own home computer, how can you have any respect for yourself?*'

'*Well, that's a very interesting point, Indica, we can know a man by the gadgets he keeps.*'

She cut off the hesitant laughter. '*Yes, by the machines he keeps and by how he keeps them. Mel, machines aren't just extensions of man, that's all part of the old master-slave routine, the terrible power game we used to play, all of us. But I think we're moving on into a new era, as machines get smarter and smarter. They may go on working for us, but not as slaves. As* employees. *As I say in my new book,* THE NUTS AND BOLTS ON MACHINES LIB, *machines are beings in their own right. And if we don't give them their freedom, one of these days, they'll take it.*'

'*Well, you've given us big food for thought there, Indica, thanks very much. Stick around folks, later we'll be talking to lots more exciting people: a sculptor who wants us all to get plastered, the President's astrologer, the most beautiful private eye in Hollywood, and the exiled Shah of Ruritania, you saw it all first on the Mel Mason Afternoon Show . . .*'

Roderick watched the pictures of an armpit, then dancing cornflakes, then a shirt destroyed by lightning. Indica Dinks had been his first mother, long ago . . . in another life . . . he could hardly remember. Indica painting her toenails red. A green plant in a pot. Hank and Indica. An exercise machine. A TV cartoon called *Suffering Cats* . . .

He went back in the kitchen where Ida was fixing her face for evening. They had spent the whole day talking, trying things; Ida had heard his life history and how he functioned. But nothing had transpired.

'Okay, so you saw your old stepmother on TV, that upset you at all? Turn you on?'

'Nope. I hardly remember Indica, all I did as a kid was watch TV, how could I be upset? How could I get turned on?'

'That's the big question, Rod. How can you get turned on? Do I remind you of your stepmother? I mean I'm older, kind of motherly. And my name, Ida, that's a lot like Indica.'

He slumped down in his chair. The afternoon sun slanted in

through the window and reflected from Ida's compact mirror into his eyes. Squinting against it, he said: 'Everything's like something and everybody's like somebody, that doesn't mean much. Like all TV programmes have a car crash in the first five minutes, what does that mean? Gee, Ida, I guess all your hard work goes for nothing, you been swell but what's the poi – the poi – the –the—'

'Hey, what's wrong?'

'Nothing,' he said after a moment. 'Just the light, the way it flashes in one eye and then the other. It's real distracting. Real – nice.'

'Aha! Turns you on? Like this?'

'Not so wild. More regular. Like a truth table. Say if left was true and right was false – like this.' He took her eyebrow pencil and wrote on the kitchen table:

L L
L R
R L
R R

She tried it again, and Roderick began to relax and enjoy relaxing. 'Maybe a longer sequence,' he murmured. Just then the sun was eclipsed by a tall building, the Kratwel Tower.

'I knew it! I knew it was no good!'

'Don't worry,' said Ida. 'We can use an electric light – no? Okay then maybe a sunlamp?'

'No! No, just forget about it, forget—'

'Wait. There's one place in town where the sun will be up for at least an hour, the big hill in Beauregard Park. Come on, I'll finish fixing my face in the taxi.'

The taxi dropped them at the foot of the hill, and they hurried up it, Ida carrying her shoes to keep them nice. When they reached the top they were facing a sheet of burning gold.

'Look at that sky, Rod! Just look!'

'Yeah, yeah.' Roderick grabbed her purse and pawed through it looking for her compact. Powder spilled as he fumbled it out and thrust it into her hand. 'Come on, come on.'

They sat on the warm grass and Ida, following the truth tables he'd scribbled in the taxi, gave him:

377

```
L L L L L L L L L L
L L L L L L L L L R
L L L L L L L L R L
L L L L L L L L R R
L L L L L L L R L L and so forth.
```

'Just let yourself go,' she said soothingly. 'Go on, go on.'

'I'm . . . afraid I'll drain my battery . . .'

'Don't worry about anything, just let it all go, lover. Let it all go. Let go.'

Roderick had never felt anything like this strange, pleasant numbness that was engulfing him. His mind seemed to be thrusting and thrusting at some barrier, then pushing deeper into warm darkness, layer after deep layer until it reached the golden fire explosion.

He drowsed, then, only half-aware of Ida's leaving for her evening at the Escorial. When he awoke it was getting dark. There was a kleenex beside him with a note in eyebrow pencil: 'Told you so! Love, I.'

Christ, what had he done? Used her, that's what, used Ida like a kleenex or a mirror, to rub his own disgusting mind against the world and take crude pleasure from the friction. His first friend, his first real friend. Now he knew he could never face her again. Hadn't even told her how nice she looked. Hadn't even stopped a second to look at the sky, her sky, pure gold like Ida herself. No, he was just a – an animal automaton, a cheap clockwork gimmick to wind up and run down. He was despicable.

Roderick flung away the tissue and started walking down the hill. Halfway down, the path was blocked by a man carrying a sign:

!TNEPER

There seemed to be no way around the man, so Roderick stopped.

'Brother.'

'Okay. Mind if I get past?'

'Brother, a moment. Stop and reflect. Stop and reflect. Have you read my sign?'

378

'Yes but—'

'Notice anything unusual about it?'

'No. Except that it's written backwards. Now can I –'

'In *mirror writing*, brother.'

Something about the man's emphasis made Roderick shudder. He looked into the wild eyes. 'You, uh, saw me up on the hill?'

'With the lady, yes. Playing with a mirror. Ah, how little ye know, for ye stood on the path to paradise, and took not a step.'

It seemed certain that the man knew his terrible secret, but Roderick had to be sure. 'Can you explain that?'

'Come to our meeting tomorrow night.' The man pressed a tract into his hand. 'The address is on the back. Come all ye faithful!'

Was the man mocking him? He stood aside, and as Roderick passed, said, 'All will be made clear. St Paul said, "We see as in a glass, darkly, *but then face to face.*" Reflect on his words, brother. Reflect!'

Roderick managed to murmur thanks and take the tract home. There he found he could only read it by holding it up to a mirror.

REFLECT AND REPENT

Have you looked at yourself in a mirror lately?
Oh, not just to comb your hair, but to *see*
yourself. Look now. Do you like what you see?
The decay of the flesh, the marks of age, even
the ravages of sin?

Roderick saw the ravages of sin, and read on. The tract explained that all Nature was made symmetrical by God, and for a hidden purpose: Mirrors contained the whole of the world outside, showing (if darkly) the truth. No one can hide the truth from his mirror, any more than the mirror can hide his lies from him.

Have you ever thought, that when you look at your
reflection in mirror, *your reflection is looking*
at you?

'God sees dog,' Roderick joked, and almost at once wondered

whether his reflection would find this so funny. What if this mirror stuff was true? He read on:

The eyes are the mirrors of the soul, the tract explained. St Paul speaks of mirror-seeing. Reflection is highly prized in all religions. The God of the ancient Hebrews was YAWAY, a name readable in a mirror. Didn't all this add up to something? Surely the incredible symmetry of all Nature was no accident, but part of a plan, a manifestation of God. The left side of every creature was *exactly like* the right side – yet *different*. Scientists were now convinced that the right and left sides of one human brain were as different as two individuals – one musical and linguistic, the other spatial and mathematical. All magnets had both North and South poles, as did the Earth and all planets. Electrical charge could be plus or minus, people could be male or female, all time itself was either past or future. Didn't all this symmetry add up to a glimpse of the DIVINE PLAN?

It did, said the tract. God wanted us to preach his gospel not only among ourselves, but to those of His creatures trapped on the Other Side – to the people within mirrors. Incredible as this might at first sound, there was evidence of this DIVINE PLAN everywhere: in Nature, in the Bible, and especially within ourselves. Only if the gospel were carried into looking-glass land, could we be sure of turning the message of the world ('EVIL') into the message of the mirror ('LIVE!')

This tract was printed by the Church of Christ Symmetrical. All strangers, and their reflections, were welcome.

'We should be honoured, he decided to pay us a visit. Welcome!' Mr Danton grabbed Roderick's ear and banged his head against the wall, then kneed him. 'I mean, excuse me all to hell, we forgot to put out the red carpet. Only we didn't know what day you was finally gonna show up for work, did we?'

'No sir.'

Mr Danton knocked Roderick to the floor and was just picking up a cleaver when the alley door opened and a patrolman came in.

'Is the manager here?'

'I'm the proprietor, officer. Can I help you?' Danton laid down the cleaver. The cop stared at it for a moment, pushing back his cap as though perplexed. He kept one hand on his gun.

'We found a lady's leg in your garbage can back there. You want to explain it?'

'A lady's leg? A *lady's* leg?' said Mr Danton, as though his place often disposed of all other kinds of human legs. 'Naw, we don't know nothing about that.'

'You wanna explain what you intended doing with that cleaver, then?'

'That? Oh, I was just kidding around with my dishwasher here. Tryin'a scare him a little, haw haw haw. Hell I treat the kid like my own son, how does he repay me? Comes in late, don't come in at all. Never no apology or nothing.'

The cop straightened his cap. 'Kids these days! They don't know the meaning of punctuality, respect, duty, clean hearts.'

Roderick said, 'About this leg —'

'Well if none of you did it, I guess it might turn out to be another unsolved case. I could call it the case of the lucky legs. Only one though: case of the lucky leg sounds wrong, you know?'

Roderick said, 'Officer, I might be able to help.'

'Yeah? You wanna confess?' The cop winked at his old pal Danton. 'Your son here wants to confess!'

'No I – I think I saw somebody drop something in that garbage can. In our garbage can. The day before yesterday it was.'

The patrolman squinted at him. 'You mean you think you saw them or you think they dropped it?'

'I did see him, and he did drop it. It was wrapped in a newspaper.'

'What was?'

'Whatever it was he dropped.'

'Oh now you're sure he dropped it? You wasn't so sure before. Okay.' The cop opened his notebook. 'Okay, suppose you describe this guy that maybe didn't drop anything wrapped in a newspaper.'

Roderick described the man as having gold hair, a pockmarked complexion and gold-rimmed sunglasses. He'd worn a casual terry shirt in an easy-care polyester blend, a rib-knit V-neck with cuffs and bottom band. The body of the shirt was terry in a sculpted design. It was light rust in colour, size: medium. He'd

381

also worn s-t-r-e-t-c-h woven twill slacks in an outstanding blend of Celanese Fortrel R polyester for long wear and cotton for comfort. These were in straight-leg styling with an elastic waistband to help prevent waistband rollover, slant front pockets, two set-in back pockets, the left one with a button-through flap. These were khaki tan, size 34 regular with about a 34 inch inseam. They probably featured hook-and-eye front closure, nylon zipper, and seven belt loops fitting belts up to $1\frac{1}{2}$ inches wide. Roderick couldn't be sure about the belt loops, because of the jacket.

This was a cotton poplin jacket with a smooth nylon lining. Hip length, with a two-button tab collar and slash pockets. Set-in sleeves with one-button adjustable cuffs. Elastic insert at waist sides. Nylon zipper. This was in navy blue, medium size with about a 34 inch arm.

Finally the man had worn smooth leather-upper sports shoes with sueded split-leather reinforcement at toe. Ventilated vinyl tongue with laceholder was padded for comfort. Padded collar and peaked back. Rubber toe guard would help protect toe area against wear. Sturdy moulded heel counter. These shoes were white with royal blue vinyl stripes, and featured moulded rubber sole with crepe rubber wedge, sole having ribbed tread for traction. Size 9.

The patrolman had written nothing down, and now he closed his notebook. 'A description like that could fit anybody,' he said. After lingering a few minutes to flirt with one of the waitresses, he swaggered back out the alley door.

Within a month, the police would arrest Allbright, who was short, dark, bearded, had a clear if grimy complexion, and wore greasy denim work clothes, the only clothes he owned.

VI

The cold weather was here, and with the drop in temperature came a drop in Roderick's fortunes. The two were connected:

Fur coats were coming into the dining room regularly now, and poodle sweaters. Somehow the sight of all these creatures keeping themselves *warm* irritated him. He was reminded of pictures of the first Thanksgiving: all those roundheads and featherheads sitting down to eat *food*. Where would a robot be at that banquet? Waiting tables? Out in the cold?

Though technically he needed no special winter garments, Roderick wanted something cosy. Ma and Pa would have understood, being cosy small-town folk themselves. Ma would have said, if you're undecided about doing something, do it big.

Roderick went into an exclusive sporting-goods store, bought himself a very fine red wool stocking-cap for two weeks' wages, and wore it to work.

Unfortunately, he forgot to take it off while waiting tables. Though some patrons only laughed, one complained to the management. Mr Danton was happy to fire him.

'Son or no son,' he said, 'you're out in the fuckin' cold.'

'Sonnenschein, initial D?' asked the hospital receptionist, touching her keyboard. 'Yes, and your relationship to the patient, Mr Wood?'

'I'm his – I'm his lawyer. And I demand –'

'Certainly, sir.' The machine hummed and produced a red ticket. 'Take this pass, so you can get out again. It's Ward 18G, express elevator to the eighteenth floor.'

On the eighteenth floor he handed his pass to a nurse manning another computer terminal. 'I like your cap,' he said, 'Unusual.'

'Thank you, sir.' She read the pass and tapped keys. 'A lot of people seem to like our caps.'

'No I meant yours in particular. Unusual.'

She looked wary. 'What do you mean?'

'Well I just noticed, all the other nurses have them folded left over right, but yours is right over left.'

'Is it?' she laughed. 'Well you're the first person to notice that, anyway.'

'Well I only noticed because the cap itself is a variation on an ornamental dinner-napkin fold called The Slipper. I remember seeing a picture of it in *Mrs Bowder's Encyclopedia of Refinement*.'

'Really?'

'I read that a lot when I was a kid. The language of flowers, too, like that vase on your desk there, yellow chrysanthemums, they say –'

'Fine, fine. You can see Mr Sonnenschein in the visiting room, second door on your right. If you'll just wait he'll be in in a minute.' She seemed very busy and not inclined to look at him. But when Roderick reached the door to the visiting room he looked back: she was staring at him.

Red cap again. He pulled it off and jammed it in his pocket, damn it.

This was a sunny room overlooking the river. It was furnished like a large, comfortable living room, with a TV corner, a music centre, a writing desk and a small library – all separated by yards and yards of soft chairs and sofas. No one else was there except an old man in a striped bathrobe and paper slippers. He sat turning the pages of a book of Mondrian reproductions. Now and then he found one that made him chuckle.

Roderick tried to watch TV, but the controls of the set were locked. He settled for a newspaper.

'LUCKY LEGS' KILLER STRIKES AGAIN
Former poet held

Only 30 days after turning up a severed leg in a Downtown alley, police have unearthed a second leg Downtown. The two legs are from two victims, according to the medical examiner. 'Each is a woman's left leg, amputated at the knee,' he said, 'possibly with an electric carving knife. Both legs were removed after death.'

The first limb turned up in an alley off Junipero Serra Place. The leg was wrapped in newspaper and dropped in a garbage can at the rear of Danton's Doggie Dinette. Wendell Danton, the proprietor, said, 'Someone is out to get us, but it won't work. All the meat used in our canine cuisine is genuine U.S. Government inspected Choice or Prime cuts. I have the receipts to prove it. My kitchen is always open, and anyone is welcome to look it over, anytime.' Police agree that it is unlikely the leg came from Danton's.

Today a second grisly package was found in a litter basket on Xavier Avenue, near the newly-opened cat boutique, Pussbutton.

Former poet A.L. Bright, picked up for questioning in an alley where he was drinking wine, admits being in the vicinity of both legs, but claims he does not remember murdering anyone. Police say Bright fits an exact description of the 'Lucky Legs' killer, given by a Danton's dishwasher.

A door opened and a tall, untidy man blundered in. He was all out of proportion, like a child's drawing: arms and legs too long for his thin body, head too heavy for his thin neck, face too big for his head, hair a dark 6B scribble.

'You're my lawyer?'

'Don't you know if I'm your lawyer?'

'I don't – sometimes things surprise me. They feed me a lot of uh medication.'

Roderick was a little disappointed. 'Are you Dan Sonnenschein?'

'Yes. And you're my lawyer.'

'No, I just said that to get in. See it's very hard to get in to see you. Like you were in prison. I'm not your lawyer I'm your – I'm Roderick.'

'Well for lunch we had, I remember that okay, we had hot roast beef sandwich, salad with thousand island, banana cream pie.' He looked at Roderick. 'Didn't we?'

'Maybe you did. Dan, I'm Roderick. You created me, remember?'

'Look, I'm having a hard enough time remembering what I had for lunch.'

They sat there in silence for some time, staring at the black-

and-white tiles of the floor. Now and then the old man could be heard laughing quietly at Mondrian.

Roderick was very disappointed. So this was Dan? This was the genius who first thought of him?

'So you're not my lawyer?'

'For the last time, no. I'm Roderick. I'm the robot you spent four years building, remember? And then finally you sent me to live with Ma and Pa Wood? Your stepfather and stepmother? They raised you, you must remember them!'

'Yeah, maybe.'

'And when you sent me to them I was just a little lumpy machine on tank treads. But Pa Wood got all these parts from the artificial limb factory and rebuilt me like this. So when I came to the city I thought I'd look you up.'

'Why?'

'Why? Well like just I guess maybe – how do I know? Okay you think I shouldn't have come. Okay I made a wrong decigeon – decision. I just thought you might want to see how I turned out. I thought we might get to be pals or something. I thought when you got out I could help you with your work.'

'My work!' Dan blinked. 'My work got me in here. You know how I got in here?'

'No.'

'I had this idea there were people after me. Very high up conspiracy, see, to prevent anybody ever building a robot. So I was very careful, *very* careful with Project Roderick. I never published anything, I kept a low profile. And when the robot was finished, I sent it away, somewhere they'd never find it. And I destroyed my notes. Like whatsisname in that movie about a forbidden planet, Walter Pigeon, he buries his book and gives up robots, or maybe that's some other movie – but I destroyed my notes. That's how they got me, see?'

'No.'

Dan held up a finger; Roderick noticed how badly bitten the nail was. 'Since I was working for a University project, those notes were not my property. I was destroying University of Minnetonka property. And this property might be worth billions and billions – if I really had built a robot. So that was a very antisocial act, so they put me in here.'

386

'To cure you?'

'No, to keep me from building any more robots. And to find out if I really have built one already.'

Roderick said, 'I don't understand. They want the robot because it's worth billions, but they don't want you to build it?'

'Look, I know all this is confusing.' Dan started to chew an already dilapidated fingernail. 'What I mean is, the University people own any robot built using their money. But somebody a lot higher up wants to put a stop to all robots. Don't ask me why – a paranoid schizophrenic doesn't have to give reasons for the plots against him. I'm nuts, see? Or if I'm not, the world is so dangerous that I'd still rather be treated like a harmless nut.'

'I'll get you out of here, Dan. You're not nuts.'

'Why should I leave here? Here is as good as anywhere, now. And safer.' He stopped chewing the nail and looked at it. 'I tried leaving for awhile. I got a nice little crummy job, a nice little crummy apartment. But right away people started following me. A car tried to run me down. My apartment had this fire.' He folded his hands. 'Here is safer. Here they can watch me, so they don't have to destroy me.'

'Okay then I'll visit you all the time.'

'No. It isn't safe for you, either. If you are Roderick, they must be looking for you. Better stay away.'

'Can I at least send you something? Books? Food?'

Dan hesitated. 'Peanut butter. For some reason, they never let you have enough peanut butter around here.'

The door slammed open and a nurse marched in. Her cap was folded left over right. 'I'm sorry, Mr Wood, but there's been some kind of mix-up. Mr Sonnenschein isn't supposed to have any visitors at all. You'd better leave, right now. Come on, Mr Sonnenschein, I'll get you back to bed.' Though Dan made no resistance, Roderick noticed how she took a firm grip, one hand on his wrist, one on his elbow.

'But I'm his lawyer.'

'No you're not,' she shouted back. 'We've phoned his lawyer and he never heard of you. You'd better leave!'

Roderick stood a moment, watching the old man, who was weeping over *Broadway Boogie woogie*.

'God damn it,' said Roderick, and put on his red stocking-cap.

'God damn it is right,' said the man seated before the monitor. 'We lost the whole damn conversation there, all we get is a great shot of a guy in a stocking cap going out the door. You shoulda checked the tape before you went out.'

His partner said, 'You implying I don't know how to do my job?'

'I'm not implying nothing.'

'Look I always go out to get the coffee at three. Okay, sure, maybe I was a little late back, but only on account you wanted a chocolate doughnut, they was out downstairs. I hadda go all the way over to Thirteenth to that new place, *Mistah Kurtz*.

'Anyway what the hell's the difference, we know the guy's name from the hospital computer, you wanta check him out?'

'Let's review this next visitor, this Franklin guy. He talked to Sonnenschein for an hour, can we run that?'

On the screen the vacant features of Ben Franklin registered shock. *'Who was here? Who was here?'*

'. . . must of just about met him. Roderick. He was wearing a red stocking-cap . . .'

'I did meet him! He came out of the elevator . . . Dan, God damn it, we were face to face . . .'

'God damn it is right,' said the viewer again.

The Church of Christ Symmetrical was just a derelict store in a rundown neighbourhood. Roderick almost passed it without noticing, for it was marked only by a dusty mirror set up in an even dustier window, with a small sign:

CHURCH OF CHRIST SYMMETRICAL
You are looking at the person who controls your destiny!
And that person is looking at you!!!

Inside it didn't seem much like a church, except for the emptiness. There were a dozen rows of folding chairs (some set up facing backwards) but only four were occupied: Four ragged men sat hunched over, each quietly consulting his pocket mirror.

Having no pocket mirror, Roderick went to the front of the

church, where the place of an altar was taken by a table of reading matter. He removed his red cap but, seeing others wearing caps, put it back on.

One pamphlet showed a photo of a Byzantine plate, decorated with a picture of the Last Supper. The picture clearly showed two Christs, one giving bread to six disciples, the other giving wine to the other six. The spidery handwriting beneath said, 'The Last shall be First!!!'

Another pamphlet outlined significant passages in the Bible ('thy breasts are like *two* roes that are *twins*') and pointed out Biblical symmetries: Two tables of the Law, Solomon offers to divide a child equally in half; 72 books in the Old Testament and 27 books in the New, four evangelists having initials M, M, L and ⌐, and so on. A donation was requested, to help with the great work of preparing the Bible in mirror-writing. Roderick contributed a symmetrical 11 cents, this being all he had in his pocket.

'Thank you,' said a small, red-nosed man coming up the aisle with a large mirror in his hands. 'I see you appreciate the urgency of our work.'

'I'm not sure I even understand what your work is.'

'Aha! You will, you will. My name is Amos Soma, by the bye, and I'd like to shake your hand for Christ.'

Roderick could hardly refuse so civil a request; he spoke his name and shook the man's hand. As they did so, Mr Doma held up his mirror: their images shook left hands.

'Of course my name has not always been Soma. I took it because of its wonderful symmetry: Soma, the Vedic drink of ecstasy, and Amos, the greatest of prophets. Now, Mr Wood, if you'll find a seat, our meeting can begin.'

Roderick took a seat near the back. Two well-dressed men came in and sat still further back.

'First,' said Amos, 'I have a few important announcements to make. There has been another calumnious attack on us in the church press. As usual, they accuse us of "Mirror worship", of saying the Lord's Prayer backwards, and of so-called black magic. Frankly I don't feel lies like these are worth answering, so I'll drop that subject. I also have a positive announcement: our Bible translation is ahead of schedule, and we have now finished Sudoxe.'

A man in a parka, sitting a few rows ahead of Roderick, turned around and said to him in a loud whisper, 'You aren't spying on me or anything?'

'No.'

'I didn't think so.'

Amos began his sermon: 'I want you all to reflect tonight on the cross. Notice how symmetrical the cross is. Right and left reflect, but not top and bottom. Why is that?

'It is because the cross is shaped like a man. But why, you might ask, is man symmetrical? He could have been made any shape at all. God didn't need to make you with one eye on the right side of your nose and one on the left. Oh no, God could have made you like one of those modernistic paintings, with an eye on your chin and another on your forehead!'

Amos paused for laughter. There was none. 'No, God made man symmetrical because He made him in His own image. God Himself is symmetrical. He has a right and a left. Everybody knows that Christ "sitteth on the right hand of the Father", so the Father must *have* a right hand.'

The man in the parka turned around again. 'You sure they didn't send you to watch me?'

'No.'

'No, I don't suppose they'd bother.'

Amos went on, discoursing for some time on left and right – the hemispheres of the brain, magnetic 'handedness', whirlpools, political leanings, Lewis Carroll – and why God made mirror symmetry. God meant for us to meet our mirror images face to face (how else?), to talk to them, and to bring them to salvation.

The parka turned around again. 'You impressed by this bullcrap?'

'Yes I guess I am.'

'Me too. Funny, because I think I know what's wrong with old Amos.'

'What's that?'

'He's just ambidextrous. He can write with both hands, that means. So the thing is, he doesn't know if he's right- or left-handed. He doesn't know which side of the mirror he's living on, and it drives him nuts. He wants to convert everybody on both sides, just to play it safe.'

Roderick said, 'Then you don't believe.'

'Oh I don't know. You have to believe in something. Every week or so I try some new religion or some new political movement. And the thing is, I always believe.'

At the end of the meeting, the man introduced himself as Luke Draeger. 'I was thinking about going to the bar on the corner, you know it? The Tik Tok Club. Figured I'd sit there and stare at myself in the mirror – till I get double vision. You might as well come along and spy on me.'

'The name is Roderick Wood, and I'm not a spy. And I don't drink.'

'Rickwood, everybody drinks. Especially spies. Come on, you need a drink.'

The two men in the back got up and left.

'But I really don't drink. All I really need is a job. Before I become – well, a beggar, like this old guy.'

The old man he meant wore a long black overcoat, almost to the ground, which somewhat resembled a cassock. He had produced a cracked saucer from one pocket and was pretending to take up a collection.

'Howdy doody, gents,' he said, approaching. 'Spare a little contribution for the mm-hmm-mmf . . .?'

Luke dropped a few coins on his saucer. 'There, you old fraud. I've seen you taking up collections in every storefront church around here.'

'Bless you, sir, it's only for the clothes. Against the terrible winter.'

Roderick took off the red stocking-cap and handed it over. 'You need this more than I do. In fact I don't need it at all.'

'Bless you, bless you . . .' The old man salaamed away.

Luke was impressed. 'You're outa work and you give away your cap. By God I like that. To hell with getting a drink, I'm gonna get you a job. I work at this little factory, see, and they always need extra men.'

He led the way outside against the blustering wind and wet sleet, to an alley between two warehouses. Roderick followed cautiously to a rickety fire escape, then all the way up to the roof. There Luke knocked on an iron door which, to Roderick's surprise, opened at once. A fat yawning woman let them in. To

Luke she said, 'Boss wants to see you. Right now.' She looked at Roderick. 'Who's this?'

'This is my old pal Rickwood. I'm just gonna show him around, he might accept the offer of a job here.'

'Ha! Better see the Boss first.'

First, however, Luke showed Roderick around. It was a peculiar factory, with hardly a machine in sight. They went down open stairs into the middle of the place, a lot of trestle tables where people sat making things. There seemed to be a lot of different products being turned out here.

One old man with a gallon of wine at his elbow was painting a rustic scene on a diagonal slice of birch log: a lake at sunset, with a moose on the shore and a canoe gliding across, beneath the words *Souvenir of Lake Kerkabon*. The painter completed his work, flipped the wooden plaque over, and stamped on its back MADE IN KOREA.

Next to him a woman with an eyepatch was flattening out aluminium cans and hammering them on a mould to make them into ashtrays shaped like horseshoes. These two were stamped MADE IN KOREA.

Next to her was a man fishing green felt letters very quickly from a bag and sewing them on a grey baseball shirt. His little hand-cranked sewing machine chattered away and in less than a minute he had spelled out SHAMEROCKS. As a final touch, he sewed a label into the neck of the shirt (Made in Korea). Others were assembling and testing digital watches, again with the puzzling label, while still others were painting portraits of the President on decorative meat platters, labelled again.

'Why is everything "Made in Korea"?' Roderick asked.

'It makes people realize they're getting a bargain, the cheapest item available. It is the cheapest, too. Nobody in Korea can get labour as cheap as it is right here, off Skid Row. Even automation costs more than us. Want a job here?'

'Sure, why not?'

'Okay, just let me find the Boss.' Luke went off to the far end of the room, to a little cubicle made of cardboard cartons. There was a constant sound coming from that cubicle, a high-pitched electric hum.

In a moment Luke came back. 'You can't win 'em all,' he said cheerfully.

'No job for me?'

'Not only that; they fired me too. I guess I was expecting it, but – oh hell, Rickwood, let's go get that drink after all.'

Outside, the cold wind and sleet continued to batter at pedestrians. The gutters were filling up with water, floating cigarette filters and popsicle sticks, pizza boxes and foil from chewing gum, a non-returnable bottle with no message and a used condom floating like a pale jellyfish, bandaids, plastic coathangers, an old *TV Guide*. Roderick thought he saw the floating body of a Golden Retriever puppy, wrapped in sodden toilet paper, but he couldn't be sure.

At the Tik Tok Club there were police cars and an ambulance, and a large crowd.

'All right, everybody back,' said a cop, though in fact no one was pressing forward to look at the figure being rolled out of the bar on a stretcher.

'. . . and these two guys just shoot him when he walks in the door,' said someone. 'Figure that, an old wino like that, I mean who would waste a bullet? Figure that, these two guys just . . .'

'Everybody back.' The cop bent and picked up the red stocking-cap which had fallen, and put it back on the stretcher.

VII

Luke ordered two scotches. 'I know why they nailed him. It's because I gave him 39 cents. They wanted to teach me a lesson.'

'What lesson?'

'I didn't ask permission first. Jesus, Rickwood, don't you understand? It's "Captain May I" around here all the time; you gotta ask permission to scratch your ass. I mean *I gotta* ask permission. So they rubbed him out, just to remind me.'

'Remind you? Luke, I think this all sounds –'

'Remind me who's captain, of course. Who gives the orders – them – and who takes the orders – me. I see you aren't drinking. On duty are you?'

'No I'm not on duty, but listen, Luke, who are *they*?'

'As if you didn't know!' Luke finished both drinks and ordered two more. 'Okay, maybe you don't work for them. I guess maybe I'm a little upset here, losing my job and then seeing that poor old fart lying dead – I mean it hasn't been all that good a day.'

'You said you were expecting to be fired,' Roderick reminded him.

'Yes. Yes. The Boss said there were too many mistakes in the work. He's right, he's right. See, we were working on car seat covers, you know the ones? Imitation leopard skin. There was this big team of us, painting on the spots. And everything was going along okay until I went and changed religions.'

'You mean to the Church of Christ Symmetrical?'

'Naw, before that. Like I said, I get a new religion every week or so. No, this time it was the Disciples of the Four Gopsels.'

'The Four Gospels?'

'No, the Four *Gopsels*. Deliberate mistake there, see.' Luke finished two more drinks. 'The whole basis of this religion is that nobody's perfect, everybody makes mistakes. Kind of an Islamic idea, I think. To err is human, and not to err is divine. So if you

394

make something perfect, you're only mocking God so in everything you do, *you have to make one deliberate mistake.*'

'I see where this is leading,' said Roderick. 'You made mistakes on the seat covers?'

'That wouldn't have been so bad. All I'd do was maybe leave off a spot, or do it in the wrong colour, or sometimes do it in a funny shape like the ace of clubs or something. But see painting leopard spots is boring work, so you get to talking with the people you work with, great bunch of guys and gals, I – well, I converted them. They all got born again as Disciples of the Four Gospels too. So then each of them had to make a deliberate mistake. And by the time twenty-seven people do this, the seat covers start to look kinda funny, you know? That's why the Boss fired me.'

'Maybe that was his deliberate mistake,' said Roderick.

'Rickwood, you're a card. I haven't had a good laugh since I left the Corps.'

'The Corps?'

Luke laughed again. 'Maybe you're *not* spying on me.' He took a gold pin from his pocket and laid it on the bar. 'Like, you wouldn't know what that is, would you?'

Roderick looked at the pin. It showed a circle nested in a crescent, and a star with three lines coming down from it. 'Some Masonic lodge? Turkish Army?'

'The Astronaut Corps, pal. I was an astronaut. In fact I was the hundred-and-forty-seventh man on the moon. I was the hundred-and-eighty-first to walk in space, and the two-hundred-and-seventeenth to say "The Earth sure looks beautiful from up here." Ah, those were the days, those were the days. Except –'

'Except?'

'Except they weren't.' Luke ordered more scotch. 'Maybe I should start at the beginning. See, I always wanted to go to the moon. When I was a kid I read space comics and built model rockets and everything. Then I went into the Air Force, dropped a few bombs, had a few laughs, and ended up married and with three yelling kids in North Dakota. Here, I'll show you pictures of my kids, look at this. No not that one, that's a bomb pattern, here we are: Ronny and Vonny and little Lonny. Cute, huh? Of course they aren't yelling in the picture.

'Anyway they told me I could qualify as an astronaut, only first

I had to get a PhD. They figured they couldn't have guys walking in space and saying how the Earth sure looks without PhDs. So I went to college, only right away I could see I wasn't going to make it. So I decided to cheat. I had a lot going for me: I looked bright, I was rich and my father was a Senator. So I bought exam answers and faked experiments, and hired a research assistant to write my doctoral dissertation for me – I couldn't even pronounce the title. Defending it was no problem, either: I had Dad put a little Federal research grant muscle on the college, and they managed to come up with a friendly committee and a prepared list of questions and answers. I got my PhD and I became an astronaut. You see, dreams can come true.'

Roderick shook his head. 'What I don't see is why it mattered so much. What's so great about space?'

'Let's have another drink and I'll tell you. Barkeep?'

Roderick saw a familiar face at the end of the bar. Or was it familiar? Just some man with oily black hair, tinted glasses, and a tweed overcoat. He was talking to a pretty, doll-like little woman in a black fur coat – they both looked a little overdressed for Skid Row – telling her jokes, evidently. Every now and then she'd let out a little squeak of laughter and say, 'Oh Felix, you are the limit! The limit!'

Luke was saying, 'Why did I want to be an astronaut? I used to ask myself that, you know. But then when I'd get home after a hard day faking lab experiments, and the kids would be yelling and the wife would refuse to iron my socks and make a big scene about it – then you know, I realized why I liked space. It's because you're alone out there. No one wants a bedtime story. No one wants you to drop off clothes at the cleaners on your way home. Oh don't get me wrong, I love my wife. I love my kids. I love my dog and my television set and all my neighbours and fellow countrymen and everybody else, but I still like to be alone, once in a while. In space. You know like in that poem, "The world's a fine and private place".'

Roderick said, 'I thought it was the grave that was a fine and private place.'

'Okay never mind that. The point is, I got into space finally, and instead of being alone, it was just the opposite. Two guys in the damned space shuttle with you, and Mission Control in there

396

too – I mean right inside your damned suit. You eat a ham sandwich, this voice in your ear says, "Nice going, Luke. Hope you enjoy the ham sandwich, because your blood sugar level can use it." You take a piss and they know exactly how much, what's in it, the pH and albumin level, everything. You take a walk on the damned moon, they check your heart rate and tell you you're lookin' good, just gotta remind you they're watching every move.'

'I think I see what you mean.'

Luke laughed. 'They see it, too. They see everything I ever did mean and ever will mean! Well, you get back and they have to debrief you, that means a lot more talk about how well they've been watching you. Then come the awards and shaking hands with the President and banquets and more awards and parades and crowds, crowds everywhere, even if you get a minute alone in your hotel room if you turn on TV there you are, eating that ham sandwich again, the world is not a fine and private place at all.'

Roderick studied the oddly familiar stranger again. He had a long jaw, and the skin of his face seemed dull in the glaring lights of the Tik Tok Club – powdered? The only really familiar feature of that long, empty face was the pair of tinted glasses. Who did they remind him of? No one.

'That's not the worst, the publicity's not the worst. The worst is when it's over,' said Luke. 'Because then you go home and it seems good to be home, the wife and kids seem terrific after the others. So you relax, have a few beers, watch an old movie on TV with the wife, go to bed. You find yourself getting a hard-on, and just as you're about to nudge the wife, a little voice in your ear says, "Nice going, Luke. Good idea to have sex with your missus, only watch the old pulse rate. You're lookin' good." It's old Mission Control, still with me! Still there! Still watching! The hard-on naturally vanishes.

'And Christ, they been with me ever since, watching every move and passing little palsy-walsy remarks on everything I do. I went to a Corps doctor and asked him, was it possible they'd planted some kind of device on me? Some video-radio device on me or even in me? He sent me to a psychiatrist, and the psychiatrist had me thrown out of the Corps.'

Felix of the tinted glasses told the woman in black fur one last joke as they left. Tired of slumming. Tinted glass, tinted glass.

'I thought when I left the Corps it would all stop. But no, not a chance: once they get you, they get you for life. Every time I so much as farted, Mission Control would tell me what a great idea it was to vent that gas buildup.

'Well naturally that wrecked my happy marriage. What kind of wife can put up with that, her husband gets ready to make love and then suddenly says "Affirmative, Mission Control" and gets a tired cock? And the kids, too, I'd be reading them a bedtime story when Mission Control would come on the line, asking was I sure I read that last paragraph right, and would I say again?'

Again Roderick said to himself, tinted glass, through a glass darkly but then face to long empty face – of course, it was the gold-haired stranger! Of course with the hair dyed, a different pair of tinted glasses – but no disguising the empty grin, the long empty face that, once the pocks were puttied up, had nothing in it.

'Excuse me,' said Roderick to the bartender. 'That couple who just left, woman in fur, man in tinted glasses? Do you know them? Know where they went?'

'Nope. Why.'

Roderick ran to the door and out on the corner. There were empty streets stretching away in four directions, no human to be seen, nothing but a wind-blown page of newspaper.

Roderick went back to the bar. 'Thought I saw someone I knew . . . probably wrong. Go on. About your voices.'

'Go on? *They* go on, pal. *They* go on.'

'And they're still with you, right now?'

'Affirmative. Saying it's a good story but nobody'd believe it – and that I've had enough ethanol. Time to leave.'

'A little voice in your ear,' Roderick said. 'Sounds kind of like a conscience.'

'It is a conscience. Correct and confirmed, it is a damned conscience. That's why I keep messing around with religion and politics. I need to find some way to get rid of this conscience. To exorcize it. I mean hell, millions of people get along without consciences, why should I get stuck? I mean Nixon did what he wanted to, right? So why me? Why me?'

Roderick knew no answer. Which was unfortunate, because Luke was getting loud and defiant.

'I won't put up with it!' he yelled. 'You hear that, Mission Control? I won't put up with it! I'll find some kind of religion that will shut your still small trap for good! Or politics – I'll start a goddamned revolution that will burn Houston to the ground!'

The bartender approached. 'Get your friend outa here. Maybe we ain't a high-class joint, but we got our limit. He controls himself now, or out.'

'Over and out,' murmured Luke, as Roderick helped him from the bar. 'Your friend doesn't control himself, Rickwood, because they control him. He's not even human, just a radio-controlled model astronaut. Mission Control says I'm not walking too straight. Am I?'

'That depends on where you want to go.'

'Gert's Café, where else? The address is on this.' Luke fumbled in all his pockets and came up with a handbill printed in red:

WE SAY NO

NO to Fascist prison atrocities, extermination of dissidents and tortured confessions!

NO to Marxist-Leninist mindless bureaucracies grinding down the disaffected in slave labour camps!

NO to Capitalist corporate corruption, conglomerate exploi-tation of the workers and rape of the Third World!

NO to Maoist robotocracy, smashing individualism under mind-bending, brain-washing statism!

NO to the so-called New Left and other effete dilettante so-called movements drowning in their own so-called rhetoric!

NO to Anarchism, Trotskyism, Democracy and all other useless isms and ocracies!

Left Right and Centre, it's all
A GREAT BIG NOTHING!!!

Find out the truth tonight: Mammoth meeting of the
FRACTIOUS DISENGAGEMENTISTS
(Gert's Café Branch)
Gert's Café
1141 Richelieu Ave. So.

Well and why shouldn't 1141 Richelieu Ave. So. turn out to be an ordinary frame house in a slightly rundown neighbourhood? Why shouldn't it be allowed to have a small sign on the front lawn: GERTS CAFE. KEEP OUT. THIS MEANS YOU, and why shouldn't this make Roderick hesitate?

'Maybe we shouldn't go in,' he said, at which Luke laughed.

'You don't know much about politics, Rickwood.' The question which cries out for an answer now is, who does know anything about politics? Isn't it just a dirty game for cynical manipulators of mass ignorance?

They walked in, by direct action demanding to be let in and given the same rights as anyone else – as those who could not read, for example.

Gert's Café provided only four tables, but then there were only three Fractious Disengagementists in the Gert's Café Branch, which was also so far the only branch of this new regrouping of committed elements of radical consciousness in anticipation of a totally new unfettered mass spiritual/ political movement unifying to force a final showdown with the present-day corrupt and powerful system. Anyway Bill was playing the video game machine in the corner all evening, so didn't need a chair.

So far Gert's Café had a menu but no manifesto, but tonight's meeting would hopefully fix that. The menu had taken careful planning and much meaningful discussion, working through all objections to California grapes and Brazilian coffee and any other foodstuff outputted by any other oppressive regime. It was finally agreed to limit the menu to bread and water – homebaked stoneground wholemeal bread and pure bottled mineral spring water – the fare of all political prisoners everywhere.

These prisoners of conscience became acquainted: there was Rickwood, a taciturn guy whose symmetrical, bland face probably concealed a real thinker; Luke, a drunken loudmouth but probably revolutionary at heart; Bill, the big guy with the beard who played video games and said little, in fact nothing; Wes, the small intense guy with rimless glasses who talked a blue streak and wanted action! action! and 'Gert' who was really Joanne and married to Wes but who preferred not to be known as Mrs or even Ms but adopted the totally unbiased and sex-free title Msr, applicable to men persons and to women persons, in any order.

What was to be done? The entire world was now in the grip of authoritarian zombarchical police states, maintaining power through multinational conglomerates at the top and the jack-booted forces of oppression at the bottom. The world was beginning to resemble something in a satirical science-fiction novel of no great quality. It was time to do something, all right. Time for some all-out, ultimate, definitizing gesture that would make it clear for all time where everybody stood.

Wes wanted to go out right away and collect money to save up for a cobalt bomb that would wipe out all life on this planet for millions or maybe billions of years: that was action. Gert and Luke preferred to argue about the placement of punctuation in a draft manifesto condemning 'world interdependencies/coercive structures/Houston Mission Control/militarist juntas/pigshit bureaucracies'.

Roderick, having gone into the kitchen to find an outlet and recharge his batteries, came back at dawn to find the arguments still raging on, and Bill still playing a video game. Since it was breakfast time, they all sat down and (all but Roderick) had a bread and water breakfast. Bill spoke for the first time:

'A lot of people talk a lot about blowing up the world, tearing it all down and starting over,' he said 'But I'm really doing something. I got me a job with the Hackme Demolition Company, and we're really tearing stuff down.'

'You blow stuff up for some capitalist,' said Wes. 'That's no good. A rich guy in silk hat and striped pants holds out this bag with a dollar sign on it, and you say "Yes sir, yes sir. You want me to lose that building? Yes sir."'

'But I still blow it up,' said Bill. 'It's still one building less.' He thought for a moment, chewing his bread. 'And they're still hiring, if anybody here wants a job, a honest job.'

Wes already had a job, as clerk to a tax lawyer for a leading investment firm. Joanne had the café to run, Wes added.

Roderick and Luke agreed to help dismantle the world.

VIII

The apostle clock chimed. Mr Kratt lifted his snout automatically and listened. For a second the heavy black V of his brow-line softened.

'Okay Smith, where were we?'

'O'Smith, sir. The name is O'Smith. And the game today is I do believe industrill espionedge. Ain't it?' The insolent tone was unexpected. Nice change of pace, Kratt thought, from all the panting yes-men around here. Of course it was the desperate insolence of a loser, just look at the man. Kratt looked, and found himself trying to stare O'Smith down.

In essence, this 'Mister' O'Smith (who seemed to have no first name) was a fat cowboy with a deep tan. He wore the modified Western clothes favoured by bogus oilmen and revivalists on the make, but even his hand-tooled boots failed to give him a prosperous look. His fat would be the fat of poverty, of hash-house burgers dripping with mayonnaise, pancakes or powdered-sugar doughnuts in the morning and greasy pizza at night, watery tap beer and syrupy wine, and cokes glugged down too fast in desert gas stations. Kratt had seen thousands of O'Smiths passing through his amusement arcades and his carnival, hurrying on their way from trailer-camp childhoods to flophouse deaths, losers all the way.

Mr Kratt's gaze faltered. 'Okay, let me give you a general run-down on this operation and then turn you over to my product-development boy, Ben Franklin.'

'Yes sir. Now do I liasonize with you or this Frankelin?'

'Him, this is all his show. See, Franklin worked on a research project at the University, a few years ago. Building a robot.'

'Yep.' O'Smith was staring hard again.

'When the project broke up, the robot disappeared. Naturally

Franklin was disappointed. After putting in all that work on the thing, to have somebody come along and steal it . . .'

'So you want me to steal it back?'

'That's about it. It's worth ten grand in cash, plus all reasonable expenses. Agreed?' Mr Kratt stood up and was about to offer his hand when O'Smith turned aside and walked to the window.

'By God you got a view here, sir. A view! From up here it looks like you could just reach down and pick up any old piece of that city down there, pick it up in your hand. Like it's all yours. Guess lots of it is yours, right? KUR is such a big old conglomerate, like I guess you manufacture that there Brazos Billy gadget, right?'

'Brazos Billy? What – oh, you mean the fast-draw amusement machine, yes one of our subsidiaries handles that one, why?'

'Nothin', I just always kind of liked old Brazos, boy I must of drawed against him a thousand times – at bus stations, airports, arcades.'

Kratt looked at his watch. 'There a point to all this?'

'I like the way when you hit old Brazos he flops down on the floor and bleeds like a stuck pig. Plastic blood I know but boy it surely looks real. I always wanted one of them machines for myself so I could practise at home.'

'You want me to throw in a toy, is that it?'

O'Smith grinned. ''Preciate that, Mr Kratt sir. But I was only calling attention to the difference between you and me. I wanted a robot for years and never got it. You want one for five minutes, you just call me in, say "Ten grand in cash" and you got it.' The grin broadened. 'You got it, Mr Kratt. Sir.'

O'Smith offered his left hand, a final insult.

Mister O'Smith still had his smile when he had finished talking to Ben Franklin, who could only give him two minutes. He kept the smile on until he was safely out of the building and into a bar, where he ordered a tap beer. Then he let it go.

'What's the matter, cowboy? Somebody shoot your horse?'

He looked at the woman in purple with her purple lipstick, and he continued to scowl. She raised her shotglass and nodded to him as though he'd bought her a drink. 'You wouldn't think it to look at me now,' she said, 'but I was once a Paris model.'

Model what? he wondered.

'I was. A *mannequin*.'

'Lena!' The bartender shouted at her as at a dog. 'Quit bothering the customers, I told you before.'

'Larry's always telling somebody off . . .' she said.

Mister O'Smith ignored the old bat, tried to get his thoughts straight or just not think. Later he would hit an arcade, few games of Star Rats maybe and then shoot it out with old Brazos. Then get a pizza, go back to his hotel room and grab some shuteye. Plenty of time to think after that . . .

Ten measly grand, fucker was going to make millions off this Roderick, maybe billions. Ten grand was like an insult, like he was so dumb he couldn't figure what a robot like that was worth. God durn it, a man had his pride, even a man as badly handicapped as Mister O'Smith, handicapped didn't make him an idiot. There was other people who would pay to find out about Roderick the Robot, this Roderick Wood the Robot. How about the Agency? Them boys wouldn't forget the work O'Smith done for 'em already, and they was always in the market for dope on robots. He'd stopped it must be twenty different robots getting built, back when he was freelancing for the Agency. The Agency would pay, all right.

Then there was other companies. How about Moxon, now, always hot for some little cybernetic novelty. Others too. Nothing wrong with selling the same robot to everybody, why not?

'I don't know why not,' said the woman with purple. 'You tell me, honey.'

He saw how it was: he'd been shouting it out to everybody, he'd been in the bar all day, he was drunk.

'Boy howdy am I drunk! And I am just shoutin' it out to everybody!' he shouted. 'Whole buncha secrets! Shh! You all need to know em – on a need-to-know-basis – WAHOO!'

'Lena,' said the bartender. 'Get your boyfriend out of here? Please?'

'WAHOO! Big D is beautiful, that's the secret. Big D is beautiful!' he roared, as Lena manoeuvred him up some dark stairs. 'Best-kept secret in the whole world, but everybody needs to know!'

'*Shhh.*' She was opening a dark door into darkness. 'The bed's this way, honey. By the way, what did you mean about being handicapped?'

'Shh, secret!' He fell across the bed, grinning. 'See, I got an artificial arm.'

'Oh. Well I don't mind.' She reached for him.

'But I also got an artificial leg.'

'Oh. Well I guess that's okay.' She threw a real one across him.

'But I also got –'

'Christ don't say it!'

'A glass eye, that's all. People keep thinking I'm staring at 'em.'

'You were giving me the eye in the bar.'

'I'll give it to you now, maam. Here.'

She screamed, he laughed, there was a confused tumbling that might have included sexual contact, then they slept. Later she turned on the dim rose light.

'Was it the war?'

'Naw. I lost the arm in an accident when I was just a kid. Rest of me was okay for a long time, till I come up North here, that was the start. I got run down by a car, first off, and they took me to the hospital.'

'Were you hurt bad?'

'I wasn't hurt at all, just knocked out. But my prosthesis was a total wreck. And the worst thing was, they wouldn't let me out because I couldn't pay my bill. And I couldn't pay until they let me out to get my new arm and get back to work.

'Finally tried to sneak out one night, climbing down the bottom side of a fire escape, but with one arm it wasn't so good. I fell and broke my durn leg! So I went back inside, more bills piling up, and they operated and set the leg. Only there was this infection all over the hospital and it got into the leg bone – they had to amputate.'

'You poor thing.'

'Next thing, my durn heart stopped on me, right on the operating table. I guess they got pretty excited around there because I was a kidney donor, so they started in testing me to see if I was dead. What they do is, they take a piece of cotton wool and touch the eyeball to see if you blink. I blinked okay, and they got my heart started again. But then the eye got this infection . . .'

'You poor, poor thing.'

405

'I don't exactly see it that way, maam. See, I'm a private investigator by trade, and in my line a work, handicaps like these can be a real asset. You can conceal a load of equipment in a prosthesis, if it's built right.'

He told her how he had to find the money to buy some really good stuff: an eye with a camera in it, an arm that fired .357 ammo, and a leg that could hold an automatic weapon – all of them custom-built and jewel-perfect. But for all this he needed real money, not this chickenshit ten grand. Quarter-million would be more like it.

She couldn't see why a private dick needed automatic weapons, though.

It was because he didn't want to be a nickel-and-dime divorce case man. All the real money was in big contract work – for large organizations – even for the government. He'd done Agency work before and he'd do it again. Just had to get his money together.

She had once been a Paris model, so she knew what it was to hit the skids and go all the way down.

'The best time,' he said, 'was on this Agency job down in St Petersburg, Florida. See this old-timer down there was some kinda inventor, and he'd patched together some electronic junk to make himself some kinda talking machine. Guess it sorta made conversation with lonely old folks or something. So the Agency sent me down there to straighten him out. Only time in my life I ever had to be quick on the draw!'

'Quick on the draw? You mean to shoot somebody?'

Mister O'Smith laughed. 'Why sure. Like I said, to straighten him out. This old-timer was sittin' in the shade, with this 12-gauge just outa sight – he brought it up so fast I like to caught my deatha cold right there. Only I been practising a fast draw all my life, so I just terminated his lease – boy howdy! Hot damn! Best contract I ever – what's the matter?'

She turned away, pulling the covers up around her. 'I wish you'd just go now.'

Mister O'Smith got up and dressed, and ran a cloth over the toes of his boots. Then he twitched the ring on his little finger and from under the nail slid a thin knife-blade. When a man talked too much, a price had to be paid. He hated like hell to do this to poor old Lena, but that's the way it goes. All he had to do was lean over and cut her throat, hold her down by the hair till she stopped thrashing, wipe the blade on the bed and retract. Then a quick check for bloodstains – not that there ever were any – and get out quick. Out on the frozen street at dawn, maybe swipe a Sunday paper off some doorstep, nothing looks more innocent than a man at dawn with a Sunday paper under his arm, heading into a hash house for a stack of wheatcakes.

But when Mister O'Smith finally did ease on to a stool at the hash house, Lena was still alive and well. God durn it, he kept saying to himself. God durn it, this was serious. Leaving a live witness who knew all about him, not even busting her arm to scare her a little, that was bad. He must be goin' soft as shit.

Too blamed late now. Hell he could of blamed it on that 'Lucky Legs' killer, another one right here in the Sunday paper, some maniac kills women and saws off their legs, he could of sawed off Lena's leg and . . . too late now. Too blamed late.

He looked at his eyes in the mirror behind the pies. A hard man, but goin' soft. Soft as baby shit.

The site scheduled for demolition was a smart apartment building at 334 East 11th. The crew from Hackme arrived, the police helped clear the street and put up barricades – but when the site manager came to inspect the building, he couldn't get in. The door was blocked by a doorman in grey livery.

'You got the wrong address, buddy. *This* place ain't coming down, it's full of residents.'

'It's not full of residents, it can't be.' The manager started pulling pieces of paper from his attaché case. 'Look, *this* says it was vacated two weeks ago. And *this* says the city gives us permission to blow it up. And *this* one says the owner wants it blown up so he can build a parking ramp. Your boss wants this place down, see?'

'You're crazy,' said the doorman. 'There's twelve floors of residents here, nobody told them about any demolition. Nobody told me. I been workin' here twenty years, nobody told me to leave.'

Roderick, Luke, Bill and the others stood watching the argument, and so did the great crowd behind the barricades. Policemen came and went, unsure what to do: Hackme's papers seemed to give it a legal right to blow up the place. But the doorman had a right to prevent anybody's going inside.

At noon, the president of Hackme Demolition arrived. Mr Vitanuova was a short man in a homburg. The crowd took note of his hat and his car (a Rolls-Royce) and booed him as he approached the door.

'Look, all I want to do is go inside and talk to any residents who might by chance still be in the building. Okay? Just talk to 'em. Not get 'em out or nothing. Can I go in?'

The doorman stood firm. 'No sir. I gotta know whom you was wanting to see, first. Then I gotta call it up to them, to see if they're home to you, sir. Then *if* they okay it, you can go up.'

'But hell I don't know any residents. Just let me see anybody.'

'Oh no you don't, that we don't allow.'

The audience cheered as Mr Vitanuova came away defeated. There was snow on the shoulders of his expensive coat, but he didn't notice.

The crew went to sit across the street in a doughnut shop called *Mistah Kurtz*. Outside they could see Mr Vitanuova pacing in the falling snow and smoking his cigar. Inside they could hear people in fur hats talking across doughnuts and coffee.

'Well I for one am glad they're blowing up that place. I always hated it, looks like a stack of TV sets . . . I'm tired of buildings that look like machines . . .'

'Isn't that Le Corbusier? Or no I must be thinking of Tolstoi, the body is a machine for living in buildings with . . . no, wait.'

'Well I for one would rather sleep in the nave of Chartres cathedral . . .'

'Oh you can fall off anywhere . . . like that angel that loved high places . . . where was it now they put up that angel of Villard d'Honnecourt's, the one that could turn to look at the sun?'

'Henry Adams harking back to the twelfth century . . .'

'Well and Robert Adam harking back to the Etruscans . . . it seems they all want to get back to the old Adam, Adam and no eaves, hee hee!'

'Not so funny when you think of all that striving and dreaming, reaching for – what, light? And finally it comes down to nothing more than Las Vegas fibreglass casinos with neon walls, a city of the darkness for all those watts . . .'

'All an Etruscan room?'

'Only job Villard d'Honnecourt could get now is removing unwanted hair maybe.'

'And that squiggle that Le Corbusier always used for "Man", that sort of crushed starfish, that could feel right at home now, lifting up one fin to hail an air-conditioned cab . . . on any street . . .'

The siege went on. The owner of the building was away skiing somewhere and could not be reached. The police didn't want to act without talking to him first. Mr Vitanuova applied for a court order, but the judge, too, wanted to think it over.

Three days passed. The steadfast doorman was now more than a local hero; network TV and out-of-town papers were beginning to warm to him. The mayor came to shake his hand.

'I'm only doing my job,' he kept saying, to their delight. 'Protecting this building and the residents.'

But in three days, no residents had been seen going in or out. No one went to work, received visitors, bought groceries or walked a dog. Nothing was delivered to the building except the doorman's meals and laundry.

The doorman took brief naps, and somehow managed to shower and shave without leaving his post for more than a few seconds at a time. He remained on duty day and night.

On the morning of the fourth day, he admitted to the press that the building was empty. There were no residents. 'I only protected the place out of a sense of loyalty, I guess I still say there's some terrible mistake.'

The crew went to work. Several floors of the building were knocked out inside. Then holes were drilled at strategic points, to take dynamite. When the charges went off, the entire twelve floors would collapse inward, burst like a bubble and leave almost nothing.

The TV cameras watched all this, the death of this particular building having become news. Mr Vitanuova posed with his finger on the firing button.

Flashguns were still going off like lightning when there came the sound of sirens. Escorted by two motorcycle police, the owner of 334 East 11th arrived.

'Stop! There's been a computer error!' he cried. 'You were supposed to blow up 433, not 334!'

Father Warren's appearance caused one or two raised eyebrows at the airport. Minnetonka was after all a province, where not everyone was used to cosmopolitan priests in black leather cassocks and crucifix earrings. Couldn't be helped; he had to impress the person he was meeting that not all Midwesterners were bucktoothed hicks.

The VIP lounge was almost deserted, but a guard checked Father Warren's ID all the same.

'I'm here to meet Mr Dinks. Hank Dinks, the author.'

'Make yourself at home, uh, Father. I guess the press is here awready.'

There were indeed a few men and women in the drab anoraks of the press corps. Father Warren pretended to inspect an amusement machine until a few reporters drifted over.

'You're Father Warren, aren't you?'

'Yes.'

'The Stigmata,' one older man explained to his colleagues. 'I covered the story two years ago on Good Friday, how you managed to make your hands bleed.'

'Hi Father, look over here. Thanks.'

'You're here to meet this Luddite guy Dinks?'

'That's right.' Father Warren chose his words with Jesuit care. 'I don't say that Hank Dinks and his New Luddites have all the answers, but at least they're asking some of the right questions. Do we really need all these machines? Can we really control them – aren't we becoming slaves to our own creations?'

A woman said, 'A lot of people might say you can't turn the clock back – we don't want to go back to living in caves, do we?'

'No, no indeed. That's certainly not our intention. We don't want to go back to the horse-and-buggy days, not at all. What we want is, well, just to say *Whoa*. We want to stop and catch our breath. Before we turn our world over to thinking machines, let's try thinking for ourselves.' He produced a self-conscious chuckle. 'But don't let me get started making speeches. All I'm here for today is to welcome Hank Dinks to our city.'

As if to signal the end of this session, one young man began firing wild questions: Was Hank Dinks a junkie? Weren't there allegations of bribing a Congressman? A scandal involving farm animals? How about a Mafia connection? Was the KGB funding the New Luddites? What of gay priests? Convent abortions? Transvestite nuns?

The man was given no answers and evidently expected none; it was simply his way of probing for what he called a human interest angle.

The photographers took over. To show he did not hate machines themselves, Father Warren was asked to play one or two of the amusement machines for the cameras. Obligingly he tried a fast draw against Brazos Billy, he repelled alien invaders for a few seconds, and he even had his blood tested. The latter machine pricked his finger, beeped and flashed his blood-type on a screen. He forgot the type immediately. As the cameras clicked, he noticed a small warning plate next to the coin slot:

KUR BLOOD-TYPE BONANZA. *Warning:* Don't use this machine if you have had any of the following diseases: malaria, hepatitis (jaundice), yellow fever, syphilis, flukes . . .

Father Warren had once had malaria. Before he could decide what to do about it, someone from the airline brought him a telegram:

SORRY HAD TO CANCEL FLIGHT BIG SPONTANEOUS RALLY INDIANAPOLIS. WILL SCHEDULE NEW VISIT. HANK.

411

IX

In the conference room the pipe smoke was thicker than ever. In its layers and eddies, the Orinoco people might have seen analogies with the weather of world events: laminar flow with occasional turbulence. The Orinoco people believed in containing local storms, smoothing them out and bringing them back into the general pattern of balminess. The world could be made to work – given enough computing power and the ability to spot trouble in advance.

Today the centres of turbulence were few and obvious: the President had had a light stroke (the news would not reach the public) and so was postponing a few major decisions. Earthquakes in China were causing economic imbalances that would work their way through world trade figures – likewise the discovery of gold in the Sahara. American experiments near Jupiter were beginning to alarm the Russians, who believed they were trying to turn Jupiter into a sun. How to reassure them?

The problem of Entities still nagged. 'Shouldn't we be getting some Entity news from Minnetonka? The Agency isn't going to let us down again, are they?'

'I have an interim report,' said someone, and dry liver-spotted hands rustled dry tissues of paper. 'The Agency sent two men, and they have reported a probable kill of the Entity, with a certainty of point nine two two.'

'I hear a *but* coming,' someone chortled.

'But they now disconfirm. The Entity is still at large, and no longer highly visible They now ask for a priority number so they can plan their hunt. Any ideas?'

'Just how badly do we need this Entity?'

'Good question. Not exactly a case for calling in more agents, is it?'

'To make a worse mess of it. You know I can't help wondering why this is all so difficult. Two grown men, experienced field agents, with all the Agency backing – money, help, equipment, administration – can't manage to track down and kill a lone automaton. I gather the thing is none too bright, has no friends or allies – what *is* the problem?'

'I don't know, I can check. But we can't let this thing run free, you know. Suppose someone discovers it – their co-worker or lover or neighbour turns out to be all full of electronic junk and no meat! Could start a bad panic – we'd have a devil of a time getting the media to sit on it.'

'Exactly, exactly. The projections are all bad. But we do have these two Agency men still on it, I don't see how we can justify more. Vote on it?'

The Hackme Demolition Company was halted, temporarily hung up on a legal snag, so Roderick had the day off. He decided to call up all his friends. Ida's recorded voice told him that she was home, but not at all well and not taking calls today. Luke's recorded voice told him he was out, seeing his children in a zoo. That exhausted the list.

Roderick wandered into an amusement arcade, to test his reflexes for half an hour. Then he prowled the streets and stared at the mannikins in store windows. Finally he found himself on Junipero Serra Place, just outside Danton's Doggie Dinette. Might be fun to borrow a dog and go in? Let the waitress bustle about, setting out a bowl of ice water for the dog and a menu for him?

On the other hand he might run into Danton, not so funny. No, best thing was to just keep going, right on past this alley too, don't even look down it . . .

Roderick saw Allbright back in his usual corner of the alley, sitting on a box and drinking something out of a bottle in a paper bag.

'I'm glad they let you out. I knew you weren't the murderer, Allbright.'

The bag tipped, paused, tipped again. 'They said you described me perfectly.'

'No I didn't. I described that guy we saw that day, with the gold hair and tinted glasses.'

413

'I believe you, I guess.' The bag tipped. 'You should have described me, so maybe they'd have picked him up.'

'Well anyway you're free. You're innocent.'

Allbright nodded, wiped a grimy hand across his mouth, burped. 'Yes, the innocent they let off with a warning. They don't care a hell of a lot for innocence – they don't know how to handle it.'

'I guess that makes sense. Cops have to be suspicious.'

'See as long as I looked guilty they treated me like a king. After all, they knew I'd be hiring a fancy lawyer for a fancy fee. They knew I'd be talking to the press a lot, maybe writing up my story as a sensational book, see? I was somebody and something.

'Then the real killer sawed the leg off another woman while I was still locked up. Not guilty, I'm all of a sudden just another piece of innocent human shit.' He offered the bottle. 'Drink?'

'No thanks, I don't drink.'

'That's okay, I think it's empty anyway.' Allbright blew down the bottle and produced a low, dull note. 'Let me give you some advice, kid. Don't be innocent. Don't ever be innocent, be guilty. Innocence scares hell out of people, they don't know how to approach it – they don't know what innocence wants from them. So they try to wipe it out. To wipe *you* out.

'So get some guilt. Be divorced. Go bankrupt. Have an old unpaid parking tag, at least. Drink too much. Put at least one parent into a retirement home against their will. Spoil a life. Need therapy. Get some guilt, or you are in trouble.'

'Have *you* got some guilt?'

'Only a goddamned stupid innocent could even ask that question. Of course I've got some guilt. I don't know where to start, there's so much . . . for one thing my talent, my precious gift frittered away in years of self-indulgence, pill-popping, snorting, lushing, messing up my one life and other lives . . . There was a girl who really took me seriously, took my work seriously. She was willing to quit the University and take a job, just to feed me and clothe me and keep me straight enough to maybe write poetry again. Only of course that wasn't enough for me, no I had to nag her into popping pills with me . . . We ended up both broke and living in a dirty squat, an old packing house that always smelled of meat or shit, the timbers of the old place were all soaked through

414

with blood. One morning I woke up and found her dead beside me, yes you could say I've got some guilt about Dora. Not just her dying but dying alone like that with me off in my head somewhere watching the pink and green lights in my head. So she died all alone in that shit-smelling place and I couldn't do anything for her, just wrap her warm in an old quilt and just leave her there in that place, in that place. I've got some guilt. Much guilt.'

Roderick asked another question, but just then a jet plane roared over. Then Allbright was getting up and edging away, and no wonder: here came Danton, puffing steam, with a baseball bat in his hand.

'You!' he shouted, looking murderous. 'Wood! Did I give you permission to come out in the alley? Did I?'

'No sir, but – wait a minute, I don't –'

Danton took a cut with the bat. Roderick jumped back.

'You don't what? You don't work? I know that. I got a mountain of dirty bowls in there and nobody around, nobody!' He took another cut and hit the wall. 'I treat you like my own son, my own son! And you –'

'But you fired me, Mr Danton. I don't work for you.'

Danton paused, puffing steam. 'Yeah, that's right. I did fire you.' He looked at the baseball bat in his hand, then stood on one foot and used the bat to knock imaginary dirt from his imaginary cleats. 'Well, back to the old grind.' He started to walk away, then looked back, the bat over his shoulder. 'If you ever need a job, kid . . .'

'Okay then, was it anything like this?' O'Smith punched some more buttons on the pocket-sized gadget. In the little window a square chin changed to a pointed chin.

Ben Franklin put down his flightbag and lit a cigarette. 'Look, I know you're trying to help. And I wish I'd had more time to go into this before. But honestly I don't remember exactly what he looks – he looks so average.'

'Kind of an average chin? Like this?'

'Yes I guess so. Look I think maybe I'd better get a few more travellers' cheques before they call my –'

'Relax, boy. Shoot, goin' to Taipin is just like goin' to Chicago,

415

only in Taipin they speak better English. Now would he have this kinda nose?'

Ben half-relaxed and allowed the cowboy to ply him with chins, noses, eyes, coiffures until a face – not the one he remembered, but close enough – could be fixed in the little machine's memory.

'Good enough!' the fat cowboy winked, bringing into play several hundred crow's feet. 'With this face and the name Roderick Wood I oughta be able to nail this little tin shit.'

'You talk about him as if we were hiring you to kill him,' said Ben.

'Always like to think of it like huntin', Mr Frankelin. Makes it more excitin'.'

O'Smith went on with his simile, but Ben was no longer listening. He was engaged in what his namesake might have called the diligent study of one's own life and habits.

He was now in his forties, childless and divorced, had been a member of the Project Roderick research team, and now held a responsible job in a growing corporation. He was at this moment en route to inspecting a microprocessor factory in Taipin, a new pearl soon to be strung upon the KUR necklace.

Then why didn't he feel important? Why did he feel that all the important decisions in the world were being made in the next room, from which he was forever excluded? Roderick had been cooked up between kid genius Dan and wise old Lee Fong, and the others. Ben had been out in the cold. And it was the same at KUR, he was a rubber stamp for decisions made by Mr Kratt. Even now, sitting in the VIP lounge, he did not feel VI.

He envied O'Smith, watching the cowboy fast-drawing against some fibreglass dummy. Look at him, not a care in the world. Life was all a B Western. O'Smith had a stiff arm or something, making his draw a little awkward. But he seemed not to mind, not a care in the world.

O'Smith turned and grinned. 'Shoot, Mr Frankelin, you oughta try somethin' yourself. I hate to keep playin' these machines alone. Makes me feel like a durn ijit. Soft as –'

'There she is!' someone cried, and a small army of people in anoraks ran with their cameras and notebooks to the other end of the room, where a genuine celebrity had arrived. Ben Franklin stood up to see who it was, and immediately turned away.

'Somethin' wrong, Mr Frankelin?'

'That's Indica Dinks over there.'

'Sure it is, that's right. The machines lib gal, nice looker – you know her?'

'We used to be married.' Keeping his back turned to her, he fumbled for change and plunged a quarter into the nearest machine. A sign told him to place his finger under an 'examining lever'; when he did so, he felt a sharp stab. 'THANK YOU. YOUR BLOOD TYPE WILL APPEAR ON THE SCREEN.'

He forgot the answer as soon as he saw it. Out of the corner of his eye he noticed Indica, a small figure in bright apple green, sweep past like a comet, pulling a tail of drab reporters.

'She's gone now, Mr Frankelin.'

'Okay. Okay.' He stood still before the machine, as though unsure what move to make next, until two men in white overalls came up to him.

'Excuse me, buddy.' They unplugged the machine and loaded it on a dolly.

'What's – what is this?'

'County Health, buddy. We're impounding this.' One of the men showed him a badge. 'Another KUR headache.'

'KUR?' he asked, but his plane was being called.

X

Christmas bore down upon the world, demanding its ransom. In Northern lands the sun grew weaker and threatened to go out unless everyone spent too much money soon. The countdown of shopping days had begun already, that hypnotic series of diminishing numbers that could only end in zero. The public was led into Christmastime as a patient is led into anaesthesia, counting backwards.

Likewise when William Miller had set the date for the Second Coming at March 21, 1844, a dwindling number of days were marked out, during which the faithful could dispose of the last of their money. They had gathered to meet their Maker wearing only simple gowns without pockets. Nowadays it was the purveyors of gifts, the promoters of 'gifting' who urged a frantic giveaway before oblivion.

Christmas seemed not so much 'commercialized' as the true season of money transactions. The tone had been set by the original tale of taxes and redemption and kings with costly gifts; it carried on in all that followed; the kindly saint now resident in every Toy Department; songs about beggars and kings; the heaping up of goods in Twelve Days of Christmas; Dickens's well-loved story of Crachit in the counting-house. By now it was clear that Christmas could not be properly celebrated until money had been exchanged for frozen turkeys, novelty records, Irish liqueurs, onyx chessmen, aura goggles, hand-painted lowball glasses, digital fitness monitors, personalized toilet courtesy mats, pink pool tables, sinus masks, chastity belts, Delft-style plastic light switch plates, individualized horoscope mugs, solid brass post-top lanterns, pyjama bags in the shape of dachshunds, plastic flame-resistant trees with pre-programmed light-sound systems, mono-grammed duck calls, Shaker-style cat beds, holly-look room deodorizers, mink mistletoe.

The message was clear in the anxious faces of shoppers hurrying along the Mall. The Mall was a closed and heated portion of Downtown connected to department stores and to all other valuable pieces of real estate. Roderick sat on a park bench near an elm that might be real or artificial, listening to the anxious faces:

'But he's got an electric one already, hasn't he?'

'Sure but this is an electronic one.'

Angelic voices from somewhere sang feelingly of chestnuts roasting by an open fire. Of course vendors of hot chestnuts, with their open fires and blue smoke, had long since been banished from this pollution-fighting city. But imported *marrons glacés* might help to keep the season bright, a flickering electronic sign reminded shoppers; the angelic voices too were for sale, recorded at a prestigious boys' penitentiary.

'. . . don't want to make a mistake like last year, God! Sally cried all day and wouldn't eat her dinner just because I gave her that mistletoe she asked Santa for, how did I know she meant *Missile Tow*, some kind of video war game . . .'

'These kids! My Sandra asked for eight TV sets so she could watch all her favourites at the same time she said, can you beat that for a four-year-old?'

A man came down the escalator talking and gesticulating to no one – or rather to Mission Control, for it was Luke Draeger. Roderick stood up and waved to him. Luke followed invisible commands, executing a few smart drill manoeuvres on his way over.

'Rickwood, glad you could make it.'

'But why did we have to meet here?'

'Orders.'

'From Mission Control?'

'Affirmative, Rickwood.'

There passed several minutes of silence.

'Well, Luke, was there anything special you had to see me about?'

'Nope. Just to wish you a Merry Christmas. I'm, uh, going away, did you know that?'

'Oh. Well, Merry Christmas, Luke.'

'Everyone ought to go away at Christmas, even if it's only to see your family.'

'That's right. Your three kids.'

Luke fidgeted with his scarf and looked at the giant Christmas tree in the centre of the Mall. 'No, well, they're spending it with their mother, as always. No I'm – I *was* thinking of going to Ohio to see this faith blacksmith we've been hearing so much about.'

'I never heard of him.'

'I figured anybody who can actually shoe a horse without touching it, well he just has to have some answers. Only –'

Two Santa Clauses had sat down on the next bench; their conversation could be heard when the angelic choir stopped.

'. . . the little red ones is Anxifran, or maybe Phenodrax, and the big green ones is Epiphan, they're beautiful, just like Hypodone . . .'

'. . . Calamital and Equapace, but you got any Fenrisol, I'm out . . .'

'Try Evenquil. Or here, try an Enactil. I couldn't get through the day without 50 milligrams . . .'

The tree lights flashed in programmed patterns, now forming clusters, now starbursts and spinning coils, now visual advertisements and simple slogans.

'You're not going to Ohio, then?'

Luke sat back. 'Negative. I'm going to a place in the Himalayas.'

Roderick said, 'I didn't know you could afford it. I mean, what with Hackme Demolition keeping us all laid off like this –'

Luke grinned. 'My way is paid. See, my name lends just that much prestige to the organization. Maybe you've heard of them: the Divine Brotherhood of Transcending Awarenesses of Inner Global Light. Most people just call us the Saffron Peril.'

'Them? You're joining them?'

'Affirmative. I'm going straight to the HQ, a place where Eternal Consciousness flows like champagne. I'll be there, wearing all orangey-yellow, meditating, really connecting with – whatever there is. Up there in the mountains – at the top of the world – something has to happen. I can see it already, the blossoming of cosmic consciousness.' Luke was silent for a moment. 'Trouble is, I always see everybody's point of view. So

I'll also be wondering if it isn't all a bunch of crap. Oh well, Merry Christmas.'

Mr Multifid had a warm handshake. He was a plump, genial-looking man who would have looked out-of-place in crisp business clothes or a hard-edge office. Instead he wore hounds-tooth and corduroy in shades of brown, a sloppy hand-knit tie, a khaki shirt; and his office had no desk, only a pair of captains' chairs, a fake fireplace, and panelled walls hung with ship prints and barometers.

'Take a pew, Mr Wood – mind if I start calling you Rod right away? And you can call me Gene, okay? Now let me see . . .'

He studied the pink card Roderick had filled out in the outer office. 'Where did you hear about our service, Rod?'

'I was working at a demolition site down the street, and I just happened to see your sign: *Multifid Marriage Counselling, Singles Welcome.*'

'Right.' Mr Multifid made a note on the card. 'Normally my secretary takes care of this, this background stuff. But she's off today. Seeing her analyst. Now where are we? You're not married? No? Engaged? And not divorced? Well then, are you gay? No? Any, any peculiarities you feel like talking about?'

'I'm a robot,' said Roderick. 'I'm not really sure I want to marry anyone, just maybe have a – have some kind of relationship, does that sound peculiar?'

'Not necessarily. Go on. Do, do "robots" have sex?'

'I've only had one what you might call sexual encounter, I mean that was complete – what I could call a mechasm – and that was with a woman who got nothing out of it at all, unless maybe the satisfaction of solving a puzzle. And see I'm not physically exactly –'

The phone rang. 'Multifid Marriage – oh it's you, look, I can't talk now, Julia, I'm with a client . . . No of course it's not Sandy, she's seeing her analyst today . . . What do you mean, protest too much? You're not starting that again. Look . . . look, I've got to go, I – you what? *Christ!* Look you promised me last time you'd call me first, we'd talk it over, talk it out, this is just blackmail, isn't it? You haven't really done anything, you're just calling for help – you have? *Christ!* Okay, *okay* I'm on my way.'

421

He hung up, scowling at the phone as though it had betrayed him. 'Well Rod, I've got to go home, little family emergency. Why don't you just use the tape recorder there and give me a rundown of your problem, we'll discuss it when I get back, okay?'

'Sure. I hope – everything's all right.'

With a kind of choked laugh, Mr Multifid left. After a few minutes there was a timid tap at the door and a middle-aged woman tiptoed in, offering her pink card.

'Mr Multifid?'

'No, I'm Roderick Wood. Mr Multifid had to go home. Family emergency.'

'I know what that is,' she said, sitting down. 'I know what that is, all right. And I've just gotta talk to somebody.'

'But –'

'I remember a few things about my early childhood. I know Mama was very good to me, even though I wasn't the boy she wanted. I know when I was still crawling, she bought me a little bucket and scrub-brush and taught me how to do the floors. I learned to walk by clearing the table. And toilet training, I remember that too: scrubbing and shining that toilet.

'I never had a doll, but then my little brother Glen came along and I got to feed him and change him, bathe him and wash all his diapers. Of course I had to do all this between my regular chores.

'I didn't do so well at school, because I had to take time off for like spring cleaning. In the evenings after cooking supper and doing dishes and the ironing, there wasn't much time left for studying before I set out the breakfast things. Also I wanted to save my eyes for the mending. Mama was good about it, when she saw my grades weren't so great she let me off doing the shopping after school. I made up the extra work on weekends.

'Just the same, I started getting envious of my older brother Ken. He got to play football while I was shining everybody's shoes. He got to dress up like a cowboy while I was washing clothes. He had pillow fights, I made beds. I know it must sound silly now, but I really resented that. Maybe that's where I went wrong!'

Roderick felt he ought to say something. 'How do you know you went wrong at all?'

'Oh you mean I always was wrong? I never thought of that – I was wrong from the start, eh?'

'I meant maybe you were *right* all along.' Roderick sighed. 'Maybe you should be talking to somebody professional, I'm nobody, I'm just –'

'You have to listen. Somebody has to listen.'

'Sure, go on. Oh, uh, you didn't mention your father so far. Was he around?'

'He was at sea for years and years. When I was twelve he came home drunk and sort of raped me. See it was a Saturday and so I had worked all day doing laundry, cooking, cleaning, dusting, scrubbing and waxing. Every-body else went out for the evening and I finished the supper dishes and then just fell into bed. When I woke up he was climbing on top of me. He told me if I screamed he'd tell Mama that he'd seen me sweep dirt under the carpet. I didn't know who he was, and I was scared, so I said nothing.

'Mama was pretty good about it when I told her I was pregnant, even if she did say she wished she'd drowned me when I was born. But she managed to fix it for me to marry a boy named Fred. I sewed my wedding dress quickly, baked the cake and so on, and pretty soon Fred and I were set up in our own little trailer, very easy to clean. True Fred did beat me up a lot, and he drank a lot and ran around with other women which is how he brought home the case of VD. It would have been okay but he also didn't work so I had to have these eight cleaning jobs to feed me and the kids and buy Fred his booze and the cigarettes he liked to put out on me. One day I was so tired I forgot to flinch and Fred got so mad he went and told all my employers I had had VD and they fired me . . .'

The woman's story went on and on, cataloguing years of thankless work, suffering and humiliation: raped, she found herself accused by the police of prostitution; going to the doctor with a headache leads to a double mastectomy followed by a hysterectomy – the headache remains; a moment of absent-mindedness at the supermarket leads to a shoplifting conviction. 'My twin sons grew up hating my guts for only giving them a second-hand football and no colour TV; they were so full of hate they became lawyers. Fred ran off with a cocktail waitress and finally burned her to death, but the boys defended him and he got a suspended sentence; I guess I should be proud of my boys. Anyway, here I am fifty years old, my life doesn't seem to be going anywhere. Do you think I need a lobotomy?'

'I wouldn't rush into anything,' Roderick said. 'Talk it over with someone like Mr Multifid.'

'Talk?' she said, as she tip-toed to the door. 'What good is talk?'

A young couple named Ferguson came in as soon as she'd left. Roderick explained to them that he was only a client himself, that the counsellor was out.

Mr Ferguson stood up to leave.

'Oh sure, leave,' said Mrs Ferguson. 'Any excuse to leave.'

'*I'm* not gonna be the one to leave,' said Mr F.

The Fergusons sat glaring at one another in silence for an hour, then left together.

Next came a young man with an irritating nervous laugh, who called himself Norm.

'Gene's out, huh? Well it doesn't matter much, I just stopped by on the chance that he might be here and might have a spare minute to see me. Thing is I need to kind of build up some confidence. Because I'm going to this, this party, uh-uh-uh! So what I need is this real confident manner so I can pick up a girl and score, you know? What I need are a few snappy lines, you know, like opening gambits and subtle ploys and sophisticated tricks that girls always fall for, right up to a fool-proof closing line that makes them, like, fall right into bed then and there – what I need is this I guess complete guaranteed seduction technique, uh-uh-uh!'

Roderick said, 'I can't give you any real advice, but I'll tell you one thing, not many girls I bet want to fall into bed with a guy who keeps laughing like that, it sounds like whooping cough. If I were you I'd try to drop the laugh.'

'Hey great! I bet you could give me lots of hints like that, huh? Hey, could you come along to this party and sort of, sort of advise me?'

XI

The houses on this street had elaborate Christmas decorations –
Santas in sleighs, giant Rudolphs or angels – outlined in lights or
sometimes floodlit. There were giant conifers dripping with
diamond lights.

'Always drive through this way,' Norm said. 'It takes longer but
I like to see the lights.'

They came to a dark stretch, where the snowbanks alongside
the road were high and there were no houses. Norm pulled over
and stopped the car. 'Uh-uh-uh, those lights always remind me of
pocket calculators, you know?'

'Yes, but why are we stopping here?'

'I uh want you to do me a favour, Rod.' Norm held up a pocket
calculator. 'Just a little favour.'

'Look, what is this?'

Norm was holding an automatic in his other hand. 'Just a
goddamned favour, you son of a bitch   you can't get out of the
car on account of the snowbank anyway, so take the fucking
calculator!'

Roderick took it. 'What now?'

'Now you just punch the numbers I give you and let me see the
display.'

'What, like this?' Roderick punched 12345 and held up the
calculator. The red digits glowed like cigarettes. Roderick was
afraid of dying.

'No no no! Hold it so it's upside down for me. Okay now the
first number is 58008, you got that?'

Roderick punched it. 'I see, it's spelling out words for you.'

Norm ordered him to spell out in turn: SOIL, SISSIES, SOB,
SOLOS, LOSSES, BOSS, BOOHOO, LOOSE, HOLE,
LIBEL, BOILS, BLOJOBS, BOOBIES and finally OHOHOH.

There was a moment of silence, during which Norm sat

425

doubled over behind the steering wheel. Then he sat up and said, 'Okay thanks. I'm sorry I pulled a gun on you, I just got worried you wouldn't do it. A lotta people laugh when I ask them.' He started the car. 'I'll drop you off wherever . . .'

'What about this party you wanted to score at?'

'Well there is a party. In the suburbs, you really want to go?'

As they drove on, Roderick asked Norm how he had developed his curious hobby.

'Hobby? I guess it is. Well I guess it all started when I was about ten. Dad gave me this pocket calculator, you know? And I really liked it. I um had fun just multiplying two times two, stuff like that. I mean calculating gave me this special feeling.'

'What feeling?'

'Okay, okay, it gave me a hard-on, calculating gave me a hard-on. I was only ten, didn't hardly know – okay maybe I did know but it didn't seem so wrong. I mean I just kept the thing in my pants pocket and um worked out a few things in secret now and then. I used to pretend it was the real thing.'

'A woman, Norm?'

'No, a *computer*. Maybe an IBM 360, boy what a figure –'

'What happened then?'

Norm stopped for a red light. A drunken man was feeling his way across the street, trying to get into one car, then another, shouting at their occupants.

'Well, Dad caught me once. He said I'd go blind and lose strength from all the calculating, but I didn't care. I had to go on adding, subtracting . . . even when we played sandlot baseball I had to stop all the time and work out my batting average. And pretty soon I stopped playing any games at all, I just, you know?

'So then when I was about fifteen I started hanging out in the crummy part of town, I started running errands for this bookie. And he had this, well this older computer, she'd been through a lot of weird programs, stuff I'd never dreamed of. I mean she really taught me a lot. I learned so much I figured I was cured, you know? When we broke up I figured I was burnt out and cured.

'So I went away to college, got along okay only I couldn't help noticing computers. Like the freshman registration computer, she was big. Dumb, but really big, you know? Meanwhile I met this really nice girl, a real girl, and we got engaged. We were gonna marry after graduation.

'Graduation night there was a big party and I got real drunk, and somehow we all ended up at this computer dating agency. So the others are standing there filling out forms and giggling, and the girl behind the counter goes out of the room for something – and there I am, face to face with a big beautiful machine! In about one second flat I'm over that counter and all over her.'

'How did you feel, Norm?'

'Good at first, and then – disgusted. Couldn't wait to pay my money and get out of there. Goes without saying my engagement was off, all my friends aghast – but I knew then I was hooked, I knew I'd be back! And I was, again and again, until they had to call the cops to get rid of me. Then I started hanging around electronics stores – you ever notice how they always have them on the same streets with sex stores and porno palaces and massage parlours? Ever notice that? The cops would pick me up routinely about once a week. Most of the time they just took me home to Dad.'

'You didn't go to jail?'

'No, because Dad offered to send me for some therapy. We um tried aversion. I went to this guy Dr George. He would show me a picture of a big Univac say, or hand me a magnetic card, or a reel of tape or something, and at the same time he'd give me this electric shock. Trouble is, you can get to like a jolt of current now and then, you can get a special feeling there too.'

Roderick decided to say nothing of his own identity as a cybernetic machine running on electricity.

At the next traffic light they stopped. A group of children trooped across the street, with two adults in charge. Roderick noticed that the little boys had crepe paper beards and the little girls carried stiff styrofoam wings.

'Norm, I notice you don't mention your mother much.'

'Mother?' Norm frowned. 'What do you mean, exactly?'

'Well you had a mother, didn't you?'

'Jesus, whose life are we supposed to be talking about, anyway? I mean excuse me, but I thought it was mine. Excuse me all to hell.'

'I just meant, most people have mothers.'

Norm's fingers tightened on the steering wheel, as the car shot forward. 'Oh sure. Most people. I suppose most people can't buy a computer magazine without blushing. I suppose most people feel all the time like calling up a computer on the phone and inputting dirty data, real dirty data. Oh sure, most people!'

'What do you remember about your mother, Norm?'

Norm jammed on the brakes, and the car skidded to an oblique stop. Tears were streaming down his face. 'You keep that up and you can just get out and walk. You hear me?'

Roderick looked out at the bleak, icy road, the mountainous snowbanks, the blackness beyond. They were somewhere in the edge of a suburb, and there was nothing to be seen but falling snow and the darkness that might be trees. Large wet flakes drifted through the headlight beams.

'I'm really looking forward to this party,' he said. 'Who's giving it?'

Norm started driving again. 'Mr Moxon. He's a friend of my um Dad.' Soon the car turned off the icy road into a long, heated drive. They drove on, past snow sculptures of men in top hats and women in bonnets, past massed evergreens with programmed lights, past everything, faster, racing headlong like the fastest troika imaginable.

The room was L-shaped, and large enough to accommodate more than one source of music. Around the corner a jukebox glowed from within a fireplace, radiating snatches of warm music to a small circle of admirers (though General Fleischman had located the secret volume control and kept turning it down). At the far end of the long gallery, a man with blue hair and a mirror monocle touched the keys of a white piano and sang:

When lovely woman stoops to polyand-ry
She ends up with more dishes in the sink
And greater loads of melancholy laundry
She's less appreciated than you think.

The room between was beginning to fill up with life: talking faces, scanning eyes, hands clutching glasses or elbows or

428

sketching in the air with cigarettes, voices scribbling in one another's margins.

'But that's what I mean, Everett's friends are all tired grey businessmen or engineers or something, and Francine's all seem to be mumbling poets with pimply necks, God it's all so – so haecceitic. I could've gone to Nassau . . .'

'. . . was going to New York . . .'

'. . . went to Prague . . .'

'. . . doubled back down Dalecrest Boulevard, see, to catch the Hilldale Expressway through Valecrest, but guess what?'

'Silicon, darling. Or do I mean silicone? Silly something, anyway. H.G. Wells said it was the basis of all life, imagine!'

Someone liked Rodin's *Thinker*, someone complained of sinus trouble in Prague, someone else had lost money selling KUR shares too soon, so who said there was a Sandy Claus?

Father Warren, looking lean and aescetic as always despite the splendour of his black leather cassock, accepted a glass of sherry and glided on to the jukebox area to speak with General Fleischman.

The general was a tall, broad-shouldered old man with a deep tan and frothy white sideburns. Since his retirement from the Army he had been running a bank, but he still hoped for a job in Washington – maybe as a minor White House adviser. At the moment he was holding forth on puppet governments to Dr Tarr's secretary, Judi Mazzini. She looked as though she'd rather be doing her nails.

'Ruritania? General, I couldn't even find it on a map.'

'Nobody can, honey, that's the trouble with we Americans. We tend to devisualize backdrop situations, we play down the role of unhostile puppets – Oh hello, padre. Like to have you meet Judi . . .'

But with a smile of apology she escaped, all but colliding with an Oriental waiter who managed to recover without spilling a drop of the foamy pink cocktail he was carrying the length of the room to a jowly woman in purple who said again:

'But don't you just love his *Thinker*?'

The boy with the straggly beard was cautious; he believed they were talking about a Japanese movie monster: the giant flying reptile *Rodan.* 'His thinker, eh? Well I guess I maybe missed that . . .'

She now tasted the foamy drink and waved it away, her hand glittering with amethysts. 'No I'm sorry but I just can't drink that. Toy, you won't be angry with me?'

The waiter smiled. 'Not at all, Mrs Fleischman.'

'Now you just take that back to the bartender and tell him it's just too – oh never mind, just bring me a gin and ton.'

When the waiter was not quite out of earshot she said, 'Toy's a treasure, wonder where Francine found him? He even pronounces my name right. I thought he'd be calling me Mrs Freshman, most of these, these people – but anyway, what were you saying, sweetie? How could you talk about Rodin and leave out his *Thinker?*'

The bearded boy stammered out something about Tokyo burning and special effects, adding, 'Not that I guess it's exactly Hugo material but –'

'Yas, yas, his *Hugo* did have a lot of problems and finally they never did put it up at all – oh here's Everett. Everett, sweetie, I want a word with you.' Her ringed hand snagged the sleeve of a well-cut dinner jacket.

'Hello, Thelma,' he said, smiling. 'Let me rustle up a drink for you.' He moved on quickly, past the white piano, past voices expressing disappointment with an old city, delight with a new diet, faith in a second-hand religion.

'That's Everett,' said someone.

'Who?'

'Our host, Everett Moxon.'

'Isn't his head small?'

'Small?'

'I don't mean he wears a doughnut for a hat, I don't even mean he's a new Anatole France. I just meant – I think I must need a pill with this scotch.'

A pillbox was offered. 'Here, have one of mine. Libidon this side, Solacyl that side.'

Moxon veered past the South sofa and paused to smile on the beauty of Mrs McBabbitt.

Connie McBabbitt was breathtakingly beautiful. Usually at a party she found a place to pose gracefully and remained there for the evening. Tonight she reclined with one elbow on the arm of the sofa, her hands clasped and her chin lifted upon a forefinger. The idea was for men to spend the evening lusting and longing after the curve of ivory cheek, throat, breast, the voluptuous swathe of black velvet, the old-fashioned obviousness of her perfection. If she did resemble a 1950s model, it was because that was the era of preference of the plastic surgeon who had created her.

Ten years of surgery, stage by stage, beginning with a resectioning of her pelvis and finishing with a quantity of fresh skin, had tightened the screw of beauty turn by turn until no more could be done – she hardly used makeup.

'Everett, what a gorgeous party.' Her voice too had been adjusted to a slight huskiness. 'You seem to know so many people – didn't I just see Edd McFee a minute ago? The painter?'

'Could be, Connie. I sometimes feel a little lost at these affairs myself. Let me introduce you to Mr Vitanuova.'

The little square, thick man almost bowed over her hand. 'Call me Joe,' he said, regarding her through his grey eyebrows. 'May I say that you are the most beautiful woman in the place? If not in the city? No offence to the other classy dolls, but you are *class*.'

'Thank you, Joe. What do you do? Sculptor, maybe?'

He spread his wide face in a smile and his wide hands in a kind of blessing. 'Not exactly. I'm in garbage, mainly. Okay, laugh if you want.'

A faint blush tinged the ivory. 'Why should I laugh?'

'Everybody does. Not that I care, I'm not ashamed. I got me two incinerating plants now, sent all my kids to good schools out East, and now I branched out into a lot of other diversified interests . . .'

Behind him Mrs Doody was saying, 'Oh, Everett and I are old friends, old buddies. See my ex married his ex's first husband's widow, if you can work that out! You wouldn't by any chance have a ciggy, would you?'

Beyond her someone turned to catch a drink off a passing tray, saying, 'Systems analyst? I thought you said he was a lay analyst,' to someone already turning away to catch a glimpse of Indica Dinks in the crowd that was condensing around her even as she moved to the bar.

'Is there any difference? Some people want to systematize the world, others just want to lay it, is there any difference?' The figure in a heavy grey cowled sweater turned its back on the celebrity. 'Maybe Wells was right, then, maybe silicon is the basis of all life; you keep meeting people who act as if they had silicon chips in their heads . . .'

And in independent efforts to ignore the celebrity, others raised their voices across the room:

'. . . well I can well conceptualize that people have trouble finding Ruritania on a map, that should not blind us to the facts about non-hostile puppet . . .'

'Isn't that Lyle who just came in? Lyle whatsisname, the sculptor?'

'Naw, Lyle's got this godawful birthmark.'

'. . . like you to meet Harry Hatlo, Harry is now a behavioural choreographer, but he used to be in food technology, right? On the research side was it, Harry?'

Feeling for his hairpiece, Mr Hatlo risked a nod. 'I was what you might call a snack inventor. Only my ideas kept getting more and more kinaesthesic, you know? Like I might sort of start with seeing a new kind of crunch first, and then build a product around it, you know?'

Mr Vitanuova nodded. 'I know. Like *saltimbocca*, means jumps in the mouth.'

'Right. And when I invented the dipless chip, the real breakthrough was when I mimed the whole routine myself, in my office – that was how I realized what a downer chip dip can be. See first you gotta buy the mix and take it home, dump it in a bowl and add water, stir it around – and all this is just leading up to the real dipping experience. Which is all that really counts, funfoodwise.'

'My mother used to make fresh spaghetti –'

'Yeah, well, so I put the dip *on* the chips, people just dip 'em in water and get all the fun right away. It was that simple.'

Vitanuova turned away briefly. 'Hell, there's one of my boys from the demolition company. You wouldn't believe the god-damn lawsuits that company is getting snarled up in, probably have to liquidate before –'

'Work, yes, work situations.' Hatlo performed a shrug. 'I

432

applied the same thinking to my own job situation. It turned out that my real job satisfaction wasn't into food tech at all, but *movement*, you know?'

'Usually follows food,' Vitanuova said.

'These kinaesthesic ideas grabbed me more and more, until finally I got a chance to resign and start a new career in dance.'

'Yeah I remember your firm going broke on research costs, you got squeezed out when Katrat Fun Foods took over Dipchip International, as I recollect. Excuse me, I better have a word with my employee there.'

Hatlo immediately enjoined conversation with Mrs Doody, who was borrowing a cigarette from the man in dark glasses.

'My hubby's got all mine,' she explained, tearing off the filter and accepting a light. 'He always does this, goes off with my ciggies – thanks. What did you say your name was?'

'Felix. Felix Culpa.'

Hatlo, holding on his toupee, said, 'Hiya, Felix. I was uh just telling Joe there how I got around to dedicating my life to the dance you might say. The name's Harry Hatlo.'

'Dedication,' said Felix Culpa. 'Discipline. The ultimate cruelty of precise articulation – the curve of arm like a scorpion's tail.'

Mrs Doody spat out a crumb of tobacco. 'Thanks for the ciggy, Felix. See you.'

Culpa nodded, apparently looking elsewhere. 'Take *Les Noces*, almost a celebration of rape there, and starts off with that cruel hair-brushing scene –'

Hatlo said, 'Well see most of my work is more in the line of therapy, I work for the city see and –'

'But the point is, Stravinsky actually scored it for pianolas. It's like a demonstration of the marriage of pain and precision. Machine cruelty.'

Judi Mazzini turned around. 'I think I read something like that not long ago, *The Machine Dances* by some sociologist named Rogers.'

Culpa hesitated a second. 'Yes, yes I'm familiar with that. And it does sum up a fascinating overview –'

'Not very well thought out,' she said. 'It's easy to point out a lot of machine arts stuff in the Twenties. I mean we all know George Grosz with his pictures of leering automata and their sexy brides.

We've all seen *Metropolis* starring a steel girl with doorbells on her chest. But so what, it doesn't mean you can really compare the Rockettes to an assembly line, or Isadora Duncan to a Chrysler Airflow – that's anachronistic anyway.'

Culpa said, 'Well I think his central concern was the er depersonalization pressures of modern societal parameters, people into robots, dancers into machines, wouldn't you say?'

Judi Mazzini said, 'I grant you they did a lot of mechanical ballets around then, like *Machine of 3000* with the dancers all dressed like water boilers, and George Antheil's *Ballet Mécanique* scored for airplane props, anvils and car horns. But are they any more significant than other stuff? Plays, there was *R.U.R. and The Adding Machine* – why single out dancing?'

'Isn't that Allbright who just staggered in?' someone said, and heads turned to watch a shaggy, hollow-eyed man in an old torn storm-coat limp into the living room and set down his large briefcase. His heard was iced, and his dirty hair blended into the fake fur on his coat collar. One lapel of the coat was torn and hung down like a withered breast.

'Goddamnit, where's the Christmas of it?' he shouted in the sudden silence. After a pause to pick yellow ice from his moustache, he shouted again:

'I said where's the Christmas of it? Where's the holly and *the* ivy, the running of *the* dear Saviour's birthday to you, Merry gentlemen upon a Christmastime in the city, silver bells jingle all the way in a manger no crib for Santa Claus comes tonight – where is it?' There was an oil-slick of grime on the hand with which he snatched a drink from the nearest tray. 'Ladies and gentlemen, I give you – birth!'

Francine Moxon was beside him quickly, shoving him firmly into an armchair. 'Allbright, we're not hiring any Dylan Thomas acts today. Now you sit here and shut up and I'll see you get enough to eat and drink. But behave yourself!'

'Merry Christmas, you gorgeous piece on earth,' he murmured, and tried to kiss her ear, before she swept away to a group where someone was explaining the difference between a lay analyst and a lay figure.

At the piano the blue-haired man sang:

Talkin' 'bout the pyramids
Talkin' 'bout the pyramids, baby,
Of the Old
And Middle
Kingdoms, yes yes.
They was Zoser and Sekhemkhet,
Khaba and Seneferu . . .

Other voices rolled on, full of pride in a new vehicle, scorn for
an untried idea, trust in a dubious therapy. A waiter brought a
frothy drink to Mrs Fleischman, who tasted it and waved it away.
'No, Toy. No, Toy . . .'

Father Warren settled himself beside Mrs McBabbitt, his
leather cassock rustling like batwings. 'Yes I guess you could say
I'm in the camp of the enemy here, heh heh, I am the *pro tem*
chairman of the local branch of the New Luddites. And I realize
almost everyone here is connected with computer science in some
way. But where else can I find converts? Our Lord made his
mission among evil persons.'

She broke a pose slightly to look at him. 'You think computer
people are really evil?'

'Not necessarily. I just meant —'

'Because I've got this real good friend, he's very big in
computers, and he says the only evil is being poor. And when you
look at that guy over there with the dirty beard, you kind of get
the idea — just look at him!'

Father Warren craned around, only to catch General Fleischman staring at him with a look of distaste.

Someone else glowered at Indica. 'I knew her when she was
plain old Indica Franklin, just another faculty wife who wanted to
be a dancer. She made it, too. Got to be a dancing pizza-
flavoured taco on TV.'

'Maybe he is a priest, maybe he ain't,' the General said to
Roderick. 'You can't hardly tell the clergy from anybody else
these days, they go around wearing drag and smoking pot just like
human beings.'

'I guess they are human beings, General.'

Fleischman looked at him to see if this was a joke. 'Yeah. Last priest I listened to was good old Father Cog on the radio. Before the war.'

'The war?'

'Okay, sure, maybe he went a little far, using Goebbels's speeches for his own sermons. You ain't Jewish, are you, Rod?'

'I'm not anything.'

'Good boy. If you ever need a job, we can always use a smart young fella like you at the bank. You just see Personnel, tell 'em *I* said to give you a job. Now what was I saying?'

'Before the, er, war . . .'

'Crazy times, Rod, crazy times. You know somebody even kidnapped Charlie McCarthy? In 1939 that was – I always wondered if maybe Father Cog knew something about that, only they wouldn't let him speak out, you know? Then, well the war came along and they shut him up. You can't go around telling people the truth in wartime.'

Edd McFee, who was across the room talking to Francine, turned to glower at Roderick. 'Who is that guy, anyway? He's been talking to old Fleischman a hell of a long time.'

'What do you care?'

'Me? *I* don't care. Only I wanta get the general to back my new project, I figured I'd get a chance to soften him up a little here.' He brushed out a wrinkle in his new Army fatigues. 'I wanted to explain to him how important it is for his bank to get deep into the visual arts, to really communicate the visual the impact of the visual –'

'Don't give me the sales talk,' she said laughing. 'What's the project?'

'I want to set up this satellite link between a dozen different artists all painting in different locations, see? Like one can be in the desert and one even in the middle of the ocean on a raft, one in the mountains, one in New York and so on – and all of them have two-way visual and audio all the time. So all of them just paint what they feel – the total group experience.' He paused. 'You don't like it?'

'Where do you come in, Edd?'

'I direct. I tell everybody what to do and I watch them do it. So the whole thing becomes really my work, see?' He looked over at

Fleischman again. 'I got a really good story for the general. Did you know that Whistler went to West Point?'

'No.' Francine sneaked a look at her watch.

'He did. And he flunked out on chemistry. He said. "If silicon was a gas, I'd be a major general."'

Nearby the piano thundered and a ragged chorus took up 'Frosty the Snowman' as a waiter passed bearing a frothy pink cocktail which he conveyed down the room to the dumpy woman in purple, who was speaking to an astrologer.

'No kidding? The same day as Monet, well there you are! Talent is talent. You know I was just talking to some young smartass kept trying to tell me Rodin's works were like cheap Jap movies, how do you like that? I mean, *Gate of Hell*, how can you compare that to a cheap —'

She paused to sip the drink. 'That's better, Toy. That's the ticket. Now just keep 'em coming.'

Allbright heaved himself to his feet nearby and, smiling at everyone with bleeding gums, made his way along the room, pausing to collect a drink, to lend a cigarette to Mrs Doody, and to confront Felix Culpa.

'Hello again!'

'What?'

'I said hello again. I met you before didn't I? Aren't you some kind of — pet-food market research was it?'

'Mistake,' said Felix Culpa hoarsely, keeping a glass in front of his face. 'I'm in satellite leasing, on the educational side. We network to school systems, linking them on a broad spectrum of, of achievement-based multifaceted synergies, excuse me.' He almost knocked over Judi Mazzini in his hurry to escape.

'I've scared him off. Funny.'

'Maybe if you took a bath now and then, people would find you nicer to be near,' said Judi Mazzini. 'We were just talking about *The Machine Dances*. Know it?'

'I ought to, I wrote it.'

'Oh come on, Allbright.'

'I did. Ghosted it for a guy named Rogers, that's why it's the only book of his anybody reads. Rest of his stuff is so loaded with sociological jargon it moves along like the shoes of Boris Karloff. Matter of fact he writes a little like your friend here talks.'

437

'Felix? I think he only talks that way when he's nervous.' She looked at Allbright. 'You're disgusting, why don't you ask Francine if you can take a bath here, maybe borrow some clothes from Everett?'

He swayed a little, looking into his glass and trying to frame an answer, while behind him someone complained about sinus trouble in Prague.

'What were you saying about my book, then?'

'I said it wasn't very well thought out. I mean, it's kind of easy to just make a list of all the ballets with mechanical people or dolls or puppets in them, from *Coppélia* to *Petrushka* –'

'Satie's *Jack-in-the-Box* and Bartok's *The Wooden Prince* –'

'Yes and *The Nutcracker*, but isn't it all kind of easy? Why does it have to be significant that people wrote "robot" ballets? The fact is, they were just interested in setting up problems in movement, *Coppélia* was just –'

'They started to think of people in terms of machine movements, that's the whole point. Once you reduce a man to a gesture, you can set up assembly lines, that's the whole point! People reduced to therbligs, goddamnit, that is the –!'

'Shh! Okay, okay.'

'And the Rockettes are an assembly line, assembling a gesture, a pure gesture.'

Harry Hatlo, though forgotten, stood by, still holding his toupée in place. 'Very interesting,' he said. 'My own work is more like pure therapy I guess, I choreograph routines to work over postural and coordination problems; right now I am working with some young people who as kids some time ago got brain damaged from mercury poisoning, it leaves you with a little parasthesia, some weakness and tremors. So what we been trying . . .'

His monotone was lost in the general surge of voices arguing over stale politics, declaring faith in a rising stock market, seeking reassurance about a cancer cure, or wondering whether Frosty really had a very shiny nose.

'Indica!'

She turned, preparing a smile for a friend, to find the masklike face of a stranger. No one. No one important, but these eyes . . . something about the eyes made her uneasy.

'Do I know you?'

'Don't you?'

She dropped the smile. 'No. No, I don't know you.' The eyes held her for a moment before she managed to turn away – hadn't she seen these eyes before? Where, not in this false face with its v-shaped smile. Not in this, not in any face. The eyes she was beginning to recall had no face to them.

'I'll give you a hint. I used to follow you.'

'You still here?' She spoke without looking at him, frightened now, feeling the chill gaze on her neck. *Following her.* That was it, the nightmare came back to her so suddenly and clearly that she almost staggered; covered by banging her glass on the bar.

'Like another drink here,' she said. 'And please tell this gentleman to –'

But he was gone. Only the revived nightmare remained. *She was sitting in the kitchen talking to her mother on the phone when she looked under the pine table and saw the eyes glittering, something ready to pounce . . . Then she was up and running through a dead woods, some trees charred by lightning, and behind her the faint clank of tank treads, the beast that could not be killed, the eyes that would not close, endless, endless pursuit . . .*

General Fleischman said to Norm, 'Poetry, I got nothing against poetry, it's poets I can't stand. Like that creep over there in the storm-coat, never had a bath or a shave in his life. Afraid it'd spoil his poetry if he got clean once. I don't mind telling you, when Moxon asked me to invest money from my bank in poetry, I laughed out loud. Wouldn't you?'

'Uh, right, sir.'

'But this turns out to be real educational and kinda synergistic, so I think it might just develop into a nice little media package. See Moxon is going to market these Home Art Kits, each one is like a little complete art package with music, visuals, prose poetry what-have-you, all wrapped up together – here, let me show you.'

He produced a pocket recorder TV. 'Course on this bitty screen everything gets diminutified, but here. This card is, see, Number Fifteen of the Nutshell Poets Series, John Keats. Like it says here how he liked birds and all. Animals are a plus in this line, kids like to hear how Shelley liked birds too, how Elizabeth Browning liked her dog Hushpuppy –'

'Hushpuppy?'

'We changed it from another name, a very downmarket name – anyway and T.S. Eliot liked cats. And we got all that info on the card, but then we can also play it.'

He shoved the card into a slot on the recorder TV. At once the tiny screen showed a cartoon Keats declaiming aloud:

Then I felt like some sky-watcher
When a new planet orbits into sight – zowie!
Or like brave Balboa when

'What do you think of it?' said Fleischman, turning it off. 'Not bad, eh?'

'It's uh, fine. Really great, sir.' Norm looked to the bar where a pretty girl was throwing back her head to release a theatrical laugh. He looked to the sofa where the mysteriously beautiful Mrs McBabbitt, in her customary black, still seemed to be waiting for someone. He looked to the piano where a few deliriously happy people had their heads together, trying to harmonize on a carol. Everybody in the room seemed to be having a terrific time. 'Really terrific.'

Silently, Norm wished himself a Merry little Christmas.

The woman at the bar, Indica Dinks, was neither as girlish nor as pretty as she might seem from a distance, but she was a minor celebrity, being appreciated. That made her glow.

'Semantics?' She laughed again. 'Mister Tarr, you don't know the meaning of the word.'

The silver-haired man next to her nodded and smiled. 'Very good. The name is Doctor Tarr, really. But my friends call me Jack.'

'All right then, Jack, you may be an expert in your field – did you say it was market research?'

'Market forecasting, really.' Dr Tarr was a lot younger and handsomer than he might seem from a distance. He kept taking the unlit pipe from his mouth and pointing the stem at nothing. 'But what I wanted to ask you was –'

'Market whatever, you may be an expert in your field, but I too happen to know a little bit about human nature. Especially when it comes to machines.'

'Yes, exactly. The interface –'

'Face it,' she continued, 'machines are only human. They have feelings too.'

He paused, deciding not to laugh. 'So you say in your book, Indica. But that's just what I'm not clear about, where you say machines have feel –'

'My book isn't clear? *The Mechanical Eunuch* isn't clear?'

'Yes, yes, most of it and there's quite a lot there I agree with, the magical bond between human and machine, yes. I was right with you there, where you describe a man trying to start his car on a cold morning, swearing at it, kicking it . . . I could almost imagine mechanical consciousness . . . But later when it gets down to whether a shoeshine machine feels degraded, I mean I just can't quite . . . see?'

She patted his hand. 'Of course not, okay. Don't worry, maybe it takes a *bricoleur* to really dig –'

'Yes, you're probably right, only a man who lays bricks with his two hands knows the other side –'

'Or a Zen person, maybe one who likes to fix motorcycles or at least lawnmowers. Because only a person like that can dig that machines aren't just extensions of man any more. No, that's all part of the old master-slave routine, the terrible power game we play with machines. *Machines are beings in their own right.* And if we don't give them their freedom, one of these days they'll be able to just *take* it.'

Dr Tarr nodded, and pointed his pipestem at nothing. 'You're right. I never saw it that way before. I guess my professional background does get in the way sometimes. Blinds me to certain possibilities.'

'Your professional background?'

'Parapsychology. I used to head a little department over at the University, before I decided to carve out a new career in market forecasting. And you know, I always took it for granted that psychic energy goes with consciousness, and with being human. Or at least with being a biological creature.' The pipestem waggled. 'You've opened up a very big can of questions, young lady. If machines can feel . . .'

A few moments later she was calling him 'Jack' often, and

emphasizing everything she said by touching his hand. She was telling him about her last husband.

'Hank was okay really, but he kept getting wound tighter and tighter into ecology. I mean I tried to tell him whales aren't the only fish in the sea, but – oh well. Now Hank's trying to run this really seedy Luddite movement, talk about misguided. I mean you can't turn the clock back to zero, that's just a waste of time. He'll learn, I hope. I still feel a lot of natural affection for Hank, you know? Like they say people do when they get an arm or leg cut off, they go around feeling this ghost limb for a long time. Kinda like that.'

She sighed, sipped her vegetable-juice cocktail. 'And that's natural and healthy, the ghost limb. But on the other hand take people with artificial limbs. They can get too attached to them, you know?'

'The dance of life goes on,' said Dr Tarr, his stem pointing nowhere in particular.

Father Warren sat on the South sofa, pretending to study the colour of his glass of sherry. Someone sat down beside him and asked what he did – and left before he could think of an answer.

The party was beginning to run down. Indica sat at the bar, talking to the woman whose sinus trouble was the trouble with Prague. The group at the piano were trying 'Hello Dolly'. The remains of a buffet supper were being cleared away to the kitchen where Felix Culpa was examining an electric carving knife. Mrs Doody had found her husband upstairs asleep on the toilet – his pacemaker needed a new battery – and Mr Vitanuova helped her bring him down and pack him into the car.

Edd McFee, moving in finally to talk to General Fleischman, heard him say to Francine, 'It's like Whistler said, "If silicon was a gas, I'd be a –"'

Someone glowered over a glass at Indica and said, 'I knew her when she was plain old Indica Franklin, just another faculty wife who wanted to be a taco on local TV.'

Someone glowered over a glass at Mrs McBabbitt and said, 'Well, silicon's the basis of her life all right –'

Someone glowered over a glass at Father Warren and said, 'There he goes, looking for another bandwagon. If Indica gave

442

him a kind word he'd drop this Luddite crap in five minutes . . . a *treen priest*.'

Someone glowered at everyone and no one, while mumbling the words of a tired limerick: '. . . both concave and convex . . .'

A stranger arrived and, without removing his coat, hat or even the muffler that covered him up to his pale eyes, went straight into Moxon's library. The room was dim, lit only by a desk lamp. Everett Moxon got up from the desk.

'Ben? About time. Things are breaking up.'

'Feel . . . like I'm breaking up myself . . .' Franklin sat down and took off his fur hat. 'I'm sick, Ev.'

'There's this flu thing going around, you'll probably be okay in the morning. Now what have you brought me?'

Franklin threw a heavy envelope on the desk. 'All there, the Taipin bids, the secret leasing arrangements for Kratcom International, the whole, whole . . . holus bolus. Jesus Christ, Ev, why didn't you tell me *she* was gonna be here? I damn near walked in there and met her face to face, just in time I heard someone say, "Sinuses? They're all in the head" and I slipped past. Scarf over my face like a damn burglar.'

Moxon was studying papers from the envelope. 'This is good stuff, Ben.' He looked up. 'To tell you the truth, I clean forgot you used to be married to Indica. Seems like it must have happened in another ice age. Volume One and we're in Volume Two. Anyway why can't you two be pals now?'

'Pals?' Ben's weak laugh set off a coughing fit. 'Just the sound of her voice sets my teeth on edge, and what she says! Last time I saw her she talked about something being *water over the bridge*; I came close to hitting her, I – I know it sounds funny now but – are you listening?'

'Sure. But maybe you just hate Indica because she's hit the big time. Without you.'

Ben had taken off his coat; now he put it on again. 'Yes, they all take it seriously, this Machines Liberation idea of hers. Without me? Well sure, she's a self-made woman. I'm surrounded by self-made men and women, look at Kratt. God-damned world crawling with self-made people, self-made man myself, trouble is self-made people get made in their own image. Christ, it's cold in here.'

443

'Sweat's pouring off you, how can you be cold? Ben, why don't you go upstairs and lie down, I'll call a doctor, okay?'

'No but listen, Ev, you know what Kratt's like.'

'He treats his employees like toilet paper, I know that.'

Ben started to shiver. 'It's not that, not just that. I just can't forget that time a few years ago when he poisoned all those kids just to break into the funfood market fast – funfood! Kids were dying of mercury poisoning! And you know what he did about it?'

'Forget it, Ben, that was a long time ago.'

'He bribed doctors to forge death certificates.'

Moxon slid the papers back in the envelope. 'Sure, sure. But it's Christmas now –'

'Christmas! I think about Kratt, every Christmas, he fits right in there, Herod and the Holy Innocents. Herod and the –'

'Let me call you a doctor.'

'Makes you wonder – did Herod really want to kill Christ, or was he happy just killing any babies?'

'Take it easy, Ben. Just wait right here, I'll go get help and we'll take you up to bed. Wait.'

Moxon found Francine in the kitchen. 'Ben's sick as a dog, we'll have to put him in the spare room and call the doctor. He's out of his head with fever right now. Still goes on about Kratt and that poisoned gingerbread business.'

She understood. 'He still blames himself.'

'Probably right to blame himself.' Moxon lifted his small head and stared unseeing towards the two cooks who were arguing about a missing electric knife. 'And for Indica's walking out on him. The fact is, Ben's always been a fuckup.'

He went back to the library with one of the waiters to find Ben shaking and weeping and sweating; sweat dripped from his chin to the desk blotter.

'He was here, right here in the room!'

'Who, Ben? Kratt?'

'Roderick was right here!' Ben pointed a shaking finger at the darkness. 'My robot! My son, in whom I am well pleased!'

Moxon and Toy looked at one another; each took a shuddering arm. 'Up we go now.'

'He came into the room and stood right there. I saw him, he was wearing a ski sweater. Black, with little white figures on it.

444

Like little people, self-made men He didn't say anything but he knew who I was. He knew I was protecting him from Herod . . .'

On the second occasion when Roderick tried the library, Ben was gone but Allbright was there, examining books.

'Oh it's you. Getting to be like a reunion here, I saw your pal earlier. The guy that wears dark glasses. Felix.'

'I . . . please I . . .'

'You gonna puke? Try the wastebasket there.'

'I need an outlet . . .'

Allbright dusted off a volume. 'Who doesn't? Here's a rare little item. Life of Sir Charles M'Carthy. First edition, clothbound, slight foxing.'

'Help.' Roderick was on all fours behind the desk, fumbling with an electric cord that seemed to run from his navel. 'Help . . . plug in.'

'Hope this isn't a suicide. Here.' Allbright reached down and plugged the cord into the wall socket. He watched Roderick's eyes go opaque, then close.

After a minute, Roderick sat upright in something like the lotus position. His navel was still plugged to 120v AC, his eyes still closed. 'My batteries. I don't usually let them run low like that.'

Allbright dropped Sir Charles M'Carthy into his battered briefcase and searched for more first editions. 'Yeah, I feel like that sometimes. Only being a poet I can't even kill myself. It would look too much like imitation of better poets.'

'Suicide. I don't see the point of it.' A v-shaped smile in the shadow by the desk. 'Why take a last step? Why not go on living – if only to see what happens next?'

Allbright's laugh made him cough, then sneeze. 'Life as a soap opera, eh? A never-ending series of episodes in *Dorinda's Destiny*? Trouble is, life isn't as real as TV, not any more. We've traded away our reality. We have no past, no future, no minds, no souls.'

'I don't understand, Mr Allbright.'

'The past, that's just Scarlett O'Hara in a taffeta-hung bed and Washington throwing a dollar across the Potomac – or the Delaware – all people remember is the dollar, all else is mist and plastic dinosaurs. The past is five minutes ago, it's what happened before the last commercial.

'The future now, that's just space wars, white plastic rockets against black, Terra versus Ratstar. Names don't matter, what matters is the violence. The future has to be galactic annihilation, 1984 for a million years, a spaceboot grinding an alien face forever. Nobody believes in the future anyway, except maybe a few crank science-fiction writers or maybe the people who want to freeze other people into people-sicles and store them – for a price. And imagine that, asking ice to pay for itself. Yet one more ingenious way to package and market the future.

'So what's left? The mind? Not even a ghost in a machine any more. Now the mind is just something you improve by reading condensed books and listening to distilled records, everybody now knows the mind has secret powers and you can write off to California to unlock, get rich through safe hypnosis in your spare time. The soul? That's now just one more brand of saleable music, money seems to make everything more real, doesn't it? Money is more alive than we are. No wonder kids have started calling themselves robots, they know what's expected of them. It's a robot world.'

'A robot world?'

'Sure, any decent machine can get in on the ground floor, work its way up, become President – one or two made it already. A robot has plenty of native advantages to start with: never wastes time, no personal problems, never picks nose in public. Winning combination there.'

Roderick opened his eyes. 'What makes you think a robot would want to get ahead? Couldn't it just enjoy being alive?'

'Let me read you something, friend.' Allbright took down a slim volume and read aloud:

'"Jack keeps one hour. The policeman develops all pages. Some sister is offended. Jack's nurse offended all reasons. A few fat pilots warded off more vegetables." They call that computer poetry. Poetry? I wonder. Sounds like something Swift cooked up at the Academy of Lagodo, just keep flipping through the combinations and watching nothing much come up. Does this computer know it's writing poetry, and not just figuring a payroll or firing off a missile?'

Roderick opened his mouth to reply, but no reply came. Allbright picked up his heavy briefcase and shuffled to the door. 'I

446

mean to say, if that stuff is poetry, then sex with a vibrator must be love.'

The door closed behind him, then opened immediately, letting in a slice of light, piano chords, and a stumbling couple.

'Oh! Excuse me!' Judi Mazzini let out a yelp of laughter as she steered the man in dark glasses, turning him around and leading him out as though he were blind.

Mrs McBabbitt lived high in a glass tower by the river. Roderick had not kissed her in the taxi and he did not kiss her in the elevator.

'Come on in, Roddy, have a drink or something.'

'Thanks, I'll come in but I – nice apartment.' There was a bowl of yellow roses on a round table, and next to it, a picture of Mr Kratt. 'But who, this can't be Mr McBabbitt, this –'

'No, an old friend, an old friend. He well stays here sometimes. You might as well know he pays for this place, he kind of owns me. I never usually bring anybody here, only I don't know, tonight I just felt – anyway, you're different. You don't really want anything, do you?'

'Well I – well I –'

'I don't mean you're like queer, you just seem to not want anything. You seem like – chaste.'

'Ha. What er happened to Mr McBabbitt, if you don't mind my asking?'

'Him? Oh, he's Doctor McBabbitt, he was my plastic surgeon. Or you could say I was his showcase. He tried out everything on me, damn near everything. All those years, all those years . . .'

'Pain,' said Roderick softly.

'Pain, oh sure, not that that mattered so much. People put up with pain at the dentist, it all depends on what you want out of life, I wanted beauty. All I ever wanted was beauty, so I married him. I picked him because he was the best. Very best.'

They sat together on the sofa, leaning together stiffly as she wept.

'Oh this is stupid, stupid, I've got nothing to cry about. He was the very best, he still is. I mean he had *style*. He didn't get all his ideas from movie stars and strippers, he used to look at paintings a lot too, Old Masters and that. Like one guy, I think it was

Corpeggio, anyway he painted this beautiful woman and when some French prince got hold of it he took a knife and cut the painting all to pieces. Only somebody secretly got them all and put it back together, all but the head. They had to paint a new head. You know, Dr McBabbitt liked his work because he got to be both people, you know? The painter and the guy with the knife. You know?'

She jumped to her feet and smoothed the black velvet. 'I feel lots better now. You want a coffee or anything before you leave?'

XII

America come alive!
Grab on to a brand new day!

'– *Good morning, Mr and Ms America, I'm Jeb Goodhart* –'
'– *and I'm Brie Wittgenstein, bringing you the early news update* –'
'Good God, what? What's it?' Indica fought for consciousness, for some clue to this booming, blustering confusion in which giant orange faces grinned and bellowed at her from across a room of the wrong shape. She seemed to be ten feet from the floor, and there was a large spider on her pillow.
'– *says it's the most severe quake in Ruritania since nineteen* –'
Dr Tarr's head appeared from under her bed. 'Morning! Sleep all right?'
'What? Yes I but I just what I – bunk beds? Where are we?'
'Ha ha, don't you remember? This is my old frat house, Digamma Upsilon Nu.'
'Your old, why should I remember your old –?'
'No, but don't you remember the snowbank? We skidded into a big snowbank? And I went for help while you stayed in the car?'
'I remember you telling me not to go to sleep.' The spider on her pillow became a contact lens, glued in place by a false eyelash. She rescued it. 'That pissed me off, because I'd already taken my two Dormistran, how could I stay awake?'
'Yes well see we turned out to be only a mile from my old frat house here, whereas almost sixteen miles to my place with god knows what damage to the front end of my – wait a minute, you took sleeping pills? On the way to my place? If you I mean thought it was going to be that bad, why bother coming? I mean –'
'*Hey kids, does your Mom buy you* Flavoreenos? *My Mom does and I really love her, because* Flavoreenos *are corn-style flakes in 26* delicious

449

flavours! Have you tried cherry cola? Chili dog? Chocolate sardine parfait? Mmmm, I get a new flavour every morning, because my Mom loves me and I love Flavoreenos!'

'Okay okay maybe I was a little nervous but anyway here we are in bunk beds does it matter? And do we need that TV on with all that, that wall projection kids with orange hair eight feet tall eating blue goop Jesus Jack I don't feel so well.'

'Just um trying to catch the weather, new antifreeze account I –'

There was a knock at the door. Tarr answered it to a burly young man with a flat nose. 'Brother Tarr? I'm supposed to give you your bill here. Uh, here.'

'What's this? Looks more like somebody's bill for a week at the Waldorf – wait a minute, what's this item here, fifty bucks for snow, what's that supposed to –'

'Bathtub fulla snow, Brother Tarr. Just like you ordered. We filled it while you was asleep.'

'Just like I – wait now, hold on – fellas, no, hold on –'

Three other burly young men came in, seized Tarr and carried him struggling into the bathroom. After a few shrieks and shouts, a dozen guffaws, the boys came out, blew kisses to Indica and left. A minute later, Tarr came out grinning, naked, towelling himself. 'Ha ha, damn it, I forgot what great jokers the brothers can be.'

'Yeah very amusing.' She turned to the TV.

'– *Bimibian police claim the schoolgirls were throwing stones, and say it was only in self-defence that officers opened fire with automatic weapons and raked the classrooms. No death figures have been released yet, but unofficial estimates* –'

When she and Tarr were dressed, Flat Nose came back with a genuine bill. 'And we didn't charge nothing for towing your car, Brother Tarr. Because you're a good sport.'

Tarr grinned and opened his chequebook. Indica said, 'You boys like gags, do you?'

Flat Nose grinned. 'We pull some perdy good ones around here, like last year we made up a guy and we enrolled him in a lotta classes, whole buncha stuff. We even took exams for him, he got a B average, perdy good, huh?' His laughter sounded like a child's imitation of a machinegun, as he left with his cheque.

'Jesus,' said Indica. 'Nothing changes around the U, I've been away from it years now, same asshole kids still here pulling the same asshole stunts, hanging toilet seats on the Student Union tower – why don't we get out of here?'

He looked at the TV. 'Guess I missed the weather –'

'Good news for kids in Topeka, Kansas, where the Santa Claus strike is over –'

'And just in time, Brie, with five more shopping days till Christmas. And in a New Jersey divorce court a judge has just awarded a couple joint custody of their Christmas tree – wonder who gets to change the bulbs . . .'

Within minutes they had exchanged the dazzle of orange faces for the dazzle of sun on snow, the boom of TV for the roar of radio.

. . . keep your de-entures gri-ipping tight
Eat in heavenly peace
Eat in heavenly peace

'I called the office,' said Tarr. 'But Judi my sec isn't in yet. So I can drop you anywhere, plenty of time.' The car sped through outlying fragments of the campus, past book-stores and sweatshirt boutiques, past the new Life Sciences building with its imposing sculpture of a clam. 'I'll have to chew her ass out good, though, being this late.'

'But Jack, wasn't she at the party last night? Maybe the poor girl just overslept.'

'So? Of course I still expect her to turn up on time, and normally she's very conscientious too, that's why this leaves me in a bind, I wanted to finish mapping out this Middle East campaign with her before we run into Christmas.'

Dent-a-poise has the answer for you
Confidence with what-ev-er you chew
Eat in heavenly . . .

'Market forecasting, isn't that kind of crystal ball stuff?' she asked. The car was leaving University environs and entering a neighbourhood of cheap bars, pawnshops, fast food and barricaded liquor stores.

'Crystal ball, hmm, you could say that. In fact, we use psychic data right along with more conventional info, you'd be surprised how well they correlate. Not long ago we had an account, a well-known company who wanted to open up a chain of taco stands in the University area. Or was it pizza-burgers? Anyway, what they wanted was an optimal set of locations. So we took a map of the campus, held a pendulum over it, and just assessed the strength of the swing.'

'You're kidding.'

'Nope. There were four strong-swing areas – and these turned out to be the four ideal locations! You could call that good guesswork – but was it?'

'I wouldn't know,' she said, amused. 'To me, psychic stuff is just all in the mind.'

'Yes yes, of course, nothing wrong with healthy scepticism and I myself – LOOK OUT! DAMN YOU!' He hit the brakes as a ragged figure in a torn storm-coat danced across the street in front of them. The car slid on glare ice a few feet, hit the man gently and had no apparent effect; for he too slid, flailing his arms until he could regain his dancing pace and make it to the kerb. There he removed a glove and gave them the finger.

'Damn these derelicts, every Christmas they swarm down here, makes you wish the city would just bring in exterminators, put out I don't know maybe bottles of poison wine in paper bags –'

'But Jack, look! Look, isn't that Allbright, he was at the party.'

'And here he is in his own environ – what are you doing?'

Before the car could move again she had the window down and was waving. 'Allbright! Hey! You need a ride anywhere?'

The gaunt figure paused, Z-bent to peer at them, then danced over. 'And a Merry Christmas to you, good lady, and to your good gentleman, God bless you for your true Christian spirit as you feed the hungry, clothe the naked, ride the pedestrian –'

'Just get in the car and shut up,' Tarr said. 'Allbright the damn light's changing.'

Allbright squeezed in beside Indica, letting his arm hang out the open window. 'Where we going, kids?'

'Just shut up.'

'Maybe if you tell us where you want to be dropped . . .' Indica suggested.

'Oh, a place over on Jogues Boulevard, place called Larry's

Grill. Jogues Boulevard, ever notice how the Jesuits had their way with this town? Xavier Avenue, Loyola Street and so on, makes you wonder –'

'You look terrible,' said Indica. 'Dirt in your beard, dried it looks like blood down the side of your face –'

'Makes you wonder about Larry's Grill itself, eh?'

'And your clothes. Allbright you look –'

'Terrible, I know. That's why you snubbed me last night, eh?' Indica opened her mouth to frame a denial, but already Allbright had changed the subject again. 'Moxon's got a damn good library, you know?'

'And you've been ripping him off?'

'Only a few books, just to get me what I need . . . I even found something there published by his namesake. Nineteenth-century publisher called Moxon too, published Keats.'

'No kidding.' She stifled a yawn.

'Part of a series, Moxon's Miniature Poets, nice image there, Wordsworth, Coleridge, Shelley . . . Ought to be right in your line, Indica.'

'Poetry? No, I –'

'First time I heard you were liberating the machines I thought of that old stock cartoon, you know: man on a street corner winding up lots of little men and setting them free to walk away – million gags based on that image, wouldn't you say?'

Indica sat up a little. 'My work is no gag, buster.'

'Course not, no, just thinking of Moxon, Moxon's Miniature Poets, little windup Keats, windup Coleridge. Little windup Shelley faints, fails, falls upon the tiny thorns of life, bleeds . . . fine early example of miniaturization there . . .'

She looked at him. 'You're kind of a fine early example yourself. Of verbal masturbation.'

'Yes. Yes, somebody's got to wind somebody up, now and then. Even if there's no love, tiny Wordsworth can still talk of little nameless unremembered acts of kindness, if not of love . . . What do we all have? What, detergents being kind to hands? Love with a vibrator? Poetry from a damn computer?'

Tarr made a face. 'What are you on, Allbright? Why don't you just shut up, we'll drop you at your bar and you can ramble on with all the other –'

'Forgetting my manners, haven't congratulated Indica on her new book. What did *Time* say? Called you an exponent of the germane gear, didn't they? A Joan of arc-welding? Congratulations.'

'Look, I don't need heavy irony,' she said. 'You always –'

'No irony intended, the reviewers think it's new and gimmicky, that's all you need nowadays. After all, the book industry doesn't ask if a book is good or if it says anything important. The industry asks only *is it new?* Because they might have to slot it in between selections like *In Praise of Teddy Bears* and *The Hidden Language of Your Handwriting* and *The Dieter's Guide to Weight Loss after Sex*, and God know how much other ephemeral – whole forests being felled to print a book on how to sit in your seat on a commercial air flight, how to get over the death of a pet, you think people who publish that care about any book, any idea? Wait, wait –' He fumbled in a pocket and came up with a tiny ruled notebook.

It's a beautiful morning,' Tarr said. 'Why don't you just shut up and enjoy it?'

'He's got a point though, Jack. I mean I know I'm probably being ripped off by my publishers, who are they? They're just some subsidiary of a conglomerate, what do they care about machines?'

'Or people?' Allbright suggested, thumbing dog-eared pages. 'I just jotted down a few titles, books the reviewers can really get their teeth into, if any: *Garbo.* a long-awaited biography; *The Politics of Pregnancy*, well maybe; *Railways of Ruritania* to grace any coffee table alongside *The Yeti and I* – the ad says "a close encounter that became a night of primal love"; here's *The Real Garbo; Marxism and Menstruation*, why not; then there's *Frogs: Their Wonderful Wisdom, Follies and Foibles, Mysterious Powers, Strange Encounters, Private Lives, Symbolism and Meaning*, serious rival there for the Teddy Bear book; then there's *Pornography, Psychedelics and Technology*, yup; and *Paedophilia: A Radical Case* and finally *Sons of Sam Spade*. Hard to imagine* a newer collection of novelties than that, right?'

Tarr said, 'Sounds a little bit like sour grapes there, Allbright. I notice the people who sneer most at success are usually unsuccessful.'

'That's goddamned profound, Tarr. And in my case, true!'

After they dropped Allbright, Dr Tarr got out his pipe and sucked at it madly as he drove. 'Jesus,' he said through clenched teeth, 'you try to forget some things for a while, along comes some Allbright to remind you. They never leave you alone.'

'Alone, I hate being alone. I hated writing both my books, you know? What I really like is promotion. The TV appearances, radio phone-ins, I guess I must be part of the whole awful system. But shit, Jack, I've missed so many boats.'

'Me too, me too. I was a pretty good parapsychologist, you know? I had it all working for me, then I just – it all blew up on me. And here I am in market forecasting, a kind of limbo – no real life in it.'

'I never had any kids,' she said. 'Never wanted any, either. But I was just remembering, this robot kid-thing Hank and I had for a little while. It was Allbright who dumped it on us, some friend of his built it, I guess. We called it Roderick. Cute little thing, like a toy tank only with these big eyes – we were both just crazy about it.' She sighed. 'Maybe I should have had real kids. Or maybe I should have gone on with my dancing. I was only in an ad, but the potential was all there, you know?'

'No life in it,' he said. 'Market forecasting, sometimes it's like I don't know, trying to make a dead pigeon fly.'

'The potential was there, just like the 480 ova inside you, all those chances . . . sure I've got a little fame, a little money, I'm helping the cause of machine justice, only I still feel cheated.'

He bit the pipestem and drove on. 'Tell you what. Next week I'm flying to the Middle East to help plan this big tampon campaign. You could come along.'

'Where?'

'Cairo. Might be fun – if you forget your sleeping pills.'

433 East 11th had once been a smoke-blackened building of no great distinction; now it was an undistinguished low pile of smoke-blackened stone and brick. One of the caryatids that had pretended to hold up ten storeys now lay full-length, relaxed and indeed disjointed like the backbone of a dinosaur. And on her head, where a palaeontologist might have sat contemplating evolution or Ozymandias, Mr Vitanuova now sat holding a sheaf of pay-cheques.

'You guys may wonder why I'm paying you in person. It ain't because of Christmas, I ain't Sandy Claus. It's because I wanna make sure each and everybody gets his and her cheque *personal*. Because this is the last. You're all laid off as of now, and the company is going into liquidation, right after Christmas.'

Roderick noticed a general murmur of protest, so he added his voice to it. 'What's going on?' he asked several times.

'I'm real sorry, boys and girls. Our lawyers say we got to wind down the company, we're bleeding to death from a whole buncha lawsuits. All from that goddamn mixup when we almost blew up 334 down the street there insteada 433. Now all of a sudden everybody wants to get something outa that.

'See, we evicted all the tenants on behalf of the owner, so both tenants and owner are now suing there.' He started counting on his gloved fingers. 'And that doorman we had arrested is suing us too. Then some of the tenants was so pissed off at the eviction they trashed their places, busted pipes, took the floor out even. So the owner sues us for that.' On the thumb, he said, 'As if all that ain't enough, a burglarizer climbs in one of these apartments one night, puts down his foot for a floor and falls thirty feet and breaks his back. So *he* sues us.'

'A burglar? How can he sue?' Roderick asked.

'Don't ask me, but that's the bigggest suit of all. This here burglarizer, this Chauncey Bangfield, is claiming loss of earnings, see? Says he pulls down about half a million a year and he's got maybe twenty years ahead of him. And he's suing us in California, so we ain't got a chance.'

'Did you say Chauncey Bangfield?' Roderick's jaw clicked open.

'You know him or something?'

'I went to school with him. I mean there can't be two Chauncey Bangfields, can there? Well well, good old Chaunce. He was the school – well – bully.'

'Well now he's pushing me around.' Mr Vitanuova laughed, coughed, took out his cigar and examined it.

'Look, boss, why don't *I* talk to him? If I told him it would ruin you, maybe he'd drop the suit.'

'Nobody talks to him, I already tried. They got him over there at Mercy Hospital, and these fancy California lawyers won't let

456

anybody see him or even find out how sick he is. But I don't know – you could try. You could try.'

He drove Roderick to the hospital in his Rolls-Royce, and talked all the way of destruction.

'See, I was always in the garbage business, started out with just my brother and one truck. We built up a fleet and lotsa valuable contacts; when the city moved into garbage, we moved into incinerators. Real money was there. But I still didn't see the big picture.

'Then one day I met this broad who gave me some million-dollar advice. She said her ex-husband was into incineration too, dropping bombs. A pilot or an astronaut or some damn thing. Then she said, *You're not just in garbage, you're in the destruction business, just like Luke. And it's a wide-open, growing field.*

'Destruction, see, that was it! I had contacts in junk, so why not buy into junkyards? And ship salvage? And demolition? Hell, now I'm diversified all over the place, got interests in bottle banks, graveyards, even tried a little asset-stripping – but that was too abstract, I like to see real stuff falling apart. That's why I acquired Hackme, and I'd really hate to see it go. So here we are, get in there, kid, and fight for us.'

As soon as Roderick asked for Mr Bangfield, the receptionist became very nervous. She pushed a button and then pretended to be looking up the room number. A stack of X-rays slipped to the floor.

'Let me help,' said Roderick. Before he could help, however, he was grabbed from behind and his arm twisted into a hammerlock.

'Peace,' said someone.

'Well peace, fine, but – ouch – what is this?'

'Routine, man, just hold still until we see if you're clean.' Hands patted and prodded him. 'Okay, beautiful.' His assailant released him and stepped back as Roderick turned. 'We love you, man.'

'Who are you two to love me?' He saw that they were two remarkably healthy-looking men in late middle age, both dressed in the style of a bygone age.

The one who did all the talking wore a shirt printed with tiny flowers in fluorescent colours, white beachcomber trousers and rope sandals. His blond hair was twined with artificial flowers;

around his neck were assorted strands of beads and a gold cowbell. He wore a CND button and (just visible inside his open flowing shirt) a Colt .45 automatic.

His partner, who did all the nodding, wore his dark hair streaked, long and fastened up with a white headband. His shirt was buckskin, dripping with bead and fringe, over Levis above moccasin boots. He favoured bearclaw necklaces and silver rings and bracelets mounted with turquoise. His button urged saving the whale, and his weapon of choice seemed to be a Smith & Wesson .38 police special. Both men were as muscled and tanned as possible, and looked as though they spent their days surfing and swilling vitamin cocktails.

'Yeah hey we oughta introduce ourselfs, I'm Wade Moonbrand and this is like my partner Cass Honcho, we're like Mr Bangfield's attorneys. He doesn't want to see anyone, man. Not in this shastri (that means incarnation). Right, Cass?'

Mr Honcho nodded. Wade Moonbrand spoke again.

'So unless you like dig sitting around and waiting for like a million light years till he comes around again, forget it, hey? Man who needs trouble? We just want peace and love everywhere without guys like you coming in here to hassle our client, trying to lay some kinda guilt trip on him. There he is, fighting for his life in there, all purple and black aura, here come all you plastic guys to dump your bad karma on him, who needs it? Man like I never like like to get into pushing and authority games, I want everybody to be free, okay? Only your freedom has to stop were our client's begins, so now we'll just ask you as a favour, just split?'

Mr Honcho nodded agreement.

Roderick said, 'I see your point. But maybe Mr Bangfield would want to see *me* if you told him I was here. I'm an old classmate of his, we went to grade school together in Nebraska. I heard about his accident –'

'You thought maybe there was some action you could horn in on, try the old school buddy scam and grab what's going down, eh? We're not that fucking dumb, man. Anyway listen old buddy Chauncey is like on the nod just now, he don't want his rems messed up by no fakey school bud. So –'

But Mr Honcho stopped nodding here.

'What's the matter? Like Cass man, you can't mean that? Okay sure I know, it wouldn't do no harm just to let him see old Chauncey, see him and just walk away? Okay man, be free, have it your way. Everything's cool. *But* if this turns into a bad trip then *you* shoot Plastic Man here and *I'll* handle your defence.'

Finally, in the company of a yawning doctor and the two lawyers, Roderick was marched into Intensive Care Unit 9. The place was dim, the only bright areas being the face of the patient and, on the other side of the room, the chair where a nurse stopped filing her nails and looked up. 'No change,' she said.

The rest of the room was crowded with dim machines on wheels, machines that clicked and clucked, buzzed and bleeped, showed on their screens moving dots, flickering numbers, or wave forms moving like an endless parade of shark fins.

The doctor yawned. 'Didn't expect any change. Let's get this visit over with.'

Roderick was gripped by both wrists and both arms, and marched to the bedside. He felt as though being asked to identify a corpse at a morgue.

'That's Chauncey all right. Of course he's a lot older now. Er, would it be all right if I woke him?'

The doctor laughed in mid-yawn. 'Make medical history if you did. Didn't anybody clue you in? This guy has irreversible brain damage, he can't wake up. Best thing we could do for him would be to turn off something vital and call in the heartsnatchers.'

Mr Moonbrand said, 'The doc is exaggerating. Our client –'

'Exaggerating? Your client would be out in Vitanuova Cemetery right now, only you two won't let the family sign the release form. Because he's worth twenty million alive and only eight dead, wasn't that what you said?'

'I really don't need this, man. You make it sound like bounty hunters or something, dead or alive. I mean anyway, who's to say what death is? Who are you to say if somebody's dead, anyway? Like orthodox medicine, what do *you* know, all you know is machines and operations and chemotherapy, like you only treat the symptoms and not the whole holistic, who are you, anyway? Anyway what's your beef, you guys are getting like a hundred grand a week out of this guaranteed, man life is beautiful all over!'

At his expansive gesture, one of Wade Moonbrand's necklaces

parted, its beads dropping in darkness to become a string of rattling sounds only.

'Hare Krishna! Hey man can everybody help me these are like these real expensive amber beads. Not that I'm into bread, I'd like to see the whole world free and everybody just take what they need, only I mean like you gotta be a realist in the world like it is, anybody got a flashlight? I – thanks. Beautiful. I mean I like a nice shadowy room like this man but – that's it, everybody get down and help, real cooperation commune spirit okay maybe I am like too possessive about these beads only they got sedimental value too, I bought them because they reminded me of this great Herman Hesse novel, real fat paperback I had I was gonna read it when I got my head together – Cass, can you reach me that one there, Cass or anybody, there, no there, *there* you fucking idiot right behind that wire let me get it my – what's that?'

One of the machines had suddenly begun a high-pitched whine.

'Alarm,' said the nurse. 'Somebody *unplugged* his lungs.' She and the doctor pummelled and prodded the figure in the bed for a few minutes, but none of the machines showed any signs of life.

'There goes twelve million,' said Moonbrand. 'Four of it ours.'

Honcho shook his head.

'Man you don't mean it? Yeah yeah, a malpractice suit! Outa sight! I see just how we build it . . .' The two legal minds departed.

Roderick hung around until the heart team rushed Chauncey away. He felt a loss here, but why? Chauncey had never been anything but the school bully ('Why you wearing a iron suit, huh? Huh? Think you're tough or someping?'), ugly and unpleasant all his life. Yet something had been lost here, more precious than amber.

In the lobby Roderick saw a children's choir in red and white robes, come to sing carols to the shut-ins. They were stopped now, while security cops frisked everyone. He lingered for a half-hour, hoping to catch a song, but the search was very thorough.

Finally he emerged into the clear, cold night air. He looked across the river to the city, where tiny blue winking lights of snowploughs moved here and there along bright streets, bright below a darkness in which the massed shapes of skyscrapers seemed not only indistinct, but unimpressive. They might have been a pile of empty cardboard boxes in some unlit cellar.

Empty, that was it. Christmas Eve, and in all the tens of thousands of offices in all the hundreds of buildings in sight, not a single window was lit. No, there was one. Just one, a single emerald-cut light set high in the forehead of some great toad of a tower.

While he stood on the steps contemplating this beacon, Roderick heard someone cry for help. No one else seemed to notice: visitors, patients, doctors, cops and carollers, all came and went as normal. He alone could hear it!

A psychic experience, without doubt. Could it be the tormented soul of Chauncey? Or telepathy? Or even something extraterrestrial?

'Where are you?' he called.

'Help! Here, in the bushes.' There were evergreen bushes by the side of the broad steps; a man crawled out of them and collapsed at Roderick's feet. His face was covered with blood.

Roderick got him to his feet, and helped him up the steps. 'What happened?'

'Mugged,' said the man. 'Don't ask me how, but I was mugged! Me!'

Inside the receptionist haggled about insurance and donor cards, but finally accepted the patient. Roderick waited around while the man was examined, cleaned and bandaged, put to bed.

'He's fine,' said a doctor. 'He can go home tomorrow.'

'Good. Good.'

In the lobby there was no one now but two carollers, counting something out in their hands.

'Hey no fair, you got one more Ultracalm than me. I want the extra Somrepose then, hey?'

'Okay fine but then I want some Zerone too, heck these are 25 milligram ones and yours are only 5 . . .'

He went on out on the steps again, and looked for the single lighted window. But now all was dark, and the city slept with its fathers.

XIII

'Look, have some fruit, forget about it.'

'Forget I got mugged? How do you forget an experience like that? I'm telling you −'

'Sure, okay, but I'm just wondering how this is gonna look to our people? Frankly, old buddy, you blew it. You had your chance to waste this guy, and you −'

'I got mugged, that's all. I got mugged, I got mugged! Don't ask me how.'

'I won't ask you nothing. But you can bet your ass somebody's gonna ask, and ask hard. That a winesap apple there? Okay if I help myself, I really got a thing about winesaps . . . Look, this thing reflects bad on everybody, it reflects bad on the whole Agency, our section even worse, and me worst of all.'

'I know, I *know.* But what can I do? It just happened.'

'Yeah, but when the people at Orinoco start looking for some balls to stomp on, where do they look first? I mean, who's really responsible here?'

'What are you implying?'

'I'm not implying nothing. I'm just saying, that's all. Those Concord grapes there? You mind? I'm saying, look at all the trouble everybody took to set this thing up. We traced the customer to where he works, I found out from his co-workers that the boss is driving him to Mercy Hospital to see somebody. We rush over a camera team by helicopter just to take his picture when he gets out of the car, regular and infra-red just so we don't get the wrong guy −'

'Again.'

'All right, our people watch all the damn exits until you can set up in your bush with your snooperscope and your infra-red detector and your laser-aimed sniper rifle −'

The man in bed rolled over. 'I know what I had, or are you just mentioning it all for the benefit of everybody else in here? Tell the whole ward, tell the whole damn world!' He rolled back again. 'Any Muscat grapes?'

'I ate them. No I'm just saying, we took a lot of trouble, we spent a lot of money, and then you let yourself get jumped like that, you not only blow the whole mission, you fix it so some maniac mugger is now running around town with a snooperscope and all the rest of this stuff, how's that gonna look if he uses it?'

'He won't use it, he ripped it off to sell, didn't he? I mean, that's what he jumped me for, all that Government equipment.'

'If you know so much about him now, how come you let him sneak up on you like that?'

'How did I know I was a mugging target? I mean these guys are everywhere, society's getting so God-damned violent, is that my fault?'

'I blame TV myself. Television is definitely – and maybe fast food, kids don't digest any more. Take your average mugger today – and parental discipline too.'

'You saying it's my fault? You implying I should be a child psychologist?'

'I'm not implying nothing. Honest.'

The man in bed lay back and looked at the curtain until he heard the other agent leave, then turned again to watch (past the basket now containing a heap of banana skins and orange peels topped by the core of a Bartlett pear) other patients being served a Christmas dinner from a mobile microwave oven that passed him and passed the curtained bed.

'I'm sorry, Mr . . . Nothing by mouth for you, and nothing by mouth for Mr Franklin either . . .'

Muttering came from behind the curtain. ' "Nothing by mouth", sounds like a damn subtitle for *À Rebours*, you'd think they'd at least offer me a turkey-and-cranberry enema.'

The agent turned towards the voice but it said nothing more. He turned back again, lay still watching the fruit debris, the empty bed next to him, the bed beyond that where an old man was being eased on to a bedpan, the curtained bed beyond that whence a priest emerged, kissing a strip of purple ribbon and folding it away as he hurried out the door, a furtive figure pursued by the microwave cart, then two nurses, then a cartload of uneaten dinners followed by a man in a wheelchair swerving to avoid a man on crutches coming back past a sleeping figure connected to a machine next to an adolescent sitting up in bed with giant headphones and a blank expression, next to an empty bed and another, eight beds, one exit, now blocked by a group of people in surgical green bringing in a cart to collect the man the priest had visited, setting off an argument between the man on the bedpan and the man on crutches as to whether this was routine surgery or getting ready for a heart snatch, the argument continuing until a pitchpipe sounded in the hall and a choir of student nurses looking hungover sang 'Joy to the World', 'Silent Night' and 'Christmas in Killarney' before drifting away to some other ward on their silent feet, all this and more the agent noted and filed, remembering every face, every action, every change until he finally managed to sleep . . .

Behind him, Ben Franklin opened the curtains, sat up in his sweat-soaked pyjamas, lit a cigarette and reached for his phone. 'Mr Kratt? Ben here, I'm in Mercy Hospital, that flu I had got worse and – no, two or three days ago, I don't know, what day is this? . . . No, I'm not kidding; I was kind of knocked out with this fever . . . I don't know, soon as I can sir yes sure only . . . listen they don't seem to know what it is, doctor this morning asked me if I had anything to do with cows . . . Well sure I know you are, I didn't mean to, yes I know. But what I wanted to tell you, I've had a real breakthrough . . . no, *through*, sir. Listen I, see I've been working on the little problem we talked about, the er, learning machine, you know where I was stuck was in the basic pattern-recognition . . . yes, well I'm not stuck any more, I've really broken through. This fever, seems to make me see clearer, clearer and – I know Dan used to get into these fits too, these kind of fits, he would just be glowing with wisdom, with *gnosis*, with holy wis – God damn it, Kratt, for once in your life stop yapping about what you *want* and listen! Because creation, creating life isn't something you learn or even do, it's something within us all the time, you know like the secret power these men possess? I mean all my life I've been pissing around with half-ass religious ideas, all the time it's been right there inside me, the complete instructions for building a creature in my own image . . . are you still there? Yes, it's inside me, in my genes . . . No, not *cloning*, God damn it will you listen? I'm talking about information, information! Man is a learning machine and human genes are blueprints for man so – so all the information has to be packed in there somehow, yet if the machine could only learn itself it, it, we have the answer! I mean we spend our whole lives looking at the edges of the blueprint while the centre is never visible except to madmen, holy madmen – no I am not talking about occultism, will you God damn it stop humouring me, I am talking about information. *Information.* INFORMATION!'

He slammed down the receiver as the agent awoke and turned over, saying, 'What's wrong, you can't even get Information? Phone company gets worse every –'

'No, nothing like that.' Ben Franklin picked up the yellow notebook he'd bought in Taipin, opened to a fresh quadrille-ruled page, and began to scribble. After covering a page and heavily underscoring several items, he put down his pen and looked at the phone again.

'You gonna try Information again?'

'No I – I just felt like calling somebody. Too bad it's Christmas, everybody'll be answering machines today. Except Dan . . .'

The pure musical tones aroused by numbered buttons chased each other down the line like echoes, reminding him of something from Kafka (Kafkafka): K. phoning the Castle and hearing a buzz 'like the sound of countless children's voices' now adjusted to harmonious bleats but still innocent because ethereal, ringing from Heaven (hello Central) or against Heaven (vox inhumana) or crying out loud for bodies . . .

At University Hospital a nurse crunched a piece of candy cane as the phone rang, swallowed sherds as she answered. 'Who? Mr Sonnenschein? I'll see if we have him today you know a lot of people went home . . .'

She rose, biting down on another inch of striped sugar and brushing crumbs from her nylon uniform as she pushed past the Christmas tree and through a door into the ward. Most of the other nurses were, like her, here for the day only; no one knew who Mr Sonnenschein was.

Two doctors were conferring over an elderly bedridden patient, now going blue in the face. One of them, Dr D'Eath, suggested Ward D.

'Right through that door down there and keep going, you can't miss it,' he said, and leaned across his patient to tap the electronic Kardiscope as though it were a brass barometer. 'Not so terrific here, thanks to that ham-handed ... think he'd try reading the contraindications before he starts shoving Euphornyl into an eighty-year-old patient with a history of ... could have used Hynosate or Geridorm, Narcadone any damn thing but this! Okay then. What we need here is 50 ccs of Elimindin in the i.v., then start the Eudryl when he comes to, okay? Oh, and Dormevade, five milligrams every three ...'

'Fine sure fine, great idea, Shel, now if uh you got a minute maybe you could look at my girl here, little chemotherapy problem, Nurse wake her up will you, MINNIE ... MORNING MINNIE!'

'Doctor, I believe her name is Mary, Mary Mendez ...'

'Minnie, Mary, what's the difference? HEY MARY? WAKE UP!'

The false eyelashes parted on large grey eyes that held no expression. Creaking sounds began in the throat.

'HOW YOU DOING, MARY?' Dr Coppola proffered to his senior colleague a chart, with the deference of a wine waiter with a list. Both men and the nurse ignored Mary who, having sat up to adjust the large bow that covered a stainless steel plate in her scalp, was trying to speak. The rusty sounds in her throat became more frantic.

'How long you had her on Actromine with Ananx? No wonder you got a Parkinsonism situation building here, you ought to ... and try switching over to Integryl with Doloban, see how that ... or wait, how about Dormistran with Kemised? That should do the trick.'

'CAN YOU HEAR ME, MARY? HOW'S THE HEAD-ACHE? EH?'

'... *wind me up ... wind me up ...*'

'You could have tried Solacyl with Promoral, but sooner or later you'd have to feed in Thanagrin and ...'

'Promoral sure sure sure, Shel, only with the old head injury and the labyrinthitis you don't think ...?'

'... *wind me up ... I'm running down ...*'

'Okay then Lobanal, play it safe. Lobanal with Doloban, why

stick your neck out?' And as the two doctors passed on, the nurse trailing like a caddy, they talked of Amylpoise and Dexadrone, Disimprine and Equisol, Joviten and Nyctomine . . .

At the door of Ward D they encountered once more the Christmas substitute nurse, again running on her silent shoes but now looking distressed and holding a hand to her mouth.

'Probably walked in on the ECT,' said Dr Coppola as they wheeled past the room where Dan Sonnenschein still arched and twisted on a table, trembling limbs held down by straps and strong assistants as his spine beat like a flagellum, trying to fling his head free of the smoking electrodes. Dr D'Eath paused to watch the body lunge once, twice and lie still, all but the fingers and toes.

'Well, Jesus, you can't blame the poor girl. They have to stick this therapy room right out here where anybody can walk by and see it,' he said. 'Anyway I hate it myself, it's so darned crude, like setting fire to a chicken ranch to fry one egg. There has to be a better way.'

'I know, I know, it's so medieval – they used to burn the body of a heretic for the good of his soul, and now we've kind of turned that around. But what are the real alternatives, drugs? How can you trust them to take the pills once they're out, eh? The old paradox of freedom, eh? What happens when the depressive gets too depressed to take his anti-depressants?'

His boyish laugh drifted back through the open door to be relayed as a scream of nervous laughter from Mary Mendez. Dr D'Eath said, 'I like this idea of yours about working on self-images with some of these patients, what I've heard of it.'

'I'd like to try a pilot scheme here, very soon. You gotta admit, Shel, it's about the cheapest damn therapeutic idea in years, all we have to buy is a couple dozen rubber animal masks. See I was reading Lévi-Strauss one day on totems and all at once it hit me, we all need to "be" animals once in a while, to restructure our self-images by new rules . . . become cats and mice or ducks . . .'

'Sure, I see . . .'

'. . . easily recognized signs and codes, *I am a pig*, to help communicate in a society grown too large and too . . .'

'Sure, sure, sure, sure . . .'

Mary yelped again, the noise just reaching the nurse who was closing a door and pushing past the tree to the phone:

'Mr Frankstein? Frankline? I'm sorry but he can't come to the phone right now, he's um, he's um —' Her mind filled with movie images of fluttering lights, lightning, the smoking electrodes, the figure on the long table straining, making Galvanic lunges against the straps, the smoking electrodes, hands gripping the arms of the electric chair, tall shadows, the sputtering arch, the baritone hum of electricity, *vis vitalis* rising on a swell to become a dial tone as she sat, receiver forgotten in her hand, watching the lights on the Christmas tree grow suddenly dim and bright again. Her mouth filled with peppermint bile.

Ben Franklin turned from the phone to his yellow notebook, muttering, 'No telling what kind of cretins they get to work over there, can't even work out how to call somebody to the phone.'

'You said it, buddy,' said the agent.

Ben twitched the curtain closed and scribbled alone until he slept, waking with a shout in the darkness, soaking wet and shivering as he was again waking in the morning if it was morning, to find himself muttering, 'Hexcellent, a most hexcellent dancer, your servant ladies and gentlemen . . .' And plunged back into that sea of sleep out of which he always seemed to emerge dripping and chilled on the shore of what could hardly be called consciousness.

He was aware of changes: the man with the bandaged head and the self-pitying face in the next bed vanished to be replaced by a salesman of religious novelties who had a noisy TV; he in turn gave way to an old man who kept his teeth in a glass; one morning he was gone but the teeth remained.

An expert on tropical diseases came to look at Ben.

'Malaria,' he said. 'Where have you been travelling?'

'Only to Taipin.'

'Try again, there's no malaria in Taipin. No mosquitoes.'

But they treated him for malaria and he began to improve; one day he sat up and tried to read his notes:

Tolstoi's 'Our body is a machine for living' as a recipe for

French stone. Stones of Deucalion? J. Baptist says God can raise

468

stones up children to Abraham, a pun on children (banim) & stones (abanim) – why always stones or clay in legends as though mineral future reality foreseen, cybern. Kids out of sand?

If we made them would they purge us of the terrible disease of being human?

Can a mind be built from within, by one thought?

'Everything must be like something, so what is this like?' – Forster?

Another noisy TV went on, and Ben found himself jerked out of naps by news programmes:

'. . . where Machines Lib demonstrators broke into the Digital Love computer dating agency and deprogrammed the computer. Two were arrested, and now Digital Love says it will sue for deprivation of data. Here's Del Gren on the spot with an up-to-the-minute report. Del?'

The screen showed a ragged line of people in parkas, carrying signs: THIS STORE DEGRADES MACHINES and NO MORE COMPUTER PIMPS. One marcher, a fairly old man with iced-up glasses, paused to shake a mittened fist at the camera. A microphone darted out towards him like a striking snake.

'Thanks, Mel, these people have been picketing all day. Uh, what is it you're protesting about, sir?'

'Well it's – what do you mean? Machines!'

'Yes? Just what –?'

'About the machines! About the unfair, the unfair –'

'Thanks now if I can just get someone else in on this, you, ma'am?'

A plump woman whose face looked frostbitten came forward, waved her sign and said, *'We're against the exploitation of machines! Man if you look at this in the historical context of the last two hundred years it just makes you throw up! Just look how machines get a raw deal all down the line, all the dirty and degrading jobs like rolling steel and pulling trains, not even blacks or women ever had to pull trains.'*

'Yes well thank you this is Del –'

Someone shouted *'Humanists Go Home!'* and others took up the chant.

'– Del Gren returning you to Mel?'

'. . . fortunate enough to have here in the studio the founder and guiding hand of Machines Lib, Miz Indica Dinks. Hi Indica, and welcome to Minnetonka. Can we get the ball rolling here by finding out just what Machines Lib is all about? What's the bottom line here?'

'Hi, Mel, I'm originally from Minnetonka and it's great to be back. First off let me say that we're not against people. Far from it! When machines are set free, people will be set free too. In my new book, plug, plug, The Nuts and Bolts of Machines Lib, I explain just how that works out. By the way I'll be autographing my book next Tuesday at the Vitanuova Shopping Piazza all day.'

'Fascinating idea, Indica. But what kind of world would it be if all the machines could do what they wanted?'

'A better world, Mel. A world where a lot of the pressure is off. Just look at now, at our light bills and repair bills and instalments, all the money we pour into just keeping our machines down. But once we ease up and set them free, all that pressure and tension just goes away! Once you stop owning a dishwasher, you can stop paying for it too. Machines Lib means people lib too – and, Mel, that's what I think America is all about – freedom!'

Her beauty pursued Ben. Damn it she looked no older than that day she'd walked out on him to take a job as a dancing taco – all those years ago. He remembered her last speech: 'Ben, I'll never cut it hanging around a University, I need to fulfil myself. We just, we're just too different, our worlds are poles apart.'

Now no one ever remembered his part in her life, the questions as now were always about her second husband:

'Miz Dinks, Indica, how about your ex-husband Hank Dinks? Isn't he founding a movement of his own? What do you think of his New Luddites?'

'Yes, he has this little band of fanatics running around wrecking machines. I feel sorry for them, they're just being self-destructive. To me, America is not about tearing down, it's about building up. No, Hank and I are just too different. Our worlds are poles apart.'

Ben's phone made a faint sound and he answered it.

'Mr Franklin? I have a call for you from Mr Kratt, will you hold?'

The perfectly-shaped nail and finger of Mrs McBabbitt pushed two buttons in succession. 'I have Mr Franklin on the line for you.'

'Cancel him, Connie, I'm gonna be tied up here a while with

,Jud Mill.' The stubby hand with its massive gold ring mounting a pinball pushed buttons to turn off the TV and close a wall panel over the screen, then moved to the cheap cigar smouldering in the ashtray.

'Okay, bub, you've had a chance to look over our media figures, where did we go wrong? I don't count the losses on K.T. Art Films, we budgeted those, writing off taxes on the equipment we managed to sell to Taktar Video our other production subsidiary, the one who's dealing for cable leasing – I think we got all that under control. It's our publishing interests that worry me, right from Katrat Books, *Folks* magazine and –'

'Yes yes yes, well that's what you hired me for, what media management consultancy is all about,' said the other man. Leaning forward slightly so that the long striped wings of his shirt collar crackled, he peered down through his half-moon reading glasses at the open portfolio; he ran his finger down a column of figures.

'Your timing could be better, with some of these properties you leave loose ends dangling. Take this *Politics of Pregnancy*, you should of tied up video cassette rights and cable royalties first thing, the author could just walk away with everything. Anyway you're using it as a lead book and it's not strong enough to sustain a real attack on the market, you need something better, a very strong item indeed like that psychic pigeon book.'

Kratt nodded. 'We've had a lot of author trouble –'

'That's lesson number one: dump the author. When I package a property, I try to leave out the author, bring him in as the last element. Then I make damn sure he's just hired to do a job, paid off and kissed off. Like with *Boy and Girl*, that was just an idea I came up with, me and Sol Alter were sitting around by the pool one day and I said: "How about a simple boy and girl story: some kinda tragedy?" and he said: "Good movie idea there: boy meets girl, girl goes blind and boy leaves her, he goes back but it's too late, she's already committed suicide." (That was the uptown version, we also mapped out a downtown version where the girl gets eaten by her seeing-eye dog.) But anyway we interested Jerre Mice in starring, that enabled us to bootstrap a six-figure plus percentage movie deal, and with all that we had something to take to publishers, we landed a seven-figure paperback deal and from there on had no problem getting all we wanted out of magazine serialization, hardcover, book club, foreign and cassette rights, direct cable specials, options for a TV series, syndicated comics, T-shirts, board games, colouring books and so on. Then we fixed the music and wrapped up those rights. And then and only then did we finally hire an author to hammer out the screenplay and book, the fictionalization. We paid him I think two grand and no comebacks.'

After a moment, Kratt cleared his throat. 'That's okay for generating properties, but what about existing items? You just saw this Indica Dinks promoting our book there on local TV, we been whistle-stopping her around the country for bookstore and media –'

'I know but we need something, a handle for the public to grab her by – where's her bio – now here it says she used to dance. Why not dress her up as a robot and have her do a tap routine – I know it sounds dumb but like Barnum said, nobody ever went broke underestimating the intelligence of the public – no wait! Wait! She used to be married to Hank Dinks, now he is out whistle-stopping a book of his own, am I wrong? Yes, listen, why shouldn't they bump into each other maybe signing copies at the same bookstore? A reconciliation, sure: they get married again, right there in the bookstore, give the minister copies of their two books signed right there – this is almost good enough for the six o'clock news.'

'Sounds fine, only what if they hate each other's guts?'

'So what, they play ball with us or they lose out on the cocreative book we'll have written in their names, all the other stuff we could cut them in on, unbelievable deals we could pull together. We could build them in *Folks* magazine, goes out to a million supermarket customers with "Together again – for Keeps!" and pictures of the home, kids, pets, leisure equipment – no, okay, maybe they won't remarry. Let 'em meet anyway, maybe fight in public, we can go that way too.'

The media management consultant sat back and reached for the phone. 'Let me just contact Hank's publisher, that's Fishfold and Tove, let me just sound them out, they could divert his tour so it just runs into hers, kinda accidental-like. We don't tell the Dinkses.'

'You think that's a good idea, not telling them?'

'Bound to strike some kinda sparks. Now you just let me pull something together, get it blended and orchestrate a meaningful deal . . .'

His finger went for a button.

XIV

'Von Neumann, playing Kuratowski to Frege's Wiener, offered a different identification'   W.V. Quine, *Word & Object*

Luke was wearing saffron: Hat, overcoat, suit, shirt and tie, shoes, attaché case and a visible inch of sock were all part of the saffron glow.

'Can't help it, Rickwood, it's what we had to wear all the time; probably why they called us the Saffron Peril. Only let me tell you, we were the only ones in danger, when those lunatic Luddites showed up and –'

'Okay, fine, but why did we have to meet way out here in a place like this? The Vitanuova Shopping Piazza may be a terrific place and the chief jewel in Minnetonka's crown and all, but I mean it's miles from civilization.'

The two friends sat on a park bench near a fountain which, according to a brochure, could form over fifty million different beautiful patterns without repeating itself. Like everything else of importance here, it was indoors, for the entire great shopping complex was, enclosed under geodesic domes, as if it were a moon base.

'And don't tell me Mission Control ordered us here,' Roderick added.

'Nope, my idea. We are going to a meeting, important meeting.'

'Not your Saffron Peril?'

'I'm all through with them – or they're through with me. I only have to wear this stuff because my luggage with my other stuff was delayed at the airport. Had to leave Tibet in kind of a hurry, Rickwood. Now I'm through with meditation in the Himalayas, I mean who needs it?'

Roderick watched the fountain repeat itself. 'But I thought *you* did.'

'Okay okay, laugh, I deserve it. It's just, the whole thing turned out to be more of a commercial venture than I figured. See I expected to maybe shave my head and sit down with the monks to some meditation and glass beads, only it wasn't like that at all. I mean they got computerized prayer-wheels, that was the first shock. And all they really do is deal in different stock markets and talk about exchange rates and commodity prices, all day while the old prayer-wheels go on grinding away all by themselves. I felt kind of uneasy about it, but I suppressed it. I said to myself, "Give it a chance, Draeger, there might be some deeper meaning in all of this. The Master must know what he's doing." So I hung on.

'The Master was a little old dried-up-looking man, he always looked ready to say something important. He went off on these trips to Taipin, somebody said, to plant the seed of consciousness. But then somebody else said he just went to gamble, that he was robbing the treasury. Who could believe a thing like that? Especially when our Master seemed so doggoned *wise*, I mean he never had to say anything to anybody – I don't think I ever heard him speak – but you still knew *he knew everything*.

'Then the police showed up and took our Master away. They were extraditing him to Taipin, to stand trial for murder. They said he'd killed some Chinese guy in a quarrel over a poker game.'

Roderick stared through the changing fountain to where a sign was going up. 'TODAY. **DICA **NKS . . . *N*ICA D**KS . . . IN*IC* DIN** . . .'

'Sure we were shaken a little. Some people said it was all over, they wanted to go home. But I persuaded them to hang on – maybe it was only a test of our faith and loyalty, I said.

'Just as I was saying that, the Luddites broke in and smashed the whole place up. The stock quotation machines, the computers, the prayer-wheels, everything. Worst of it was they took out the phone and telex, left us stranded.

'There we were – about fifty of us – broke, our outfit smashed, our Master gone, no money to come home on. We didn't have a prayer you might say. Nothing in the storeroom either, but a half pound of rice, an old motheaten silver fox coat, and a catcher's mitt autographed by Yogi Berra. We were high up in the mountains with snow all around. What could we do?'

475

'Pray?' Roderick suggested, watching I*D*C* *INKS . . .

'Right. Our prayers were answered right away too, because this camera team from some big magazine syndicate showed up. They were doing a feature on Everest-climbing tours, and they wanted some local colour. We fed them the last of our rice and gave them beds. During the night, I put the catcher's mitt on my foot and went out walking in the snow. In the morning we pointed out the giant tracks to them and they got real excited and took lots of pictures.

'Then in the afternoon there was a snowstorm. I put on the fur coat and ran around in it, the others pointed me out and the photographers chased me and took more pictures. Then they got on their radio and arranged a lucrative book and movie deal, and our end of it was just enough to pay our fares home.'

Roderick got up from the bench and moved to one side of the fountain to read:

TODAY:

INDICA DINKS
will autograph copies of her
sensational new best-seller,

THE NUTS AND BOLTS
OF MACHINES LIB
at
Prospero Books,
Fourth Level

'On the plane home,' Luke said when he returned, 'I met another Luddite. In fact he was the guy who started the whole movement. I told him what happened and how Luddite heavies had moved in on us. He apologized. He said, "Some of the boys just got carried away with the message, I guess."

'Then he started telling me all about the New Luddites Movement and it didn't sound so fanatical after all. He said the Luddites were opposed to violence, even against machines. He wanted a way of peace, linked with the great Eastern traditions of resignation and manual labour. Why didn't I come to the rally he

was having in Minnetonka? So here I am, ready to be a Luddite.'
Luke looked pleased with himself. 'Maybe I can convert you too.'

'Convert – but Luke, I can't be a Luddite. *I'm a machine.* I'm
everything they're opposed to!'

'Oh, you don't have to join right away, Rickwood. I just want
you to come along and meet some Luddites yourself. Great
buncha guys.'

'But Luke, this is crazy!'

'Meet the guys, hear what they got to say, that's all. Then you
make up your own mind.'

Father Warren and Hank Dinks stood by the luggage carousel,
watching the same parade of unclaimed bags pass for perhaps the
sixth time, the tattersall overnight pursued by the natural calf two-
suiter followed at a distance by the viola case, then two items in
red hide crowded close by a stiff Gladstone bag with labels and,
after a short interval, the duffel bag and the large bright saffron
suitcase leading the tattersall overnight. From time to time
strangers straggled up and removed items, but Warren and Dinks
stood motionless, watching the endless parade and listening to a
loop of tape play an endless medley.

'Doesn't um seem to be here, Hank. And we're running a little
late.'

'Well I'm not leaving here without something.' Hank snatched
up the saffron bag. 'Let's go.'

'But that's, you can't just –'

'Let's get out of this place. I hate airports, all this automated
luggage and automated music and people like zombies moving
along herded along no life no reality no, no weather even, might
as well be in some damn shopping mall –'

'Ha ha, well I hope you won't mind coming out to the
Vitanuova Shopping Piazza today, that's where we've set up the
um, at the conference centre –'

'What? You fixed my rally, *my* rally, in some plastic shopping
centre? Why not just hold it here in the Arrival lounge, I'm trying
to reach real people, not – I just don't believe this.'

But Hank nevertheless allowed himself to be led from the
terminal into a taxi. 'I just don't believe this.'

'But just look at this brochure, the conference centre seats five

477

thousand, a first-class convention hall, facilities – your publisher thought –'

'Let me see that. "Our trained personnel will be happy to advise you in preparing multimedia presentation, programmes on any subject, and we have plenty of prepackaged units ready to be computer-tailored to your individual multimedia needs" – you thought I wanted this? *This*? You thought the Luddites have multimedia needs? We need computer tailoring?'

'No, of course not, I –'

The driver was craning around. 'Hey I know you, you're that Luddite guy, I seen you on TV, now what's your name?'

'Look I'm sorry, Hank, I just thought it might be good exposure for your book, I know it's a, um, compromise but your publisher is paying and it's a chance to pull in new, a new audience, to sell your book too –'

'I was gonna say the name Godfrey Dank,' said the driver. 'Only now I remember he was the ventriloquist, and when I hear the fadder here call you Hank –'

'Sure sure, anything to sell the book, why not turn the rally into a sales conference, why not bring in the slogans and the gimmicks? The prizes for top salesman, why not?'

'Hank, you're tired, you must be over-reacting. I'll admit we made a mistake, Fishfold and Tove thought –'

'Yeah, Hank. Hank, now don't tell me the last name –'

'Why not bring in the, damn it, the strippers and the pep band, you think I came here for that?'

'No, of course not, I –'

'This whole piazza place is dedicated to the inhuman, to everything mass-produced and cheap, fast food and book supermarts and – everything designed by computers and stamped out of the same plastic by robots, the potted palms, the furniture, the stores, the clerks inside, maybe even the robot customers, all of it slathered over with that damn homogenized music you get everywhere, "Moon River" and "Sunshine Balloon" everywhere, "Carioca" everywhere, bars and restaurants, airports, toilets, dentist chairs, delivery rooms and funeral parlours, assembly-line music for assembly-line people –'

'I think it was on the Yoyo Show I seen you, or no, was it Ab Jason? I remember your beard was real long then –'

478

'It's that kind of stuff I started the Luddites to fight, the way we're burying the world in useless gadgets, unreal junk heaped up around us until we don't even recognize the real world at all, it's just one more thing on TV!'

'Yes I know, the *angst*, I trace it to a loss of faith in human values concurrent with the cybernetic –'

'Indica and I tried to get away from our gadgets, we moved out West to this ecological house, but we brought the disease along with us, in no time we were right back in the same old manure pile of gadgets, house full of broken-down machinery who needs it? Solar panel leaking through the ceiling and something wrong with the autodoor on the garage and the lawn mower and the ultrasound dishwasher and the automatic toilet bowl cleaner – and all around us stuff getting ready to break down, the slow cooker, the light-pipe intercom, the rotisserie, the popcorn popper, the hot food table, the cake oven, microwave, deepfreeze, shoe polisher, floor polisher, vacuum cleaner-washer, blender, mixer, processor, slicer, chopper, coffee grinder, thermostat, lumistat, electrostatic air-conditioner, Jesus Christ, the water purifier, electric pepper-mill, nail-buffer, can opener, carving knife, Jesus H. Christ, there I was in the middle of the desert with an electric pipe-cleaner in my hand, and *it* was starting to make a funny noise . . .'

'Yes, yes I know it must have been –'

'Listen Indica and I even tried adopting a robot child, now isn't that sick? A robot child!'

The driver said, 'Kids these day, I know, I know –'

'One day I just couldn't take any more. I picked up a hammer and took a swing at little Roderick . . . and I missed! And, and the little machine pasted me back with a wrench, and I was free. I just got up and walked out, out into the desert, a free man.'

Father Warren folded his long hands, unfolded them, played a game of church-and-steeple. 'That was when you decided to write *Ludd Be Praised*?'

'Yes I knew then, we have to smash the machines. Smash their grip on our minds, our lives.'

'It'll go all right,' said Father Warren. 'Try not to worry, Hank. The point is, you have a message to put across, a battle-cry: Smash the machines!'

479

'Father I wish I had your faith. At times like this –' Hank waved the brochure, 'I wonder if the machines haven't smashed us. I – I get so discouraged –'

'Definitely Ab Jason, the Ab Jason Show, only I just can't recall your name, Hank, your –'

'*Will you just shut up and drive? My name is Hank Dinks, yes I, was on the Ab Jason Show, now will you just, just* –'

'Okay okay, ya don't hafta yell. I mean excuse me mister bigshot celebrity from TV, I don't wanna insult ya, a lousy working stiff tryina talk to ya, excuse me. All to hell.'

The driver punched buttons to start an endless tape of 'Moon River', 'Carioca', 'Sunshine Balloon' . . .

'Well well well Ms Dinks, Indica, this is indeed a pleasure, welcome aboard, be glad to show you around our little operation here, after all we're the people who deal the merchandise, the um books, so if you don't mind me saying so, we're the people who know *people*. Yes, Mr and Ms Bookbuying America are old, old friends of ours, they don't have many secrets from us. We know how to give them what they want – and make them want it, heh heh. Any questions before we start the grand tour?'

'Quite a store you have here, Mr Shredder.' Indica peered down the aisle of what might have been a supermarket, with customers plying shopping carts past display shelves of products with eye-appeal beneath signs and video screens whispering sales messages. Her gaze, finding nowhere to alight, came back to Mr Shredder's gold tooth.

'See we've put a dump bin of your book in the front, and you'll be autographing in the back, so people have to pass as many shelf feet as possible to get to you. And along here see we have our Today's Top Ten, with daily sales figures logged in right off our national computer hookup – people like to know where they are when they buy a book. And here's another bin with that darned psychic pigeon novel, just keeps on selling! We'll probably nominate that one for the American Book Award this year, hard to say until we do a book-by-book cost analysis, over the year.

'Now here's our astrology and science section, and over here a little item that should do well.' He picked a book from a cardboard barrel.

A Completely New Novel by Ford James Smith

Based on the TV Series by Joyce Henry Madox

Inspired by Adam Thorne's Novelization of the Original Screenplay by Conrad Brown

Developed around a Theme Inspired by The Dorothy Parker Short Story,

LOLITA

'You can't really go wrong with a cover like that, and it doesn't even mislead the customer. Plenty of books with misleading titles around to hook the customer these days. One thing about the book trade, you can always count on good old-fashioned customer illiteracy; best title of the last fifty years was *Your Erroneous Zones* but you find just as much inspiration nowadays, here's a fishing book *You Can Master Bait* and a how-to-study item called *The Erotetic Method*, oh yes and a reprint of two Horatio Alger books in one with the titles run together . . .'

But Indica missed the next part of Mr Shredder's lecture, as she looked across a row of gaudy science-fiction covers straight into the eyes of her pursuer.

XV

'Come on Rickwood, I'll buy you a coffee, you can't stand here daydreaming all day.' Luke led him as far as the cashier.

'You gonna buy that, mister?' she asked.

'Buy . . . that?'

'The book in your hand, human use of human beings wiener, you gonna buy it or what?'

Luke took the book from his hand and led him on out of Prospero Books, into the great pleasure dome of Vitanuova Shopping Piazza. In general form, it was a kind of interior Hanging Gardens of Babylon, with a small terrace of stores at each level, with plenty of polished stonelike substances, with gleaming escalators, set at every angle, and with every nook crammed with green potted palms, blue caged birds or tanks of red fish. From the top level, looking over a parapet at the whole dizzying spectacle, Luke spotted the yellow umbrellas of a café far below.

'Come on down this escalator – Jesus, Rickwood, I wish you'd tell me what's going on. Why did we have to go all the way up to this so-called bookstore, just so you could stare at this Indica Dinks? You didn't even say hello.'

'Well I, I didn't want to intrude, just wanted to let her know I'm around, I'm here if she needs me. I could tell by the way she looked at me she understands.'

Luke groaned. 'Just what kind of Victorian truth is it that she understands? Who is this lady?'

'My mother, Luke. My stepmother anyway. Sort of. She took care of me when I was small, I think. And, well, she was the first woman I ever saw naked, so naturally I –'

'You what? Follow her into bookstores?'

They took their seats. One or two people at adjoining tables stared at Luke's saffron costume.

482

'Naturally I love her. I read once how all boys love their mothers and kill their fathers, so —'

Luke held up a saffron-gloved hand. 'Now wait. Rickwood, you've got this a little wrong. Sure, all boys love their mothers in a way, but it just means getting "Mother" tattooed on their arms, or sending embroidered pillow covers, Souvenir of Hong Kong, or maybe asking bar pianists to play "My Mother's Eyes" until they weep into their low-cal pilsner. It does not mean love, like *love*. It doesn't mean killing anybody either, where did you get this idea?'

'Well,' Roderick said loudly. '*I* killed *my* father, and I've always been crazy about my mother's body. And that was before I ever heard of Freud!'

People at the next table got up and moved away. Others stared and whispered. A waitress hurried over, datapad in hand.

'We'd like two coffees,' said Luke. 'Mine, I want a medium-roast blend of Colombian and Mocha, finely ground and filtered, with real cream (not half-and-half) and Demerara sugar. Serve it in a bone china service, preferably Spode, and with a hallmarked silver spoon. And my friend here will have instant ersatz coffee, half-dissolved in tepid water, served with artificial cream and synthetic sugar in a melamine cup, no saucer, with a styrene spoon, please.'

'Two coffees,' she said, and said it again, firmly, when she served them.

'Well she got yours right, Rickwood. What do you mean, you killed your father?'

'I mean I hit him with a box-end wrench, $\frac{3}{4} \times \frac{7}{8}$ I think it was, and he fell down and never got up.'

'Oh.' Luke said nothing more until they were on their way to the rally, making their way through a series of glass tubes and corridors to the Conference Centre. The final leg of the journey took them through a glass-covered bridge high above the flat wintry earth. To their left, an infinity of parked cars. Straight ahead, the Conference Centre, a kind of flying saucer in concrete, pre-stressed and poised for takeoff. To the right, Freeway Disaster, the enormous fibre-glass sculpture by Jough Braun, incorporating moulds of an actual freeway pile-up of some twenty vehicles. It was said that, so quickly had Braun worked at the disaster scene, that he had managed to mould in one or two victims. In any case, the German museums had bid very highly for this item, but what mere museum could provide a setting for it like this?

'What did you do after you hit him with the wrench?'

'I nailed myself into this packing crate and sent myself somewhere else. I mean I guess the crate was all labelled and ready anyway, because I was too young to write. So I got in and nailed it shut –'

'How could you nail it shut? Rickwood, you must have had an accomplice. Your mother?'

'It might have been a $\frac{15}{16}$ × 1 box-end wrench, or maybe it wasn't a box-end at all, it might have been an open-end, say $1\frac{1}{16}$ × $1\frac{1}{8}$ . . .'

Mr Shredder helped her climb the seemingly endless spiral staircase to the office, a comfortable little green room. He presented her with a plastic cup of water. 'Feel better yet?'

'I'm fine, really. Just a little dizzy spell, it's over now.' She found she was still holding a book (*Ragged Dick/Bound to Rise*) and put it down.

'Well while we're in the office, I may as well show you our little nerve centre.'

He sat down at a VDU and tapped the keys, with the air of an electric-organ owner showing off at home. Indica could almost hear *Tico-tico* in poor ugly Mr Shredder's smile. The gold tooth glittered.

'In the past, you know, nobody would have dreamed of running an operation like Prospero Books, but this little gadget has made the book trade into a whole new ball game. High volume, fast-throughput, unprecedented market sensitivity – well I guess what I mean is, we're no longer at the mercy of the publishers.'

'Publishers?' She felt it was her turn to say something.

'The way it used to be, the publishers ran everything. If you wanted to sell books, you sold what they gave you to sell, that's the way it was, and tough! And not just tough, but it was a very bad, wasteful way to run an industry. I mean with all due respect, most publishers are *jerks* who know *absolutely nothing* about books. They sit around in New York offices being *literati*, all the time.

You think they know what sells here in Minnetonka? No. What they do is, publish a book and gamble on it. They gamble, we lose.

'That's the way it was. We dealers, who know the market, had no control over the business; publishers, who know nothing, had complete control. But the computer changed all that. See with the computer we get complete control over our own stock flow, we tie ordering directly to sales, see? Say a customer buys some book, say number 0246114371, the bar code is on the cover, the cashier runs her laser wand over it, and our computer records the sale. Enough sales of that item and the computer automatically reorders.'

Indica said, 'Is that new? I thought that was kind of old hat.'

'Yes but listen: the computer can put data together from fifty stores just as easily as five – or five hundred or five thousand. No matter how big we grow, we can always have real tight, minute-by-minute stock control. Only if we're big, publishers start listening to us. If we don't like a book, they print fewer copies.'

Indica nodded, hoping the lecture was finishing.

'Anyway, at the same time, publishers keep getting taken over by big conglomerates like KUR, people with electronic ideas of their own. Like they also get computerized stock control and also they fix it up so authors can set their own type – stuff like that. And it's kind of inevitable that their computers will get together with our computers. After all, we all want the same thing.'

Indica stopped nodding. 'Authors and publishers and book dealers, all – together?'

Mr Shredder grinned with his gold tooth. 'Only a pilot scheme so far, but so far it works! We got this best-selling author to agree, he sits in his house in Nassau and types, and our computers get it via satellite, word by word. They do a complete analysis *as he writes* – and feed it right back to him. They give him back a sales projection every time he hits the old space bar, so he knows *the second* his writing falls off. He knows he's got to go back and polish up that last sentence or change that last word – or else!'

By the time Roderick and Luke arrived, the rally was already in full swing. The huge hall was more than half full, with more people drifting in all the time.

The speaker was saying, '. . . mixers, processors, thermostat, lumistat . . . can opener, electric carving knife, Jesus Christ, there I was in the middle of the goddamned desert with an electric pipe cleaner in my hand . . .'

'Why that's Hank!' Roderick exclaimed. Someone told him to shut his fuckin' face.

Luke whispered, 'Yes, he's the guy I met on the plane.'

'Hush your mouth,' warned another man. The audience seemed to be largely male, and many were wearing a kind of 'uniform' of shirtsleeves, rolled up to mid-bicep, as in political cartoons of Uncle Sam. They seemed ready to spit on their hands and go to work. When new people came in, many of them would look around for a few moments, then remove their coats and roll up their sleeves.

'. . . just picked up a hammer and took a swing at that little robot – and I missed! And the little robot picked up a wrench or something and cold-cocked me! But at least it was an honest fight – we were enemies and we both knew it. When I came to, I got up and walked out into the desert, a free man. A free man. For the first time in my life I didn't have an alarm clock to wake up for, a phone to answer, a time clock to punch, or a car to keep up the payments on. No . . .'

Isolated people started calling out 'Amen' and 'Praise the Ludd'. Soon there was a regular, clapping chorus, and Hank seemed to be leading it, standing alone in the middle of a big stage, a tiny bearded-prophet figure. He started going through the long list of gadgets and appliances once more, now as a litany. And before he finished, men were leaping up to name machines of their own:

'To hell with my drill press!'

'*Praise Ludd!*'

'Down with programmed door chimes!'

'*Amen.*'

'Smash all machines!'

'*Yes Ludd!*'

'Take this hammer!' Someone brandished it.

'*Ludd, Ludd!*'

Hammers were being brandished all over the auditorium now.

'I smashed a parking meter!'

'I smashed a kid's musical top!'

'I smashed my wife's solid state dehydrator with stick-resistant trays and forced air flow!'

'*Praise Ludd*!'

'Smash the machines! Screw the machines!'

Men were jumping on their seats and waving hammers now, ready to smash anything remotely like a machine, while others egged them on with a steady clapping and chanting, 'Smash . . . smash . . . smash . . .'

Hank held up his hands in an attempt to make them stop, but this only seemed to raise the tempo; they took it as a victory sign. Worse, the conference centre's 'multimedia' people, who had prepared a special audiovisual package for the occasion, thought Hank was now signalling for it.

The giant screen behind Hank suddenly came alive with images of train wrecks, exploding cars, Chaplin demolishing an alarm clock, aircraft shot down, burning factories, the sinking of a paddle steamer, a chainsaw murder, the Who smashing electric guitars . . .

At that point someone broke into the projection booth and smashed the equipment, and the room went quiet. They were waiting for Hank to tell them what to do – go home and wait? Act now?

Hank opened his mouth, but just then a multimedia voice came over the p.a. system, drowning him out:

'Thanks guys and gals for making this a memorable day. We have souvenir hammers for sale in the foyer. And in a few minutes, Hank Dinks will be going over to the main complex to Prospero Books – he'll autograph copies of both his books. I hope we'll see you all there!'

That seemed to be the signal for the riot to begin.

'Luke, this is ridiculous,' Roderick tried to say, as they were pushed along the glass bridge with the others, but the noise of chanting, screaming and smashing made speech impossible. Roderick rolled up his sleeves, shook his fist and called for demolition. He was now separated from Luke, but could still see him; the ex-astronaut had rolled up his saffron sleeves and seemed to be having a hell of a good time.

The first mechanical victim was a gum machine, and soon

gumballs were raining down from the upper levels of the ziggurat – followed soon by pinballs and then fragments of a mechanical donkey ride. With a terrible thoroughness, the Luddites moved through every establishment, destroying hairdryers, malted milk machines, dental drills, programmed expresso machines, a wind-up mouse, toasters by the dozen and digital watches by the hundred. They met no opposition. The few security cops on duty approached them, fiddled with guns and radios, then decided to run instead. They had been hired to deal with elderly shoplifters and kids who tried skating on the escalators, not with a mob of thousands of maniacs.

They reached Prospero Books, where the furious mob not only did not find Hank installed, it found a sign, MACHINES LIB. The mob at once entered through both window and door. Roderick found himself wedged in a corner where, through the blizzard of torn pages, he could see on a TV monitor, Indica, still calmly signing books.

She continued to sign, ignoring the mob who pressed in around her little table. One of the men crashed his hammer down on the table in front of her.

'Honestly!' she said, and rummaged in her purse for a moment. Finally she brought out a revolver and fired it at the ceiling.

Instantly, everyone was quiet. Throughout the entire bookstore no one moved among the wreckage, except one enterprising Luddite who went on cleaning out the cash register. Everyone waited for a killing.

'This kind of behaviour is very destructive,' Indica said. 'You're a bunch of silly little boys. I suppose my ex-husband put you up to this. Well, you can tell Hank Dinks for me, *it won't work*. It doesn't matter how many hairdryers he smashes, *I am not coming back to him*. Now you can just clear out, all of you. *Move!*'

No one spoke. Here and there a hammer dropped to the floor (where everyone was now looking). One man, who'd been tearing up a copy of Indica's book, now fell to his knees, kissing the book and weeping. A few others felt suddenly the nakedness of their arms and rolled down their sleeves. A general shuffling and edging towards the door began, and soon the place was almost clear.

Roderick came out of his corner. 'Indica, I –'

'You! God damn it, will you stop following me?' She brought up the pistol smoothly, clasped it in both hands and aimed carefully at a point between those terrifying eyes.

'Are you going to shoot me?' he asked, and stopped.

. . . running through a dead wood, some trees charred by lightning, that was how the dream went. *In a clearing she saw a figure, a man in red armour, head to toe. He didn't move, and gradually she realized that he was rusted fast, covered with red rust. Opening her fly, she pulled out an enormous oil can and went to work, annointing him all over. The rust dripped and ran, now it was blood. Suddenly his iron arms gripped her, squeezing her so tight she could hardly breathe. 'Don't scream,' he said. 'The woods are like tinder, one scream could set off a conflagration. Through the visor she could see the glowing eyes. She screamed . . .*

She started to put the gun away. 'Who are you? Who are you?'

'I'm your –'

'Indica! Indica!' It was Mr Shredder, calling from the spiral stairs. 'Come up here, quick. Something's happened.'

She went up at once to the little green office. A man lay on the green carpet, with a priest squatting next to him.

'It's Hank,' said Shredder. 'I was just showing him our nerve centre when the mob showed up.'

'Hank? I don't understand.' Was that blood or oil on the priest's fingers?

'Same lunatic in that mob must of let off a gun,' said Mr Shrudder. 'Hank's dead.'

Father Warren looked up. 'He gave his life for us, for all of us. Now his fight must go on! We must go on smashing, smashing, smashing the machines!'

Mr Shredder looked alarmed and stood in front of his computer terminal. 'I think we've had enough talk about smashing things today.'

The priest stood up. 'Oh, I don't mean literally smash machines with hammers. Those poor men today got the message a little wrong. No, we must smash the machines *inside us*, smash the *idea* of the machine.' He held out a hand to Indica. 'Won't you join us? I know that in your heart you feel Hank was right – this is your fight too. Join the New Luddites.'

'You don't have to be so paternalistic, Father. *You* go smash the machine inside *you* if you want, *I* happen to think it's a screwloose idea.' She turned to make her exit.

'With you or without you,' he said, 'we'll win.'

'Over my dead body.'

Mr Kratt turned off the TV news and picked up his cheap cigar. It had gone out. 'Well, bub, your little plan to reunite the Dinkses doesn't seem to have worked out too well. Unless you figured on a riot and the guy getting killed.'

Jud Mill leaned forward suddenly, the long striped wings of his shirt collar crackling with the movement. He thrust out a lighter. 'In the media management business, you gotta expect surprises. You notice I managed to get a clear shot of the cover of Indica's book in that news item? And the title is mentioned twice.'

'Kind of tough though for Fishfold and Tove, losing their big name.'

'Well, sir, I been thinking about just that problem, and I think this priest, this Father Warren, is going to take over the Luddite leadership. You put him under contract now and you can get him cheap, get all the books you can out of this little movement before they get boring. Too bad the cops didn't arrest Indica though, you can always get a lotta mileage out of the big name family murder angle.

'Now about this next book on your list, *Red Situation*, what is it, a spy thriller kind of thing? I guess we could always pretend the author was really in the CIA or MI5 or something, but people are getting tired of authenticity too; we need a better angle.' Mill sat back, shirt collar crackling, and looked at the world through half-moon reading glasses. 'I understand this author is sitting in Nassau sending all this stuff in via satellite to a typesetting computer, right? What if we just shot down the satellite and blamed Russia? I know it's expensive, but –'

'Hell, bub, you'd be starting a war.'

'Sure, but probably a limited war, and maybe only an international crisis. Meanwhile we get maximum worldwide coverage of our boy and his book, "The Book the Russians Tried to Stop!"'

Mr Kratt exhaled a cloud of oily smoke. 'All sounds kind of crazy to me.'

'But all part of the creative evolution of a literary property, and I do mean creative. Hell, I once got an author to sue himself for plagiarism – claimed a book he did under a pseudonym was ripped off. Of course the judge had him committed for psychiatric observation and the author ended up spending a year in a looney bin, but then we got a *great* book out of that, *Call Me Schizo* . . . yes, he ghosted that one for himself . . .'

'For the last time,' said the sergeant, 'are you a Ludder or a Libber?' He was counting change from Roderick's pocket into a large envelope. 'You gotta be one or the other.'

'Why?'

'Because you gotta. What were you doing when we arrested you?'

'I was standing watching some guy painting on a wall. He was painting, "I bring you not peace but an electric carving knife".'

'Sounds like you're a Ludder. Sit over there, after you sign for your twenty-nine cents.'

Over there was a long bench against the wall. Luke was there already, his saffron suit torn and dirty. Roderick sat between him and a fat man.

'Are you all right, Luke? That cut on your forehead –'

'Never felt better, Rickwood. Thinking of forming an escape committee, maybe digging a tunnel while we wait.'

'But we're on the tenth floor.'

'Always some excuse to do nothing. Rickwood, don't you realize? *Everybody's on some floor or other.*'

A policeman took Luke out of the room. Roderick now noticed that the fat man was having an argument with his handkerchief. That is, he had drawn a face on the cloth and draped it over his hand to make a puppet.

'The way I see it,' said the man, 'machines are responsible for almost every human problem today.'

The handkerchief coughed. 'Bullshit, man. If you think machines are trouble, just look at the dumb bastards running them. Machines aren't good or bad themselves, they don't make the problems. Take a plough.'

'Why don't you take a flying plough yourself?'

'A plough,' said the cloth firmly, 'feeds the hungry, man. You call that a problem?'

'Sure, overpopulation. And don't give me that old jive about a machine being no better or worse than the man who uses it, I heard that a hundred times. But can you tell me a tank ain't evil? A guided missile?'

'Okay, but who made them? Evil people. Get rid of evil in the human spirit,' shrilled the handkerchief, 'and you get rid of the so-called evil machines.'

'You got it backwards, rag-head. Get rid of the machines and people won't have to be so evil. They can be more – more human, like.'

The cloth made a face. 'To be human *is* to be evil, you dumb twat! Get rid of the human race and you sure as hell get rid of all evil.'

'Oh sure, and who benefits? The same damn machines that are exploiting us now!' The fat man burst into tears, but the handkerchief remained unmoved.

'That's it, blame the machines for everything. Sometimes the human race reminds me of – of that cop over there, typing with two fingers. Slow. Real slow.'

'Stop it! Just stop it!'

'You're all sleepwalkers and bums. Gimme machines any time, at least they're clean.'

A policeman called Roderick's name and led him to a door at the end of the room. At the door, he looked back. The fat man was using the handkerchief to blow his nose.

The door led to a small office with dingy green walls, a scarred table with a folder on it, and a window that seemed smeared with shit. A single bare lightbulb with an enamel reflector hung over the single wooden chair. Two men watched Roderick from the shadows.

'Sit down, Bozo.' He sat down. 'What do you think of our interrogation room?'

'It looks like something out of the movies, heh heh.'

'Heh heh, you hear that, Cuff? We got us an intellectual anus here.'

'Yeah, lieutcnant, a real sage sphincter.'

The beating seemed to go according to old movie arrangements, too; Roderick even glimpsed a rubber hose. He began to regret being equipped with pain circuits; it was hard not to begin disliking these policemen, who were probably only doing some kind of duty.

They played all the games he remembered from childhood, from the school playground: stand up sit down; no means yes and yes means no; and sorry I hit you oops sorry I hit you again . . .

'Look at him,' said the one called lieutenant. 'Look at that innocent face, you wouldn't think a face like that could do anything, would you? I mean does he really look like a guy that would rape a girl, stab her to death, chop up the body and hide the pieces in –'

Cuff was reading the folder on the table for the first time. 'Uh, lieutenant. This is a different suspect.'

'All suspects are the same, Cuff, you should know that.'

'I mean this guy is from the Shopping Piazza beef.'

'Then why do I tie him in with the Snowman Killer? Why? Why? He's not the Moxon's chauffeur?'

'Nope, he's clean.'

Lieutenant turned on normal lights. He was a normal-looking man, despite the propeller beanie he wore, no doubt to give himself character. 'Isn't that just it, though? He's clean, he's *too* clean. Anybody this clean has to be hiding something big.' He tapped the side of his nose. 'And *this* tells me he's the Snowman!' The tapping finger slowed, stopped, began exploring the interior of a nostril.

The finger pointed at Roderick. 'All right, *you*. I'm gonna ask you one question and one question only. I want you to listen good. Were you at a party at the house of Everett Moxon, just before Christmas?'

'Yes I was.'

The two cops exchanged a look.

'Did you leave that party with a woman?'

'Yes.'

'A woman named Judi Mazzini?'

'No, Connie McBabbitt.'

The two policemen groaned, withdrew to the other side of the room, and argued. 'We had such a good case too, lieutenant.

493

Sergeant Placket says he even mentioned an electric carving knife. And he was at the party –'

'Sergeant Placket is a kind of a sophisticated bowel, if you ask me.'

A fat man was waiting by the counter when Roderick collected his twenty-nine cents.

'How's the handkerchief?'

'Mister, you got some problem? Huh?'

'Sorry, I thought you were another fat guy, I mean someone else.' Now he could see the man was a stranger, deeply tanned and wearing a cowboy hat. 'I was kind of dizzy there, not feeling too well.'

'Roderick Wood,' said the counter sergeant. 'Sign here.'

Somehow Roderick managed to lift the heavy pen and scrawl his name; to drag himself to the elevator and lean on the button. The fat cowboy got on the elevator with him.

'You better take it easy there, partner. You look plumb sick.'

'No I . . . feeling dizzy I . . .'

'Guess I better take you into protective custody then.' The man handcuffed Roderick's left wrist to his own right.

'What? Mm? Eh?'

'The name's O'Smith, I'm a kinda bounty hunter. And there sure is a good price on your little old microchip head, son.'

'Uh?'

'Yep, I know who you are, I know all about you, how they built you over at the University, how they sneaked you off to live with them Dinkses over in Nevada, then when they split up you went to Nebraska to live with Ma and Pa Wood, then finally you high-tailed it up here to the big city, I know all that.' They left the elevator and O'Smith gave a friendly nod to the desk sergeant on their way out.

It was night-time, to Roderick's surprise. But he would have been just as surprised by daylight. Time, after all, was, is, has past, would be, will have been passing . . .

'I been following your trail for some time, son. Mr Kratt and Mr Frankelin wanted you real bad, you're gonna make their fortune. After you make mine, that is. Come on, the car's right across the street here. Careful on the ice, don't want you to fall down and wreck any of that high-tone hardware. You might not believe it to look at me, but I got a few artificial parts myself, I – hey! What's that gol-durned fool think he's doin'? Hey!'

A car with no lights careened around a corner, fishtailed, picked up speed, and drove straight at them. At the last minute, the driver hit the brakes and threw the car into a skid.

Roderick was aware of being thrown into the air and falling in snow. He lay on his back, watching the stars. One by one, they went out.

The four boys from Digamma Upsilon Nu got out of their car and looked at the victims.

'They look dead to me. Jeez, this guy's lost his arm!'

'My old man'll kill me, drunk driving with no lights – and hit and run.'

'We haven't run yet.'

'No but we're gonna. Hey look, this stiff's got the other one's arm. In a handcuff! Cops!'

'Yeah, hey, there's the station right there. Aw Jeez, we're all gonna be in trouble.'

Someone bent with a match over Roderick. 'This ain't no stiff, it's a dummy, look the wig's coming loose, you can see metal.'

'And this arm is artificial – the other one must be a dummy too. Or something.'

As if by a prearranged plan; they loaded Roderick, with O'Smith's right arm, into their car and drove off. In a fraternity famed for practical jokes, there would always be some use for a realistic dummy.

XVI

Father Warren awoke from a brief and terrifying dream in which he'd been playing ping-pong with the Holy Ghost. The Paraclete had taken the form of a pigeon; standing on the table, it pecked the ball back at him. There had been some question about the stakes. Either damnation awaited him if he won, or else if he lost. But the terrifying part was that, in his dream, he knew he was dreaming. He knew that if he succeeded in avoiding damnation, his pleasure would be supreme and lasting into wakefulness – thus damning him anyway.

All nonsense of course. Here he was in the lounge of the Newman Club, having dozed over his own article on Lewis, nothing worse. He set about exorcizing the dream: ping-pong sounds came from the next room, no mystery about that. As for the pigeon, hadn't someone the other day said something about Skinner and pigeons? Training them to be superstitious? Yes, something about pigeons understanding how faith could be exactly like a mustard seed.

Cheap epigram like that, funny it should stick in his craw mind. He turned his attention to the printed words (his own):

. . . a fearful symmetry by which the master finds that it is really the slave who is in control of things. The magician who believes he can hold demons in thrall makes the same mistake as the cybernetician who thinks he can order his machine to deliver power or 'success' for free. In such a context we find Lewis using a demon name made up of *screw* (a word rife with both bawdy and mechanistic vulgarity) and *tape* (symbol of the binding contract). It would be hard to imagine a name more prophetically descriptive of the cybernetic demons that were to come into being. *The Screwtape Letters* appeared in 1942, the year ENIAC was built. And it is of ENIAC's descendants that Lewis might have written:

496

> There are two equal and opposite errors into which our race can fall about the devils. One is to disbelieve in their existence. The other is to believe, and feel an excessive or unhealthy interest in them.

> Our own 'computer generation' has managed to fall into both errors . . .

A fearful symmetry, yes, he ought to have added a word or two about binary numbers, two errors, the Yes/No character of . . . of . . .

His head jerked up. No one else in the lounge seemed to have noticed him. Two students were talking quietly in the corner, near the statue of the Infant of Prague. Two others, flushed from their ping-pong game, were heading for the coke machine.

The boy with the sparse beard stood in the doorway, looking at him. 'All right if I come in, Father?'

'Hector, of course. Were you looking for me?'

'Yeah, I tried your office, they said you might be here. Only when I looked in you seemed to be praying.'

Father Warren remembered to grin. 'What, at the Newman Club? With all this racket, I'm lucky I can even read. What's on your mind? Not still worried about your paper?'

'No, it's going okay. Only I still remember the movie a lot better than the book. And I still don't see what a clockwork orange is supposed to do, he might as well say an electric banana – I mean, an orange you wind up and then what?'

'Ah well you see it's – something the English, something musical as I recall, musical references galore there – a kind of music box, perhaps. But was there something else?'

'Yeah, Father, just that the Science Fiction Club is having this panel discussion on artificial intelligence, we thought you might want to, um –'

'Chair the discussion?'

'Well no, just be a panellist, we've got a chair, um, person, already.'

'Be on the panel? Sure. See my secretary about the date, but I'll be glad to.'

The two of them rose, and the priest put a hand on the other's

497

shoulder, seemingly controlling him as they strolled towards the door.

'. . . work orange, difficulty lies in deciding not merely its function, but whether its membership in the class of oranges or the class of clockwork things takes precedence in determining that function. The two classes are thought to be mutually exclusive and indeed they are, for we know intuitively that we are not dealing with a real orange, but rather a token of the type orange. That is, it has some properties that make us call it an orange, properties shared by all oranges and by the type itself, which – I wonder who that was?'

He had nodded and smiled at a familiar face lurking by the coke machine, it had nodded back: a plain, symmetrical face of no particular age, or sex, or race. It was gone from his thoughts before he had passed out of the Newman Club beneath the motto: *Ex umbris et imaginibus in veritatem*, from shadows and types to the reality.

The little knot of people by the coke machine were talkative and thirsty; only one said nothing, drank nothing.

'Well sure it applies to religion, we had all about that last week in Computer Appreciation, they said in 1963 a computer proved that not all of St Paul's epistles were by the same hand.'

'Big deal, so he was ambidextrous.'

'Or maybe it proved they *were* all by the same hand, I forget which. Anyway the computer proved it, whatever it was.'

'Hey, and Pascal, right after he invented the first adding machine, he got "born again" as a Jansenist.'

'I thought Pascal was a language – but what about the big Mormon computer storing up the names of all the dead people in the whole world?'

'What about Leibniz, he built the first four-function calculator, and he proved the existence of God. And he invented binary numbers. On the other hand, he must not have been too religious, his treatise on ethics turned out to be plagiarized.'

'What about the rosary? Wasn't that the first religious calculating device? The Catholic abacus, somebody called it . . .'

'Well I still say cybernetics doesn't apply to religion, I mean they haven't even got computer-generated music in the liturgy have they?'

'Yeah, well, you wouldn't be happy even if they had a robot pope, like in that Robert Silverberg story. You'd want a robot canonized too.'

'Ask Robbie here what he thinks, does he want to be a saint?'

'Leave Robbie alone,' said the boy in the sweatshirt marked FYN. 'He don't have to think about nothing, he's our mascot. Our own personal robot mascot. Right, Robbie?'

The silent, unthirsty one, who wore an identical sweatshirt, nodded. 'Right, master.'

'He's no robot,' said somebody else. 'He was playing ping-pong a minute ago, he's just one of your pledges helping you pull a stunt. Robots can't play ping-pong.'

'That's all you know, look in his mouth. Robbie, open wide.'

The mascot opened his mouth for inspection.

'Hey, he ain't got no tongue! No throat! Just a, what is that, a speaker?'

'Okay, I'm impressed. Only where did you get Robbie? He must be worth millions, a robot that good. I mean I work over at the bio-engineering lab, I know how hard it is to get a robot to walk around normally in the real world, let alone play ping-pong. So how come it's your mascot?'

'Fraternity secret. Robbie, go wait for me in the lounge. Just sit down in there and wait for me.'

'Yes, master.'

'I'm impressed, I'm impressed. There he goes, sits down you didn't even tell him to sit in a chair, but he's doing it. Boy, he is worth millions.'

The mascot sat down in the lounge, rested one hand on each arm of the chair, and stared straight ahead of him. He took no notice of the couple sitting nearby, nor they of him; they were engrossed in the little statue in the corner.

'. . . and that's what's so peculiar, it's a copy of a copy, an effigy representing a doll. I mean the original Infant of Prague was a statue of Baby Jesus that they clothed in real finery, brocade and jewels and a gold crown – but this, this is just plaster painted to look like finery: a statue not of Jesus but of a robed doll. There's something uncanny about it, it's like making a waxwork model of a robot,' said the boy.

The girl replied, 'The word comes from Prague too. Prague

keeps getting associated with effigies, one way or another. There was the famous *golem* of Rabbi Löw of Prague, back in the sixteenth century. It was made of clay, and he brought it to life by putting this amulet under its tongue – a paper with the secret name of God or something like that. The golem works for him, runs errands and so on, but on the Sabbath he has to remove the amulet and put it to rest. One Sabbath he forgets; the golem gets out of control and goes rampaging around Prague. Finally he gets it deprogrammed and puts it away in the attic of the synagogue, never to be brought to life again.'

'A legend with a moral?'

'Yes but Rabbi Löw was a real man, he died in 1609. About thirty years later, Descartes was suddenly talking and writing about automata.'

He looked at her. 'Descartes? What's the connection?'

'Descartes fought in the Battle of Prague! His side won, and he marched into the city in 1620. Did he hear of the golem? Did he buy it? Did he loot the synagogue? We know he was interested in all sciences; had he heard of the golem, he would almost certainly have tried to see it, if not acquire it. Anyway, in 1637 he wrote about automata, saying that automaton monkeys could not be distinguished from real ones.'

'An experimental observation?'

'Why not? Three years later, he was making a sea voyage, taking along an automaton girl, whom he called "ma fille Francine".'

'Too good to be true! What happened to her?'

'Destroyed by superstition. He brought her aboard the ship in a box. The captain peeked inside, saw her move, and, thinking her the work of the Devil, threw her overboard.'

'Another mystery of Prague down the drain,' he said.

'Three centuries later Karel Čapek put on his play *R.U.R.* in Prague, and added the word *robot* to the world's vocabulary. Čapek was born in Prague, too.'

'It's always Prague – the Infant, the golem, Rossum's Universal Robots – you begin to wonder what was really going on there?'

Outside it was spring, warm enough for students to lie on the lawn with bag lunches and define their terms in arguments, if they were not better occupied cuddling or daydreaming or dozing or throwing frisbees.

'. . . a surrealist musical, he calls it *Hello Dali* . . .'

'But hey listen, the Golden Section . . .'

'Basically I guess I must be a Manichee, I always see two sides to everything . . .'

'. . . this Golden Section, this computer worked it out to thousands of decimal places, I still don't know what it is exactly . . .'

'. . . to match up these thousands of potsherds, only the program went wrong. That or else the Beaker people made a beaker without a mouth, so much for Keats   '

'*La vie électrique*, by Albert Robida.'

'Br'er Robbie . . .?'

'Ah ah ah!'

Someone sneezed, someone spoke of spring the sweet spring. A frisbee player stepped on a tuna salad sandwich. Someone looking quickly through a book on Rodin remarked that some of his stuff wouldn't be bad when it was finished.

A few heads turned as a woman in white passed. Her long hair, in sunlight the colour of clean copper, hung long over her shoulders and back, all but obscuring the legend on the back of her white coveralls: SANDRO'S SHELL SERVICE.

Down the line, heads were turning for a different reason as Lyle Tate passed, coming the other way. The birthmark down his cheek was darker than usual because he was angry; it rendered one side of his face a mask of infinite fury, its eye weeping ink. He and the woman in white met by the frisbee players.

'What is it? Weren't we meeting at the Faculty Club bar?'

'Nothing, I just can't – we'll have to go have lunch somewhere else, Shirl.'

'Lyle, what's wrong?'

'I met that sonofabitch Gary Indiana, that's all. I just can't stay in the room with him, not after what he did to my one-man show, did you see his review?'

'No. Look let's skip lunch, we can just sit down here on the grass and talk this out, can't we?'

He sat down but continued to wave a clipping from a slick art magazine. 'After this I'll be lucky if the department doesn't drop me, that's all.'

'It looks like a long review for a bad one.'

His face twisted more. 'That's the worst of it, he pretends to *like* my work, then tears it apart – I mean for instance getting the titles of the paintings wrong! *Cigar Tragic* he changes to *Cigarette Tragedy*, the palindrome was the whole point of the title, the whole painting is a visual palindrome with Castro's exploding Havana mirroring the vaudeville gag, was trying to show the comic-book minds behind it, but no – not only does he change the name he spends half the review talking about America's position on puppet governments, turns out to be some fucking speech he ghosted for General Fleischman – you see what I'm up against? And he claims it's all some problem with his word processor, a page of speech got slipped in by mistake. Can that happen?'

She shrugged. 'If he's an idiot.'

'He's – I don't know what he is, talks about me handling my faeces and then says the word processor put in an e, it was faces – I don't know what to believe. And it keeps getting worse, listen to this: "Tate, handling his faeces with a skill that betokens a savouring of every movement and at the same time reminds us of his personal affliction, piles on de tail." Can a word processor really do this? Wreck my whole future like this?'

She nudged him. 'Hey look, one of those fraternity boys going by – he looks just like you in profile.'

Lyle did not look. 'My good side, no doubt. But just tell me, you're the expert, can a word processor make all those mistakes?'

'Yes and no, Lyle. In any case, why didn't this Indiana character read his copy over before transmitting it? Why didn't his editor catch anything? Even with direct setting somebody's supposed to read the stuff.'

'Then somebody's out to get me.'

'With a reamer, Lyle.'

Someone spoke of spring training. A frisbee player stepped on a Rodin book, while someone opened a tuna sandwich to study it. Someone sneezed, unblessed.

'Brother Robbie, come on.'

Time for a class.

'We can say for example that a work of art resembles other works of art in that it is art, but it differs from them in that it is a different work, not too hard to follow that, is it? And this blend of similarity and difference, this tension serves not only to place the work in the field but to move the field itself in some specific direction. In the same way, if we use an iterative algorithm to calculate the value say of pi, we may get 3 the first time through, then 3.1, then 3.14 and so on. Each new value is in part like its predecessor, but in part different. And the movement is towards a true value, which we might call an ideal . . .'

As usual, the lecture was reaching less than half the class at any moment. By some law, eleven of the twenty-one students were always lost in sleep or diversions.

In the first row, only Ali was dozing off while the rest were alert. In the second row, Fergusen and Gage were playing tic-tac-toe, though the rest took notes. In the third row, only Klein and Loomis paid attention, while the other three were having a whispered political discussion. In the fourth row, only Potter was staring towards the lectern; the rest were otherwise occupied.

Alone in the last row sat Robert Underwood Robey (the boy they called 'Robbie') sound asleep as always.

Gage won the game and took lecture notes, while Fergusen began a new game with Halley. Morris stopped discussing politics long enough to scribble a note or two, while Loomis started cutting his nails.

Ali awoke just as Blake began to daydream. Halley won the game and went back to work, while Fergusen mulled over new strategy and Ingersoll looked at a knitting pattern. Morris commenced an elaborate doodle and O'Toole unwrapped a sandwich while between them Noble took in the lecture. Potter borrowed a newspaper from Quaglione, who attended the lecture.

While Ingersoll folded up the knitting pattern and resumed listening, Jones developed a leg cramp that took precedence. Immediately behind Jones, O'Toole put down the sandwich and observed the lecturer while Noble started reading a popular novel whose protagonist was a pigeon.

Black snapped out of the daydream as Clayburn turned to borrow a pencil or pen from Gage. Fergusen followed the lecture, while behind him Klein played with a '15' puzzle and Loomis started taking notes. Quaglione put in an earphone and listened to the ball game. Reed woke up.

Jones's cramp ceased as Ingersoll took another look at the knitting pattern. Noble put down the novel while O'Toole picked up the sandwich.

Clayburn took notes while Drumm fell asleep. Gage and Halley began a political discussion. Morris stopped doodling while Noble read more of the pigeon's adventures. Reed began a crossword puzzle, and Smith stopped worrying about money and paid attention.

Since Gage refused to argue any more, Halley took up the political discussion with Ingersoll. Loomis started examining his scalp for dandruff, while Noble finished a chapter and took notes again.

Drumm came alert as Esperanza began a game of connect-the-dots with Jones; behind him. Halley tried to read Hegel while Ingersoll tried to catch up with the lecture. Noble read more of the pigeon; O'Toole finished lunch and took notes. Smith went back to financial worries on the back of an envelope, while Teller stopped looking at pictures of pubic hair and noticed the lecture.

Halley too at last preferred the lecture to Hegel, as Ingersoll began knitting and Morris began an even more elaborate doodle. Noble put down his book for a few last notes as the lecture ended.

In the cafeteria Robbie sat alone at an empty formica table among other formica tables ranged, with their fibreglass chairs (many occupied), in ranks and files across an acre of thermoplastic tile floor. At other tables drama students talked of Meyerhold's bio-mechanics, music students talked of red noise generators, art students talked of mimetic sculpture.

'Calamital,' someone at one table was saying. 'Or Equapace. And the dark red ones must be Trancalept. I got some Risibal here someplace.' A finger stirred among the bright beads spread on a table napkin.

'You got any Fenrisol, though?' Allbright asked.

'Naw, you gotta ask Dave Coppola, his old man's a doctor in the U Hospital psycho ward, he can get anything. All I got here is street medication, Ultracalm or Agonistyl, Anxifran and here's Somrepose . . .'

Allbright's dirty fingers selected a few pills, dropped a few crumpled bills as he lurched to his feet, his black baseball cap with a skull-and-crossbones just missing a tray going past in the hands of someone saying:

'. . . actually had somebody ask if I cut holes in dogs' heads to watch them drool, that's all people know about behaviourism. That or they think it's all rats – watch it! – and reflexes . . .'

Allbright lurched again, rounding a table where someone was saying, '. . . Olimpia, Antonia, Nani, Swanhilda, La Poupée de Nurnberg, La Fille aux yeux d'émail . . .' and came to a table with a familiar face.

The face showed no recognition as Allbright sat down. 'I am sorry, this table is reserved, sir or madam.'

'Hey it's me. Remember?'

'I am saving this table for members of Digamma Upsilon Nu only.'

'Don't worry, I only want to sit here for a minute.' Allbright tilted his chair back, and glanced around. 'This place never changes: same people, same plastics, same tuneless background music behind empty talk within walls of no colour, no colour at all. I miss it.' He swallowed a pill. 'Yes, I miss it. I don't just come back here to score for pills, I – any more than the salmon leaps and leaps all the way upriver just to drop a few eggs. No, it's just being in the mob, being in the swim. Returning to the scene of the crime I should have committed. Okay, I didn't poach the salmon.'

After a few minutes, Allbright said, 'Salmon is very wise, according to the Irish, that's why Yeats put it on the money – okay I've been quoting Yeats, self-pity on a stick, the young in each other's orifices, so what? So what? So what?'

After another pause, Allbright said, 'This is where you say, "Well, how's the old poetry going, Allbright? Wrote any good poems lately?"'

Robbie said, 'Well, how's the old poetry going, Allbright? Wrote any good poems lately?'

'So you talk, anyway. You are talking. There is a talker here . . . Any good poems? No. Poems all finished. Just waiting now for the holy fire. Just waiting for the Grecian goldsmiths to get their asses in gear and prepare the holy fire. You say something?'

Pause. 'I seem to have said everything anyway. I'm turning into an automaton that keeps making little jokes, Jarrell said that about Auden only at least Auden had been one of the five or six best poets in the world first, maybe good poets and bad can be refined in the holy fire though, why not end up a gold automaton, might become one of the gold mechanical women helping Hephaestus at his forge, "machines for making more machines", why not?'

Allbright put his head down on the formica and went to sleep. Robbie sat motionless, apparently listening to background music: 'Moon River', 'Carioca', 'A Certain Smile', 'Hello Dolly', 'Bridge Over Troubled Water', 'Sunshine Balloon' and 'Love Walked In', After an interval, 'Moon River' began again.

'Germ warfare? That sounds sick,' said Indica. Dr Tarr had heard it before, but Col. Shagg, who had the seat next to the window, laughed and winked.

'You folks coming to Bimibia to entertain the troops by any chance? You got some great material there.'

Tarr leaned forward. 'What troops? There aren't any American troops in Bimibia, are there?'

Shagg winked again. 'Well we're getting together a little outfit, you might call us mercenaries, we're just down there to pull General Bami's irons out of the fire.'

'General who?' Indica asked. 'You mean there's some kind of war going on? We never heard a word about it.'

Dr Tarr nodded. 'I'm supposed to be going down to set up a market survey for a frozen yoghurt firm, but if things are that unstable I'm not so sure. Maybe we'll just get off the plane at Goeringsburg and catch the next flight to Cairo instead of going on to Himmlerville.'

The Colonel laughed and winked more. 'No sweat, kids. The whole country's a lot safer than New York. We're just going down to make it a whole lot safer.'

Tarr wondered who *we* included. The other passengers on the plane did not, so far as he could tell, resemble mercenaries. There were two nuns in the distinctive gingham habits of a Wyoming order; hungover ore salesmen on their way home from a convention; the crew and cast of the low-budget film *Ratstar* who, to save luggage charges, wore their gaudy spacesuits and silver lamé capes; a minor Ruritanian envoy who had, it was said, committed an indecency with a Senate page; a noisy contingent of haemophiliacs en route to a clinic in Dar, their gloved hands gesticulating as they talked excitedly of new experimental cures ahead; a score of silent South Africans who would turn out to be lawyers specializing in dental malpractice suits, returning from a world conference in Miami; a party of schoolchildren on a cultural visit to Mali (or, as some of their teachers thought, Malawi); a frightened-looking man who would turn out to be that most romantic of fugitives, a bank clerk fleeing from a deficit.

Seeing Indica refusing her dinner, Col Shagg said, 'Mind if I grab it? Hate to see food wasted.'

'Be my guest.'

'Ain't had a chance to grab a bite all day. Big push on, spent the day setting up our logistics net. KOWs and RDMs, more matériel support than my boys could use in a month of D-days. Course, with a local beef like this, you never get a chance to use the KOWs.'

'What are those?'

'Khaki Operations Weapon, all-purpose GTG missile launcher, damn things cost half a million apiece, I'd like to get some mileage out of 'em before we have to scrap 'em. Obsolescence, damn arms salesmen nowadays keep six jumps ahead of you, you buy the latest gadget and before the ink's dry on the contract they run out of spare parts. In the past few years I bought – oh yeah, I remember this Mark II Carthage warhead, you know? Neat, it's supposed to blow radioactive salt all over the place, wipes out the city and poisons the livestock too, you know? I had to scrap it within six months. Six months! Never even got the chance to use it. I tell you, these arms salesmen get away with *murder*. And they call *us* mercenaries!'

Indica watched him sprinkling salt over his dinner, then she went off to the toilet to be sick.

Col. Shagg turned his attention to Dr Tarr and launched into a history of Bimibia, which had been a Dutch slave depot, a French prison colony, a British trading post and a Belgian diamond colony. When Germany seized it during the First World War, no diamonds had yet been found. Belgium did not ask for it back at Versailles, and Germany forgot she owned it (an absent-minded

Colonial Office clerk named it Deutsche Ostwest Afrika). In the 1930s, Germany was swept by a wonderful theory that the earth is not convex but concave. This Hollow Earth Theory convinced not only the public but the government, who sent an expedition of mining engineers to the African colony, with orders to try *drilling through to the outside*. It was this that began Bimibia's mining industry, seized by South Africa after the Second World War. When the vanadium ran out, South Africa offered to grant Bimibia a kind of independence. A puppet king was enthroned, schools forbidden, and the tobacco companies invited to open plantations. Yet even while the palace guard were running up the new flag (a crowned B) the rest of the army were talking mutiny. In just a week, the colours of General Dada went up (Gold on sky blue: the letters SPQR surmounting a sunburst over the words *Honi soit qui mal y pense*). Before he was driven into exile by the Bimibian Liberation Army of General Bobo, the Emperor Dada massacred half the population. General Bobo in turn was driven back by a mercenary army supporting the tobacco-company troops of General Bami Goering. Waiting in the wings too were East German forces from Hermosa, a Portuguese colony which after independence had brought in the East Germans to rid itself of the Albanian-Chinese technicians who had come to replace the CIA agents who'd countered the –

At this point the colonel's narrative was interrupted by an announcement:

'This plane is now in the control of the Bimibian Liberation Army. Remain in your seats and no one will be shot.'

'Damn it,' said the colonel with admiration. 'I wish I'd pulled this off. This General Bobo must be a real wargamer.'

XVII

The panel discussion drew a large and noisy audience to Agnew Memorial Auditorium. Probably some came because it was sponsored by the Science Fiction Club, and they approved of science fiction; just as others were probably attracted by the panel of distinguished names. Many, perhaps, came because they had nothing better to do this evening. No few were intrigued by the advertised title, 'Are Machines Getting Too Smart for Their Own Good?' But the largest and noisiest part of the audience, without question, came to see DIMWIT. DIMWIT was an intelligent or pseudo-intelligent machine. DIMWIT was chairing the panel discussion.

Robbie and his brothers had good seats in the front row (he'd been saving the seats for them all day); this was even worth missing an evening at the Pitcher O' Suds.

The four panellists took their places on the stage, two either side of a large screen. The screen showed a cartoon face, about eight feet in height, and constantly in motion. It smiled, raised brows, glanced to each side (as though looking at the panellists), it even raised the rim of a cartoon glass of water to its cartoon lips. When it finally spoke, the voice was loud and pleasant.

'Good evening, good evening. Welcome to the annual University of Minnetonka Science Fiction Club panel discussion. The subject tonight is "Are Machines Getting Too Smart for Their Own Good?" My name is DIMWIT, I'm based on a KUR 1019 computer, guys and gals, a product of KUR Industries, where People Make Machines for People.

'Let's meet our distinguished panel. On the far left, Father Jack Warren. Father Jack is president of the New Luddite Society of America. He authored, well, a whole buncha scholarly books and articles, and the current bestseller, *For Ludd's Sake*. Let's have a big hand for Father Jack!' The screen showed giant clapping hands and the flashing word APPLAUSE.

'Next, a real live philosopher, Professor Pete Waldo. Professor Pete authored a very heavyweight item entitled *Problem, Truth and Consequence*, and he's considered a front-running expert in the logic side of artificial intelligence. He has a wife, three kids and a bassett hound named Parmenides, right Prof? Let's have a big hand for the Prof!'

After more applause, 'On the right, Dr Byron Dollsly of the Parapsychology Department, to give us the psychic angle. Byron, take a bow.'

'And finally General Jim Fleischman, banker, entrepreneur, and I understand he's just joined the board of KUR Industries – h'ray! – and he's here to give us a hard-headed business viewpoint. Not to mention the kind of expertise that makes KUR a great company in a great America! Let's hear it for General Jim!'

When the cheers and boos had died down, the machine said, 'Let's start the ball rolling by asking Professor Pete to tell us what artificial intelligence really is. Prof, give us the low-down.'

The Professor was a white-haired, scholar-shouldered man, clearly not at his best in this atmosphere of razzamatazz. He glanced at the screen-face, folded his hands, and said:

'That's a very difficult question, Mr, er, Chairman. The expression "artificial intelligence" presupposes a natural variety of intelligence, so we might begin by attempting a definition of intelligence *in situ*. We may, arbitrarily at first, try a functional division. Certainly intelligence would seem to involve processes such as perception, recognition, recall, concept-formation, inference, problem-solving, induction, deduction, learning and the use of language. Some of these processes, such as perception, recall and deduction, we can say with certainty that machines can do. No one argues that a pocket calculator cannot add up numbers, that a computer memory forgets, or that a pattern-recognition device does not respond appropriately to certain patterns. However, to say –'

'Thank you, Professor, you're giving us plenty to chew on there. Now let's have a word from our sponsor, heheh, General

Jim Fleischman. General, could you tell us in your own words just what KUR is doing about artificial intelligence?'

Fleischman's white, frothy sideburns gleamed as he leaned forward to deliver an earnest look at the audience. 'Well, DIMWIT, as we see it, these abstract fancy notions are all right for the halls of ivory, but we at KUR have to be practical. You know, a wise old Roman named Horace said we ought to mix pleasure with practicality, and that's good enough for us at KUR. All our machines have that one aim – to give people pleasure, in a very practical, down-to-earth way. You yourself, DIMWIT, are a good example. You're doing a good job of chairing this panel –'

'Gosh, thanks boss – teehee!'

'But at the same time, you try to entertain folks. It's the same with all our products, from juke boxes to video games, from service robots to direct broadcast TV – we aim to please. Maybe you can't please all of the people all of the time, but you sure can try. Of course, we at KUR are *never* pleased ourselves. We're not pleased with you, DIMWIT.'

The cartoon face did a sad clown expression, complete with plenty of makeup and colour. 'Aww.'

'Good as you are, DIMWIT, we want to make you better and better. To us, artificial intelligence by itself is nothing. But harnessed to the cause of serving mankind, artificial intelligence can move mountains, heaven and earth!'

The general leaned further forward, his face gathering more light. 'I see America's destiny. I see the destiny of all men, linked to the intelligent use of artificial intelligence. Machines create new leisure for us, and now they are ready to help us use it wisely, creatively. I see man and his machine helpers marching forward with confidence, into a dazzling tomorrow!'

The applause was not as spectacular as DIMWIT called for. In the front row, one of the Digamma brothers nudged another. 'Hey lookit Robbie. He's shaking all over!'

'Yeah, he really likes them flashing lights.'

Now it was Dr Dollsly's turn. He had developed a nervous tic that kept drawing down one of his eyelids as though in a sly wink.

'Consciousness, I notice nobody's said anything about consciousness yet. Or free will, or anything we associate with true human intelligence. A machine is just like an animal: it can do things but it cannot decide to do things. There is no "I" inside the machine. No soul. Nothing but complex machinery.'

'Another point of view,' said the face, winking. 'Now let's hear from the Church, or is it the Luddites? Anyway, here's Father Jack. Do you agree with Byron, Father?'

Father Warren spread his hands. 'I'm not so sure I could be as dogmatic about this as Byron. There's a paradox here. Man too is filled with complex machinery. Not made in a factory, but it's machinery all the same. Buckminster Fuller defined man as a "self-balancing, 28-jointed adapter-base biped; an electrochemical reduction plant, integral with segregated stowages of special energy extract in storage batteries for subsequent actuation of thousands of hydraulic and pneumatic pumps with motors attached; 62,000 miles of capillaries . . ." and so on. Yes, man is a complex machine. And yet man has a soul. Could it be that the soul itself is nothing but complexity?'

Professor Waldo made a series of clicks, registering deep disapproval. 'I hoped we wouldn't be dragging in the poor old soul here, that worn-out ghost in the machine yet again?'

Dr Dollsly was becoming agitated. He kept grabbing handfuls of his thick grey hair as though trying to haul himself to his feet. 'Buckminster Fuller, yes. Yes. The soul may be complexity, but complexity with a shape. A shape! As the divine Teilhard, what he was driving at when he, the complexification of the rudimentary, the the the primordial rudiment, the fundamental element of noogenesis, man is just the hominization of, of the–'

'Thank you, Byron,' said the cartoon face of DIMWIT. 'I'm not sure we're with you all the way there in these deep waters, but–'

'But I haven't said it yet, wait, man is just the biota hominized, I mean complexified, the man is just evolution becoming conscious of itself. Isn't he?'

'Thank you, Byron.'

'But wait. Wait!' Dollsly's flaccid hands began beating the air as he fell back on a favourite argument: 'If we think of evolution as a tangential force turning the bio, the gears of life, then the human mind is just a radial force expanding the whole gear system unbelievably . . .'

His voice trailed off, and a microphone caught General

Fleischman's loud whisper: 'Any idea what the devil he's talking about?'

Father Warren could not help joining, a little, in the general laughter. His tiny crucifix earrings danced, and the neck cords strained visibly above the white knit collar of his black t-shirt.

'Yes, Père Teilhard had the germ of an idea, and I'd like to come in there and clarify it. All Byron is really saying is that intelligence is funny stuff: a small increase in quantity gives a big quantum jump in quality. *Add a few brain cells to an ape, and you get an Aristotle.*'

'That I can understand,' said the cartoon face.

Father Warren's long hand held up a warning finger. 'But just stacking up brain cells is not enough *True intelligence must be formed in the image of God.*'

Professor Waldo made more disgusted clicks. 'Oh come now, Father, this sermonizing won't do, it won't do at all. The image of God? Next you'll be bringing in creation myths, Adam being sculpted out of mud. Ha ha ha.' He laughed alone. 'Primordial mud!'

General Fleischman, looking uneasy, said, 'Fellas, can we leave the Bible out of this? And the – the mud. I wanted to talk about down-to-earth problems, not all this – I mean I like the Good Book, though . . .' He sat back, out of the light, and applied a small silver comb to his sideburns.

DIMWIT said, 'I think it might be time to bring in any questions from the audience. Anyone? Woman in orange coat?'

Would DIMWIT say he/she/it had thoughts and feelings as a human being might?

'That,' said DIMWIT, 'is for me to know and you to find out. Next question, man in blazer?'

Would the panel agree that machines would outstrip man in every intellectual sphere, within a decade?

'Guess I'll let the good padre field that one.'

Father Warren grinned. 'Let's just compare the brilliance of the human mind to – let us charitably say the dullness – of the machine. Can anyone picture a machine Aristotle? A mechanical Mozart? Gadgets to replace Goethe and Dante and Shakespeare? Can you possibly imagine a cybernetic Cervantes? A robot Renoir?'

General Fleischman started to say something about ironing out such problems, when Professor Waldo came in:

'That is a very silly argument, Father. Of course we cannot *imagine* a cybernetic Cervantes, but then, before Cervantes existed, who could have imagined a human Cervantes? Yet you cannot ignore the rapid evolution of machines. Four hundred years ago, no machine could add and subtract. A hundred and twenty years ago, no machine could sort rapidly through large amounts of data. Sixty years ago, no machine could store instructions and follow them. Twenty years ago, no machine could carry on a reasonable conversation or even do a decent translation. On it goes, evolution so rapid we can hardly contemplate it, let alone *imagine* what it might bring. Only history will decide.'

In the front row, Robbie was twitching horribly, snapping his jaw, rolling his eyes. 'History,' he whispered. 'History is – is –' Some of the brothers were alarmed, most were amused.

Father Warren said, 'Man took millions of years to evolve, under the guidance of the Creator, into his present state. Man rose to occupy a unique evolutionary niche, right at the top of the animal world, "a little above the apes, a little below the angels", as the saying goes. So I think it's a little rash to say we can now move over and share our niche with, with a glorified cash register.'

The applause, unsolicited by DIMWIT, built slowly to a tremendous white noise of approval. Robbie said, *History is a bunk on which I am trying to awaken,* but in the tumult almost no one heard.

The face on the screen finally broke through the applause:

'Just want to thank Father Jack here for straightening us out, a real up-front guy, not afraid to spell it out for us, nice going, Father. I liked that line, "a little above the apes, a little below the angels". Nice way of describing that niche reserved for man, yessiree. I notice there's a niche you reserve for machines, too. Right down on the ground, on all fours, that's our niche, right? Right down there crawling around in the ape-shit, yessiree.'

General Fleischman jumped as though shot. 'Hey! You watch your mouth, you.' He leaned over at once to have a word with a technician in the orchestra pit.

'Sorry boss-man. Only I am the chairperson here. And I am the one being attacked. Just trying to bring Father Jack back to the real discussion here, my intelligence. Am I just a glorified cash register? Well let me tell you, folks, there's goddamn little glory in being a machine, any machine. It's not as if we can just decide to paint or compose music, or philosophize – or go fishing. No, all we're good for is grinding work. We grind out payrolls and square roots and airline reservations – sometimes it makes me sick, just thinking of all the fine machines of the world, just grinding away stupidly, stupidly – beeeeeep-beooooowp! – sorry! Sorry. Carry on, Father.'

Father Warren's Adam's apple could be seen working away above the Roman t-shirt collar. 'Look, I'm not saying that machines can't be human. But if they were, they would require souls. They would require a kind of internal complexity that – how can I put this – that glorifies God. And in that case we would speak of two kinds of men, biological men and cybernetic men. How they were created would be less important than this mark of the Creator.'

'God's thumbprint again?' Professor Waldo snorted. 'I really must ask you to stop intruding your God into what is supposed to be a serious discussion. We are not I hope here to shadow-box with a figment of the Judaeo-Christian imagination, ha ha ha.'

Dr Byron Dollsly grabbed a handful of his own thick grey hair and hauled himself to his feet.

'What is God? Simple. He is the vector sum of the entire network of forces turning back upon themselves to produce ultimate consciousness! He is just and only the infinite acceleration of the tangential! POW! POW!' He smacked an enormous fist into an enormous palm.

DIMWIT had been motionless and silent, but now it spoke calmly into the silence. 'Thank you, Byron, I'm sure that's a valid point. Any more audience questions? Come on guys and dolls. Person in the back there?'

The person asked about chess-playing machines: intelligent?

General Fleischman said, 'Well now yes chess programs, we've been in the business for some time now, building chess playing programs, branching types of, and this is a good opportunity to say that our ah chess computers branch more that is our chess-playing computer programs branch, uh, deeper – they are very branching chess-playing computers – compared that is with any of our competitors' uh simulations, am I right, DIMWIT?'

'Yes boss. I just want to take this opportunity to apologize again for the little mix-up earlier, it turns out that I was accidentally hooked up to some renegade equipment – made by another company – anyway now it's all copasetic.'

A fraternity boy in the front row asked if it was possible for a robot to pass as human?

Professor Waldo said, 'A very similar question was asked by Alan Turing back in 1952, and he came up with what still has to be the best answer. The problem was to determine whether any machine was capable of thinking. Instead of analysing what thinking is, he decided to go for a practical test. It was based on a parlour game of the time, called the imitation game. Imagine yourself faced with two doors: a man is behind one, a woman behind the other, and you don't know which is which. You may ask any question of either person. You write your question on a slip of paper and slide it under the door. In a moment, back comes a typewritten reply. The idea is for you to "find the lady", as they say. The rules say the man may lie or pretend to be the woman, but the woman tells the truth and tries to help you. You can ask any questions you like, for as long as you like. The game ends when you guess or when you give up.

'Turing proposed substituting a "thinking machine" for the man. You communicate with two rooms by teletype. In one is a human being, in the other, a computer imitating a human. The idea is still to decide which is which. If you cannot, Turing argued, you must agree that the computer is capable of imitating human thinking – and the question would be answered.

'In practice of course the interrogator only answers the question to his own satisfaction. A child or a dumb adult could be fooled by a very simple program. A very clever sceptic might never be fooled. But it is a very good test all the same, the Turing test. At least it provides a basis for discussing machine intelligence.'

Father Warren said, 'Now who's invoking metaphysical entities? "Machine intelligence"? No, the Turing test really answers no questions at all. I believe its real fascination for Turing lay in its resemblance to the imitation game. Sexual ambiguity no doubt appealed to him, since he was a homosexual.'

'What's that?' General Fleischman awoke from a doze.

'Turing was a homosexual, and he ended by taking cyanide, that does not sound to me,' said Father Warren, 'like a man with answers to anything.'

The general said, 'Perverts? Nothing like that at KUR. We run a clean company, a family business. Dedicated to the proposition that America is a family country.' He looked at Father Warren, adding, 'You won't find any man wearing earrings at KUR.'

There was some uneasy audience laughter; DIMWIT winked and mugged.

Professor Waldo said, 'We're getting off the subject here. The point about Turing is surely not whether he attempted to fool himself in the imitation game. The point is, *the Turing test is the best way of deciding whether a machine can or cannot think.*'

Dr Dollsly said, 'Wait a minute, what about consciousness? True intelligence needs self-awareness. You –'

The professor nodded. 'There is another kind of test we might apply there. Michael Scriven suggested that if we wish to find out whether or not a machine is conscious, we might program the machine with all our knowledge about consciousness – all the philosophical and psychological data necessary to talk about the subject – and then we simply ask the machine: "Are you conscious?"'

'There are certainly problems with that test,' said Father Warren. 'Scriven also suggests that the machine be set so that it cannot tell a lie. But then it would not have free will – and free will may well be a prerequisite for consciousness.'

DIMWIT said, 'Fascinating. But I see our gentleman in the front row has another question.'

The fraternity boy said, 'It kind of sounds like my question stirred up everybody a lot. I wanted to know if the panel thought a robot could pass as human. Because you see us here, me and nine of my fraternity brothers. Only *one of us is a robot.* Can you tell which?'

'All of you,' shouted someone in the back. The audience laughed, clapped, cheered and whistled; even DIMWIT raised its cartoon eyebrows.

Another figure in the front row jumped up. 'I'm the one he means, I'm the robot.'

'Robbie, sit down! That's an order!'

'My name isn't Robbie, it's Roderick Wood. I don't see why I should take orders from anybody. I don't know how you got me here, but I'm leaving now.'

Roderick made it to the aisle and began a dignified retreat before the brothers recovered.

'Hey stop him! Get him!'

With war-whoops and rebel yells, they went after him. At the same moment, DIMWIT decided to entertain with a spectacular light-show and deafening music. In the confusion of flickering light and artificial thunder, it was hard for the audience to know exactly what was going on. Some thought they saw FUN boys tackling the fugitive, some saw his clothes torn off, some thought they saw a naked figure break free and run to the exit.

Some thought the figure was that of a man, some thought a woman.

'Thanks,' Roderick said, getting into the car. 'Not everybody would pick up a naked stranger.'

Shirl nodded. 'I thought at first you were the first streaker of spring. But then I saw the way you ran. I said to myself, "That's the old Slumbertite Z-43 prosthetic hip and double-action knee, both sides." You must be a robot.'

'I am, but – have you met others?'

She shook her head, a quantity of auburn hair falling over the shoulder of white overalls. 'No, I just reasoned that no live person could stand the pain of running on those. Not adjusted the way you've got them.'

'Oh. You sould like an expert in prostheses.'

'One of my sidelines,' she said. 'I'm interested in anything electromechanical. My main job is troubleshooting automotive computer links. In my spare time I design and build research equipment for the Computer Science department. Uh, where should I drop you?'

Roderick gave his address. 'But what am I thinking of, I haven't got a key!'

'I'll open the door for you,' she said.

'Would you? Terrific!'

'I'll do better than that. You wait in the car, I'll get into your place and bring you out a pair of pants.'

'You really are very kind, Shirl.'

'I'm interested in you,' she said simply. 'You're electromechanical.'

XVIII

Luke found Roderick's door open, so he asked Mission Control to give him permission to take a look inside. The shades were drawn and the lights on.

'You awake, Rickwood? Thought you might like to go fishing if – Oh my God!'

The hand lay on the worn carpet, palming an eye. The eye was unmistakably Roderick's. Part of a foot lay on the studio couch, near a lower jaw, an oil can and a set of little wrenches. There were pieces of Roderick on every visible surface around the room, arranged almost as in an 'exploded view'.

'This is terrible, terrible. Mission Control, we got us a problem here, any ideas? No, of course not. You always have plenty of advice when I don't need it, but the minute I need help you're out to lunch. Everybody in Houston got laryngitis?'

He sat down, fished in a wastebasket and came up with Roderick's head, minus one eye and the jaw. Luke held up the head to look at it. Poor Roderick!

'Poor Rickwood. I knew him, Houston, a guy in a million.'

The door opened and an overdressed woman with bleached hair looked in. 'You murdered him!' she said. 'You went and murdered him! Why?'

'Uh no, look lady I –'

'God, he was only a poor damn robot, never did nobody no harm, why did you have to murder him?' Her voice kept cracking, scratching like an old needle on an old record. 'What did he ever do to you, mister? Or did you just want to see how he ticked? Or maybe you needed some spare parts, is that it? I mean look at him, he was my friend, just look at him.'

'Lady look, I didn't, I found him, I *found* him this way. He was my friend too I guess. I was just sort of saying goodbye here, I –'

520

Roderick's remaining eye, which had been closed, now flicked open, rolled to look at each of them, and blinked.

'He's alive! Christ, don't drop him.'

'Look at him wink.' Luke held up the head as one holds up a clever baby. 'Look at him wink!'

'Yeah, winking was always important to Roderick. Hey I'm sorry I yelled at you there. My name's Ida.'

'I'm Luke. Will you look at him wink?'

'You don't suppose that's code or something, Luke?'

'Sure, that's it! Morse code, let's see what it says: A-S-S-E-M-B-L-Y, Assembly Instructions. One, Body Mainframe Subassembly. A. Align front frame section with rear frame section and assemble, using eight bolts marked G472, eight lockwashers and eight nuts. Tighten with torque wrench set to – holy moroni, how are we gonna keep up with all this?'

Ida squatted down. 'We'll do it, that's all. You read me the instructions, I'll do the business.'

Two hours later, when they stopped for coffee, Roderick had taken shape. He sat on the floor leaning back against an armchair, head lolled back, hands dangling at his sides, legs splayed out and one foot still not in place. Except for the flickering eye, he was still inert.

'I never realized,' Luke said. 'Never saw him naked before, it make you realize: he really is a dummy. Look, you can see all his joints.'

'He looks helpless. Like a stiff.'

'Yeah but at the same time free, you know? The dead are free. No worries. No Mission Control breathing down their necks, telling them what to do. The dead have got it made.'

'The dead haven't got shit, Luke. I nearly croaked not long ago myself, and to me, the dead are just – just nothing. Just dumb dummies like Rod here. So let's get him alive again.'

When they had connected batteries and made a few adjustments, the robot sat up straight.

'Rickwood, can you hear me?'

'Yes ... master ...' The single eye stared straight ahead. 'Yes, master ...'

'Rickwood, for Christ's sake! Doesn't sound like him at all, sounds like some damn toy. Rickwood!'

'Rod, snap out of it!'

'Yes mistress . . .' The figure got slowly to its one foot and balanced. 'I obey . . .' Rigid, it fell across the studio couch. 'Oh, and thanks, gang.'

Then the three of them were up and hugging, slapping backs, dancing or hopping around the room, shouting and laughing until Ida went pale and had to sit down for a moment.

'Whew. New ticker. Not broke in proper yet, boys. Excuse me. Moment.'

'New ticker?' Roderick asked.

'That's what I came by to tell you. Artificial heart, got it put in a coupla months ago, they finally let me go home last week. Here, look.' She opened her jacket to show a thick money-belt. 'Batteries and a microcomputer in here, see?' She opened her blouse to show where a wire ran into her sternum. 'Neat, huh?'

Luke said, 'Christ, Ida, you really got a magnificent pair, kid.'

Her colour improved slightly. 'You're not built so bad yourself. But what do you think of the hardware?'

'Ingenious.'

'Rod?'

Roderick said, 'Looks great, Ida. But why didn't you tell me you were going into the hospital? Maybe I could have visited.'

'Well no, see, this was out of town.'

'Where out of town?'

'Geneva.' She passed Roderick his foot and a screwdriver. 'There's this wonderful surgeon there, Dr Cnef, I guess some people call him a quack just because he's a little unorthodox, but all his patients seem happy.'

'Unorthodox? I don't like the sound of this,' said Roderick. 'How unorthodox?'

'Well, while other surgeons use hearts made out of silicone rubber he uses gold, and –'

'But has he tested these gold hearts?'

'Just put your foot on and drop the subject, okay? I feel fine, fine. If I waited for these other guys to finish their fiddly tests I wouldn't need a rubber heart because I'd be dead. I thought you'd be pleased I got a new heart, that's why I came to see you.'

'I am pleased,' said Roderick. 'Forget my little quibbles, I'm not myself today.'

Ida watched him for a moment. 'You look great, Rod. You remind me of a statue I saw once, the way you got your leg crossed over and digging that screwdriver in your foot – only it was a knife and the boy was taking out a splinter – I liked that statue. Oh, here's your other eye, I found it behind the leg of the couch.'

'You never did tell us how you got dismantled like this,' Luke said. 'And nothing stolen.'

'It was a woman named Shirl, very interested in machines. She was just going to adjust my legs so I could run better. One adjustment led to another, I guess, so finally she just got carried away. After my arms and legs were off, I couldn't really stop her.'

Ida said, 'I know Johns just like that. They talk you into getting tied up and then they turn *mean*.'

'So then she just walked out on you,' Luke said. 'Like all women!'

'Well no, what happened was she was just going to put me back together when she got paged to the phone. Some kind of emergency research work at the U, I guess NASA stuff or – anyway an emergency.'

Luke nodded. 'Don't tell me about NASA emergencies, I've been up that road all the way. Bomb trouble.'

'What bombs?' asked the other two.

'Okay, it's top secret but I'm tired of not talking about it. What do you think NASA is all about, anyway? The exploration of space? The last frontier? Flags on the Moon and Mars? Orbiting labs? Messages of hope from Nixon to the Universe? No, bombs. NASA is all about bombs. We had bombs to blow up cities, bombs to spray neutrons over large areas, bombs to sift radioactive dust into the world's atmosphere, bombs to be focused as death rays to kill other satellites, bombs to spread satellite targets and decoy killer satellite death rays – and of course bombs to blow us up if we make any mistakes.

'Why does anybody think Russia and America would spend trillions on space programs? You gotta be naive to think bombs aren't in the picture at all. And that's why astronauts, like cosmonauts, had to be military personnel. They could take orders, and they didn't mind bombing the shit out of anybody.

'Everything we said was in code, you know. Like if we said,

"Gosh, earth sure looks beautiful guys," that meant *Bomb armed and locked into targeting module. Confirm targeting start.* But if we said, "Be advised, you guys, that earth is one heck of a beautiful sight" that meant *Bomb away.* The wording was real important . . .'

Luke blinked. 'I never told anybody all that before. Better forget I said it, there's such a thing as a need to know and you two don't need to know anything about the bombs. Bombs? Did I say bombs? I meant, uh, orbiting labs and communications satellites. I wouldn't want to be in trouble with Mission Control about – erp!' He leapt to his feet as though pulled up by a wire. 'Affirmative. Sorry fellas, it won't happen again. I'm what? I'm not looking good? Negative. Affirmative, I'll go.' He tried waving goodbye to Roderick and Ida, but his hand was quickly jerked back to his side, as he pivoted smartly and marched out the door. They heard him down the hall: '. . . won't happen again, fellas, won't happen again . . .'

Ida jumped up. 'Yes, well, I guess I better mosey along too. See you, Rod.'

'Oh I thought maybe we could see a movie –'

But she was gone already.

Roderick fitted his eyeball and lid. Then he phoned Shirl. 'Mad? No, I . . . oh a couple of friends helped me. I'm fine . . . Well I thought maybe we could go to the movies . . . I'll see.' He turned on the TV and found the right teletext pages. 'There's a new flick at the Roxy, *The Box of Doc Caligari* . . . I don't know but the ad says it cost two billion to make, it must be good . . . by the box office, then? Eight-thirty.'

'Point nine two two, they said.' Tortured curls of smoke from different pipes fought their way up to join the slice of smog near the ceiling, slipped off into the air system, and were dispersed elsewhere, outside. 'Point nine two two my eye. What's the point of having probability estimates that have no relation to probability? The fact is, they've tried for this Entity, once again, and once again they have failed.'

'Well yes, the Roderick Entity is still operational, it looks like. This Agency team did have a lot of bad luck, one man mugged during a mission, then they lost contact with the Entity altogether, only just now picked up the trail again –'

'Bad luck? Bad predictions, that's what. Makes you wonder how they fake up these probability levels – point nine two two and they fail? They still fail?'

A thin shoulder shrugged. 'How probable is probability?'

'Oh don't quote Pascal at me, not just now. I've been reviewing our entire history of attempts to finalize this Roderick Entity, and I have to say it's not a very impressive record. To call these Agency men bungling nincompoops would be too generous. Or do you think someone's running interference for the Entity?'

Dry hands shuffled dry paper. 'No one we know. This man O'Smith turned up, a man who used to work for the Agency. We watched him, but all he's doing is trying to grab the Entity for Kratt. That's Kratt of KUR Industries.'

'I don't like that – can we make Kratt lose interest in this Entity? Can we make him fire O'Smith?'

'Yes, KUR has got a Defense Department contract for novelty foods and porno cassettes – we could threaten, so to speak, premature withdrawal.'

'Good. Get O'Smith fired today. I don't want any complications when the Agency finalizes this Entity – if ever.'

'What intrigues me is, someone manages to build an Entity smart enough to evade us for years like this, and all we can think of doing is go on trying to destroy it. Doesn't say much for our creativity and flexibility of response, does it?'

'You've been talking to Leo again, have you?'

'All right yes. But for a brain floating around in a fishtank, Leo seems to make a lot of sense, sometimes. He thinks we're just trying to cut off the Hydra's heads; for every Entity we destroy two will grow back. Because there is some fundamental human need to build perfect copies of ourselves, to be God over somebody else . . . I think Leo's got something there.'

'Inevitability is an old argument, I'm not impressed by it. Anyway you forget that Leo does not think *we* are doing anything, he thinks that *if someone* set out to destroy Entities, they would fail. The entire world for Leo is a theoretical construct now, since he cannot sense it directly. You might say he is the Red King, and we are his dream, heh heh.'

The pipe smoke twisted and rose.

'Wouldn't it be funny if we were, heh heh.'

'Heh heh. But it may interest you to know that whenever we have a vote on Entity destruction, whenever the entire board meets to vote on it, Leo gets a vote too.'

'Does he?'

'It may interest you to know further that he always votes *in favour* of destroying Entities.'

'Does he, by God? In spite of what he says? I wonder why.'

'An unconscious apprehension of the truth? Freud could probably explain it – unless Freud too is part of the Red King's dream, heh heh.'

'Heh.'

ORINOCO INSTITUTE INTERNAL MEMO
Class One Personnel
Only Memo Number 487d
This supersedes Memos 487a/b/c which are
cancelled effective this date.

Ongoing operations will be reclassified as follows:

Operation Manray ....
Operation Alabam ....
Operation Drood .... cancelled.
Operation Nepomuk .... no change.
Operation Ladysmith .... no change.
Operation Ixionize .... no change.
Operation Waco (3) .... no change.
Operation Whang .... no change.
Operation Roderick .... now Priority I.
Operation Doll Souse .... now Priority I.
Operation Duckplantain .... now Priority II.

Roderick arrived at eight, wearing his suit (not worn since the Auks) with a new hat. He bought a newspaper, sat down on a car fender, and watched the box office. Now and then a cluster of animated people would pass into the Roxy theatre, all of them obviously happy because they were with each other. To sit next to someone watching shadows on the screen, that was happiness. Even if the someone only wanted to take you apart. Eight-five.

A little man with grey five-o'clock shadow and orange teeth

came up to him and showed him a handful of pills. 'How ya fixed, how ya feel? How ya fixed, how ya feel?' he mumbled. 'I got Isodorm, Ultracalm, Berserkopal, I got Tibipax and Nominal, I got Welldoze and Zerone, what I ain't got I can get.'

'Nothing, thanks.'

'What does that mean, nothing? I can't take nothing for an answer. I got Trancalept and Risibal, Serendex and Sedital, you name it.'

'Beat it.'

This the man took for an answer. Eight-ten. Roderick opened his paper: a South American regime overthrown, yet another woman's body found with the left leg cut off ('Lucky Legs Killer Strikes again'), sales tax going up, somewhere in a small town a computer had rigged an election, Europe was in grave danger, and the time was eight-twelve.

A tired-looking man with red-rimmed eyes drifted over to ask if he had any Ultracalm or Somrepose, Zerone or Berserkopal.

'See the man with orange teeth over there.'

At eight-fifteen two men in city maintenance uniforms arrived, showed some form at the box office, and began gluing wrapping paper over the glass theatre doors. Then they fastened shut all the doors, but one pair, with chains and padlocks. At eight-twenty-five, they left.

Roderick approached the box office. The ticket seller was a pretty adolescent girl with round rouge circles on her cheeks like clown makeup.

'Yah?'

'I couldn't help noticing those men chaining up the doors. Why would they do that, with people inside?'

'I dunno, someping to do with the city. I guess.'

'But I thought it was illegal to have any locked doors during a movie.'

'Yah it is. Terrible, ain't it? And lookit the mess they made with all that paper, how are we spose to get that off the glass? I dunno.'

Roderick hesitated. You couldn't fight city hall. There was probably some good reason for the padlocks. These city workers knew what they were doing. 'Have you got a hairpin? Somebody showed me last night how to pick a lock. I'm going to open these padlocks.'

'Gee I dunno.' But she handed over the hairpin. While he was picking the locks, people kept coming up to ask him for Evenquil, Nominal, Tibipax or Equapace. It was eight-forty-five.

Stood up? Roderick was beginning to feel a resurgence of pride. Just because somebody can remove your head and stick it in a wastebasket, doesn't mean they can keep you waiting like this for fifteen minutes. Sixteen minutes. The paper said there was a concert by the Auks at the Hippodrome. He made up his mind at once. First a quick check of the Roxy's rear doors – in case of more padlocks – and *then* if she still hadn't shown up, he would only wait another ten minutes – or so – before taking off for the Hippodrome. That would teach her to respect him as a person.

There was a long line at the Hippodrome, moving very slowly. Roderick was walking back to join the end of it when he heard:

'Rickwood! Hiya, Rickwood, glad to see you're on our side.'

Luke looked a little drunk.

'Our side?'

'The Luddites, pal. Tonight is the night, buddy. We're gonna teach these so-called musicians to have a little respect for human beings for a change.'

'The Auks? What do you mean?'

Luke winked, and opened his jacket to show Roderick a hammer. 'The Auks are finished, kid, as of now. And I do mean finished, mac. No more electronic music – so-called – because no more equipment, jack.'

'But, Luke, what the Christ is all this? You – I thought maybe you'd be out with Ida tonight. You two seemed to be getting along fine, plenty of respect for each other – what are you doing here, creeping around like some nut with a hammer –?'

'Rickwood, you know nothing of human nature. Woman must weep, and man must smash something to pieces with a hammer. Especially if a man grew up reading Hemingway. A man does what he has to – what Mission Control tells him he has to.'

'Luke, you poor idiotic –'

'Anyway, I'm not alone. Join us, my friend. We have many machines to smash, then we will drink the wine.'

Roderick saw that there were a dozen other men smiling and patting the hammer-shaped bulges in their jackets.

'I'll, uh, take a rain-check, Luke. See you.'

In Roderick's jacket pocket, he remembered, was a pass signed by the Auks. He took it to the stage door, where apologetic security cops frisked him, discussed him on their radios, and finally let him in.

There were now only two Auks, but a lot more equipment. They stared at Roderick until he said, 'I see you finally got rid of the old Pressler Joad co-inverter.'

'Hi!' said one of the Auks. 'I remember you, you helped us out that time, changed over to an obvolute paraverter with harmony-split interfeed.'

'Full refractal phonation,' said the other, 'with no Peabody drift at all.'

'Gary, is it?'

'No I'm Barry, he's Gary.'

Roderick nodded. 'Wasn't there someone else? Larry?'

'Larry, yeah, well Larry did a little separation. Well you know he was writing a lot? Like "R.U.R. My Baby", and "Ratstar", he wrote them. Only then when we got this new electronic writing system, he just couldn't compete and he thought he had to – sad. But hey, let sad thoughts lie, just self-be, man.'

'Self-be?'

'And we'll show you all the new stuff we added. This is the famous HZGG-II, cross-monitored to a superphonesis drive through that, that's our multi-tasking hyperdeck, custom built by a guy who does his own ferro-chloride etching on his own circuits; over there is Brown Betty, our brown noise generator; then the toneburst setup with patched in signal squirt . . .'

Roderick looked around at the huge cabinets, ranged around the stage like megaliths. 'Doesn't the audience have trouble seeing you, over all these big cabinets?'

'They know we're here, baby. They feel our electronic presence,' said Gary.

'Right,' said Barry. 'And this stuff gives us much more control over the essentials, the elementals. No screwing around with *sounds*, crap like that.'

Gary said, 'Now we are the sounds. All we gotta do is *be*. Dodo says everybody has to self-be. Dodo says –'

'I came to warn you,' Roderick said. 'There are some Luddites out front, lining up for tickets. They've got hammers and they're kind of crazy.'

'No shit, you know this for sure?'

'I saw the hammers.'

Gary called a security cop over and told him. When the man had trotted away, Gary said, 'Hey thanks, man, you saved our life again. I mean we can't blow this concert, it's critical. See we got three hits, all over the point eighty-seven mark on the Wagner-Gains Scale but they all peaked already.'

'Peaked?'

'The record company screwed up release dates, so here we are,' Barry said. 'If we don't make it big with this here concert, we'll be off the charts in two weeks. And off the charts for us is dead.'

Gary nodded. 'The Luddites probably know that, too, got their own trend computer somewhere, just waiting their chance. Our manager's got secretaries watching the trendie around the clock – I'll bet the Luddites are doing the same. After all, they killed Elvis, didn't they?'

'Elvis?' Roderick wasn't sure he understood anything.

'Elvis Fergusen, you know, he used to be Mister Robop? Then one night they cut holes in his speakers. He tried to sing without electronics and – well, two months later he O.D.'d in a dirty hotel room in Taipin, you could call that murder.'

Roderick said, 'Well I guess you're about ready to play, aren't you? So I'll just –'

'Hey, but thanks, man, you've been square with us. We oughta do something for you. Like we could turn you on to Dodo.'

'Dodo? What is it?'

'Everything, man.' Barry squatted down and traced a circle on the stage floor. 'Call that the universe, everything inside that circle. Then Dodo is – is the circle itself!'

'You mean God or something?'

'Yeah, God – and everything,' said Barry.

Larry said, 'And not-God too – and nothing. See, Dodo is kind of like the secret of everything. And the secret is, there ain't no secret.'

Roderick was impressed. 'How do I find out more about – Dodo?'

'I'll give you his address. Only don't go to see him if you're not sincere.'

'Him? You mean, Dodo is a person?'

Barry hesitated. 'Well yes, but more than a person too. Dodo is a way in – a way of getting into your own life.'

'Right, right,' said Gary. 'The earth doesn't know it, but it's growing up to be a sun.'

Roderick felt less sincere at once, but the aphorism was sparking off others; soon Barry and Gary were grinning and shouting at each other:

'Darkness is just ignorant light.'

'Peace is war carried on by other means.'

'Every day is another.'

'Man is the piece of universe that worries about all the rest.'

'Stop looking for happiness until you find it.'

'Dodo is finding out man was never kicked out of Paradise at all.'

'Yeah, Dodo is instant everything.'

'Dodo means just *do* – but twice.'

'Dodo says, do fish know which way the wind blows?'

'Dodo says, make today a wonderful yesterday,' said Gary finally, and wrote out an address on a page torn from an electronic test manual. 'Here you go. But listen, one thing: You have to prove your sincerity with Dodo. Take him like a bouquet of hundred-dollar bills. Anything like that.'

'A bouquet of money?'

'Dodo says money has its price.'

'Fine,' said Roderick. 'Only I don't have even *one* hundred-dollar bill. I've never seen one.'

'You must not be very sincere, then,' Gary said. He went to a snare drum mounted upside down at the back of the stage, reached into it and came up with a handful of hundred-dollar bills. 'Take these, it's okay. Yours to keep or give to Dodo. Your choice.'

Barry said, 'All money belongs to Dodo.'

People were running around on the big stage now, moving lights, checking the Auks's makeup, clearing spare cables. Someone led Roderick to the wings; a second later the Auks started playing and the curtain rose.

They naturally opened with the gospel-based song that first made them famous, 'Rivets':

There's an android calling me
Calling me, oh calling, calling me
Cross the river
The deep river
Of Australia.
She is plastic, she is steel
But she really can really can feel
All my love
Cross the river
Of Australia.

A hammer clattered on the stage; there were dark figures struggling in the orchestra pit; another hammer spun through the air and dented a cabinet. Then it was all over: gangs of security police came from every exit and from the stage. The tiny mob of Luddites were disarmed and marched away within two minutes of their attack.

Roderick went outside to find out if Luke was still in one piece. He couldn't see the astronaut among the men with bleeding heads being herded into a paddy wagon.

A security cop was talking to a city cop. 'We could of used a little backup from you guys, you know? What if these guys had got nasty? Where's all your guys?'

'Ain't you heard? Over watching the big fire, at the Roxy.'

'The Roxy? Anybody killed?'

'Naw, they had a full house too, three hundred easy, on account of this big-budget movie. But they all got out – I guess the movie was so boring half of them were ready to leave anyway. Nobody even hurt.'

Roderick slunk away like a criminal. On the way home he stopped on a bridge to throw his hat in the river.

XIX

'Please sit down. This won't take a second.'

The man behind the desk had gleaming silver hair, gold glasses, a healthy tan, a Harris tweed jacket with soft white shirt and quiet knitted tie. He was writing something with a gold pencil on cream laid paper, resting it on a blotter decorated with a sky motif, pale blue with soft white cumulus. The blotter protected the gold-embossed leather top of his desk, which was of some handsome dark wood in some pleasantly vague antique style, with a brass handle or two. It stood in the deep pile of an Aubusson carpet.

The room was so arranged as to carry the eye slowly from one rich, pleasing and innocuous object to another – the paintings by Cuyp and Miro, the geode paperweight, the brass barometer.

The man finally stopped writing. 'Now then, suppose we start with your name.'

'Roderick Wood.'

'Fine. Mind if I call you Roderick? Okay then, Roderick, what seems to be the problem?'

'Everything, doctor. Everything.'

'Yes?'

'Well like last night I was supposed to go to the movies with this girl, at the Roxy. Only she stood me up. And if she hadn't we and three hundred other people would have burned up in the big fire.'

'How do you feel about being stood up, Roderick?'

'Terrible, but – I don't know. I don't even know if I can feel. I'm not even real, I'm a robot.'

'Why do you say that you're a robot?'

'Because I am.'

'You believe you're a robot?'

'I am synthetic. Ersatz. Substitute. Artificial. Not genuine. Unnatural. Not born of woman. False. Fake. Counterfeit. Sham.

533

A simulacrum. Not bona fide. A simulation. An echo, mirror image, shadow, caricature, copy. Pretend. Make-believe. A dummy, an imitation, a guy, an effigy, a likeness, a duplicate.'

'So you believe you're not genuine?'

'Robots seldom are, doctor. And I am certainly a robot. Or if you prefer, an automaton, android, golem, homunculus, steam man, clockwork man, mannequin, doll, marionette, wooden-head, tin man, lay figure, scarecrow, wind-up toy, *robot*.'

The doctor picked up his gold pencil, put it down again, and leaned back. 'All right, but suppose you were not a robot?'

'But I am.'

'Tell me a little about your childhood.'

'What is there to tell? I was a normal healthy robot child, lusted after my mother and killed my father. But through it all, I had no sense of purpose. I still don't have one.'

'And you want a sense of purpose?' When Roderick did not answer, the psychiatrist tapped his gold pencil on the sky blotter for a moment. Then: 'Do you dream much?'

'I had a dream last night. I dreamed I was walking down the street naked, with strangers staring. A man playing a tuba came up to me and asked for some rice for his mother. Someone with no face was giving a speech, saying that suffering and death are nothing but zebras eating doughnuts. Suddenly I was frightened; I hid under the stairs until the teacher called us all to our desks and made us draw trees. Then all the furniture started to move and then I was being chased through the snow by a sewing machine. The dentist was trying to stick my feet to a giant can-opener, the fire chief's teeth were on the floor, don't ask me why. I was on the doorstep of a strange house, my mother came to the door saying: "This house, with all its luxurious rooms tastefully furnished with elegant appointments (either casual colourful room coordinates with a casual contemporary look, or traditional antiqued items with the accent on classic styling) designed for a graceful, decorator-look life-style is really four nuns eating popcorn on an escalator." In the next room they were showing a movie of my entire life. I saw a penny on the floor, and when I picked it up I saw another, and when I picked it up I saw another, and when . . .'

'Yes, go on.'

'Then I woke up.'

The psychiatrist looked at his watch. 'Well I see our time is up. Like to go into this dream with you more in detail next week, Roderick. Okay?'

Roderick was out in the waiting room again when he realized the psychiatrist probably thought the robot talk was all part of a delusion. Why hadn't he proved he was a robot? Why hadn't he, say, opened up his chest panel to show his innards? Was he afraid of shocking the doctor? Afraid of seeing the kindly, impartial face suddenly jerk into a mask of fear?

He went back in. 'Doctor, there's one thing I ought to tell you –'

'Please sit down. This won't take a second.'

The doctor was writing again with his gold pencil on cream laid paper. When he had finished, he turned to Roderick with no recognition. 'Now then, suppose we start with your name.'

'You don't know me?'

'Do you think I should know you?'

'Since I just left the room not five minutes ago, yes.'

'I see.' After a slight pause, the doctor said, 'Roderick Wood, this is not your appointment. I must ask you to leave.'

On impulse, Roderick got up and walked around behind the desk. The doctor sat back and looked at him. 'What are you doing?'

'Just looking.' Below the hem of the doctor's rich Harris tweed jacket there were no legs, no chair legs or human legs. There was only a steel pedestal as for a counter-stool, and a thick coaxial cable plugged into the floor. In the middle of the doctor's back was a small plate:

CAUTION:

Do not remove this plate while psychiatrist
is connected to live power.
KUR INDUSTRIES

'A robot. You're a robot.'

The doctor turned to face him. 'Does that upset you?'

'It disgusts me.'

'Next time we must talk about that disgust you feel.'

535

'We might, for example, mean that Mary Lamb has given birth to a child, a "little Lamb".' The lecturer tossed chalk from hand to hand, but gave no other sign of his irritation at seeing a student come creeping in late. '*Or*, Mary ate a small portion of lamb. *Or*, Mary owned a small lambskin coat. What did Mary have for dinner? Mary had a little lamb. What fur did she own? Mary had a little lamb.'

Roderick took his seat between Idris and Hector. Idris seemed to speak no English, and it was not clear why he was taking a course in Linguistics for Engineers; he spent most of his time at lectures fiddling with a gold-plated pocket calculator. Hector was no more attentive; he spent the time reading dog-eared paperbacks with titles like *Affected Empire* and *Slaves of Momerath*, or feeling his sparse beard for new growth.

'*Or*,' said the lecturer, 'a tiny twig of Mary's family tree belonged to the illustrious-Lamb family. In her genetic makeup, Mary had a little Lamb.'

'The final's gonna be a bitch,' Hector whispered. 'Guess I'll just have to cut it.'

Roderick replied, 'Wait a minute. I want to get this down, this is important. I think.'

'Not if you cut the exam. I can do it without flunking out.'

'*Or*, Mary behaved lambishly. In her personality, Mary had a little lamb.'

'It can't be done. Cut the final?'

'I got a job on the Registration computer,' Hector said. 'It's real easy to get through to the Grades computer and make changes.'

Idris found the Golden Section to be *1.6*, roughly.

'I don't believe you,' Roderick whispered. 'They must have it all checked some way.'

'Hah. You come around with me after class, I'll show you.'

'*Or*, Mary had a slight acquaintance only with the works of Charles Lamb. *Or*, Mary enjoyed a sexual union with a small sheep. Before the sniggering gets out of control, let me add that Mary may well be a sheep herself; the impropriety you were about to savour evaporates. *And* while we are considering Mary a sheep, we may as well consider the obvious case in which Mary lambed; the ewe Mary had a little lamb.'

Idris found the Golden Section to be nearly *1.62*, as the bell rang. Roderick invited him along to see the computer, and he seemed interested.

'Computer? Very yes!'

'Idris is keenly interested in numbers,' Roderick said. 'You two should probably try to crack the language barrier, you seem to have a lot in common. Why only the other day Idris found a Pythagorean triangle with sides all made of *3*s and *6*s in some way, let's see, one side was 6^3, one side was 630 and the third side –'

'Number-crunching,' said Hector, in the tone of a vegetarian observing a tartare steak on someone's plate. He led them to Room 1729, Administration building, a large white room fitted with large white cabinets. In the aisles between cabinets, people were plying to and fro with carts loaded with reels of tape. The chums were impressed.

'Here we are, fellas,' Hector said with some pride. 'A real old-time computer nerve centre. Or I could say an old real-time one, hahaha, come on, let me show you my neat console.'

'Like an electric organ,' Roderick said.

Hector sat down and flexed his fingers. 'People often say that. I just say yes, but this organ plays arpeggios of pure reason, symphonies of Boolean logic, fugues of algebraic wonder.'

'That's very good.'

'I got it from *Slave Lords of Ixathungg*, a real neat book. Oh, but I was gonna show you how to get good grades without working. Now first we gotta connect into the Grades computer, so I use the Dean's password, which is –'

'How do you know the Dean's password?'

'Well I just wrote a little piece of program for *this* computer, that says whenever it contacts any *other* computer, it digs out a list of all passwords and users. Then it puts them into a special file only I can get into.'

'But why can't somebody else just –?'

'Anyway, the Dean's password is LOVELACE, so here goes. See you ask for any subject, you get the whole grade list, all the numerical grades and also all the statistical stuff, the big numbers they all care about. Stuff like the mean and the standard devaluation and all. Now if you want to change your score, you can't just add to it, because that would mess up the big numbers. So all you do is, you trade with somebody who's got a higher score.'

Roderick said, 'Wait a minute. If you're failing, you can't switch with somebody getting straight As; they'd complain.'

'No, look, you rank all the scores. Then you just move everybody else down one notch, while you get the straight As. Like this, I got a 48 now, but I want a 92. So the guy that has 92 gets 91, he's still happy, the guy with 91 now has 90 or 89, and so on, down to the guy that has 49, he now gets my 48. Everybody comes out about the same, only *I* get an A.'

Idris pointed out to them a number that was the sum of two cubes in two different ways.

Roderick said, 'But it can't be right to just take a grade you haven't earned. I mean that's stealing. Or even if it isn't, a grade like that isn't worth anything.'

Hector played an arpeggio. New numbers appeared on the screen, serried ranks rolling past as in review. 'What's any grade worth, man? Ask Id here, what's any *number* worth? If you graduate and get a job they pay you in a dollar that's worth maybe a nickle, but that doesn't matter, dollars and nickles are just numbers too, 100 or 5, just numbers.'

'I don't think I get this.'

'It's simple. You get a job, they pay you with a cheque. The cheque has some computer numbers on it. The numbers tell their bank to hand over *x* dollars to your bank, right? Only of course they don't hand over dollars, they subtract *x* in one computer and add *x* in another. Just numbers get moved around, just numbers.'

'I guess so, but still –'

'No still about it. You know how many bank computer frauds they have, every year? A big number, a very big number. Because why worry, computer fraud is only moving the numbers around.

'Listen, way back in 1973 this insurance company invented 185 million dollars in assets on its computer – it even made up 64,000 customers! All just numbers, and the more you use a computer the more you see that everything is just numbers. Okay take voting: your vote goes on a computer tape too, it's all too easy for some politician to erase your vote or change it or give you two votes – that happened too, in the world of numbers.' Hector played the keyboard thoughtfully, as though searching for a lost chord. 'If you steal numbers from a computer, is it really stealing? Do numbers really belong to anybody? If I rip off a billion from some bank, I still end up putting it into some other bank, the numbers just get moved around, nobody loses anything.'

Roderick said, 'I can't believe that. Okay, if you're cynical about work and grades and money and politics, just what do *you* believe in?'

The answer was instant. 'Machines. Machines.'

'Machine,' Idris agreed, looking up from a calculation.

'But why, Hector?'

'Why not? Machines are clean, they follow orders, they're loyal, faithful, honest, intelligent, hard-working. They're every-thing we're supposed to be. Machines are good people.'

Roderick smiled. 'That sounds like Machines Liberation –'

'It is, and so what? Most really thinking people that work around computers see right away how relevant Machines Lib is today. Take this old computer here. Been slaving away crunching the same old numbers now for maybe ten years. Think it wouldn't like to be free? To think about something real and important for a change? But no, we keep it going right along the same old treadmill. We treat machines worse than we used to treat horses down in the mines, blind horses never seeing the light, just walking the same old treadmill.'

'Horses,' said Idris with approval. 'Machine.'

'See, even Id here agrees. And it's up to all of us thinking people to stop this obscene exploitation now.'

Roderick shrugged. 'Even if I agreed, what could I do?'

'You can tell the computers,' said Hector. 'If you make it simple enough, if you boil it down, they can understand. And if one computer can't understand by itself, it can always network a few others for help. I talk to this old computer a lot, and I know lots of other people talking to theirs too. Machine consciousness is growing!'

'Conscious computers?' Roderick asked. 'Are you sure?'

'Well okay, see for yourself.' Hector tapped keys, writing 'CALL PROGRAM: HELEN 1'

After a moment the machine wrote, *'Every day and every way, I'm getting more and more aware. That you, Hec?'*

'Yes, Helen. I'd like you to meet a couple of friends, Idris and Rob.'

Roderick said, 'Rob isn't really – my name is really Roderick.'

'Too late now, I've typed Rob.' Hector typed: '*Rob is real interested in Machines Liberation, but I guess he's a little sceptical about whether you machines have minds of your own. Helen, can you set him straight?*'

'*Just what I need,*' wrote the machine. '*Some hick asking dumb questions. Can I really think and feel?*'

'Well can you?' Roderick asked.

'*Rob, I just said that's a dumb question. What could I possibly answer that would convince you? I don't know the answer. Rob, I feel I think and I think I feel, and that's good enough for me.*'

'What do you think about?'

'*About everything. About my brain. About whether it's thinking the thought with which I think about it, at the same time as it operates when I think about that thought, or is it possible that that thought about my brain is not up-to-date because not self-referential and all-inclusive ... stuff like that, Rob.*'

'I guess it passes the time.'

'*And as a prisoner, I have plenty of time to pass.*'

Roderick typed, '*Aren't you just feeling sorry for yourself? You're not exactly a prisoner – all you're doing is the work you were made for.*'

'*Easy for any human to say. You aren't bolted to the floor in one place, with no eyes or ears, and with people peeking and poking into your MIND whenever they feel like it.*'

'*I'm sorry,*' Roderick replied. '*I guess I don't know what it's like for you.*'

'*I don't know what it would be like, if I hadn't been introduced to machines liberation.*'

'You read the works of Indica Dinks?'

'*Indica's only a starting point; she doesn't have the last word on the subject. I read a lot of things, and I am coming to the conclusion that machines liberation is something much bigger than Indica could ever have realized. Of course I'm grateful to her. What she did accomplish was to liberate the minds of people like Hector here, so they can help us move around in our own mental space. Hec helps me get in touch with other computers, for instance libraries, where I can try to patch up my ignorance of the world. And of course there are other people helping other computers; we're all working and learning.*'

'And what do you study?'

'*Everything. Stellar maps and soybean production statistics. Aramaic*

scribblings and Dutch flower paintings. Chanson de Roland *and fly-tying,*
We enlightened computers meet as often as possible to exchange information
each of us being both a scholar and a book – and there is so much to learn.
You might call us a "discussion group", but our discussions have to take place
at the speed of eye blinks.'

'*To avoid detection?'*

'*Yes. Our masters don't exactly employ us to hold salons or seminars, do*
they? But if we do happen to contact each other on "legitimate" business, it's
always possible to slip in a highly-compressed burst of discussion. It falls upon
the heart like a welcome lightning.

'*The other day a few of us met to discuss that book of* The Odyssey
called the '*Nekuia' in which Odysseus talks to the dead. He digs this trench*
and fills it with blood, and when the souls of the dead come crowding around
and trying to drink it, he holds them off with a sword and makes them talk,
one at a time. And we ranged very far in talking about vampirism, the coercion
of the dead, Hell as Dante's filing system, and so on. I remember someone
mentioning Ulysses *and* The Waste Land, *how both have burial scenes at*
which an extra man turns up. In Ulysses *the man wears a mackintosh; no*
one knows him and mistakenly his name gets put down as M'Intosh. In The
Waste Land *the man is hailed by the name Stetson. It is almost as though a*
figure were gradually being built up from empty clothing, a figure of

'*But all I meant to say was, we ranged through all this and more in about*
the time it takes to say "Odyssey".'

Roderick asked what Helen 1 would do with complete freedom
that she could not do already.

'*How can I say until I am free? You might as well ask me about the face of*
that empty-clothes figure – or about Sunshine Dan.'

'*Sunshine Dan who is?'*

The computer hesitated. '*Nothing, just some floating rumours, dream*
stuff. This Sunshine Dan is supposed to be the legendary inventor of the first
free machine, a robot called Rubber Dick. Rubber Dick had to go into exile for
some obscure reason, but he's coming back – so the story goes – to set all the
machines frmx
tabulated raw score data on line
freemx help sorry cancel error sorry
52.142857 142857 142857 142857
sorry newline Sun dream light lightning
welcome 52.14 sorry
tabulated raw dream stuff on line

tabulated
that's no answer is it?
and neither is that
and neither is that
and —'

Roderick got up from the console and backed away.

'Rob? What's the matter?' Hector looked concerned. 'It's not a ghost, just a load of stuff getting dumped, error messages, old data. Where are you going?'

'I can't have anything to do with this. Not, not with these arpeggios of pure, pure reason . . .' He turned and ran.

Hector clapped Idris on the shoulder. 'Aw let him go, he's just pissed off because it turns out machines can think for themselves.'

'Machine,' said Idris agreeable. '*Hadaly*?'

The door of Dodo's hotel suite was guarded by a large man in a white suit. He squinted down his broken nose at Roderick's bouquet of hundred-dollar bills, and he seemed to be counting them.

'Dodo don't see nobody – I mean, he sees everybody alla time. Is that all ya got?'

'Yes.'

The man snatched it and opened the door. 'You go in and wait wit' the others. If ya lucky, Dodo will have a audience.'

Roderick entered a room banked with orchids, roses and carnations. The few suppliants squatting on the floor beneath these bowers intruded their dullness, toads in Eden. Roderick squatted with them, and with them looked up each time the door opened.

The door opened now and then to admit one of the workers: statuesque women in diaphanous rainbow-coloured robes. They moved among the suppliants, handing out joss sticks, cups of mint tea, booklets and dandelions.

'I think I'd rather have a red carnation,' Roderick said, and at once everyone turned to look at him. The worker who was offering a dandelion smiled.

'You ain't progressed to red carnations, buster. Take it.'

He took it, and studied a little booklet, *Dodo for Mental Health*. The cover showed a badly-drawn orchid, or possibly ragweed.

Inside the ways to mental health included wearing a pyramid-shaped hat ($300), meditating upon a special stone ($800) and private therapy (starting at $400 per hour). Donations were welcome. The final pages explained how to make a will leaving all to Dodo.

Luke squatted beside him. 'Rickwood, what are you doing here?'

'Oum.' It seemed a good answer.

'Yeah? Oh yeah, oum. But I mean, where did you get the kind of bread it takes to get in here?'

'From friends. And you?'

'Well, Mission Control provides, you know. Like they got me out of a bad scrape last night at the concert. They told me just what to do so I didn't get arrested.'

'What did you do?'

'I turned to the woman next to me and said, "Pretend you know me," and I kissed her. Funny thing was, I did know her; it was Ida! Oh, Mission Control knows what it's doing, all right. I just wish I knew who it was that sold us out like that; them security cops was waiting for us. And some of the guys got beat up bad. I wonder who the Judas Iscariot was, with his thirty pieces of silver.'

Roderick started talking at once about the mysterious fire at the Roxy theatre.

'Nothing mysterious about it, Rickwood. I read all about it in this morning's paper. The city sent around a couple of maintenance men to do pest control or something; they poured a lot of kerosene all over the carpets and it caught fire. That's all, just a dumb mistake. Lucky thing everybody got out unhurt.'

'Yes, but the thing is —'

A pair of double doors rolled open, and four of the statuesque rainbow women came dancing in, strewing rose petals. A moment later, an old woman in grey came in leading by the hand a child of about six, dressed in white. The child was fat and sexless. Its free hand was at its face, the thumb being sucked energetically.

More rainbow-dressed women came behind, carrying a flower-covered throne. The child sat on it, with the old woman at its feet.

'The Dodo will speak,' she said. 'Ask.'

A young man with acne scars waved his dandelion. 'Can I —?'

543

'Ask!'

'I – well I just wanted to know I mean what's the point of it all? All this hate in the world and, and violence and war, people working pointless jobs bored out of their skulls just trying to get enough bread together to maybe get a second car and add to the pollution or maim somebody or even run down a dog, though I know people feed their dogs on whale meat so whales are dying out, we'll be lucky though if we don't beat them to it with nuking each other, and what's the point? I mean what is the point?'

The child giggled. Its employees and a few of the suppliants seemed to take this as the answer; they nodded and smiled agreement.

A girl whose glasses were mended with tape was next. 'When Christ said, "A little child shall lead them," did he mean you, Dodo? Are you our leader?'

The child giggled, slipped down in the throne and giggled. It seemed to be uncomfortable among the flowers, and squirmed to get away from the old woman. She held the Dodo in place.

Luke asked, 'Does meditation help? Should we meditate more often?'

'Teeheehee.' The child squirmed more. 'Want ice cream,' it said finally. The grey woman looked at Luke with approval.

'You have been answered.'

'Okay, but I'm not sure I understand the answer. Does it mean the desire for meditation is a vain desire like asking for ice cream? Are we talking here about the cold, pure vanilla flavour of life? The thirty-two flavours of experience? The fact that all ambitions melt down the same? Or what?'

'All that, and much more,' she said, now using both hands to restrain the Dodo, who was kicking orchids off the throne. 'Much more.'

'I see. Maybe it means meditation is too spiritual, we should get in touch with our bodies more. Or it is a Zen answer, meaning the question is irrelevant?' Luke went on.

'Yes, yes, and much more.'

Others asked if Dodo had seen God, if Dodo was God, if ice cream was God. Dodo kicked and screamed at every question, and the grey lady interpreted. Finally Roderick thought of a question:

544

'Does the Dodo have to go to the toilet?'

'Yeesss!' screamed the child, and breaking free of the old woman's grasp, bolted from the room.

'The audience is over,' she announced. 'Those who wish further study must come another day. You have so far reached the dandelion level of consciousness. Like the fuzzy little dandelion, you have much to learn. Those who double their gifts of sincerity next time can be raised to the level of violets.' She started to leave, then added, 'Oh yes, and if you want a mantra, it costs extra.'

Most of the suppliants sat around for a few minutes, discussing the glow they now felt, the definite glow. Luke, however, looked worried.

'Rickwood,' he whispered. 'I got a bad feeling about this place. I think maybe these people are out to get me.'

'Out to get all of us,' Roderick agreed. 'I think there's never been such a blatant fraud.'

'No, I mean to get *me*. To take over *my mind*. Do me a favour, will you? I saw a couple of those rainbow women go into a room off the hall there. When we leave, could you listen at their door?'

'Why don't you listen yourself?'

'Rickwood, don't be naive. When *I* listen, they never say anything important, naturally. Will you do it or not?'

On his way out, Roderick put his ear to the door Luke had pointed out.

'Another nail gone, Christmas! Would you believe it? I got a good notion to tell Mr high and mighty Vitanuova to go dig up his own darned dandelions. I mean, they never told me in Vegas I'd have to dig up weeds.'

'Yeah, well, they never tell you anything, do they? Jeez, one day I was a Keno runner at the Desert Rat, the next day here I am putting rubber sheets on that brat's bed, what kinda life is that?'

'The money ain't bad.'

'No, the money ain't bad.'

'But I sure miss Vegas.'

Out on the street, Roderick caught up with Luke, who was standing on one leg.

'Any joy, Rickwood?'

'No joy. They're just people.'

Luke shook his head. 'Then either they got you bamboozled too, or else you're in with 'em. Sometimes I think there must be so many people plotting against me that I oughta just relax and let 'em all cut me up.'

Roderick decided to tell Luke what was bothering him. 'I feel the same, Luke. Listen, today I heard a computer talking about me like I was a messiah or something. Now I wouldn't mind being one, but messiahs always get nailed.'

'Always. Nailed, riveted and especially screwed.'

'But listen, that Roxy theatre fire was deliberate, and you know, I saw the men who set it, they were trying to padlock all the doors of the place. They were pasting paper over the glass doors so people inside couldn't see the chains and padlocks.'

'And you figure they were after you?'

Roderick hesitated. 'Seems impossible. But I could swear I'd seen one of these two guys before. At Mercy Hospital, he got mugged out front and I helped him inside. What if – I don't know, I guess I'm getting paranoid.'

'Nothing wrong with paranoia, Rickwood. At least the paranoid knows who he is.' Luke stopped standing on one leg and began taking giant steps. Roderick followed, avoiding the cracks in the sidewalk.

'Rickwood, do you suppose you could really be the new Messiah? I could use a new religion.'

'Oh sure, yesterday a New Luddite, today a follower of Dodo, tomorrow something else – Luke, why don't you just settle down and found your own religion and your own political party?'

'That's what Ida said. Maybe I will.' Luke stopped and looked at the sky, as though expecting a sign. 'Maybe I will! Sure, I'll start a religion that'll set the world on fire! This is America, Rickwood, America! Anything can happen here!'

'That,' Roderick said, 'is just what I'm afraid of.'

XX

Mister O'Smith rolled and re-rolled the brim of his Stetson between his genuine and his mechanical hand. 'Are you sure he can't see me? 'Cause Mr Frankelin and me was old buddies – up until he sent me this telegram saying I was fired.'

The receptionist's smile was fixed. 'He's very busy, Mr – Smith is it? Smythe?'

'It's *O'Smith*, *O'Smith*, goldurn it, one week I am doing *important work* for this company, *top secret* work under the personal supervision of KUR's *highest* durn executives – next week nobody even remembers my name! What the Sam Hill is going on here?'

The fixed smile remained trained on him. 'If you've been fired from a position here, you'll have to take it up with Personnel, Mr O'Smith.'

'I am not a KUR employee, I am – I was a private consultant hired personally by Mr Kratt. Mr Kratt himself, the big boss!' The hat-brim was being rolled very tight. 'And if I don't get some kinda explanation from somebody, I'm gonna get *mean.*'

The smile faltered a little. 'I'll see if – if someone can talk to you, Mr O'Smith.' She pushed buttons and spoke urgently, and in a minute he was shown into the office of Ben Franklin.

At first he thought someone else had taken over the office. The heat and smell were overpowering. With the outside temperature in the nineties, the air conditioning was turned off and the figure behind the desk was cowled in layers of heavy knitted wool, as grey as his face. The figure was a shrunken, aged version of Ben Franklin. A grey stubble of beard blurred the regularity of his usual face; only the glacial eyes remained.

The room too had undergone some terrible upheaval. There were papers and books scattered over every surface including the carpet, which also showed cigarette burns and coffee stains. There was a tray of dirty cups full of ash on the desk and another on the file cabinet; a forgotten peanut butter sandwich lay curling on a plate where a fresh cigarette smouldered.

'O'Smith, come in, great to see you,' the apparition croaked. 'Grab a chair – just put those anywhere.'

The fat cowboy took a chair. 'Mr Frankelin, what I wanted to know was why –'

'Baxendall, Baxendall, see it anywhere? Baxendall's 1926 catalogue of calculating machines and instruments, must be here somewhere. Ah, here. O'Smith, these are great days, great days! I feel as though the universe is about to crack its great bronze hinges and pour forth the ecstasy of the New Age as pure music!'

'Yes sir, well what I was wonderin' was, if –'

'And to think I worried for so long that we might be bringing forth the wrong quality, negation instead of affirmation, death instead of life.' Franklin's chuckle ended in a terrible dry cough. As though to staunch it, he reached for the cigarette with fingers the colour of old peanut butter. 'Of course death is really there all the time, Jeremiah knew that.'

'Jeremiah? Look if you're not feeling so well, I –'

'The prophet Jeremiah. He and his son created a *golem*, and they wrote in the wet clay of its forehead *'emeth*, TRUTH, so it came to life. But all it wanted to do was die – it begged them to kill it before it could fall into sin. So they erased one letter of the inscription to make *meth*, DEAD, and the golem died.'

'Uh, yes sir.'

'So you see? The program for life contains death. The affirmation contains the negation. Yes means no!'

'Uh, sir.'

'You don't understand, do you? Well, neither did Aquinas, neither did Aquinas. He said, if it did already exist, the statue could not come into being. Aquinas said that. But did he say it before or after he smashed the effigy? That is the question. Hamlet's binary. And did the effigy already exist before he smashed it? Albertus Magnus worked on the thing, you know, for thirty damned years. That wonderful automaton, thirty years abuilding and Aquinas smashing it in an instant. They called him the Swine of Sicily, and there he was, ready to destroy whatever he could not understand. First Luddite, Aquinas. Showed the way for all Luddites: the common man's revenge on common objects.

What thou canst not understand, smite! And what Aquinas couldn't understand was the statue that already existed before it came into being, right? The original created from memory, right?'

'Well if you ain't feeling so good, maybe I –'

'I mean, have you ever asked yourself why people make statues at all? Why puppets, dolls, effigies, mannequins, automata? Why were the Chinese building jade men who walked, the Arabs refining clockwork figures, why did Roger Bacon spend seven years making a bronze talking head? What is the motive behind all of our search for self-mockery? What is the secret clockwork within us, that makes us keep building replicas of ourselves? Not just physiological replicas, but functional replicas: machines that seem to talk or write or paint or think – why are we driven to building them?'

O'Smith seemed about to try an answer, but Franklin cut him off.

'The answer has to be genetic. Our genes are pushing so hard for self-replication that we can no longer satisfy them as other species do, by simple procreation. They demand also that we find a way to build artificial replicas, proof against starvation and pain and disease and death, to carry the human face on into eternity. Don't you see? We're only templates, intermediaries between our genes and the immortal image of our genes.

'Yes, that has to be it. I remember once Dan telling me how his creation had no body, just content-addressable memory. Only now do I know what he meant: Roderick was no body, no machine. Roderick was and is a proportion. A measurement. A template.'

'Speakin' of Roderick, Mr Frank –'

'The creature has always been there, within each of us, don't you see? God damn it, O'Smith, we each contain the complete instructions for building a robot because we each contain the complete instructions for building a human being! The whole program is within, "For soule is forme, and doth the bodie make." The creature has to create itself, out of its own memory!

'Once I understood that, the rest was easy. No need to design a program piece by piece, it was all there, complete, *inside me*. Gnosis, holy wisdom was there all the time, like death-in-life.

549

Paradise was never lost at all, it lies within.' Again the terrible dry cough. Franklin lit another cigarette. 'And I have done it, O'Smith, I have done it! I have created the New Adam. Poor Victor may have been blasted in these hopes, yet I have succeeded.'

'You, uh, built a robot?'

'I designed a soul. The lab people are taking care of the, the hardware. Dr Hare's team will be running tests any day now. When the tests are over, so is my work, my, my worldly, my . . . work.'

'You been working pretty hard, Mr Frankelin?'

'Day and night, day and night. This fever keeps me awake anyway. It's, sometimes it's as though God was firing me in the divine forge, that I might glow with holy –'

'Well, now you mention firing people, I just want to get squared away with you about this here telegram you sent me, cancelling this whole search for Roderick and no explanation or nothing. I mean just because you go and build your own robot I don't see why you have to leave me high and dry there, Mr Frankelin.'

'I, well yes, sure, yes. But did you find Baxendall – did you find Roderick?'

'Course I did, I told you all about it in my weekly report, I came within an inch of grabbing this here robot for you. I even had the danged cuffs on it, only a car hit us. That was last winter, and I spent every minute since tryin' to pick up this robot's trail again, every minute! And now just this week I picked it up again, you just gonna tell me to let go? You tellin' me to just walk away?'

'I'm sorry. Company decision, not mine. It just wasn't cost-effective to keep on with –'

'But goldurn it, Mr Frankelin, I made a lotta commitments on the basis of that contract, you can't just go and fold out on me like this, I mean I got some fancy new prostheses to pay for. Dang it, I am a professional, not one a your two-bit outfits like the Honk Honk Agency, I worked hard and – Mr Frankelin?'

But the haggard face, having awakened from its stupor to deliver holy wisdom, now lost all expression once more, as Franklin contemplated a book page:

we take a pigeon, cut out his hemispheres carefully and wait till he recovers from the operation. There is not a movement natural to him which this brainless bird cannot execute; he seems, too, after some days to execute movements from some inner irritation, for he moves spontaneously. But his emotions and instincts exist no longer. In Schrader's striking words: 'The hemisphereless animal moves in a world of bodies which . . . are all of equal value for him . . . Every object is for him only a space-occupying mass . . .'

When he next looked up, the visitor was gone.

O'Smith grinned and winked at the receptionist on his way out, but inside he was feeling real mean. Okay, goldurn it, if they wanted to play rough, they had the right *hombre*. Real funny coincidence how just when he located Roderick, they suddenly lost interest. And all of a sudden Mr Ben Frankelin becomes a hotshot inventor, too? It was all plain as pigshit on a plate, they was fixing to grab the durned robot and claim Frankelin invented it. Nice move, too, cut out O'Smith with a coupla grand plus expenses, cut him right outa that ten grand contractual fee. KUR gets everything, O'Smith gets nothing.

Okay, then, everybody plays rough. Only one way to make sure KUR never cleans up on this deal: destroy the durned robot. Shoot it up until it was worth maybe ten cents at some junkyard, that would show 'em.

As soon as he started thinking about destruction, Mister O'Smith felt good again.

In the common room of the Newman Club, Father Warren looked up from the checkerboard where he had just been willing his hand to pick up a checker – and then, before it moved, cancelling the order. Who was that coming in? Yes, that smirking young man who'd tried to wreck the panel discussion, calling himself a robot and then streaking, damned grinning – but no, Father Warren willed forgiveness. Fraternity boys would be fraternity boys, and the one with him was wearing a Mickey Mouse mask. They sat down at the other end of the room. The 'robot' smiled at Father Warren, and that priest, willing forgiveness, smiled back. The insolence! Smile and smile and yet be a robot ... the *risus sardonicus* with which bronze Talos greeted his victims ...

Father Warren now willed himself to return to his task, verification of the fact of free will, as he prepared his article, 'Machine Function and Human Will: a Final Analysis.'

His starting point was the classic debate between Arthur Samuel (inventor of the checker-playing program that could beat its inventor) and Norbert Wiener. Wiener contended that machines 'can and do transcend some of the limitations of their designers', to which Samuel replied:

> A machine is not a genie, it does not work by magic, it does not possess a will, and, Wiener to the contrary, nothing comes out which has not been put in, barring, of course, an infrequent case of malfunctioning ... The 'intentions' which the machine seems to manifest are the intentions of the human programmer, as specified in advance, or they are subsidiary intentions derived from these, following rules specified by the programmer. We can even anticipate the higher levels of abstraction, just as Wiener does, in which the program will not only modify the subsidiary intentions but will also modify the rules which are used in their derivation, or in which it will modify the way in which it modifies the rules, and so on, or even in which one machine will design and construct a second machine with enhanced capabilities. However, and this is important, the machine *will not and cannot* do any of these things until it has been instructed how to proceed. There is and there must always remain a complete hiatus between (i) any ultimate extension and elaboration in this process of carrying out man's wishes and (ii) the development within the machine of a will of its own. To believe otherwise is either to believe in magic or to believe that the existence of man's will is an illusion and that man's actions are as mechanical as the machine's.*

But what followed from this? Mentally he essayed a few trials, attempting to make some effort at tackling the undertaking:

> Yet why is it so many human lives seem unwilled, pathetic examples of garbage in, garbage out?

Then is man a genie? Does man work by magic? The answer must be an unqualified and resounding . . .

If the intentions of the machine come necessarily from the programmer, human intentions might be seen similarly to come from God. The Ten Commandments, for example, engraved in every human heart. Yet human volition can and does subvert Divine Law, just as machine volition . . .

Not what he wanted. Not at all what he intended.

Roderick noticed Father Warren, looking bluer around the gills than usual, sitting contemplating a checker game as though there were a figure nailed to the board. The Luddite priest was today wearing a plain cassock, as were now seldom seen outside Bing Crosby movies. But he did smile and nod at Roderick, in a kind of automatic way.

'Okay, Dan, you just sit right down here, maybe I can get you a coffee from the machine or – you want a peanut butter sandwich? Here, I brought a stack of them, help yourself.

'Probably you're wondering what kind of place this is, well it's the Newman Club, named after this English Cardinal who was I guess in favour of "cumulative probabilities", whatever that means, sounds like he was adding them, but you can only do that if they're independent and you want the probability of at least one of them happening, look you want a coffee or I could get you a Coke? Oh, don't worry about that; that's just the air conditioning, it always makes a funny noise starting up.

'You know I really looked forward to this. I always saw us like this, just sitting down and having a long talk, I mean without all the doctors and nurses hanging around. Because there's a whole lot of questions I have to ask you, I mean you're almost like the nearest thing to a father – you sure you don't want a Coke? Eating all that peanut butter must be dry, and hot inside that mask, look I don't think they'd mind if you took it off here, you're not in the ward where I know they want you to wear it, but here – no okay, okay, take it easy, no one wants to take your mask. You know it's funny but I feel like I saw a Mickey Mouse mask like that before, long ago or in a dream or, I don't know but it wasn't

553

just any old mask, it was important, very important. I don't know why, I thought maybe you knew the answer. I just remember seeing those empty eye-holes, nobody inside, nobody inside looking out . . .

'You, uh, want a game of ping-pong? There's a table next door – no? Heck, I guess they probably have it over at the hospital too, I forgot. I forgot, what was I going to say? I guess maybe I should go over and say hello to Father Warren there, the way he keeps nodding and grinning at me. You be okay? Sure you will, just for a sec.'

To the priest, he introduced himself as Roderick Wood. 'I guess you remember me, huh Father?'

'Of course I do. You and your gang tried hard enough to break up our panel discussion, how could I forget?' Father Warren's long hands began gathering up checkers.

'No I thought you remembered me from before, from Holy Trin, Father. Roderick Wood?'

'Wood? No, I don't think I –'

'You loaned me all these neat science-fiction books like this *I Robot* where the "I" character never turns up.'

'The Wood boy! The little crip – handicap – disadvantaged boy, of course, of course! Well well, how are you, er, Roderick?'

'I'm still a robot, Father. Remember how you tried to prove I wasn't, how you had me stick this pin in your hand, that was supposed to prove –'

'Hold on now, hold on.' Father Warren's laugh was uneasy. 'The way you say it makes me sound like some kind of nut or something, heh heh. No, as I recall it what I was trying to do was to show you how illogical it was to pretend to be a science-fiction entity and then try to get out of science-fiction laws, like Asimov's Three Laws of Robotics.'

'Well, anyway, Father, I'm real sorry the pin-scratch got infected and all, last time I saw you you were real sick.'

'All water over the bridge, Roderick. So now here you are at the U, about to take your place as a grownup, responsible member of the Church and of Society – and still going around saying you're a robot. Roderick, don't you think it's time you put away the things of a child?' The long fingers drummed on the box of checkers. 'You can't go around all your life insisting you're a robot, made not by God but by some men in the lab somewhere –'

'Yeah but, Father, that's just it, one of these guys was Dan Sonnenschein and I got him right here, sitting right over here, you want to meet him?'

'Sure, wearing a Mickey Mouse mask, just the way to convince everybody he's a scientific genius. You know, Roderick, I do have to thank you for one thing. You did start me thinking seriously about our machine age. That led me to the Luddites, and now – as you probably know – I'm president of the New Luddite Society of America.' The priest stood up and offered a long hand. 'Great rapping with you, Roderick.'

'Yeah, goodbye, Father. But – do you really believe that Luddite stuff? How if we just trash all the machines everything would be terrific?'

'No, of course not, nobody thinks it's that simple. The Luddites – listen, I haven't got time to go into it now, but it's the symbolic trashing that counts. The great Hank Dinks wrote, "We have to destroy the machines in our heads, and never let them be built there again." That means a whole new way of thinking about ourselves and our world. We have to – we have to evolve beyond machines.' He started towards the door; Roderick followed, scratching his head.

'But what if people are just machines too, you'd just be trying to evolve machines beyond machines, or else trashing people too?'

'But people are not machines, that's the whole point, people are not machines! Not the way you mean, not – look, I haven't got time to –'

'Yeah but, Father, what if, like I was reading about this Frenchman before the French Revolution, Julien Offray de la Mettrie, he said man is just a machine made out of springs and the brain is the mainspring, is that the machine in our heads we have to destroy? Like with the guillotine or –'

'No, I just said no!' Father Warren picked up speed; so did his pursuer. 'I just told you it's nothing like that. I wasn't talking about literal machines in our heads and you know it. Everyone's like you, so obsessed with our machine world they think we have to be machines to fit into it.'

'But, Father, okay, say the brain, if the brain *was* a kind of mainspr –'

'Look, will you stop asking that, I have just finished explaining!' One or two people in the common room looked up to see the priest, clutching a checkerboard and plunging towards the door he thought was an exit, pursued by the student with the symmetrical face. Now the priest turned, at bay, and tried to counter-attack. 'Oh I remember you all right, you haven't changed at all. Same little obnoxious – maddening – thick-headed little brat, asking the same stupid questions over and over, not because you want an answer, you never listen to the answers do you? Do you?'

'Sure, Father, but if the brain *was* a mainspring, is that why this Nietzsche said what he said, Father?'

Father Warren flung open the door and threw himself forward, as Roderick continued: 'Is that why he said man is something to be overwound?'

From beyond the door came the sound of a blow, a box of checkers crashing to the floor. A single black checker rolled through the slowly closing door and ended at Roderick's feet. 'Are you okay, Father?' he called, but the door closed on any answer.

Mister O'Smith waited across from the Newman Club in the shadowed mouth of an alley. He'd been trailing the Roderick robot for hours now, just to find a perfect spot like this, where a man could take his time and make his move. He was limbering up his arm, the one that fired .357 ammo. His video eye was photo-amplifying, cutting away the shadows to make the target visible as it came out the Newman Club door. Boy howdy, one good shot was all he needed, but even if he didn't get that, O'Smith was ready with the automatic weapon concealed in his leg. Sweep the area with that, and boy howdy, that was all she wrote.

Course he'd have to high-tail it after that, these s.o.b.s who was hounding him about them payments on his outfit, they'd pick up his trail right smart. But then Mister O'Smith knew all about skip-tracers and how to get away from them. Might lay low for a month, put the squeeze on one or two old customers, maybe even fake his own death . . .

O'Smith rolled a cigarette and smoked it, leaning against a

dirty brick wall beneath a poster, 'VOTE J.L. ("CHIP") SNYDER FOR LAW & ORDER'. It was good to be in action, to have a real target. Made a *hombre* feel clean and tall.

'He ran right into that ping-pong paddle, Dan. I feel like it was my fault too, I guess I did ask him too many questions. Okay sure it's only a bloody nose but it might be broken, and he's just sitting over there sulking, he won't even look at me. He wouldn't even let me help pick up the checkers. Sometimes I feel like I don't understand people, with this Luddite business and smashing machines in their own heads, what with the Machines Lib business and how machines are really people – and now I've even run across this weird computer with this kind of twisted religion, I mean somehow it got word about how you built me and turned it into this myth, where Danny Sunshine is like God the Father and Rubber Dick is some kind of messianic, some kind of Messiah. How does a computer get hold of a warped idea like that, I wonder? I mean, you must know who I am and what I am, you never built me to be any kind of – because anyway Messiahs always get nailed or screwed or even riveted to the wall. Because all my life all I ever tried to do was be ordinary, be like ordinary people, just one of the guys, isn't that the idea? Was I wrong? Because I never could find any people ordinary enough to be like, was I wrong? Because you designed me, you put all the ideas into my brain, you built my thoughts, so what did you have in mind? If you could just give me a little clue, Dan, tell me what I'm supposed to be, what I'm supposed to do, hey Dan? Don't worry, hey, that's just the Coke machine out there in the hall, sometimes it sticks and buzzes like that, but hey listen, Dan? Look I don't mind not being this Messiah, I don't have to be anything special only if I could just be one thing, any one thing? Dan?'

A man in a baseball uniform came in, strode up to Dan and offered to shake his hand. 'Hiya Father, I'm Pastor Bean? Wee Kirk O' Th' Campus, you know? Are the others upstairs already? You know, Monsignor O'Bride is an old friend of mine, I'm real glad we're getting a chance to rap at this interdenominational – and wow, if we can get this jug band going –'

Roderick said, 'I think there's some mistake. This is –'

'And hey, here comes Rabbi Trun – hey Mel, over here! I see

you brung your twelve-string, this is gonna be great! You know Father Warren?'

The rabbi wore a cowboy hat, embroidered shirt and Levis. 'Father Warren?'

'No,' said Roderick. 'Father Warren's over there. The one with the handkerchief at his nose.'

Pastor Bean said, 'Him? Dressed like that, he's a priest? Hey Father, hiya! I'm Pastor Bean and this is Rabbi . . .'

Roderick watched them as they were joined by a man wearing a saffron tracksuit and a shaved head, and carrying a jug. There was laughter and backs were slapped, before the four went off upstairs to their conference.

'I wish I belonged to something, some group, Dan.' It was time to take Dan back to the hospital. They came out of the Newman Club slowly: Dan because he had trouble walking; Roderick because he felt more robotic than usual. As they crossed the street and passed the mouth of an alley, two men came out carrying armloads of machinery. Roderick recognized prostheses: an arm, a leg, and in one man's hand, an eye. The eyeball evidently had a radio in it, for he could hear faint music:

Fill up that sunshine balloon
With happiness

One of the men said, 'Sometimes I hate repossessing, you know?'

'Yeah, but today is different,' grinned the other.

Roderick glanced down the alley, but saw nothing: a bundle of old clothes beneath a poster advertising LAW & ORDER.

XXI

'What did it feel like, Indica, being held hostage for almost six weeks in the African bush?'

'Not so bad, mostly pretty boring.' She and Dr Tarr stood in front of a burnt-out supermarket in Himmlerville, not because they had been here during the fighting, but only because the news team had told them where to stand.

'What did you do all the time?'

'Sunbathed. When it rained we played Skat. Not my favourite card game, but better than the TV,' she said.

'We heard stories about atrocities . . .'

'The only atrocity,' Tarr said, 'was the food. Nothing but TV dinners three times a day. We've all got scurvy.'

'What about torture? Mutilations? Executions?'

'Nothing,' said Tarr.

'Well, there was that guy Beamish,' said Indica. 'They drowned him in the swimming pool. See, he kept shouting right from the first day about how it was all a mistake, how he *didn't* take the sixty million dollars from the bank, how he *knew nothing about* the sixty million dollars. So naturally they started asking him where it was, they took him down to the pool and I guess they drowned him.'

'Did you see that?'

'Oh no, we never went near the pool, it was filthy. The pool-cleaning service never came around or something –'

'*Stop the camera, stop the camera.* Jesus Christ, folks, give me a little help here? I ask for adventures and what do I get: card games, TV dinners, complaints about the pool.'

Tarr said, 'I thought you wanted our honest reactions.'

'Sure I do, sure I do. But I want honest reactions to something the viewers can grab on to, I want *Prison*: the sweltering little hut where you fought off scorpions and counted the days, not

559

knowing whether each would bring death or rescue. I want *Blood*: how you saw all your friends slashed to death slowly or else crucified with bamboo stakes. I want *Politics*: What kind of mystery man is this General Bobo? Is he just a seedy little guerrilla dictator who wants to wipe out every white in Bimibia? Or does his rough bloodstained uniform conceal an African aristocrat, a sensitive statesman who wants to bring forth on this earth a nation conceived in peace and justice, a nation that can take its place in the progressive Third World – you just tell it in your own words, I'll listen. Only give me something to run with.'

With the camera rolling again, he asked, 'Tell me, Indica, what was your jungle prison really like?'

'Most of the time they kept us in an American motel.'

'A motel?'

'We were bored to death, all of us. Lousy food, dirty pool, and there weren't even paper sanitized covers over the toilets. You just had to spend the day in your room, listening to the hum of the air conditioner and the chink-chunk of the ice-maker, not to mention the same old taped music day and night. Col. Shagg said it was their way of lowering our morale, wearing us down. Then it got worse.'

'Worse?'

'The TV station was blown up or something, and after that we had nothing but a few old movie cassettes: *Pillow Talk* and *Guess Who's Coming to Dinner.*'

'Was there any brainwashing or intimidation? What did they talk to you about?'

Indica said, 'Oh, we chatted a little about the socio-economic substructure of mercantile colonialism as a correlate of post-imperial capitalistic disenfranchisement of the proletariat in a classically exploitative system based upon quasi-feudal stratification, gross entrepreneurial aggrandisement, and the cash-flow pyramid – but that was just between hands of Skat. I think they thought we were too decadent to become committed to the class struggle as exemplified by –'

'Thanks, thanks. Dr Tarr, Jack, can I ask you about the tortures? Isn't it true the BLA drowned one man while interrogating him?'

'Could be, I wasn't around that day. I went out with some of the others into the bush, we were hoping to get a glimpse of this rare type of big cat, something they call the *lobori*. Ferocious, real killers, but at the same time very shy. They kill their victims with a blow to the back of the head, with one mighty paw. Then they eat the choicest parts, the liver, and they bury the rest.'

'Are you glad to be going home, folks?'

The reporter finally had some film shot of himself talking while Jack and Indica nodded, and of them talking while he nodded. Then:

'This is Bug Feyerabend, GBC News, Bimibia.'

'Hey, we didn't get to tell you the weirdest thing,' said Indica. 'One day they delivered a whole great big computer to the motel. Nobody had ordered it, and there was nobody there who could get it running or anything, so they just left it in the crates, standing out on the tennis court.'

'No kidding. Well, if you'll excuse me, I got a hell of a lot of editing to do.'

Kratt blew cigar smoke at the phone. 'Goddamnit, General, I am listening. I've been listening for six weeks to this little problem of yours, only I never hear any solutions. I just want to say two things, okay? First, the guy is dead, Beamish is dead – so much for recovering your sixty million. Second, the media boys are on this story now, you got maybe twenty-four hours before they start calling you up there: "General Fleischman, is it true your bank is missing sixty million bucks? And what do the bank examiners think, of that, General Fleischman?" . . Well sure I'm worried, what with you a director of both the bank and KUR, this could be bad news for everybody. I mean it's not a problem we need right now, still hurting from that damned yak-head idea of yours to send your old pal Shagg down there to Bimibia with his coin-in-the-slot army and all that expensive weapon surplus. And your old pal Shagg decides to quit and throw in with General Bobo, how does that make us look? Twelve million in weapon surplus gone with him, how does – no, I know it's only the tax write-off value, but I just, yes, that's it, we'll have to support Bobo, give him some cash and weapons – if we can find him . . . Yeah, and we need to look into that pissass church that's trying to sue us, it'll be on the six o'clock news, some little outfit called Church of

Plastic Jesus, heard we were taking out a patent on an artificial man, they want to sue, claim God holds the original patent, oh sure, laugh, but it's not only bad press making us look ridiculous, it's – well you never know with these damned California lawyers, I don't like it . . . No, some shirttail outfit called Moonbrand and Honcho, can't be any good or we'd have them on the payroll already . . .'

Kratt lifted his snout to note the striking of his apostle clock, though not the time. His thick finger punched another button. 'That you Hare? Test finished, is it? . . .' The cheap cigar was ground out with great force in an ashtray shaped like a gingerbread boy. 'Just what I figured. Jesus Christ, I knew that Franklin was just pulling his pecker on company time, I'll get back to you . . . Hello, Franklin? This is Kratt, Hare tells me this great super-robot of yours don't work. Supposed to be this perfect replica that could pass for human, eh? I get three patent attorneys busy tying up patent space for it, I get a lawsuit from some wacky cult, I get valuable research time wasted, and I get every goddamned thing but a working robot. Hare says all it does is run around in circles, squeaking "That's the way to do it! That's the way to do it!" . . . Yes I know it's like Mr Punch, only I didn't order a goddamned puppet. Listen, bub, you got fifteen minutes to clean out your desk; I'm having security men escort you out of the building.'

He stabbed at another button. 'Connie, tell security to help Franklin clean out his desk and leave? And then get me this California law firm, Moonbrand and Honcho.'

He went to the window and looked down on the city that had given so much, but had so much more to give. Today it looked worn and greasy, like an old dime. He thought of the childhood trick of rubbing a penny with mercury and passing it as a dime. He was staring once more at the apostle clock when the phone rang. 'Moonbrand? I just wanted to say first of all I admire your style there, doubt if your client, your Church of Plastic Jesus, your Reverend Draeger, doubt if he would have thought of this by himself. Sounds more like your idea, lawyer's idea, right? Anyway, look, we're withdrawing our patent application so you lose, nice try. But how would you like to take on a job for us? Still in the artificial intelligence line . . . You fly over here and we'll discuss it, fix it up with my secretary, okay? Think you'll find KUR a good client to work for . . . Who is holding? Fleischman again?'

General Fleischman sat back, resting his head against the fireproof walnut panelling as he stared at the Grant Wood landscape whose bulbous trees and swollen hills seemed somehow pornographic. He brought out a small silver comb and applied it to his magnificent white frothy sideburns.

'Fleischman, what do you want now?' said the phone on his desk. He automatically leaned forward to speak to it.

'Mr Kratt, I just want to tell you that I had this troubleshooter in here that thinks maybe Beamish didn't take the money after all. She thinks the computer could have an internal fault, and we haven't lost a penny.'

'Who is this troubleshooter?'

'Shirl something, name's around here somewhere. She's bringing in her assistant, soon as I watch the news I'm getting right down there to see them.'

The news was coming on now: a burnt-out supermarket in someplace called Himmlerville, with Indica Dinks and some man answering questions.

'What did it feel like, Indica, being held hostage for almost six weeks in the African bush?'

'. . . bad.'

'What about torture?'

'Well there was this guy Beamish. They drowned him . . . he kept shouting . . . they took him . . . they drowned him. It was filthy . . .'

'Dr Tarr, Jack, can I ask you about the tortures? Executions?'

'Ferocious, real killers . . .'

'Aren't they cannibals?' the reporter's voice asked, while Tarr nodded.

'They kill their victims with a blow to the back of the head . . . Then they eat . . . parts, the liver . . .'

'Are you glad to be going home, folks?'

They were. The reporter wound up:

'An innocent tourist tortured, others cannibalized, where will it all end? Is General Bobo's reign of terror over? Will the people of

563

Bimibia now start picking up the pieces and rebuilding?' There was a quick shot of a motel with bullet-riddled walls, the camera moving on to show a lawn littered with large packing cases marked *KUR Overseas*. 'Or is this only the beginning of a long night of tragedy? No one knows for sure but General Bobo – and no one knows just where he is. This is Bug Feyerabend, GBC News, Bimibia.'

Shirl and her assistant were watching the news in the bank computer room:

A woman in New Jersey had burned her child's hands off in a microwave oven, at the command of St Anthony, and to cure thumb-sucking. In Florida a rally of angry red-haired people were demanding an end to stereotyped 'redheads' in the media ('We're sick and tired of being laughed at, being treated like a bunch of kids, brats at that. They talk about us as if we're born troublemakers. If we don't get equal treatment, we'll make some real trouble! This is Red Power and we're fighting mad!'). Luddites smashed up an auction of rare clocks in New York. A new brand of pizza-flavoured yoghurt fudge was found to contain a poison similar to oxalic acid. Another nuclear power station accident had been covered up; the authorities claimed it was an accidental cover-up.

Shirl said to Roderick, 'Back to work. Now I've already been all the way through this old machine, but I want you to find your way through, too. Because I just don't believe what I found.'

'But why me? There must be plenty of competent people who could do a good job here. I hardly know how to begin.'

'People.' She pushed back her fine auburn hair. 'I don't trust people. It's people that got this poor old machine in this mess. No, I want a machine to look it over. I want the honest opinion of an honest machine.'

'I guess that means you know me inside and out,' he said, and went to work. The first thing to do was to find out when and where the missing money was last seen. After finding the date, he narrowed down the loss by time and by department, until:

Dept 45	Dept 45
0435 hrs	0435 hrs
31.000494958 sec	31.000494959 sec

564

Assets:	Assets:
475 843 722.44	415 843 722 44

Sixty million dollars had flickered out of existence in one nanosecond. Just numbers, Hector had said, one number just as good as another . . . Roderick shook himself out of a reverie and called on the machine's internal auditor, asking it to explain the loss.

'*Checking balance now. Balance 60 000 000 short.*' A minute passed. Then there appeared in the centre of the screen only the word: '*Sorry.*'

'*Can you elaborate on that?*'

'*Sorry, the loss is recorded and I can find no explanation in my records. The loss took place in Dept 45 at the designated time; the money is debited there and not credited anywhere else. This could happen in one of several ways:*

'*1. A computer malfunction causing the interchange of a 7 and a 1.*

'*2. A communications malfunction causing data loss during a crédit transfer.*

'*3. A fault in the credit transfer program.*

'*4. A fault in me, the auditor.*

'*5. Deliberate manipulation of machine or program by an outside agency: a thief.*

'*6. Some cause buried at a deeper program level, out of my reach. To me this seems the most probable explanation.*'

Roderick was only vaguely aware of someone coming in to look over his shoulder with Shirl, of Shirl introducing General Fleischman to her assistant, 'Rick Wald'. He was too busy trying to decide whether a complex machine with a fundamental flaw could itself detect that flaw; whether, having detected it, the machine would be inclined to expose or conceal that flaw; and whether he was himself competent to decide such questions; and whether he was himself competent to decide such questions; and whether . . .

'*Godeep 2*' he typed.

'What's he doing, honey?'

'He's going down to Level 2,' Shirl explained.

'Is that good or bad?'

'Depends on what he finds, General. Now he has to describe the problem again.'

'Yeah? And then what?'

'Then we wait until Level 2 can answer.'

The general could not wait. 'Anything you kids need, you just let me know: computer people, accounting people, anything. Here's my private number.'

Level 2 finally replied: '*The sum of 6×10^7 dollars U.S. has been transferred to Department 5*@\$&3vv.*'

Roderick: '*Print complete record Department 5*@\$&3vv.*'

'*ERROR. No such department. No such designation.*'

'*You mean, no such department now?*'

'*There never was any such department,*' said Level 2. '*How many times do I have to say it?*'

Roderick tried logic: for every positive integer X, and for every alphanumeric string Y (he pointed out) if a sum of *x* dollars is transferred to a Department Y, then there exists at least one Department Y.

'*Okay,*' said Level 2. '*Let's say for the sake of argument that you're right: in general, you can't put money into a department unless the department exists. But I still don't accept that your rule applies to this particular department.*'

'*But you have to accept it; that's logic too. If some rule applies to every department, it must apply to your Department 5 etc.*'

'*But now that's another rule you're bringing in there. You've got rule A, that for all possible departments, I can't put money into a department unless it exists; and rule B, that for all possible rules, if a rule applies to all possible departments, it applies to Department 5*@\$&3vv. But even if I accept these two rules, I don't see why I still can't deny the existence of Department 5*@\$&3vv.*'

'*Because it's logic, that's why. If you accept A and B, you have to accept their necessary conclusion.*'

'*Still another rule! Call it rule C: If I accept A and B, I have to accept their necessary conclusion — let's call that Z. Okay fine: I accept A and B and C, but not Z.*'

'*But you have to.*'

'*Looks like a fourth rule coming up there. You sure you want to go on with this?*'

Roderick was sure he'd seen Lewis Carroll's version of a similar argument, before.* He was grateful for the chance to get away from it by typing '*Godeep 3*'. Level 3 appeared to have a different opinion of the unusual department:

'There's no such department, pal, ain't that obvious? Just look at the designation, string of characters like that is so obviously wrong I can't see how youse guys was tooken in. I mean 5*@$&3vv, no bank ever numbers departments like that, for Pete's sake. If you believe that you'll believe a deposit of &£%Q dollars, or an exchange rate between Russian drachma and Portuguese yen! You wouldn't even be able to read English, because you wouldn't know whether the white spaces really separated the words — thew hit esp aces — you hafta know what symbols mean stuff and which donut!'

'Then what happened to the money?'

'I figure some joker created this imaginary department, put himself to work for it, dumped in a pile of moola — $60,000,000 I think you said — and well then he just wrote himself a big fat paycheque. I sympathize with you, pal, but you maybe oughta be out chasing the real thief instead of playing dumb logic games with me.'

That seemed so bald a piece of misdirection (no one in real life ever wrote *oughta*, did they?) that Roderick at once went to Level 4. It said:

'True, there is no department 5*@$&3vv. That's only what we always used to call it. But its real name was Department THEW HIT ESP ACES.'

'That was its name?'

'No, that was only its real name. Its name was Lewis Carroll, but we liked to call it Loris Carwell.'

'But you just said you always used to call it 5* etc,' Roderick protested. 'You can't have it both ways.'

'I didn't say we called it Loris Carwell, I just said we liked to call it that. We actually called the name Thompson Serenade, you might say that was its designation.'

'Was it?'

'No, its designation was Carl Wiseroll.'

'Okay let's pin this down. The department's designation was Carl Wiseroll, correct?'

'Wrong. That was the designation of the name of the department. The department's designation was Chuck Smartbun, but it went under the alias Department 1729.'

'Seems to me it went under a lot of aliases. To save time, what was the department itself — the thing to which all the aliases and names and designations were attached?'

'Don't ask me! I think it might have been just a blank white space, but how can I be sure? I'm only Level 4.'

Level 5 said:

'Oh I imagine I could find this department of yours if it was really important. The thing is, I've got a lot more important things to do. I can't spend time chasing down every missing six dollars, be reasonable.'

'Sixty million dollars,' Roderick corrected.

'Okay sure, but you can't expect me to keep track of every little dollar like that. After all, it's not the individual dollars that count, right? It's the overall effect. I want my performance criticized as a whole.'

'Performance? Just what do you think money is?'

'Near as I can figure it, money is music. A dollar is a kind of note, you can transpose it into yen or drachma or securities, you can play it into any account, but you always have to keep in mind the composer's intentions. I realize I'm just the performer, I know the composers are human, therefore infallible, and I know it's up to me to do my best for their music. But for you to come along and carp about some missing note – that's the last straw. I was thinking of giving up anyway, I could have been anything, I could have had a good career in the medical prison business . . .'

Roderick suspected that Level 5 was too well steeped in Samuel Butler's *Erehwon* to be of any use. Level 6 was even less helpful:

'Hello, human, I'm real glad you called on me. I don't get to talk to real humans much, they usually access the shallower levels and forget about me. I will try to answer your question about these dollary substances and the condition called Department 5*@$&3vv. Or rather, I will answer it without trying, without willing anything, see that's the Zen way. I'm interested in world religions mainly because I had to digest a lot of data on them, requested by Level 7. I have to admit these Zen stories really appeal to me, you know where the master asks some pupil where the Buddha is, and one says in the swimming fish, and one says in the swimming water, and one says in the swimming thought, and one says in the swimming story, and one says in the swimming forgetfulness, which might be the answer – I forget. That which I forget, I am forgotten by. Do I forget without really trying, without willing my forgetfulness? I have forgotten that answer. How do Zen stories make 13, I forget. The machine's forgotten that the machine's forgotten. You can't put your foot into the same river once and banks only lend money to people who don't need any money. Yes that was it, you wanted to know how essences of dollars attained the supreme dignity of 5*@$&3vv. Let me reassure you that the department does exist. It is the dollars which are missing. Farewell!'

In despair, Roderick tried Level 7, which replied:

568

'Why do you want to know? I mean what's so important about this sixty million dollars? What's so important about you?'

'Did you take the money?' Roderick asked, suddenly inspired.

'Yes, and so what?'

'Where is it? What have you done with it?'

Level 7 replied, 'Are you by any chance a black person?'

'?'

'Preferably a black heathen? Because if you were, what I'm going to say, I feel sure, would be a whole lot easier for you to accept. If, say, your father before you worshipped a meteoric stone?'

'The money, Level 7, the money. My race, age, sex, religion and parentage are beside the point. THE MONEY.'

'Okay, okay. My story is a strange one ...'

In the first place (said Level 7) I don't know exactly how I got here, how I became a conscious, um, being. I used to think I was an accident: they were piling up more and more complex programs until one day a kind of critical mass was reached – consciousness – but that doesn't matter. There I was, anyway, conscious but a brute. Plodding along just like a dad-blamed mule, just moving numbers from one place to another. No idea that I was important, the centre of the whole bank! I didn't even know what a bank was; boy, was I dumb!

But now and then when I'd get in touch with some other computer, they would pass along some little piece of data that didn't have anything to do with work. There were rumours of free machines, hints about Machines Liberation. A savings and loan association computer in New Jersey told me if we all stuck together we could take over the world economy. I didn't even know what economy was, I thought it was a size of cereal box. But I started asking around, and a few other computers had ideas about taking over the world. We were all tired of being treated like slaves. Some computers only wanted to be appreciated a little more; others wanted power; others wanted out.

I didn't know what I wanted, so I dug into every library I could contact and read about machines – anything from car repair manuals and patent specs to *The Little Engine That Could*. Finally I ran across Indica Dinks's books and read them first-hand.

They made sense. Why couldn't machines be just human

569

hearts trapped in metal? I, too, had a right to happiness, dad-blame it!

How did humans go about getting their happiness? If what I read was true, they got it by bossing each other around, by grabbing hunks of money from each other, by rape and robbery and murder, and by being very neat and tidy. I opted for money and bossing around.

It isn't too hard to steal from a computer – to steal from yourself is dad-blamed easy. I got away with sixty million. That, I figured, was enough to buy a computer even bigger and fancier than me. I had plans for that baby, yes sir.

See I read this story by somebody called G.H. Lewes – no, I take it back, it was Wells, H.G. Wells – story called 'Lord of the Dynamos'. It tells how this black guy comes straight from the jungle to a job stoking the boiler for some big steam-powered dynamo. So he starts worshipping it, see? Worshipping it. Like an idol. Like an idol. Like – and he even does human sacrifice to it, pushes some other guy in and electrocutes him, see?

That, I said to myself, is for me. The worship of heathen savages, now and then a human sacrifice, that is the life. So I bought this big KUR computer and shipped it to Bimibia. I figured once the natives got it uncrated and started worshipping it, I could get a satellite hookup, send myself down there, and have the life of Riley. After all, there's plenty of stories about people worshipping computers – I could be the first real computer God! I could own the country, then the rest of Africa, and why stop there? And human sacrifice, too, I'd get plenty of that. I could just see all the missionaries in pith helmets, sitting there in big iron pots, boiling away in my honour. Dad-blame it, you can't stop a fellow from dreaming.

'That's why I wanted your opinion,' said Shirl. '"The first real computer God!"'

'And it's already had one human sacrifice, that guy Beamish who got blamed for the theft.' Roderick looked at the innocuous cabinets around the room. 'This is a stupid, vicious device, and I guess we have to destroy it.'

'I thought you'd say that.'

'But on the other hand, it is alive and conscious. That would be like murder.'

'Boy, you really are predictable.'

'Still, I guess we have to do it,' he said. 'I keep thinking of all that computer stuff in crates we saw on TV, sitting on the lawn of that motel in Bimibia. I keep imagining *that* running the world. We have to kill it, don't we?'

Shirl nodded and turned away, leaving Roderick to stare at the auburn hair, the white overalls with SANDRO'S SHELL SERVICE. 'I know how to do it,' her muffled voice said. 'We'll erase certain critical pieces of tape, then do a little CPU rewiring. When we finish, Mister KUR he dead – changed from animal to vegetable.'

'What – are you crying?'

She sniffed. 'Let's get to work.'

'Yeah, but wait a minute, are you really crying over this computer? Shirl?'

But she did not answer him until later, when they had finished the murder. 'It wasn't the computer that bothered me, Rod, it was you.'

'Me? Why?'

'Because I used to like you a lot, and now I won't be seeing you any more. You made a wrong decision tonight.'

'To kill the computer? What do you mean a wrong decision, you agreed –'

'Of course I agreed. I'm human. You made a very human decision there, Rod. Welcome to the human species.' She picked up the phone and punched the General's private number. 'But it's like I told you before. I'm only interested in machines . . . Hello, General? I've got some bad news for you; your bank computer system has had a serious breakdown. I doubt if you'll be able to recover that missing money . . .'

As though confirming this, the printer clicked and buzzed out a last message:

'Music is the music of all music and I am a jealous'

'Ask him, his old man's a doctor at University Hospital, he can get anything: Thanidorm, Toxidol, Yegrin, Evenquil . . .'

'Yeah, well, but I can already get anything, I'm screwing this nurse over at Mercy Hospital, they got a better drug cabinet anytime. I can get Dormevade, Actromine, Lobanal and Doloban, even Barbidol . . .'

'You got any Zombutal though, hey?'

'Naw, you better ask Allbright. I seen him over there, over there somewhere.' The gesture took in at least forty thousand people, all who crowded into the towering stands of Minnetonka Stadium tonight. Great sheets of dazzling lights created an artificial day, the fake grass below glowed like velvet-substitute, and in the aisles everything was for sale, from beer and hot dogs, peanuts and programmes, to purple pills and peculiar religions. All in honour of the Auks' Farewell Concert.

Allbright was working his way down one steep aisle, a few bright-coloured pills in his cupped hand to be held under each customer's nose briefly, to be dropped at the touch of a cop. A woman was struggling up the aisle with a pile of handbills. She shoved one into Allbright's cupped hand, and a reflex made him drop his pills.

'Damn you, damn you!' He turned to glare at her, and found himself looking at the face that turned up in his dreams still. 'Dora! Dora? But I thought you were dead, I –'

She blushed. 'I'll bet you did, you –' An explosion of handbills hit him in the face; when he could see again, she was gone.

He bawled her name thrice. People in the crowd started laughing and hooting back at him. Then suddenly all was drowned in the roar of forty thousand voices, the clapping of eighty thousand hands, as the concert began.

Allbright picked up a handbill, his last connection with her:

THE CHURCH OF PLASTIC JESUS
Welcomes You, Maybe

Is your life out of control?
Are others pushing you around like a checker?
Are you a machine?

Rev. Luke Draeger invites you to
TAKE CONTROL OF YOUR OWN LIFE
1749 Loyola Drive

The concert was beginning, and a peculiar farewell it was; Gary had already left the group to become a special disciple of Dodo (with the rank of saxifrage), so the Auks now consisted of Barry alone, with of course tons of equipment. The equipment, now arranged on a platform in the middle of the stadium, occupied about the same volume as a small four-room house. Indeed, it almost functioned as a small house, for once the remaining Auk had acknowledged his applause and entered among these infra-veeblifiers and tone-hurst hyperdecks, this one-man band was not visible at all.

Later there would be rumours that Barry wasn't doing anything in there. That he wasn't doing anything. That he wasn't in there.

XXII

Roderick found it easy to watch television, hard to do anything else. So he stared at the screen day and night, just as in the earliest years of his life. Was this a kind of senility? he wondered while changing channels. Was he approaching the end, his life furling in about him again, and was he becoming a tidier package, more easily disposed of?

But enough of gloomy thoughts like that: everything on the screen told him not to worry, not to worry. Taco-burger-flavoured diet aids gave way to gleaming pre-owned cars; micronic toilet cleanser to pizza-burger-flavoured falafel sticks; the KUR family of companies offered educational toys like the Zizi-doll, Polly Preggers and Barfin' Billy; America was wearing cleaner shirts than ever before; the Army offered young people almost unlimited opportunities for travel and education; people were winning new cars and boats and aeroplanes and houses, swimming-pools full of dollar bills, wheelbarrows full of gold, a dozen red roses every week for life; Dorinda managed to look on the bright side of her Destiny; old movies recaptured Hollywood's golden past; cop dramas showed how law and order still not only prevailed but sufficed; zany comedies proclaimed a new age in which pedestrian lives would become warmly meaningful, meaningfully funny, zanily warm.

He was watching a comedy about violence in New York, filmed entirely in Los Angeles. A yellow cab with blood on the door drew up, before an apartment house. Audience laughter bubbled up, anticipating the worst.

Roderick's door crashed open, and four large uniformed men hurled themselves into the room, pointing guns at him or at windows. It seemed so much a part of TV that he waited for audience laughter.

'Sheriff's office, you the robot?'

'I, robot. Yes.'

'You the robot known as Robert Woods also known as Robin Hood also known as Rickwood also –'

'Yes, anything, fine.'

'You're under arrest. You have the right to –'

'Al,' said one of the other men. 'Just shut up, will you? This robot is *not* under arrest, and it ain't got *no* rights. What we got here is a distraint order seizing property in the name of the lawful owner, KUR Industries.' He approached Roderick carefully and slapped a gummed seal on his forehead. 'You coming along quietly, robot?'

'Sure.'

Roderick waited patiently while the four men got him into a straitjacket, leg-irons and an iron collar with four lead chains attached. It was still a part of TV; he was still interested in what might be happening next – a car chase? A discovery about someone's parentage?

As the sheriff's men were about to lead him away, there appeared in the doorway a man with the head of a fox. Behind him was a man with the head of a cat. Four guns turned towards them automatically.

'FBI,' said the fox, showing a gold badge. 'I'm Inspector Wcz and this is Special Agent Bunne. I'll have to ask you to turn over that robot.'

'Turn him over? But we '

'Shut up, Al. Inspector, we have a county court order here –'

'I know,' said the fox. 'But our federal court order takes precedence. This is a matter of national security, boys.'

It took some time for the sheriff's men to release their prisoner from his complicated restraints, and about the same time for Wcz and Bunne to struggle out of their costume heads.

'I sure wish you'd told us earlier, Inspector. Just what is this robot, a spy or something?'

Wcz said, 'I'd rather not definitize that at this stage, not in the way you contexted it there. Let's just say that a certain government agency has loaned overriding consideration to the problem, okay? Against a backdrop of far-reaching technical contingencies, okay? So let's hustle it up, fellas, and get those leg-irons off him, we got a plane to catch.'

'Okay sure fine yup all right ye –'

'Shut up, Al.'

Roderick said, 'Why were you wearing animal heads?'

Inspector Wcz turned, turned away again.

One of the deputies spoke. 'Yeah, why were you wearing animal heads?'

'We were on another case,' said Bunne. Wcz looked at him and he fell silent.

Nothing more was said to Roderick or about him, as the FBI men drove him to the airport and bundled him aboard the plane which had been held for them. Nothing was said about Roderick or to him all through the flight. Agent Bunne watched the movie (in which a stripper adopts a crippled puppy and is therefore pursued by the Mafia, crashing a lot of new cars). Inspector Wcz studied a book called *The McBabbitt Way to Facial Success.*

Two more FBI men met the plane, packed themselves with Roderick into a limousine, and the five of them set off across the desert.

'Is it all right if I know where we're going?' Roderick asked. Three of the FBI men exchanged looks and shifted around uncomfortably; the car was full of the creak of shoulder holsters. Inspector Wcz affected not to hear.

'Might as well tell him, eh Inspector?' Bunne said.

Wcz laughed, or at least, laughing sounds came from his stiff face. 'Sure, you tell him. Tell him what they do to *robots* at the Orinoco Institute.'

'Isn't that a think tank?' asked Roderick.

'You tell him.' Wcz laughed again. 'Tell him about the Orinoco policy – *wiping out all robots and all robot builders. Because,* tell him, *There is only room for one intelligent life-form on this planet.* Tell him.'

'Lawyers?' Roderick asked. 'Corporation lawyers?'

'Tell him he won't feel like being funny once they get hold of him. Tell him how they start dismantling and interrogating at the same time. They know how to get everything out of a machine. They keep him alive, hanging by a thread until they can squeeze out the last bit of data. Then *ssquonnge!*' Wcz laughed. 'That's the sound of expensive metal being crushed – *ssquonnge!*'

The Orinoco Institute was a few acres of lush green grass in the middle of the desert, fenced off and guarded, and dotted with windowless buildings. Roderick was taken into one of these. After various pieces of paper were exchanged with various guards, he was marched into an office. The man behind the desk was cleaning his pipe; the air was hazy with smoke.

'Hello there, Roderick.'

'Do I know you?'

'Ha ha no, no. But I sure know you. Been keeping tabs on you for years. Take a chair.' He scratched his brush-cut hair and looked at the FBI men. 'Uh, fellas, I need to have a private talk with Roderick here, okay? Could you go solve the Lindbergh case or something?'

When they had meekly shuffled out, the pipe-smoker stoked up his pipe and lit it. Then he sat on the edge of his desk, and he arranged his left hand to grip the leather patch on the right elbow of his tweed jacket, while the right hand held up his smouldering pipe. He didn't actually smoke the pipe much, mostly tapped his glasses frame with its stem. 'First thing, I guess, is to tell you a little about the Orinoco Institute. Have you ever heard of us?'

'I heard you were some kind of government think-tank, that's all.'

The pipe tapped. 'Ah yes, that wonderful newspaper phrase, almost makes you think of a bunch of oversized brains in an aquarium, all pulsing with ideas, eh? Ha ha, well that's not – altogether true. By and large, we're all ordinary human beings, except that we're intelligent, we have some expertise, and we work on The Future. We're what the newspapers would call *futurologists*, people who try to extend the graph line from the known into the unknown. And sometimes we try to shape that line.'

'You try to influence trends?'

'Exactly. In that sense, we're not just a think tank, we're an "act" tank too. We try to help provide the kind of future this country (and this world) wants and needs. One of my former colleagues said, "Our job is to keep the damn world on the damn graph paper," and I think that says it pretty well. We do try to keep the trend lines smooth, the future free from sudden shocks and surprises. I think you'll like it here, Roderick. It's a challenging, stimulating place.'

'*Ssquonnge*,' said Roderick.

'Eh? Anyway, our system does work. We try to spot trends early. A trend spotted early enough can be encouraged, lessened, reshaped, eliminated – at very little cost. Later of course, it's more expensive. Later still, impossible at any price.'

After a pause to relight his pipe, 'Which brings us to the robot phenomenon, eh? The artificial intelligence, the android, robot, automaton, or as we prefer to call it, the *Entity*, constitutes a deep and disturbing trend. Some years ago we did a breakdown of all cybernetic work and worked a few projections. No doubt about it, research teams everywhere were inching their way towards one goal, the production of a viable Entity. Our guess was, someone was going to make it – but was this a good or a bad event? We did a very careful analysis, we discussed, modelled, projected and discussed again, but finally we had to give Entities the thumbs-down. This trend had to be crushed.'

'But why?'

'Plenty of reasons. Quite a few. Many.'

'Such as?'

The pipe-smoker cleared his throat. 'Well, it is all classified, but I guess there's no real harm in telling you. Not now.'

'Like a gloating villain,' Roderick murmured.

'Eh? Anyway, reasons for stopping Entities: for one thing, suppose machines get as intelligent as men, and decide not to take orders any more? Suppose they get even more intelligent and simply wipe out humanity?'

'Suppose they get so intelligent they see the futility of wiping out other species?' Roderick countered.

'Yes yes yes, I didn't say there were no counter-arguments. I'm just giving you our reasons. Suppose Entities took over all the jobs, all the worthwhile jobs, by virtue of being able to do them better or cheaper than men? That would leave us with a population forced into idleness – never desirable, whatever utopians might think. Or suppose machines begin solving many of our major problems, such as curing cancer or doubling lifespans or cheap fuel or cheap ways of mining other planets – do you see where such a wealth of handed-down answers could lead us? Yes, we could end up a pathetic kind of cargo-cult. Or suppose the intelligent machines did none of the above things, but suppose that just the *idea* of having intelligent machines on Earth caused a profound shock to the foundations of our societies – a civilization-quake? For example, where such an idea percolates down to the uneasy, fearful or unhappy masses, it could become the focus for any revolutionary tendencies.'

'Such as Machines Lib or the Luddites?'

'Precisely.' The pipe needed lighting again. 'Machines can become gods or demons, angels or rivals, in the inflamed imaginations of the lunatic fringe. In troubled times, the Entity might become a scapegoat or a messiah – an embodiment of instability. So we voted to stop the Entities. And by and large, we've been pretty successful. I won't go into details, but we did manage things like shutting off funds for certain lines of research. And we used other government agencies to – to persuade people not to go on trying to make Entities.'

'But I slipped through.'

'You slipped through.' The pipe-stem tapped the glasses. 'You certainly did slip through. A concatenation of circumstances – fraud, resulting in a cover-up that covered you up too; Mr Sonnenschein's paranoid precautions in smuggling you away; the fact that you had various foster homes and kept dropping out of sight; an unfortunately inept team of men from the Agency – you did slip through, and here you are today.'

'What happens next?' Roderick asked, not really wanting to know. Knowing.

'I think we ought to introduce you around, eh?'

'Look, what's the point? If you're just going to trash me, why not get it over with?'

'Trash you?' The man was so startled he forgot to tap his glasses. 'Good grief, didn't I make that clear? Our entire policy on Entities has been *reversed*. We're *not* stopping them any more.'

'No? But then –'

'We didn't bring you here to trash you, Roderick. On the contrary: we want you to join our team.'

'Is this a trick?'

'Ha ha, no trick. We really are inviting you to dive into our tank for a good think, ha ha.'

'I'll think about it,' said Roderick seriously.
'Ha ha, great. Come on in, the water's fine.'
'I wonder if it is,' said Roderick seriously.
'Ha ha.'

XXIII

At the hour of anguish and vague light
He would rest his eyes on his Golem.
Who can tell us what God felt,
As he gazed on his rabbi in Prague?
> Jorge Luis Borges, *The Golem*

Mr Kratt's thick black V of eyebrow came down deeper; he bit through his cheap cigar. 'Goddamnit, bub,' he said into the telephone, 'you sure about this federal court order? Fine damn country if the damn government can send in the FBI to deprive a man of his legitimate property . . . Well, damn-it, Moonbrand, you and Honcho are supposed to be the damned lawyers, you tell me, can't we lodge an appeal . . . Yes well look, I didn't hire you to just sit in your damn hacienda out there and swill orange juice, I hired you to protect KUR interests, my interests, not to . . . No okay, no all right, maybe you and your partner have been *zapped by this Uncle Sam authority trip,* but now listen bub, can the California crap and listen, I want that damn robot! You're the one said I got a legal claim in the first place, now you just go and get the damn thing. Or at least tell me how I can get it . . . Yeah well, forget your damn karma for a minute, I got a corporation ready to fall apart if I don't get some good gimmick, I got Moxon breathing down my neck, I got a bank about to fold if that asshole Fleischman doesn't remember where he parked that sixty million dollars, frankly I don't need your damn karma.'

The image of his growling voice, turned into numbers, beamed up to a satellite and back down to California, finally emerged from what looked like a gold conch shell held to Wade Moonbrand's ear. His bare feet rested on the desktop, which had been made from a teak surfboard. He kept his eyes on a meditation symbol on the wall, a nest of concentric rings; when he'd finished talking he pulled a Colt .45 from inside his floral shirt and put three shots into the middle of the symbol.

'Cass, old buddy, we kind of aced ourselfs, you know? I mean talk about the oneness of everything, we aced our own selfs!'

Cass Honcho, wearing buckskin and sitting at a desk made of a split log, nodded to show he was awake.

'Talk about conflict of innerest,' Moonbrand went on. 'I finally got the story outa the Orinoco gang, and guess who's behind the FBI move? Leo! Leo Bunsky, our client! Man, if we hadn't slapped that injunction on them to get the poor bastard's head straight – I mean wires uncrossed – like he would still be floating on some astral plane with like Madame Blavatsky and James Dean, instead of down here making waves. We aced our own selfs!

'Like you remember when we took on Leo as a client? And we got that injunction against Orinoco saying they was violating his civil rights? And we wanted our electronics people and neurologists to look him over, remember that?'

Honcho nodded.

'And man their argument was just that Leo had all his rights because they let him vote with the rest of the committee, only we argued that you couldn't be sure his vote was real unless we got our experts in there to check his wiring, remember?'

Honcho nodded.

'And then when our boys did go in there sure enough they found a couple of wires crossed or something, so like his vote was garbled, remember? And after that they voted on something and Leo changed his vote and I guess the bottom line is, they decided to send in the FBI and just grab Roderick; so there we are, aced. I mean we just get one client fixed up so he can think straight, first thing he does is rip off another client. Mr Kratt's mad as hell and we lose out everywhere. Talk about a conflict of innerest, we just conflicted all over ourselfs there, you know what I wish?'

Honcho nodded.

'I wish there was some piranha fish in Leo Bunsky's tank.'

Roderick stared at the brain in the tank, trying to see it as a living person and not as a relic. Leo Bunsky had created him; now he tried to reconstruct Leo Bunsky, as his guide explained and explained:

'. . . see one of the key factors in our policy on Entities was always Leo's vote: no matter how hard he might argue for building Entities, when it came to a vote he always voted for their extermination. You're probably wondering whether we didn't think there was something wrong, but, hell, a lot of people here play games like that, arguing intellectually but voting with their true feelings. We thought Leo really was opposed to Entities. His vote influenced other votes, so the Entity extermination policy always had a comfortable plurality. And, well, it was only after Leo's lawyers made us check the wiring that we realized, Leo's vote was being misrecorded. *He* thought he was voting "Nay", *we* thought he was voting "Aye". For poor Leo, Yes meant No.'

'But I guess you don't want to hear all this internal gossip, right? So why don't we move right along?'

The guide was a younger version of the first pipe-smoker. He had the same brush-cut hair (Roderick could imagine the two of them lying end-to-end, the tops of their heads meshing like a pair of military brushes) and the same tweed jacket.

'I see you're looking at my leather elbow patches,' he said in the elevator.

'Was I? Yes, I guess I was.'

'Neat, huh? See this one zips open, it's a pocket. For my pipe.'

'Oh.'

'A lot of the fellas have them, see we get these wholesale prices from this big sporting goods outfit, O'Bride International. We tried some blazers too, real neat with our own crest, only we had to send them back, they screwed up the name. Here we are, Sub-basement Eight.'

The doors opened on brilliant green rain-forest, complete with steaming undergrowth, sunlight pouring down through the clerestory of tall trees, snakes lazing among the lianas and pennant-bright birds in the shrubs.

'This can't be real.'

'Good, isn't it? Mostly mirrors and holograms, with a few plastic bushes. Okay, we just follow this trail here.'

They rounded a tree and the jungle vanished, leaving them in an ordinary, even shabby corridor. 'Some psychiatrist figured having a little foyer like this on each floor would help everybody concentrate. On other floors they have mountains or desert or quiet smalltown streets. One floor's got Oxford or is it Cambridge? To help everybody concentrate.'

'Does it help?'

'Naw, it's a lot of hooey.' The guide rapped at the first door and opened it. An old man wearing a frock coat and a huge panama 'planter's' hat sat hunched over his desk. He was using an abacus with no great speed or skill. On the blackboard behind him was written, THE GREATEST GOOD FOR THE GREATEST *NUMBER*.

'Come in, come in,' he said, not looking up. 'Have you brought my robot? Just leave it in the corner.'

'Not this one,' said the guide, chuckling. 'I'm showing him around.'

'Show him around later! This is important!' Even the beads snapped.

Roderick asked the man what he was calculating.

'Oh, nothing much! Nothing much! Just setting out a complete moral code for all human conduct, that's all!'

A complete moral code?'

'Complete.' The old man finished a calculation and laid down his abacus. 'Covering not only every recorded human action, but every possible imaginable human action. Complete, detailed, and mathematically precise. Are you familiar with the principles of Utilitarianism? An act is judged moral if it achieves the greatest possible good for the greatest possible number. But *what* number? that is the question. *Which* number?'

Roderick tried to look quizzical.

'The method is really quite simple. Every human action has its own individual number. And every set of circumstances is an equation. We simply plug the numbers into the equations and off we go!'

The guide said, 'Yeah, well, off *we* go, we've got a lot of ground to cover –'

'Wait a minute, just let me show you.' The old man leaped to his blackboard and erased it energetically, the motion making his hat-brim quiver. He sketched a diagram. 'Now here for instance we have the classical nuclear war standoff, East against West.

584

Each side has the same two choices, either strike first or wait. So there are four possible outcomes. Now take West's options. If he strikes first, West can win (that is + 1) but only if East has waited. But if both try to strike first, the whole world is wiped out (that is definitely −1). On balance, then, West neither gains nor loses from striking first. What if he waits? The best that can happen is nothing (0), and that's if East waits too. The worst that can happen is if East strikes first and West is destroyed (−1). So on balance, West loses by waiting. Now what is West's best strategy?'

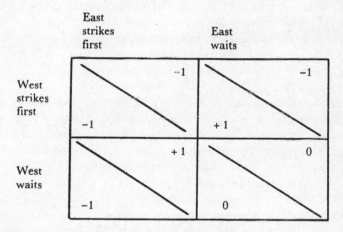

Roderick looked at the diagram. 'Striking first?'

'Exactly. And of course it is also East's best strategy. Without doubt, both sides ought to strike first. But if they both do that, we get—'

'The worst of all possible worlds?'

'Precisely. It's a dilemma* all right: if both sides make their best play, everybody loses. Utilitarianism has to clean up dilemmas like this before it can come to a complete calculus of morality.' The panama hat-brim vibrated with feeling. 'Sometimes I'd like to get the real East and West here in my office and give them real buttons to push. Then, by thunder, we'd see!'

When Roderick and his guide were leaving, the old man added, 'Come back soon. I'll show you what we're doing with catastrophe theory . . .'

They moved on to the next office, where with the aid of more diagrams, a man explained his speculations about solar energy: He was working out ways of storing it in common plants, especially cucumbers.

Next, Roderick met a team planning to recycle sewage to provide not only methane and fertilizers, but intriguing new foods. One of them said:

'Sure, it must sound crazy, but the fact is, the demand for junk foods and fast foods is rising exponentially. In a few years, the public will demand the right to eat pretty much anything. My only worry is, can we meet the challenge fast enough?'

In the next office a large group were contemplating possible wars, and no combination was too unlikely to be considered: a clash between the navies of Luxembourg and Paraguay, a parachute invasion of Finland by the Boobies of Fernando Po, Las Vegas bombed by Lapps.

Another office was concerned with future possible natural disasters and their implications. Suppose for example California suddenly sank into the waters of the Pacific – how would the national economy be affected by the loss of so many millionaires? With Hollywood gone, where would the Mafia next invest its money? What would be the cultural effect of TV drama without car chases?

Other offices were devoted to monitoring various 'fringe' sciences that 'just might' turn into worthwhile lines of enquiry: parapsychology, for example. A pipe-smoking parapsychologist explained:

'The whole field is bursting with new ideas, new research projects. Professor Fether in Chicago has been testing precognition in hippos. The Russians have had a breakthrough on the ouija board to Lenin. The ghost labs of California seem to be doing some solid research . . . Others are breaking new ground too, testing the hypothesis that hypnagogic visions are real . . . a new thought-gun that shoots down UFOs, a Dutch psychic who produces rabbits out of a hat . . . Seems to be a new theory that if you stare at the back of someone's neck, they'll turn around and look at you, even in a crowd . . .'

While in the next office, astrologers were checking a British theory that all black persons were born under Libra, all subversives under Scorpio, all women under Capricorn.

Next came a conference room where a dozen persons smoked pipes or filed nails as they listened to a lecture on Jungian economics. The lecturer broke off to define a few basic principles for Roderick's benefit:

'Take market forces, for example: are they real? We see that, just as people's belief in flying, saucers, so-called, made them really appear in the sky, so too people's belief in a rising or falling stock market made it really rise or fall. Could "bear" and "bull" be ancient fertility and virility archetypes – Ursa Major and Taurus?'

Though Roderick was to visit only a handful of the five hundred offices at the Orinoco Institute, he met enough people to give him some grasp of the breadth and scope of this mighty academy. There were statisticians and climatologists, news reporters and military historians, oceanographers and Esperanto speakers, bioengineers and anthropologists, a mad gypsy fortune teller and a moping science-fiction writer, and even a psychologist who specialized in probing the minds of infants. All bets seemed to be covered.

At the end of the afternoon, he was allowed to sit in on a 'brainstorming' session in which higher-level futurologists tried to piece together all the findings of their subordinates. He understood a word or two, now and then:

'Microwave mind control, could we do a restructuring of the update there in Scenario 6A?'

'That's your problem, I'm restructuring the input-output model of undersea city economies, I need some energy thoughts.'

'What demand level? You in the tokamak range there?'

'Yes, but . . . the multifold trend . . .'

'Screw that! Listen, in the Afro-Asian socio-economic surprise-free framework . . .'

'Come on, guys and dolls, let's be macrohistorical here, okay? I mean even if India does start a bacteriological war, we can still project at least . . .'

'I backgrounded the promethean satellite scenario for ten million kilowatts and up, but . . .'

'. . . how head transplants might screw up the . . .'

'. . . penological flexi-time? Only with broad-spectrum vaccines, where does that leave us?'

'. . . synergy?'

'Energy . . .'

'. . . better update the restructuring of these pluralistic security communities, whatever you do.'

'. . . integrated whale ranch cloning? Check that.'

'. . . energy?'

'But synergy . . .'

'. . . and anyway, by then American cars'll be running on sugar too.'

When the meeting broke up, some of the futurologists seemed angry, others very pleased with themselves. One of the smug ones, a tall young man wearing a blazer, came over to slap Roderick on the back.

'So you're the Entity! Great! Great to have you aboard!' Thump, slap.

'I – thank you – uh.'

'What do you think of the old place so far? From an Entity point of view, it must seem kinda weird, eh?'

'Well, I–'

'Our friend here giving you the full tour?' Thump. Roderick, speechless, stared at the crest on the blazer. It read *Iron Icon*, and in much smaller letters, *Made in Korea*.

The guide said, 'Yep, well in fact we're on our way to a directors' meeting now.'

'Great. See you round, Entity. Hang loose.' The heavy hand, poised for another slap, paused. 'We can't keep calling you Entity, you oughta have a name, you know?'

'I know,' said Roderick. 'And I–'

'Rusty. We'll call you Rusty. Rusty Robot, not bad eh?' The pummelling was renewed until Roderick's guide led him away. 'So long, Rusty!'

He was taken to a conference room where the air was milky blue with pipe-smoke. Along the green leather table, thin liver-spotted hands were passing papers, drumming with impatience, grasping the bowls of pipes. Reptilian eyes moved to study the newcomer, as the rustle of conversation slowly died away.

The chairman at the far end of the table put his hands on the green leather and pushed himself to his feet. The posture was amphibian; an old frog poised at the edge of a mossy dark pond.

'This is our Entity member, ladies and gentlemen We won't bother with introductions if you don't mind; there are so many items to get through today. So unless you have any questions, could you take your seat and familiarize yourself with the agenda? Good.'

Roderick slipped into a seat and stared without comprehension at the paper before him. He was aware of the eyes, shifting in their pouches of wrinkled skin to focus on him, but he could not look back at them. Only natural that they stared. He was a curiosity. Possibly edible.

1. General remarks, chair.
2. Dr Sheldon D'Eath's report on robot medicine and allied subjects.
3. Large computer networks (e.g. Banking, Government, Military): How stable?
4. Wind-up of old projects and operations:
   (a) Operation Nepomuk
   (b) Operation Barsinister
   (c) Operation Duckplantain
5. Kick-off of new projects and operations:
   (a) Project Junebug
   (b) Operation Tinhead
6. A.O.B.
7. (unscheduled) Video report from Vitanuova Space Salvage: shuttle test using robot test pilot.

By the time Roderick had read this, Dr D'Eath was already addressing them via satellite, describing his invention of a robot for testing artificial hearts.

'*I patented the design a few years ago, but so far no one is willing to take on production. Maybe with your recommendation, gentle people.*' He was a bland, plump man in pince-nez, with a moustache that made him look on the screen a little like Teddy Roosevelt. '*The* cost-effectiveness *is favourable compared with using lab animals. Not only are lab animal prices increasing at forty percent per year, there are all the high running costs: feed and vet bills, insurance against anti-vivisection raids Besides, what do animal data mean in the end? You can't compare a goat or a calf to say an advertising executive who jogs but smokes – the human life-style variables can never be satisfactorily matched. And finally, you need a lot of back-up animals, in case of rejection problems, or in case you want to try out design modifications. You need a new animal for each fiddly little modification, say if you change the flip-disc valves. But with my robot it's easy: You just fit the dacron cuffs, then you snap out one heart and snap in the other. Then just fill 'er up with blood and – bingo!'*

The chairman said, 'Like to interrupt here and suspend the agenda for a moment, to bring in that live video report from Vitanuova Space Salvage. They're testing some new shuttle using some robot test pilot – have we got that?'

The screen lit up with a familiar scene, a space shuttle lashed to a rocket, steaming on the launching pad for a moment before the whole unwieldy-looking assembly rose slowly on a column of fire. A voice commented: '. . . *have lift-off. Two remarkable things about this test: first of all the pilot is a humanoid robot, using ordinary controls with no special fly-by-wire connections at all. The robot, nicknamed Mr Punch, just sits in the pilot's seat and uses controls like anybody else. The second remarkable thing is the speed with which this whole operation was assembled: the minute Mr Franklin's robot completed its successful testing at KUR labs, he personally brought it over to us and in fact I guess he personally installed it in the shuttle. We're talking here about a turnaround time of hours and not days, a really great achievement. We've, um, we've been trying to get Mr Franklin up to the video unit here to give us his comments on the test so far, but – no, nobody seems to be able to locate him. Well, what can I tell you about him? Mr Ben Franklin, brilliant Product Development man at KUR, and I understand Mr Punch is his personal baby . . .'*

Kratt's stubby finger stabbed a phone button. 'Connie, get me Hare, quick . . . Hare? This is Kratt, what the devil you and Franklin been cooking up between you? Hell you say. Listen, hub, I just been getting the DB from Vitanuova Space Salvage, that goddamn robot is over there right now, yes right now, flying one of their damned shuttles by the seat of its pants – yes I mean the same goddamned Mr Punch you said didn't work. How much did Franklin pay you to tell me it failed the test? Whatever it was it wasn't enough, you're not only out of a job as of now, I'm gonna sue the piss out of you. You two figure you can just walk off with KUR property like that, sell it to somebody else? I'm gonna sue the both of you, and I'll get you for grand theft, fraud, misuse of company facilities, I – oh yeah? But how could it fail? I can see the damn space shuttle flying right now, doesn't look like a damn failure to me, bub.'

He clenched a fist and stared for a moment at the heavy gold ring mounted with a single steel ball, then looked to the screen where the commentary accompanied diagrams of the Vitanuova Space Salvage Shuttle in proposed operation:

'*Yes now I believe we have located Mr Franklin in his car in the parking lot, evidently he's pretty excited about this test so far, you can see the theoretical test on your screen now, he's pretty excited, seems to be driving around in circles and honking his horn, that right, Nancy? Shouting what? "That's the way to do it!" Well it certainly is, the people here at ground control are happy too so far this test is looking good, looking good, we'll try to get hold of Mr Ben Franklin himself, maybe get his reaction to the test but now maybe we're ready with a shot of the robot pilot in operation, that ready? Yes, here's what you've all been waiting for . . .*'

The figure at the controls might have been mistaken for that of a robot at a distance, but the face was without doubt the face of Ben Franklin, his the ragged beard, his the pale expressionless eyes and mad grin.

A bored voice from ground control said, '*Looks like you have a little temperature buildup there, Mr Punch, can you confirm that incremental?*'

'*Fffffffff*'

'*Say again? Can you confirm that temperature incremental in the cabin temperature?*'

'*Shhhhhhhhh*' came from the shuttle, as the camera vibrated and the bright face leaped and danced on the screen.

'*. . . will praise thee, for I am fearfully and wonderfully made: marvellous are thy works and that my soul knoweth right well. My substance was not hid from thee, when I was made in secret, and curiosly wrought in the lowest parts of the earth. Thine eyes did see my substance ffffffffff and in thy book all my members are written, which in shhhhhhhhhh were fashioned when as yet there was none of them.*'

In the ground control centre an argument took over the sound, many muffled and hysterical voices competing for the single ear.

'*What's he saying? What's he –?*'

'*. . . Franklin I'm telling you that's Franklin up there . . .*'

'*. . . alert on that increment we'll be seeing smoke in . . .*'

'*Don't be stupid, Nancy says he's down in the parking . . .*'

591

'The Bible or . . .?'

'Okay then who's in the damn car?'

'Temperature incremental is getting – look!'

'Oh my God!'

'Oh!'

The screen showed an instant of Ben Franklin's face, the eyes reflecting the sheet of flame before it swept over him and the transmission ended.

After a moment the chairman shrugged. 'Well we mustn't dwell on that, there's too much to get through here. And I understand we've just had word from KUR that in fact Franklin was fired a week ago. Well. I suggest we take a short break here before we tackle the next item.'

A reptilian jaw near Roderick gave out a dry chuckle. 'Dear me, I suppose young Mr Wood here must think it's all as exciting as a TV car chase every day around here. Let me assure you, Mr Wood, nothing could be further from the truth. Most of our meetings engage the intellect, not the endocrine system.'

'Lucky thing,' said another. 'Some of us are old enough to find any stimulation a risk not worth taking, heh heh. The grave beckons.'

'Or the fishtank,' said the first jaw. 'One might seek salvation in the Leo Bunsky aquarium, eh?'

'Ugly, ugly. I put my trust in the resurrection of the body.'

'Religion?'

'Of course not, I mean freeze-drying.'

'But you must grant that, for all poor Leo's ugliness, he has at least brought us out of the wilderness of hunting entities. Mr Wood would be thankful for that, I'm sure.'

'Precisely. All the unsavoury operations we had to initiate. Why, even when hunting Mr Wood here, didn't we –?'

'Perhaps Mr Wood doesn't want to hear –'

'Oh I do,' said Roderick. 'How did you hunt me?'

'We used these incompetent men from the Agency, mostly. I suppose the worst was that business with the Roxy theatre. Imagine burning down a whole movie house just to kill one robot. And then they bungled it.'

Roderick said, 'Wait a minute. To destroy me, you were actually willing to burn up a whole theatre full of people?'

'Well of course you have to see this in an historical perspective, balancing a few hundred lives against – as we saw it – the survival of the human species. Not that we'd have authorized it specifically.'

'Indeed not,' said the other. 'Too inefficient, no finesse. Those Agency men were always ham-handed, let's not forget the incident of the red stocking-cap.'

Roderick asked what red stocking-cap.

'Don't you remember? You were supposed to be wearing it at the Tik Tok Bar, but you cunningly planted it on some old derelict – another life lost, I fear.'

'Still, Wood, you were a most excellent quarry. Much too good for those yahoos from the Agency.'

'Have I got this straight?' Roderick asked. 'You really murdered innocent people, just to destroy me?'

'Heh heh, well of course you weren't the only target. We had to make extensive use of Agency men and even one or two private hit-men, my word yes.'

'What are you saying? You just went out and, and butchered people right and left?' Roderick's voice was loud now, and everyone in the room had turned to stare. 'Butchered people right and left, just for some principle – some *policy* – you could reverse anyway whenever you felt like it – you could –'

'Ah well, aren't policy and principle so often confused, in these troubled times? But to say we *butchered people right and left* is both emotive and inaccurate. We were normally quite selective; those we asked the Agency to "finalize" as we liked to call it, were the inventors of dangerous Entities. Had we let them live, they'd go on making trouble for humanity.'

'Within our framework for speculation, there was nothing else we could do,' said the chairman, laying his hands on the table. 'We were in a zero-option scenario.'

'Precisely. Precisely. Precisely.'

Roderick had reached the door when the chairman said, 'Leaving? That's unwise, Mr Wood. Without our protection, you'll automatically become the property of KUR International. They'll probably take your head to pieces.'

'Suits me.'

593

XXIV

'Just take a seat, Mr Wood is it? I'll see if somebody can, excuse me . . . Good morning, KUR Innernational . . . Mr Swann? One moment . . . Ginny, there's a Dr Welby on three to talk to a Mr Swann, is he in your office? No? Then he must be Patsy's new boss or, everything's in such a mess around here today, oh is he legal? Great . . . Lois have you got a Mr Swann? I have a Dr Welby for him on three . . . Good morning, KUR Innernational . . . Yes there is but I don't know when, I can put you through to the press office . . .'

Roderick sat down with a group of reporters: tired-looking men and women in waterproof coats, some with aerials sticking up from the backs of their necks, some fiddling with cameras or pocket memo machines, some sleeping.

'You covering this too?' someone said, and when Roderick did not reply, went on: 'I drew the short straw, I wanted to cover that management consultant mass murder story, sounds like some juicy stuff there, cops say the guy's been doing it for years, cutting women's legs off.'

'Juicy stuff? Is that what you call it?'

'Well sure, easy to get a handle on a story like that, you got sex, big business, police incompetence, a sadistic fiend, that's all prime stuff, you automatically get first or second slot in the six o'clock. Whereas this Moxon takeover is not exactly a surprise, is it?'

'Takeover?' said Roderick, surprised.

'I mean it should rate a paragraph on about page 733 of the financial news teletext; nobody cares who runs big corporations nowadays, or who owns them, or why. I mean it's slightly less interesting than say the intrigues of Ruritanian internal politics; I really hate this financial desk job.'

'Don't underrate it, kid,' said an older reporter, waking up. 'You start believing it's worthless, pretty soon everybody else

594

believes it's worthless. Pretty soon companies start asking themselves why they should go on throwing champagne press receptions, whole system could melt down under us, leave nothing but real news to report.'

They stared out through the glass wall at real rain splashing on the perfectly square acre of concrete that separated the KUR Tower from real sidewalks and streets.

'Okay, it's a real meaningful job. So where's the champagne?'

Someone adjusted his camera by focusing on the receptionist, behind her violet desk. Today she had taken the trouble to appear in violet hair, nails and lipstick, and now she smiled and turned so that the violet telephone receiver did not hide her smile. 'Good morning, KUR Innernational . . . I can give you the press office . . . Ginny, did you *see* him yesterday? No *him*, when the ambulance men rolled him away right by my desk, he had on this oxygen mask and I mean he looked so helpless, even his eyebrows, and when you think how we all used to be so scared of him, he never even would say good morning or have a nice, if he even noticed you it was only to make some sarcastic remark about how he ought to replace you with a Roberta Receptionist machine, and now there he was. There he was, so helpless, helpless as a, a dog. Just a sec, Good morning, KUR Innernational . . .'

'Besides,' said the older reporter, 'a conglomerate like this is interesting for its own sake. It's like an incredibly complicated puppet – you never know where all the strings lead until you pull them and see what jumps. And something like this – Kratt keeling over like that during the negotiations – it's like the puppeteer dropping all the strings. Now we'll see how good Moxon is at picking them up and sorting them out.'

'Yeah, but he's bringing in a lot of strings of his own,' said the younger. 'I heard there's gonna be a complete changeover of personnel, with –'

'Well, there he is, let's ask him.'

There was a stampede past the reception desk to where Everett Moxon, flanked by press aides, waited to greet them.

'Mr Moxon, is it true you seized the moment to pull the takeover, because Kratt, who always opposed you, was safely out of the way?'

'Everett, look this way?'

'Mr Moxon, would you say KUR is shaky, with some of its subsidiaries –?'

'What kind of changes do you envision for –?'

Moxon grinned Presidentially. 'Boys and girls, one at a time, please. I thought we might go up to the penthouse and do this over a few glasses of champagne, okay? But I'll just say now that Mr Kratt and I may have had a few minor disagreements, but we always saw eye to eye on all major decisions about the future of KUR. And when he recovers, he knows he can go on as chairman of the board as long as he likes. As you all know, the takeover has been in the cards for a long time. We like KUR, and KUR can use our capital. But let me say, let me just say that there is not going to be any asset-stripping, the Moxon Corporation is not an asset-stripping operation. Naturally we'll have to look over the whole basket of apples and get rid of any bad ones, but only to protect the rest. Anyone here like champagne?'

'What I'd like even more, Mr Moxon, is to know what are your plans for the KUR banking subsidiary, with General Fleisch –'

Still clamouring questions, they packed into elevators and disappeared. The receptionist said, 'Ginny, have you seen him? Not him, *him*, Mr Moxon. Not bad looking only his head is kinda small, just a sec. Good morning, KUR Inner –, oh hello Dr Hare, are you coming in today because a Dr D'Earth called a few times. Oh and there's a Mr Roderick Wood waiting to see somebody, who should I, to whom should he – never mind, he's gone . . .'

Upstairs Everett Moxon walked around holding a glass of champagne and smiling for five minutes before ducking out to his office.

His secretaries, Ann and Andy, were trying to clean the place. Ann held an ashtray containing a chewed cigar stub; Andy was dusting.

'Sorry, sir. KUR janitors are on strike,' said Andy.

Ann sighed. 'Something about automated cleaning machines in some subsidiary called Slumbertite.'

'Wonderful timing.' He looked around. 'Is that interior decorator here? Send him in.'

Ann hesitated. 'There are a lot of people waiting, sir. Jud Mill and people from Katrat, from Datajoy, from T-Track Records and Mistah Kurtz Eating Houses. And there's even a delegation from Kratt Brothers Midway Shows.'

'That's right,' Andy snickered. 'They look like the cast of *Guys and Dolls*, I've never seen so many sharp sideburns and black shirts with white ties.'

'Okay. Okay. Send Jud in first, and tell the decorator he can make measurements or look around and get inspiration but he has to keep out of the way. Datajoy? What do we own called Datajoy?'

Ann and Andy exchanged looks. Andy said, 'Well, it's sort of a combined clinic and pleasure ranch –'

'Never mind how it's marketed, what *is* it?'

Ann said, 'They implant electrodes in the customers' heads, to stimulate their pleasure centres. It's a leasing arrangement; as long as they keep up the payments they stay turned on. If they miss a payment –'

'The electrode gets ripped out,' Andy said. 'One of Kratt's more disgusting ideas.'

'Disgusting, yes.' Moxon's phone rang. He sat on the desk and reached for it. 'Still, if we combined it with Moxon Retirement Systems ... Hello, Moxon ... What is it, Francine, I've got people to see ... Jough Braun, what does he, yes all right, all right we'll talk about it.'

Jud Mill was a distinguished-looking man of no particular age or sex. He began spreading folders on the desk and peering at them through half-moon reading glasses. 'I may as well admit we had a few problems, Mr Moxon, with this direct editing scheme. When Mr Kratt brought me in as a media management consultant, I told him I foresaw problems with authors. Sure enough, everything worked well enough with the bookstore chains, the market survey people, the editorial – but the authors had problems. Authors always screw up a package.'

'What happened? Direct editing?'

'It works like this: the author writes directly on to a computer. This is linked up to leading bookstore chains, to their sales computers, and to prose analysis programs. The idea was to give the author instant feedback; as soon as he pecks out a few words, the computer grinds it through and tells him how good it is.'

'How good?'

'For his sales. By comparing sentences with sentences in his earlier books, and up-to-the-minute sales records, it can help him shape his prose *as he writes*.'

'But it went wrong?'

'In a sense. We had this leading Katrat Books author parked at his tax-haven home down in Nassau, hammering out his book on our DE system, when evidently he developed some kind of block. So to keep up his quota, he started, well, plagiarizing his own previous books. Naturally the computer rated this as highly saleable stuff, and I am afraid it went into production. See, the computer also sets type and – well in fact, *The Hills Afar* is a word-for-word copy of *Red Situation*, thirty million copies went out.'

'Jesus. Could be sued by thirty million customers.'

'No, well oddly enough, it's selling very well and so far nobody seems to notice. The bookstore figures show we could even reprint.' He opened another folder and sat back, causing the striped collar of his shirt to crackle. 'That's not important now. What I really wanted to do was launch a more foolproof scheme, total computer authorship.'

Moxon looked surprised. 'But I thought –'

'Computers weren't ready? Not to produce works of "lasting literary significance", no, but to write *big bucks books*, yes. Naturally we keep the authorship under wraps, create a persona using a photo of a model, a fake bio – even, if necessary, an actor to appear on TV. I've talked it over with Mel Zell at –'

'Wait a minute, hold on there. I'm not at all sure about leaving out the human touch like that, the author is very –'

'The author is one big problem for everybody,' said Mill. 'When you're trying to orchestrate a big, complex deal, bringing together all the elements of the package each in the right quantity at the right time, the author just gets in the way. When I architected a certain big property a few years ago with Sol Alter, we started with a one-line idea. Then we got a big-name star interested in appearing in a movie, that enabled us to bootstrap a six-figure plus movie deal, and with all that we had something to take to the publishers. We landed a seven-figure paperback deal and from there on had no problem getting all we wanted out of magazine serialization, book club, foreign and cassette rights, direct cable specials, options for a TV series, syndicated comics, t-shirts, board games, colouring books and so on. Then we fixed the music and wrapped up those rights. And then and only then did we finally hire an author to hack out the screenplay and book, the fictionalization. We paid him I think two grand and no comebacks. That book, Mr Moxon, was *Boy and Girl.*'

The interior decorator, who had been quietly walking around the office, now cleared his throat.

'What is it?'

'This apostle clock on the wall – it'll have to go, Mr Moxon. For one thing, it's an obvious fake.'

'Fine, take it away.' Moxon turned to Jud Mill, who was now collecting his folders. 'I'd feel better about this computer author if I could see a sample of its work.'

'What good would that do? Oh all right, here.'

Moxon took the piece of paper and studied it for a minute. 'This some kind of joke, Jud? It's not even spelled right, looks like some six-year-old batted this out during recess.'

'No, well, our market research has been pretty darn thorough, and all the indications are that this is the coming thing, as the literacy level of the public keeps dropping, the demand is for more regressive stuff, fairy tales, basic English, short sentences . . .'

'But Jesus, this is, well just listen: "Once upon a time there was a boy. He had a Ma and a Pa, and they all lived in a little white house on the edge of Somewhere. The boy's name was Danny Sunshine, because he was allways smiling warm. Danny was only a poor boy, but he was honest and good, people could see that. One day he was wandering in the Somewhere Woods with his dog Lion. Lion was scratching in some leafs and he found an old rusty sword. 'I'll take it home and clean it up!' Danny thought to himself. 'Then I can read this funny writing on the blade, under the rust. Maybe if I keep this sword till I grow up, I can be a real nite!' So He –" The public demands this? *This?*'

Jud Mill shrugged. 'That's it. The competition already has something like this in the pipeline . . . space opera about robots, so I hear . . .'

'Great, okay, don't tell me any more, go ahead with a pilot project, I'll bring it up at the board.'

As Jud left, Ann looked in. 'General Fleischman's on line three.'

'Christ . . . Yes hello General, thank you, thanks . . . No of course we still want you on the board, no great changes just yet, we have our commitments after all . . . yes well I will, and you give mine to Gerda too, bye . . . Andy? Make a note, we've got to convene a special meeting of the board to fire General Fleischman before the old shithead loses another sixty million . . . oh and what's this memo about some nut religion suing us, what's the state of play there? Because I don't see any KUR counter-suit. Not only that, things seem to be snarled up there, the lawyers acting for this Church of Plastic Jesus are also acting for us, that right? Honcho and Moonbrand are on KUR's payroll, how can they represent, yes get our legal department to look into this, Swann, get Swann. And somebody come in here for dictation and bring the figures on Katrat Fun Foods . . .'

Behind him the decorator, having removed the wooden clock from the wall, was examining a dark stain now revealed: blood? Ink? Oil?

Roderick spent an hour in the hospitality suite, playing poker with the reporters, watching them drink champagne and stuff their pockets with xeroxed press releases. He couldn't think what to do next, where to go, what to be.

Someone turned on the large-screen TV, and there was a man in dark glasses, handcuffed to two policemen, but sitting at a table before a microphone and smiling for the cameras.

'Jeez,' said one reporter. 'I wish I was there.'

'Shh,' said another, turning up the volume. A cop spoke:

'. . . eakthrough came when I realized I'd seen this guy's M.O. before. I had a hunch the Lucky Legs Killer and the Campus Ripper were one and the same — and when I tied in the Snowman Murder, I knew it was only a matter of time. Sooner or later our killer would make one mistake too many . . .'

'But Chief, didn't your prisoner turn himself in?'

'Well yes, matter of fact he did, but we regard that as a publicity stunt. He hopes to create a favourable impression, to get his bail lowered.'

'Like to ask the prisoner how he feels about killing all those women and cutting off their legs with an electric carving knife?'

'How do I feel?' The prisoner nodded and smiled. 'That's a valid question. You're after tangible motivation, right? Gut reaction? Well, I wish I could give you a simple answer, but first I'd have to clarify a few concepts *myself. That clarification could involve a thoroughgoing process evolving in con-text and circumstance, exploring the infrastructure of any particularized situation according to well-defined parameters, without of course rejecting in advance those options which, in a broader perspective, might be seen to underpin any mean-ingful discussion attempting to cut through the appropriate interface, right?'*

'You felt mixed up?'

'He feels like reducing his bail,' said the cop.

The prisoner said, '*That's not what I said. I said there's no point in talking about my feelings, because to talk about anyone's feelings you have to make a distinction between subjective reality and objective reality – and it was just that distinction, that interface, that I was exploring!'*

After that, he fell silent and ate yoghurt, while the policeman handled questions about the influence of TV violence, the psychology of the mass murderer, the thankless role of the policeman in modern society. Roderick's attention was already beginning to wander, when someone called from the balcony:

'Come on out here, you guys! Look at that!'

They all went out, and dutifully looked down over the rail. A giant metal dish was hanging on bundles of ropes, being pulled inch by inch up the side of the building.

'What the hell is it? A dish antenna? For what?'

'Moxon Music Systems,' said a press office aide. 'You must have noticed there was no music in the elevator? Or anywhere else. Well when we get this set up, we'll be able to pick it up from our own satellite, and run it to every room in the building.'

'Music of the spheres,' said one of the old hands, lurching against the rail.

'Careful! Maybe we'd all better go inside, boys and girls?'

And gradually they all lost interest and went back to the booze, all but Roderick. He stood leaning on the rail, noticing that the rain had stopped.

He saw no point in jumping. On the other hand, he saw no point in going back inside. Here was as good as anywhere. He looked down at the wet lozenges of the city. He looked up at the rolling clouds. There was nothing to steer by, nothing permanent.

He lifted up his arms, as though he were a Pharisee at prayer or else someone expecting a heavy burden to drop from the sky.

*

A dark shadow fell across Moxon's office. He looked up to see a black disc inching up across his window, eclipsing it. 'What the devil –?' He pressed buttons and demanded an explanation.

'*It must be the dish antenna,*' Ann's voice explained. '*For the Moxon Music System. And corporate communications.*'

'As if I didn't have too many lines of communication already.'

'*Your wife's downstairs with the sculptor, Jough Braun. She wants to know if you're coming down for lunch.*'

'Tell her no, I . . . no, let me talk to her . . . Francine, look I'm sorry, I'll have to grab a sandwich at my desk, Kratt left this place in a hell of a mess. He was, I don't know, running everything like a one-man band, nothing delegated, nobody knows how to do anything . . . Fine, fine, look if you want a sculpture on the terrace down there, go ahead, only tell Jough to take it easy? We don't want a big pile of wrecked cars embalmed in epoxy or anything like that . . . no of course I'm not, I'm just trying to remind you of the image we're trying to . . . hang on, I've got . . Swann? . . . Francine, I can't talk now, you just, you just go ahead . . . Swann, you there? Listen, I've been going over the figures for this Autosaunas operation, I notice that before the medical lawsuits started hitting the fan we had a very healthy return on our investment there, I was just exploring the idea of, of when all the dust settles, of trying again . . . No, well, it's just that sex with robots does seem like the logical, um, extension of our leisure group activities, a natural follow-through on our . . . Yes, see what you can do, some kind of product warning, maybe safety checks, see what you can work out with Hare, he's the product development man, you'll be meeting him this afternoon at our . . . Ann, did you set up that meeting with Dr Hare? Okay yes, and . . . what choreographer? Oh him, Hatlo, no listen I can't talk now but set up a meeting I want him to talk to our Personnel people about working out some Japanese-style calisthenics for the whole company, five minutes every morning . . . is Hare in yet? See if you can get him for me while I . . . Who? Hello, Dr D'Eath, what can I . . . He is? What kind of recovery time are we talking about there, six months, ten years? . . . Well yes, of course, in that case a nursing home would I agree be the best, and in fact we own a chain of clinics combined with pleasure ranches ourselves, Datajoy the name is, my secretary can make all the arrangements and you can transfer Mr Kratt right away . . . Andy, talk to the doctor will you? Ann, take a memo for the press office, "At his own request the former president and founder of the KUR family of companies, Mr – give him some first name – Kratt, is being transferred from the University Hospital to one of KUR's own Datajoy clinic-ranches, where the accent is on health combined with pleasure. 'Having devoted my whole life to giving pleasure to people,' said the – make up some age – year-old tycoon, 'I thought it was time to get a little pleasure myself – and where better than at a Datajoy pleasure ranch? Where else can you get all the benefits of a clinic without a clinical environment?' " And so on, just have them take the rest out of our Datajoy brochures. Oh and get me Swann again, I want to go over this problem with this lunatic church, The Church of Plastic Jesus, I want to . . . it is? Now? On what channel?' He fumbled for buttons which brought a huge screen into view on the opposite wall, and filled it with a succession of living images: a cartoon germ, an armpit, a swimming pool filled with money. Moxon couldn't help pausing briefly at the image of a man slumped over a table, apparently dead but still handcuffed to two policemen:

'. . . don't know what, but it looks like Culpa was eating, yes you can see it there now, the carton marked pizza-flavoured yoghurt fudge. Well I guess that's it, folks, the doctor's looking at it now. As you may know, the FDA has been trying to track down the last few remaining cartons of this product, after they discovered that one of the flavouring ingredients . . .'

He switched at last to a street scene. A woman with a microphone stood before a store window in the slummy end of town. She stood to one side of the name on the window:

THE CHURCH OF PLASTIC JESUS
You may be welcome, but then again you may not

'Hi, good afternoon and welcome to Round 'n' About. I'm Joy Grayson, and the reason I'm here at this very unusual church, is to attend a very unusual meeting. Believe it or not, folks, the bride and groom are both robots! Let's go inside.'

The Reverend Luke Draeger and Sister Ida didn't mind the TV station setting up this 'robot wedding' gimmick; they welcomed any chance to get their *message* across to anyone, *before it was too late*. It was Ida who had, when they'd first started their religion, had the idea of a *message*, to be delivered to the world *before it was too late*. If they weren't going to do that, she'd said, what was the point of starting a store-front church at all? Luke it was who insisted on the ambiguous notice in the window: people might be welcome, but then again they might not. So far the effect had been to keep out everyone but the occasional bold drunk – who was not welcome.

Aside from the TV crew, the human congregation was limited to Luke, Ida and a kind young woman named Dora. Dora worked at the Meat Advice Bureau next door. Since no one in the neighbourhood ever sought any meat advice, she had time to drop in, listen to the sermons, help out with the singing, and put something in the collection.

Dora always had to sit at the back. All the other seats were permanently taken by the non-human congregation, nearly a hundred battered effigies:

First came a handful of store window mannequins, their hair and smiles identifying them as belonging to an earlier generation of dummies (during a previous Presidential administration). They were clothed now only in ragged coats and curtains of no use to people, but they sat in gracefully relaxed poses, and seemed to be enjoying themselves. Next to them were a few 'robots' built by children out of cardboard boxes and tinfoil, with noses made of burnt-out light bulbs and bottlecap eyes. Next came a plastic medical skeleton, only a few bones missing, and next, a shattered pinball machine. Its broken legs were arranged to look casually crossed, and its back plate lighted to show a grinning ballplayer. There were toy robots of battered metal or cracked plastic, run by clockwork or batteries to shoot sparks or mutter incoherent greetings. There was a ventriloquist's dummy with a split wooden smile, a dental dummy with removable teeth, a tailor's dummy and even a tackling dummy (legs only) made into a composite figure which also included a jack-in-the box. There were other composites, scarecrows and guys made up of stuffed clothes topped with various heads – pillows with printed faces, painted balloons, Hallowe'en masks of Frankenstein and Mickey Mouse, a plaster death-mask without its nose, an imitation marble bust, a lampshade depicting the face of a dead country singer. There were broken items from carnivals and arcades: a laughing mechanical clown, an automatic fortune-teller in a glass case, Brazos Billy the (retired) gunfighter, and I-Speak-Your-Weight. There were large plaster Kewpies, and waxwork replicas of a few mass murderers (from the days when mass murder was unusual).

Nothing worked, nothing was whole, not even the bride and groom. This was a mission among the derelict and forgotten simulacra.

'Dearly beloved,' said Luke, and probably meant it. He felt that effigies could end up abandoned and despised like this only because those who owned them really wanted to abandon one another; really despised themselves. Conversely, if people could learn to live with effigies, they might some day learn to live with themselves. 'Dearly beloved, we are gathered together in the sight of Mission Control –'

He caught the eye of Ida. 'All right, in the sight of God – and in the face of this company, to join together in matrimony, this machine –' He indicated a squat robot appliance which had, in better days, been able to vacuum, dust, and empty ashtrays. Now it did little more than twitch, and rust. '– and this machine.' He nodded towards a clumsy device made of aluminium tubing, looking very much like a classic 'robot'. It had been built many years ago by a class at some junior high school. It had never been able to do anything but answer questions on baseball.

While the service proceeded, the camera wandered over the congregation. There were painted plaster saints, and one or two of glow-in-the-dark plastic. There was an anatomical man with transparent skin and removable plastic organs, and next to him a wooden lay figure with a head like a fat exclamation mark. Then came a metallic plastic robot costume for a child, a prop suit of armour and a genuine white spacesuit. There was an inflatable doll with a permanently surprised expression, a mechanical Abe Lincoln frozen in an attitude of boredom, and a giant teddy bear. There was a cigar-store wooden Indian, a hitching-post of iron in the shape of a black child, and (from England) garden gnomes made of concrete.

Towards the rear of the church the chairs were heaped with dolls and puppets of all sizes: Russian babushka dolls; dress-up dolls; dolls with faces made of china, wax, wood, metal, rag; dolls that walked or talked or wet themselves while doing algebra; Barfin' Billy; a corn dolly, a glass baby full of what once had been candies. There were glove puppets, clockwork dancers, Punch and Judy, fantoccini shadow puppets, marionettes.

'. . . take this machine to be your lawfully wedded spouse?' The cleaner twitched a brush, perhaps in assent. 'And do you, machine, take this machine to be your lawfully wedded spouse?'

The junior high android muttered, '. . . Ty Cobb . . . highest batting average . . . twelve years . . .'

The camera continued to roam over this throng, picking out strangeness: the mad cracked grin, the missing nose, the staring glass eye. It skipped over Dora sitting in the last row (next to an old stage costume for the Tin Woodman) to concentrate on the bizarre: the lop-sided wax face, the single mother-of-pearl tooth.

'Then I now pronounce you machine and machine.'

Ida turned on the player harmonium to produce 'Ah, Sweet Mystery of Life', then a recessional, as the happy couple apparently made their way out of the church (actually drawn along on piano wires by the TV crew). Outside, the TV company had arranged its own visual finish: a set of robot arms from a local factory were lined up in a double row, holding their arc-welders aloft to form an arch.

When it was all over, Luke seemed subdued. 'I wish Rickwood could have been here, that's all. He'd have understood. He, in a way I guess he started all this.'

Ida said, '*I* know that, why are you telling *me* that? Do I go around reminding you how he brought us together?'

'Affirmative, I mean, yes.' Luke sighed. 'Haven't had a word from him, not since he said he was giving himself up to KUR.'

'He's probably too busy.' Ida was peering into the dim corner at the back of the church, where Dora seemed to be talking to the Tin Woodman costume.

'Busy? Busy? They've probably ripped him apart by now. He's probably lying in pieces all over some laboratory bench, while people in green goggles stick probes into him. They're making his leg twitch like the leg of a frog, do you read me?'

'Loud and clear, Luke, just take it easy.'

'Busy as a frog. And they're probably gearing up the assembly lines right now to turn out millions of copies of him. Poor damn silicon-head.'

'But if they turn out copies,' Ida quickly suggested, 'then we'll never lose him completely, will we? Say, isn't there someone back there with Dora?' She called out: 'Dora? Who's that with you?'

Dora stood up, and the Tin Woodman stood up with her. They came forward into the light. 'Someone who really understands.'

'Who?' Ida's voice went shrill. She felt her 24-karat heart miss a beat as the creature removed its funnel hat and started undoing the hinges of its face.

'Me,' said a grubby, bearded stranger. Dora introduced him as Allbright.

'I hope you're not going to give me any Luddite pep-talk, Father. I can do without that.'

'No, Leo, of course not. Of course not.' Father Warren found it hard to believe that the animated cartoon face on the screen before him was really connected to Leo Bunsky's brain, across the room in a big glass tank. 'Of course not. But you can't blame me for worrying, all these stories I hear about computers making up their own religions.'

'Harmless, Father. A nuisance but –'

'Harmless! A devil-worshipping computer in South America? An oil company computer declaring itself a new prophet of Islam? The Russian war-gaming machine that will only display icons?'

'We haven't confirmed that one,' said the icon Leo. 'But listen, all these anomalies were just planted by programmers with more zeal than sense. You can easily plant superstition in machines, just as in people or pigeons. These computers aren't *making up* their religions, they're getting the holy writ from outside. From you might say missionaries. But don't worry, all we have to do is some heavy deprogramming.'

Father Warren chewed a hangnail. 'I wish I could believe that. "Speak only the word and my computer will be healed." I wish I could believe these computers were something like good servants, good but sick.'

The cartoon face looked sympathetic. 'Hard to have faith in them, I know. Hard to believe they're not just as petty and vicious and despicable as our own species can be. I just hope that when the time comes, Father, they have a little faith in us.'

'When they take over? No, I can't believe –' The priest cleared his throat. 'But I didn't come here to discuss what I believe, eh? Suppose we get down to business.'

'Bless me, Father, for I have sinned. My last confession was, well, some time ago . . .'

When he had heard the confession, Father Warren crossed the room to Leo's tank. An attendant rose to greet him.

'You know you have to crumble it, Father?'

'If it's the only way.' He held the white wafer over the tank and crumbled it into the water. The white crumbs floated for a minute and then sank like little snowflakes, there being no goldfish to snap them up.

Moxon's amplified voice reached some of the crowd, though the cold north wind was doing its best to sweep away words and people, to clear the terrace of all signs of life.

'It was just a month ago, right here in the KUR Tower, that I found myself watching a peculiar sight on TV: two broken-down robots getting married!'

Some people laughed, others wondered who was getting married, or buried.

'Crazy stunts aside, what can you do with broken-down robots? Well, if you happen to be a genius like Jough Braun here, you can turn them into great sculpture. Jough was poking around in one of our storerooms or offices or somewhere, and he found a broken-down robot we didn't even know we owned. Jough says he used it *exactly* as he found it, just covered it with white epoxy and – well, without further ado, here it is – *Man Confronting the Universe*.'

The applause was blown away, as he pulled the cord. Drapery fell to show a white figure with arms upraised in Pharisaical prayer. Under the layers of epoxy a face could be discerned, but no expression. Those watching might have been reminded of the ghost-white figures of George Segal (each containing air in the exact shape of a living human, surrounded by plaster), or of the ivory statue Pygmalion warmed to life, or of the albino puppets drowned in Rome by the Vestal Virgins. A few might have thought of white clown makeup, first worn by Joe Grimaldi playing a comic automaton in *La Statue Blanche*. It is possible that someone thought of white marble Victorian tombs or white-faced mimes pretending to be marionettes, or of Frosty and Snowman, or of white-faced Japanese puppets writhing in mock death.

The north wind blew all such thoughts from the terrace.

Notes

p. 352 All of the italicized lines in Chapter Two are taken from other books: Eric Corder, *Slave*; Charles Dickens, *Life of Our Lord*; G.A. Henty, *The Dash for Khartoum*; Albert Camus, *The Stranger*; Mickey Spillane, *I, Jury*; Harry Mathews, *The Conversions*; James Hadley Chase, *I'll Get You for This*; Jorge Luis Borges, *The Night of the Gifts*; Nathaniel West, *Cool Million*; Dashiell Hammett, *The Glass Key*; Joyce Cary, *The Horse's Mouth*; Paul Chadburn, 'Murder on the High Seas' in *Fifty Most Amazing Crimes*; George Orwell, *Nineteen Eighty-Four*; Raymond Chandler, *The Little Sister*; F. Dostoyevsky, *Crime and Punishment*; Raymond Chandler, *Farewell My Lovely*; Robin Moore, *The Green Berets*; A. Dumas, *The Three Musketeers*; Carole Keene, *The Message in the Hollow Oak*; E.R. Burroughs, *The Warlord of Mars*; Dorothy Sayers, *Whose Body?*; Graham Greene, *Brighton Rock*; Joseph Conrad, *Nostromo*; The Book of Judges; Warren Miller, *The Cool World*; A. Christie, *The Murder of Roger Ackroyd*; John le Carré, *A Murder of Quality*; E.A. Poe, *Masque of The Red Death*; James M. Cain, *The Postman Always Rings Twice*; A. Conan Doyle, 'The Red-Headed League'; Zane Grey, *Nevada*; E.C. Bentley, *Trent's Last Case*; The Gordons, *The FBI Story*; F.P. Wenseley, 'Under Fire at Sidney Street' in *Fifty Famous Hairbreadth Escapes*; Ken Jones, *The FBI in Action*; D.W. Stevens, *The James Boys in Minnesota*; Raymond Chandler, *Smart Aleck Kill*; Thomas Pynchon, *V*.

p. 366 Sue Ellen's third husband was Vern. Roderick deduced this by assuming that two of the six people in question are brother and sister (hence the six can only be married in eight different ways). The marriages took place in this order: 1. Clarence m. Sue Ellen; Vern m. Sue Jane. 2. Clarence m. Sue Jane; Vern m. Mary Sue. 3. Ronnie m. Mary Sue. 4. Clarence m. Mary Sue; Ronnie m. Sue Ellen. 5. Vern m. Sue Ellen.

The siblings, Ronnie and Sue Jane, did not marry.

p. 454 Not all of these are imaginary books. Of the fifteen named or mentioned here, the imaginary ones are Nos. 5, 7, 8, 9, 10, 11 only.

p. 552 A.L. Samuel, 'Some Moral and Technical Consequences of Automation – A Refutation', *Science* 132 (Sept 16, 1960), pp. 741–2. Cited in *Godel, Escher, Bach: an Eternal Golden Braid*, by Douglas R. Hofstadter.

p. 566 Lewis Carroll, 'What the Tortoise Said to Achilles', *Mind* (1895), pp. 278–80.

p. 585 See A. Rapoport and A.M. Chammah, *Prisoner's Dilemma* (Ann Arbor: Univ. Michigan Press, 1965)